Making a Difference

Making a Difference

Canadian Multicultural Literature

Edited by Smaro Kamboureli

Toronto New York Oxford
Oxford University Press
1996

Oxford University Press
70 Wynford Drive, Don Mills, Ontario M3C 1J9

Oxford New York
Athens Auckland Bangkok Bombay
Calcutta Cape Town Dar es Salaam Delhi
Florence Hong Kong Istanbul Karachi
Kuala Lumpur Madras Madrid Melbourne
Mexico City Nairobi Paris Singapore
Taipei Tokyo Toronto

and associated companies in
Berlin Ibadan

Oxford is a trademark of Oxford University Press

Canadian Cataloguing in Publication Data

Main enry under title:

Making a difference : Canadian multicultural literature

Includes bibliographical references and index.
ISBN 0-19-541078-5

1. Canadian fiction (English) - Minority authors.
2. Canadian fiction (English) - 20th century.
3. Canadian poetry (English) - Minority authors.
4. Canadian poetry (English) - 20th century.
I. Kamboureli, Smaro

PS8235.M56M35 1996   C810.8'08   C96-930452-8
PR9194.5.M56M35 1996

Design: Max Gabriel Izod
Cover Illustration: *The Poets Garden # 1* by Harold Klunder

Since this page cannot accommodate all the copyright notices,
pages xiii-xvi constitute an extension of the copyright page.

1 2 3 4 – 99 98 97 96
This book is printed on permanent (acid-free) paper ∞.

Printed in Canada

CONTENTS

ACKNOWLEDGEMENTS

Compiling this anthology has been the most arduous project I have so far undertaken, but the many tasks I had to perform have also taught me a lot and given me enormous pleasure. During the project's long period of gestation and preparation I benefited from the advice, help, and moral support of many colleagues and writers.

The encouragement of Brian Henderson, formerly with Oxford University Press Canada, was instrumental in my decision to undertake the compilation of this anthology.

For the headnotes that introduce the selections my warm thanks to many of the contributors who sent me biographical information and statements. Special thanks are due to Roy Miki and Daphne Marlatt, who provided me with information about Roy Kiyooka.

I am grateful to Sue Mitchell, Diana Rutherford, Darlene Hollingsworth, Lisa Power, and Puri Chadwick, the support staff of the Department of English, University of Victoria, for typing and collating the various drafts of the manuscript and doing so with particular care and with great appreciation for the material. Their good cheer and ingenuity helped me survive numerous computer mishaps.

I am thankful to Phyllis Wilson, Managing Editor of Oxford University Press, Canada, for her patience and attention.

I can't begin to express enough gratitude to my faithful friends Evelyn Cobley and Phyllis Webb, who indulged me, in ways that only the best of friends know how to do, when I despaired at the difficult choices I had to make.

I owe a special thanks to Lola Lemire Tostevin for her exquisite hospitality in Toronto and for her wit during those late-night long-distance calls that kept me going in the face of various frustrations.

I am immensely grateful to my friend Lorna Jackson who was my constant sounding board during the entire process and who, as my research assistant, made my tasks of searching and proofreading infinitely easier.

Phyllis Webb came to Victoria from Salt Spring Island especially to help with proofreading, and I owe her particular thanks for that.

My parents, and my brother and his family, although a continent and an ocean away, remained a constant source of inspiration and never neglected to remind me that I do have there a home and supporters.

And finally, I owe my most deepest and pleasurable debt to my husband Robert Kroetsch for understanding my fears of completion and for making it possible for me, through his unfailing patience and endless support, to complete this project.

In its early stages, this project was assisted by a Social Sciences and Humanities Research Council of Canada grant.

S.K.

IQBAL AHMAD. 'What Little Sophie Did' from *The Opium Eater and Other Stories* (Cormorant Books, 1992). Reprinted by permission of the publisher.

LILLIAN ALLEN. 'Nothing But A Hero' and 'With Criminal Intent' from *Women Do This Every Day: Selected Poems*, Toronto: Women's Press, 1993. Reprinted by permission of the author.

JEANNETTE ARMSTRONG. 'History Lesson', 'Magic Woman', 'Wind Woman', and 'Indian Woman' from Jeannette Armstrong's poetry collection *Breathtracks* published by Theytus Books (ISBN 0-919441-39-4). Reprinted by permission.

DAVID ARNASON. 'The Sunfish' copyright David Arnason, reprinted by permission of the publisher, from *Fifty Stories and a Piece of Advice*, Winnipeg: Turnstone Press, 1987.

HIMANI BANNERJI. 'Paki Go Home', 'a letter for Iraq', 'death by trivia', and 'Apart-hate' are reprinted by permission of the author.

VEN BEGAMUDRÉ. 'Mosaic' from *A Planet of Eccentrics* (Oolichan Books, 1990). Reprinted by permission of the author.

SANDRA BIRDSELL. 'Flowers for Weddings and Funerals', copyright Sandra Birdsell, reprinted by permission from *Agassiz Stories*, Turnstone Press, Winnepeg.

NEIL BISSOONDATH. 'On the Eve of Uncertain Tomorrows'. Copyright © Neil Bissoondath 1990. Reprinted with permission of the author.

DIONNE BRAND. *From* 'No language is neutral', 'hard against the soul II', 'hard against the soul III', 'hard against the soul V' from *No Language is Neutral*. Copyright © Dionne Brand 1990. Reprinted by permission of Coach House Press.

DI BRANDT. 'foreward', 'when I was five . . .', 'but what do you think . . .', 'missionary position 1", 'missionary position 2", copyright Di Brandt, reprinted by permission of the publisher, from *questions I asked my mother*, Winnipeg: Turnstone Press, 1987.

BETH BRANT. 'This Is History' from *Food and Spirits*, by Beth Brant. Vancouver: Press Gang Publishers, 1991.

AUSTIN CLARKE. 'Doing Right' from *Nine Men Who Laughed*, copyright 1986 by Austin Clarke. Published in Canada by Penguin Books. Reprinted by permission of the author via the Bukowski Agency.

GEORGE ELLIOTT CLARKE. 'Look Homeward, Exile', 'Blank Sonnet', 'The Symposium', 'King Bee Blues', and 'To Selah' from *Whylah Falls* by George Elliott Clarke (Polestar Book Publishers, 1990). Reprinted by permission of the author and Polestar Book Publishers.

RIENZI CRUSZ: 'Sitting Alone in the Happy Hour Café', 'From Shovel to Self-propelled Snow Blower: The Immigrant's Progress', 'In the Idiom of the Sun', 'In the Shadow of the Tiger (3)', and 'A Door Ajar' from *Still Close to the Raven*, TSAR Publications, 1989. Reprinted with permission of TSAR Publications.

ANTONIO D'ALFONSO. 'Im Sachsenhausen', 'The Loss of a Culture', 'The Family', and 'On Being a Wop' from *The Other Shore*, copyright 1986, 1988 Antonio D'Alfonso and Guernica Editions Inc. Reprinted by permission.

CYRIL DABYDEEN. 'Lady Icarus', 'Multiculturalism', and 'I am not' are reprinted by permission of the author.

PIER GIORGIO DI CICCO. 'Waking up among Writers', 'Latin Ontario', and 'Symmetries of Exclusion: Duo-Genesis' from *Virgin Science* by Pier Giorgio Di Cicco. Used by permission of the Canadian Publishers, McClelland & Stewart, Toronto.

MARY DI MICHELE. 'Life is Theatre or O to be an Italian in Toronto . . .', 'Afterword: Trading in on the American Dream', and 'What is Desire' are reprinted by permission of the author.

SAAD ELKHADEM. 'Nobody Complained' is reprinted by permission of the author.

GEORGE FALUDY: 'Goodbye, My America' from *Learn This Poem of Mine By Heart*, Hounslow Press, 1983. Reprinted by permission of Hounslow Press.

PATRICK FRIESEN. 'Sunday afternoon', 'bible', 'evisceration', and 'breaking for light', copyright Patrick Friesen, reprinted by permission of the publisher from *Flicker and Hawk*, Winnipeg: Turnstone Press, 1987. 'the forge' is reprinted by permission of the author.

HIROMI GOTO. 'Night' is reprinted by permission of the author.

ZAFFI GOUSOPOULOS. 'Four Greek Men' is reprinted by permission of the author.

FREDERICK PHILIP GROVE. 'The First Day of an Immigrant' is reprinted by permission of A. Leonard Grove, Toronto.

KRISTJANA GUNNARS. Excerpt from *The Prowler* is reprinted by permission of the author.

CLAIRE HARRIS. 'Black Sisyphus' is reprinted from *Travelling to Find a Remedy* with the permission of Goose Lane Editions. Copyright © 1986 by Claire Harris. 'No God Waits on Incense' from *The Conception of Winter* copyright © Claire Harris. Reprinted by permission of the author. Excerpt from *Drawing Down a Daughter* ©Claire Harris, 1992 is reprinted with permission of Goose Lane Editions.

MARWAN HASSAN. Excerpt from *The Confusion of Stones* © Marwan Hassan (1989). Reprinted by permission of Cormorant Books.

ANGELA HRYNIUK. 'mouthful', 'the thief', 'from destination to destiny', and 'no visual scars' from *no visual scars* (Polestar Book Publishers, 1993). Reprinted by permission of the publisher.

JAMILA ISMAIL. Excerpt from *scared texts* is reprinted by permission of the author.

ARNOLD ITWARU. Excerpt from *Shanti* is reprinted by permission of the author.

GEORGE JONAS. 'Wakes up next morning to the strains of O Canada on the radio' by George Jonas from *The Happy Hungry Man* (Anansi, 1970), copyright © George Jonas, reprinted by permission of the author. 'In Any City', 'Once More', and 'From the Book of al-Maari' are reprinted from *The East Wind Blows West* (Cacanadadada Press, 1993). Reprinted by permission of George Jonas and Cacanadadada Press.

JANICE KULYK KEEFER. 'Nach Unten' is reprinted by permission of the author.

THOMAS KING. 'The One About Coyote Going West' is reprinted by permission of the author.

ROY KIYOOKA. Excerpt from *Transcanada Letters* (TalonBooks, 1975), 'since you and I forsook the rites of marriage', 'since I wrote the night sky down', 'the pear tree a siamese cat named cooper and me', and 'dear lesbia'.

A.M. KLEIN. 'Autobiographical' and 'Doctor Drummond' from *Complete Poems,* edited by Zailig Pollock, University of Toronto Press, 1990. Reprinted by permission of University of Toronto Press Incorporated.

JOY KOGAWA. Excerpt from *Obasan* (Penguin Books Canada, 1991) is reprinted by permission of the author.

RACHEL KORN. 'The Words of My Alefbeyz' and 'Home' from *Generations* (1984). Reprinted by permission.

HAROLD SONNY LADOO. Excerpt from *No Pain Like This Body* is reprinted with the permission of Stoddart Publishing Co. Limited, Don Mills, Ontario M3B 2T6.

YASMIN LAHDA. 'Beena' from *Lion's Granddaughter and Other Stories* by Yasmin Ladha. Reprinted by permission of NeWest Publishers Ltd., Edmonton, Alberta, Canada.

EVELYN LAU. 'Marriage' copyright © 1993 by Evelyn Lau, from *Fresh Girls and Other Stories*. Published by HarperCollins Publishers Ltd. First published in slightly different form in *NeWest Review*.

IRVING LAYTON. 'Whom I Write For', 'The Search', 'The Improved Binoculars', 'Terrorists', and 'At the Belsen Memorial' from *Collected Poems* by Irving Layton. Used by permission of the Canadian Publishers, McClelland & Stewart, Toronto.

C. ALLYSON LEE. 'Recipe'. Reprinted by permission of the author.

SKY LEE. 'Bellydancer: Level One'. Reprinted with permission from *Bellydancer*, by Sky Lee. (Vancouver: Press Gang Publishers, 1994).

VERA LYSENKO. 'The Fairy Tale Spinners' (from *Yellow Boots*, 1992) is reprinted by permission of The Estate of Vera Lysenko, Canadian Institute of Ukrainian Studies Press, and NeWest Publishers Ltd.

DAPHNE MARLATT. Excerpt from 'Month of Hungry Ghosts' from *Ghost Works*, by Daphne Marlatt. NeWest Publishers, 1993.

ASHOK MATHUR. 'Into Skin' is reprinted by permission of the author.

ROY MIKI. 'the rescue', 'September 22', 'in flight, 1/4", and 'membrane translate' from *Market Rinse*. Reprinted by permission of the author.

ROHINTON MISTRY. 'Swimming Lessons' from *Tales from the Firozsha Baag* by Rohinton Mistry. Used by permission of the Canadian Publishers, McClelland & Stewart, Toronto.

DANIEL DAVID MOSES. 'Admonition to an Ice-Skating Child', 'Paper', 'The End of Night', and 'Bearwalk' are reprinted by permission of the author.

MICHAEL ONDAATJE. Excerpt from *In the Skin of a Lion* (Vintage Canada) © Michael Ondaatje. Reprinted by permission of the author.

FRANK PACI. Excerpt from *Black Madonna* by F.G. Paci is reprinted by permission of Oberon Press.

MARLENE NOURBESE PHILIP. 'Discourse on the Logic of Language' and 'Blackman Dead' are reprinted by permission of the author.

IAN IQBAL RASHID. 'A Pass to India', 'Another Country', 'Could Have Danced All Night', and 'Hospital Visit: The Heat Yesterday' are reprinted by permission of the author.

NINO RICCI. 'Going to the Moon' is reprinted by permission of the author.

NICE RODRIGUEZ. 'Big Nipple of the North' from *Throw It To the River* by Nice Rodriguez, Women's Press, 1993. Reprinted by permission of Women's Press.

LAURA GOODMAN SALVERSON. 'The Coming of Thor' from *The Viking Heart*, McClelland & Stewart, 1975.

BILL SCHERMBRUCKER. 'Chameleon' from *Chameleon & Other Stories* (TalonBooks, 1983) is reprinted by permission of the author.

SHYAM SELVADURAI. 'Pigs Can't Fly' from *Funny Boy* by Shyam Selvadurai. Used by permission of the Canadian Publishers, McClelland & Stewart, Toronto.

GERRY SHIKATANI. 'After a Reading of Isan', 'Bird of Two Forms', 'The Three Coins', and 'Haiku' are reprinted by permission of the author.

MAKEDA SILVERA. 'Her Head a Village' is reprinted by permission of the author.

JOSEF ŠKVORECKÝ. 'The Army of Creativity Contest' from *The Republic of Whores* by Josef Škvorecký. Copyright © 1971 Josef Škvorecký. Copyright © in the English Translation 1993 Paul Wilson. Reprinted by permission of Alfred A. Knopf Canada.

J.J. STEINFELD. 'Ida Solomon's Play' by J.J. Steinfeld from *Forms of Captivity and Escape* (Thistledown Press Ltd., 1988). Used with permission.

ANDREW SUKNASKI. 'Philip Well' from *Wood Mountain Poems* (Macmillan of Canada, 1976), 'West to Tolstoi, Manitoba (circa 1900)', 'Vasylyna's Retreat', 'In the Beginning was The', 'Letter to Big Bear', and 'The Faceless Goodbyes' from *In the Name of Narid: New Poems* (Porcupine's Quill, 1981). Reprinted by permission of the author.

YESHIM TERNAR. 'True Romance with a Sailor' is reprinted by permission of the author.

RENATO TRUJILLO. 'Rain', 'Hunger', and 'Unsolicited Mail' are reprinted from *Behind the Orchestra* with the permission of Goose Lane Editions. Copyright © 1987 by Renato Trujillo.

ARITHA VAN HERK. 'Of Dykes and Boers and Drowning' is reprinted by permission of the author.

M.G. VASSANJI. 'The London-returned' from *Uhuru Street* by M.G. Vassanji. Used by permission of the Canadian Publishers, McClelland & Stewart, Toronto.

FRED WAH. 'waiting for saskatchewan' and 'Father/Mother Haibun #4" from *Waiting for Saskatchewan* by Fred Wah (Turnstone, 1985). Excerpts from *Music at the Heart of Thinking* (2, 10, 50, 51, 52, 55) by Fred Wah (Red Deer College Press, 1987). Reprinted by permission of the author.

HELEN WEINZWEIG. 'L'Envoi' is reprinted by permission of the author.

ARMIN WIEBE. 'Oata, Oata'. Copyright Armin Wiebe, reprinted by permission of the publisher, as it first appeared in *The Fiddlehead,* from *The Salvation of Yasch Siemens,* Winnipeg: Turnstone Press, 1984.

RUDY WIEBE. 'A Night in Fort Pitt or (if you prefer) The Only Perfect Communist in the World' is reprinted by permission of the author.

JIM WONG-CHU. 'tradition', 'baptism 1909", 'curtain of rain', and 'equal opportunity' are reprinted by permission of the author.

Every effort has been made to determine and contact copyright owners. In the case of any omissions, the publisher will be pleased to make suitable acknowledgement in future editions.

INTRODUCTION

SMARO KAMBOURELI

Making a Difference: An Anthology of Canadian Multicultural Literature at once celebrates what has been called minority literature in Canada and attempts to change our understanding of what minority literature is.

What makes this anthology of Canadian literature different is its gathering together of both poetry and fiction by authors who come from a wide range of racial, ethnic, and cultural backgrounds. Beginning with F.P. Grove and Laura Goodman Salverson, the first non-Anglo-Celtic writers to achieve recognition in Canada, and including First Nations authors, this anthology belongs to the genealogy of Canadian literature, a body of writings that come from a variety of traditions that used to be kept separate from the so-called main tradition.

One of my primary intentions has been to create a space in which contributors to the anthology might dialogue with each other, without suspending their differences. Through their poetry, their fiction, and their statements about their writing that are cited in the headnotes, this anthology enables these authors to speak with each other across boundaries that are marked by many differences. Be they differences of race, of ethnic origin, of gender, of place, of ideological affiliations, or of thematic concerns and aesthetics, they characterize this literature in remarkable ways. Each of the seventy-one contributors speaks in her or his particular accent. I use the word accent here not so much as the language marker announcing that the origins of someone—like me, for example—lie outside Canada, but rather as a sign of particularities, of differences that do not become absent or are not rendered silent. The writers in this anthology make a difference because, when read together, they invite the reader to consider the social, political, and cultural contexts that have produced Canadian literature in general and their work in particular. As a collage of voices, *Making a Difference* fashions an image of Canadian culture that reveals how we have come to our present moment in history.

This history speaks of arrivals and departures, trajectories whose starting points contain, more often than not, conflict. It is a history of the legacy of colonization, but also a history of the 'discovery' of Canada as a new home whose 'newness' constantly calls forth the spectre of the past, the nostalgic replay of other geographies. It is also a history of persistent attempts to compose a unified vision of Canadian culture against the reality and cultural understanding of many Canadians, a history that bursts its seams. It is, in other words, a history haunted by dissonance. This history, which is paradoxically one of plenitude and of disquieting gaps, is what the subtitle of the anthology intends to evoke.

Canadian Multicultural Literature. In some respects, one word too many. For Canadian literature is, should be thought of, as reflecting the multicultural make-up of the country. That I feel compelled to spell this out, that I do so at a time when, for example, some of the contributors to this anthology have won some of the most coveted Canadian literary prizes, suggests that Canadian literature—Canadian literature as an institution—is still not as diverse as it should be. Prizes do not by themselves establish the literary significance of an author; still, they confer on authors a validity, they sanction the kind of affirmation that the Canadian literary establishment has long denied Aboriginal writers and writers of non-Anglo-Celtic backgrounds. *Making a Difference* intends to reflect the changed—and changing—state of cultural affairs in Canada.

◈ ◈ ◈

In explaining how I came to select and represent the writers included in this anthology, I can only begin by resorting to the cliché offered by other anthologists. No sooner is an anthology complete than it begins to address its own gaps; it can only exist within the ellipses it creates.

While working on this project, I remained profoundly aware of the fact that inclusion is synonymous with exclusion. The irony that an anthology of this kind is, in many ways, a response to earlier cases of exclusion informed my wish to compile an anthology that would represent Canadian writing while calling into question representation itself. In many respects, this is an impossible task, perhaps even a preposterous ambition. Yet, if I were to reconstruct what prompted me in the first place to compile this anthology, the questioning of representation would figure prominently as both one of my primary goals and one of my guiding principles. I believe that we reside forever within the realm of representation: we represent ourselves through language and through our bodies, but we also see ourselves represented by others. No image, no story, no anthology can represent us or others without bringing into play—serious play—differing contexts, places, or people.

Making a Difference attempts to question representation in a number of ways, perhaps most significantly by challenging the concept of minority. All the contributors, by virtue of their race and ethnicity, belong to the manifold 'margins' that the Canadian dominant society has historically devised. Yet, if we consider these authors in the various contexts that have produced their writing, it becomes apparent that 'marginalization', from an individual as well as a collective perspective, is impossible to define in any stable way.

These authors' experiences with Canadian publishers, the reception of their work, their personal histories in Canada, how they position themselves with regard to their cultural differences, the diverse treatment of their racial and ethnic groups by the Canadian dominant society, how (if at all) these experiences are translated into literature—all these and other related issues argue persuasively to one conclusion: that the concept of marginality has no inherent meaning in itself. As Russell Ferguson says,

> When we say marginal, we must always ask, marginal to what? But this question is difficult to answer. The place from which power is exercised is often a hidden place. When we try to pin it down, the center always seems to be somewhere else. Yet we know that this phantom center, elusive as it is, exerts a real, undeniable power over the whole social framework of our culture, and over the ways we think about it.[1]

Minority literature, then, is nothing other than a construct, an expression of the power and literary politics of any given time.

This is why we see in *Making a Difference*, for example, a writer like Lee Maracle alongside a writer like Michael Ondaatje. Maracle might be one of the most prolific and widely read Native authors, but she began her writing career by publishing her own books because no Canadian publisher would publish her. Ondaatje, on the other hand, has long enjoyed a national reputation and has recently achieved international status. Similarly, Marlene Nourbese Philip and Dionne Brand are often now included in courses on Canadian literature and have become the focus of recent critical studies, but their lives and writing careers clearly reflect the discrimination and racism they have encountered in Canada. In contrast, Evelyn Lau has had her work published by mainstream presses, and resists writing out of, or identifying with, her ethnic community. In a different way, Frank Paci has been writing fiction for years, but only recently, after the success of Nino Ricci's first novel, to which his work has been compared, has he become more widely recognized. Difference, then, is always a matter of intensity, and is weighed differently in given historical moments. Its meanings are variable, shifting, even provisional.

My selection of contributors was intended to reflect, in part, a counterreading of what we have come to call mainstream and minority literatures in Canada. Multicultural literature is not minority writing, for it does not raise issues that are of minor interest to Canadians. Nor is it, by any standard, of lesser quality than the established literary tradition. Its thematic concerns are of such a diverse range that they show the binary structure of 'centre' and 'margins', which has for so long informed discussions of Canadian literature, to be a paradigm of the history of political and cultural affairs in Canada.

I did not want this anthology to be an instance of tokenism, and this was yet another factor that has informed my selections. By holding onto what the 'otherness' of writers—be it ethnicity, race, or gender—is in relation to the dominant culture's self-image, tokenism assigns a single meaning to cultural differences. It masks the many nuances of difference. On the one hand, it homogenizes the diversity that multiculturalism is intent on embracing; on the other, it disregards the fact that a writer's identity and the meaning of a poem or a short story cannot be defined in any single way.

Since the late 1980s, in response to the currency that multiculturalism has achieved in the political, social, and academic arenas, anthologies, critical studies, and course syllabi have gradually begun to include authors who have been traditionally excluded from mainstream representation. These gradual and tentative changes have been necessary steps toward revising our understanding of what constitutes Canadian literature. Yet many of these attempts, however well-intended, have resulted in further consolidating the minority position of the selected writers. Representing Canada's multiculturalism with a spattering of only one or two authors, making such writers visible only by viewing them as representative of their cultural groups, does virtually nothing to dispel the 'marginality' attributed to those authors.

I have attempted to avoid such pitfalls by considering the contributors to this anthology as Canadian writers, and not as representatives of cultural groups. The tendency to read multicultural literature through the racial or ethnic labels affixed to its authors more often than not reinforces stereotypical images of the authors themselves and of their cultural communities. Labels are vexing and sneaky things because they are intended to express a stable and universal representation of both communities and individuals. By implying that there is a specific essence, say, to the writing of First Nations authors, labels prematurely foreclose our understanding not only of the complexity inherent in individual communities but also of the various ways in which authors position themselves within their cultural groups and the Canadian society at large. As Jeannette Armstrong has written,

> First Nations cultures, in their various contemporary forms, whether an urban-modern, pan-Indian experience or clearly a tribal specific (traditional or contemporary), whether it is Eastern, Arctic, Plains, Southwest or West Coastal in region, have unique sensibilities which shape the voices coming forward into written English Literature.[2]

The particular relations of writers to culture, the complex contexts within which they write, are always inscribed in the literature itself. And this is the reason why this anthology is not organized by cultural groups.

Even when a community claims a writer as its spokesperson, or when a writer voluntarily takes on that role, she or he must write out of a space of difference. The difference is made by the writing act itself, by a writerly belief in language as an act of the imagination, by a faith in the power of language, irrespective of its forms and contours, to effect change, to make us perceive ourselves and those around us *otherwise*.

Roy Kiyooka once said that, for him, 'to survive in this culture was essentially a quest for language as the modality of power about which you could be present in the world.'[3] In searching for potential contributors, this is what I have looked for: how these writers make themselves 'present in the world', how they articulate their relation to language and to culture. That many authors in *Making a Difference* share the same cultural background is, in many respects, a fortuitous result of my selection process. That the writing of those who have a common heritage often echoes similar themes and just as often reflects different concerns, attests that cultural boundaries are porous, that cultural representation is contingent on the authors' singularity of imagination. No single form of literary representation can adequately reflect a community's complexity. Indeed, the variety of authors that come from and write about individual groups resists any notion of a sole authentic image of those communities.

Thus, both Himani Bannerji and Rohinton Mistry come from India, but their writing gestures toward different spaces. This reflects not only the richness and diversity of Indian culture, but also their individual sensibilities. Armin Wiebe, Sandra Birdsell, Rudy Wiebe, Patrick Friesen and Di Brandt are all known as Mennonite writers, but their Mennonite experiences are coded differently in their writing. Furthermore, it would be reductive to read their work only through the signs of Mennonite background and, as a result, ignore all the other elements that contribute to the complexity of their writing. Communities have a social and cultural coherence, but they are also characterized by fluidity. No constellation of literary images can sin-glehandedly mould a community's particular ethos. We must read the distinctive ways in which authors identify with, or resist, their communities in the context of other historical factors that permeate their work.

As Thomas King says, 'when we talk about Native writers, we talk as though we have a process for determining who is a Native writer and who is not, when, in fact, we don't. What we do have is a collection of literary works by individual authors who are Native by ancestry, and our hope, as writers and critics, is that if we wait long enough, the sheer bulk of this collection, when it reaches some sort of critical mass, will present us with a matrix within which a variety of patterns can be discerned.'⁴ It is my hope that *Making a Difference* will have a similar effect, that its readers will develop an incremental understanding of who its contributors are and what they tell us about the history of our multicultural tradition.

My selection process has also been informed by my desire to represent Canadian multicultural literature by bridging the gap between established and emerging authors. Many contributors—like Austin Clarke, Joseph Skvorecky, Joy Kogawa, Aritha van Herk, M.G. Vassanji—have produced substantial bodies of work that have influenced both our overall appreciation of their writing and some of the ways in which we approach Canadian literature. Presenting these authors alongside, for exam-ple, Zaffi Gousopoulos and Corinne Allyson Lee, who have so far published only in literary magazines, or next to authors like Hiromi Goto, Yasmin Ladha, Nice Rodriguez, and Ashok Mathur, who have so far published only one book each, reflects my attempt to give the reader a broad view of what Canadian multicultural literature has to offer at this point in time.

My intention to represent Canadian multicultural literature while questioning the label of minority attached to it has also led to my decision to organize the contents of this anthology according to the birthdates of authors. This arrangement, I believe, affords the reader a historical overview while, at the same time, dispelling the notion that multicultural writing is only a recent phenomenon. I would like to stress that I am not offering *Making a Difference* as an anthology that claims to redress all the gaps of cultural difference in the Canadian literary canon. No anthology could pur-port to do that. Any anthology that intends to offer a historical overview can only function as an allegory of literary history, can only map out yet another narrative path by which we can enter that history. Like all anthologies, *Making a Difference*, too, has gaps, but what it does not include, I hope, is balanced by the various ways in which I have tried to remain alert to change and limits.

How we function as subjects of our own representations and how we figure as objects in the representations of others; how culture is defined and who implements those definitions; what or who devises the boundaries that determine how cultural dif-ference—be it celebrated or curtailed—is represented—all these questions have been central to the making of this anthology. In my selection process I was guided by the belief that multiculturalism disputes certain kinds of representation, the kinds that are built around the principle of sameness, of cohesiveness, of linear development.

The seventy-one contributors represented here are introduced by headnotes that include both biographical information and, with a few exceptions, comments by the authors themselves. Although there was no difficulty collecting material about the lives and writing careers of most of these contributors, in some cases gathering information proved to be a real challenge. This accounts for some of the inconsistencies that appear in the kinds of information and material provided. Furthermore, I have encountered some discrepancies in dates and other facts in the various sources that I have consulted. I have tried to resolve those problems to the best of my ability.

The authors' statements cited in the headnotes come from interviews, from their essays (included in the bibliography that appears at the end of this volume) or, in many cases, from comments written by the authors. Beyond the need to introduce the basic outline of individual careers, the headnotes are designed to let the contributors speak for themselves about their writing. I am, of course, responsible for the specific comments that I cite, and I am aware that I mediate these writers' own self-representations. But representation, as I have already tried to explain, is a matter of construction, always something that stands in for something else.

Some of the comments I cite address issues about which many of the contributors have often spoken. I have taken this to reflect a persistent concern on their part and on the part of their audiences, and thus I have included such comments. How they became writers, how they approach their subject-matter, what they think of language or the function of literature are some of these issues. I have also included statements which show the diversity of the cultural and social spaces from which these writers come, and which demonstrate that Canada, historically and culturally, has been both a troubling and an exciting place to inhabit.

Thus while some of the contributors speak of their resistance to labels like ethnicity and of the relationship of their cultural origins to their writing, they do so in different ways. The narrative that emerges from these comments is, then, one of contradictions, of differences. What is consistent is the anxiety many of these authors share about any homogenous image of Canadian culture, their concern with the tendency of readers and the media to represent their identities and their writings in minority terms, irrespective of the power with which some of these minority spaces are invested today. Like the literature included in this anthology, these comments illustrate that the differences that permeate Canadian multiculturalism are not to be seen as barriers but as signs of complexity.

❖ ❖ ❖

The literature in *Making a Difference* offers different soundings of the social and cultural body of Canada. Since its beginnings, the making of Canadian literature has coincided, in many respects, with the making of the Canadian state. Far from being a Canadian phenomenon alone, this overlap shows how literature, like other cultural expressions, measures the pulse of a nation. What might be particularly Canadian, however, is the kind of anxiety that has continued to characterize both what Canadian literature is and what constitutes Canadian identity. This is not surprising since Canada as a state is, relatively speaking, new. And it also explains David Taras's claim that 'there has been throughout Canadian history a passion for identity.'[5] Few would dispute this. What is disputed, though, is the overwhelming tendency to define Canadian identity in collective and unifying terms, this despite, or perhaps because of, the legacy of colonialism and the overpowering evidence that Canada has always been a place of diversities—racial, ethnic, and linguistic.

The binary structure which *Making a Difference* attempts to dissolve, that of 'centre' and 'margin', is part and parcel of Canada's colonial history, of its attempt to construct a Canadian identity that is modelled after the image of the colonizers. This, too, is consistent with the patterns of colonialism elsewhere. For in the history of Western domination, the paradigm of 'centre' and 'margin', as Gyan Prakash writes,

> surfaces precisely at the point where the encounter with cultural difference is organized into the colonizer/colonized polarity, where the historicist notion of history gathers 'people without history' into its fold, and where the metropolitan culture speaks to the marginalized in the language of its supremacist myths.[6]

In Canada's colonial history, 'the encounter with cultural difference' was, for all intents and purposes, a non-encounter. The British and French colonizers saw themselves as settlers, as arriving in a land that was taken to be more or less empty. The presence, cultural differences, spirituality, and languages of the Aboriginal peoples, the people who live in what we now call Canada, were not seen as having any inherent value. The land they inhabited, and which they continue to inhabit, was deemed to be ready for the taking. And this remained the case for a long time.

Canadian history, until relatively recently, perpetuated this image of Canada as a land that was 'discovered', not a land that was colonized. As Olive Patricia Dickason says,

> Canada, it used to be said by non-Indians . . . is a country of much geography and little history. . . . How can such a thing be said, much less believed, when people have been living here for thousands of years? As [Aboriginals] see it, Canada has fifty-five founding nations rather than the two that have been officially acknowledged. . . . Canada's history has usually been presented not as beginning with the first Europeans, the Norse, who arrived here in about AD 1000, but with the French, who came . . . in the sixteenth century.[7]

The myth that Canada was 'discovered' was intended to hide the fact that what we now call Canada has always belonged to other peoples, peoples with their own distinct languages and cultures.

Jeannette Armstrong's comments in this collection indicate the unequivocal presence of the rich and diverse cultures of Aboriginal peoples. She grew up in the nurturing environment of 'a traditional family . . . with a long history', a history that includes 'the total purity of our language', the Okanagan language that has 'been handed down through thousands of years'. But her Okanagan people have been one of the First Nations groups fortunate enough to maintain their language. As Armstrong says,

> I remember as a teenager that I began to understand the value of being who I

am, an Okanagan woman, a person who has been educated and taught things that other people did not have access to. Many of our people were coerced and brutalized for speaking their language and practicing their culture until their memory grew distant and dim.

The early constructions of Canada as a unified nation were synonymous with the kind of colonial practices that Armstrong talks about—the imposed invisibility of First Nations peoples through such institutions as residential schools.

Some legislation and empirical conditions might have changed since then, but the prevailing notions of Canada as a nation, of Canadian identity, and of Canadian literature are still sequestered within this legacy of colonialism. As Lee Maracle has said, 'Unless I was sleeping during the revolution, we have not had a change in our condition.'[8] In this respect, the circumstances of Maracle's protagonist in the story included in this anthology must be seen not only as isolated events taking place in the life of a single woman, but as part of the continuum of Canadian history. As the narrator of the story tells us, Bertha's 'memory retreats to another time', a time when 'Bertha was not called Bertha', when the 'home' for which Bertha longs is a place that can be conjured up only through happy but also troubled memories:

Home was a young girl rushing through a meadow, a cedar basket swishing lightly against dew-laden leaves [. . .] while her mind enjoyed the prospect of becoming . . . becoming, and the words in English would not come. She remembered the girl, the endless stories told to her, the meanings behind each story, the careful coaching in the truth that lay behind each one, the reasons for their telling, but she could not, after fifty years of speaking crippled English, define where it was all supposed to lead.

The stories that Bertha was told as a child were, are, part of the oral tradition of the First Nations peoples, the cultural heritage that the official history of Canada has systematically ignored. In the story, Bertha is defeated by the burden of her memories, by the ways in which she and her people have been disenfranchised. Yet the memory of her life, her attempt at 'whispering her sorrow in the gentle words of their ancestors', is passed on to a young girl.

This passing on, this linking of the past and the present with gestures that speak at once of cultural genocide and cultural pride, of elision and perseverance, forms part of the continuum of Canadian history. It is a continuum that persists against the gaps that mark the official history of Canada. This is the continuum within which Lee Maracle, like other First Nations authors, writes: 'I can spiral out into the world,' she says, 'to reconceive of place. I can stretch time. I can erase the artifice of separation that divides today from yesterday and yesterday from tomorrow. In this place all time is the same time. In this place images speak reality—paint truth in believable pictures.'[9]

The various attempts over time to define Canada as a cohesive nation, to invent a homogenous Canadian identity—an identity minus the identities of the Aboriginal peoples, and later the identities of new immigrants—has not been the only pattern that has determined the course of Canadian history. Despite its aggressive tactics, the colonial construction of Canadian identity has not remained unchallenged. During the course of Canadian history there have always been attempts to redefine this construction of a cohesive identity, even to displace it.

Ironically, some of these challenges stemmed, and in a way continue to do so, from the very force and exploitative tactics through which the colonial establishment attempted to consolidate its position. The Chinese Immigration Act of 1923, following earlier discriminatory legislation against Chinese immigrants, which, with few exceptions, prevented the arrival of Chinese people in Canada, is one example among many that discloses the early perception of a dominant Canadian identity to be dominant only insofar as other identities were systematically kept out of or at the periphery of Canadian society.

The comments and the writing in this anthology by Jim Wong Chu and Sky Lee reinforce the fact that the inherited notion of a unified Canadian identity has only imaginative coherence. And as Sky Lee's first book, *Disappearing Moon Cafe*, suggests, this kind of imaginative coherence has not been a strategy employed by mainstream societies alone. As Kae, the novel's narrator, finds out, her Chinese-Canadian family harbours a secret—or many secrets—that hold the key to how a community might internalize the racism that constructs its position as 'other' to dominant society. Due partly to the Chinese traditions that they bring to Canada and partly to the pressures they experience in Vancouver, Kae's ancestors try to conceal the knowledge that their Chinese patriarch had a child, and a male one at that, with Kelora, a Native woman. Their elaborate attempts to maintain for a long time a pure image of their cultural origins has disastrous effects on the younger generations. Yet the novel also shows the importance of hidden histories, the need to disperse the notion of cultural authenticity. This is the kind of imperative that tells us that cultural identity, as Stuart Hall has put it, 'is a matter of "becoming" as well as of "being".'[10]

The homogenous image of Canadian identity, Canada as 'a white man's country', is still an image we have to come to terms with by rereading and rediscovering the histories hidden behind it. As Elliot L. Tepper writes,

> the process of integrating a more complete history of Canada into public consciousness is at its earliest stages. . . . Settlement history in general seems to plod methodically, and haphazardly, from 'European' to French to British to Other, an enduring image which has been politically useful but empirically incomplete.[11]

Yet, the unified image of Canadian identity has always exhibited fissures and shown itself to be fragile, full of anxiety to maintain, and redefine, its tenuous hold on power. We have come to see the constitutional debates, the recurrence of which characterize the modern history of Canada, as a syndrome that has afflicted many Canadians with 'constitutional fatigue'. This should not prevent us from seeing what they really mean: that Canada is a state in continual process, in a constant state of re-vision. The Meech

Lake Accord and the Charlottetown Agreement, under the aegis of Brian Mulroney's government, were two of the most recent attempts at 'nation building'. They instigated yet another round of talks and soul-searching about what Canadian means. Most recently, the 1995 Quebec referendum had, in different ways, the same effect. Such political events, and the many Royal Commissions that precede and follow them, point to one thing. The unity of Canadian identity is a cultural myth, a myth that can be sustained only by eclipsing the identities of others.

We are at a point now where the presumed uniqueness of Canadian identity is only that—a presumption. *Making a Difference* is testimony to the fact that we can no longer harbour the conceit that Canadian identity is homogenous.

◈ ◈ ◈

Beginning with the 1971 policy of multiculturalism, introduced by Pierre Trudeau, and later with Bill C-93, the 'Act for the preservation and enhancement of multiculturalism in Canada' legislated in 1988, we have entered a new and formative period in Canadian history, what we can call the multicultural stage of Canadian cultural politics. According to K. Victor Ujimoto, 'Canada was the first and only nation in the world to establish a Multiculturalism Act.'[12] This might be so, but it is interesting to remind ourselves how the official acknowledgement of Canada's multicultural heritage was framed.

The federal policy of multiculturalism was the result of the work of the Royal Commission on Bilingualism and Biculturalism, whose Report covers six volumes (1967-1970), including one entitled *The Cultural Contribution of the Other Ethnic Groups* (1969). The Commission's 1963 mandate was, as reported in its 1969 volume, to 'make recommendations designed to ensure the bilingual and basically bicultural character of the federal administration', and to find ways of 'promoting bilingualism, better cultural relations and a more wide-spread appreciation of the basically bicultural character of our country and of the subsequent contribution made by the other cultures'.

The Report's recommendations led to the 1969 Canadian Official Languages Act. By establishing French and English as the official languages of the country, this Act further reinforced the notion that the French and the British were the two founding nations of Canada. Still, the Act did very little to appease Quebec's anxiety about the sovereignty of its culture (in 1977 French was declared the single official language in Quebec), and accomplished little more in the rest of Canada. In English Canada, many of the objections were voiced in the western provinces, where there is a long-standing resistance to bilingualism and where ethnic groups, at the time notably Ukrainian-Canadians, felt further marginalized by the Act.

Indeed, the 1971 White Paper, Trudeau's policy of multiculturalism, and the subsequent Bill C-93, which passed while Brian Mulroney's government was getting ready for the 1988 elections, did nothing to realign the colonial ideology of official history. The White Paper was intended to preserve the heritage of 'the other cultures'; it reiterated that there are two official languages, but stressed that there were 'no official cultures'. In a similar fashion, Bill C-93 declared that, 'whereas ... English and French are the official languages of Canada', it proposes to 'recognize and promote the understanding that multiculturalism reflects the cultural and racial diversity of Canadian society', and promises 'to preserve, enhance and share their cultural heritage'. The 1971 policy does not mention the First Nations peoples, and the 1988 Act specifically excludes them. The Canada Clause of the Charlottetown Agreement intended to rectify this omission by acknowledging the status of cultures other than those of the two official languages, but the Agreement was rejected (not necessarily for reasons related to multiculturalism) in the 1992 referendum. These are just a few of the factors that led to the official policy of multiculturalism. The legislative Acts as well as the events and political agendas that have given rise to them register some of the recent ways in which Canadian identity has wavered from one form of representation to another.

It is apparent that the history of Canadian multiculturalism is not a simple, linear narrative. It is a narrative that has many beginnings, a narrative that unravels in many directions. No matter what narrative thread we resolve to follow, some of the inherited perceptions about Canada have been decidedly altered. The land we now call Canada was already multicultural, and multilingual, before the arrival of the first Europeans. As J. McGee shows in his *Loyalist Mosaic* (1984), even the United Empire Loyalists who settled Upper Canada consisted of diverse ethnic groups. And George Elliott Clarke, in his comments cited in this anthology, makes it clear the origins of the Black people in the Maritimes go back to 1783 and 1815, when the Black Loyalists and Refugees arrived in Nova Scotia. The fact that the Dominion Parliament introduced an Immigration Act in 1906 intended to control the influx of Asian immigrants to Canada is not only an example in a series of discriminatory practices that belong, in effect, to the history of Canada's multiculturalism, but is also further evidence that the cohesiveness of Canadian identity has always been imaginary.

But not everyone would necessarily agree with this position. Multiculturalism signifies different things to different people, and has not been embraced with the same enthusiasm by all Canadians. Indeed, as Vic Satzewich points out,

> if multiculturalism is under attack from some for being too successful in promoting cultural pluralism, it is ironic that it has also come under attack by others for not promoting enough pluralism. That is, the traditional critique of multiculturalism has been that it promoted only symbolic ethnicity, or those aspects of non-anglo ethnic cultures which did not threaten the anglo-saxon dominated status quo.[13]

For some Canadians, then, the tolerance they see multiculturalism advocating threatens their understanding of Canadian history and augurs against the development of a cohesive Canadian identity, which they think should be the goal of the nation. For others, it is the very notion of tolerance to which they object, for tolerance alone does not promise that those who have traditionally been constructed as 'others' will be able fully to practise who they are as individual subjects. Along the same lines, multiculturalism has been attacked for offering a policy of containment, a policy which, by legislating 'otherness', attempts to control its diverse representations, to preserve the long-standing racial and ethnic hierarchies in Canada. The question of preservation has also been tackled in a different way, for some Canadians believe that the mandate of Bill C-93 to 'preserve' and 'enhance' the cultural heritage of Canadians other than those of Anglo-Saxon and French descent tends to promote stereotypical images of their cultures, and advocates a kind of ethnocentrism that might further prevent their integration into mainstream society. Thus while multiculturalism is expected to facilitate the process of decolonizing the inherited representations of Canadian history, the literary tradition, and other forms of culture, it is also seen as essentializing race and ethnicity, namely assigning to racial and ethnic differences, as well as their various expressions, attributes that are taken to be 'natural', and therefore stable.

In the field of literature, many of the contributors to *Making a Difference* have played a direct or indirect role in shaping our understanding of these arguments. As for myself, I believe that within this complex web of historical changes, cultural differences, and politics there still remains the fundamental question of what constitutes Canadian identity. But in the 1990s this question has been reconfigured, and, I think, irrevocably so. For we can no longer afford to think of Canadian identity in singular terms. Its imaginary cohesiveness has already collapsed upon itself. Nor can we afford to cavalierly dismiss the current interest in cultural differences as a mere fad, or an obsession. The recognition of cultural differences in the 1990s marks yet another beginning in Canadian multicultural history, the beginning of an attempt to understand how distinct identities can converge and dialogue with each other within Canada, how boundaries of difference must be repositioned—not in relation to the signs of 'centre' and 'margins' but in relation to new and productive alignments.

Making a Difference: Canadian Multicultural Literature is an instance of such a dialogue. The writing and the comments of the contributors in *Making a Difference* help animate some of Canada's multicultural realities. Students reading this anthology will discover how Canadian multicultural literature tugs at the seams of the fabric that is Canadian culture. They will see that for these writers, and for many others who could not be included in this collection, who we are as Canadians is contingent upon how we move from one context to another, how we cross the thresholds of memories, how we embrace or, for that matter, keep away from the differences we encounter, how we negotiate our histories in the context of other histories.

These kinds of convergences and negotiations have been the focus of an abundance of publications about multiculturalism, immigration experience, and the issues that pertain to the First Nations peoples within such disciplines as sociology, anthropology, law, political sciences and education. Yet Canadian literary criticism has shown a belated interest in these issues. Since the late 1980s, however, the increased publication of ethnic and Native anthologies and bibliographies, the various conferences and gatherings of writers aimed at resisting both the stereotypical reception of their work and the way they have been, if at all, represented in curricula, and the fact that now both large and small presses publish authors once considered to be only 'minor', have dramatically altered the amount and kinds of critical response to their work. As Enoch Padolsky says,

Twenty or thirty years ago literature in English Canada consisted primarily of writings by British-Canadian writers and a few individuals from a small number of Canadian ethnic minority groups (e.g., Icelandic, Jewish, Ukrainian). Today, Canadian literature reflects a much broader proportion of a changing Canadian society and both the number of writers and the group experiences represented have expanded dramatically. Not surprisingly, this increasing diversity is having an impact on the way Canadian literature is perceived, and a number of critical, theoretical, and institutional issues have arisen because of it. At the moment these issues are in the process of being absorbed into a literary critical scene which also reflects other kinds of theoretical and critical challenges (e.g., feminism, post-colonialism, new historicism) and though changes in Canadian literary scholarship with regard to ethnic minority writing are clearly in the wind, the resolution of these new issues still lies in the future.[14]

I have stressed the construction of identity as a primary concern in multicultural literature. But I am also arguing that the representation of the differences, as Padolsky points out, must not be seen exclusively in terms of the question of identity, no matter how identity is configured. The authors in *Making a Difference* write by following the trajectories of their imaginations, and these lead them along many and diverse paths.

✵ ✵ ✵

'The imagination has a history,' says Guy Davenport, a history 'as yet unwritten, and it has a geography, as yet only dimly seen.'[15] It is the imagination of the writers included in this anthology that *others* our perceptions of reality, that invokes the figure of identity, that shows their geographies and their communities, their concerns with love, family, gendered bodies, to be unlimited. Unlimited in that these writers show the histories of these spaces and images to be forever written, unlearned, revised, transplanted, invented. 'For,' as Iain Chambers says, 'to write is, of course, to travel.'[16] Reading through the poetry and fiction of the seventy-one authors in this anthology is indeed like taking a journey. It is a journey that takes us to many places, but also a journey that takes many forms and shapes. As the narrator of Yasmin Ladha's story says, directly addressing us as readers, 'Between you and me, there is no glint of a badge. Badges are razor sharp. Between you and me, the ink quivers.'

Much of the writing in *Making a Difference* involves actual travel, the kinds of departures and arrivals that accompany people of any diaspora. Diaspora—the dispersal of a people around the world—necessitated as it is often by major historical upheavals, carries along with it seeds from the original land that help the people on the move and their descendents to root themselves in the new place. The experience of displacement, the process of acculturation or integration, the gaps between generations, the tensions between individuals and their communities—these are some of the themes that inform diasporic literature. Sustaining a link with the past, paying homage to histories that one cannot afford to forget—or perhaps writing out of what they know best, as some writers would put it—is another important feature of diasporic writing.

For example, the poetry included here by Rachel Korn, A.M. Klein, and Irving

Layton is deeply rooted in the experiences of the Jewish diaspora. Within this context, the short story by J.J. Steinfeld is a literal dramatization of the Holocaust experience of the female narrator's mother. As she rehearses her role in her one-woman play, she both relives her mother's experiences and tries 'to escape the character' she plays. But she knows that, in many respects, this is not just a one-woman drama: the past, she admits, is also a 'tangible character' in the drama. Her acting is an acting out of the past, an attempt to come to terms with the demons of history. Both this woman and the female narrator of Helen Weinzweig's story are born in Radom, Poland, not a mere coincidence in the context of this literature, but a significant detail that helps us locate it historically. Art, this time painting, and movement between a marriage and a love affair are the ways in which Weinzweig's character attempts to deal with her memories.

In a different way, the fiction of Harold Sonny Ladoo and Arnold Itwaru directly addresses the places from which they come. They show their settings to be storied places, places layered with the impact of colonialism, colonial desire, and its detrimental effects, especially on women. The function of language as a means of control is Marlene Nourbese Philip's point of entry into her critique of colonialism. The different kinds of discourse that she uses in her poetry are aimed to reveal that tracing the genealogy of a self must also involve uncovering the genealogy of language, an issue that also characterizes Jamila Ismail's poetry.

Indeed, language—language not as a mere instrument of communication but language as that which constructs the articulations of ourselves—is a recurring concern for many of the writers in this anthology. The title of Dionne Brand's long poem, *No Language Is Neutral*, sections of which appear here, makes it clear that any neutrality attached to language only helps to conceal the various gestures of elision by which representation operates. 'No / language is neutral seared in the spine's unravelling. / Here is history too,' she says. And if this history, as I read her, is structured like a language, it is because the 'grammar' of the black people's experiences that she writes about bears the unmistakable signs of enslavement: 'talking was left for night and hush was idiom / and hot core.'

Fred Wah's desire 'to touch the sight of the letter oral tactile,' to chase his fleeting memories of his father's writing hand as it moves the 'silver, black, gold nib' of a pen across a page, to understand how language inhabits his body, is a desire that reflects our passage 'through the language of time'. He makes us aware of how we are, in a certain way, 'histographs', because the representations of ourselves reside in, and are always inscribed by, history, a concern manifested in different ways in Kristjana Gunnars's and Aritha van Herk's prose.

The writing act as a specific manifestation of language is another way in which language appears in this literature. Many of these poems and stories are, literally, scenes of writing, scenes in which we see a writer at work. In the journal entries that record Daphne Marlatt's first return to the place where she was brought up, she wonders how to 'get' everything 'down'. So we see her watching over her own writing act: 'How completely i learned to talk Canadian (how badly i wanted to). . . . Wonder how it sounds to you?' she says in a letter she writes back home. How to get everything down is the same question that seems to preoccupy the protagonist of Makeda

Silvera's story, a black woman who tries to be a writer while also trying to fulfil most of the roles expected of a woman.

Pressures similar to those that Silvera's protagonist experiences permeate much of the writing in this anthology. The questions of how gender is constructed, how the representation of gender impinges upon desire and sexuality, how who we are as men or women relates to where we come from are addressed in various ways by such authors as Claire Harris, Mary di Michele, Di Brandt, Yeshim Ternar, Sandra Birdsell, M.G. Vassanji, Ian Iqbal Rashid, Ven Begamudré, and Shyam Selvadurai. Ashok Mathur's story focuses these concerns on his protagonist's body, a body that is not transparent in that it cannot easily be read as male or female. Beyond questioning the conventional representations of gender difference, this story also brings to the fore one of the most significant issues in multicultural literature, that of racialization. Concern with racialization, the construction of images of ourselves or of others by relying on the loaded and biased ideological definitions of racial categories, one of the processes that leads to racism, surfaces in much of the writing in this anthology. Corinne Lee, Roy Miki, Joy Kogawa, and Himani Bannerji are some of the writers who directly address this issue.

If some of the writing in this anthology, as I have suggested, deals with themes that directly pertain to the diasporic experience, there are also authors here who write from a diametrically opposed experience: the knowledge of not having been separated at all from their lands, but having been systematically denied the right to their places and cultures. The writing of Beth Brant, Daniel David Moses, Thomas King, Jeannette Armstrong, and Lee Maracle, and many other First Nations authors and storytellers who could not be included here, is a reminder to other Canadians that we have all been travellers, that, somewhere in our personal or familial histories in the recent or distant past, we all belonged somewhere else. And what is most pertinent about this reminder is that the first foreign travellers who came here came under the pretence of coming to an empty land. At the end of Beth Brant's creation story, 'First Woman touched her body, feeling the movements inside. She touched the back of Mother and waited for the beings who would change her world.'

⊞ ⊞ ⊞

Making a Difference: Canadian Multicultural Literature is a gathering of voices that offer the reader only a sampling of what Canadian literature is about today. Beyond my own attempt here to introduce some of the contexts and concerns of this literature, it is the task of the readers to discover for themselves what these authors invite us to share with them.

'"Cultures" do not hold still for their portraits,' says James Clifford.[17] *Making a Difference* is a living and changing portrait of Canadian literature, a portrait that invites the reader in as one of the subjects. We portray ourselves by reading together.

NOTES

1 'Introduction: Invisible Center' in *Out There: Marginalization and Contemporary Cultures*, eds Russell Ferguson, Martha Gever, Trinh T. Minh-ha, and Cornel West (New York: The New Museum of Contemporary Art; Cambridge, Mass.: The MIT Press, 1990), p. 9.

2 'Editor's Note' in *Looking at the Words of our People: First Nations Analysis of Literature*, ed. Jeannette Armstrong (Penticton, B.C.: Theytus Books Ltd, 1993), p. 7.

3 As cited in Roy Miki, 'Inter-Face: Roy Kiyooka's Writing, A Commentary / Interview' in *Roy Kiyooka* (Vancouver: Artspeak Gallery and the Or Gallery, 1991), p. 48.

4 'Introduction', *All My Relations: An Anthology of Contemporary Canadian Native Fiction* (Toronto: McClelland and Stewart, 1990), p. x.

5 'Introduction' in *A Passion for Identity: An Introduction to Canadian Studies*, eds Eli Mandel and David Taras (Toronto, New York: Methuen, 1987), p. 10.

6 *After Colonialism: Imperial Histories and Postcolonial Displacements*, ed. Gyan Prakash (Princeton, New Jersey: Princeton UP, 1995), p. 4.

7 *Canada's First Nations: A History of Founding Peoples from Earliest Times* (Toronto: McClelland and Stewart, 1992), p. 11.

8 'The "Post-Colonial" Imagination', *Fuse* 16, 1 (Fall 1992): 13.

9 'The "Post-Colonial" Imagination', p. 14.

10 'Cultural Identity and Diaspora' in *Colonial Discourse and Post-Colonial Theory: A Reader*, eds Patrick Williams and Laura Chrisman (New York: Columbia UP, 1994), p. 394.

11 'Immigration Policy and Multiculturalism' in *Ethnicity and Culture in Canada*, eds J.W. Berry and J.A. Laponce (Toronto: U of Toronto P, 1994), pp. 97, 98.

12 'Multiculturalism and the Global Information Society' in *Deconstructing a Nation: Immigration, Multiculturalism and Racism in '90s Canada*, ed. Vic Satzewich (Halifax, Nova Scotia: Fernwood Publishing, and Social Research Unit, Department of Sociology, University of Saskatchewan, 1992), p. 351.

13 'Introduction', *Deconstructing a Nation*, p. 15.

14 'Canadian Ethnic Minority Literature in English' in *Ethnicity and Culture in Canada*, p. 361.

15 *The Geography of the Imagination* (San Francisco: North Point Press, 1981), p. 4.

16 *Migrancy, Culture, Identity* (London and New York: Routledge Press, 1994), p. 10.

17 'Introduction: Partial Truths' in *Writing Culture: The Poetics and Politics of Ethnography*, eds James Clifford and George E. Marcus (Berkeley, Los Angeles, London: U of California P, 1986), p.10.

FREDERICK PHILIP GROVE

(1879-1948)

In his second book on Frederick Philip Grove, *FPG: The European Years* (1973), Douglas O. Spettigue says 'There is still much too little known about our literary forefathers; it will take our joint efforts to do them justice.' The notion of Grove as one of our Canadian 'literary forefathers' was at the time a rare instance of claiming an immigrant author as a forefather of the Canadian literary tradition. Whether he is one of 'us', or a 'stranger', as Ronald Sutherland once called him, Grove has long been a major, albeit controversial, figure in Canadian literature. From the first book he wrote in English, *Over Prairie Trails* (1922), which chronicles his winter-time commuting as a teacher in Manitoba, and his first Canadian novel, *Settlers of the Marsh* (1925), to his later novel, *The Master of the Mill* (1944), Grove's writing has commanded critical attention ranging from exaggerated or qualified praise to rejection. He won the Lorne Pierce Medal in 1934, was elected a Fellow of the Royal Society of Canada in 1941, and received the Governor General's Award for his fictionalized autobiography, *In Search of Myself* (1946). This kind of recognition, however, did not lessen Grove's feelings of neglect.

Beyond the ongoing critical debates about the literary value of Grove's fiction, arguments about him have also revolved around his identity and origins. Until Spettigue resolved the mystery of 'who Grove really was', what we knew about Grove derived from his own autobiographical narratives, which proved to be largely fictional. Both in his writing and in his life, Grove kept reinventing his identity and origins. He was not, as he claimed to be, a Swedish national born in Moscow, nor was he the son of a wealthy landowner who, upon leaving Europe, emigrated first to Canada. And he was a novelist and a translator of literary titles before he became a writer in Canada.

Grove, a German national, was born Felix Paul Greve in Radomno, Prussia, a border town now in Poland. He was brought up and educated in Hamburg. Living in a style beyond his financial means, he had to borrow money, was charged with fraud, and ended up spending a year in prison. Failing to earn a living that would have allowed him to repay the debts he had accrued, Grove faked a suicide in 1909, and found his way to America. He was accompanied by Elsa Ploetz (a.k.a. Baroness Elsa von Freytag-Loringhoven, also a writer) whom he eventually abandoned somewhere in Kentucky before he came to Canada. Assuming the name Fred Grove, he worked as a schoolteacher in the Mennonite regions of Manitoba, where he began to write. He moved to Ottawa in 1929, and, a year later, to a farm near Simcoe, Ontario, where he made a failed attempt to raise cattle.

As was made obvious by the great success of his three lecture tours across Canada in 1928 and 1929, Grove's audience at the time was well aware of what his life choices and writing represented. In Margaret Stobie's words, 'Here was an ideal subject for the Canadian Clubs—an immigrant who had tried life in the United States, spurned it, and chosen Canada; a New Canadian who could give voice to the silent strangers, who could reveal their needs, trials, and dreams to their would-be helpers.' With public lectures such as 'Canadians Old and New' and 'Assimilation', Grove participated in the vigorous debates of the twenties about immigration. In a tone that was ironic and extremely confident, Grove chastized the 'old' Canadians for not making the 'newcomers . . . feel at home'. Acknowledging the values inherent in the indigenous literary traditions of immigrants, Grove passionately argued that, 'If assimilation means the absorption of one race by another, the absorbing race not to undergo any change by the process, then there is no such thing as assimilation.'

The struggles of early immigrants that Grove wrote about in epic and tragic terms, and the frankness with which he approached the living conditions of women immigrants, make his writing exemplary of many of the patterns that characterize migrant experience. Interestingly enough, his immigrant characters rarely, if at all, reflect a nostalgia for their origins or a need to align themselves with other members of their ethnic group. For example, the itinerant life of Phil, one of Grove's invented selves, in *A Search for America* (1927), expresses a kind of individualism modelled after Rousseau and Thoreau, rather than a desire to assert ethnic difference; indeed, Phil is often indifferent to, if not contemptuous of, the other immigrants he encounters. This is not the case, however, in the short story that follows, where Niels, a character who is also the protagonist of Grove's *Settlers of the Marsh*, finds encouragement in the presence of another Swedish immigrant.

The First Day of an Immigrant

About six miles west of the little prairie town of Balfour, twelve miles south of another little town called Minor, hard on the bank of the Muddy River which gurgles darkly and sluggishly along, there lies a prosperous farm, a very symbol of harvest and ease. Far and wide the red hip-roof of its gigantic barn shows above the trees that fringe the river which hardly deserves that name, seeing that it is no more than a creek. The commodious, white-painted dwelling, with its roofed-over porch and its glassed-in veranda, however, reveals itself for a moment only as you pass the gate of the yard while driving along the east-west road that leads past it, a few hundred feet to the north; for the old, once primeval bush has been carefully preserved here to enclose and to shelter the homestead; and the tall trees, with their small leaves always aquiver, aspen leaves, while screening the yard from view, seem at the same time to invite you to enter and to linger.

The east-west road cuts right through the property, leaving the level fields, at least the greater part of them, three hundred and twenty acres, to the north, while the yard nestles to the south in a bend of the little river which, curiously, makes the impression as if it were introduced into this landscape for the sole purpose of enfolding this home of man. Beyond the river, there is the remainder of another quarter section the greater part of which serves as pasture. Huge, sleek, gaily coloured cows and frisky colts, accompanied by anxious mares, have at all times access to the black-bottomed water.

The gates to both sides of the road—the one leading to the yard, and the other, opposite it, to the fields—stand open; and a black track leads across the grey-yellow highway from one to the other. There, humus from the field is ground together with the clay of the grade into an exceedingly fine and light dust, perfectly dry, which betrays that many loads have already passed from the field to the yard.

It is a beautiful, crisp, and sunny morning of that reminiscent revival of things past which we call the Indian summer. A far corner of the fields, to the north-west, is bustling with the threshing crews. Engine and separator fill the air with their pulsating hum; and the yellow chaff of the straw comes drifting over the stubble and crosses the road and enters even the yard, threading its way through the trees which, apart from the trembling leaves, stand motionless, and through the entrance that winds in a leisurely way through their aisles. Slowly the chaff filters down, like fine, dry, light snow.

Now and then a wagon, drawn by heavy horses and heavily laden with bags of grain, passes slowly over the road; and every now and then an empty wagon—empty except for a pile of bags on its floor—rattles out in the opposite direction, going to the scene of operations in the field. From the gate a diagonal trail leads through the stubble to the engine; it is cut a few inches deep into the soft soil and worn smooth and hard by many haulings.

That happens just now; let us jump on at the back and go with the driver, an elderly, bearded man of unmistakably Scottish cast: broad-shouldered and heavily set, his grave, though not unpleasant face dusted over with grime and chaff. The wagon, being without a load, rattles along; the horses trot.

Twice the driver has to get out of the trail in order to let a load pass on its way to the yard. To the left, the ground now slopes down a grassy slough in which here and there a clump of willows breaks the monotony of the prairie landscape; no doubt this slough holds water in spring; but at present it is perfectly dry. At its far end, beyond the threshing outfit, an enormous hay-stack rises on its sloping bank.

Now we are in the field of operations. All about, long rows of stooks dot the stubble, big stooks of heavy sheaves. Hay-racks drive from one to the other, one man walking alongside and picking up the sheaves with his fork, pitching them up to another who receives and piles them on the load. Here the work proceeds in a leisurely, unhurried way which contrasts strangely with the scene ahead. The horses do not need to be guided; they know their work; a word from the man on the load is enough to tell them what is wanted.

We have reached the vibrating machines now, joined by a huge, swinging belt. But our Scotsman has to wait a few minutes before he can drive up to the spout that delivers the grain, for another teamster is filling the last of his bags.

Two or three hay-racks, loaded high with sheaves, stand waiting alongside the engine that hums its harvest song. The drivers are lazily reclining on their loads while they wait for those who are ahead of them to finish. They do not even sit up when they move a place forward; the horses know as well as their drivers what is expected of them. Here, the air is thick with chaff and dust.

The few older men in the crew set the pace; the younger ones, some of them inclined to take things easy, have to follow. Those who are alongside the feeder platform, pitching the sheaves, do not make the impression of leisurely laziness.

The engineer, in a black, greasy pair of overalls, is busy with long-spouted oil-can and a huge handful of cottonwaste. The 'separator-man' stands on top of his mighty machine, exchanging bantering talk with the pitching men.

'Let her come, Jim,' he shouts to one of the men, a tall, good-looking youth who works with a sort of defiant composure, not exactly lazily but as if he were carefully calculating his speed to yield just a reasonable day's work and no more; a cynical smile plays in his young, unruffled face. 'Let her come,' the separator-man repeats. 'Can't choke her up.'

'Can't?' challenges Jim's partner, a swarthy, unmistakably foreign-looking man.

And from the opposite side of the feeder-platform another foreigner, a Swede, a giant of a man, six feet four inches tall and proportionately built, shouts over, 'We'll see about that.' He is alone on his load, for, as usual, the crew is short-handed; and he has volunteered to pitch and load by himself.

And this giant, the Swede, starts to work like one possessed, pitching down the sheaves as if his life depended on choking the machine. The Ruthenian, on the near side, follows his example; but Jim, a piece of straw in the corner of his smiling mouth, remains uninfected. He proceeds in his nonchalant way which is almost provoking, almost contemptuous.

All about, the drivers on their loads are sitting up; this is a sporting proposition; and as such it arouses a general interest. Even the Scotsman follows proceedings with a smile.

But apart from these, there has been another looker-on. The outfit stands a few hundred feet from the edge of the slough which stretches its broad trough of hay-land slantways across this end of the field; and there, among some willows, stands a medium-sized man, with a cardboard suit-case at his feet and a bundle hanging from the end of a stout cane that rests on his shoulder. He is neither slender nor stout, five feet and eleven inches tall, and dressed in a new suit of overalls, stiff with newness, his flaxen-haired head covered with a blue-denim cap that, on its band, displays the advertisement of a certain brand of lubricating oil. His clean-shaven face is broadened by a grin as he watches the frantic efforts of the two men on their respective loads. His is an almost ridiculous figure; for he looks so foreign and absurd, the more so as his effort to adapt himself to the ways of the country is obvious and unsuccessful.

But he watches idly for only a very few seconds. Then he drops bundle and cane and runs, circling the engine, to the side of the Swede. There he looks about for a moment, finds a spare fork sticking with its prongs in the loose soil under the feeder-platform, grabs it, vaults up on the load of the giant, and, without a word of explanation, begins to pitch as frantically as the other two. The loads seem to melt away from under their feet.

The grimy separator-man on top of his machine laughs and rubs his hands. His teeth look strangely white in his dust-blackened face; his tongue and gums, when they show, strangely pink, as in the face of a negro. 'Let her come, boys,' he shouts again, above the din of the machine, 'let her come. Can't choke her up, I tell you. She's a forty-two. But try!' From his words speaks that pride which the craftsman takes in his tools and his output. He looks strange as he stands there, in the dust-laden air, on the shaking machine; his very clothes seem to vibrate; and in them his limbs and his body; he looks like a figure drawn with a trembling hand.

A fixed, nearly apologetic grin does not leave the face of the unbidden helper. There is good-nature in this grin; but also embarrassment and the vacancy of non-comprehension.

The elderly Scotsman who came out a little while ago has meanwhile driven up to the grain-spout and is filling his bags. He keeps watching the newcomer, putting two and two together in his mind. And when his load is made up at last, he detaches himself from the group, casting a last, wondering look at the man who is pitching as if he were engaged on piece-work; for, when the Swede has finished his load, this stranger has simply taken his place on the next one that has come along.

Then the Scotsman threads once more the diagonal trail across the field, staying on it this time when he meets another wagon, for the man with the load, such is the rule, has the right-of-way; and finally, when he reaches the gate, he drives through it and across the road, and on into the welcome shade. For the length of a few rods the entrance leads through the gap between the huge, park-like trees, and then it widens out into the yard. Right in front stands the house, a large, comfortable, and easy-going affair with a look of relaxation about it, though, no doubt, at present nobody there has time to relax, for, red from the heat of the ranges, women are frantically preparing the noon-day meal for the many-mouthed, hungry monster, the crew. The huge and towering barn, painted red, occupies the west side of the yard; and beyond it, a smaller building—it, too, painted red—is the granary for which the load is bound.

In its dark interior a man is working, shovelling wheat to the back. He is tall, standing more than six feet high, broad-shouldered but lean, almost gaunt. His narrow face is divided by a grey moustache which, as he straightens his back, he rubs with the back of his hand in order to free it from the chaff that has collected in its hairs. He is covered all over with the dust of the grain.

When the wagon approaches, he looks out and asks, 'How many, Jim?'

Jim is backing his load against the open door. 'Twenty-four,' he answers over his shoulder.

The man inside takes a pencil suspended by a string from a nail and makes note of the number on a piece of card-board tacked to the wall. Thus he keeps track of the approximate number of bushels, counting two and a half to the bag.

Jim, having tied his lines to the seat, tilts the first of the bags, and the man inside receives it on his shoulder and empties it into the bin to the left. That bin is already filled to one third of its height.

Jim speaks. 'Got a new hand, Dave?' he asks.

'Not that I know of,' replies the man inside with a questioning inflection.

'Fellow came about an hour ago, climbed up on a load, and started to pitch. Good worker, too, it seems.'

'That so?' Dave says. 'I could use another man well enough. But I didn't know about him.'

'Looks like a Swede.'

'Better send him over.'

So, when Jim, the Scotsman, returns to the field, he shouts to the stranger, above the din of machine and engine. 'Hi, you!' And when the stranger turns, he adds, 'Boss wants to see you,' nodding his head backwards in the direction of the yard.

But the stranger merely grins vacantly and, with exaggerated motion, shrugs his shoulders.

The others all look at Jim and laugh. So he, shrugging his shoulders in turn, drives on and takes his place behind the wagon at the spout.

Two more hours pass by; and still the stranger goes on with his unbidden work. The sun, on his path, nears the noon. Meanwhile the stranger has been the partner of all the men who drive up on his side of the outfit: but only one of them has spoken to him, that giant of a Swede who was the first man whom he helped. This giant is clean-shaven and dressed with a striking neatness, yes, a rustic foppishness which shows through all the dust and chaff with which he is covered. He does not wear overalls but a flannel shirt and corduroy trousers tucked into high boots ornamented with a line of coloured stitching along their upper edge. Those of the others who address him call him Nelson.

'Aer du Svensk?' he has asked of the stranger. 'Are you a Swede?'

'Yo,' the stranger has replied in the affirmative.

And further questions have brought out the fact that he has just arrived from the east, on a through-ticket reading from Malmoe in Sweden to Balfour, Manitoba, Canada. 'You'll find lots of Swedes up there,' the agent had told him at home, at Karlskrona in Blekinge, whence he hails.

Nelson grins when he hears that tale. Three years ago, when he himself left Sweden, he was told the same thing; but when he arrived, he found that the Swedish settlement was small and considerably farther north. Thus he has become wise in the tricks of the steamship-agent's trade. 'Did the boss hire you?' he asks, speaking Swedish, of course, while they proceed with the work in hand.

'No. I haven't seen anybody yet. But I do want work.'

'Better see him at noon. What's your name?'

'Niels Lindstedt.'

'Come with me when the whistle blows,' says Nelson as he drives away.

The brief conversation has cheered Niels greatly.

'I am in luck,' he thinks, 'to meet a Swede right away, a friend to help me in getting started.'

In Balfour, where he had landed very early in the morning, he had almost lost courage when he had found that nobody understood him. But at the hardware store a man—the same who had made him a present of the cap he was wearing—had made signs to him as if pitching sheaves, meanwhile talking to him, tentatively, in short monosyllables, apparently asking questions. Niels had understood this sign language sufficiently to know that he was trying to find out whether he wanted work in the harvest fields; and so he had nodded. Next the hardware dealer had made clear to him, again by signs, that his clothes were unsuitable for work; for he had been dressed in a black cloth suit, stiff and heavy, the kind that lasts the people at home a lifetime, so strong that even years of wearing do not flatten out the seams. He had shown him the way to a store where he had acquired what he needed, till he thought that now he looked exactly like a Canadian. Then he had once more returned to the hardware store, and the friendly man had put him on the road, pushing him by the shoulder and pointing and shouting directions till he had picked up his suitcase and the bundle with the clothes he had been wearing and had started out. When, after a few hundred yards, he had looked back, the hardware man had still been standing at the corner of his street and nodding and waving his arm, for him to go on and on, for many miles. And he had done so.

Most of the men with whom he has been working are foreigners themselves. Niels knows the English or Canadian type sufficiently already to recognize that. Some are Slavonic, some German; though they, too, seem to have Russian blood.

Niels exults in the work. After the enforced idleness of the passage across the ocean and the cramped trip in the train, it feels good to be at work in the open. He wonders whether he will be paid for what he does. He is hungry, for he has had no breakfast; and so he hopes he will get his dinner at least. Probably, he thinks, that will be all he is entitled to. He has heard, of course, of the fabulous wages paid to the workingman in America. But possibly that is no more than idle talk. As hunger and the consequent exhaustion lay hold of him, he begins to view things pessimistically.

The size of the field about him dazes him. The owner, he thinks, must be some nobleman. Will a field one tenth, one fiftieth of the size of this one some day be within his own reach, he wonders? The mere thought of it sends him once more into a fury of work; again he pitches the sheaves like one possessed.

Then, suddenly, startlingly, the noon whistle blows from the engine; and when he sees Nelson, the giant, just arriving on top of a load of sheaves, he runs over and helps him to unhitch his horses.

'Come on,' says Nelson and starts off, running and galloping his horses, in order to snatch a ride on a hay-rack which is returning empty to the yard. The rack waits for them, and they climb on, Nelson leading his horses behind.

When the team is stabled in the huge barn where Niels looks about and marvels, the two go over to the granary and find Dave Porter, the boss. Dave looks Niels over and asks a few questions, Nelson interpreting for his new friend.

A few minutes later the newcomer is hired at current wages of four dollars a day till threshing is over; and if he cares to stay after that, at a dollar and fifty a day for plowing till it snows or freezes up. Niels gasps at the figures and has to recalculate them in Swedish money, multiplying them by four: sixteen and six Kroner a day! There must be a mistake, he thinks; he cannot have heard right. The wages must be for the week. But when Dave turns away and Niels asks Nelson, the giant laughs and says, 'No. No mistake.'

So they turn and walk over to the house for dinner.

Niels is quick to learn; and by the time he has had his dinner and gone over the yard with Nelson while they are waiting for the horses to finish theirs, he has picked up much of the new country's lore.

In the granary where they return Niels shows him the figures jotted down on the piece of card-board which show that already the huge bins hold eight thousand bushels of oats, four thousand of barley, and three thousand of wheat. Niels is awed by the enormity of these quantities. There is a strange sort of exhilaration in them. He merely pronounces the figures and has to laugh; and something very like tears comes into his eyes. Nelson chimes in with his throaty bass. No, Niels does not feel sorry that he has come out into this west.

Yet, when the horses are taken out again and the two new friends once more find room on an empty hay-rack, to return to the field, there is a shadow on his consciousness. At dinner, in the house, he has become aware of a certain attitude towards himself, an attitude assumed by those who were unmistakably Canadian. After all, this is not home; it is a strange country; and he is among strange people who look down upon him as if he were something inferior, something not to be taken as fully human. He does not understand that, of course. He has heard Jim, the cynical, good-looking young fellow say something to a number of the men who, like Niels himself, were apparently recent immigrants. Jim had contemptuously addressed them as 'You Galishans!' And it had been clear that they resented it. Niels does not quite see why they should; if they are Galicians, why should they mind being called by that name?

But he also understands that what they really resent is the tone in which it was said.

He wonders as he looks about while the horses trot briskly over the stubble whether in a few years' time this country will seem like home to him, as apparently it does to Nelson, his newly-won friend.

And with that he turns his mind away from his critical thoughts and back to his dreams. He sees himself established on a small farm of his own, with a woman in the house; and he sees the two of them sitting by lamp-light in a neat little living room of that house while from upstairs there sounds down to them the pitter-patter of little children's feet—his own little children's, romping before they crawl into their snug little beds.

That is his vision: the vision that has brought him into these broad plains. And that vision is destined to shape his whole life in the future.

LAURA GOODMAN SALVERSON ◈

(1890-1970)

The daughter of Icelandic immigrant parents, Laura Goodman Salverson was born in Winnipeg but spent her early years moving with her poor family from place to place, crossing the American and Canadian border more than once. Her nomadic life continued after her marriage in 1913 to George Salverson, an American-born railway employee of Norwegian descent. Although as a child she often felt embarrassed because of her parents' ethnic differences, Salverson's devotion to her art and her pride in her Icelandic heritage can be traced back to their encouragement. Despite the deprivations she experienced as a child, and her interrupted education because of her frail health and her family's moves, she was a voracious reader from early age, and decided to 'write a book . . . and . . . write it in English'. She was ten when she began to learn what she called 'the greatest language in the whole world!' And she kept her promise to herself by writing the first Canadian ethnic novel in English, *The Viking Heart* (1923), which established her reputation as one of the most talented Canadian writers of the time.

A narrative that records with almost documentary accuracy the mass migration of 1400 Icelanders to Canada in 1876, this novel announced Salverson's persistent concern with the theme of immigrant dislocation and the dilemma of maintaining one's ethnic traditions or opting for integration that run through her other two novels, *When Sparrows Fall* (1925) and *The Dark Weaver* (1937). The latter won Salverson her first Governor General's Award. She received a second Governor General's Award for her autobiography, *Confessions of an Immigrant's Daughter* (1939).

A regular contributor to such magazines as *Maclean's* and *Chatelaine*, Salverson enjoyed national and international recognition (the Institute of Arts and Letters in Paris awarded her a gold medal in 1939) early in her career. However, perhaps because her other books, including *Lord of the Silver Dragon: A Romance of Leif the Lucky* (1927), *The Dove of El-Djezaire* (1933), and *Immortal Rock* (1954), were written in the manner of the historical romance, her reputation later dwindled. Although she is considered to be a forerunner of Canadian prairie fiction, her work has received only scant attention in recent years.

The selection that follows, a chapter from *The Viking Heart*, is about the birth of Thor. Although a third-generation Canadian, Thor's Canadianness is achieved, later in the novel, only after he dies at Passchendaele an ironic and symbolic death as an Icelander.

THE COMING OF THOR

> White as a white sail on a dusky sea,
> When half the horizon's clouded and half free
> Fluttering between the dun wave and the sky
> Is hope's last gleam in man's extremity.
>
> —*Lord Byron.*

All day the wind had swept angrily about the little house in the clearing, whistling down the chimney and rattling the panes of the little windows. Now it was beginning to snow. The white flakes whirled about in furious eddies, reluctant to descend to the brown earth. The big trees, sentinels around the patch of cleared land, rocked their branches drunkenly, muttered ominously among themselves. It had been a wild day and the coming night promised no respite.

This storm-beaten house, some sixteen by twenty feet in dimension, with its pole and mud roof and its gloomy log walls, was the hard-earned home of Bjorn Lindal. He had been in the new settlement, which was spreading from the lake front all along the Icelandic River, only about two years.

His neighbours considered him an upright and ambitious man. They said among themselves that they were surprised a man who spoke English so well should not stay in Winnipeg, whence he had come, rather than go into the wilderness of this colony. His wife they had considered a bit odd at first—a silent woman, with eyes that were far too disconcerting to please them and with far too fine an opinion of what a back-woodsman's wife should be. They had whispered of her eccentricities among themselves but had generally been disinterested enough in her presence.

It was not until she had nursed Mrs Johnson—never called anything but Finna in the manner of the Icelander who addresses every associate by his Christian name—with efficiency and true neighbourliness, that she and her 'queer' ideas were accepted as part of them.

They learned that she had suffered much. That she had been separated from her parents immediately upon coming to Winnipeg from the Old Country, and that for many months she had had no tidings of them. Then there had come news to the farm where she had worked of a frightful epidemic which had broken out among her countrymen at Gimli. For months no further communication had been possible. Then, after nearly two years of weary waiting she had learned that both father and sister had died of the plague. Her mother had been spared, but only to enter upon a long, trying invalidism, the result of hardship and the ravages of smallpox.

The new neighbours of the Lindals grew tender and ashamed of past criticisms when it was whispered that the young Borga, taking her small earnings, had set out on foot in the dead of winter upon the sixty-mile journey to Gimli, that she might spend with her mother the last few months of life remaining to that tortured body with its unbroken spirit.

Over coffee cups, on delightful occasions when the toil-worn women of the neighbourhood got together, there was also repeated the joyous gossip of Mrs Lindal's love affair.

'But a long hard time they had of it, the poor darlings!' Finna, the enthusiast and leading gossip, usually commenced. 'Four long years they never met—picture it! And to think that they were still faithful! Not that I wonder Bjorn couldn't forget her,' she would hastily amend, loving Mrs Lindal dearly. 'Nor was it that he put off going to see her. But you see, like a foolish fellow, he went on a hunting trip with some free trader who made glittering promises of a lot of money to be made; he was gone for over a year, and picture it——! The Trading Post judged his furs all poor. Then he was taken sick with one of these new-fangled fevers they get in this country and when he could go in search of Borga she had already gone to Gimli. It's just like a book the way they finally met! Borga returned to Winnipeg and had gone to work in St Boniface after her mother died. Picture it,' she would emphasize her tale, 'how it was for the poor girl, twenty rooms to care for and only eight dollars a month, and no mother! And maybe what's worse—though I shouldn't say it who's a mother myself—no hope of seeing her young man again. But on Easter the Lord somehow moved the old crank she had worked for to let her go to church in the evening. Mrs Lindal had so wanted to see the new church on Pacific and Nina—I've heard it's a very fine church—and there they met!

'Oh dear, oh dear—but picture yourself how it must have been. But even then they couldn't get married for five years. Both wanting to start out grand with a stove and a kettle and a mattress and what not.'

So had the coming of the Lindals been an event in the life of the colony and no less an experience in the lives of the Lindals. For the first four years of married life they had lived in Winnipeg and Borga had worked out as long as she could. But after their two little girls were born, Bjorn decided it would be wiser to take a homestead. He had saved a little money and could start in what was then considered a promising way.

But now upon this stormy day, an event old as life, yet ever new, was impending; an event which was destined to change the current of their lives.

Inside the one-roomed cabin at first glance all seemed peaceful. The big stove, shining and black, gave out a grateful heat, and a fantastic, fitful light flickered in the gleaming tins hanging on the opposite wall. There was a long pine table with benches pushed under it standing nearby and a large cupboard, well-made and neatly painted. In the far end of the room was a bed, and opposite this a bunk. Between these two stood a chest of drawers and at the foot of the bed a 'kofort', an Icelandic trunk. With the exception of a few old odd chairs, there was nothing else in the way of furniture. But on a shelf upon the wall over the chest of drawers was a row of ragged books and a good clock. These were the Lindal treasures.

The two little girls, Elizabeth, a grave, dark-haired child of five with her mother's expressive eyes, and Ninna, a golden cherub of three—her father's idol—squatted beside the fire munching bits of bread. Their mother sat hunched upon a chair by the bed; aware that once again her hour had come. Taut and expectant, listening to every sound and shuddering to hear the rising wind, she moved heavily to the stove to replenish the fire. Again and yet again she crossed to the window, blowing upon the frosted pane to peer out into the black night. What could be keeping him! Surely no evil had befallen? Why, tonight of all nights, must he be so late?

The grateful sound came at last—a heavy grinding of wheels on the frozen earth and the creaking of leather—familiar sounds that told her Bjorn was safe. He did not come to the house immediately. That was not his way. He would be unharnessing the tired oxen; putting them under shelter for the night. But now she wanted him— needed him as never before. She thought of sending little Elizabeth to call him. But the small voice would be lost in the howling wind. She must wait. Only a matter of minutes now. Hang on to the tortured nerves. Hang on tight—and pray.

Bjorn entered at last, covered with snow and stiff with cold. All day he had been cutting firewood in the North Quarter, but he quickly forgot his own weariness at sight of Borga's drawn face. He pushed aside the children who had run to meet him and hurried to his wife. 'My dear, you're not well—Borga!—you don't suppose—but what have I been thinking of!' As his agitation mounted Borga tried to smile at him.

'Don't worry, Bjorn. It's all right.' She was breathless. 'I'm afraid you'll have to go for Finna.'

'Yes, of course,' his voice was strained, his eyes anxious. 'Is there nothing I can do before I go——'

She was seized with pain and could not answer him. When the spasm passed she pointed to the stove. He understood and hurriedly crammed the firebox to capacity. Then, with a final word of comfort for her, he plunged into the storm.

Love lends wings to the clumsiest of feet; in an incredibly short time Bjorn had covered the two-mile trip to Finna's isolated homestead. Now they were back, half frozen but victorious over wind and weather and icy trails. Poor Finna, very close to exhaustion, puffed a little as she shook off her frosted reefer but a glance at her patient put all else out of mind. She had come none too soon. Borga lay across the bed tortured with pain that only women suffer. What was worse she had a queer, fevered look which Finna thought unnatural. She was right in her fears. This was to be a battle where the valour displayed might have honoured any military field. A battle such as the pioneering mothers of our country faced again and again without hope of either laurels or praise.

Finna, dripping with sweat, and filled with aching compassion, worked with her patient, trying everything she knew, and none of it was of the slightest avail. Bjorn was as a man demented, pacing the floor like a caged lion, pestering the poor woman with endless questions. Impelled to do something, he stoked the fire until the little room became a furnace of heat. In desperation Finna ordered him out for water. He filled every vessel in the house! Then, beside himself with the thought of Borga's suffering, he rushed into the woodshed and by the light of the lantern started sawing the wet green logs he had just dragged home.

The wind had slacked a little but the snow fell in a steady thickening shower, blanketing the earth in a winding sheet of white silence. Bjorn shuddered and went at his task as though his life depended upon it. He did not want to think of what was happening in the house. He had never visualized such pain. It was monstrous! Indecent! Dreadful to feel so helpless! His bitter thoughts were arrested by a sharp call from the house. The saw dropped from his nerveless hand and he stumbled forward.

In the red glare of light from the open doorway Finna stood as if rooted in a gateway of flame. It lent her a terrifying aspect—terrifying as her words. 'Bjorn, Bjorn— I'm quite beside myself!' she cried, 'I've done all I can—it's not enough. Then it came to me there is a midwife from Winnipeg. At the Fjalsteds. She might help us—she's GOT to help us, Bjorn!'

She fetched his greatcoat while he harnessed the oxen, and made him drink a mug of hot coffee before he started. 'Man dear, drink it down,' she told him, 'You'll need it . . . there now! let me help you with that muffler. It's a long cold night before you, Bjorn. Take care you don't freeze. It won't do Borga any good to have a cripple on her hands as well as a new baby when she's up again.'

When she's up again! It was a small crumb of comfort to the frightened man.

'Here, mind you take the whip!' Finna thrust it at him. 'I'm not for sparing cattle, God save us, in a time like this.'

When he was gone she leaned against the door for a moment, hands pressed over her swollen eyes. 'Oh, dear Lord, if you ever hear a poor woman like me, prove it now . . . give speed to those poor creatures' feet.'

There was need enough for that frantic prayer. Bjorn had five miles of almost snow-bound, newly-broken trail before him. Faith may move mountains, but oxen move only so fast.

To Borga fighting her agonizing battle, and to the frightened woman waiting beside her, moments were endless, hours an eternity. Borga, stupefied with pain, did not hear the returning team, but Finna, with that unnatural keenness which nervousness gives to the ear, heard the muffled thud of their feet an incredible distance off. She rushed into the storm to meet them. Impossible to wait quietly the remaining moments till they reached the house. She must satisfy herself that this was Bjorn and see if the stranger were with him. The creaking wagon drove up, and she saw that this was so.

The midwife climbed out and hurried into the house with only a simple greeting. Finna helped her off with her snow-covered wraps. The woman was half-frozen; she held her purple hands a few moments over the hot stove, then hurried to the bed. Borga was moaning pitifully, her strength badly spent. She had no further control over her nerves nor the groans that escaped her. The midwife saw with despair that her patient had long ago reached the stage where the over-worked muscles refused to do their appointed task. Borga was no longer a human machine, where mind and nerve and muscle labour rhythmically together. She was a body wracked with useless pain and fast slipping into a state of coma, the dearly bought anaesthetic of nature.

The midwife tried every means in her power to revive Borga's strength. She bathed her face and neck and hands in cold water. She gave her a stimulant and frequent sips of water. She applied compresses to try to increase muscular activity, but everything proved futile. Finally she turned to Finna hopelessly and admitted her defeat. Finna shrieked and threw up her hands imploringly. Bjorn, who had been sitting by the stove in a paralysis of fear, could bear no more. He was wild with terror. He paced the cabin like a panther. All this commotion awakened the little girls who mercifully had been sleeping through this night of horrors, and Ninna, setting up a shrill cry, ran in her fright to her father. But he had become a primitive thing—a creature caught in a net of impending destruction and driven frantic with his helplessness. He caught the frightened child roughly by the shoulder and shaking her fiercely, flung her aside. Just so in its fury might a captured brute tear at any stray object within its reach. The tiny Ninna, too surprised for tears, fled back to her bed and crawled into the sheltering quilts.

Bjorn looked after the flying figure, stupidly passing his hand across his brow. What he had done! Had he suddenly gone mad? A faint groan from the bed, more fearful in its frailty than stronger sound might be, whipped him into fuller consciousness.

He begged the women to do something. He implored fortune—or heaven—or the universe—or any power that be, to show mercy. He cursed the providence which for generations had forsaken his people. He cursed the world in which such things might be and cursed himself for coming to such a wilderness. The two women gazed at him, distracted, yet fascinated by his fury. He turned upon them wildly.

'For God's sake don't stand there doing nothing,' he shouted. 'Must she die like that in this God-forsaken hole? Isn't there ANY way to save her?'

Finna threw her apron over her head and rocked from side to side drearily. The midwife, the calmest person in the room, having been through similar experiences elsewhere, shook her head.

'Not without instruments,' she told him reluctantly.

'NOT without instruments——' he repeated this over and over, staring at her as if trying to grasp its meaning. There flashed through the harried mind of Bjorn a vision of two shining silver instruments. Two long, bowed bits of cold metal he had once seen in a doctor's case. Two magic bows of deliverance that have within their sharp embrace the power of granting life.

At once Bjorn ran to the cupboard hunting frantically through the various boxes and shelves till he found what he wanted. He faced the midwife with two silver soup spoons. They were old, long of handle, and worn to a thinness which allowed of their bending—heirlooms which had been brought to this country by his aunt.

'Look,' he said to the astonished women, holding aloft the two improvised forceps.

'Oh dear, oh dear, his mind's leaving him—maybe gone—poor man,' Finna whimpered.

But the midwife, having the open mind of a true physician which welcomes any new suggestion, saw at once the possibility, wild though it appeared.

She became at once self-possessed. A general. She ordered Finna to find some jug or jar for boiling water. There were no antiseptics of any kind, but believing that anything was better than nothing, she threw soda into the water and then plunged the spoons into it. She found a clean apron and put it on. She ordered more water. She made certain of blankets and rags, of scissors and cord, then these simple and doubtless unscientific preparations being made, she scrubbed her hands as best she could and set to work.

They worked like Trojans over the inert Borga, and at last, to their inexpressible joy, they were rewarded by that anxiously awaited sound, a baby's first greeting to the world.

'God save us, if it isn't a boy! Picture yourself what Borga will say,' Finna cried, almost in hysterics, then flew to warm the blanket.

Bjorn sank on his knees beside the bed and buried his head in the pillow beside Borga. He was shaking as with ague and wondered mutely how much one might endure and yet live. Finna, with tears streaming down her face, hushed the crying infant against her breast. And beside her patient stood the midwife, on her face that look of exultation which every hard-earned victory brings. On a chair at her side lay the two bent spoons.

Some hours later a very white and very big-eyed Borga whispered to her husband, smiling a wisp of a smile, 'He is my little storm child—Let us call him Thor.'

RACHEL KORN

(1898-1982)

Although Rachel (Rahel) Korn lived and wrote in relative obscurity in Canada, she was one of the most prominent poets to write in Yiddish, and won some of the most prestigious prizes for Yiddish literature, including the Segal prize. Born in Galicia (a region of the Austrian Empire annexed by Poland in 1919), Korn fled, with her daughter, to the Soviet Union after the German invasion of Poland, while many members of her family, including her husband, were killed by the Nazis. After some time in refugee camps she settled in Moscow, where she found a supportive environment within the circle of Yiddish writers.

Upon her return to Lodz, Poland, at the end of the war, she became an active member of the Yiddish Writers' Union, which she represented at an International PEN conference in Stockholm. She never went back to Poland, but emigrated to Montreal in 1949, where she lived until her death in 1982.

Her first poetry book, *Dorf* ('Country', 1928), was published in Vilna, one of the intellectual centres of Yiddish culture before the war, and it marked the beginning of a much-celebrated career. The two volumes of poetry she wrote next were about to be published in Kiev, but were among the many Yiddish manuscripts and books the Nazis destroyed. Like other Yiddish writers who became part of the Jewish diaspora, Korn published her work in various Yiddish cultural centres: *Haym un Haymlozikeit* ('Home and Homelessness', 1948) was published in Argentina; *Bashertkeit* ('Providence', 1949) in Montreal; *Vun Yener Zeit Lied* ('Beyond Poetry', 1962), and *Varbitene Vor* ('Changed Reality', 1977) in Tel Aviv—the latter being the last book she published.

A lyric poet who maintained an attachment to nature both as a place of spiritual uplifting and as a source of metaphors, Korn also wrote short stories and critical essays. Miriam Waddington, who has translated some of Korn's poetry into English, remarks that Korn's 'concerns are wide-ranging. . . . But whatever she writes comes from a woman's sensibility combined with a powerful intellect that expresses itself through her mastery of form in language and rhythm, through her amazing use of metaphor, and the deep emotional penetration of her themes.'

Korn's poetry in English translation has been published in two separate volumes, *Generations*, edited by Seymour Mayne and translated by various translators (1982), and *Paper Roses: Selected Poems of Rachel Korn*, translated by Seymour Levitan (1985).

THE WORDS OF MY ALEFBEYZ

The words of my *alefbeyz**
smelled of wild poppies and periwinkle
ripe wheat and hay,
but they were branded with a number at Treblinka,
charred in the smoke of Belzec and Maidanek.

Mourning a last sigh,
cradling an unsaid prayer,
they are the messengers of the ghetto kingdom,
survivors of bloodbath and betrayal.

They inscribe me on synagogue walls
in unheard supplication.
Carved into me,
I am the gravestone of my people.

When was it, how many years ago?
Under the blossoming cherry—
a wood bench, a table, a prayerbook,
points and lines like a new bridge
leading to the old shores of *tanakh*,**

and all at once, as if struck by the scent of milk and honey,
three—
a wasp, a fly, a bee—
settled and drank at the edge of the book.

Stillness, only the humming wasp and bee,
when Shmuel, my teacher,
lifted the letters with his narrow ruler,
unchained each one from the long line.

The blue sky looked at the page
through the white petals of the tree,
gave a fatherly wink
to the doves on the roof,
and all rose circling one by one,
weaving a wreath of fluttering white wings
around my head
as if each dark word
on the half-yellow page
was a seed sown by God
for their greedy beaks.

Stillness now too—the quiet of evening
and only the page I write
stirring under my hand,
offering a home to my half-forgotten childhood
and my wandering.

Translated by Seymour Levitan

alefbeyz — Hebrew alphabet; *alefbeyz* is the Yiddish pronunciation
**tanakh* — Holy Scriptures

HOME

How many years have passed
since I stepped across the threshold
for the last time?

A bridal canopy of turbid smoke
has spanned itself
above my one-time home
with its wrought-iron rail,
and they who led me down the aisle to my beloved
are Belzec and Maidenek.

And I,
fugitive from under that black pall
am homeless still,
a wanderer,
nomad, with no guide,
a leper
scarred by adversity and pain.

My needs are few,
a corner,
a roof for my sorrow
which trembles
beneath the chilling glance
from alien eyes.

How many years have passed
since I crossed my own threshold
for the last time?

My days and nights grown dim
with premonition
that my home hangs
suspended on a spider-thread
of memory.

Translated by Shulamis Yelin

A.M. KLEIN

(1909-1972)

'The true poet is he who, nourished upon the ancestral heritage, yet—if only in the slightest—deviates therefrom. Rooted in the common soil, he turns his eyes to new directions.' These words by A.M. Klein capture the ways in which he practised his poetry: by immersing himself in his Jewish heritage while renewing it by showing how it relates to the larger humanistic tradition.

A.M. (Abraham Moses) Klein was born in Ratno, in what is now Ukraine, and immigrated to Montreal with his family in 1910. The orthodox Jewish milieu in which he was brought up and his solid Jewish education had a profound influence on Klein's belief in the role the poet has to play in his community. In his 20s, he joined Young Judea, a Zionist youth movement, and later he became the Associate Director of the Zionist Organization of Canada, acted as the editor of *The Canadian Zionist*, worked as a speech writer for Samuel Bronfman, and was a contributing editor to *The Canadian Jewish Chronicle*. In 1949 his experiences on a research trip to Israel, Europe, and Northern Africa, commissioned by the Canadian Jewish Congress, led to his only novel, *The Second Scroll* (1951). Its complex and tightly structured narrative can be seen as a 'scripture' that comprises both the theological and secular histories of Klein's heritage, while evoking the modernist tradition as practised by James Joyce, a writer Klein admired and about whom he wrote.

A student at McGill University, he was associated with the *McGill Fortnightly Review* group of poets, and began publishing his poetry in both Canadian and American magazines. After he received his B.A. (1930), he studied law at the Université de Montréal. Following his graduation in 1933, he prac-

tised law for many years. *Hath Not A Jew* (1940) and *Poems* (1944) announced his lifelong commitment to exploring the victimization of Jews and celebrating their rich tradition. *The Hitleriad* (1944), in its mock-epic style, offers an indictment of Nazism by offering a satiric portrait of Hitler. *The Rocking Chair and Other Poems* (1945), which won the Governor General's Award, was highly acclaimed by critics and poets. Some of the poems in it, earlier published in the magazine *Poetry*, received the Edward Bland Prize, an award given by black Americans to poetry of social importance. This collection, focused as much on Jewish themes as on his Québécois environment, expressed Klein's belief that there was much that the Jewish and francophone communities of Quebec shared at the time: 'a minority position; ancient memories, and a desire for group survival. Moreover the French Canadian enjoys much—a continuing and distinctive culture, solidarity, *land*—which I would wish on my own people.' At the same time that these poems bear the strong signature of Klein's ethnicity, they express a universalist vision both about the function of the poet and the ways in which history can be redeemed.

In 1954, after the first signs of a psychological illness, he stopped practising law, and eventually stopped writing and withdrew from life. In recognition of his major contribution to Canadian literature, Klein received the Lorne Pierce Medal in 1957. Posthumous publications by Klein include *A.M. Klein: Literary Essays and Reviews* (1987), edited by Usher Caplan and M.W. Steinberg, *The Short Stories of A.M. Klein* (1983), edited by M.W. Steinberg, and *A.M. Klein: The Complete Poems* (1990), edited by Zailig Pollock.

AUTOBIOGRAPHICAL

1
Out of the ghetto streets where a Jewboy
Dreamed pavement into pleasant bible-land,
Out of the Yiddish slums where childhood met
The friendly beard, the loutish Sabbath-goy,
Or followed, proud, the Torah-escorting band,
Out of the jargoning city I regret,
Rise memories, like sparrows rising from
The gutter-scattered oats,
Like sadness sweet of synagogal hum,
Like Hebrew violins
Sobbing delight upon their eastern notes.

2
Again they ring their little bells, those doors
Deemed by the tender-year'd, magnificent:
Old Ashkenazi's cellar, sharp with spice;
The widows' double-parloured candy-stores
And nuggets sweet bought for one sweaty cent;
The warm fresh-smelling bakery, its pies,
Its cakes, its navel'd bellies of black bread;
The lintels candy-poled
Of barber-shop, bright-bottled, green, blue, red;
And fruit-stall piled, exotic,
And the big synagogue door, with letters of gold.

3
Again my kindergarten home is full—
Saturday night—with kin and compatriot:
My brothers playing Russian card-games; my
Mirroring sisters looking beautiful,
Humming the evening's imminent fox-trot;
My uncle Mayer, of blessed memory,
Still murmuring Maariv, counting holy words;
And the two strangers, come
Fiery from Volhynia's murderous hordes—
The cards and humming stop.
And I too swear revenge for that pogrom.

4
Occasions dear: the four-legged aleph named
And angel pennies dropping on my book;

The rabbi patting a coming scholar-head;
My mother, blessing candles, Sabbath-flamed,
Queenly in her Warsovian perruque;
My father pickabacking me to bed
To tell tall tales about the Baal Shem Tov,—
Letting me curl his beard.
O memory of unsurpassing love,
Love leading a brave child
Through childhood's ogred corridors, unfear'd!

5

The week in the country at my brother's—(May
He own fat cattle in the fields of heaven!)
Its picking of strawberries from grassy ditch,
Its odour of dogrose and of yellowing hay,—
Dusty, adventurous, sunny days, all seven!—
Still follow me, still warm me, still are rich
With the cow-tinkling peace of pastureland.
The meadow'd memory
Is sodded with its clover, and is spanned
By that same pillow'd sky
A boy on his back one day watched enviously.

6

And paved again the street: the shouting boys
Oblivious of mothers on the stoops
Playing the robust robbers and police,
The corn-cob battle,—all high-spirited noise
Competitive among the lot-drawn groups.
Another day, of shaken apple-trees
In the rich suburbs, and a furious dog,
And guilty boys in flight;
Hazelnut games, and games in the synagogue—
The burrs, the Haman rattle,
The Torah-dance on Simchas-Torah night.

7

Immortal days of the picture-calendar
Dear to me always with the virgin joy
Of the first flowering of senses five,
Discovering birds, or textures, or a star,
Or tastes sweet, sour, acid, those that cloy;
And perfumes. Never was I more alive.
All days thereafter are a dying-off,

A wandering away
From home and the familiar. The years doff
Their innocence.
No other day is ever like that day.

8
I am no old man fatuously intent
On memoirs, but in memory I seek
The strength and vividness of nonage days,
Not tranquil recollection of event.
It is a fabled city that I seek;
It stands in Space's vapours and Time's haze;
Thence comes my sadness in remembered joy
Constrictive of the throat;
Thence do I hear, as heard by a Jewboy
The Hebrew violins,
Delighting in the sobbed oriental note.

DOCTOR DRUMMOND

It is to be wondered whether he ever really
saw them, whether he knew them more than type,
whether, in fact, his occupational fun—
the doctor hearty over his opened grip—
did not confuse him into deducing
his patients' health and Irish from his own.

Certainly from his gay case-histories
that now
for two-tongued get-togethers are elocutional,
one would never have recognized his clientele.

Consider this patrician patronizing the *patois*,
consider his *habitants*, the homespun of their minds and motives,
and you will see them as he saw them—as *white* natives,
characters out of comical Quebec,
of speech neither Briton nor Breton, a fable folk,
a second class of aborigines,
docile, domesticate, very good employees,
so meek that even their sadness
made dialect for a joke.

One can well imagine the doctor,
in club, in parlour, or in smoking car,
building out of his practice a reputation
as raconteur.
But the true pulsing of their blood
his beat ignores,
and of the temperature of their days, the chills
of their despairs, the fevers of their faith,
his mercury is silent.

GEORGE FALUDY

(b. 1910)

By the time George (György) Faludy arrived in Canada in 1967, he was already one of the most important Hungarian poets in exile. His prominence was secured with the 1937 publication of *Villon Balladái* (*Ballads of Villon*). Despite, or perhaps because of, its great appeal and influence, the book was burned in Germany by the Nazis in 1943, and was confiscated four years later by the Hungarian Communist government. Until 1987 when he signed 'contracts with Hungarian publishers for editions of 50,000 copies each', that was Faludy's last book to appear in Hungary.

Born in Budapest, Faludy studied at the Universities of Berlin, Vienna, Graz, and Paris. His resistance to totalitarianism and bourgeois complacency, which forced him to go into exile, began while he served in the Hungarian army, where he was accused of engaging in anti-Nazi activities. Following his immigration to Paris in 1938 and subsequently to Morocco, he moved to the United States in 1941. While there, he enlisted in the American army, and was stationed at many locations in the United States.

His American sojourn led to his writing poetry in which he views the New World culture in America with critical irony. The poem included here is an early example of the poetry he wrote before returning to Hungary from New York in 1946. An ode, it employs Walt Whitman's grand style, but the exuberance of Whitmanesque rhetoric is parodically reversed to castigate the insidious anxieties and consumerism of daily life that Faludy saw as a threat to American culture.

Of the ten years that he lived in Hungary after his return as literary editor of *The Voice of the People*, three and a half were spent in detention. Accused of espionage on behalf of the Americans, he was imprisoned for six months in the secret headquarters of the Budapest police. Following this, he did three years of forced labour in a camp at Recsk (1950-53). He discussed those experiences, as well as his life in France, Africa and the United States, in his autobiography, *My Happy Days in Hell* (1962). After escaping from Hungary during the revolution of 1956,

he spent the next ten years in Europe, living in London, Italy, and Malta.

Hungarian friends in Toronto 'lured' him there in 1967 'with the promise of an academic position, which turned out to be non-existent'. Failing to find employment in Canada, he found himself lecturing at Columbia University in New York, while he continued to live in Toronto. Commuting between these two cities for three years, Faludy had ample opportunity to observe, and write about, the differences between their two cultures and life-styles. As many of his poems in *Learn This Poem of Mine by Heart* (1983) and *East and West: Selected Poems* (1978) illustrate, Faludy bemoaned the eroding impact of technology on American culture, and the tastelessness and crassness that assaulted his aesthetic and social sensibilities. The morality of Faludy's cultural stance toward the disintegration of civic order is summed up by the persona of Georgius, in the poem 'The Letter of Georgius, Byzantine emissary', published in his *összegyüjtött Versei* ('Collected Poems', 1980): 'The wall won't defend the burghers of the town / If the burghers do not defend the wall.'

Although 'Toronto is not Athens under Pericles,' as Faludy said, he wrote about his Canadian life with a brightness that often belied his general reproach of the contemporary human condition. After his wanderings from country to country, and having 'held five different passports', Faludy had no qualms in stating that Canada 'is the most marvellous decent society I have ever lived in. Not perfect, God knows, but *decent*.' *Notes from the Rainforest* (1988) records, in the form of diary entries and in a meditative style, his thoughts about, among other things, the cultural differences between Canada and the United States.

Faludy, who wrote poetry only in Hungarian, received honorary degrees from the University of Toronto (1978) and Bishop's University (1983), and was twice nominated for the Nobel Prize for Literature. Other Canadian publications by Faludy include *Twelve Sonnets* (1983), *Selected Poems 1933-1980* (1985), and *Corpses, Brats and Cricket Music* (1987).

GOODBYE, MY AMERICA
after Walt Whitman

1.

I outbellow you, O boat's fog-horn. O ocean, the hue of slate,
　　Like fog over asphalt,
Long Island appears there, slate-grey,
　　As it stands erect above the distant horizon,
As if to take its leave of me.
O continent, I am taking my leave of you, O country, where I
　　could remain, were it not that I had to go,
O country, where I was received as a guest, I rise now to my
　　feet to take my leave.
　　　　If I had one, I would tip my hat.

2.

O arid Arizona, O magical Colorado,
　　O New Jersey of slag-heaps,
O rock-bound Massachusetts, O wind-swept Indiana,
　　O Missouri of the lightning-bolts,
O endless plains of Kansas, and you who pained me so,
　　O Magyar-like Ohio,
You, the states over which I wandered, feared and loved,
　　Over which I suffered and succumbed:
O you, the Great Lakes of bored grey waters,
　　With these winds from Canada,
The forests of the Carolinas, the trailing moss among the trees,
　　So like the Gothic cathedrals,
Thrice-shaded coast of Maine, its green pine forest sloping
　　By greenish rocks into a sea of greenishness,
O pebbly-sea'd Nevada: O Salt Lake, its crimson mountains
　　like isles amid the snow,
Louisiana's coast, muskeg of the marsh,
　　Like mouldy skins forgotten in fields,
Downy Montana, sheep in their millions
　　On mildly shelving pasture-lands,
Violet-hued Wyoming, where solitary I might wander
　　Over passes unsuspected by birds,
And then you, immense Manhattan!

3.

O people, Scots, Swedes, Dutch, Philippinos,
　　Albanians, Portuguese,
You thriving Anglo-Saxons, you eight-children'd Italians,

You vanishing Indians,
You Negro cotton-pickers, you Polish shopkeepers,
    You Chinese laundrymen,
You Jewish cab-drivers, you Norse sailors,
    You half-breed quarrymen, Irish cops,
You, who have airplanes spray your fields of fruit
    And have garages for your cars,
Workers, awaiting your trains and clutching in your hands
    The handles of lunch-buckets, you,
You, who at bars down your whiskeys and never once greet
    The moon for the neon-signs,
Who occupy rented rooms and loiter on streetcorners,
    The sticky asphalt of summer evenings,
You, who naked in your sleep stare at the awesome
    Windowless walls of night, bleak and blank,
Who in salmon-shaded shirts ride across the prairies,
    With lassos in hand,
You, who angle for trout in the bluish creeks
    Of a Pennsylvania dusk,
You, rocking on the verandah of your family home,
    Pipe clutched between your teeth,
Or hurrying from your red-brick house to your place of work
    On broad Main Street,
(No difference which Main Street, since you made them all
    Similarly distasteful),
You, who love a steak larger than a plate,
    And about speeding without limit,
You, who loaf about in open shirt, with loose socks—
    Comfort above all else—
And, feet on the table, you drink, hugging one another's
    Shoulders, laughing and laughing,
You who picnic by driving into the country on Sunday
    And turning your car into a field,
You, who always rush about as if life were a sport
    And you, who prefers
To sport on the road of technology
    You dash along
As if it would carry you ever-upward—O races by the thousands
    Well-nourished and well-looking,
Beaming and busy, clean and uncomplaining,
    Good-hearted and most helpful,
From all of you I take my leave.

4.
Insolent capitalism! Abattoirs, smoke-stacks,
    Fields of oil and mineshafts!
Lift-bridges, canals, threshing-machines, blast-furnaces,
    Tugboats and railroad cars!
And you, bold youth! O universities by the hundreds,
    O volleyball games in the evening,
O Palo Alto gardens, wherein I could pluck grapefruit
    From my sleeping-bag,
And where blimps of silver by the dozen course above the palm-grove,
    In the reddish dawn!
O you, dear San Francisco, Telegraph Hill, Golden Gate Bridge,
    Sweet smell of olive trees,
Those weekends on the ocean, those noisy crowded cable-cars
    With their tipsy Marines!
O electricity in every home! And those who gave me lifts in their cars,
    Whenever I stood on the roadside,
People most dear, who drove a hundred miles out of their way to show me
    A mountain peak, like a family heirloom!
My bathroom, and sallow Long Island, with its record-players
    And blaring radio sets!
My Manhattan of pincushions, where skyscrapers and towers
    Out-thrust each other!
Washington! As if infants' hands had mixed up mud and marble
    And made of them a green park!
O beryl of Green River! O greyish Hudson!
    O the azure of the Colorado River!
The deep Mississippi, jaundice-coloured, whirlpooled,
    Its surface a treacherous peace,
All along its shores: ramshackled Negro shacks with shadows
    Leaning over the waters,
Within them, through the dirty windows, glass figurines of flowers,
    Erect on broken-down chests of drawers.
O slender, chattering girls! After them, summer louts!
    O kids, red of cheek,
Afraid of nobody, who are angling in the mouths
    Of sleeping uncles their dentures!
O Negro mammy in your bandana! Labourers in leather vests,
    O briefcases flying by!
O bathing beauties of Hollywood! Hags of henna-coloured hair,
    Ancient gentlemen with knotted white ties:—
From all of you I take my leave.

5.
O the past, O the pioneers, Revere riding through the night,
    And Lincoln, Lincoln, Lincoln,
King George the Third and his taxes, which were found unjust,
    And Lincoln, Abraham Lincoln, who . . .
The rising of Washington and of Abraham Lincoln
    Who, in Springfield, Illinois,
When he was elected President and stood there,
    Taking leave of his townsfolk
Between the rows of sumach trees before the yellow station,
    Big and unbeautiful,
And Mary Todd, eyes raised to her husband, bursting with joy,
    All the while Abraham Lincoln spoke thus
And Walt Whitman, the poet, the white-bearded, the beautiful,
    Who lamented the death of Lincoln,
Teddy Roosevelt with his big stick, and the famous Edison,
    But Abraham Lincoln it was who spoke thus
While he stood between the rows of such trees
    By the big yellow railway station,
Lincoln six-feet-tall, who never would have become President,
    Had not Mary made his life intolerable,
And Woodrow Wilson the bungler, and his rebellious Congress,
    And the Depression of the Thirties,
But it was Lincoln who said, taking his leave of Illinois,
    On his way to the White House
And the war will last long and grow bloodier and bloodier,
    But end in the defeat of feudalism,
And in the liberation of the slaves,
    Or to express it with more precision,
Make slaves of the miners and factory-workers
    So that in place of the whip,
The horror of the big city, the penny dreadful,
    And prosperity would make the slave
Happier and happier, but it was Lincoln who said,
    Taking leave of Illinois,
That in the end everything that man plans
    Sinks and stinks,
That in the end, everything that man creates
    Is faulty and transitory,
That everything in the end is senseless and will pass away,
    Like all man's doings,
And so, therefore, we must believe that all our work is necessary
    That it is worthwhile to live,

One must believe this until the end, the bitter end,
    It was Lincoln who said that to them.

6.
Permit me to bid you adieu, buddies—not lofty generals,
    Gleaming with medals,
Never unaccompanied or unattended, whose names appear regularly
    In the newspapers—
But you, who lugged the machine-gun and the mortar,
    The cauldron and the spade—
And the officers' possessions—and yet asked not their advice
    During the fighting,
You, who crawled in the mud and whose resinous sweat trickled
    Into our eyes,
And into the pools of the jungles and who asked not
    Praise for every enemy killed,
O anonymous buddies! You waded in seas up to your chins,
    To land at Tarawa
While machine-guns riddled you with holes and the landing vessels
    Overturned on the reefs,
Who passed through the sulphuric hell of Iwo Jima,
    And you, who, at Guadalcanal,
Feverish with malaria, fought though the snipers
    Were on high up the palm-trees,
Who swam in the waters of Manila Bay, across the Irrawaddy,
    In the brine of the Sea of Japan,
And at Chinwangtao, on the Yellow Sea, where the sharks played
    Hide and seek around your ankles.
O unnamed buddies! Who set sail across great oceans,
    Joking and singing,
And leapt onto islands, in your pocket the snapshot of your sweetheart,
    From island to island,
Who strolled so far away from home, with pocket radios,
    With electric razors,
Who died modestly, making no great fuss,
    Taking leave of life,
Who lie under Saipan's Coral Reefs, Luzon's yellow loess,
    The clay of New Guinea,
Who shattered into hundreds of pieces when crashing
    Into the slopes of the Himalayas,
O marine pilots, who lie buried inside their wrecked planes,
    Or under the waves,
Who fell into volcanic holes, you who rest now
    In sea, in earth, in fire,

And you who rest nowhere and never again shall see
    Lovely Main Street,
Broadway, or hear your sweetheart say goodbye to you.

And to you, who once more are living at home,
    And have the power to forget,
You, who work, drive cars, bathe and fish,
    For whom nothing has happened—
O America the happy, O America the young, O America, you,
    unlike you,

The country where I am going will be in terrible torment,
Will be a desolate ruin, a foul shack, home for rats and ravens,
Bedlam made by raving half-wits and fanatics,
Where quarrels are everlasting and life is lessened—
O America, happy, O America, young,
    I take my leave of you.

O monumental mountains! O prairies and plains,
    Where beckons a future still,
Where I could live for myself alone, and no one would ever ask me:
    What's your address? What's your politics?
O whipped cream and chocolate fudge! O pleasant train journeys,
    O leisured lifetimes!
O wolf-whistles! O snappy conversations!
    O endless laughter!
O country, so hard to leave, so impossible to forget,
    O country, where I was received as a guest, O country,
Where I could stay, were it not that I had to go,
On which I now look back and which a hundred times I will evoke,
    I take my leave of you.

Aboard ship on the Atlantic, having
left Long Island behind, 1946

VERA LYSENKO

(1910-75)

Vera Lysenko, who also wrote under the pen name Luba Novak, was born in the North End of Winnipeg, home for many generations to immigrants of diverse ethnic backgrounds. Her parents, Peter and Anna Lesik, emigrated in 1903 from their hometown of Tarashcha, south of Kiev, because of religious persecution. Vera Lesik took the Ukrainian pen name Lysenko, a sign of her desire to assert her ethnic ancestry and resist assimilation—this despite the fact that her family remained outsiders to Ukrainian communities because they were Stundists, a Protestant sect.

Lysenko belongs to the generation of Ukrainian-Canadian writers who began writing in English after the Second World War. Indeed, the 1954 publication of her first novel, *Yellow Boots*, is seen by some critics as the event that initiated that shift in language among Ukrainian-Canadian writers. Out of print for many decades, this novel was reprinted in 1992, accompanied by an introduction by Alexandra Kryvoruchka.

An excellent student, Lysenko, with the assistance of a Province of Manitoba Scholarship, studied English at the University of Manitoba, and graduated in 1930 with an Honours B.A. She was one of the first Ukrainian-Canadian women to receive a university education, and that marked the beginning of her intent to break new ground both as an ethnic Canadian and as a woman. Her upbringing in a working-class neighbourhood in Winnipeg and her experiences as a single woman seeking employment during the Depression period instilled in her a determination to fight against social injustices. She worked as a nurse and teacher in Edmonton, but she also tried, after moving to Eastern Canada, an array of jobs ranging from saleswoman and factory worker to domestic servant, translator of French novels, and journalist. It was in her journalistic articles that Lysenko's social consciousness first found expression. As Kryvoruchka says, Lysenko's *Chatelaine* article, 'The Girl Behind That Bargain' (1936), 'stripped away the façade of glamour in the fashion industry and revealed that the companies amassed huge profits while female employees were paid starvation wages.'

A proto-feminist, an astute social critic, and a writer with a decidedly strong ethnic consciousness, Lysenko undertook to write the first history of Ukrainian-Canadians, *Men in Sheepskin Coats: A Study in Assimilation* (1947). Its publication gave Lysenko wide recognition for her significant contribution to Canadian history, but also hurt her reputation. An ambitious and thorough project that required financial assistance, the book was sponsored and eventually edited by two Ukrainian-Canadians who were active members of the Communist Party of Canada. Given the attack on the book by Watson Kirkconnell (an established academic at the time and widely known for his polemical arguments) and the Cold War climate of that period, Lysenko found herself signing an affidavit that certified that she had never been a member of either the Communist Party or other left-wing associations. Traumatized by the experience, Lysenko stopped publishing for a number of years, and later on decided to turn to fiction.

Men in Sheepskin Coats is at once an exposé of the history of Ukrainian-Canadians and a study of the cultural diversity of Canada. Lysenko stresses in it the wealth of social and cultural experience brought to Canada by the various groups of immigrants, and laments the fact that their contributions are not recognized. At the same time that she argues for the protection of 'their national identity against high-pressure "assimilationist" policies', she envisions a Canada where 'a genuine artistic renaissance' will be possible only if Canadian culture 'embraces in its entirety the manifold life of all the national groups which constitute its entity'.

The fable-like style and ethnographic elements of *Yellow Boots* reflect what Lysenko believed ethnic writers ought to do, namely explore their ancestral heritage. The novel's female characters pass on the legacy of ethnic origins through storytelling, songs, and folkloric customs, as is shown in the short chapter that follows. The character of Lilli is on the receiving side of that tradition. She grows up learning both to oppose her father, who continually asserts his patriarchal power by claiming her as his property, and to sing, thus resisting the old order while preserving what she values about her ethnic origins. Lysenko published a second novel, *Westerly Wild* in 1956.

THE FAIRY TALE SPINNERS

The house was still now, with the magic stillness of a spring afternoon, serene beneath the chirping of the kitchen clock. The girl was lulled by the sunshine into a peaceful mood of expectancy. Something marvellous was about to happen, born of that peculiar mood of childhood most receptive to fantasy. On such an afternoon, magic slippers commenced to dance, animals developed human personalities, golden mountains gleamed. . . .

In the few days which had elapsed since the crisis, the girl had gained enough strength so that she could be left alone in the house with Granny Yefrosynia, all the others having gone out to the spring work. The old lady sat now at the loom weaving a tapestry. Granny had one white curl, like a chicken feather, poking out from her shawl. Circling her throat, a necklace of many coins made music with every movement. Her features had once been clean-cut, as though sculptured by a chisel, but with age had become blurred in outline, like a melted candle. About her waist was a six-inch striped wool belt, from which hung numerous small leather bags in which Granny kept her treasures, such as tobacco, roasted pumpkin seeds, herbs. In one bag was a handful of earth from her native village. 'What is it to be, then, a story?' questioned Granny.

'Yes, Granny, a story!' the girl clasped her hands with pleasure. To hear Granny tell a story—that was really something! Stories poured out of the old lady's mind 'like grain out of a sack', as Grandfather Nestor used to say when the girl, as a small child, had visited the old couple in their house near the village church.

Granny now began to tell the story of the Cranberry Flute, which concerned the secret murder of a beautiful girl by her jealous stepsister. The girl was transformed into a cranberry bush growing by the side of the road. A couple of travelling merchants, as they passed through the country, noticed the beautiful plant and cut a flute from the branches. The traveller began playing on the flute and the flute sang out:

Gently, gently, traveller, pray,
Lest upon my heart you play,
For a treacherous sister's knife
Took from me my youthful life.

And so the dreadful secret was revealed to the world. When the father of the girl heard the song, he said, 'What kind of flute is this? It plays so beautifully that it makes my heart ache. Give it to me and let me play it.' And the flute sang out with a human voice.

As Granny sang, the girl listened critically. She knew by instinct that the quavering sentimentality of Granny's voice was not adapted to this particular song. She heard, hovering about her, another tune—a high, youthful cry of anguish reproduced musically, capturing the tone of a flute. When Granny sang the song a second time, she protested, 'That is not the right tune, Granny.'

Granny stopped abruptly. She did not relish interruptions. 'Well, you sing it, then,' she snapped.

The girl hummed the tune in her mind, a high note of youthful anguish and entreaty.

Granny listened appreciatively, tapping her feet. 'Yes, yes, I forgot,' she murmured. 'That is the way it goes. Thank you for reminding me, dearie.' Although Granny had never before heard the tune as the girl had sung it, she did not inquire into its origin, but accepted it, as all folk tale spinners accepted improvements on the original. The girl herself did not know she had composed a tune—she had heard the tune and knew it must be the right one. Stories, for her, were accompanied by melodies heard only in her mind—the running of a rabbit, the cry of a flute, the siren song of water nymphs.

It was this enchantment which lingered on that afternoon, which gave the girl the feeling that she herself, under its magic influence, was changing somehow, that some transformation was taking place in her. People sometimes imposed upon one an uncongenial personality which did not fit one, but which one had to wear, nevertheless, temporarily, like an unbecoming cloak, while another was being tailored for one.

'Now,' said Granny, 'I have something for you.' She took a scrap of scarlet silk from a bag at her waist and gave it to the girl. 'That silk,' said Granny, 'is from the dress of a gypsy.'

'Who are the gypsies, Granny?' The girl rubbed the silk between her fingers.

'Folk who have no home, but wander about the earth.'

'Am I a gypsy, Granny?' asked the girl.

'Lord forbid!' exclaimed Granny, but she seemed uneasy.

'Then why do the gypsies wander?'

'They were cursed by God.'

The girl was struck by an idea. 'Granny,' she confided, 'Granny, I would like to grow. I am too small.'

'Yes,' reflected Granny. 'You could walk between the raindrops and not get wet.'

'If I were not so small,' continued the girl, 'then father and mother would let me stay home, and I would not have to wander.'

Granny regarded the girl with a shrewd look. 'You will grow,' she said positively. 'You have many years for growing yet—one hundred and two years, haven't you? In that time, my dear, you might become a giantess.'

Comforted by this logic, the girl leaned back on her pillow. She felt closer to the intense humanity of Granny than to her mother and father, and wished that Granny would always live with them, instead of staying as an occasional visitor, as now. Her mother was an alien person, enclosed between two boards of stiffness and morbidity, but Granny could enter the child's world of fantasy and create something new and beautiful out of scraps, whether of cloth, food or words. Who could be unhappy in the presence of Granny?

Granny believed intensely in her stories, and the tales she told formed a gigantic story book, rich and full of life. The legend of the Cranberry Flute had travelled the seas and continents, and yet had an immortal hold on the imagination, this story of the human voice transferred to a musical instrument on the death of a girl. Distilled through the primitive mind of Granny it opened the door for the girl to the magic of poesy and legend.

IRVING LAYTON

(b. 1912)

'Because many poets have averted their eyes from this radical evil [the sight of a happy man], they strike me as insufferable blabber-mouths. They did not retch enough; were too patient, courteous, civilized. A little brutality would have made them almost men,' says Irving Layton in his foreword to his volume of selected poetry, *A Red Carpet for the Sun* (1959), which won the Governor General's Award. What these poets lack is precisely what defines Layton as poet: an overbearing exuberance; an unabashed display of sexual bravado—that he often identifies with the Dionysian element; a deep commitment to what he values, which often translates into a cocksure attitude about things aesthetic and political. 'I am not at ease in the world (what poet ever is?),' he says; 'but neither am I fully at ease in the world of the imagination. I require some third realm, as yet undiscovered, in which to live. My dis-ease has spurred me on to bridge the two with the stilts of poetry, or to create inside me an ironic balance of tensions.'

One of the best but also one of the most controversial poets in Canada, Layton was born Israel Lazarovitch in Tirgul Neamt, a poor village in northern Romania, at a time of rising anti-Semitism. This, combined with his family's poverty, led to their immigration in Montreal a year after Layton's birth. Layton attributes his literary sensibility to his 'extraction'. 'My father was an ineffectual visionary,' he says; 'he saw God's footprint in a cloud and lived only for his books and meditations. A small bedroom in a slum tenement, which in the torrid days steamed and blistered and sweated, he converted into a tabernacle for the Lord of Israel. . . . Had my mother been as otherworldly as he was, we should have starved. Luckily for us, she was not; she was tougher than nails, shrewd and indomitable. With parents so poorly matched and dissimilar, small wonder my entelechy was given a terrible squint from the outset.' His family background certainly left its mark on young Layton, and he periodically dedicated himself to reading about Jews, but, as poet Joe Rosenblatt once said, 'Layton's a fool. . . ; he's an ignorant man in terms of what Judaism is all about.'

An avid reader from his teenage years on, Layton went to Baron Byng High School, from which he was expelled and from which he graduated only after A.M. Klein's intervention. He received a B.Sc. in agriculture (1939) from MacDonald College, Ste Anne de Bellevue, Quebec, and an M.A. in political science and economics (1946) from McGill University, and in 1969 he moved to Toronto to teach at York University until his retirement in 1978. He often visited Europe, where he lived for short periods in Greece, France, and Spain.

In the 1940s, Layton was actively involved with the poetry movement in Montreal led by the literary magazines *First Statement* and *Northern Review*, and was one of the forces behind Contact Press that published some of the innovative poets at the time. Beginning with the publication of his first book, *Here and Now* (1945), Layton was heralded as one of the most important poets of the 1950s and 1960s. But his prolific, and often indiscriminate, output—'to sustain his image as a genius', for a long time he published a book a year—and his controversial ideas and attitudes have also established him, ironically, as a 'miserable clown', the image he himself attributed to poets who do not understand 'the joy and wonder that is poetry'. Writing out of a 'messianic' belief in exposing the 'disorder and glory of passion', '[t]he modern tragedy of the depersonalization of men and women', the 'hideously commercial civilization', Layton has written powerful poetry, but also a poetry that has been driven by disputable passions such as his misogyny: 'Modern women', he said, 'I see cast in the role of furies striving to castrate the male; their efforts aided by all the malignant forces of a technological civilization that has rendered the male's creative role of revelation superfluous.' Such ideas as well as the fact that his later publications often repeat his messages has led reviewers and critics to view his recent titles in disparaging ways.

Still, Layton remains one of the most anthologized and internationally known of Canadian poets. Translated into many languages, Layton was nominated for the Nobel

Prize. His many titles include *In the Midst of My Fever* (1954), *The Cold Green Element* (1955), *The Improved Binoculars* (1956), the American edition of which was edited by William Carlos Williams, *The Swinging Flesh* (1961), *Droppings from Heaven* (1979), *The Gucci Bag* (1983), *Dance with Desire* (1986), and *Final Reckoning* (1987). *Fortunate Exile* (1987) is one of his many volumes of selected poems. His other books include *Engagements: The Prose of Irving Layton* (1972), *Taking Sides* (1977), prose, *An Unlikely Affair* (1980), letters, and *Waiting for the Messiah* (1985), a memoir.

WHOM I WRITE FOR

When reading me, I want you to feel
    as if I had ripped your skin off;
Or gouged out your eyes with my fingers;
Or scalped you, and afterwards burnt your hair
    in the staring sockets; having first filled them
with fluid from your son's lighter.
I want you to feel as if I had slammed
    your child's head against a spike;
And cut off your member and stuck it in your
    wife's mouth to smoke like a cigar.

For I do not write to improve your soul;
    or to make you feel better, or more humane;
Nor do I write to give you any new emotions;
Or to make you proud to be able to experience them
    or to recognize them in others.
I leave that to the fraternity of lying poets
    — no prophets, but toadies and trained seals!

How much evil there is in the best of them
    as their envy and impotence flower into poems
And their anality into love of man, into virtue:
Especially when they tell you, sensitively,
    what it feels like to be a potato.

I write for the young man, demented,
    who dropped the bomb on Hiroshima;
I write for Nasser and Ben Gurion;
For Kruschev and President Kennedy;
    for the Defense Secretary
voted forty-six billions for the extirpation
    of humans everywhere.

I write for the Polish officers machine-gunned
    in the Katyn forest;
I write for the gassed, burnt, tortured,
    and humiliated everywhere;
I write for Castro and Tse-tung, the only poets
    I ever learned anything from;
I write for Adolph Eichmann, compliant clerk
    to that madman, the human race;
For his devoted wife and loyal son.

Give me words fierce and jagged enough
    to tear your skin like shrapnel;
Hot and searing enough to fuse
    the flesh off your blackened skeleton;
Words with the sound of crunching bones or bursting eyeballs;
    or a nose being smashed with a gun butt;
Words with the soft plash of intestines
    falling out of your belly;
 Or cruel and sad as the thought which tells you
    'This is the end'
And you feel Time oozing out of your veins
    and yourself becoming one with the weightless dark.

THE SEARCH

My father's name was Moses; his beard was black
and black the eyes that beheld God's light;
they never looked upon me but they saw
a crazy imp dropt somehow from the sky
and then I knew from his holy stare
I had disgraced the Prophets and the Law.

Nor was I my mother's prayer;
she who all day railed at a religious indolence
that kept her man warm under his prayershawl
while her reaching arm froze with each customer
who brought a needed penny to her store;
added to another it paid the food and rent.

An ill-matched pair they were. My father
thought he saw Jehovah everywhere,
entertaining his messengers every day
though visible to him alone in that room

where making his fastidious cheese
he dreamt of living in Zion at his ease.

My mother: unpoetical as a pot of clay,
with as much mysticism in her as a banker
or a steward; lamenting God's will for her
yet blessing it with each Friday's candles.
But O her sturdy mind has served me well
who see how humans forge with lies their lonely hell.

Alien and bitter the road my forebears knew:
fugitives forever eating unleavened bread
and hated pariahs because of that one Jew
who taught the tenderest Christian how to hate
and harry them to whatever holes they sped.
Times there were the living envied the dead.

Iconoclasts, dreamers, men who stood alone:
Freud and Marx, the great Maimonides
and Spinoza who defied even his own.
In my veins runs their rebellious blood.
I tread with them the selfsame antique road
and seek everywhere the faintest scent of God.

TERRORISTS

Insulted, forsaken exiles
harried, harassed, shat on
learning
　　　　Justice is heard only
when it speaks through the mouth
of a cannon

learning
　　　　Right lies waiting
to fly out of a gun barrel

learning weakness is the one crime
history never pardons or condones

Uselessly you bruise yourselves, squirming
against civilization's whipping post;
Black September wolfcubs

terrify only themselves

The Jewish terrorists, ah:
Maimonides, Spinoza, Freud,
Marx

The whole world is still quaking

AT THE BELSEN MEMORIAL

It would be a lie
to say I heard screams
I heard nothing
It would be a lie
to say I saw ribs
like the bones
of beached ships
I saw nothing
It would be a lie
to say I sniffed
the odours
of decomposing crystals
or of bodies
that are left to lie
in the wind and rain
I sniffed nothing
nothing at all
It would be a lie
to say
emaciated ghosts
of little children
brushed against me
and that I reached out
my hands
to touch them
There were no emaciated
ghosts
and my hands
remained in the pockets
of the summer suit
I was wearing
The taste of death
was on my tongue

on my tongue only
When it pierced my neck
I was turned into stone
towering and black
Come:
read the inscription

HELEN WEINZWEIG

(b. 1915)

Of Polish-Jewish ancestry, Helen (Tenenbaum) Weinzweig was born in Radom, Poland, and arrived in Toronto at age nine in 1924. Although a voracious reader, she abandoned her formal education during the Depression, and began to work at odd jobs (salesperson, receptionist, nursery school teacher) until she decided to become a writer. A product of her childhood environment—'orthodox life in a Jewish ghetto in Poland'—she experienced another sort of separation in Toronto. In her own words, 'either through nature or nurture—my circumstances from the time I arrived in Canada were, to understate it, inauspicious—I became what is now termed a loner. I had no sense of belonging to community or to country.' This lack of connectedness was perhaps the reason why as a reader she favoured literature from countries other than Canada, England, or the United States.

She married the composer John Weinzweig in 1940, and began writing in 1960. Her first novel, *Passing Ceremony* (1973), announced her sense of drama, the

logic and tension of her language, and her use of ambiguity and paradox—elements which characterize most of her fiction, and which she attributes partly to her reading of books translated into English. 'Culturally,' Weinzweig says, 'if the writer's literary experience has been in another language, she must think in that language, and "translate" it into English. As a writer I find myself "translating" even my own language of English when I rewrite a text in order to incorporate colour or, perhaps, another culture.'

'Translation' is also important in Weinzweig's work as a metaphor for the process of understanding gender relationships, the complexity of desire, and the difference between fantasy and reality, as is reflected in her second book, *Basic Black with Pearls* (1980). This novel was awarded the City of Toronto Book Award in 1981, and was translated into Italian in 1994.

The short story that follows is taken from *A View from the Roof* (1989), a collection of short fiction which was nominated for the Governor General's Award.

L'ENVOI

. . . Tell me, father, what I did wrong and I will never do it again . . .

The young girl seated on the cart beside the pedlar, or, perhaps behind him on top of whatever goods he was carrying—that nine-year-old girl must have had such a thought, not concretely, for the young are protected from premature awareness. It can be assumed that her mind was dealing with everything or with nothing as a result of confusion as she looked up at her father's pock-marked, bearded face. Then the pedlar brought the birch switch down on the horse and the cart rumbled off.

The girl did not know then, nor could she ever say, why she was sent away to live in a distant city amongst strangers. That day in 1912 she was sent to Lublin to live with her grandmother. Whose mother, her mother's or her father's? She never explained: it was as if the details of the transitions in her life were of no significance: one was born in this or that place, into this or that family, poor or poorer, one prevailed or one died.

Nor did she ever recall whether she left in the dead of winter, when hunger and cold were at their most abysmal; or whether it was in the heat of summer, when the wells dried up and the dirt streets gave off a dust one tasted; or if it was in a season in between. They drove off very early in the morning, probably, to get a good start on the day since the pedlar would be making many stops at farmhouses and small villages to sell whatever it was he had in the back of the cart—pots, pans, linens, shoes and hats. Perhaps the sun was shining.

She was sent away from her home in Radom in Poland. Home consisted of two rooms, dark and dank, with an earthen floor. The ears always strained for the clang of horses' hooves. The terror of an unsheathed sword. A sound in the night of a stumbling, drunken peasant, demanding money and jewels that 'every dirty Jew has hidden'. Wakefulness induced by bedbugs. Vermin. Sores that would not heal. Sudden death. (I know, because I was born in that same place years later.) Memory, too, must have suffered indignities for she could remember nothing of the journey. If no one told her why she was being sent away from her mother, father, two brothers and three sisters, then she was forced to exist without the memory of words. Something should have been said—the truth, a lie, an approximation even—for in the absence of words a presence slips in to fill the emptiness and haunts forever.

Scenes of preparation for leaving home can be imagined. For weeks her head had been doused with kerosene to kill lice. Her brothers and sisters, sensing something portentous going on, watch covertly. Her gentle small mother (from a faded sepia photograph) kneels on the floor to bathe her eldest daughter the night before. The water is in a tin tub on the floor. The mother frequently raises a wrist to adjust a shabby, brown wig that keeps slipping over her eyes as she bends over her child's body. The girl's one dress is clean. Perhaps shoes are found for the journey. And her father, tall and handsome, his face turned to the wall in a corner of the same room, phylacteries wound about his arm, fingers the fringes of a prayer shawl and remains deep in a dialogue with God.

(I remember my grandfather always, it seemed to me, at prayer, intoning litanies, stroking his beard and swaying as he prayed. Otherwise, he was silent, a man distanced by futility and religion.)

Surely, as a final paternal gesture the girl's father held her, even if only to help her up on the seat. Surely he said something to his friend, the pedlar. For the man who bore the child away was not a stranger. He was her father's best friend. They had been friends since boyhood, having studied at the *Yeshivah* together. As young men, in order to avoid military service, they had administered to one another the blows that broke the bones of the index finger of the right hand. The pedlar, seated with the reins in his hands, assured his dearest friend that he would take good care of the child and deliver her safely to her widowed grandmother.

At the last moment the father no doubt spoke:

'Be good. Listen to your grandmother.'

She kept her eyes on her father's face, photographing the high forehead, straight brows, the skin ravaged by smallpox, the beard thick and black. The girl must have felt an urge to run and scream, but the passivity required of her at that moment was fixed forever. At that moment, also a volcanic energy was born, hidden from sight, seething with a fiery rage, to erupt without warning throughout her lifetime.

*

I suppose Julius will always be nervous at a preview opening of an exhibit. Tonight, at his sixth one-man show, he has been backed into a corner at the far end of the gallery, between two of his canvases; he looks pale and ill at ease. The Gallery Donegani is very long and very narrow and it is impossible to step back from a painting without colliding with someone who is also stepping back from a painting on the wall opposite. To view the exhibit, people soon learn to move to the right only, sideways. Earlier, Julius was interviewed by a tv reporter and was centred for a few minutes under the tv camera lights. All this time I have been standing firmly to the right of the open doorway, brushed against but not disturbed. A few people recognize me as Julius' wife, but since the wine has been set out at the other end, they do not linger.

Everyone we know or have ever known (except Jim, who couldn't make it, but sent a wire of congratulations) has come to the opening. Julius is in that fortunate position, creatively speaking, where his artistic growth is at the exact meeting point with the public's recognition of his work. And while I am pleased that Julius no longer has to suffer anonymity, I cannot help but worry how long do an artist and his public stay at this meeting point? Who goes on to by-pass the other? Julius is clasping and unclasping his hands like parting lovers. I think he would feel more comfortable if he had something in his hands. His hands seem to have a will of their own; he satisfies them by giving them brushes to hold, paint to mix. During the night, in his sleep, his hands clutch the pillow's edge, a sheet, a blanket.

I am drunk, lonely and desperate. It is on such occasions, when I should be self-contained with pleasure, that a perversity takes hold and I keep drinking the cheap wine, and I say to the nice young man who has been very attentive and has brought me glass after glass; and who, moreover, is asking *my* opinion—it is at times like these that I hold forth and say,

'Control? Oh yes. You are indeed perceptive to have discovered Julius' tremendous control over his work: control over his ideas, over form, over content, over technique. Total control. Yes, indeed, most amazing. But,' I whisper confidentially, 'nature punishes over-specialization by giving the organism what it wants. Consider the oyster. It can survive only within a certain range of temperature and degree of salinity in the water and depends on the food passing by. This controls the entire future of the species, because once he's attached to his culch, the oyster cannot move an inch. Where,' I ask earnestly, 'where will all this control lead?'

The new art critic for the *Toronto Planet* (it was) appropriated my casual remarks as his own considered critical opinion. Julius raged. 'That man is stupid . . . the fool . . . he missed the whole point . . . there's no such thing as "too controlled" for God's sake . . . might as well call my work too artistic . . . the idiot doesn't know that control is crucial to all great art goddamnit . . . '

*

For a short while after the exhibit Julius' hands held me at night and we became as we had been once. Then he began to work in his studio again and forgot everything. He forgot the show's success, the amount of money that was coming; he forgot *The*

Planet's art critic; and he forgot me. More than once he has told me that 'an artist must forget; he must have no memory.' Memory, I suppose, can be disturbing, since memory and emotion often go together, sometimes to no apparent purpose, so why permit memories to intrude on one's life . . . ? So I surmised.

Then Julius picked up his paint brushes again in the day and clutched the bedding at night. Familiar life was resumed, which included a visit from Jim, my husband's best friend. Their bonding, as that kind of close tie is termed nowadays, goes back to childhood, through all the rites of passage. The fact that Jim and I are lovers has not affected their friendship.

At two on Friday afternoon I picked up Jim at the airport, drove to his hotel, we made love until six and then I drove him to our house for dinner. The traffic crawled at that hour and we had time to catch up on the lives of our children since he was here almost six months ago. I have two grown sons who call him Uncle Jim; he has eight children whom I have seen only in snapshots, living as they do in the three American cities where their mothers' divorces were granted. In front of my house, before we got out of the car, Jim cautioned, as he always does:

'We mustn't do anything to hurt Julius.'

When Jim comes into town he and Julius are together as much as possible. Even when the three of us are in our car, Julius and Jim sit side by side in the front and I sit in the back. My affair with Jim is more a matter of propinquity than of passion. We three are such good friends that sometimes I imagine myself as Jeanne Moreau, loved by Jules *et* Jim.

*

Every summer Julius leaves his third floor studio and sets up his work in the living room, which also faces north. Each summer we are thrown together a great deal in that part of the house I consider mine. It is becoming difficult to share space with my husband. To make matters worse, instead of going about my daily routines, I find myself hanging about while he paints. He has grown a beard. 'Don't hide your face, I love every mark on it,' I used to plead whenever, in the past, he wanted to grow a beard as other painters did. 'Every scar makes me think of ordeals and victories.' 'Aw, come on, it was only a bad case of adolescent acne.' But just the same he was pleased and took a shave.

I spend hours watching Julius as he contemplates a canvas on the wall before him; he holds the brushes in one hand and strokes his beard with the other. I have not been able to take my eyes off the beard and the pocked skin above it. All summer long I have been watching the beard grow, as it went from a bluish skid-row shadow, to a black stubble that Julius dug his fingers into constantly, then to its ultimate thick blackness which is in strange contrast with his thinning brownish hair. I worried about the bare patches just under the lower lip; then, with relief, I saw the bald spots fill in with soft hairs. Here and there at the edges, especially towards the ears, some grey appeared. It is now September, and Julius is back in his third floor studio, yet I am still not used to the sight of that beard. The worst time is in bed at night when, if his beard brushes against my arm, my face or neck, my skin shrivels.

'Jim is coming today. He's going to stay here.'

'Great!' Julius said. 'I've got four new pictures to show him.'

'He's not coming on business, nor to see you—he's coming to see *me*.'

'What exactly does that mean?'

'It means that I phoned him to come right away. I must talk to him.' In the absence of a response, I added. 'I've got to talk to someone; I can't stand it any more.'

'"It" again. What is "*it*" this time?'

'Your beard. I hate it. I wish you'd shave it off.'

In his silence I heard: 'And then what? If I give in to you again, you will be satisfied for a while, I will work, you will keep busy; then for no reason you will get bitchy and I will have to stay out of your way, especially in bed.'

Behind his departing back I hurled my silent reply, 'Since you refuse to talk to me openly so that together we might make a discovery of some sort, I shall continue to be unfaithful to you. You might as well know that in a scale of one to ten, Jim is eleven in bed: *you* are about four and a half.'

Either Julius did not know or he did not want to know that in the middle of the night I left our bed. For the rest of that night I lay beside Jim in the spare bedroom. Jim knows a great deal about women, about their 'needs', which is his term for that impossible longing for intimacy.

'You must understand that Julius loves you,' he assured me, 'it's just that he can't turn off his creativity.'

'I'm with him all the time too, and he can turn me off very easily.'

Jim embraced me. It is his way of saying, 'Now, be reasonable . . .'

The three of us had breakfast together as if nothing had happened in the night. I looked closely at my husband to see how he had slept, but neither his eyes nor his expression showed signs of suffering. After the third cup of coffee, the two men rose and went up to the studio. Jim carried a case of beer. Late in the afternoon Jim came down into the kitchen. He stood beside me at the sink, serious, concentrating on the potato peels.

'Julius asked me to tell you that he will give you $50,000 and 10 percent of all his future sales if you'll get out.' Now he was watchful and stood well back of the knife in my hand. 'His words, not mine.'

'Julius hasn't got $50,000. He's just starting to sell. That's your money he's offering me.'

'He's my best friend.'

'You're *my* best lover.'

'I feel like a flea between two pit terriers.'

'Tell me what I have done wrong that he wants to send me away.'

'He feels that in some way you are undermining him. Julius says he can't paint. He has to work. It's as simple as that. Oh come on . . . it's not the end of the world . . . you need to live your own life . . . maybe this will be for the best . . . think about it.'

'There's nothing to think about. This is my home. He can't make me leave.'

Suddenly I was overcome by the recurrence of an old dread, a mysterious anguish that paralyzes me. Jim took the knife out of my hand. He made me sit down. He drew up another chair so close to mine that his long legs were on either side of my chair. He took both of my hands in his and held them between his thighs.

'My entire life,' I said, 'my entire life has been spent trying to forge one human tie with one person in this whole wide world who would want me.'

I had just begun. Injustice, humiliation, overweening desires—I opened a bin of unclaimed emotions. Jim let go of me. He was curt.

'Keep it light. Keep it light. Let's not get serious.'

'Jim,' I told him, 'deep down you're shallow.'

In the narrowing of his eyes I saw already the determination of a man hardened by many partings.

Out of habit I served dinner and out of habit Julius and Jim sat down to eat. I broke the silence. I turned to Jim:

'You've always liked Julius' work, haven't you?'

'Oh yes, right from the start when we were students at the Ontario College of Art. Everyone recognized he was the real thing, the born painter; the teachers left him alone.'

'Then why,' I asked, my tone silken, 'do you, as the great international art consultant, choose all that crap that goes into lobbies of skyscrapers and all that mediocrity hanging on the walls of executive offices? You have never bought one of Julius' paintings.'

'Oh, those people . . . ! They're not ready for experiments.'

All this time my husband was abstracted, hardly listening. Now he looked up, as if he had just thought of something:

'. . . you never asked me to submit anything . . . '

Jim said, 'Don't you see what she's doing . . . divide and rule . . . '

I said, 'Don't you see what *he's* been doing? He picks your brains. He finds out what you dismiss as suitable only for motels and *buys* it! He peddles paintings as if they were pots and pans. He's nothing but a pedlar.'

Jim got up to leave. The way he looked at Julius, the way his hands went up into the air and then disappeared into his pockets, left me with a final image of a drowning man just before he goes under for the last time.

Every morning now I am up early to prepare a substantial breakfast for my husband. Then Julius leaves for the studio loft on King Street that I found for him. I've not seen what he's been working on. At breakfast we listen to the radio news; we share the morning paper; we have our old desultory chats about matters which do not directly concern us.

'Are you interested in seeing the van Gogh exhibit,' I ask, 'if I can wangle a couple of tickets?'

'Well . . . '

'It's all right. I just wondered. What are you working on these days?'

'"Breakfast Number Four".'

'Seriously . . . '

'Seriously.'

'Abstract expressionism . . . ?'

'Something. Walter was over yesterday. He likes the new series. Wants a show next year.'

'You can use the house this weekend, if you want to. I'll be away.'

'Well . . . it means dragging things back and forth. Maybe some sketches.' He puts down the paper. 'Artists and intellectuals are not safe in this world.'

'I know a man who is an authority on Russian military history.'

'Listen, if you get a chance, will you check our account at the bank. Maybe I ought to open my own account near the studio. There's a branch at Bathurst and Queen.'

'Leave it. They know us here and will cover if we overdraw.'

'All right. See you at six.'

We go out into the hall together. In the winter I wait until he puts on overshoes and hat and scarf and overcoat. Sometimes he takes a lunch and I carry it to the front door. Then we have a parting kiss; I am getting used to the feel of his beard.

Julius leaves and I go into the living room, the curtains are sheer and although I can see out, no one can see me from the street. As the days and months go by I keep a morning watch at the window. I watch as Julius crosses the road and then stands on the sidewalk opposite and looks up at his former studio. I observe that his beard is short and neat and his moustache is trimmed, giving him the look of a French *boule-vardier*. I wait until he is out of sight, then I start the day.

JOSEF SKVORECKY

(b. 1924)

Josef Skvorecky, with his wife Zdena Salivarova, also a writer, left Prague to go into exile in January 1969, only a few days after Jan Palach's self-immolation in Prague, 'the gloomiest time since the invasion itself'. When he returned to Prague after the 'velvet revolution' in 1990, it was to receive from President Vaclav Havel the order of the White Lion, Czechoslovakia's highest award for foreigners. By then, Skvorecky was a Canadian citizen, founder, together with his wife, of the Toronto press Sixty-Eight Publishers (1972), which has been called 'the most prominent Czech publishing house in the world', and a writer of international standing. For Skvorecky, who lived under the totalitarianism and communism of Czechoslovakia, forced to publish under the names of the writers with whom he occasionally collaborated, 'real politics always involve[s] danger. . . . Canada and the United States and most of Western Europe don't have politics; life in these societies is free of politics.'

Skvorecky was born in Nachod, where, following his high school graduation in 1943, he worked in the Messerschmidt factories. Images and experiences from this period found their way into some of his most well-known novels, *The Cowards* (1972), the first novel he wrote but which was published ten years later only to be immediately banned, *The Bass Saxophone* (1977), and *The Engineer of Human Souls* (1984). The latter, partly set in Canada, was the first translation (by Paul Wilson) to win the Governor General's Award for fiction in 1985.

After he received a Ph.D. in philosophy (1951) from Charles University in Prague, he served two years in the army, an experience that found its way into his novel, *The Republic of Whores*, completed in 1954 but published for the first time in French in 1969. As Skvorecky says, 'I have an incurable tendency to base my opinions on experience and solid reading, not hearsay and ideology.' The 'history' of the protagonist Danny Smiricky (who appears as a character in some of the other novels), Skvorecky says, 'is in fact the history of my people'. As the following selection from this novel illustrates, Danny, morally and intellectually detached from the new social order that the army represents, is more interested in women than in the political implications of the Stalinist fifties. This novel was translated into English in 1993.

In addition to his many novels, Skvorecky has also written screenplays, film scripts, literary criticism, and non-fiction that includes a history of jazz. He has also translated into Czech many American writers, among them Henry James and Ernest Hemingway.

A year after his arrival to Canada, he became a professor of English at the University of Toronto, which awarded Skvorecky and his wife honorary degrees in 1992. He is also the recipient of the Neustadt Prize from the University of Oklahoma (1980).

Skvorecky, who writes non-fiction in English, uses what he calls 'American or Canadian Czech' for his novels, 'the Czech most North American Czechs use'. A writer whose relationship to Canada is marked by his strong émigré sensibility, he 'think[s] that if an ethnic culture is going to survive beyond the second or third generation it will do so whether it is officially supported or not'. Although he has remained 'tied to the old country'—'I'm still a Czech,' he says—he calls Toronto, where he has lived since his arrival to Canada, 'home'. His most recent book is *The Bride of Texas: A Romantic Tale from the Real World* (1995), a novel about Czechs in the American Civil War.

FROM *THE REPUBLIC OF WHORES*

THE ARMY CREATIVITY CONTEST

Danny did not report to his commanding officer as ordered. It was late Friday after-noon, and he felt the tug of Prague. Not only was Lieutenant Pinkas spending the weekend at home with his family, but Danny had read in an army newspaper that in the auditorium of the Nth Division there was going to be a gala evening that night for winners of the Army Creativity Contest. The winner in the poetry division was Robert Neumann, Lizetka's husband, so it was clear that he wouldn't be home with his wife. And though the tank commander was now under the spell of a new and quite different poetry—the poetry of tracer bullets and stars above the shooting range—he didn't want to waste this new chance to try the marital fidelity of that strange woman, Lizetka.

To avoid possible complications with Captain Matka, he used the underground railway that the men of the Seventh Tank Battalion usually took to freedom. As soon as his shift in the guardhouse was over, he went straight to the attic in battalion head-quarters where the wardrobe was kept, donned his walking-out uniform, determined from the duty officer that the CO was at supper, picked up an exit permit from the duty officer, forged the captain's signature on it, then called on Private First Class Dr Mlejnek, the battalion scribe. Using a skeleton key, Dr Mlejnek opened the steel strongbox containing the unit's official stamps, and took one and stamped the falsi-fied document, thus confirming its authenticity. Then the tank commander took refuge in the gathering dusk along the path that led among the barracks to the rail-way station. Despite the splendid forgery, he left the base not via the main gate but by a less hazardous route across the small park behind the baths, and through a hole in the fence below the tracks. He crossed a shallow stream and, sticking close to the hedgerows between the fields, finally reached the highway to nearby Lysá.

It was evening now and growing dark, and trucks from the base drove past him. He could have hitched a ride, but there was plenty of time before the train left for Prague, and he felt like walking. The road led westward towards the town over a ridge of undulating hills. The evening was warm and full of colour, like the recent night when he'd carried the basket of plums home for the lieutenant's wife. Like every autumn night for the past ten or fifteen years, this night held a poetic enchantment that was related as much to his glands as to the weather. His mind was buoyed by his success with Janinka, but, rather than being filled with tender thoughts of her, he felt charged with a dynamic sense of determination to press his luck with the tantalizing, exasperating Lizetka.

When he reached the first houses on the outskirts of town, night had fallen and the streets were dimly lit by a few isolated streetlamps. A military police jeep was parked in front of the Žižka Inn. Beside it, two abject and rather drunk soldiers were just being relieved of their passes by a lieutenant in a smartly pressed uniform. A corporal wearing a service armband stood discreetly in the background, trying to convey to the victims through body language that there was nothing he could do about it. The lieutenant tried to catch out the tank commander, but wilted when he saw that all the signatures and stamps on his papers appeared to be in order. He merely told Danny to straighten his tie and tighten his belt, then drove off into the darkness in search of further victims.

Thus Danny was able to board the Prague express, and at half past eight he was ringing the doorbell of Ludmila Neumannová-Hertlová, known to all her suitors as Lizetka.

* * *

There was a rich variety of faces on the stage. The voices orated and declaimed or mumbled and whined. Some authors, adopting the parade-ground manner of a sergeant-major, bellowed their poetry into the smoke-filled hall, while others were barely audible and were lost in the creaking and scraping of chairs.

The voices and faces varied; the subject matter displayed greater discipline.

> *I'd rather walk with you on Petřín Hill*
> *And tell you of my love and my fidelity—*
> *But, so that you may bright and peaceful live,*
> *I and my gun stand guard o'er your tranquillity.*

The form was as regular as any medieval sonnet or ballad. The first two lines expressed genuine longing, and the next two lines an offering, a libation, to redeem the social irrelevance of the longing in lines one and two. The private who had just delivered this variation was so fat that he could only be guarding the tranquillity of his loved one from behind a typewriter in the office of some command post or other. He left the podium to a smattering of indifferent applause.

The next contestant was a corporal with thick glasses, who, in a deliberate but penetrating voice, made this claim:

> *A young girl's kisses are sweeter*
> *Than the powder the cannon reek of;*
> *But the world is divided, did you know?*
> *And the enemy his chance does seek, love.*

The soldiers and officers gathered in the divisional auditorium listened to all this with Christian patience mixed with military restraint. They were, after all, the army's intellectual elite. Some of them rested their foreheads in their hands, feigning intense interest in the poetry and the lessons they might derive from it and apply in their daily work. Others lounged casually on their chairs and leered at the members of the Women's Army Chorus in their attractive, well-fitting uniforms. Some whispered comments to each other after every poem, others remained silent, fending off sleep.

> *My hand is frozen hard to the steel*
> *And the icy frost bites into my cheek.*
> *For all our loved ones around the world*
> *I guard our border, week after week.*

These lines were murmured in a scarcely audible voice by an engineer who looked like a fly on spider's legs. When he'd finished, an officer with two brightly polished medals dangling from his chest, the Fučík Badge and the Badge of Physical Fitness, leaned over to Robert Neumann and said, 'Feeble, wouldn't you say?'

'Good beginning, lousy ending. No juice,' said Robert expertly, and he was saved from making further critical comment when an exhausted member of the chemical warfare unit behind him fell asleep and tumbled off his chair. The bemedalled officer turned around reproachfully, leaving Robert Neumann to this thoughts, which were coloured by a strange mixture of his habitual gloom and sudden bursts of euphoria over his own poetic triumph. But the more he listened, the more the gloom began to predominate. A triumph in this competition, he realized, would be of questionable value indeed, especially in the eyes of Ludmila. He watched the next contestant on the podium click his heels together, thrust his chest out, and begin to recite rapidly:

> *You write me letters, darling mine:*
> *When will you come home to me?*
> *And I stand here on watch, and guard*
> *Our future and a better time.*

To Neumann, the future appeared bleak indeed. That morning he'd received an anonymous letter from a colleague of Ludmila's, Jarmila Králová. Last week, at twelve-thirty in the morning, Králová had seen Ludmila on the steps of the Golden Well nightclub, with a man who had his arm around her waist. The man was Dr Karel Budulínský from the Ministry of Domestic Commerce. Robert knew Dr Budulínský. He considered him a family friend, and in Ludmila's presence he would read him his real poetry, not the verses he composed for the army. The letter made him feel doubly bitter, for he now knew with more certainty than ever that any husband of Ludmila's must necessarily be a man without male friends. Surrounded by masculine camaraderie, he felt oppressed by loneliness.

This feeling remained with him even during a convivial speech delivered by the National Artist Josef Bobr, a fat novelist whose words, so full of cordial sincerity, glorified the present and, somewhat illogically, attributed to an even more glorious future a feeling of envy that it couldn't have been that glorious past. The National Artist droned on, reading from notes, and the loudspeakers turned his voice into a hollow, soporific monotone. In the back of the hall, the body of the soldier from the chemical warfare unit fell off the chair and again crashed to the floor, and the decorated officer whirled around once more, ready to admonish.

The National Artist went on to glorify the literature of the present, which would preserve for that happy future a truthful and undistorted picture of the breadth, depth, and colour of the age, whose palette appeared to him—again somewhat illogically—in various shades of salmon-pink.

Finally, ogling the female comrades in the Army Chorus, he called out: 'Thank you, comrades, thank you, soldiers, for the beauty and strength your poetry pours into our souls—into us, your readers. Thank you for the encouragement and the inspiration with which you endow us, poets and writers. Thank you and hurrah! Hurrah and thank you, comrades!' And the women from the Army Chorus, their nylon knees gleaming below the hems of their skirts, began to sing a song of praise for the armoured assault units, in professional four-part harmony.

* * *

Lizetka lived in a modest family house her parents had built during the Depression. The door was answered by her father, a stage manager at the National Theatre, who said, 'Come in, Mr Smiřický. Liduška's not at home.'

He led the tank commander into an overheated kitchen where Lizetka's mother was listening to Radio Free Europe on an old console radio. The device was sputtering and squawking unpleasantly, but through a screen of mechanical noise induced by the jamming station a distant, piping voice could be heard announcing the failure of Communism to collectivize the villages.

'Good evening,' Danny said, and the woman nodded pleasantly and flashed him a gold and white smile. For two years now, this soldier had been instigating her daughter to commit adultery. The mother's generation might well still believe in platonic adoration, but the mother herself had sprung from the bosom of the working people, who had never seriously entertained such notions. 'Please sit down,' she said, 'and listen to this.'

Danny sat down and listened. Mr Hertl lay down on the settle under the window, put his muscular arms under his head, and began listening too, trying to follow the weak voice through the grating noise of the jamming. Sometimes the voice was drowned out altogether, but then it would become stronger, almost comprehensible. Bored by what was obviously a nightly ritual, Danny watched the restless canary in its cage. 'The Communists resorted to repression,' the voice was saying. 'Any farmer who did not give to the Communist authorities the quota of goods set by the Communists. . . .' Then the voice faded.

Mrs Hertlová nodded vigorously. 'That's exactly what they did with my father's farm.'

She looked at the tank commander and he nodded in agreement.

The voice was now entirely submerged in background noise, and the buzzing increased until the speaker began to pulsate dangerously. Mrs Hertlová turned down the volume. 'Communist swine!' Mr Hertl muttered from his couch.

The jamming faded slightly. 'They were defenceless,' said the voice. 'Communist thugs in leather coats with revolvers in their pockets drove around the villages on motorcycles and terrorized. . . .' The voice faded.

'The bastards! The sons of bitches!' came the voice from the settle.

'A dirty business,' agreed Danny.

'Just like in our village,' said Mrs Hertlová.

A loud crackle surged out of the apparatus and the voice of Radio Free Europe thundered around the room. 'Did the confiscated grain end up in Czech bakeries? Was it turned into bread for the Czech people? Not at all, dear listeners at home in Czechoslovakia. The rye harvested in Hana, the wheat grown from the golden soil of

Bohemia, were turned into perogies for the fat Communist cats in Soviet Azerbaijan. . . .'

Another loud crackle and the radio set trembled with a new, aggressive wave of jamming. Mrs Hertlová turned down the volume again, so that silence framed the bitter cry from the settle: 'Those Commie pigs are stuffing their faces!' The stage manager's own face, inflamed with rage, rose like an angry moon above the edge of the table, and he stared at Danny with bloodshot eyes. 'Where the hell are we living?' he roared. 'Mr Smiřický, I ask you, where are we living? Is this what we end up with? Is this what we've busted our gut for?'

'They're a bad lot,' said Danny gently.

'They're thieves!' cried Mrs Hertlová. 'Stealing from people—*that* they know how to do.'

'Mr Smiřický!' The stage manager's face radiated despair. 'Think about it, just think about it. Is this what we wanted? Is this what we spent twenty years building a country for? And we call ourselves a nation!' He fixed his burning eyes on the tank commander as though he were accusing him personally of the disaster that had descended upon their well-tempered state.

'You're right,' said Danny.

'Shut your mouth, Mr Smiřický.' Mr Hertl scowled ferociously. 'We're all guilty! We've done this with the nation of Jan Hus and T.G. Masaryk and Jan Žižka! That's the kind of whores we are. Drop the H-bomb on us. Drop the cobalt bomb on us!'

'It's true, we've gone to the dogs,' said Mrs Hertlová. 'We've abandoned God, and now you might as well write us off.' She sighed. 'Before, when the—'

'Do you hear that, Mr Smiřický?' said the stage manager, interrupting his wife. 'And now they're always searching your flat to make sure you haven't stolen anything.'

'It's a miserable business,' said Danny.

'It's a bloody *crime*, that's what it is,' yelled the stage manager. 'But just you wait. This can't go on for ever. And then heads will roll, friend or foe. What, I'll say. You say you're my friend, I'll say. Maybe you were once, but not any more. String him up, I'll say. I'm a Christian, Mr Smiřický, but without the slightest compunction whatsoever, Mr Smiřický, I'll hang every Commie I can get my hands on. And I know who is and isn't a Commie. I'm in charge of dues in our Party cell, and I've got the goods on everyone. No one will be able to deny he was a member, and I'll show no mercy, Mr Smiřický, I swear I won't.'

'That's exactly what they deserve. Show no pity,' said Mrs Hertlová.

'That's a fact,' said Danny. 'By the way, do you know when Lída's coming home?'

* * *

The merciful and impenetrable Originator of All Things did, after all, grant some solace to Robert Neumann, for into the half-circle of svelte young ladies in the chorus stepped a beauty with bright green eyes. She was welcomed by spontaneous applause, for she needed no introduction; she had starred in several movies that everyone had seen, usually playing a sexy young bricklayer or lathe-operator. Now, in a honeyed voice, she announced that she was going to read the grand-prize winner in this year's Army Creativity Contest—a poem by Sergeant Robert Neumann called 'Farewell to the Army'. Neumann felt a ripple of exultation.

His winning entry had been inspired not, as the poem pretended, by the approaching end of his army service, but by despair. The actress seemed to sense that its melancholy was of an intimate rather than socio-military nature, for she endowed the verses (Ludmila had called them 'fripperies') with a warm, moist fog of practised eroticism. Into the microphone she whispered:

> *Beneath my footsteps rustle leaves*
> *And the bony crackling of icicles.*
> *Like flakes of winter, two glittering butterflies,*
> *Tears flutter into your eyes.*
> *Your tenderness silences the boys. . . .*
> *How much better, comrade, do I understand*
> *All that we once banished with pleasantries.*
> *But after we leave, and put on other garments,*
> *We will still and always be as once we were*
> *In those years when, rifle in hand,*
> *We stood guard for our Czech land.*
>
> *At the guardhouse, intent on our love,*
> *We wait, the first time without belt and badge,*
> *And shyly we will lead her*
> *Through an autumn of burnished copper:*
> *The earth her comely luck will yield,*
> *And we become her shield.*

Robert Neumann was moved to real tears by his own sentimentality. The rest of the audience was drawn to the speaker herself. Not all of them, though; during the performance, the weary member of the chemical warfare unit fell out of his chair a third time, and on orders from the decorated officer he was escorted from the hall by the soldiers on duty.

Somewhat later, all the winners were sitting around a long green table laden with food and drink, in the small salon in division headquarters, listening to the head of the division's cultural program.

'And so, comrades,' said the colonel, whose name was Vrána but whom the men called Colonel Dryfart, 'the artillery made an especially strong showing this year, both in the number of awards and in the number of poems submitted. And that is a special reason for joy, comrades, because our aim is to cultivate, not outstanding individuals, but a reliable collective. Our slogan was, is, and will always be "The masses, above all!"'

A private at the end of the table shouted, 'Hurrah!', but the rest merely looked at him and his battle-cry hung in the air in an embarrassing silence. The speaker was so surprised by this unexpected interjection that he stopped talking. Everyone looked down. Finally, a lieutenant from the Army Song and Dance Ensemble said, 'Wonderful! Wonderful work, cannoneers.'

'Yes indeed!' said the National Artist. 'So the artillery muse was the most creative of all?'

The colonel laughed. 'That's right, comrade,' he said. 'Out of sixty-five poems received, thirty-eight were from men in the artillery. And of the twenty awards, twelve were given to artillery men!'

'Including the laurel wreath of victory,' interrupted a major from the Song and Dance Ensemble, 'which was won by a cannoneer as well.' He smiled at Robert Neumann as though he owed his high rank to him. 'I'm particularly pleased by that since I was originally a cannoneer myself.'

Neumann smiled too—at the major with his mouth, and at the actress (who returned his smile) with his eyes. They had been introduced after the concluding ceremonies and she was now sitting next to the prize-winning novelist. Neumann had already succumbed to the ancient fallacy that one can compensate for bad luck with one woman in the company of another woman without making matters worse.

'And what about poetry from the armoured division, Comrade Colonel?' said a sergeant with tank corps insignia.

'What about the engineers?' roared a large man on the other side of the table.

The colonel examined a sheaf of papers. The prize-winning novelist looked over his shoulder while stifling a yawn with a pudgy hand. He smiled apologetically at the actress; she smiled back at him, then shifted her smile to Robert Neumann, who flashed a flirtatious smile back at her.

He had decided that, should the opportunity present itself, he would sin that evening, at least in word and thought. He wasn't quite ready yet, he realized, to sin in deed.

Then someone invited the National Artist to tell them what he thought of the competition in more detail than he had been able to provide in his speech. The novelist settled into his chair like a lump of jelly and began to speak. 'I must say, comrades, the level of the competition astonished me. I had certainly not expected to find such a wealth of young talent.'

'What did you like most about the competition?' the Song and Dance major asked humbly.

'What did I like most?' The National Artist was silent for a moment. He was the kind of writer that people in reactionary literary circles liked to call 'an old whore'. He understood literature, but he didn't place a great deal of importance on his own integrity, and therefore literature, even genuine literature, no longer gave him any pleasure. Gazing around the table, he declared in a voice of thundering authority: 'The spirit of the competition, comrades! What a beautiful and joyous picture this competition gave us of the spirit of our young soldiers. In that torrent of genuinely fresh young poetry—and most of it, to a certain extent, was relatively very good poetry, almost—there was not a hint or a suggestion of the self-indulgent melancholy, the despair, the lack of faith, even the disgust, that used to be the main subject of young poets in the old bourgeois times.'

Both high-ranking officers continued to nod, and a diminutive lieutenant rescued Bobr from having to expand on that observation. 'I agree, comrade,' he said. 'I've observed that in our own unit, with every passing year, the comrades who come to us are somehow better, somehow—well, new socialist men. What I mean is, it seems that work is continually becoming, well, more and more—joyful—somehow.'

'Yes, yes,' said the National Artist quickly. 'You've put that well, comrade.' The lieutenant flushed with pleasure. 'Work is indeed a more joyful thing nowadays, both for you in the army, and for us in the Union of Writers. When I think,' and the novelist settled his blob-like body more comfortably into his chair, 'when I think of the situation in literature in this country back in the bourgeois, capitalist republic—well, it's shameful even to talk about it.' For a moment he appeared to be dreaming, and he was—about those balmy days when, as the star writer of a private publishing house, he had been given the cushy job of editor, with the duty of working once a week for three hours and being paid three thousand pre-war crowns for the privilege. He heaved a sigh that could have been interpreted as sorrow, and went on: 'The things people wrote then—and published!' He waved a paw in the air to fill his rhetorical pause. 'It was vile. It was the deliberate, programmatic dehumanization of man. Poets just mucked about with feelings, and they were petty feelings at that. It was pure existentialism!' He pronounced this with the same kind of disdain Lysenko had used in denouncing the fruit-flies used in genetics experiments. 'Ah, but today, in our socialist fatherland, when I hear the variety, comrades—this poem is about love, that one about work, or about standing guard—I am delighted. Truly delighted.'

The colonel stopped nodding his head and said, 'I think I speak for everyone present when I say that your praise has deeply touched and warmed us all. But now, perhaps Comrade Bobr would like to give our soldier-poets some more detailed pointers—'

'Why of course, naturally, comrades,' said Bobr quickly. 'That's what I'm here for.' He cleared his throat. 'It goes without saying that your work has its weak points as well as its strong ones.' And with that, he plunged into a list of the negative aspects of the poetry submitted. For a long time he spoke without being specific. Then he focused his remarks on the work of a corporal who, so far, had managed to be inconspicuous. 'Take these lines, for instance, comrades,' he said. *'You footlockers, beacons of Hope! Soldiers adorn you with the faces of women.* This is not a good line. *You footlockers*—yes, it broaches an interesting subject, a novel subject. But—*beacons of Hope?* Hope? What hope? And hope for what? Can you feel, comrade, how vague, unoriginal, and unrealistic that expression is? It completely spoils the line. Learn from our classical writers like Jan Neruda, or from foreign comrades such as Pablo Neruda, comrade.'

He fell silent and the Song and Dance major seized his opportunity. Poetry fell within his area of competence, after all. 'Would you allow me, comrade?'

'By all means,' said Bobr scornfully.

'I only want to add to what the Comrade National Artist here has said. This matter has to be looked at politically, too. We must realize, Comrade Corporal,' and the major turned to the non-com, whose hollow face radiated undisguised terror, 'we must realize that such a poem will fall into the hands of many comrades, right? And that poem will have an influence on them. Words too are weapons, comrade, and we who work with the masses must make sure they are good weapons, useful weapons, well-oiled weapons. And this is what you write: *You footlockers, beacons of Hope.* As the Comrade National Artist pointed out, it is a non-concrete, naturalist image. And I would add to what the comrade here said, comrade: from the political and ideological point of view it is a very suspect line.' The major glared at the corporal so disapprovingly that the young man's head sank and his hollow cheeks flushed crimson with shame. 'It is not at all a politically correct line!'

* * *

Danny was still waiting for Lizetka at twelve-thirty, long after her parents had gone to bed. Her boudoir, with its intimate lighting, reminded him of the disarray of a soldier's bedroom just before reveille. A large icon of the Virgin Mary and a period etching of Henry the Eighth stared down with dead eyes on the messy pile of books, dresses, underwear, fruit, and cigarettes strewn on the round, glass-topped table, and on the rumpled couch under the window, where she slept. There was an open clothes closet in the corner of the room, and a summer dress and a crumpled petticoat lay casually across a chair. Several nylon stockings and a sluttish blue satin bra hung on the armrest of another chair. Various other items were scattered on the floor. Everything was exactly as it had been since her husband was called up.

The tank commander opened the door to the next room. There, everything was stiffly tidy. The corner couch was reflected coldly in the glass doors of the bookshelves. If Lizetka's nature was reflected in the shambles of her den, here was a picture of the soul of her poor sod of a husband.

He went back to her room, emptied one of the chairs onto the floor, and pulled a few letters from the pile of things on her bedside table. He took one and began to read it:

> *My darling,*
> *I keep wanting to write you but I can't. You have to understand that, surrounded by all this emptiness, one simply doesn't have the courage; one fears everything. I've composed so many letters to you in my head since you left, but so far not a single one have I written down. I have often thought—not without understanding—of your special saintliness and decency.*

Yes—a saintliness called frigidity, a decency called narcissism. He didn't bother to look at the signature; his experienced eye judged the letter to be the work of the first of his successors, Kurisu, a student of Japanese. *So she didn't put out for him either,* he thought with satisfaction. *At least I have dubious precedence in that, as a* primus inter pares, *I was the first to demonstrate to her that a Catholic marriage need not exclude platonic infidelity, in the hope, of course, that with a little help from a Catholic devil, her platonic infidelity would one day become actual, physical infidelity. I haven't managed to bring her to that point,* he sighed, *but on the other hand I have been able to turn her into a perfect little platonic whore.*

He began reading the next letter:

> *Lizette, it is rather awful. I write you, and my worst problem is a chronic ill-*
> *ness of the soul called boredom. There is no escape, there is no way out except*
> *the one along which we walk, but that, perhaps, has neither beginning nor*
> *end.*

The quasi-existential sentiments betrayed the writer as Maurice, another of his colleagues in platonism, who had grown up in Vichy France during the Second World War.

> *Do you think we may have met sometime in another life, my wise queen? I*
> *write you, Karina, and I don't know if you are alive.*

Well. He reached for another. This one wasn't a letter, just a crumpled piece of paper. On one side, drawn in an artless hand, was a crude red heart with a red arrow pointing at it, and beside it, in shaky English: *It is your heart and beats only for me?*
Beneath that, in Lizetka's hand: *Yes!!*
And the response: *It is not difficult to love you—you most charming girl!*
And below that, from Lizetka: *Attention! My man see you!*
Well, here was someone new. He sounded like a real jerk. Why didn't he learn decent English? On the other side of the paper, however, they reverted to their mother tongue. *Didn't I put that rather cleverly? And my husband didn't suspect a thing.* Beneath that: *You're the Beauty and he's the Beast.* And then: *That's why I have to sweet-talk him all the time, otherwise he'd leap out and eat you, Budulín.* And with that the dialogue ended. Perhaps Budulín had, in fact, been eaten at that point. If he had, a willing replacement would certainly have jumped in.
Danny rummaged around in the pile of papers and came up with a small notebook. He opened it at random and read:

> *This afternoon, went into town and arrived at the Adria an hour late.*
> *Maurice was there, annoyed. A long walk to Barrandov. Maurice teed off at*
> *first, then pleasant. Tells me about his problems. Wonderful supper, then we*
> *dance. Maurice talks about divorce. Walk down the hill to the trolley-stop. I'm*
> *awfully sleepy. Maurice sticks with me all the way to Radlice. In bed by about*
> *two.*

> *Tuesday: Rise at 7:45. Terrible rush. Mother has words again. Half-hour late*
> *for work, but the Queen wasn't there yet, just Lexina. We gab a bit, talk about*
> *Pecka. The Queen arrives about ten, carrying some cakes. We all indulge, feel*
> *sick. Then to lunch, and a gentleman starts talking to me, tell him I went to*
> *school in Switzerland and he starts talking French to me. I get embarrassed*
> *and tell him it was German school. Says he desperately wants to see me again,*
> *he's from the Min. of For. Trade. So we make a date for next week. Then in*

the Church of the Little Jesus of Prague I pray for Robert and for myself, and
for the strength to stop being this way. Back to work about two and I go
straight for a bath. I lie in the tub and downstairs they're playing records with
a Jewish cantor singing. They're wonderful. I try reading a book called The
Egg and I *in the bath, but I get it wet and stop. Out of the bath at four. The*
Queen didn't show up at all this afternoon. Milan calls, Lexina brings me the
telephone in the tub. Then Budulín calls and I go to his place and we drink
absinthe.

So Budulín didn't get eaten after all, Danny though glumly. He put the notebook
aside and wondered what he was doing waiting there. *I suppose it's because I love her.*
Well—more likely because she never came across. So it's either vanity or it's love. And what
about Janinka? Ah, Janinka. . . . I guess it must be because Lizetka didn't come across.
In which case it's probably love, too.
Pleased with this reasoning, he succumbed to military weariness and fell asleep.

* * *

The disgraced corporal's name was Josef Brynych. In civilian life he had been a clerk
in a tobacco warehouse, and he had never written poetry before. The poem about the
footlockers had occurred to him one night when he was on guard duty. The guard
post was a wooden shack with a single bench of rotting planks, and the corporal
couldn't sleep. Bored to savagery with the four-hour pause between rounds, he read
the only material allowed in the guard post—a two-week-old copy of the tank division daily, *Armoured Fist*. He ploughed through everything, from an editorial entitled
'How to Continue Mass Cultural Work while Fulfilling the Summer Plan for Target
Practice with Heavy Machine-Guns' to the masthead—everything, including the
phone numbers. As he scanned those four printed pages again, in the final stages of
terminal desperation and believing that he had read every single letter, something
caught his eye, something he would normally have ignored altogether because it
promised even less amusement than he dared to expect from the people's democratic
press. It was a brief text arranged in short lines of unequal length—in other words, a
poem. Exhausted by insomnia, irritated by the snoring of the other guards on the
bench, tired of trying to lure an over-experienced mouse out of its lair with a piece of
bacon, and crushed by the sight of the guard commander, who was going against regulations by sleeping on the table, Corporal Brynych was driven to read the item, titled
'Poem Written on a March' and signed with the name Lt Jan Vrchcoláb. He read:

The merry song flies up like a raptor
And falls, strumming the heavens.
What could be apter?
Our platoon
marches, singing a tune.
I sing and think of you,
My heart's captor.

His tired brain stopped for a moment to consider the line *and falls, strumming the heavens.* He involuntarily tried to imagine what the merry song of an infantry platoon would sound like strumming the heavens. He imagined something soaring, then rubbing against a firm but yielding substance, then tumbling down to earth again. Then he tried to remember the last time his platoon had sung at all, let alone merrily. He reconsidered the poem and discovered that along with the rhyme *platoon* and *tune* he could add *saloon*. The possibilities began to interest him. He cast about for an appropriate line until he found one. The poem, written by Jan Vrchcoláb and improved by Corporal Brynych, now went like this:

> *The merry song flies up like a raptor*
> *and falls, strumming the heavens.*
> *What could be apter?*
> *Our platoon*
> *Marches, singing a tune.*
> *I sing and think of you,*
> *And of our favourite saloon,*
> *My heart's captor.*

The corporal's imagination was stimulated. After some thought, he transformed the poem yet again, so that it now read:

> *Grey boredom flies up to the heavens*
> *And falls directly on you.*
> *Our platoon*
> *Couldn't give a sweet fuck.*
> *I yawn, think of you,*
> *And curse my luck.*
> *Somewhere, in a warm saloon,*
> *Some young buck*
> *Is making you swoon.*

He found this highly entertaining. He looked through the other verses of Vrchcoláb's poem, and his eye fell on a notice printed underneath it announcing that the deadline for the divisional round of the Army Creativity Contest was July 15. He decided to enter something. He pulled a filthy diary out of his pocket and began to think about a subject. The first thing that came into his head, God knows why, was his footlocker with the picture of Blaženka and the village square in his hometown inside the lid. Then he thought that this awful boredom would soon be over, and he imagined himself sitting again in the aroma-filled kitchen in Blaženka's house, grinding coffee in the antique coffee mill while Blaženka, in a blue apron, made supper, and her mother, Mrs Jarošová, called him Mr Pepa, and Mr Jaroš winked at him and said, 'Some gal, eh? Sugar and spice, she is!' And Blaženka would blush and glance at him, her blue eyes dancing with the promise of pleasures to come after the wedding, and the wedding would be right after Christmas. Thus filled with poetic thoughts, Corporal Brynych produced the first four lines of his poem:

> *You footlockers,*
> *Beacons of Hope!*
> *Soldiers adorn you*
> *With the faces of women.*

He sent off two copies, one to *Armoured Fist*, the other to Miss Blažženka Jarošová, Sales Clerk, c/o Pramen Grocery Enterprises, Modřanky, p.o Rakovník. From Blažženka he got an enthusiastic letter, and after some time a notice appeared in *Armoured Fist*. Among the poems given an honourable mention in the divisional round of the Army Creativity Contest was one by Corporal Brynych, Josef. And now he was sitting here while the officers tore his poem apart.

* * *

The rattling of a key in the main door woke Danny, and a few moments later Lizetka was standing in the light from the table lamp. She was wearing a nylon jacket and slightly rumpled checked skirt. She smiled, but it wasn't a warm smile. 'Ahoj, Lízinka,' he said.

'Well, company,' she replied. 'Greetings, Comrade Tank Commander. You haven't come to see us for some time. What's up?'

'Nothing,' he said. 'Isn't it more like there's something new here?'

But she'd already put him out of her mind. She went to her writing table and began leafing through some papers. He felt as useless as a wax statue.

'So tell me, my friend,' she said absently. 'What's been going on at the base?'

'I got into some trouble before I came,' he said mechanically, looking intently at her bottom in its checked skirt. Was it vanity or was it love? Sex appeal, most likely. He started telling her the story of Lieutenant Malina and Sergeant Babinčáková. Lizetka went on leafing through her file.

'Are you listening, Lizetka?' he asked, irritated.

'I'm listening.'

'It's a strange kind of listening.'

'I'm paying attention.'

'I'll bet you don't even know what I'm talking about.'

'There was this Sergeant Babinčáková in the guardhouse and you had guard duty—no, prisoner escort duty—and Second Lieutenant Malina went to bed with her in her cell.'

'Well, all right,' he said grudgingly, and continued the story. But he had no taste for it. Lizetka began writing something in the file.

'Líza, couldn't you at least pay attention to me?'

'I told you, I'm listening.'

'Then couldn't you look at me while you listen?'

She turned to him. 'You want me to come and sit in your lap? For God's sake, Daniel, you sound just like Robert.'

The tank commander felt anger rising in him. Coming from Lizetka, there was no greater insult.

'If this is how you make him feel, I'm not surprised.'

'Not surprised?' she said, raising her eyebrows. 'There was a time when you were surprised.'

'There was indeed,' he said harshly.

'And those times are gone?'

He said nothing. As always, harshness had no effect on her. As always, Danny was the first to soften.

'In that case,' she said, 'thank God I didn't marry you.'

'Don't say that.'

'I repeat: thank God. I only regret I married anyone at all.'

'Last time, you said that if Robert got killed while he was in the army, you'd marry me.'

'That was last time. Not now.'

* * *

'Hope, Comrade Corporal? Hope for what?' the major was asking. 'And on top of that, you gave it a capital "H". Now, when a young comrade reads a line like that, what is the first thing that occurs to him? We know soldiers miss their loved ones and those close to them. But we mustn't reinforce these tendencies at all. In fact, Comrade Corporal, these tendencies must be wiped out. We don't want soldiers to spend their evenings sitting on their footlockers and mooning over photographs of their girlfriends and sighing. We want them in the mass cultural activity room, singing our mass songs and dancing our mass dances, right? This poem of yours, comrade, does not make our task any easier. No indeed, comrade. In fact, comrade, this poem of yours defeats our purpose.' The major's head was tilted threateningly towards Corporal Brynych, and every 'comrade' sounded like the salvo of a firing squad. The tobacco-warehouse clerk felt cold sweat dampening his back. Jesus, he hadn't asked for this.

'But otherwise, comrade,' said the National Artist, who obviously felt sorrier for the young poet, 'your poem isn't bad. You know it's not because it got honourable mention, after all.'

But the tobacco-warehouse clerk didn't care about the poem; what he was worried about was the report he'd take home from the army. So he just nodded mechanically at the novelist, while glancing anxiously at the major, his heart gripped with fear that mostly had to do with whether Blaženka would still want him if he had to leave the tobacco warehouse and work in the mines.

Corporal Brynych was just opening his mouth to apologize, to explain that he hadn't done this intentionally, when a notorious poetic hack of the Seventh Tank Battalion named Sergeant Maňas spoke up.

'Since we're already on the subject of the political impact of the work we heard tonight,' he began, 'allow me to draw your attention to one thing. The comrade cor-poral here was quite correctly and justifiably taken to task because the political content of his poem was different than he may have intended in his possibly, indeed perhaps undoubtedly, sincere effort. In this regard, I should like to draw attention not so much to the first four lines, but to the conclusion of his poem, comrades.' He stopped talking and turned his eyes thoughtfully towards the ceiling, where not long ago a soldier who had been a sign-painter in civilian life had rendered a fresco of rosy-cheeked soldiers embracing rosy-cheeked miners, smelter workers, farmers, and the working intelligentsia, whom he had painted wearing white lab coats and glasses; a private in a trooper's helmet was being given bread and salt by a rosy-cheeked but unembraced girl while, seated in a cloud, the Commander-in-Chief of the Czechoslovak Armed Forces, General Čepička, looked benignly down.

Sergeant Maňas took a deep breath, tore his eyes away from the joyous apparition on the ceiling, and went on: 'Just take the two concluding quatrains, comrades.

> *You footlockers.*
> *When tears of rain come down*
> *Upon your cracked paint*
> *Outside the barrack gates,*
> *We will carry a piece*
> *Of life home in you,*
> *And autumn will swallow us*
> *In a grey curtain of rain.*

'This captures one thing very well, I believe,' Maňas said. 'The mood of nature in autumn. But suppose we enquire after its political impact. What is the final impression? Is it happy? Optimistic? Is there a sense of pride in being a soldier? Joy at the prospect of returning to civilian life? I don't think so. I think the basic tone of this poem is melancholy. And it is an unjustified melancholy, one that is consistent neither with the attitude of our soldier to his basic military service, nor with his attitude to his private life. In short, it's a melancholy that has no place in the psychological armoury of our units.'

Others now jumped into the debate. A corporal remarked that sometimes melancholy was simply one of the undeniable facts of life, to which the Song and Dance major replied that, if this was the case, then they had to struggle against it. One poetic soul declared that the feeling of melancholy carried within it a kind of vengeful power, and that all revolutionaries were melancholy. Maňas easily deflated that heresy by labelling it an idealistic error and challenging anyone to name him any melancholy revolutionaries—and if anyone did, to prove that they had been melancholy. A politruk from the tank division declared that the comrades in his units had no reason to be melancholy at all. A Sergeant Pankůrek began to develop the idea that, besides its intellectual content, a poem had values that might be called cumulative—that is, they enriched life and created a treasury of variegated emotions. To this the Song and Dance major replied that life was now rich and variegated enough without melancholy. By this time Corporal Brynych was so terrified that he no longer noticed what was going on around him.

When the debate finally ended, in absolute victory for Sergeant Maňas and his opinions over Sergeant Pankůrek and his, the debaters suddenly remembered the person whose versified creation had started the discussion in the first place. But when they looked around, they discovered that Corporal Josef Brynych was no longer among them.

He was on the asphalt road leading back to his barracks, and he was composing in his mind a pledge he would make that, upon completing his basic military service, he would volunteer for work as a miner in the brown-coal mines of Kladno.

*　*　*

'I still love you, Líza,' said the tank commander. When he said it, he was convinced that it was absolutely true.

'Don't talk nonsense, darling,' said Lizetka. 'Don't try to make a fool out of me, all right? When was the last time you were here?'

'That has nothing to do with it. We've had weekend manoeuvres two weeks in a row.'

'And how many letters have you written me?'

He felt a pang of alarm. It was an odd thing: since that night above the shooting range he had completely forgotten his romantic correspondence with Lizetka.

'I haven't had the time,' he said weakly. 'I was dog-tired after all those manoeuvres. But I love you, Lizetka. I always have and I always will.'

'Baloney,' she said. 'This Corporal Babinčáková or whatever her name is has got your head spinning. Or is there someone else?'

'Lizetka, I swear to you the only reason I haven't written is those manoeuvres. I can prove it.'

'What are you going to do, bring me a note from your CO?' she said.

'Lizetka, get a divorce and marry me!'

'What a catch you'd be! Besides, I can't get a divorce.'

'I know, the Holy Mother Church won't allow it.'

'Don't blaspheme.'

'Jesus Christ,' groaned Danny. 'Are you that afraid for the state of my soul?'

'Yes.'

'And for yours?'

'That too. But that's my worry. I don't want you on my conscience.'

'And what if I kill myself because of you?'

'You?'

'Yes, me.'

'You're far too much of a momma's boy for that.'

'Jesus Christ.'

'And don't take the Lord's name in vain. That's a real sin.'

'Mortal or venial?'

'If you do it over and over again, it's mortal.'

'And what about you? Don't you sin over and over again?'

'What?'

'You know, all those guys you keep stringing along—Maurice, Kurisu. Somebody called Budulín. And don't forget me—'

'I don't want anyone to be sad. And you were the one who started it. I couldn't turn you down, and from that time on I haven't been able to turn anyone down. It's all your fault.'

'Oh, sh–' said Danny, and then caught himself in time. He wasn't on military turf now. 'You think you don't make me sad?'

'Do I?'

'I sure don't get what I want.'

'You know I can't do that. But I do everything I can.' She yawned. It was a cruel thing to do. 'Come on, Danny. What you suffer from is foolishness. I mean, is it so important? It doesn't matter who you do it with. You can do that with Babinčáková. The important thing is the soul—isn't that what you always said?'

Danny was trembling. *You bloody fool,* he said to himself. *You stupid bloody fool. She's damn right, and you're a bloody fool. Isn't it nice with Janinka? Nicer than this damn purgatory? God, God, God! God damn!* But the only thing he could think to say was, 'Lizeta, let me stay with you.'

'Oh no,' she said. 'Take this eiderdown and go next door.'

'Let me stay with you. I won't do anything.'

'No, no, darling, I want to sleep. You'd just annoy me.'

'I wouldn't.'

'Oh, yes you would. I know you.'

'I really wouldn't, Lizeta. Believe me.'

'No, no. Here's the eiderdown. Now, go take a walk.'

He took the eiderdown and carried it into the next room. He again remembered Janinka. *My God, is this me? Am I the same guy who made love to Janinka? Fuck it!* he thought—for in spirit the whole world was military turf.

He threw the eiderdown onto the shiny couch and went back into her room. She was still in her skirt, but her jacket and blouse lay on the chair. She let him stand there while she changed into her pyjamas, using a whole array of sly disrobing techniques so that he didn't see much of anything. Perhaps her problem was not so much frigidity as exhibitionism. It was clear that, after this striptease, his only possible goal was to sleep with her.

'One sin after another,' he said bitterly.

'But none of them mortal,' she retorted. Her eyes were indifferent, but they were also bright with some kind of . . . desire? Oh God! She slipped under the covers and turned off the light. He tore off his tunic, his trousers, and his shirt, and crawled in after her.

'No, Danny, go away.'

'Lizeta! Let me stay with you!'

'No. You'll touch me and I don't want that. I really don't.'

'I won't,' he said, and he could feel her body through the pyjamas, as hot as an iron. 'I won't touch you—or if I do, just a little,' and he slipped his arms around her and felt her soft breast in his hand.

'See how dumb you are?' she said angrily, and turned her back on him.

'Líza!'

'Leave me alone and go to sleep.'

He knew nothing would come of this. He certainly couldn't rape her—he'd tried it once and it had got him a two-week stay in the eye department of the army hospital. So he just snuggled close to her and placed his hand on her smooth, round shoulder. *It can't be any worse in that hell of hers. This heartless, indifferent body beside me will drive me mad.* He heard her regular breathing. She had fallen asleep. *I'll go mad, I'll go mad.*

But he didn't go mad. He fell into a light sleep, and in it he committed that sin with her. She, of course, took part immaterially, being a dream, but as far as his glands were concerned, the act was physical. He wondered why so much inconsequential stupidity surrounded something so simple to cure. He wondered if she and the sanctimonious religion she espoused were right after all: to become spiritual, to liberate oneself from. . . . And then he too fell asleep and became a liberated spirit and it was like a sweet death—sweet because, in his sleep, he didn't know that from this death he would soon awaken.

* * *

Robert Neumann paid no attention whatever to the entire controversy. In the cluster of bodies that formed after the discovery that Corporal Brynych was missing, the actress threaded her way expertly through the crowd and addressed him in a sociable voice:

'I wanted to congratulate you once more. Your poems read so well, did you know that?'

He wanted to reply that he didn't, or rather that he did—he couldn't make up his mind which—but before he could say anything, she went on, 'I'll bet you recite them out loud as you write them, am I right? Poets don't often do that, and that's why their poems don't read very well. But yours read wonderfully well. I mean it.'

As she was taking a breath, he managed to slip in a remark. 'It's mainly because of the wonderful way you read them.'

'Thank you, but I still think that's how you can tell real poetry—it reads well out loud. Isn't that so?'

Before he could say what he thought, she went on, 'Won't you give me some more? I'd like to recite some on my road trips, with your permission of course. You will? That'll be superb. You know, we tour a lot to army units outside the city, and it would be wonderful if I could read some of your poems. Do you agree?'

He could only manage a nod.

'The air's very close in here, don't you think? It's beautiful outside, almost summer weather. Wouldn't you like to go outside?'

He went, of course. In less than a minute (and he hadn't committed a single sin, in thought, word, or deed) they were sitting on a bench beside the wide asphalt road, bordered by a mosaic of white stones that shone a message into the starry night: FORWARD TOWARDS AN EXEMPLARY FULFILMENT OF THE AUTUMN EXERCISES. Despite the actress's garrulous interest in Robert Neumann's poetry, she soon had him talking about his private life. He found relief with her—not physical relief, but the kind that, in theory, the confessional was meant to provide. The difference was an important one. In the confessional, you accused yourself. Now, without even knowing how, Neumann suddenly found himself accusing his wife, and instead of undoing the buttons on the actress's Chinese silk blouse somewhere in the thick bushes across the road, he provided her with the unhappy history of his marriage with the much-admired Ludmila. It felt like a great miracle of compassion, like balsam on his wounds applied by a sensitive and understanding female soul.

In fact, Alena Hillmanová was cleverly exploiting the frustration of the progressive Catholic poet to gain an interesting insight into the love-life of her far too tight-lipped cousin, Daniel Smiřický.

* * *

The far too tight-lipped cousin was awakened next morning, in the bed of the technically faithful Ludmila Neumannová-Hertlová, by a loud noise. It was the father greeting the new day with a shout: 'Goddamned Communist swine!' But the presence of a man who had every appearance of being the lover of his married daughter didn't bother him. Danny, however, was not Marxist enough for the world to appear to him as a simple problem, resolvable through easily graspable laws. He listened calmly to the angry door-slam that marked the stage-manager's departure for work. Ludmila was sleeping like a baby, her fists clenched and her mouth, which seemed so sensual awake, now puckered as if ready to draw milk from a mother's breasts. He got up, put on his clothes, and shook her gently.

With great effort she opened one eye.

'Lizetka, when will I see you again?'

'Come to the office,' she mumbled, and closed her eye again.

He tiptoed out of the bedroom and the house, and spent the morning introducing himself around at a new and very large state publishing house where his cousin, the actress, had connections. He discovered that while he had been in the army, intellectual inflexibility had invaded publishing to a greater extent than he could have imagined, with disruptive results. In filling out the questionnaire for the post of editor of Anglo-American literature, he listed Hemingway among his favourite authors, but omitted to mention Howard Fast. In his final year at university, Hemingway had still been considered a progressive author whose only sin was to have crudely distorted the truth about the Spanish Civil War and vilified its real heroes. Since then, as the rather grave man who was interviewing him pointed out, Hemingway had been promoted. He was now a spy and an American intelligence agent. Danny reflected gloomily that this would probably ruin his chances for the job, but the grave man went on to inform him that everything evolves, including people and their opinions, and that no doubt he too, influenced by the female comrades in the Anglo-American 'Collective' (this was how they referred to editorial departments now), would develop and change. After being introduced to the comrades in question, he had no doubts about it either. One of them, a blue-eyed blonde with a round face, could single-handedly ensure his evolution in any direction she might wish.

That afternoon Danny went to see Lizetka. She worked, or more precisely was employed, in an office called Cultural Enterprises of the Capital City of Prague; Danny never did manage to find out what the organization actually did. During his visit, an old man with the title of Head of the Chess Circle stopped by, but he was quickly swept out of the office.

The office was located behind a glass partition in what had once been a vaudeville hall. Ludmila sat behind a large desk displaying a huge appointment book with almost nothing in it, an empty notepad, and a telephone. She shared the office with a peroxide blonde of about thirty called Mrs Králová, whose husband was about to be appointed to the permanent Czechoslovak mission to the UN in New York. She was supposed to be Ludmila's superior, but in his relatively frequent visits to the glassed-in office Danny had almost never found her in. Today was an exception, however, and perched on Králová's desk (which had *two* telephones) was the third employee of the organization, a slender, pretty, impudent-looking girl by the name of Lexina. A man in a pale blue business suit slouched in the corner staring at her, but he had nothing to do with the affairs of the office. When Danny walked in, Králová was just speaking.

'Naturally Vašek was teed off,' she said, 'so he goes to the section chief, who's fed up with him, but Vašek and Čepek from Security are hand in glove, and Čepek is in solid with Kopejda, so the section chief promises to arrange it for him, and before Vašek makes it back to the NV a telephone order's already arrived that Budárek is to take over the Karlín operation. Budárek isn't a bit pleased, and oh, by the way, Vašek set this little surprise up for him through Mikulka, so Vašek seemed to be out of the picture. Budárek doesn't even blink, but he checks himself into the General Hospital with kidney trouble or something, because the head doctor is somebody called Šofr who Budárek once did a favour for, and now he's waiting to see how the thing shakes out. Naturally, Vašek was teed off—'

Whatever this outfit did, relationships between its employees were clearly very complex. It turned out, Králová said, that someone called Pecka was about to get the sack because there was ten thousand missing from the till, which under normal circumstances would have been replaced by grants, if only Hampejz hadn't been after Pecka's job. And Hampejz was in hot water because of those missing French originals, so he had to leave the SD though he'd only been there three months, but he'd certainly push Pecka out because Vosáhlo was keeping an eye out for Pecka, except that now they'd demoted Vosáhlo, so Pecka was up the creek and would probably end up in the DO instead of Čuriková, who got involved with Milič and the word leaked right up to the minister, who was Milič's wife's father. . . .

As the tank commander listened to all this, the fellow in the blue suit was shamelessly eyeing Lexina, and Lexina was shamelessly letting herself be eyed, while popping chocolates into her mouth from a box on the table. Danny felt as though he'd just awakened from some idyllic, pastoral dream in which simple, uniformed shepherds were herding simple, uniformed sheep and then, two years later, driving them back into the terribly complicated world where human beings were locked in a constant struggle for good, better, and still better jobs. This complex new society was criss-crossed, it seemed, by a fine network of friendship and hostility, of favours rendered and owed, of sympathy and antipathy, of kinship and relationships that reminded him of nothing so much as a bloody family feud. He was astonished at how much mental effort went into calculating the possible combinations and estimating strengths and weaknesses, and how much depended on knowing things that might serve for blackmail. And all of this was, for some inscrutable reason, financed from state treasury.

As Králová talked and talked, the tank commander watched Lizetka. Her skirt beneath the table was high enough for him to see under it. He also looked at the long legs and pitch-black eyes of Comrade Lexina, and the usual mixture of thoughts began tumbling around in his head, most of them ill-humoured and sullen. The world, it seemed to him, was no more than a few points of light drowned in a dark mush of displeasure.

At last the fellow in the pale blue business suit looked at his watch, straightened up, and announced that he had to be going.

'Jeepers!' said Comrade Lexina, checking her watch. 'Five-thirty! Darling, would you put me down for two hours' overtime?'

'Now look, Lexina,' giggled Králová, 'just get out of here. It was only an hour and a half, and that's what I'm going to put down. You won't catch me stealing from the state.'

* * *

Lexina and the fellow in the pale blue suit were barely out the door when the telephone rang for the first time since Danny had arrived. Králová picked up the receiver and said in a tired, official voice, 'Králová, CECC.' Then her eyes opened wide. She winked at Ludmila, covered the mouthpiece with her hand, and whispered loudly, 'Kustka!'

She spoke in her official voice again: 'Comrade Kovářová has just left.'

A thin voice could be heard speaking on the other end, and then Králová said, 'I don't know where. She left by car with Comrade Dr Hillman from screenwriting.' As she said this, she kept looking at Ludmila, her eyebrows dancing a strange routine, while Ludmila's replied in kind. 'Would you like to leave a message?' she asked sweetly, and when, instead of an answer, there was a sharp click in the receiver, she hung up and said, 'I guess not,' and both women burst out laughing.

'Lexina's going to have to deal with that one,' said Králová.

'I keep telling her he's going to lay into her some day.'

'It's just what she needs, my dear. She's almost as big a bitch as you are.' Králová took a sidelong look at the tank commander, then stood up, still giggling, and said, 'Well, I'm on my way, young people.'

The tank commander suddenly realized that the fellow in the pale blue suit was his cousin's husband, whom he'd never met. He stood up quickly and said goodbye to the affable boss of his platonic mistress.

As soon as she'd vanished through the door, Lizetka said with great feeling, 'The cow! She's a real swine, isn't she? She's all giggles and honey, but she stabs me in the back every chance she gets.'

'Why would she do that?'

'Why? How should I know? What kind of question is that, anyway? You talk like you've just come from the moon.'

It was exactly how the tank commander felt. He said goodbye to Lizetka (she had to go somewhere to arrange something, but she declined to say what and where) and they agreed to meet again at ten-thirty in front of the Ministry of Culture. She was in a good mood and had invited him to something she called a 'special screening for study purposes'.

* * *

The special screening for the minister, his girlfriends, and their lovers, and for a narrow circle of film experts and their mistresses, featured an American film called *The Valley*. The screening was held in a tiny rococo salon in the Wallenstein Palace which had been painstakingly restored in brilliant gold leaf and pink wallpaper. There were silver candelabras with flickering orange electric lights turned low, and as soon as Lizetka and the tank commander had taken their seats in the beige and pink armchairs, the lights were extinguished and the credits began to roll across the screen.

The minister preferred musicals, since he liked young women, but sometimes, perhaps to whet his appetite, he declared a fast and showed westerns instead. Such was the case today. A lion filled the screen and, wreathed with the slogan ARS GRATIA ARTIS, roared out his ancient invitation to entertainment. The audience, however, had come to study.

The movie was about a stagecoach travelling through Monument Valley, where it was attacked by a marauding band of Indians. It dealt with the relationships between the people on the stagecoach, and showed the Indians as creatures with a raw animal thirst for blood. Intellectually the film was extremely reactionary, but the direction was outstanding because it offered the specialists in the audience a whole range of wonderful formal ideas. The acting was pure naturalism.

The film experts, who had come to the late-night screening directly from the première of a new Czech film called *Heroes with Callused Hands*, studied these elements intensely. In the dimness of the salon, they stared wide-eyed at the crude charm of the love scenes. A famous director, his brow furrowed in concentration, smacked his lips audibly at an original close-up shot looking straight down the barrel of a Colt six-shooter whose cylinder slowly revolved on the screen. Danny was the only one who simply let himself be carried away by the story. The hoofbeats of horses thundered and the stagecoach lurched and rattled among the rocks, pursued by hordes of red men dressed in feathers and armed with bows. Despite a long-cultivated skepticism, Danny felt deeply anxious about the fate of the beautiful girl in the stagecoach, and Lizetka obviously felt the same, for when the redskins let loose their first salvo of arrows, she grasped his hand. This brought him back to reality. When the need is greatest, he thought bitterly, divine intervention is usually close at hand—in the movies, at least. Then a cluster of men in US Cavalry hats popped up on the horizon. Danny squeezed Lizetka's hand and she returned the squeeze. 'After them!' yelled the minister joyfully, and the prize-winning director added, 'Hip! Hip! Hip!' 'After them!'

roared several experts, and Lizetka jerked her hand out of Danny's and added her voice to the swelling expressions of partisan support. Now the shots came rapidly: horses' hoofs crashing like hammers on the stone-hard ground, pistols firing, terrified faces inside the stagecoach, and the painted faces of the Indian cut-throats were rapidly intercut with the determined Yankee faces of the cavalrymen. The salon thundered with applause and the stamping of feet. The specialists rose whooping to their feet, the women shrieked, the minister clenched his fists and emitted incomprehensible but energetic grunts. A sharp, piercing falsetto rose above the hellish pandemonium: 'Hurraaaaaaaaaaaaaaaaaaaaaaah!'

Danny got to his feet, kissed Lizetka's indifferent hand, and walked out of the projection room. He had to catch the night train that would get him back before reveille the next morning. He was already facing one disaster—the one in the guardhouse—and he didn't want to add to that another breach of the orders set for the army by the people who were the source of all power, and the only ones who enjoyed all the rights and privileges of the state.

RIENZI CRUSZ

(b. 1925)

Born in Galle, Sri Lanka (formerly Ceylon), Rienzi Crusz studied at the University of Ceylon, where he received an Honours B.A. The recipient of a Colombo Plan Scholar fellowship in 1951, he studied at the School of Librarianship and Archives, University of London, England. After his arrival in Canada in 1965, he continued his studies in the library sciences, receiving a B.L.S. from the University of Toronto. He holds an M.A. from the University of Waterloo where he has been Senior Reference and Collections Development Librarian since 1969.

Anthologized and widely published in Canadian literary magazines, Crusz's poetry is often about the immigrant experience. Although, as he writes in 'In the Idiom of the Sun', 'I must hold my black tongue,' his poetry is permeated by ironic imagery that juxtaposes his native culture to that of his adopted land. Through strong rhythms and a caustic wit, Crusz attempts to construct an 'idiom of the Sun', a language that invests his 'black tongue' with layers of colonial history and traces of Canada's postindustrial society. As Arun Mukherjee remarks, Crusz has constructed the 'mythic persona' of 'The Sun Man' that 'occurs in several poems': '[t]he persona allows Crusz to amalgamate the two segments of his life in a meaningful way while it works as a readily available device with which to build further.'

Crusz's collections of poetry include *Flesh and Thorn* (1974), *Elephant and Ice* (1980), *Singing Against the Wind* (1985), *A Time for Loving* (1986), *Still Close to the Raven* (1989), and *The Rain Doesn't Know Me Any More* (1992). The tension between nature and industrialized culture, the exploration of a self that is constantly changing, and a preoccupation with the act of writing are recurring elements in these books. While his poetry often contains lush imagery evoking his Sri Lankan past, Crusz never resorts to a comforting sense of nostalgia. His double perspective as an immigrant and a 'black man' compels him to keep in mind the complexity of cultural and racial differences.

SITTING ALONE IN THE HAPPY HOUR CAFÉ

and meeting civilization head on
with a doughnut, hot coffee, a cigarette.
At the centre table,
suddenly thinking of horseshoes.
What if somebody mistakes me
for a target,
begins to practise his Western art?
Cigarette smoke snakes above my head,
makes a highway,
collapses.

I'm being watched.
Blue eyes suddenly a torment,
a torrent of waterfall,
beauty with a knife between its teeth.

So once again,
I must close my black eyes,
feel my legs climbing,
climbing
towards the sun.
Each crag, jutting root,
now a rung of mercy.

I must move, move
away from this darkness unasked for,
or make that second discovery
of fire: love
for the tall man with thrusting blue eyes
seeing nothing
but a blur of shadowed skin
a spot on his morning sun.

FROM SHOVEL TO SELF-PROPELLED SNOW BLOWER: THE IMMIGRANT'S PROGRESS

Two days into the Promised Land
and my eyes dance:
Supermarket and Mall,
those shopping faces thick with neon,
plastic cards breathing under their breasts.
One block, and the GOLDEN OX rises
with MOLSON froth and snaking smoke,
afternoon men angular in beer laughter.
I am in TV's arms.
I laugh with the HONEYMOONERS,
the Cuban and his Lucy,
trace blood along the FUGITIVE's trail.
No one can mention the forecast: tomorrow
100% precipitation / freezing rain.
So down the shimmering street I go
with only my sun head and ADIDAS,
to learn how the feet suddenly slide,
shudder with instant pain,
the body lumps to horizontal woe.
3 broken ribs, some hefty pain,
I've learnt the beatitudes of ice,
something sacred, something cold,
demanding respect, a paraphernalia

of horned boots, cowl and padded vest,
for body nicely flexed to winter's mould.

After twenty winters in my bones,
shovelling my sidewalk snow,
a self-propelled snow blower I've called Pablo
now does my chores,
                        vertical as my front door,
and I'm happy.

IN THE IDIOM OF THE SUN

It would have been somewhat different
in green Sri Lanka, where I touched
the sun's fire daily
with my warm fingertips.

I wouldn't have hesitated
to call you bastard
and for emphasis, might have even
thrown in the four-letter word.

The blood would have shuddered a little
under your Aryan skull,
but you would have held my honesty
like a temple flower in full bloom,
forgiven my unholy idiom.

Here in this white land,
the senses forged to iron silence,
the mind trapped in a snow boot,
I must hold my black tongue.

The blood has wintered,
and icicles hang like cobwebs
from the roof of my cold mouth.
I can now only spit frozen eyed,
and gently demur.

IN THE SHADOW OF THE TIGER (3)

Postcard   Colombo, 8 August, 87
Kingross Club   11:30

This Sunday morning was a beaut!
Fries and Beck's beer went down like magic
the sea was rough the children thrashed
like fish on the beach my nerves were cool,
beered cool!
Kingross Club has its kings. You can tell
from the size of their bellies, and the grins
on the black faces of the waiters

love you   rienzi

P.S. Guess what? Tamil Tigers blew up
some 300 people near the Pettah bus stand
with a powerful car bomb. Maybe we should call
Sri Lanka Beirut No. 2

Ciao   rienzi

A DOOR AJAR

Everything is green, and the wash
of blue down here, the coral alone
white, twisting its thin warm arms
round my skin.
Air bubbles, globes that burst
to feed my heaving lungs,
have skins in nothing but gossamer blue.

But I must come up
for air—leave the sharks
curving like lightning in their dance,
their teeth sucking water after
the red ambush of hunger.

Everything is good down here
but we flail our arms
for the blue kingdom of air,
our heads electric

for the sun's nostalgia, the photograph,
the pappadam and ice cream man,
the green land we left
our childhood faces in.

ROY KIYOOKA

(1926-1994)

'[W]hatever my true colours, I am to all intents and purposes, a white anglo-saxon protestant, with a cleft tongue,' said Roy Kenzie Kiyooka in 1981 while addressing the Japanese Canadian/Japanese American Symposium in Seattle. Born in Moose Jaw, Saskatchewan, Kiyooka was a *nisei*, a Canadian-born child of immigrant Japanese parents. His cleft tongue 'bears the pulse of an English'—'inglish', he called it—'which is not my mother tongue'. At five, Kiyooka had to put aside the Japanese he spoke at home, at once an act of 'survival' in an environment where the pressure was to assimilate, and the beginning of Kiyooka's recognition that he had to 'hold my own', to 'come to an articulateness by which I could stand in this world of literate people'.

Called a 'cultural autodidact', Kiyooka, who grew up in Calgary and never finished high school, was a 'multidisciplinary artist'. A painter with a national and international reputation already established by the late 1960s, a poet beginning with the publication of his first book, *Kyoto Airs* (1964), sculptor, photographer, collage-, music-, and film-maker, and an inspiring and dedicated art teacher, Kiyooka resisted the demands and conventions of the mainstream art world. 'I don't even feel beholden to my own generation . . . people don't know how to get a handle on me. I think the most critical thing about my activity is the interface between myself as a painter and myself as a language artificer. But what has to be understood is how the two inform each other.'

Kiyooka, like the other Japanese-Canadians at the time, lived through the turmoil that followed the bombing of Pearl Harbor. As he wrote, '[n]eedless to say it abruptly ended my education and our plain city life. I had the obscure feeling that something formless dark and stealthy had fallen upon me during my sleep but when I awoke nothing outward seemed to have changed, even though my childhood friends began to fall away from me. I might add that it's a loss I've never fully recovered from.' His father and older brother lost their hotel jobs, and the family left Calgary to settle in the small town of Opal, Alberta, where they found farm work. From 1942 to 1946, Kiyooka worked there 'except for off-season work' that took him to the killing floor of the Swift Canadian plant in Edmonton and to the fishing plants of Great Slave Lake, where he 'was part of a motley crew of seasonal workers comprising West Coast Japanese fishermen Icelandic and Baltic fishermen and all the First Nation's People who were recruited by McInnes Products. . . . *all this and more for less than fifty cents an hour . . .*'.

In 1959, at the Emma Lake Artists' Workshop in Saskatchewan, Kiyooka encountered the American artist Barnett Newman, who influenced his shift from figurative to abstract painting. By the late 1960s he had exhibited in many galleries in Canada and overseas, had won the silver medal at the 1966 São Paulo Bienal, and had his painting represented in major galleries. Kiyooka taught art in many places across Canada, including the University of British Columbia from which he retired in 1991.

transcanada letters (1975), his first long book, gathers together many letters/poems to family and friends during the years that he traversed Canada, 'with a hostage of snapshots'. By its size and design alone, this book speaks of Kiyooka's desire to break through boundaries and to record the process of experience and language in all its minute shifts. Much of his writing begins in or deals with Japan, which he visited many times. Many of his early poems appeared in *Imago*, edited by George Bowering, and *White Pelican*, edited by Sheila Watson. Kiyooka's early publications include *Nevertheless These Eyes* (1967), *StoneDGloves* (1970), and *The Fontainebleau Dream Machine: 18 Frames From a Book of Rhetoric* (1977). Most of Kiyooka's writing directly engages—in form, content, and design—the visual. *Pear Tree Pomes* (1987), illustrated by David Bolduc, was nominated for the Governor General's Award, and was the last collection of poetry published before his death. Still, 'since the early 80s,' in his own words, 'i've ventured willy-nilly into self-publishing under the logos of the "Blue Mule" a maverick photo gallery i kept for a few years on Power Street . . . all the . . . book/s have been printed, collated, and bound in my own good time in editions of 26 plus 10, with no thought for further editions. "the future of forethought is present-tense." i write the passages of time, . . . i go on trying to hold, in my mind, an actual world of kinship/s.' Two of these titles are *Hieronymus Bosch's Heretical* *April Fool Diverti-mementos & Other Protestations* (1986) and *March: Prose: Works: A Concatenation of Pacific Rim Vernacular/s a hank of seaweed flotsam in brine* (1986). In recognition of his cultural contribution, Kiyooka received the Order of Canada in 1977.

FROM *TRANSCANADA LETTERS*

10/ 15th/ '69
Kyoto City, Japan

dear Gladys

> . . . . accustom'd as i am to central heating——
> its a real drag to be numb with cold. not that its
> really that cold but that we have no heat. like
> inside or outside the same temperature. or aggravated
> as when winter sun glows but dont penetrate in.
> Im sittin' here with a thick wool blanket across my lap.
> my stocking'd feet sit upon a petrol foot-warmer.
> Im wearing a thick wool jacket on top of more than
> the usual underclothes. plus a heavy overcoat on
> top of all this. and its just mid-October like Indian Summer
> back home, etc. or we're all sitting around the low
> kitchen table our legs tuckt under the quilted apron whc
> hangs to the floor. under the table
> theres a small electrical heating element. its
> i suppose a miniature central heating system (with a
> small perimeter of warmth)—bolster'd with cups of hot sake
> electronic energies off the colour'd teley.
> then as often as not i'll have a late-night bath the kind
> where you soap first then rinse off before getting in
> to the hot hot water—to soak up the heat. and any number
> can use the same water with no accumulation of grey
> scum 2/3rds of the way up the tub. Phil Whalen told me
> he fucken near froze to death last winter (his 1st winter
> here. he sd he didnt get sick didnt even get a cold——
> just felt as tho he might freeze to death, daily.
> and when theres a storm outside your window think how
> nice it is to be able to go abt bare-arsed
> if you shld want to. and to hell with the romantical

theories of how great literature gets written in
draughty stone castles. gee Glad-eyes aint central heating
one of the so called marvels of these stoned ages!

> . . . thru successive re-visions
> yours truly continues to be
> as they say most unruly.

FROM *PEAR TREE POMES*

since you and i forsook the rites of marriage

intentionally without—facing up to the signals of mutual
disenchantment—we found ourselves side-stepping
each other's nakedness to fall asleep in a heap of mired feelings
til the early bird traffic on prior street summoned us
to another 'good morning—did you sleep well' breakfast
on the run . there's a lady with a champagne voice on co-op radio
singin' the ol' after midnight blues and whoops!—there's
that ol' heart-ache again . what i want to know is how come you
with your bright gists and me with my pointed beard didn't
make the perfect match . how come we ended up playing
that ol' deaf and dumb game when it was as plain as this prose
that the pear tree's forkt branches foretold the truth .
since you left i've been taking a hot water bottle to bed
> how about you with your tepid toes?

since i wrote the night sky down i've been out for

a late night bowl of barbecue duck noodle soup at kam's garden
and since i got home i put the ol' blue mule band on and
yes—i've dreamt up this 6 a/m dawn just for you . i'm just
an ol' night bird ready to do the lindy hop with any ol'
hurdy-gurdy man or woman . 'birds' who don't invest in the same
dawn tend to end up sharing a different nest . since you
left i've been keeping an early morning vigil .

the pear tree a siamese cat named cooper and me

seem to have made a compact with these fall days—
one which has something to do with an improbable stiffening of
the ligaments and joints plus an oftimes acerbic-laugh

sandwicht between thin slices of callit-a-wanton-hunger
you said put a grey pallor on our relationship . unlike the other
two, i didn't want to admit to my infirmity . thus
the pear tree basks in the rotund sun striking my cheek while
stroking the fur of the paws-up-in-the-air siamese cat
lying on the light-struck carpet under my feet .
thus language—mirroring the eddys of our indiscretions—
deposits the trio and their common ailments at the
foot of the heapt-up midden . crumpled bent unrepentant

dear lesbia

—i'm thankful i didn't have to choose
between you and the pear tree though i must admit i
didn't think i'd have that choice made for
me : nor did i think of it as a deliberate intent on
your part til the very end when it became
impossible to tell 'who' fell out of synch with 'whom'
let alone 'why' . bird bird of my once
fabled pear tree—there's one less song haunting
the morning alley since you flew off to
another nest in another neighbourhood . do fly by if
you have a spare wing and share a pear.
you know that i know a pear tree isn't anybody's property .
and if i may say so neither are you . nor i

SAAD E.A. ELKHADEM

(b. 1932)

Saad E.A. Elkhadem (Sa'd al-Khādim) was born in Cairo, Egypt, in 1932. After studying at Graz University, Austria, where he received his Ph.D. (1961), he began his academic career at the University of North Dakota. He moved to Fredericton in 1968 to take up a position as professor of German and comparative literature in the Department of German and Russian at the University of New Brunswick. An editor of many critical studies, and the author of eight scholarly books, Elkhadem has also translated many literary titles from German into Arabic (including works by Bertolt Brecht and Friedrich Dürrenmatt) and from Arabic into English.

A fiction writer and playwright, Elkhadem has published in Cairo two volumes of plays, a collection of short stories, and four novels. Although he writes in Arabic, most of his fiction has appeared in bilingual editions in Canada, translated into English by S. El-Gabalawy. His publications include *The Ulysses Trilogy* (1988), and the 'micronovels' *Canadian Adventures of the Flying Egyptian* (1990), *Chronicle of the Flying Egyptian in Canada* (1991), and *Crash Landing of the Flying Egyptian* (1992). The last three titles form what his translator S. El-Gabalawy calls an

'avant-garde trilogy' about a 'Flying Egyptian', an Egyptian immigrant writer in Canada who, through an array of self-reflective devices, attempts to write a story that is at once about the experience of immigration and fiction. Elkhadem himself calls his trilogy a series of 'micronovels', an accurate definition that reflects the ways in which Elkhadem compresses the form of the novel into what would normally fall between the length of a short story and a novella. There is an ironic intent behind this compacting of experiences: for example, as El-Gabalawy says, the narrator of the third book of the trilogy 'attempts to sum up the accumulated events of a lifetime in fewer than two hundred words as a means of defining his identity'.

Although not formally experimental, the short story included here reflects a similar kind of irony. The brassy voice of the immigrant narrator speaks of how defeated he feels by the Canadian immigration and employment systems, but also of how determined he is to resist having his identity erased. This story appeared originally in the anthology *Arab-Canadian Writing: Stories, Memoirs, and Reminiscences* (1989), edited by K.A. Rostom.

NOBODY COMPLAINED

These minutes. Don't you worry. I have all the time in the world. I hope this is not the same Smith I met in Cairo. A son of sixty bitches. May Allah destroy his mother's home. Impolite. Rude. Arrogant. The white race. He gave me the key to all seven gates of paradise. Someone with your qualifications should have no problem finding a job in Canada. May Allah damn his mother's grave. Somebody forgot to tell him about the high rate of unemployment in this cursed ice box. You could teach biology. Dammit. Hasn't he ever heard of certificate one, two, three, and God knows how many more? And your young wife will learn the language in a few months. The government will pay her thirty dollars a week. This is more than fifteen pounds. English or French. Canada is bilingual, you know. No, I don't know. The poor girl couldn't take it any more. And they hated us in Montreal. We can't speak it. We don't want to speak it. The waitress whispered to the cook and both laughed at her. Nobody soaks his bread in the spaghetti-sauce. The poor girl wept all the way home. It was cold. It was really cold.

'Mr Khalil. Ibrahim Khalil. This way please.'

Clean. Quiet. A shiny percolator surrounded by paper cups. In Egypt they drink tea. A dirty boy squeezes himself between the desks balancing a big plastic tray on his little hand. Half-filled glasses. Black, cold, and over-sweetened. The flies land for a sip then jump back to the boy's face. This is not the Smith I knew. They said he accepted all kinds of bribes. I couldn't pay him anything anyway. Seventeen pounds don't go a long way. The poor man's month has ninety-nine days. Seventeen pounds. Less than forty dollars. At least I was working. Now I do nothing and get more. The poor girl couldn't bear it any more. An unemployed hand is a filthy hand. We are beggars no matter how you call it. Charity. Alms. I am going back. Poor girl. The doctor found nothing wrong with her. Depression is very common among . . . what I mean is . . . there is no need to worry. But I worried. Mr Smith ignores me. Does he think of us when he is at home with his wife and children? Numbers. Nothing more than numbers. Poor numbers. Lazy numbers. Stupid numbers. Crazy numbers. I had a strange number from Egypt today. No, honey. This is India. The Egyptians don't have elephants. They have camels. Yes, I guess both of them have alligators. I suppose so. Crocodiles and alligators are one and the same. Then he gets his steak. He wouldn't soak his bread in any sauce. The poor girl. Then he watches the hockey games. And the numbers wait patiently in the cold filing cabinet. In the morning he gets them out of their hiding, spreads them on his desk, and asks them to perform a few amusing tricks. Then comes the coffee hour, the lunch hour, and the get-ready-to-leave hour. He never forgets to collect the numbers, to rearrange the numbers, and to bury the numbers. He is through with this one. I hope he found something for him.

'Mr Khalil. Mr Abraham Khalil?'
'Ibrahim Khalil, sir.'

Many remarks in red. I am no communist. Nasser gets weapons from Russia. Charity. Alms. But I am no communist. A few in green. Saint Patrick's Day is not a holiday. I stayed at home anyway. Mary brought a case of beer. She cooked a chicken and Chinese rice. Near East or Far East. It is practically the same. Then she pulled me to the bed. But she had to mention my wife's clothes. Dammit. The Salvation Army never gave me anything. I know them piece by piece. I love them all. The odour of her body. The scent of her perfume. I bought her a small bottle for her birthday. But she had to spoil everything. Beggars shouldn't smell good. I threw it out of the window. The poor girl.

'Ibrahim you say?'
'Yes, sir, Ibrahim Khalil.'

'T' not 'e' you stupid bastard. Don't say a word. Don't annoy the man. A crazy name anyway. Probably a Muslim. These people marry four, you know. No wonder nobody wants him to teach his kids. Of course they don't observe Christmas or celebrate on New Year's Eve. Smile. He might find something for you. I'll accept anything. Security guard. Waiter. Even garbage collector. An unemployed hand is a filthy hand. Poor girl. Mary says let them pay you. It is their mistake. All the beautiful pictures and attractive brochures. Her husband stayed three years on welfare. Nobody complained. But I can't get used to it. I don't want to get used to it. Another month like this and I'll lose my mind. Exactly as she did. The poor girl. And I can't go back home any more. All the lies. No, not lies. Everyone exaggerates a little. It was a big automatic car. Why should I tell everyone that I paid a hundred and fifty. Twenty-five a week. And the telephone. Don't they wait five years to get a new telephone? They have never heard of credit cards or of cable television.

'Are you still at the same address?'
'Yes, sir.'

Mary wanted me to move to her place. But the clothes stood in the way. The poor girl. I'll write her to come back. As soon as I find a job. Maybe today.

'Telephone number the same?'
'Yes, sir.'

If he finds something for me. I'll buy a big case of beer. And we will celebrate. Mary and I. Then I'll write her a letter. Better a telegram. Everything OK. Come at once. It takes a month till they bill me. And we will move to a better place. All the clothes will be waiting for her. Why not? A child will keep her busy. She is sitting now in the sun worrying about nothing.

'I am afraid the situation hasn't changed at all. You understand. Maybe next week. You understand?'
'Yes, sir. I understand.'
My God, I can't take it any more.
'Thank you for coming. Have a nice day.'
'Thank you, sir.'

Dammit. Filthy or not, who cares. Let them pay. Now to the liquor store. I need something strong. Mary is waiting for me. And she has no filthy hands. The Salvation Army may pay me something for all these clothes. The poor girl. Maybe next week. I'll wait till next week. The situation may change.

AUSTIN CLARKE

(b. 1934)

'This year I became eligible for Canadian citizenship, but I do not intend to apply for it. Not because I undervalue this status which is so highly prized by so many immigrants from all over the world; rather, because I *do* value its privileges highly, but realize that I would be accepting in theory a status that Canada does not intend to give me in practice—because I am a black man,' said Clarke in 1963.

Seventeen years later, and by then a Canadian citizen, Clarke won a nomination as a Progressive Conservative candidate for the provincial elections in Ontario. He was not successful, but his candidacy, together with the other political and cultural positions he later held, including Vice-Chairman of the Ontario Film Review Board (1983-85), suggest that, despite the fact that the 'system' still 'assault[s]' him, Clarke has found it possible to negotiate racial politics and art. As he says, 'There was a time when I revelled in the characterization of a black writer. . . . Now I am simply a writer and if someone knows me he knows I am black. I am not writing things simply of interest to blacks.'

Not unlike some of the fictional characters in his first collection of short stories, *When He was Free and Young and He Used to Wear Silks* (1971), Clarke views the marginalized position of blacks in Canada as reflecting not only the bitter legacy of colonialism and the pervasiveness of racism, but also the inner and outer corruption and exploitation of communities forced to live under literal or psychological segregating conditions. His novel *The Prime Minister* (1977) and his memoir, *Growing Up Stupid under the Union Jack* (1980), a winner of the Cuban prize Casa

de las Americas, directly address these issues.

Born in St James, Barbados, Clarke did not begin to write until after he arrived in Canada in 1955. A high school teacher on leave, he attended Trinity College, University of Toronto, where he studied Economics and Political Science. He did not complete his degree; he began writing instead. After a number of odd jobs, Clarke worked as a freelance reporter, and as a freelance broadcaster for the CBC, for which he produced documentaries and literary programs that dealt, as Clarke writes, 'with the social and cultural problems of black people in the United States, Britain, Canada and the West Indies'. Following the success of his first novels, *The Survivors of the Crossing* (1964) and *Amongst Thistles and Thorns* (1965), he taught at various universities in the United States, including Yale, Brandeis, and Duke. He returned to Toronto in 1977, after serving as Adviser to the Prime Minister of Barbados (1973-76), as Cultural Attaché with the Embassy of Barbados in Washington, D.C. (1974-75), and as General Manager of the Caribbean Broadcasting Corporation (Barbados, 1975-76). The three novels *The Meeting Point* (1967), *Storm of Fortune* (1971), and *The Bigger Light* (1975), a trilogy about Toronto, established Clarke's reputation as the most prominent black writer in Canada. His most recent books are collections of short stories, including *Nine Men Who Laughed* (1986), *In this City* (1992), and *There Are No Elders* (1993). Although most of these stories are set in Toronto, Clarke remains preoccupied with his place of birth and with the 'psycho-racial implications' of immigration and exile.

DOING RIGHT

I see him and I watch him. I see him and I watch him and I start to pray for him, 'cause I see him heading for trouble. Making money. 'In five or six years, I want to have a lotta money. Only when I have a lotta dollars will people respect me.'

I had to laugh. Every time he say so, I does-have to laugh, 'cause I couldn't do nothing more better than laugh.

'Look at the Rockefellers. Look at the Rothschilds. Look at the Kennedys.'

I was going-ask him if he know how they mek their money, but before I could-ask, he would be off dreaming and looking up at the ceiling where there was only cobwebs and dust; and only God knows what was circulating through his head every time he put himself in these deep reveries concerning making lots o' money and talking 'bout the Rockefellers, the Rothschilds and the Kennedys.

I was still laughing. 'Cause the present job he had, was a green-hornet job. He was a man who went to work in a green suit from head to foot, except the shoes, which was black and which he never polish. His profession was to go-round the St Clair–Oakwood area putting parking tickets 'pon people cars. Before he start all this foolishness with Wessindian cars, he uses to be on the Queens Park beat for green hornets.

A big man like him, over two hundred pounds, healthy and strong, and black, and all he could do after eight years, is to walk-'bout with a little book in his hand, putting little yellow pieces o' paper on people windshields. He like the job so much and thought he did-doing the right thing that in the middle o' the night, during a poker game or just dipsy-doodling and talking 'bout women, he would put-back-on the green uniform jacket, grabble-up the peak cap, jump in the little green car that the Police give him, and gone straight up by St Clair–Oakwood, up and down Northcliffe Boulevard, swing right 'pon Eglinton, gone down Eglinton, and swing left 'pon Park Hill Road, left again on Whitmore, and all he doing is putting these yellow pieces o' paper on decent, hard-working people cars. When he return, he does-be-laughing. I tell him he going-soon stop laughing, when a Wessindian lick-he-down with a big rock.

'I have fix them! I have ticketed one hundred and ten motto-cars today alone! And the night I leff the poker game, I ticket fifty more bastards, mainly Wessindians.'

I start to get real frighten. 'Cause I know a lotta these Wessindians living in them very streets where he does-be ticketing and laughing. And all them Wessindians know who the green hornet is. And being as how they is Wessindians, I know they don't like green hornets nor nobody who does-be touching their cars. So I feel that any morning, when one o' these Wessindians come home from a party or offa a night-shift and see him doing foolishness and putting yellow tickets 'pon their motto-cars, I know um is at least *one* hand brek. Wessindians accustom to parking in the middle o' the road, or on the wrong side, back home. And nobody don't trouble them nor touch their cars. And since they come here, many o' these Wessindians haven't tek-on a change in attitude in regards to who own the public road and who own the motto-cars.

So whilst the boy still ticketing and laughing, and putting his hands on people cars which they just wash in the car wash on Bathurst, I continue worrying and watching him.

One night just as we sit down to cut the cards, and before the cards deal, he come-in grinning, and saying, 'I ticket two hundred motto-cars today alone!'

'One o' these days, boy!' I tell him.

'When I pass in the green car and I see him, I know I had him!'

'Who?'

'I see the car pack by the fire hydrand. The chauffeur was leaning back in the seat. One hand outside the car window. With a cigarette in tha' hand. The next hand over the back o' the seat. I look in the car, and when I look in, I nearly had a fit. I recognize the pipe. I recognize the dark blue pin-stripe suit. I recognize the hair. With the streak o' grey in um. And I mek a U-turn in the middle o' the road . . .'

'But a U-turn illegal!'

'I is a green hornet, man!'

'I see.'

'I size-up the car. And I see the licents-plate. ONT-001! I start getting nervous now. 'Cause I know it is the big man. Or the second most biggest man in Toronto. I draw up. The chauffeur nod to me and tell me, 'Fine day, eh?' I tell he, 'A very fine day, sir!' And I get out. I bend-over the bonnet o' this big, shiny, black car . . .'

'Limousine, man. A big car is call a limmo.'

'Well, um could have been a limmo, a hearse be-Christ, or a' automobile, I still bend-over the bonnet and stick-on one o' the prettiest parking tickets in my whole career!'

'The Premier's car?'

'He mek the law. Not me!'

'And you think you do the right thing?'

'My legal bounden duty. Afterwards I did-feel so good, like a real police officer and not a mere green hornet. And I walk-through Queens Park on my two feet, looking for more official cars to ticket. And when I was finish, I had stick-on *five* parking tickets in their arse . . . One belongst to the Attorney General, too.'

'The same man who does-defend Wessindians?'

'I put one 'pon Larry Grossman car, too.'

Well, that whole night, all the boy talking 'bout and laughing 'bout, is how he stick-on tickets on these big-shots cars, or limousines. And to make matters worse for the rest o' we, he win all the money in the poker game, too. I feel now that the boy really going-become important, maybe, even become a real police, and make pure money. Or else going-lose a hand, or a foot.

But we was feeling good, though. 'Cause the big boys in Toronto don't particular' notice we unless um is Caribana weekend or when election-time coming and they looking for votes or when the *Star* doing a feature on racism and Wessindians and they want a quotation. So we feel this green hornet is our ambassador, even if he is only a' ambassador o' parking tickets. So we laugh like hell at the boy's prowess and progress.

And we does-wait till a certain time, on a Friday night, nervous as hell whilst cutting and dealing the cards, to see if the boy going-turn-up still dress-off in the green uniform, meaning that he hasn't get fired for ticketing the big-shots cars. And when he does turn-up, dress from head to trousers in green, we know he still have the job, and we does-laugh some more. But all the time I does-be still nervous, as I seeing him and watching him.

Then he start lossing weight. He start biting his fingers. He start wearing the green uniform not press, and half dirty. He start calling we '*You* people!'

I getting frighten now, 'cause he tell me that they tek-him-off the Queens Park beat.

So um is now that he up in St Clair–Oakwood, and I feel he going-put a ticket on the *wrong* motto car, meaning a Wessindian car. And at least one hand brek. Or one foot. And if the particular motto-car belongst to a Jamaican, not even the ones that have locks and does-wear the wool-tams mek outta black, green and red, I know um could be *both* foots and *both* hands!

I see him and I watch him.

'I have live in Trinidad, as a police. But I born in Barbados. I leff Trinidad because they won't let me ticket one hundred more cars and break the all-time record. I went to Guyana after Trinidad. I was a police in Guyana before Guyana was even Guyana and was still Demerara, or B.G. They make me leff Guyana when I get close to the record. Ten more tickets is all I had to ticket. From Guyana, I end up in Dominica. Same thing. From Dominica, I went to Antigua, and um was in Antigua that a fellow came close to licking-me-down for doing my legal duty, namely ticketing cars. In all them countries, I ticket cars that belongst to prime ministers, ministers of guvvament, priests, civil servants and school teachers.'

I see him and I watch him. I see him getting more older than the forty-five years he say he was born; and I see him drinking straight rums, first thing every morning lately, because he say, 'The nerves bad. Not that I becoming a' alcoholic. I only taking the bad taste o' waking up so early outta my mouth. I am not a' alcoholic, though. It is the pressure and the lack o' sleep.'

But he was drunk. Cleveland was drunk drunk drunk early early early every day. He had to be really drunk after he outline his plan to make money, to me.

'Remember the Rockefellers, man!' he tell me. 'This is my plan. I been a green hornet for nine years now. They promise me that if I ticket the most cars outta the whole group o' hornets, they would send me to training school to be a police. First they tell me I too short. I is five-four. But most criminals is five-three. Then they tell me that my arches fallen. Jesus Christ! What you expect? After all the beats I have walk in Trinidad, Guyana, Antigua, Dominica and Grenada, my arches bound to fall! And eight-nine years in this damn country pounding the beat ticketing cars! But they can't beat me. Not me. This is the plan I got for their arse. Tickets begin at five dollars. Right? There is five dollars, ten dollars and fifteen dollars. Right? Twenty dollars for parking beside a fire hydrand or on the wrong side. Right? Now, I write-up a ten-dollar ticket. And I change the ten to a forty. The stub in my book still saying ten. But the ticket on the car that saying ten also, I going-change from ten to a forty. Then I rush down the vehicle registration place on Wellesley Street where they have all them computers. And I tell the fellow I know from Guyana something, *anything* to get him to look up the registration for me. And then I get in touch with the owner o' the said vehicle and subtract ten from forty and . . .'

'You mean subtract ten years from forty!'

'You don't like my plan?'

'I think your plan worth ten years.'

'Okay. What about this other one? People don't lock their cars when they park. Right? Wessindians is the biggest criminals in regards to this. Right? A fellow don't lock his car. And um is night. And I got-on my green-hornet uniform. Right? Meaning I am still operating in a' official capacity . . .'

I see the boy start to smile, and his face spread and light-up like a new moon. The face was shining, too, 'cause the heat and the sureness that the plan going-work this time make him sweat real bad. But I watching him. I know that Wessindians don't have much money, because they does-get the worst and lowest jobs in Toronto. Only a certain kind o' Wessindian does-have money in their pocket. The kind that does-work night-shift, especially after midnight, when everybody else sleeping; the brand o' Wessindian who I not going-mention by name in *case* they accuse me of categorizing the race. And being a reverse racist. But *certain* Wessindians, like hairdressers, real estate salesmen and fellows who know race horses backwards and forwards, good good good *plus* the unmentionable brand, namely the illegal immigrants, the illegal parkers and them who hiding from the Police, them-so would have money to burn, inside their cars that not locked.

The boy eyes smiling. I see dollar bills instead o' pupils. I even hear the money clinking like when a car pass-over the piece o' black rubber-thing in a gas station. *Cling-cling.* 'Gimme just three months,' he say. 'Gimme three bare months, and I going-show you something.'

Just as I left him and walking 'cross Northcliffe Boulevard going to Eglinton, I see a green-hornet fellow standing-up in front a fellow car. The fellow already inside the car. The fellow want to drive off. But the green hornet standing up in front the man car. The fellow inside the car honk the horn. And the green-hornet fellow take out his black book. Slow slow. And he flip back a page. And hold down a little. And start to write down the car-licents. The fellow honk the car again. The hornet walk more closer. He tear off the little yellow piece o' paper. And getting ready to put it on the man brand-new-brand grey Thunderbird. Just as the hornet was about to ticket the man for parking next to a yellow fire hydrand, the fellow jump out. A Japanee Samurai wrestler wouldda look like a twig beside o' him. Pure muscle. Pure avoir-dupois. Pure *latissimus dorsae*. Shoes shining bright. White shirt. Stripe tie. A three-piece grey suit. Hair slick back. And long. Gold 'pon two fingers on each hand. Gold on left wrist. More gold on right wrist. The hornet par'lysed now. A rigor mortis o' fear turn the whole uniform and the man inside it to pure starch or like how a pair o' pyjamas does-look when you left um out on the line in the dead o' winter.

'Goddamn!' the man say.

'You park wrong,' the hornet say.

'Who say I park wrong?'

'You park illegal.'

'Who goddamn say I park illegal?'

'Look at the sign.'

'Which goddamn sign?'

'The sign that say No Parking between four and six. And No Stopping Anytime.

You not only park, but you stop. You stationary, too.' The Indian green-hornet man's voice get high and shaky. 'You have therefore park'.'

'Ahmma gonna give you two seconds, nigger, to take that goddamn ticket off my car, motherfucker!'

'What you call me? I am no damn nigger. I am Indian. Legal immigrant. I just doing my job for the City of Toronto in Metropolitan Toronto. *You* are a blasted Americman negro!'

Well, multiculturalism gone-out the window now! All the pamphlets and the television commercials that show people of all colours laughing together and saying, 'We is Canadians,' all them advertisements in *Saturday Night* and *Maclean's*, all them speeches that ministers up in Ottawar make concerning the 'different cultures that make up this great unified country of ours,' all that lick-up now, and gone through the eddoes. One time. *Bram!*

The goliath of a man grabble-hold of the hornet by the scruff o' the green uniform, the peak cap fall-off all like now-so, the little black book slide under the car, the hornet himself lifted up offa the ground by at least three inches, and shaking-'bout in the gulliver's hands, pelting-'bout his two legs like if he is a muppet or a poppet; and when I anticipate that the fellow going-pelt him in the broad-road, the fellow just hefted him up a little more higher offa the ground, and lay him 'cross the bonnet of the shining Thunderbird, holding-he-down like how you does-hold-down a cat to tickle-he under his chin; and the fellow say, 'Now, motherfucker! Is you gonna take the goddamn ticket off mah Bird?'

I pass 'long quick, bo', 'cause I know the Police does-be up in this St Clair–Oakwood district like flies round a crocus-bag o' sugar at the drop of a cloth-hat; and that they does-tek-in anybody who near the scene o' crime, no matter how small the scene or how small the crime; and if um is Wessindians involve, pure hand-cuffs and pelting-'bout inside the back o' cruisers till they get you inside the station. And then the real sport does-start! So I looking and I looking-off, knowing that a green hornet, even if he look like a Pakistani or a' Indian, but is really a Trinidadian, or a Guyanese and only look a little Indian, going-get help from the Police. Not one police. But five car-loads o' police. All like now-so, the road full up with Wessindians and other people, and these Wessindians looking on and laughing, 'cause none o' them don't like green hornets, not even green hornets that come from the Wessindies!

I pas-'long quick, bo'. I got to face the Immigration people in a week and I don't want nothing concerning my past or present to be a stain through witnessing violence, to prevent them from stamping *landed immigrant* or *immigrant reçu* in my Barbados passport! I may be a' accessory before the fact. But I was still thinking of my friend, the other green hornet, so I look back to see what kind o' judgement the Thunderbird-man was going-make with the Indian gentleman from Guyana, who now have no peak cap, no black notebook, one shoe fall-off and the green tunic tear-up. And as my two eyes rested on the scene *after the fact* I hear the Charles Atlas of a man say, 'And *don't* call the motherfucking cops! I got you covered, nigger. I knows where you goddam live!'

I hope that this goliath of a man don't also know where my Bajan green-hornet friend does-live! I hope the Thunderbird don't be park all the time up here! And I start to think 'bout getting a little message to my friend to tell him to-don't put no tickets on no grey Thunderbirds, or no Wessindian cars, like Tornados, whiching is Wessindians favourite cars. And I start to wonder if he know that a Wessindian does-treat a Tornado more better than he does-treat a woman or a wife; and with a Wessindian, yuh can't ask his woman for a dance at a dance unless you expecting some blows. Even if he give you permission to dance with his woman, don't dance a' Isaac Hayes or a Barry White slow-piece too slow and too close, yuh . . .

I waiting anxious now, 'cause I don't see the boy for days, these days. I feel the boy already start making money from the scheme. I walk all over St Clair–Oakwood, all along Northcliffe, swing right 'pon Eglinton, mek a left on Park Hill Road, a further left up by Whitmore and find myself back 'pon Northcliffe going now in the opposite direction, and still I can't rest my two eyes on the green hornet. Fellows start telling me that the boy does-be going to the races every day, on his lunch break from ticketing people cars, and betting *one hundred dollars on the nose* and *five hundred to show* on one horse, and leffing the races with bundles o' money. And laughing like shite.

I walking-'bout day and night, all over St Clair–Oakwood, and still no sight o' the boy.

Then, *bram!* I start hearing horror stories.

'I come out my apartment last Wednesday night to get in my car, and my blasted car not there! It gone. Tow-way!' one fellow say.

A next fellow say, 'Be-Christ, if I ever catch a police towing-way my car!'

'I don't like this place. It too fascist. Tummuch regulations and laws. A man can't *breathe*. I can't tek up my self and lodge a complaint with the police 'cause I here illegal. No work permit, yuh know? No job. Now, no car! You park your car, and when you come out in the cold morning to go-work, at a lil illegal job, no fucking car?'

'I was up by a little skins one night. I tell my wife I going by Spree. I tack-up by Northcliffe at the skins apartment. I really and truly did-intend to spend only a hour. Well, with a few white-rums in my arse, one thing lead to the next. And when I do-so, and open my two eyes, morning be-Christ brek, and um is daylight. My arse in trouble now, two times. Wife and wuk. I bound-down the fire escape, not to be seen, and when I reach ground, no blasted car!'

Stories o' motto-cars that get tow-way start spreading through the St Clair–Oakwood neighbourhood, just like how the yellow leaves does-fall 'pon the grass a certain time o' year. Stories o' fellows getting lay-off, no work permit, getting beat-up, can't go to the police, in case, and getting lock-out, all this gloom start spreading like influenza. The fellows scared. The fellows vex. The fellows angry. And they can't go and complain to the police to find out where their cars is, 'cause, yuh know, the papers not in order. As man! And the lil matter o' *landed* and *reçu* and so on and so forth . . .

They can't even start calling the police 'pigs' and 'racists' and 'criminals.' And all this time, nobody can't find the green-hornet boy at all.

Well, a plague o' tow-way cars rest so heavy on my mind, even though I don't own no wheels, seeing as how I is a real TTC-man, that I get real concern. 'Cause drunk or sober, blood more thicker than water . . .

'*As man!*'

I hear the voice and I bound-round. And look. I see cars. I see Wessindians. I don't see no police, but I frighten. I see a tow-way truck. And I still don't see nobody I know. But I think I recognize the voice.

'*As man!*'

I bound-round again, and I see the same things.

'Over here, man!'

God bless my eyesight! Um is the green-hornet man. My friend! Sitting down behind the wheel of 'DO RIGHT TOWING 24 HOURS.' I do-so look! I blink my two eyes. I seeing, but I not seeing right. I watching, but I having eyes that see and that watch but they not watching right.

'Um is *me*, man!'

The tow-way truck real pretty. It have-in short-wave radio. Two-way radio. C.B.C.-F.M. Stereos. *And* C.B. It paint-up in black, yellow and white. The green-hornet boy, dress-off now in overalls and construction hat, cock at a' angle on his head, cigar in mouth and shades on his face, like if he is a dictator from Latin Amurca.

'Remember the plan? The plan I tell you 'bout for making money? Well, I went to my bank and talk to my bank manager and squeeze a loan for this outta the bitch.' He tap the door of the tow-truck like if he tapping a woman. 'And I had a word with a fellow who was a green hornet like me. I is still a green hornet myself, but I works the afternoon shift. This fellow I know, the ex-green-hornet, couldn't take the abuse and the threats to his person of being a hornet, so he open up a little place up in Scarborough where he *enpounds* the cars I does tow-way. And me and he splits the money. I brings in a car, and quick-so, um lock-up and enpounded. If a fellow want-back his car, fifty dollars! You want piece o' this action?'

I get real frighten.

'You want to get cut-in 'pon this action?'

'But-but-but-but . . .'

'You see that pretty silver-grey Thunderbird park beside that fire hydrand? I watching that car now, fifteen minutes. I see the fellow park it, and go in the apartment building there. I figure if he coming back out soon, he going-come-out within twenty minutes. I got five more minutes . . .'

I start getting real frighten now. 'Cause I see the car. And the car is the same car that belongst to Goliath, the black Amurcan fellow. I so frighten that I can't talk and warn my green-hornet friend. But even if I couldda find words, my tow-truck friend too busy talking and telling me 'bout a piece o' the action and how easy it is to tow-way cars that belongst to illegal immigrants and get money split fifty-fifty, and that to remember the Rockefellers . . .

'. . . and I had to laugh one day when I bring-in a Cadillac,' he tell me, still laughing, as if he was still bringing-in the Cadillac. 'Appears that my pound-friend had a little altercation or difference of opinion with a Murcan-man over a car once, so when I appear with the silver-grey Caddy, he get frighten and start telling me that nobody not going-maim him or brutalize him or cuss his mother, that before anything like that happen, he would go-back home to Guyana first and pick welts offa reefs or put-out oyster-pots down by the Sea-Wall . . . Look! I got to go. Time up!'

I see him, and I watch him pull off from 'side o' me like if he didn't know me, like if I was a fire hydrant. I watch him drive up to the shiny grey Thunderbird car, not mekking no noise, like if he is a real police raiding a Wessindian joint after midnight. I see him get-out the tow-truck, like if he walking on ashes. I see him let-down the big iron-thing at the back o' the tow-truck. First time in my eleven years living here as a semi-legal immigrant that I have see a tow-truck that didn't make no noise. I see him bend-down and look under the front o' the Thunderbird. I see him wipe his hands. I see him wipe his two hands like a labourer who do a good job does-wipe his hands. I see him go-round to the back o' the Bird and bend-down. He wipe his two hands again. I see him size-up the car. I watch him put-on the two big canvas gloves on his two hands. I watch him cock the cigar at a more cockier angle, adjust the construction hat, tek-off the shades and put them inside his pocket, and I see him take the rope that mek out of iron and look like chain and hook-um-on 'pon the gentleman nice, clean-and-polish grey 1983 Thunderbird. I seeing him and I watching him. The boy real professional. I wondering all the time where the boy learn this work. He dance round to the tow-truck and press a thing, and the Bird raising-up offa the road like if um ready to tek-off and fly. I see him press a next thing in the tow-truck and the bird stationary, but up in the air, at a' angle, like a Concorde tekking-off. I see him bend-down again, to make-sure that the chain o' iron hook-on good. I see him wipe his two hands in the big canvas gloves a next time, and I see him slap his two hands, telling me from the distance where I is, watching, that it is a professional job, well done. I think I see the dollar bills registering in his two eyes, too! And I see him tug the chain tight, so the Bird would move-off nice and slow, and not jerk nor make no noise, when he ready to tek she to the pound to *enpound* she.

And then I see the mountain of the man, tipping-toe down the metal fire escape o' the apartment building where he was, black shoes shining in the afternoon light, hair slick back and shining more brighter from a 'process', dress in the same three-piece suit with the pin-stripe visible now that the sun was touching the rich material at the right angle o' sheen and shine, and I see, or I think I see the gentleman take off a diamond-and-gold ring two times, offa his right hand, and put them in his pocket, I think I see that, and I see how the hand become big big big like a boxing glove, and I watching, but I can't open my mouth nor find voice and word to tell my former green-hornet friend to look over his left shoulder. I seeing but I can't talk o' what I seeing. I find I can't talk. I can only move. A tenseness seize the moment. I do *so*, and point my index finger like a spy telling another spy to-don't talk, but look behind. But at that very moment, the black Amurcan gentleman's hand was already falling on my friend's shoulder . . .

RUDY WIEBE

(b. 1934)

'I've never really thought of writing as a way of achieving identity or national unity, or anything political. I've always felt that the only way a national literature—if such a thing exists—could develop is for everyone to write out of their own kind of experience, their own kind of imaginative world, and together you build,' said Rudy Wiebe in 1991. '[P]laces rather than regions', and the rewriting and revisioning of history have been the primary concerns of the many novels and short stories he has produced. *Peace Shall Destroy Many* (1962), his first novel written as his Master's thesis (University of Alberta, 1960), and *First and Vital Candle* (1966) deal with the history as well as with the religious and cultural beliefs of Mennonites who settled in western Canada, whereas *The Blue Mountains of China* (1970) traces, in the epic style that was to become characteristic of much of his later fiction, the experiences of diasporic Mennonite communities.

Wiebe was born in the Mennonite community of Speedwell-Jackpine, near Fairholme, Saskatchewan, the first child to be born in Canada of Mennonite parents who arrived on the prairies in 1930, having been dispossessed of their land in Russia. Until he began attending school, in Fairholme, and later on in Coaldale, Alberta, he spoke only German. After he graduated from the University of Alberta with a B.A. in English (1956), he received a Bachelor of Theology degree from the Mennonite Brethren Bible College in Winnipeg, Manitoba, and studied for a year at the University of Tübingen, Germany. Until his early retirement in 1990, Wiebe was a professor of Canadian literature and creative writing at the University of Alberta.

A writer who believes 'in *place*, not *race*', Wiebe has received two Governor General's

Awards for fiction: one for *The Temptations of Big Bear* (1973), and another for his most recent novel, *A Discovery of Strangers* (1994). These novels, as well as *The Scorched-wood People* (1977) and the short-fiction collections *Where Is the Voice Coming From?* (1974) and *The Angel of the Tar Sands and Other Stories* (1982), display the imaginative control with which he sets out to radically question the hegemonic views of Canadian history, especially the history that deals with First Nations peoples. Although he has often found himself involved in controversies that have arisen around the question of the 'appropriation of voice', Wiebe, having been brought up in a world where '"The English" were always something very different from us', does not share 'the imperial concept of history as it expressed itself in Canada'. As he says, 'that imperial world, which is part of the expression of Canadian suppression of Native Indians and taking over their land, to me is just as strange and just as repulsive now as it is to a Native Indian.'

His other publications include the novels *My Lovely Enemy* (1983) and *The Mad Trapper* (1980), and his non-fiction book, *Playing Dead: A Contemplation Concerning the Arctic* (1989). His fiction has been translated into nine languages, including French, Spanish, German, and Japanese. Whether they are set on the prairies or in the arctic territories, Wiebe's narratives demonstrate his belief that '[t]he here-and-now alone cannot give us the strength which a knowledge of our antecedents would provide: we can only be non-entities without the confidence our ancestral dead can give us.' His most recent book is *River of Stone: Fictions and Memories* (1995).

A NIGHT IN FORT PITT OR (IF YOU PREFER)
THE ONLY PERFECT COMMUNISTS IN THE WORLD

Late one November evening in the thirty-third year of the reign of Queen Victoria, a solitary horseman might have been seen riding along the hills that parallel the North Saskatchewan River. He had been riding west since before daybreak, but now long after sunset the giant sweep of the frozen river suddenly confronted him, forcing him south, or as nearly south as he could surmise from the stars that glittered occasionally, momentarily, between storm clouds. And the wind which had been threatening snow all day now roared, it seemed, with a malignant fury up the cliff down whose steep slope he could not risk his exhausted horse, though he knew that he must somewhere, somehow get across the valley if he was to find shelter at Fort Pitt, the only white settlement along three hundred miles of river between Fort Carlton and Victoria House.

The night before the rider and his small party had endured among bare poplars in the fold of a creek; when they emerged that morning onto the prairie before dawn to continue their journey, they discovered the entire sky brilliant with aurora, torn sheets of light gently glowing and leaping into blaze above them and smouldering away again. The man had stopped his horse, watched, stunned; felt himself shrink as it were into and then grow incandescent in that immense dome of brilliance until sunrise burned it into sheer light, and he became aware that his Indian guide and Métis companion had vanished into the apparently flat earth; leaving nothing but the line of their passing in the hoary grass. The quick winter afternoon was already darkening before he caught up with them in their relentless track. The radiance of aurora still informed him and he told them they had veered too far south; sunset perhaps verified his perception, for after the long day's ride they still had not encountered the river. He refused to accept another night in the open and swung onto this weary mount. His men had already unburdened theirs, preparing to weather the storm they insisted was driving up from the west in a brushy hollow. So they watched him ride west alone, the prairie so open he could inevitably be found if lost, as impatient and as superior with all necessary knowledge as every white man they had ever met, riding into darkness following stars.

And now in stinging snow the stars were lost, though it did not matter since he had found the North Saskatchewan River. Well, it did matter, because he knew that every Hudson Bay settlement was on the north bank; he must cross over the river or he would miss Pitt, he could ride as far as he had already ridden in a month, another five hundred miles across prairie into the glacial mountains themselves and not encounter a white man. As if at the thought, his horse stopped. No urging could move it so he slid off, straightening his long legs against the ground with a groan. The horse turned its long, squarish head to him, nudged him, breaking the icicles off its nostrils against his buffalo coat and then finding the warmth of his armpit. Perhaps this hammer-headed bay from Fort Carlton could become as good a companion to him as Blackie had been—the storm shifted an instant and he realized they were on a point of cliff. Perhaps a tributary cut its way into the river here as steeply as the main river. Where was he? Even if he got down into the valley, if Fort Pitt was built half a mile back from the river in a bend like Fort Carlton, he would never find it. He sheltered his crusted eyes against the whistling snow that enclosed him: the air seemed as solid as any frozen prairie. He would walk on it easily as dreaming out into the sky. . . .

The cheekstrap of the bridle hit his frozen face when the horse moved. He felt that, his arm slid onto its neck.

> He knew he could not lose this one certain warm body also, his mittens clamped onto its stiff mane and so suddenly he was led forward and down, sideways and down, the incline almost vertical and shifting like relentless sand, but that one body was solidly with his, there, whenever they slipped they slid closer together, their six feet all one and always somehow set certainly into the side of what incline of what might be rock or frozen clay, deadly as ice, but so reliable, so trustworthy he would never let go of this horse, never leap aside even if river ice parted into water as it had when he leaped from Blackie sinking, scrambled to safety while seeing his horse sink into blackness and there was its beautiful head bursting up, its front legs, neck arched, and knees clawing ice with its deadly shod feet, trying to climb up into the bright air by sheer terror, nostrils flaring bloody and the ice smashing now again and again in ringing iron, and he turned away, sprinted for his rifle—he was an English soldier, soldiers can always offer the ultimate mercy of running for their bloody rifles— and he knelt there expert sharpshooter on the white, deceptive ice until the shots hammered back at him tripled from the cliffs and the long water ran flat again and implacably empty; on his knees, crying.

But his hammerhead bay led him so easily down . . . down five hundred feet or a thousand—instinctively he was counting steps, an officer must always carry some facts, even if they are estimated—and they scrambled out between broken boulders (or were they frozen buffalo?) and there was river ice again, certainly, hard as the cliff here and he was still clutching the horse. But with his arms and legs now, completely, and it moved with his frozen face in its mane, he could smell prairie slough hay, hear scrub oaks at Fort Garry scarlet as cardinals in October light, the chant of *Te Deum* prayed by monks in a roofless Irish ruin, and he became aware that the sting of snow had quietened: there was an upthrust, darkness moving beside him, a dense blackness and he loosened one hand, reached out: it was most certainly the usual twenty-foot spruce palisade. Never anything in stone like the permanent ruins of Ireland. And a gate in the wooden wall; hanging open. Perhaps the Indians here were all dead, the gates hanging so open.

The bay followed him through that hanging gate like any dog and the storm was so abruptly quiet he felt himself breathing. High peaked roofs, gabled, around a square, he could not distinguish a light or a sound. Perhaps smallpox had discovered them all, Indian and Métis and white alike, as in Fort Carlton. Winter would keep the bodies perfectly, death already blossomed over them like spring flowers. He limped across the open square to avoid what lay at the edge of every shadow, what might move, dreadfully: a door, darkness in the centre building. He seemed to have reached the heart of something, corpses were keening all around him, at the very hoared edges of his fur cap and he wheeled around, listening. But there was only his own small breathing, nothing but the horse snoring, bent low like grass behind him. So he turned back to the door and began to pound on it. Nothing. The plank door would not budge to his fists, its cracks blacker than its wood, and he tilted forward, hands, face clutching the frame, they were all dead, O open up, *o miserere mei* . . . he heard a sound. Inside. Against his face an opening, of light, the skin of a face, a young woman's face. Impossibly beautiful.

Such materializations are possible out of the driving blackness of a prairie blizzard, lantern-light and such sudden woman's beauty as perfect as it is unbelievable? He found himself bending forward slowly, past the worn planks of the doorframe, tilting slowly into her light, his frozen cheek, his still tactile tongue . . . and felt . . . nothing. Those eyes, the black brows and exquisite nose, was it white, that skin in the golden light? Was it believable though impossible?

It is possible that when Lieutenant General, the Right Honourable Sir William Francis Butler, Knight Grand Cross of the Order of the Bath and member of the Privy Council of Ireland died in his bed in Bansha Castle, County Tipperary, on June 7, 1910, died as his daughter then wrote, 'of a recent affection of the heart . . . that was brought to a crisis by a chill', it is possible that on his deathbed thirty-nine and a half years later Sir William could still not decide: was that face he instantly loved at Fort Pitt on the North Saskatchewan River in the North-Western Territories of Canada on November 18, 1870, loved as only the truest Victorian male who believed all his life that Jesus Christ and Napoleon Bonaparte were the greatest men in all of human history could love, a latter day romantic when romanticism was still acceptable in a male if he was also practical and above all heroic, dear god, was a man who championed the innocent and detested the brutalities of war all his life while becoming one of Victoria's most honoured and decorated soldiers, a member of Field Marshal Wolseley's brilliant Officers' Ring that fought for the Empire on four continents, and who dreamed for forty years of 'the Great Lone Land' as he called the Canadian prairie and never saw again and idealized every Indian person he lived near for those few months in 1870 and 1871 when they were either dying of smallpox or more or less starving despite their unselfish greedless tradition of sharing everything, which makes Indians, as he wrote then, 'the only perfect communists in the world, who, if they would only be as the Africans or the Asiatics it would be all right for them; if they would be our slaves they might live, but as they won't be that, won't toil and delve and hew for us, and will persist in hunting, fishing, roaming over the beautiful prairie land which the Great Spirit gave them: in a word, since they will be free—we will kill them'; this Butler who on the same journey contemplated the parklands of the Saskatchewan, observed their remarkable similarity to the English downs and found it 'mortifying to an Englishman' that they were, as he so concisely put it, 'totally undeveloped': this Butler was forced over an unseeable landscape by a November blizzard to be confronted by a woman's face, her thick black braids hanging to her hips; wearing a loose nightgown.

The nightgown was probably not thin. More likely it was heavy flannel since any Hudson Bay fort at the time (they were really nothing of forts but rather clusters of log buildings surrounded by log palisades, all of which could and did, as easily by accident as by design, burn to the ground) was badly heated by cavernous openhearth fireplaces, doubtless she wore that heavy flannel of solid red or delicate floral design which the Company traded with the Cree and which those people suspended as gift offerings to the Thunderbird on the Centre Tree of their thirst dance lodges in June. And here it would hang as gracefully, draping between braids, shoulders and arms and nipples and hips a slender revelation. And the very handsome, six-foot-two and always brave and presently very hoarfrosted Lieutenant Butler, late of her Majesty's 69th Regiment in India and the Fenian Raids in Quebec across the Canadian border from New York, and most recently renowned as Intelligence Officer of the Colonel Wolseley Red River Expedition against the Métis founder of Manitoba, Louis Riel: frozen or not, Butler must fall instantly in love.

As he stood there, erect and frozen, clamped to the handsawn plank of the door-frame, his faithful pony having discharged its final faithful duty of carrying him to safety and about to collapse in faithful exhaustion behind him, did Lieutenant Butler say, 'Madam, I very nearly gave up hope of ever reaching succour'?

And did she reply as stiffly, 'O sir, our rude abode is but little better than the storm, nevertheless . . .'?

And he, accepting her hesitation: 'Madam, if I may be so importunate . . .'?

And she, accepting his: 'O sir, of course, do come in sir, come in out of the storm'?

And did she turn to send the dark servant woman standing behind her scurrying to the kitchen to revive the fire that was no more than embers in the hearth?

Perhaps that was how Fort Pitt, named after the great Prime Minister but doomed never to be as famous as Pittsburgh, named after his father the Great Commoner, perhaps that was how Fort Pitt offered itself to him. Or did she exclaim out of the lamplight, 'O la sir, what a storm brings you here!' and he, bursting into laughter, reply, 'What you see is mere weather, my fine wench. There will yet be greater storms than this!' Staring so closely down into the luminous whiteness of breasts her night-gown made but small attempt to contain.

Her father, Hudson Bay Factor John Sinclair, had only a brutal litany of disease and starvation and death to offer him at Fort Pitt. He always kept the palisade gate locked—some damn Indian had tore it loose—every building locked, they were under seige and if thirty-two of sixty people at Fort Carlton was dead, including the factor, and half the McDougall missionary family at Victoria dead too, then Pitt had been saved because he wouldn't let one goddamn Indian into the place, trade or no trade, locked them all out, and he had been damn quick in summer when he first heard the smallpox spreading and he got some blood out of a Saulteaux Indian vaccinated at the mission in Prince Albert and used that to vaccinate everybody—well, damn near everybody—in Pitt and he had kept every Cree locked out, every bloody one of them: Butler could barely restrain himself. Use them, use them any way you can, use their very blood . . . but he sat at the kitchen table devouring (with perfect Army manners, of course) the mound of buffalo steak and potatoes Mary (now properly dressed, of course) served him before the pine fire blazing on the hearth—where was the mother, the inevitable Indian, at best Métis, mother? The free traders, muttered Sinclair into his rum, had destroyed the hide and fur trade anyway, what did they care about Indians, just soak the buggers in whiskey, steal all they could from them today and to hell with tomorrow, so now even at Pitt, the very heart of buffalo country, the beasts were gone, not enough robes this summer to make three decent bundles and he'd have nothing at all to eat except potatoes if Big Bear, that ugly little bastard that never got sick, hadn't dragged in ten to trade and he'd risked taking them even though half of Big Bear's band was spitting blood, they caught it fighting the Peigans near the border who got it from the American Bloods, hell, they said it was the U.S. Army deliberately infecting the Indians down there to wipe them off the face of the earth because it was costing them damn near a million dollars each to shoot them! The smallpox was sure cheaper, about as cheap as wolfers throwing strychnine all over the prairie, and about as effective. There'd soon be nothing but corpses stinking up the whole goddamn stinking North-West.

Butler looked at him carefully: Sinclair was typical enough, a poor Scot forced to spend his whole life remembering home from the other side of the world, living who knows how in what overwhelming monotony of daily life and endless, endless miserable seasons repeating themselves, too old now for even the occasional Indian woman to rouse him, and suddenly a government official appears out of the night at whom he could momentarily blurt whatever he wanted, an official not on the summer boats but riding an assignment in the dead of a deadly boring winter on orders from the Lieutenant Governor of the Territories—there was one at long last—someone who had been within breathing distance of all those invisible Hudson Bay lords in London barely seven months before, who had often smelled the 'goddamn heather' and seen the Queen herself who had finally survived her grief for Albert and was now the emerging mother of a world empire: what poor lonely sot of a homesick Scot wouldn't seize such an opportunity to snore every pessimistic worry he had aloud into his grog?

To be starving in Pitt, Sinclair suddenly roared, is like freezing to death in Newcastle! This is buffalo country, one herd moved over these hills for seventeen days and nights in '62, over two million, there was no end of them summer or winter and he'd fed every fort from Rocky Mountain House to Vermilion and the Pas, every goddamn fur dragged out of this country and every bloody ounce of stuff dragged back into it in every bloody York boat—every fuckin' trader had Pitt pemmican in his gut and now Big Bear brings in ten jesus carcasses and he has to burn the hides and boil the fuckin' jesus christ out of the meat! But at least that old bugger knew what he was doing, telling his people to leave the fort and scatter in the bush and maybe the winter would be cold enough to kill the white man's disease, though what they would live on, even their dogs and miserable horses so far gone . . . .

Butler saw Mary Sinclair turn like a flame in front of the fire. After a month of half-fried bannock and pemmican—which had all the taste of boiled shoeleather—her baked potatoes were beyond any remembered cream and butter, dear god their very aroma—and she facing solitary winter darkness, a lifetime of that incredible skin drying up in cold and mosquito-and-blackfly heat, such a shape hammered slack by year after year pregnancies. At her bend by the hearth for another rack of buffalo rib he felt his body thaw and stretch completely, his powerful legs, toes flaring so fluidly, a kind of tensile vividness she awoke in his hands hard from cold and clenched reins all day, a touch of, somehow, flesh and resistance needed; despite heavy cotton the length of her leg, her curved thigh, her quick smile past her shoulder, her extraordinary face even when seen sideways or upside-down. Her father snored, fat arms flat on the table: every night such a lullaby and every night lying somewhere innocent, somewhere in this clumsy building, every night she was here naked against cotton and he rolled in his deerskin sack on the frozen prairie, sweetest jesus why is there no comfort in the world ever *together*?

The Métis servant came sluffing down the stairs. The bed for the gentleman was warming with hot stones between buffalo robes, would he go up? It was Mary who spoke, Mary who led him up the narrow stairs through her own shadow to the door, opening it without so much as a glance: she gave him the lantern and was gone, not a gesture of her lithe body even at his stumbled goodnight, and thank you again . . . the hall was empty before he grasped her going. Wind moaned in crevices. Well, doubtless to help the Métis woman hoist her father back into bed again. He stripped quickly, blew out the light. The stones were too hot, the robes total ice; he felt his body slowly shrinking into a huddle. Be I as chaste as ice, as pure as snow, I shall not . . . he sensed a footstep and sat up: she was there, he knew. But it was several seconds before the rustle she made told him she was lifting the heavy cotton nightgown over her head.

Could he say anything when she came in beside him, he the Irishman of endless easy words, when she laughed aloud so gently at all his sweaty underwear? And she peeled it off him, chuckling again at the memory of his goodnight, did he think Pitt was a hotel and she a chambermaid? Hot stones in bed were no better than camp-fires: you were always roasted on one side and freezing on the other. He may have had a small hesitation.

The bed . . . is too narrow.

Wide enough for one is wide enough for two.

And her skin fit completely around him, her head warm as opening lips in the hollow of his neck. If despite twelve years of Her Majesty's army his body still did not know what to do, she doubtless helped him to that too; and perhaps his own skin and various tongues in that black room taught him something of her invisible shape.

Perhaps this happened to William Francis Butler in Fort Pitt in the North-Western Territories of Canada on the night of November 18, 1870. Perhaps, if he was *really* lucky and Mary Sinclair was, thanks to her mother (certainly not her father), one of the world's perfect communists.

There is of course another story; the one Mary Sinclair told forty years later. Before the rebellion, she said, when I was only a young girl, an English officer came to Fort Pitt. He was tall and very good looking and he talked and talked and he could talk so well I thought perhaps I could love him. He told me about his home in Ireland, he came out of the snow and storm one night like someone from a different world and then when his men arrived after him he rode on to Fort Edmonton and I could only think about him. But he came back again, and he asked me to marry him. He asked me to go live with him in the Old Country. There I was, a child of the Saskatchewan, what would I do in another country? Perhaps I cried a little, but I sent him away. And after a while I did not think about him so often.

I sent him away. That is how Mary Sinclair later told it; but not Butler. He wrote a book, and he mentions her only in the same sentence as 'buffalo steaks and potatoes'. For these in Fort Pitt, he writes, 'I had the brightest eyed little lassie, half Cree, half Scotch, in the whole North-West to wait upon me,' and he mentions this 'lassie' not at all on his return journey from Fort Edmonton at the end of December, 1870, when bitter cold and a lack of sled dogs forced him, so he writes, to wait at Fort Pitt for seven days. Did she then also with steak and potatoes wait upon him? Serve him? Such a handsome Victorian soldier wrapped in tall furs on government assignment would perhaps not have remembered that she sent him away, especially not after he discovered in Ottawa a mere four months later that all the 'excellent colonial ministers', as he calls them, had large families and that 'an army officer who married a minister's daughter might perchance be a fit and proper person to introduce the benefits of civilization to the Cree and Blackfoot Indians on the western prairies, but if he elected to remain in single cussedness in Canada he was pretty certain to find himself a black sheep among the ministerial flock of aspirants for place.' Premier John A. Macdonald's only daughter Mary was handicapped beyond any possible marriage, and the most beautiful girl on the prairies could certainly not have helped Butler be an 'aspirant for place' in lumber Ottawa so, despite letters as excellent as excellent colonial ministers could make them for his excellent service, the tall officer returned to the heart of Empire still a lieutenant, still without a permanent government appointment, still without a steady war in which to achieve the fortune that could purchase his promotion; he could not know that soon the kingdoms of hot Africa would provide him with a quarter of a century of men he could, with his enormous organizational efficiency, help to kill. In Fort Pitt on the North Saskatchewan in November and December, 1870, during cold so severe no Englishman could imagine it, a beautiful young woman 'waited upon me,' as he said; sent him away, as she said.

Or is a fourth story possible? Did they dream together, narrow bed or not? Did they see those enormous herds of buffalo that once flowed along the rivers there, such a streaming of life never again seen anywhere on the surface of the earth or even in the depths of the sea? And in the darkness did they see the long, hesitant parade of the Cree chiefs approaching Treaty Number Six that ordered them thereby to cede, release, surrender and yield up all that land forever, and behind them the one chief who would not, the chief Big Bear as the whites called him, but perhaps better translated 'Too Much' or 'More Than Enough Bear' who would ask them all how could one person give away forever what they had all forever had, who had more than enough of everything except the power to persuade his people of his defiant vision until Fort Pitt was burning, was becoming a great pillar of smoke bent over the river and the empty hills and all that flour and rancid treaty pork they had never wanted, had abhored as soon as ever they saw it, surrounded them, rained on them, dripped black and stinking out of the very air they were forced to breathe?

She knows that darkness alone can offer what he longs to accept. Smell and touch and the tongue in the ear, yes, taste itself, yes, yes—but not sight. Eyes for him are impossible.

The fire locked inside each palisade log, the factor's house, the spruce walls close about their narrow bed springs into light, fire lifts Fort Pitt, transforms it into air and its place, here, on this earth, is lost to any memory, the valley and the hills changed as they are already eternally changed beyond the going of the animals and some day the Hutterite farmers will break though the bristly poplars, domesticate them into wheat fields and a plough furrow along the bank of the still relentless river one day reveals a shard of blue willow china; its delicate pastoral a century's confirmation of her waiting upon him, of her serving him?

Behind the double darkness of his clenched eyes he sees again the length of his rifle barrel and the black hair whorled behind Blackie's straining ear: the blood explodes exactly there! They had to cross today, the daily plan is irrevocable, iron shoes or not on thin ice or no ice they must cross, and his groans, his endlessly contained and most irregular, totally unplanned, tears.

They may have dreamed something together. Possibly they dreamed the scarlet riders of the police he would recommend the Canadian government establish to force English law upon the western plains, the police whose thin implacable lines would weave the red shroud of the old Queen's authority over every child of the Saskatchewan until Inspector Francis Jeffrey Dickens, the great novelist's third son who aspired to his appointment by patronage, not by excellent merit of excellent colonial service, would at Fort Pitt become the most infamous officer in the history of the world-famous force. Force indeed.

Or they dreamed again the gaunt Cree dying, scraping their pustulated legs and arms and breasts and infants' faces along the gates, the doorframes, the windows of the locked fort to force the white man's disease back upon him, to somehow smear him and his own putrefaction. And perhaps they also dreamed Big Bear walking so emaciated among his people, his magnificent voice persuading them they must scatter to the woods and the animals, that only on the solitary land would they be given the strength to destroy this invisible, this incomprehensible evil that rotted them, his words and his great scarred face proof of his lifelong power over the white diseases, his name certain and forever More Than Enough Bear for everything except the white words on the white paper, words that would one day endlessly whisper to him behind the thick, sweating walls of Stony Mountain Penitentiary.

Was it Big Bear who helped her say to him then: go away.

Only she could dream that. It is impossible for Lieutenant William Francis Butler to dream such a hopeless dream; even in a narrow bed in Fort Pitt, even in Mary Sinclair's warm and beautiful arms.

GEORGE JONAS

(b. 1935)

George Jonas is one of the better-known Hungarian-Canadian writers. Born and educated in Budapest, Hungary, he arrived in Canada as a refugee in 1956. At the time of the Hungarian Revolution, he was one of the young writers who 'drew up a program of demands—the famous Eighteen Point Programme which was published in the *Literary Gazette*'. Jonas considers identity labels like 'Hungarian' to be 'a stumbling block when people try to approach [his] poetry in this way. It's worth that I was born in Hungary, but it's not worth getting hung up on,' he says. He believes 'it's unfortunate that so many Canadian writers are preoccupied with discovering their identity, and with proving themselves. The mainstream is wherever you happen to be.' For Jonas, 'nothing can give [him] the ecstasy that poetry can,' but he 'can be bored by poetry in exactly the same way as a cartoon husband in *The New Yorker*, whose wife is dragging him to the opera.'

He has published four collections of poetry: *The Absolute Smile* (1967), *The Happy Hungry Man* (1970), *Cities* (1974), a collection reflecting his shifts from one urban centre to another, and *The East Wind Blows West* (1993). 'Poetry comes more from the inside than from the outside,' says Jonas. Although he remarks he is 'not a great believer in environmental determinism, beyond the obvious

effects,' he cannot afford to 'clos[e his] mind to the evidence of history. I'm too empirical,' he states, 'to be able to behave in an entirely ideological fashion.' Poetry, for Jonas, 'demands to be written. And it's fairly rare. . . . To some extent a poem writes itself.' However, his European background—'the mystique of aristocracy', 'the mystique of cynicism'—often informs the ways in which his poetry has been received.

As a radio producer, he has worked with CBC and has written television and radio plays, including *Of Mice and Men* (1963), *The Agent Provocateur* (1966), and *The Scales of Justice* (1983). He has also written plays for the stage, including *The Sinking of the Mary Palmer* (1972) and *Pushkin* (1978), as well as librettos for two operas by Tibor Bolgar, *The European Lover* (1966) and *The Glove* (1973). Jonas is also the author of two non-fiction studies: *Vengeance* (1984) and, together with Barbara Amiel, his former wife, *By Persons Unknown: The Strange Death of Christine Demeter* (1977). The latter, a lengthy account and analysis of the facts about the murder of a Toronto woman by her Hungarian-born husband, received the Edgar Allan Poe Award for Best Fact Crime Book. Jonas's concerns with how the legal system often erodes, instead of protecting, human rights is also reflected in his novel, *Final Decree* (1981).

WAKES UP NEXT MORNING TO STRAINS OF O CANADA ON THE RADIO

Let me put it this way:

If I were a German
I could say to myself Mozart & Rilke
But I would also have to say
Goebbels & Bergen-Belsen
Words I could not pronounce lightly.

If I were a Frenchman
I could say Molière & Camus

But I would also have to add
Napoleon & Petain & The Maginot Line
In an embarrassing footnote.

As a Belgian I would have to reconcile
Verhaeren with the Congo,
And as an Englishman subtract
The Boer War & The Playing Fields of Eton
From Milton & Yeats
Which may leave me with very little.

As a Russian I'd have to work hard
Fixing my thoughts rigidly on Tolstoy
And trying to forget all about Djerzhinsky,
And if I had to call the U.S. of A. my home
It might be more than my selective memory could handle.

But being a Canadian
By conscious and considered choice
I have to remember no one & nothing
Which in this 1969th year of grace
Suits me just fine.

In Any City

In any city at any hour of the day
We pray.

With narrow, calculating eyes
We are getting off streetcars in front of churches.
Not too far from stock markets and parliament buildings
We attempt to placate God
By giving pieces of candy to filthy children.
Generally
For each ten men we destroy
We restore one;
For each dollar we extort
We return a nickel to the priest
And a penny to the poor.

Luckily our God is a Jew
A shrewd kindly old Jew who knows his children well.
Our way of doing business is his way.

His motto too is live and let live
And a little honest profit is all he expects
On which to keep his Kingdom going.
A slight depression now and then cannot be avoided
In his difficult line.
If he can make us do our bit
And be in some vague fear of him all the time
He is satisfied
And in the end he opens for us
The gates of his heaven.

Of course, there will be a few even he cannot help.
A few who are unable to find a place in this soap opera of a world
Misfits, who are not at home, no matter what,
In this fat, happy, cause-and-effect, give-and-take universe,
A few vicious saints who want all or nothing.

These lost souls are out of the reach of God.
He cannot give them all because he too has to stay in business
So he gives them nothing.
With a sad flick of his beautiful patriarchal finger
He sends them flying after a while
Into the outer darkness.

ONCE MORE

Kirov was shot, Solon will rot in jail,
even the smallest hold-up man will hang,
Eichmann has died seven times, but the real,
the real murderers all live in my street.

They go to work each day at eight o'clock.
Some take the bus, some drive, and many walk.
They have a child or two, they like a smoke,
their wives wear rings, Sunday they cut the grass.

They talk about the business, the weather,
there is a faint click as they lock the door.
Only a few of them would hurt a fly
and all of them support a family.

Will they be caught? Is theirs the perfect crime?
All I see is the circle of the time,
all I know is I have to be prepared.

Caution causes me to glide through the walls
at night and stand beside them just to see
how long they have to wash their hands before
they turn the light out and they go to sleep.

FROM THE BOOK OF AL-MAARI

Burning stakes blossom from the footsteps of Redeemers;
the Koran fashions daggers carried by true believers;
the atheist has faith in what his eyes disclose,
the Sufi, what he sees when both his eyes are closed.
It is a Buddhist doctrine that all doctrines must fail;
the Hebrew knows nothing in exquisite detail;
the Brahmin fears the risk which in his next life he runs;
the hedonist trembles, for his life comes only once
and briefly. In the great insane asylum
of this revolving earth chaos creates the rules.
There are believing and unbelieving fools.

(after George Faludy)

JOY KOGAWA

(b. 1935)

'We have within us the political person and at times I think that person is yanked out of silence to speak,' said Joy Kogawa in 1989. For her, it is not so much a matter of balancing the tension between political action and silence, but rather a matter of recognizing the source from which language stems. Following her first collection of lyric poems, *The Splintered Moon* (1967), Kogawa shifted her ground in both thematic and writerly ways. Her second poetry collection, *A Choice of Dreams* (1974), marked the beginning of her exploration of her ancestral origins: the poems are a powerful articulation of the sensibilities and sentiments she 'discovered' as a Canadian when she visited Japan. Her exploration of what this double legacy of origins entails was eloquently expressed in her first novel, *Obasan* (1981).

This novel is based on Kogawa's own experiences as a child born in Vancouver, who lived there until the Second World War, when her family, like all other Japanese-Canadians, was uprooted. Her characters follow the route that Kogawa's father, an Anglican minister, was forced to take. The family was sent to Slocan, one of the internment camps in the interior of British Columbia. They moved to Coaldale, Alberta, in 1945, where Kogawa finished school, and subsequently to Toronto, where she studied music and theology. She moved back to Vancouver where she married, but returned to Toronto in the late 1970s after her separation.

As the excerpt from the novel included here illustrates, much of the impetus in *Obasan* revolves around the first-person narrator, Naomi, and her maternal aunt, Emily. The two women, although profoundly aware of what the labelling of their community as 'enemy aliens' means, have different ways of articulating their pain and revisiting their past. Naomi embraces the passive silence of her elderly aunt Obasan, who has become a surrogate mother to her, while Emily dedicates her entire life to unearthing all the documents necessary to demonstrate what is already apparent to all the Japanese-Canadians, namely the racism directed against them. As Kogawa has said, Naomi 'doesn't say anything, she doesn't do anything. . . . Whereas Aunt Emily acts. I think that we have within us the Aunt Emily and the Naomi.'

The novel has played a considerable role in alerting Canadians to past injustices committed against the Japanese-Canadians, and contributed, along with Kogawa's own activism, to the redress sought by them from the Canadian government. The sequel to *Obasan*, *Itsuka* (1992), meaning 'someday', offers a fictionalized version of those events. *Obasan* received many awards, including the *Books in Canada* First Novel Award, the Canadian Authors Association Book of the Year Award, and the Before Columbus Foundation American Book Award. A third novel, *The Rain Ascends* (1995), has just appeared.

Kogawa's other books include two poetry collections, *Jericho Road* (1977) and *Woman in the Woods* (1985), as well as an adaptation of *Obasan* for children, *Naomi's Road* (1986). A translation of the latter has appeared in Japanese, and an expansion of it ('*Obasan* without Aunt Emily') has been adopted as a textbook for Japanese junior high schools.

FROM *OBASAN*

The ball I found under the cot that day was never lost again. Obasan keeps it in a box with Stephen's toy cars on the bottom shelf in the bathroom. The rubber is cracked and scored with a black lacy design, and the colours are dull, but it still bounces a little.

Sick Bay, I learned eventually, was not a beach at all. And the place they called the Pool was not a pool of water, but a prison at the exhibition grounds called Hastings Park in Vancouver. Men, women, and children outside Vancouver, from the 'protected area'—a hundred-mile strip along the coast—were herded into the grounds and kept there like animals until they were shipped off to road-work camps and concentration camps in the interior of the province. From our family, it was only Grandma and Grandpa Nakane who were imprisoned at the Pool.

Some families were able to leave on their own and found homes in British Columbia's interior and elsewhere in Canada. Ghost towns such as Slocan—those old mining settlements, sometimes abandoned, sometimes with a remnant community—were reopened, and row upon row of two-family wooden huts were erected. Eventually the whole coast was cleared and everyone of the Japanese race in Vancouver was sent away.

The tension everywhere was not clear to me then and is not much clearer today. Time has solved few mysteries. Wars and rumours of wars, racial hatreds and fears are with us still.

The reality of today is that Uncle is dead and Obasan is left alone. Weariness has invaded her and settled in her bones. Is it possible that her hearing could deteriorate so rapidly in just one month? The phone is ringing but she does not respond at all.

Aunt Emily is calling from the airport in Calgary where she's waiting for Stephen's flight from Montreal. They'll rent a car and drive down together this afternoon.

'Did you get my parcel?' she asks.

The airport sounds in the background are so loud she can hardly hear me. I shout into the receiver but it's obvious she doesn't know what I'm saying.

'Is Obasan all right? Did she sleep last night?' she asks.

It's such a relief to feel her sharing my concern.

Obasan has gone into the bathroom and is sweeping behind the toilet with a whisk made from a toy broom.

'Would you like to take a bath?' I ask.

She continues sweeping the imaginary dust.

'Ofuro?' I repeat. 'Bath?'

'Orai,' she replies at last, in a meek voice. 'All right.'

I run the water the way she prefers it, straight from the hot-water tap. It's been a while since we bathed together. After this, perhaps she'll rest. Piece by piece she removes her layers of underclothes, rags held together with safety pins. The new ones I've bought for her are left unused in boxes under the bed. She is small and naked and bent in the bathroom, the skin of her buttocks loose and drooping in a fold.

'Aah,' she exhales deeply in a half groan as she sinks into the hot water and closes her eyes.

I rub the washcloth over her legs and feet, the thin purple veins a scribbled maze, a skin map, her thick toenails, ancient rock formations. I am reminded of long-extinct volcanoes, the crust and rivulets of lava scars, criss-crossing down the bony hillside. Naked as prehistory, we lie together, the steam from the bath heavily misting the room.

'Any day now is all right,' she says. 'The work is finished.' She is falling asleep in the water.

'It will be good to lie down,' I shout, rousing her and draining the tub. I help her to stand and she moves to her room, her feet barely leaving the floor. Almost before I pull the covers over her, she is asleep.

I am feeling a bit dizzy from the heat myself.

Aunt Emily said she and Stephen would be here by four this afternoon. I should clear up the place as much as I can before they arrive. Find a safe place for all the papers.

This diary of Aunt Emily's is the largest I have ever seen. The hard cover is grey with a black border and 'Journal' is written in fancy script in the middle. What a crackling sound old paper makes.

It has no page numbers and most of the entries begin 'Dear Nesan'. It's a journal of letters to my mother. 'Merry Christmas, Dearest Nesan, 1941' is printed in a rectangular decorated box on the first page.

Should I be reading this? Why not? Why else would she send it here?

The handwriting in blue-black ink is firm and regular in the first few pages, but is a rapid scrawl later on. I feel like a burglar as I read, breaking into a private house only to discover it's my childhood house filled with corners and rooms I've never seen. Aunt Emily's Christmas 1941 is not the Christmas I remember.

The people she mentions would be my age, or younger than I am now: her good friends, Eiko and Fumi, the student nurses; Tom Shoyama, the editor of the *New Canadian*; Kunio Shimizu, the social worker; my father, Tadashi Mark; Father's good friend, Uncle Dan; and Father's older brother, Isamu, Sam for short, or Uncle as we called him. Obasan is fifty years old in 1941.

In the face of growing bewilderment and distress, Aunt Emily roamed the landscape like an aircraft in a fog, looking for a place to land—a safe and sane strip of justice and reason. Not seeing these, she did not crash into the oblivion of either bitterness or futility but remained airborne.

The first entry is dated December 25, 1941.

Dearest Nesan,

In all my 25 years, this is the first Christmas without you and Mother. I wonder what you are doing today in Japan. Is it cold where you are? Do your neighbours treat you as enemies? Is Obaa-chan still alive?

When you come back, Nesan, when I see you again, I will give you this journal. It will be my Christmas present to you. Isn't it a sturdy book? It's one of Dan's Christmas gifts to me.

I'm sitting in the library, writing at the desk which has the picture of you and me beside the ink bottle. There are so many things to tell you. How different the world is now! The whole continent is in shock about the Pearl Harbor bombing. Some Issei are feeling betrayed and ashamed.

It's too early yet to know how the war will affect us. On the whole, I'd say we're taking things in our stride. We're used to the prejudice by now after all these long years, though it's been intensified into hoodlumism. A torch was thrown into a rooming-house and some plate-glass windows were broken in the west end—things like that.

The blackouts frighten the children. Nomi had a crying bout a few nights ago. I don't tell you this to worry you, Nesan, but I know you will want to know. There was a big storm during the last blackout. Nomi woke up. That peach tree is too close to her window. When the wind blows, it sways and swings around like a giant octopus trying to break in. Aya had the spare bed in Nomi's room just as you arranged before you left, but since she's had to stay so much longer, she's moved in the main bedroom and Mark sleeps in the study downstairs. Aya slept through the whole storm but Mark woke up to find Nomi sitting on his pillow, hitting the Japanese doll you gave her. He tried to take the doll away from her and she started to cry and wouldn't stop. He said it's the first time she's ever really cried. She doesn't understand what's going on at all. Stephen does, of course. He went through a phase of being too good to be true but now he's being surly. He told Aya to 'talk properly'.

All three Japanese newspapers have been closed down. That's fine as far as I'm concerned. Never needed so many anyway. It's good for the *New Canadian* which is now our only source of information and can go ahead with all the responsibility. Our December 12 headline is 'Have Faith in Canada'. Thank God we live in a democracy and not under an officially racist regime. All of us Nisei are intent on keeping faith and standing by. We were turned down for the Home Defense training plan but we're doing Red Cross work, buying War Savings bonds, logging for the war industries and shipyards, benefit concerts—the regular stuff.

There have been the usual letters to the editor in the papers. Rank nonsense, some of them. The majority are decent however. The RCMP are on our side. More than anyone else, they know how blameless we are. When the City Fathers proposed cancelling all our business licences they said we did not rate such harsh treatment. Isn't that encouraging? But now the North Vancouver Board of Trade has gone on record to demand that all our autos be confiscated. What would doctors like Dad and the businessmen do? If they take something that essential away from 23,000 people the rest of British Columbia will feel some of the bad side effects. Remember the boat that Sam and Mark finished last winter with all the hand carvings? It was seized along with all the fishing boats from up and down the coast, and the whole lot are tied up in New Westminster. Fishing licences were suspended a couple of weeks ago as well. The dog-salmon industry, I hear, is short-handed because the Japanese cannot fish any more. But the white fishermen are confident that they can make up the lack in the next season, if they can use the Japanese fishing boats.

There was one friendly letter in the *Province* protesting the taking away of the right to earn a living from 1,800 people. Said it wasn't democracy. But then there was another letter by a woman saying she didn't want her own precious daughter to have to go to school with the you-know-who's. Strange how these protesters are so much more vehement about Canadian-born Japanese than they are about German-born Germans. I guess it's because we look different. What it boils down to is an undemocratic racial antagonism—which is exactly what our democratic country is supposed to be fighting against. Oh well. The egg-man told me not to worry.

It's the small businesses that are most affected—the dressmakers, the corner store etc.—because the clientele are shy of patronising such places in public. Lots of people have been fired from their jobs. Business on Powell Street is up slightly since most of us who usually go to the big department stores like Woodwards don't any more.

A couple of Sundays ago the National President of the Imperial Order of Daughters of the Empire, who obviously doesn't know the first thing about us, made a deliberate attempt to create fear and ill-will among her dominion-wide members. Said we were all spies and saboteurs, and that in 1931 there were 55,000 of us and that number has doubled in the last ten years. A biological absurdity. Trouble is, lots of women would rather believe their president than actual RCMP records. It's illogical that women, who are the bearers and nurturers of the human race, should go all out for ill-will like this.

Are you interested in all this, Nesan?

I've knit Dad and Mark a couple of warm sweaters. Dad is back in full-time service in spite of his heart. When gas rationing starts he won't be able to use the car so much. It's so sleek it's an affront to everyone he passes. I wish he'd bought something more modest, but you know Dad.

He has to report every month to the RCMP just because he didn't take time to be naturalized, and didn't look far enough ahead to know how important it was. Politics doesn't seem to mean a thing to him. I feel so irritated at him.

But worse than my irritation there's this horrible feeling whenever I turn on the radio, or see a headline with the word 'Japs' screaming at us. So long as they designate the enemy by that term and not us, it doesn't matter. But over here, they say 'Once a Jap always a Jap', and that means us. We're the enemy. And what about you over there? Have they arrested you because you're a Canadian? If only you'd been able to get out before all this started. Oh, if there were some way of getting news.

The things that go on in wartime! Think of Hitler ship-loading people into Poland or Germany proper to work for nothing in fields and factories far from home and children—stealing food from conquered people—captive labour—shooting hundreds of people in reprisal for one. I'm glad to hear that the Russian army is taking some of the stuffing out of Hitler's troops. War breeds utter insanity. Here at home there's mass hatred of us simply because we're of Japanese origin. I hope fervently it will not affect the lives of the little ones like Stephen and Nomi. After all they are so thoroughly Canadian. Stephen and the Sugimoto boy are the only non-white kids in their classes. Mark says Nomi thinks she's the same as the neighbours, but Stephen knows the difference. Came crying home the other day because some kid on the block broke his violin. Children can be such savages.

There is a lapse of over a month until the next entry.

February 15, 1942.
Dearest Nesan,

I thought I would write to you every day but, as you see, I haven't managed that. I felt so sad thinking about what the children are having to experience I didn't want to keep writing. But today I must tell you what's happening.

Things are changing so fast. First, all the Japanese men—the ones who were born in Japan and haven't been able to get their citizenship yet—are being rounded up, one hundred or so at a time. A few days ago, Mark told me he felt sure Sam had been carted off. I took the interurban down as soon as I could. Isamu couldn't have been gone too long because not all the plants were parched though some of the delicate ones had turned to skeletons in the front window. I tried to find the dog but she's just nowhere. I looked and called all through the woods and behind the house.

Grandma and Grandpa Nakane will be so upset and confused when they find out he's gone. You know how dependent they are on him. They went to Saltspring Island a couple of weeks ago and haven't come back yet. I know they're with friends so they must be all right.

We know some people who have left Vancouver. Dad says we should look around and get out too, but we just don't know any other place. When we look at the map it's hard to think about all those unknown places. We were thinking of going to Kamloops, but that may be too close to the boundary of the 'protected area'.

It's becoming frightening here, with the agitation mounting higher. It isn't just a matter of fear of sabotage or military necessity any more, it's outright race persecution. Groups like the 'Sons of Canada' are petitioning Ottawa against us and the newspapers are printing outright lies. There was a picture of a young Nisei boy with a metal lunch box and it said he was a spy with a radio transmitter. When the reporting was protested the error was admitted in a tiny line in the classified section at the back where you couldn't see it unless you looked very hard.

March 2, 1942.

Everyone is distressed here, Nesan. Eiko and Fumi came over this morning, crying. All student nurses have been fired from the General.

Our beautiful radios are gone. We had to give them up or suffer the humiliation of having them taken forcibly by the RCMP. Our cameras—even Stephen's toy one that he brought out to show them when they came—all are confiscated. They can search our homes without warrant.

But the great shock is this: we are all being forced to leave. All of us. Not a single person of the Japanese race who lives in the 'protected area' will escape. There is something called a Civilian Labour Corps and Mark and Dan were going to join—you know how they do everything together—but now will not go near it as it smells of a demonic roundabout way of getting rid of us. There is a very suspicious clause 'within and *without*' Canada, that has all the fellows leery.

Who knows where we will be tomorrow, next week. It isn't as if we Nisei were aliens—technically or not. It breaks my heart to think of leaving this house and the little things that we've gathered through the years—all those irreplaceable mementoes—our books and paintings—the azalea plants, my white iris.

Oh Nesan, the Nisei are bitter. Too bitter for their own good or for Canada. How can cool heads like Tom's prevail, when the general feeling is to stand up and fight? He needs all his level-headedness and diplomacy, as editor of the *New Canadian*, since that's the only paper left to us now.

A curfew that applies only to us was started a few days ago. If we're caught out after sundown, we're thrown in jail. People who have been fired—and there's a scramble on to be the first to kick us out of jobs—sit at home without even being able to go out for a consoling cup of coffee. For many, home is just a bed. Kunio is working like mad with the Welfare society to look after the women and children who were left when the men were forced to 'volunteer' to go to the work camps. And where are those men? Sitting in unheated bunk-cars, no latrines, no water, snow fifteen feet deep, no work, little food if any. They were shunted off with such inhuman speed that they got there before any facilities were prepared. Now other men are afraid to go because they think they'll be going to certain disaster. If the snow is that deep, there is no work. If there is no work, there is no pay. If there is no pay, no one eats. Their families suffer. The *Daily Province* reports that work on frames with tent coverings is progressing to house the 2,000 expected. Tent coverings where the snow is so deep? You should see the faces here—all pinched, grey, uncertain. Signs have been posted on all highways—'Japs Keep Out'.

Mind you, you can't compare this sort of thing to anything that happens in Germany. That country is openly totalitarian. But Canada is supposed to be a democracy.

All Nisei are liable to imprisonment if we refuse to volunteer to leave. At least that is the likeliest interpretation of Ian Mackenzie's 'Volunteer or else' statement. He's the Minister of Pensions and National Health. Why do they consider us to be wartime prisoners? Can you wonder that there is a deep bitterness among the Nisei who believed in democracy?

And the horrors that some of the young girls are facing—outraged by men in uniform. You wouldn't believe it, Nesan. You have to be right here in the middle of it to really know. The men are afraid to go and leave their wives behind.

How can the Hakujin not feel ashamed for their treachery? My butcher told me he knew he could trust me more than he could most whites. But kind people like him are betrayed by the outright racists and opportunists like Alderman Wilson, God damn his soul. And there are others who, although they wouldn't persecute us, are ignorant and indifferent and believe we're being very well treated for the 'class' of people we are. One letter in the papers says that in order to preserve the 'British way of life', they should send us all away. We're a 'lower order of people'. In one breath we are damned for being 'inassimilable' and the next there's fear that we'll assimilate. One reporter points to those among us who are living in poverty and says 'No British subject would live in such conditions.' Then if we improve our lot, another says 'There is danger that they will enter our better neighbourhoods.' If we are educated the complaint is that we will cease being the 'ideal servant'. It makes me choke. The diseases, the crippling, the twisting of our souls is still to come.

March 12.
Honest Nesan, I'm just in a daze this morning. The last ruling forbids any of us—even Nisei—to go anywhere in this wide dominion without a permit from the Minister of Justice, St Laurent, through Austin C. Taylor of the Commission here. We go where they send us.

Nothing affects me much just now except rather detachedly. Everything is like a bad dream. I keep telling myself to wake up. There's no sadness when friends of long standing disappear overnight—either to Camp or somewhere in the Interior. No farewells—no promise at all of future meetings or correspondence—or anything. We just disperse. It's as if we never existed. We're hit so many ways at one time that if I wasn't past feeling I think I would crumble.

This curfew business is horrible. At sundown we scuttle into our holes like furtive creatures. We look in the papers for the time of next morning's sunrise when we may venture forth.

The government has requisitioned the Livestock Building at Hastings Park, and the Women's Building, to house 2,000 'Japs pending removal'. White men are pictured in the newspaper filling ticks with bales of straw for mattresses, putting up makeshift partitions for toilets—etc. Here the lowly Jap will be bedded down like livestock in stalls—perhaps closed around under police guard—I don't know. The Nisei will be 'compelled' (news report) to volunteer in Labour Gangs. The worse the news from the Eastern Front, the more ghoulish the public becomes. We are the billygoats and nannygoats and kids—all the scapegoats to appease this blindness. Is this a Christian country? Do you know that Alderman Wilson, the man who says such damning things about us, has a father who is an Anglican clergyman?

I can't imagine how the government is going to clothe and educate our young when they can't even get started on feeding or housing 22,000 removees. Yet the deadline for clearing us out seems to be July 1st or 31st—I'm not sure which. Seems to me that either there are no fifth columnists or else the Secret Service men can't find them. If the FBI in the States have rounded up a lot of them you'd think the RCMP could too and let the innocent ones alone. I wish to goodness they'd catch them all. I don't feel safe if there are any on the loose. But I like to think there aren't any.

March 20.

Dearest Nesan,

Stephen has been developing a slight limp. Dad's not sure what's wrong with the leg. He suspects that the fall he had last year never healed properly and there's some new aggravation at the hip. Stephen spends a lot of time making up tunes on the new violin Dad got him. The old one, I told you, was broken. It's lucky our houses are so close as I can get to see the children fairly often, even with the miserable curfew.

Your friend Mina Sugimoto takes her boys to play with Stephen a fair amount but she's acting like a chicken flapping about with her head cut off since her husband left.

Last night over a hundred boys entrained for a road camp at Schreiber, Ontario. A hundred and fifty are going to another camp at Jasper. The Council (United Nisei) has been working like mad talking to the boys. The first batch of a hundred refused to go. They got arrested and imprisoned in that Immigration building. The next batch refused too and were arrested. Then on Saturday they were released on the promise that they would report back to the Pool. There was every indication they wouldn't but the Council persuaded them to keep their word. They went finally. That was a tough hurdle and the Commission cabled Ralston to come and do something.

On Thursday night, the confinees in the Hastings Park Pool came down with terrible stomach pains. Ptomaine, I gather. A wholesale company or something is contracted to feed them and there's profiteering. There are no partitions of any kind whatsoever and the people are treated worse than livestock, which at least had their own pens and special food when they were there. No plumbing of any kind. They can't take a bath. They don't even take their clothes off. Two weeks now. Lord! Can you imagine a better breeding ground for typhus? They're cold (Vancouver has a fuel shortage), they're undernourished, they're unwashed. One of the men who came out to buy food said it was pitiful the way the kids scramble for food and the slow ones go empty. God damn those politicians who brought this tragedy on us.

Dan has to report tomorrow and will most likely be told when to go and where. A day's notice at most. When will we see him again? Until all this happened I didn't realize how close a member of the family he had become. He's just like a brother to me. Nesan, I don't know what to do.

The Youth Congress protested at the ill treatment but since then the daily papers are not printing a word about us. One baby was born at the Park. Premature, I think.

If all this sounds like a bird's eye view to you, Nesan, it's the reportage of a caged bird. I can't really see what's happening. We're like a bunch of rabbits being chased by hounds.

You remember Mr Morii, the man who was teaching judo to the RCMP? He receives orders from the Mounties to get 'a hundred to the station or else and here's a list of names'. Any who are rich enough, or who are desperate about not going immediately because of family concerns, pay Morii hundreds of dollars and get placed conveniently on a committee. There are nearly two hundred on that 'committee' now. Some people say he's distributing the money to needy families but who knows?

There's a three-way split in the community—three general camps: the Morii gang, us—the Council group—and all the rest, who don't know what to do. The Council group is just a handful. It's gruelling uphill work for us. Some people want to fight. Others say our only chance is to co-operate with the government. Whichever way we decide there's a terrible feeling of underlying treachery.

March 22, 1942.
Dear Diary,

I don't know if Nesan will ever see any of this. I don't know anything any more. Things are swiftly getting worse here. Vancouver—the water, the weather, the beauty, this paradise—is filled up and overflowing with hatred now. If we stick around too long we'll all be chucked into Hastings Park. Fumi and Eiko are helping the women there and they say the crowding, the noise, the confusion is chaos. Mothers are prostrate in nervous exhaustion—the babies crying endlessly—the fathers torn from them without farewell—everyone crammed into two buildings like so many pigs—children taken out of school with no provision for future education—more and more people pouring into the Park—forbidden to step outside the barbed wire gates and fence—the men can't even leave the building—police guards around them—some of them fight their way out to come to town to see what they can do about their families. Babies and motherless children totally stranded—their fathers taken to camp. It isn't as if this place had been bombed and *everyone* was suffering. *Then* our morale would be high because we'd be *together*.

Eiko says the women are going to be mental cases.

Rev. Kabayama and family got thrown in too. It's going to be an ugly fight to survive among us. They're making (they say) accommodation for 1,200-1,300 women and children in that little Park! Bureaucrats find it so simple on paper and it's translated willy-nilly into action—and the pure hell that results is kept 'hush hush' from the public, who are already kicking about the 'luxury' given to Japs.

I'm consulting with Dad and Mark and Aya about going to Toronto. We could all stay together if we could find someone in Toronto to sponsor us. People are stranded here and there all over the B.C. interior. I want to leave this poisoned province. But Aya wants to stay in B.C. to be closer to Sam. I'm going to write to a doctor in Toronto that Dad knows.

March 27.

Dan's been arrested. The boys refused to go to Ontario. Both trainloads. So they're all arrested. Dan had a road map friends drew for him so they suspected him of being a 'spy' and now he's in the Pool.

Nisei are called 'enemy aliens'. Minister of War, or Defense, or something flying here to take drastic steps.

April 2, 1942.
Dearest Nesan,

If only you and Mother could come home! Dad's sick in bed. The long months of steady work. Since the evacuation started he's had no let-up at all. Two nights ago, one of his patients was dying. He tried to arrange to have the daughter go to the old man's bedside but couldn't. Dad stayed up all night with the man, and now he's sick himself.

I'm afraid that those kept in the Hastings Park will be held as hostages or something. Perhaps to ensure the good behaviour of the men in the work camps. Dan was cleared of that idiotic spying charge and is helping at the Pool. The cop who arrested him was drunk and took a few jabs at him but Dan didn't retaliate, thank heavens. I'm applying for a pass so I can get to see him.

Dan has a lawyer working for him and his parents about their desire to stay together, especially since Dan's father is blind and his mother speaks no English at all. The lawyer went to the Security Commission's lawyers and reported back that he was told to let the matter drift because they were going to make sure the Japs suffered as much as possible. The Commission is responsible to the Federal Government through the Minister of Justice, St Laurent. It works in conjunction with the RCMP. The Commission has three members—Austin C. Taylor, to represent the Minister of Justice, Commissioner Mead of the RCMP, John Shirras of the Provincial Police.

Only Tommy and Kunio, as active members of the Council, know what's going on and they're too busy to talk to me. The *New Canadian* comes out so seldom we have no way of knowing much and I've been so busy helping Dad I can't get to Council meetings very often. There's so much veiling and soft pedalling because everything is censored by the RCMP. We can only get information verbally. The bulletins posted on Powell Street aren't available to most people. Besides, nobody can keep up with all the things that are happening. There's a terrible distrust of federal authorities and fear of the RCMP, but mostly there's a helpless panic. Not the hysterical kind, but the kind that churns round and round going nowhere.

My twenty-sixth birthday is coming up soon and I feel fifty. I've got lines under my eyes and my back is getting stooped, I noticed in a shop window today.

Mina Sugimoto heard from her husband. Why haven't we heard from Sam? Stephen asked me the other day 'Where's Uncle?' What could I say?

April 8, 1942.

Ye gods! The newspapers are saying that there are actually Japanese naval officers living on the coast. It must be a mistake. Maybe they're old retired men. I heard someone say it was just that they took courses when they were kids in school and that's the way schools are in Japan. I'd hate to think we couldn't tell a fisherman from a sailor. Maybe the articles are true. I wonder if there's a cover-up. Surely we'd know if there were any spies. But gosh—who can we trust? At times like this, all we have is our trust in one another. What happens when that breaks down?

A few days ago the newspaper reported Ian Mackenzie as saying 'The intention of the government is that every single Japanese—man, woman and child—shall be removed from Vancouver as speedily as possible.' He said we were all going to be out in three or four weeks and added it was his 'personal intention', as long as he was in public life, 'that these Japanese shall not come back here.'

It's all so frightening. Rumours are that we're going to be kept as prisoners and war hostages—but that's so ridiculous since we're Canadians. There was a headline in the paper yesterday that said half of our boats 'of many different kinds and sizes' have been released to the army, navy, air force, and to 'bona fide white fishermen'. I wonder who has Sam's beautiful little boat. It was such an ingenious design. They said they were hopeful about all the boats because one plywood boat passed all the tests. The reporter found someone he called a 'real fisherman', a man from Norway who had fished all his life and used to have a 110-foot steam fishing boat when he fished off Norway and Iceland 'close to home'. That's one man who's profiting by our misery. He's quoted as saying 'We can do without the Japanese', but he's not loath to take our boats. Obviously white Canadians feel more loyalty towards white foreigners than they do towards us Canadians.

All this worrying is very bad for Dad. He's feeling numbness on the left side. I'm trying to keep him still but he's a terrible patient. He's very worried about Stephen—the limp is not improving. Dad is so intense about that boy. He's also worried about Mark, says his coughing is a bad sign and he's losing weight too fast. A lot of his patients, especially the old ones, are in a state of collapse.

I hadn't been to meetings of the Council lately. Too occupied with the sick ones around me. But I'm trying to keep an eye on what's happening. The Nisei who were scheduled to leave last night balked. I don't know the details. We haven't heard whether they're in the jug or the Pool or on the train. It's horrible not being able to know.

April 9.

It seems that all the people who are conscientious enough to report when they have to, law-abiding enough not to kick about their treatment—these are the ones who go first. The ones on the loose, bucking the authorities, are single men, so the married ones have to go to fill the quota. Lots of the fellows are claiming they need more time to clear up family affairs for their parents who don't understand English well enough to cope with all the problems and regulations.

I had a talk with Tommy on the phone. He said they can't do much more than they're doing without injuring a lot more people. 'All we've got on our side,' he said, 'is time and the good faith of the Nisei.' At times I get fighting mad and think that the RCMP in using Morii are trusting the wrong man—the way he collects money for favours—but in the end, I can see how complaining would just work even more against us. What can we do? No witnesses will speak up against him any more. I'm told our letters aren't censored yet, but may be at any time.

April 11.
Dear Nesan,
    Dad had a letter the other day from his friend Kawaguchi at Camp 406 in Princeton. It's cheered him up a lot. You remember Kawaguchi? His wife died a few years back. He left his kids with friends and he's asking us to see what we can do to keep Jack's education from being disrupted. He says 'I think we should always keep hope. Hope is life. Hopeless is lifeless . . . .'
    This morning Dad got out of bed and went to the Pool bunkhouse for men (the former Women's Building). He was nauseated by the smell, the clouds of dust, the pitiful attempts at privacy. The Livestock Building (where the women and kids are) is worse. Plus manure smells. The straw ticks are damp and mouldy. There are no fresh fruits or vegetables. He ate there to see what it was like. Supper was two slices of bologna, bread and tea. That's all. Those who have extra money manage to get lettuce and tomatoes and fruit from outside. Nothing for babies. He's asking for improvement and so is the Council.
    Dad saw Dan. He earns about two dollars a day at the Pool helping out—minus board of course. There are a handful of others working there as well, getting from ten to twenty-five cents an hour for running errands and handling passes, etc. Dad, being a doctor, has a pass to come and go freely. The fact that he retired a few years ago because of his heart means the Commission is not pressing him into service in the ghost towns.
    We'll have to rent our houses furnished. Have to leave the chesterfield suite, stove, refrig, rugs, etc. We aren't allowed to sell our furniture. Hits the dealers somehow. I don't understand it, but so they say.
    It's an awfully unwieldy business, this evacuation. There's a wanted list of over a hundred Nisei who refuse to entrain. They're being chased all over town.

April 20.
    I have gone numb today. Is all this real? Where do I begin? First I got my pass and saw Dan at last. He's going to Schreiber in two days. I didn't feel a thing when he told me. It didn't register at all. Maybe I'm crazy. When I left, I didn't say good-bye either. Now that I'm home I still can't feel. He was working in the Baggage—old Horse Show Building. Showed me his pay cheque as something he couldn't believe—$11.75. He's been there an awfully long time.
    After I saw Dan, and delivered some medicine for Dad, I saw Eiko and Fumi. Eiko is working as a steno in the Commission office there, typing all the routine forms. She sleeps in a partitioned stall—being on the staff so to speak. The stall

was the former home of a pair of stallions and boy oh boy did they leave their odour behind! The whole place is impregnated with the smell of ancient manure. Every other day it's swept with chloride of lime or something but you can't disguise horse smells, cow, sheep, pig, rabbit, and goat smells. And is it dusty! The toilets are just a sheet-metal trough and up till now they didn't have partitions or seats. The women complained so they put in partitions and a terribly makeshift seat. Twelve-year-old boys stay with the women too. The auto show building, where the Indian exhibits were, houses the new dining room and kitchens. Seats 3,000. Looks awfully permanent. Brick stoves—eight of them— shiny new mugs—very very barracky. As for the bunks, they were the most tragic things I saw there. Steel and wooden frames at three-foot intervals with thin lumpy straw ticks, bolsters, and three army blankets of army quality—no sheets unless you brought your own. These are the 'homes' of the women I saw. They wouldn't let me or any 'Jap females' into the men's building. There are constables at the doors—'to prevent further propagation of the species', it said in the newspaper. The bunks were hung with sheets and blankets and clothes of every colour—a regular gypsy caravan—all in a pathetic attempt at privacy—here and there I saw a child's doll or teddy bear—I saw two babies lying beside a mother who was too weary to get up—she had just thrown herself across the bed. I felt my throat thicken. I couldn't bear to look on their faces daring me to be curious or superior because I still lived outside. They're stripped of all privacy.

Some of the women were making the best of things, housecleaning around their stalls. One was scrubbing and scrubbing trying to get rid of the smell, but that wasn't possible. And then, Nesan, and then, I found Grandma Nakane there sitting like a little troll in all that crowd, with her chin on her chest. At first I couldn't believe it. She didn't recognize me. She just stared and stared. Then when I knelt down in front of her, she broke down and clung to me and cried and cried and said she'd rather have died than have come to such a place. Aya and Mark were sick when I told them. We all thought they were safe with friends in Saltspring. She has no idea of what's going on and I think she may not survive. I presumed Grandpa Nakane was in the men's area, but then I learned he was in the Sick Bay. I brought Eiko to meet Grandma but Grandma wouldn't look up. You know how yasashi Grandma is. This is too great a shock for her. She whispered to me that I should leave right away before they caught me too—then she wouldn't say any more. Nesan, maybe it's better where you are, even if they think you're an enemy.

Eiko has taken the woes of the confinees on her thin shoulders and she takes so much punishment. Fumi is worried sick about her. The place has got them both down. There are ten showers for 1,500 women. Hot and cold water. The men looked so terribly at loose ends, wandering around the grounds—sticking their noses through the fence watching the golfers. I felt so heavy I almost couldn't keep going. They are going to move the Vancouver women now and shove them into the Pool before sending them to the camps in the ghost towns.

The other day at the Pool, a visitor dropped his key before a stall in the

Livestock Building, and he fished for it with a wire and brought to light manure and maggots. He called the nurse and then they moved all the bunks from the stalls and pried up the wooden floors, and it was the most stomach-turning nauseating thing. So they got fumigators and hoses and tried to wash it all away and got most of it into the drains. But maggots are still breeding and turning up here and there, so one woman with more guts than the others told the nurse (white) about it and protested. She replied: 'Well, there are worms in the garden, aren't there?' This particular nurse was a Jap-hater of the most virulent sort. She called them 'filthy Japs' to their faces and Fumi gave her what for and had a terrible scrap with her, saying 'What do you think we are? Are we cattle? Are we pigs?' You know how Fumi gets.

The night the first bunch of Nisei refused to go to Schreiber the women and children at the Pool milled around in front of their cage, and one very handsome Mountie came with his truncheon and started to hit them and yelled at them to 'Get the hell back in there.' Eiko's blood boiled over. She strode over to him and shouted 'You put that stick down. What do you think you're doing? Do you think these women and children are cows, that you can beat them back?' Eiko was shaking. She's taken it on herself to fight and now she's on the blacklist and reputed to be a trouble-maker. It's people like us, Nesan—Eiko and Tommy and Dan and Fumi and the rest of us who have had faith in Canada, who have been more politically minded than the others—who are the most hurt. At one time, remember how I almost worshipped the Mounties? Remember the Curwood tales of the Northwest, and the Royal Canadian Mounted Police and how I'd go around saying their motto—*Maintiens le droit*—Maintain the right?

The other day there were a lot of people lined up on Heather Street to register at RCMP headquarters and so frightened by what was going on and afraid of the uniforms. You could feel their terror. I was going around telling them not to worry—the RCMP were our protectors and upholders of the law, etc. And there was this one officer tramping up and down that perfectly quiet line of people, holding his riding crop like a switch in his hand, smacking the palm of his other hand regularly—whack whack—as if he would just have loved to hit someone with it if they even so much as spoke or moved out of line. The glory of the Redcoats.

April 25.
Dearest Nesan,

Mark has gone.

The last night I spent with him and Aya and kids, he played the piano all night. He's terribly thin. Dad has been too ill to see him but he says Mark should not be going to the camps.

Is it true, Nesan, that you were pregnant just before you left? Mark said he wasn't sure. Oh, is there no way we can hear from you? I'm worried about the children. Nomi almost never talks or smiles. She is always carrying the doll you gave her and sleeps with it every night. I think, even though she doesn't talk, that she's quite bright. When I read to her from the picture books, I swear she's following the words with her eyes. Stephen spends his time reading war comics that he gets from the neighbourhood boys. All the Japs have mustard-coloured faces and buck teeth.

April 28.

We had our third letter from Sam—rather Aya did. All cards and letters are censored—even to the Nisei camps. Not a word from the camps makes the papers. Everything is hushed up. I haven't been to meetings for so long now that I don't know what's going on. Sam's camp is eight miles from the station, up in the hills. Men at the first camps all crowd down to the station every time a train passes with a new batch of men. They hang from the windows and ask about their families. Sam said he wept.

The men are luckier than the women. It's true they are forced to work on the roads, but at least they're fed, and they have no children to look after. Of course the fathers are worried but it's the women who are burdened with all the responsibility of keeping what's left of the family together.

Mina Sugimoto is so hysterical. She heard about a place in Revelstoke, got word to her husband and he came to see her on a two-day pass. She wanted them to go to Revelstoke together but of course that wasn't possible. He wasn't able to make it back to road camp in the time limit so now they're threatening to intern him. In the meantime, Mina has gone off to Revelstoke, bag, baggage, and boys. I'll try to find out what happens to them for you, Nesan.

Eiko has heard that the town of Greenwood is worse than the Pool. They're propping up old shacks near the mine shaft. On top of that local people are complaining and the United Church parson there says to 'Kick all the Japs out'.

Eiko, Fumi, and I have gotten to be so profane that Tom and the rest have given up being surprised. Eiko says 'What the hell', and Fumi is even worse.

What a mess everything is. Some Nisei are out to save their own skins, others won't fight for any rights at all. The RCMP are happy to let us argue among ourselves. Those of us who are really conscientious and loyal—how will we ever get a chance to prove ourselves to this country? All we are fighting for inch by inch just goes down the drain. There are over 140 Nisei loose and many Japanese nationals (citizens of Japan). The Commission thinks the nationals are cleared out of Vancouver but oh boy, there are a lot of them who have greased enough palms and are let alone.

April 30.

We got another extension and are trying to get a place here in B.C. some-where—somewhere on a farm with some fruit trees. We may have to go to some town in Alberta or Saskatchewan or Manitoba. I have to do some fast work, contacting all the people I think could help in some way. Dad doesn't want to leave B.C. If we go too far, we may not be able to come back. With you in Japan and Mark in Camp, Dad feels we should stay with the kids—but everybody has the same worry about their kids.

Stephen's leg was put in a cast. Dad thinks that rest will heal it. He says Grandma Nakane's mind is failing fast. She didn't speak to him when he was there today. He thought she'd be all right if she could see Grandpa Nakane but he wasn't able to arrange it. Dad's worried about both of them. I'm trying to get them out of there but the red tape is so fierce.

May 1.

I have to work fast. The Commission put out a notice—everyone has to be ready for 24-hour notice. No more extensions. Everything piled on at once. We're trying to get into a farm or house around Salmon Arm or Chase or some other decent town in the Interior—anywhere that is livable and will still let us in. Need a place with a reasonable climate. Some place where we can have a garden to grow enough vegetables for a year. Somewhere there's a school if possible. If there's nothing in B.C., I think we should go east and take our chances in Toronto. Fumi and Eiko and I want to stick together.

Monday, May 4.

Got to get out in the next couple of weeks. Dad's had a relapse. The numbness is spreading. He doesn't think it's his heart.

There's another prospect. McGillivray Falls, twenty miles from Lillooet. Going there would eat up our savings since that's all we'd have to live on but at least it's close to Vancouver and just a few hours to get back. There's no school. I'd have to teach the children.

It's because so many towns have barred their doors that we are having such a heck of a time. The Commission made it clear to us that they would not permit us to go anywhere the City Councils didn't want us. Individuals who offer to help have to write letters saying they undertake to see that we won't be a burden on the public. Who among us wants to be a burden on anyone? It'd be better if, instead of writing letters to help one or two of us, they'd try to persuade their City Councils to let us in. After all we're Canadians.

Eiko and her mother might go to a ghost town to be closer to her father. Also most likely she'll have to teach grade-school. The pay is two dollars a day out of which she'd have to feed and clothe the four younger kids and try to keep them in a semblance of health. Honest, Nesan, I wonder if the whites think we are a special kind of low animal able to live on next to nothing—able to survive without clothing, shoes, medicine, decent food.

Aya just phoned that there's no electricity at McGillivray. What does one do without electricity? There are so many complex angles in this business my head aches.

Another thing that's bothering Aya is the cost of transportation and freight. We can take only our clothes, bedding, pots and pans, and dishes. We've sold our dining-room suite and piano. Mark didn't sell anything. Aya's house was looted. I haven't told her. It's in such an out-of-the-way place. When I took the interurban on Friday to see if the dog might have shown up, I was shocked.

Almost all the hand-carved furnishings were gone—all the ornaments—just the dead plants left and some broken china on the floor. I saw one of the soup bowls from the set I gave them. The looting was thorough. The collection of old instruments Mark talked about was gone too and the scrolls. No one will understand the value of these things. I don't have the heart to tell Aya.

We're all walking around in a daze. It's really too late do anything. If we go to the ghost towns, it's going to be one hell of a life. Waiting in line to wash, cook, bathe——

I've got to go to sleep. And I've got to pack. If we go to McGillivray, Fumi, Eiko, and family are coming with us. We have to go in a week or two. The Commission won't wait.

May 5.

Dearest Nesan,

We've heard from Mark. Crazy man. All he thinks about are Stephen's music lessons. He sent two pages of exercises and a melody which he thought up. He wrote about some flowers he found which he stuck on the end of his pick and says he thinks about you as he works. I read the letter three times to Dad. Dad says Stephen's health is more important than his music right now. Nomi is fine. She's so silent though. I've never seen such a serious child before.

I got a letter from Dan as well. His address is Mileage 101, Camp SW 5-3, Jackfish, Ontario.

We've had three different offers since yesterday. Mickey Maikawa wants us to go to his wife's brother's farm in Sicamous. We're considering it. Everything is confusion and bewilderment.

Eiko has heard awful things about the crowding and lack of sanitation in the ghost towns. People have been freezing in tents. She's dead set against them now. She and Fumi and I are still trying to stick together. But you never know when we'll have to go, or which way our luck's going to jump. Every day's a different story, from nowhere to go to several choices. I want to go east. Rent at McG. Falls was reduced to $80.00 per year.

May 14.

Dear Nesan,

Aya, kids, Dad, and I have decided to go to Slocan. We hear that's one of the best of the ghost towns. It used to have a silver mine, or maybe a gold mine—I'm not sure. There are just abandoned old hotels there now and a few stores. I don't know the size of the white population but it's not very large.

The family—or what's left of it—intends to stick together one way or another, and after days and nights of discussion, chasing this elusive hope or that, worrying, figuring, going bats with indecision, with one door after another closing then opening again—we finally realize the only thing to do is give in and stay together wherever we go, and moving to Slocan is the easiest.

Rev. Nakayama, who's already in Slocan, wrote and told me about a small house that Dad and I can have to ourselves, close to the mountains and away from the crowding. It makes all the difference. I'm so glad I thought to ask him for help. We'll be able to manage something for the kids—build an addition if we have to.

Now that the decision is taken, I don't want to be upset all over again. I don't want to go through all the hopes and the uncertainty of trying to find a loophole to escape from. I'm resigned to Slocan—and anyway, Rev. Nakayama says it's a nice place. It even has a soda fountain. So I'll settle for that until they say it's okay for us to join Mark and Sam and Dan again somewhere. Grandma and Grandpa Nakane have orders to go to New Denver. We've tried everything, I've cried my cry, I've said good-bye to this home. All fluttering for escape has died down. Just wish us luck, Nesan. We'll wait until that happy day when we can all be together again.

Now I must get to serious packing and selling and giving away and the same thing at your house.

I asked too much of God.

May 15, Friday.

There's too much to do. Dad's unable to help though he tries. After we get to Slocan things should calm down. The furor will die down when there are none of us left on the Coast. Then we can discuss moving to Ontario. It's time that defeated us for the present but we won't give up yet. Not by a long shot.

Dan's new address—Dalton Mills, c/o Austin Lumber Co., Dalton Ontario.

We got a letter today from the doctor in Toronto offering us the top floor of his house. That would be wonderful, but heck! how I'd hate to impose on anyone. Imagine being dependent like that. I think it was fated for me to taste the dregs of this humiliation that I might know just what it is that all the women and children are enduring through no fault of their own.

Once we're in Slocan, chances of going east are better than here. The officials are terribly harassed with the whole thing and exasperated with individual demands for attention. So, Slocan City, here we come.

Goodness, I think I'll keep my golf clubs.

May 18, 1942.

Dear Nesan,

It's flabbergasting. I can't believe any of it. Here's what happened.

I was all packed for Slocan and Dad was reasonably okay. In the middle of helping Aya, I thought—just as a last gesture and more for my own assurance than out of any hope—that I'd write to Grant MacNeil, secretary of the Commission. So I wrote asking for written assurance that I could continue negotiations from Slocan about going to Toronto. That's all. Just the word that there was hope for us all to get to Ontario. No further aspirations. I was too tired to start all over again anyway. Mailed the letter around noon from the main post office on Friday. A little after three o'clock, Mrs Booth who works there phoned to say that they'd got the letter and I was to come right away. I couldn't believe it. I dropped everything and ran. Mrs Booth, speaking for Mr MacNeil, said they were not giving any special permits but they'd make this one exception and told me to return next day with bank accounts, references, etc. I was so excited and happy, I assumed that included Dad and Aya and the kids. Next day, Mrs Booth said the permit was only for the Kato family. One family only. I told her Stephen and Nomi are my sister's kids but she said something about Commission rulings and their name is Nakane and then she asked about the Nakane family and I had to say they were nationals and I think that settled it. But she said she would look into the business of the kids. I was so frustrated not having Mark or Dad or Aya to confer with. It seemed to me at that point that I should opt for Toronto with Dad and then negotiate having everyone else come to join us.

Do you think I did the right thing, Nesan? Eiko says I did and that we should try to keep as many out of the ghost towns as possible. So I went back and told Dad and he didn't say anything one way or the other. Just kept nodding his head.

When I discussed it with Aya, she was adamant about the kids. She says you entrusted them to her and they're her kids now until you return and she won't part with them. It's true they're more used to her than to either me or Dad. And as for being so far away, Aya says ten miles or ten thousand miles makes no difference to a child.

The whole point of all our extensions was to find a way to keep together, but now at the last minute everything has exploded. Aya is being very calm and she doesn't want any discussion in front of the kids. All she's told them is that they're going for a train ride.

Fumi is resigned to not coming with us. Eiko's mother wants to go to Slocan, but I can tell Eiko wants out. I don't know what Fumi is going to do now. I think she's going to Kaslo with Rev. Shimizu's group.

I'm going to the Custodian tomorrow and then to the Commission again. Maybe the permit won't be given at the last minute. What if I transfer the Slocan papers to someone else and then don't get the Toronto permit? There could be trouble with all these forms and deferments.

Well, I'm going to go ahead, repack everything and hope. The mover, Crone, is sending our boxed goods, beds, and Japanese food supplies—shoyu, rice, canned mirinzuke, green tea. I'm taking the Japanese dishes, trays and bowls. Can't get any more miso now.

I'll just have to live on hope that Aya and kids will be all right till we can get them to Toronto. I tell myself that at least they'll have their own place till then.

What will it be like, I wonder, in the doctor's house? I'll wire them as soon as I get the permit and we'll head their way for the time being. Do we eat with the family? First thing I'll do when I get to Toronto is go out *at night*.

In Petawawa there are 130 Nisei interned for rioting and crying 'Banzai', shaving their heads and carrying 'hino-maru' flags. Damn fools.

May 21.

Dearest Nesan,

Aya and kids are leaving with others bound for Slocan tomorrow. RCMP came in person to order Kunio off to camp. Rev. Shimizu and Rev. Akagawa had to leave immediately.

Yesterday I worked so hard—tied, labelled, ran to Commission, ran to bank, to Crone movers, to CPR, washed and cooked and scrubbed. Dad is saying good-bye to the kids now. They're spending the night in the church hall at Kitsilano. I'm going over there too as soon as I pack this last item.

Merry Christmas, Nesan.

This is the last word in the journal. The following day, May 22, 1942, Stephen, Aya Obasan and I are on a train for Slocan. It is twelve years before we see Aunt Emily again.

CLAIRE HARRIS

(b. 1937)

'I have always known that I was a writer,' Claire Harris has said. She began writing in 1974 during a year-long leave of absence from her teaching in the Separate Schools in Calgary, Alberta. She spent that year in Lagos, Nigeria, studying at the University of Nigeria, where she received a Diploma in Mass Media and Communications. Her stay and studies there proved to be a crucial experience: Nigeria's 'entirely different culture forced me to pay attention', she says, and to realize that her 'task' as a writer is 'to return Africa to its place at the centre, the heart of Western Civilization'. Her recognition of what her subject matter is comes from her painful awareness that 'Africans in North America, and of course, Europe, have suffered a traumatic loss. The nations which inflicted and continue to inflict that loss have never acknowledged their crime. . . . There can, of course, be no healing while one group continues to see the other as inherently less than acceptable. There is no acceptance of our joint inheritance, no recognition of the scar tissue embroidering it.'

Harris, who was born in Port of Spain, Trinidad, emigrated to Calgary in 1966, after completing her studies at the University College, Dublin, Ireland, where she received a B.A. Honours (with a major in English and a minor in Spanish), and at the University of the West Indies, Jamaica, where she received a Post-Graduate Diploma in Education. Retired now as a teacher, Harris has been active in promoting Canadian literature to Canadians, especially through *Poetry Goes Public*, a project that involved the circulation of poetry posters by major poets in public spaces, including buses, and through her work as a member of the Writers' Guild of Alberta, as poetry editor of *Dandelion* (1981-1989),

and as founding editor and manager of *blue buffalo* (1984-1987), an all-Alberta literary magazine.

Her poetry, which has appeared in numerous literary magazines and anthologies, includes *Fables from the Women's Quarters* (1984), which won the Commonwealth Award, Americas Region, in 1985; *Translation into Fiction* (1984); *Travelling to Find a Remedy* (1986), winner of the Writers' Guild of Alberta Award for poetry in 1987 and the Alberta Culture Poetry Prize; *The Conception of Winter* (1989), which received an Alberta Special Award in 1990; and *Drawing Down a Daughter* (1992), which was short-listed for the Governor General's Award for poetry in 1993. Selections of her poetry as well as her essay 'Why Do I Write?' are included in *Grammar of Dissent* (1994), edited by Carol Morrell and gathering together Harris's work with that of two other Canadian writers from the Caribbean, Dionne Brand and Marlene Nourbese Philip. Harris is also the co-editor with Edna Alford of *Kitchen Talk* (1992), an anthology of women's writing.

Her poetry is written in a variety of styles—short lyrics, long sequences, haiku, prose narratives, texts that often claim all the space of a page—which reflect, as Harris says, 'the different ways of approaching things'. 'To mirror the profound disharmony' of our world, Harris writes, 'collages would have to take form, languages would have to knock against each other, genres would have to dissolve.' As the poems that follow illustrate, Harris is intent on re-examining how we are the products of our culture, how racialization and gender construction inform the ways in which we think we understand our culture as well as the cultures of others.

BLACK SISYPHUS

To propitiate the dreaming god at his centre
for months my father drove down green uneven

roads to the capital where tar flowed under
noonday heat in daily manouevres around new obstacles

to take form again in cold pale morning
he drove those roads in mutters searching through

the crumpled pathways of his brain while his
voice rose and stumbled in the sibilant argument

he enjoyed with life he could not be
convinced that being human was not enough

that there was no bridge he could cross
he would not 'forget de man' nor 'leave

him to God' these were his sky/trees/
his streets to name was he not greeted

by all he passed naming from a wilderness
of loss his fathers created this island garden

he would not be cast out again he
rode his right to words pointed and named

the road from one way of life to another is hard
*those who are ahead have a long way to go**

missionary zeal could not stomach such clarity
they damned him thundered fire brimstone the sin

of pride thus my father and his letters
raced weekly to the centre the apology

won he stood nodded bowed strode in his own
echoing silence out of lowered eyes/bells/incense

the worn organ's cough out of village voices
wheeling in cracked Kyries

to stand on the church steps muttering:
it is enough to be a man today

his fingers kneading my six year old hands
as if they would refashion them

*Transtromer, 'From an African Diary' (1963)

NO GOD WAITS ON INCENSE

for Rosemary

while babies bleed this is not the poem i wanted
it is the poem i could   though it is not that insistent
worm   it will not burrow through deaf ears
lay its eggs in your brain   yet it is all
for change
and it is not that beautiful weapon
it will not explode in the gut
despite your need   this poem is not that gift
it brings you nothing   you who insist on drinking
let your buckets into green and ruined wells   haul
in darkness   village women will lead you smiling
step back polite in the face of skulls
this poem will not catch you as you fall
not a net   no   it is nothing this poem
not a key   not a charm   not chicken soup
and it is no use at all   at all
nothing at all
it won't beat a drum   it can't dance   it can't
even claim to be written in dust if this morning
the Bow sky-sheeted in light   the silver air is bright
with balloons   yet it talks from a dark bed
this poem   though no
woman can lie curled beneath its covers
can hide before boots
can hope to be taken for bundles of clothes   can hope
not to cry out when the knife probes
pray her blood not betray her   nor the tiny sigh
no   this poem   not even a place where anyone is safe
it can nothing   still nothing still nothing at all
at all   in the night and disinterested air this poem
leaves no wound

FROM **DRAWING DOWN A DAUGHTER**

Gazing at piles of newspapers   she is wondering
why anyone bothers   when the voice comes
booming out of her past   'I'm saying this once
I don't care whether they're racist or not   you will
get all the education I can buy
ignorance is the luxury we can't afford'

she thinks of the *Sun*   *Globe and Mail*
ahistorical gropings in the *Lawyers Weekly*
she smiles wishing she'd known then 'ah   but it's
a luxury *they* cultivate'
and she laughs to think how he would have fumed
gathering to herself their furious
encounters   words whirling reckless around
their heads   bouncing off polished floors
ricocheting off walls to bruise innocent
bystanders   but they battened on the hail   dodging
weaving among Morris chairs they rode whims
ideas   never consenting to dust

Girlchild   i wish you something to be passionate
about   someone to be passionate with   a father for instance
natural opponent of any right thinking girl

and where the hell is yours

i'm telling you   Girl you have to watch men
you leave the islands to come to Canada
you meet the man in Canada
he's born in Canada   his grandfather's born in Canada
you marry him in Canada
now he wants to live in the islands!

look my flight is called . . . yes . . . I know
we'll settle this when I get back
keep that kid where she is for a week or so   my lady!

some are born to murder   some have murder thrust upon them

she turns back to newspapers
litany of the world's woes
earth's destruction

celebration of its terrors
    we have become cheerleaders
she thinks of Daigle
                of Bush
tyranny
        greed   our game

O Girl   even the comics are cynical

she wonders   if she had refused this child   would he
O Baby   no! your father is an honourable man   well
most of the time anyhow

restless she stands   stretches   considers cleaning
the room   again   nesting syndrome   Girl we've read
all the right books   she strokes her belly
lifts the Great Mask to her shoulders   covers
her body with its bleached grass skirts
holding out her arms she sings from *Solomon*
'Yes   you are black! and radiant
the eyes of many suns have pierced your skin'

she goes back to cold news   the tea   the notebook
she writes:

Daughter   there is no language
i can offer you no corner that is
yours   unsullied
you inherit the intransitive
case   Anglo-Saxon noun

she thinks of Africa

she should have insisted on Yoruba   not given in to the
angry gaze   the wanting to be rid of this North American
threatening to squeeze herself in to his ancient space

did he fear her lilt
that she would have taken over his
language   made it chip
to the beat of calypso

a woman without forest gods without red earth or sullen
rivers without shame or any tongue to exchange for his
harsh imperatives   the quick curd consonants

Child   all i have to give
is English which hates/fears your
black skin
           make it

d

a   c

n   e

s

i   g

to sunlight on the Caribbean

she sighs   settles to papers that assume the North's
moral right to impose   here she votes   shares spoil

how sweet it is
                to shield
    even
           from ourselves
our own
        intimacy
with evil

she rustles through her notebooks   finds last year's poem
on this year's famine   too bored   too depressed to write
another

Here on this bank of the Bow   white sky
arching over us   white snow below
i write this tale for you   Daughter   this account
as a *Matter of Fact*
enter it
      as we enter
          pure space of being
              moving to what is
                  radiant black
where we can be   truly
where great doors   of ebony and beaten brass
hard carved   fables   that blossom
to touch   and courage   compassion   truth
feathered stars   bones   whirl to the drums

here sweet hips intricate   veined feet design
                         worlds

here   under   cool   ixora   thickets   music   and   her   sisters
engage time in intricate forms so full of seriousness   from
their fullcarved lips wordspills   sun burnishes
skin   knits spring & curl of hair tight to the skull where
grace lies careless on sloping shoulders

Girlchild we wear a skin
                                            sleek
     sassy
                                      tough
                   sinuous
black n brown
                              pink n purple space
               flags
our indomitable
                                        secret self
               free
in the spirit pool
                         out of which we are

Drink often   remembering there
is mystery   inspite of perception
truth despite the word

BILL SCHERMBRUCKER

(b. 1938)

Writing for Bill Schermbrucker is an act of 'absolute necessity'. 'I mean this,' he says, 'both personally and politically. . . . I write in order to experience and define my own identity; and Canada needs writers to continue the process of establishing what it is, and who Canadians are.'

Born in Eldoret, Kenya, Schermbrucker descends from German, Dutch, and English ancestors, some of whom arrived in Africa in 1720. After receiving a B.A. in Latin and English (1957) from the University of Cape Town, he taught school in Cape Town and Nairobi and, following his Post-Graduate Certificate in Education (London, England, 1960), at Kikuyu and, as a part-time lecturer, at the University of East Africa. The short stories of his first book, *Chameleon and Other Stories* (1983), including the selection that follows, take place in Kenya at the time of the Mau Mau and the events that led to independence, and emerge out of his experiences as a teacher: 'Accent, like clothing style, may change,' he writes, 'but memory does not vanish. . . . With nobody around to confirm, deny

or enlarge on what I say, the sound of my own stories becomes terribly authentic in my head. People sometimes ask me if the stories are autobiographical. The answer is: "No, no— *much* clearer!"'

A resident of North Vancouver, Schermbrucker arrived in Canada in 1964 with a Canadian Commonwealth Scholarship to study at the University of British Columbia. He received an M.A. (1966) and a Ph.D. (1974), with a special focus on the Australian novelist Patrick White. He has been an instructor of English at Capilano College since 1968, and he has served as editor of *The Capilano Review* (1977-82). The author and editor of textbooks, Schermbrucker's other literary publications include *Mimosa* (1988), a novel which received the Ethel Wilson Prize for fiction, and *Motortherapy & Other Stories* (1993).

'Although Canada is technically a state,' Schermbrucker says, 'it lacks any clear and agreed sense of itself that encompasses all the different selves that make it up.' For him, it is the task of Canadian writers and other artists to create an 'awareness of ourselves'.

CHAMELEON

Around Nairobi, it rains just about every afternoon between the middle of April and the end of May. They are swift, heavy downpours, beginning with cracks of thunder around three-thirty, which are usually over in an hour or two. Then the sky clears.

As a child, I used to like to go out into the sunlight after the rain and see the changes in the peaceful, dripping garden. A jacaranda that had been swollen in gorgeous array would now be spidery naked in the middle of the lawn, with a ring of purple-blue blossoms beneath it. A bed of zinnia seeds would suddenly be springing with green shoots. Huge flocks of irridescent plum-coloured starlings would congregate in a wheeling cloud, then land all together in a eucalyptus tree, scattering raindrops and seed twigs onto a carpet of dead leaves. And precisely at sunset, the entire two acres of lawn would seem to wriggle upwards and fly, as the ants emerged through the Swazi grass and shook out their long wings, to begin helicoptering over to the lights of the house which the servants would now start turning on.

Like sleep, or a dip in the pool, the rains refreshed me, and I would come in to supper from the garden filled with excitement, often with a chameleon, swaying and hanging on to my steady finger. They were easy to find in that last hour of sunlight, because the falling rain was marching orders to them, and it was in that slow, wobbling move from one plant to another that their previous colouration gave them away. It takes a chameleon fifteen or twenty minutes to go from the white-veined grey of old croton bark to the pastel green of Barberton daisy leaves, or the emerald streaks of the grass. I'd stand and watch as, about once a second, he'd throw his feet forward, diagonally paired, in desperate strides. Then, as he reached the new plant, or the edge of the lawn, I'd crouch and set my finger in front of him. He'd stop, wobbling with momentum, revolve his black-pointed eyes all round, and finally stretch forward and clutch on to my skin with a little dry claw, the feel of which compares to nothing else I've known—a dinosaur's touch, perhaps, to a giant a thousand times his size.

Slowly, he'd feel me through his scaly dry skin; then, after another circuit of the eyes, he'd stretch the other foreleg and one hind leg onto my finger, and finally, curling his tail for insurance to the grass, he'd get all four legs onto the finger, then give a sideways swing to his head with its one, or two, or three horns, looking puzzled, as though thinking: 'I . . . don't . . . remember . . . this.' But it would be too late for him to change his plans. I'd stand up and carry him carefully into the house.

'Put that thing away,' my father would growl wearily, 'and sit down to supper.'

The only safe place for him, while we ate, was a plant. But my mother had none growing in the house, and she told me it was cruel to set them on red, which was the colour of most of our cut flowers: cannas, bougainvillea, poinsettias and roses. So I had succeeded in growing my own avocado in a bucket in my bedroom, and there my chameleon was safe. Later, as I lay reading till lights-out, I would watch him, checking each time I turned a page or caught a movement out of the corner of my eye.

What *would* happen, I wondered, if you put him on red? What if you set him on the multicoloured spines of a shelf of books? Would he swell up desperately, trying for the impossible, and burst? I knew that female chameleons burst upon giving birth, and I never brought one into the house. I was put off by the thought of waking to feel a swarm of tiny chameleons in my hair, or of little squishes under my shoe. And I didn't want to be cruel, either. I believed what my mother had told me, but it interested me to know all the workings of chameleons.

Their eyes, for instance: each one revolved independently in the huge eye-sockets, so how could the brain record an image of what they saw? The one tiny black bead in the centre of the skin-covered mound would be fixed on me in the bed, while the other one circled the wall behind the lampshade, looking for flies. Which of the two images did the brain pick? (Or did they have split vision, like the split screen in the movies?) At age ten, my own eye problem had finally been named and explained to me by an unfashionably talkative ophthalmologist. Instead of binocular vision, I had an alternating *strabismus*, switching from eye to eye. But this explanation was not completely satisfactory, and I would lie in bed after lights-out, thinking about these puzzles. How does the brain learn to choose one dominant image over the other; how does it know which—and especially with a chameleon, whose eyes can look in different directions and move at different speeds from one another? And if the human brain *does* choose one image anyway, and if in normal people the secondary image creates an illusion of 3-D, then how come *I* could catch a ball in the air?

The doctor sighed. My eyes, he said, moved together, but were out of line. They were lazy and preferred to work one at a time, so each eye deliberately looked at a different thing, and my brain picked which to see, and suppressed the other. I thought of the Bible: 'Let not thy left hand know what thy right hand doeth.' Like having two TV cameras going and punching in which view to send to the screen. 'But listen,' I told the doctor, and raised my arms, stick-up fashion, 'I can see both my hands.'

'Well, yes, but. . . .' It dawned on me in a panic that medical science knew less about my eyes than I did.

But eventually, I began to enjoy the condition. I was twelve years old and a specialist. My father would notice a business associate staring at my face, and remark: 'Oh, he has a small eye problem. It's . . . well, let *him* tell you about it . . . he knows how to explain it.' So the defect led to a new social skill, which I practiced arrogantly. Even recently, when a Motor Vehicle official complained about my vision ('You did all right on the board, but Jeez, you don't have any depth perception *at all*!'), I began a haughty lecture on my alternating *strabismus* and his out-of-date machinery. He cut me off at last ('Is that right, eh?') and stamped my renewal, and I walked out, gloating like a kid.

At twelve, though, I was still worried. They called me Squinteyes at school. And staring at my chameleon's slow movements on the avocado, I wondered about his life. Maybe the reason the chameleon moved so slowly, swaying unsteadily from foothold to foothold along a branch like a runner in slow motion film—maybe the *real* reason—was that he lived in a world of such confusion, a brain in which one whole hemisphere of sight revolved in random directions over the image of another, at independent speeds, or one moving and one still. So that for him, just to take a step, just the simple automatic act of moving his foot from here to there, was a problem of immense complexity, heating and shorting-out the circuits of his poor overloaded cortical centre. Watching a chameleon move was like watching a drunk trying to walk and remember a phone number at the same time. I took pity on the muddle-sighted creature.

But he could still eat. After biding his time on the thin avocado branch, after settling his intent and his aim, he could unroll his long sticky tongue with the speed of an arrow, and pick a fly off the wall before its wings took the first hint of danger. One instant the fly was on the wall, six inches away, and the next, the chameleon's thin, prehistoric lips were clamped half shut on crushed wings and a struggling abdomen. Then a gulp, and it was gone from sight, into the pouch of the chin. I never saw a chameleon miss.

Every boy finds pets, and in Africa there were many choices. The son of a famous archaeologist was said to keep poisonous snakes, which among us made him more legendary than his father. A monkey or a mongoose was special, if you could get one, and if you could persuade your parents to cooperate. Otherwise, it was the ordinary dung and rhino beetles, or the big black and yellow rose beetle you could fly on a length of thread, or tortoises (which shat so horribly you had to keep them outside, and they'd tunnel under anything), or bush babies. If you were lucky enough to live on a farm, you could have a run made from chicken wire, for one of the miniature antelope, a dik-dik or a duiker. There were lots of imported pets, too, like bantams and fantail pigeons. Nobody had tropical fish then, though everyone kept tadpoles and watched them become frogs. Dogs and cats were treated in the British way, not so much pets as members of the household. My brother developed an intense interest in tree frogs, which he kept on coffee branches in a huge budgie cage on the front verandah, and fed with many insects. For a while, I got interested in mice, and carried them in my pockets to school, trading whites for blacks to crossbreed, and getting very lively reactions from teachers when one would creep out the back of my collar and sniff the air while I bent over a book. When my mother died, I somehow associated her cancer with my white mice and I got rid of them quickly. That left chameleons. They were my constant pets.

You can't escape chameleons in Africa. They lie squashed on the roads (and I guess it was seeing pregnant females, squashed by a bicycle tire, their tiny young lying all around them, that gave us the idea that they burst). When you cut flowers, especially from white or yellow shrubs, to put in the huge glass Gould battery jars, you often didn't notice you were carrying a chameleon on a stem you'd cut, till suddenly that cold, scritchy hand clamped lightly on the skin of your knuckle. Or, standing dead still in the thornbush, smell of gun oil, safety catch off, waiting to catch sight of the guinea fowl you could hear but not see . . . you'd recoil in sudden fright from a clammy touch on the ear, where a snake might be hanging, and swing around and see, with huge relief, the arched body of a chameleon, dangling by the tail, clawing slowly at the air.

Perhaps it is the fact that they are reptiles—vague similarity to snakes and the poisonous blue lizard, *kokomonda*—that makes chameleons an object of loathing, fear and strict taboo to the Agikuyu and some other African tribes. My people were tolerant of white kids terrifying black kids, but after I'd done it a few times, advancing with a chameleon on my finger and a sadistic smile on my nine-year-old's face, towards children who opened their eyes wide and fled from a path into the bush, or coming to the kitchen door and creating panic among the servants, I somehow learned enough respect to quit the practice. I used to warn the inside servants if there was a chameleon on the avocado in my room, and they kept clear of it.

But even though I respected the taboo, it continued to puzzle me. Couldn't they see that the thing was harmless? Sometimes I would entice Kakui to come near enough to watch me feeding a chameleon grasshoppers, bumping its lips with the trapped insect till it finally opened and swallowed with that characteristic slow crunch and gulp. 'See, Kakui, it can't bite a person, just insects.' I'd pinch the base of the tail and the chameleon would open its mouth, and I'd put my finger in and let it bite down, the little bony serrations harmless as a newborn puppy's gums.

'Sssssss!' Kakui would go, breath indrawn against clenched teeth, and his lips pulled wide. He never got used to this. 'Come on, try it,' I'd say, and he'd back off.

And then I want away to university, and travelled, and became an actor and a teacher, and chameleons faded out of my life for a while.

Some years later, I got a job at a black school outside of Nairobi. One day, after a class on imagery in *Macbeth*, I stood chatting with my students on the lawn and I saw a chameleon.

'Wait here,' I said, and went over and picked it up. I held it behind my back and called: 'Wanjohi!' (a young man who was later to take a double first at Oxford and is now a senior economic advisor to an African government). 'Come here a minute, would you?'

He stood in front of me. 'Listen,' I said, 'I'm not trying to offend you, but I have something behind my back which you don't like. I want to understand why.'

'What is it?'

'It's a chameleon.'

He stepped back.

'Wanjohi!' I said. 'You're not from the bush, man. You know the animal is harmless. Why cling to a primitive belief?'

I brought my hand to the front, and he stared at the chameleon. His lips began drawing back, and I retreated a step to give him ease. 'Come on,' I said, 'tell me. You *know* it's not dangerous.'

'Come on, Wanjohi, tell him,' someone called flatly from behind him.

Eventually, Wanjohi said, 'Aagh,' as though clearing his throat. 'Just put it on a tree, suh.'

I did that, and came back to the group of uncomfortable students. 'Look!' I said, pointing to my finger. 'Cancer! Warts!'

'*Ah, no!*' They were angry with me now. Several turned aside, offended.

'I am not able to *explain* it,' Wanjohi said emphatically. 'Of course, we *know* . . . what there is to know. But I *feel* it still.'

I felt ashamed of myself. 'I'm sorry, Wanjohi. I apologize.' I put my hand on his shoulder.

'It's all right, suh.' He recoiled from my touch.

But I couldn't leave it alone. In another senior class, I began a discussion of religious taboos. 'Take the hyena,' I said, and one or two people sniffed in derision. 'As we know: very strong *thahu*. If someone sees the dung near a hut, the hut must be burned, the family must move. Well, it makes sense. They're carrion, so their dung means there's a dead body around, and in earlier times that would be good reason to move. Today, with sanitation, we can take less drastic steps if we wish. The *thahu* developed because it has survival value for a tribe; naturally the emotional taboo lingers on into modern times as a cultural hang-on. What puzzles *me* is the *thahu* which doesn't seem to have any survival value, such as ch—'

'But if I may ask?'

'Yes, Kamau?' (He was a young man for whom I had a special fondness, since he was inquisitive and a rebel.)

'If you understand that we are not pleased by hyenas, why on the hockey field when you are coaching us, do you shout and call us *nyangau?*'

'There are two words for hyena, *fisi* and *nyangau*—and *fisi* is the more offensive. Isn't it?'

'Agreed.'

'Then,' I smiled, trading on his strong sense of humour, 'at the same time that it is meant to spur you on by insulting you, I use the less offensive word, so you could also consider it a term of endearment.'

'I see.' His eyes gleamed with challenge and impatience. 'Thank you.' *One day,* Mzungu, *one day*!

And it came. First the violence, eventually illumination.

Kamau's rebellious nature was easy to forgive. He was young and intelligent, and at a time when perhaps only sixty or seventy students throughout the country were advanced as high as he was up the educational pyramid, he was ambitious. He was about seventeen, and had already written several plays, one of which was regularly produced by the students, a sophisticated comedy of manners called, 'I Love You, But You're Stupid'. It had raunchy lines in it, as well as some cracks against the British. These parts were cut or quickly slurred over whenever the school's grim principal or vice-principal were present, and everyone else knew that the only time the full script was presented (together with the odd wisecracks at current events) was in performances which the students sometimes gave in their home villages. I had been invited to one of these local shows, and allowed to hear some of the censored material, while other lines that obviously were too hot for me were rattled off quickly in Gikuyu, bringing roars and shouts from the crowd, and curious looks at me. In his way, Kamau was helping prepare the ground for revolution, and becoming quite well known in the process. It didn't surprise me that, with his mind on such things, he found the school's regulations petty. You weren't supposed to drink or smoke, or meet women from the Girls' School in the bush. Here you were, a future literary hero of the revolution, and you were supposed to try to give the appearance of adhering to imported rules of conduct that were originally laid down for good little boys and girls in England. So I was sympathetic when the house prefect would report to me that Kamau had been smoking in the dormitory, or had come in drunk, or was known to be meeting a girl in the bush. 'Thank you,' I'd say, 'I'll speak to him.' Then I'd haul Kamau in for a lecture.

'Listen, man, you've got a year and a half to go. If you want to finish school, you're going to have to play the game. If you want to live it up, at least be discreet, for Christ's sake, and don't go breaking the rules right in the goddamn dormitory.' And Kamau'd sit nodding, staring at the floor, saying, 'I know, I know, but it's *hard*! Well . . . I'll try.'

And he did. He'd get up in the morning, even with a hangover, and pull on one of the rough maroon workshirts, and take part in the common chores, washing floors, or sweeping, or cutting new sidelines in the playing fields. I'd detour sometimes to pass him working at a menial chore, and ask, 'How's it going?' He'd look up sulkily and groan, and I'd shrug. He'd shrug, too, and eventually smile. Sometimes in the chapel, when some puritanical master was preaching the dignity of labour, or the virtue of humility, I'd look over rows of faces and see Kamau, wall-eyed, dreaming.

So, there'd be complaints in Staff Meeting: 'Kamau is arrogant and cheeky. He's not a good influence.'

'Oh, come on,' I'd say, 'he's also very young and imaginative. He works hard at the things he cares about. Look at his marks. Look at his plays! For the rest, he's trying. He's really trying.'

The principal, watching this debate solemnly, would turn finally to me and end it: 'Well, *you* say so. All right.'

Thus, I became Kamau's buffer zone. And once, when he had been awarded a Saturday punishment, to mow the grass in front of the school's imposing theatre building, and he refused to put on a work shirt, the prefect finally sent for the master-on-duty, who finally sent for me. I found them glaring at one another in the Staff Room, white man and black; teacher versus student; puritan, libertine; civil servant and artist. The work shirt lay on the table like an old rag. The prefect stood beside it, waiting.

'This boy has got to be caned,' Roger said, 'because he refuses to obey an order.' His words were clipped and harsh, as he struggled to depersonalize his anger. 'I have called you as a witness. However, I would prefer that you administer the punishment yourself.'

Although I knew that a beating must always be done in the presence of a staff witness, I had never seen one before, and had not been expecting this.

'No,' I said, 'I'm not going to do it.'

'Then I must.'

'Kamau,' I said very quietly, 'please put on the work shirt.'

He stared out the window, where visitors in bright dresses and shining shoes were strolling the grounds, then back at me, deadpan and hard.

Roger fumbled with the key to the principal's office, his hands shaking. The bang of the door swinging open made Kamau and myself both blink suddenly. I appealed to him again, with my eyes and a whisper: *'Put it on!'* And the prefect added. 'For goodness' sake, man.'

'You put it on!' Kamau said. The prefect folded his arms and sighed.

He stood with his hands on the wall, for the beating. The first time Roger hit him, he cried out, 'Aaaa!' and began squirming and rubbing himself, and glaring wildly at the floor, at Roger, at the cane. 'You don't have to hit so *hard!*' he yelled. Roger stood shaking, his face fixed and trance-like, waiting for Kamau to take his hands away.

The second blow was worse. Kamau fell to the floor, rubbing his bottom in a frenzy, and screaming. I was numb with shock. I had been beaten myself at school and put up with it in proper British silence.

On the third hit, Kamau leaned weakly against the wall and began to cry steadily, like a child. 'All right, Kamau,' Roger said, 'you can go now.' Shakily, we signed the book and left.

For a while after that, there was no trouble. Then the complaints began again, and I'd send for him again.

'Make up your mind, Kamau. If it's too hard, get out. You've got your School Certificate. You don't absolutely *need* Higher. Go to Nairobi and get a job. Write plays in your apartment at night. And be free.'

'You know *damned-good-and-well*—' his emotions rising swiftly into his bright eyes, and his lips thrust forward aggressively—'You know *damned-good-and-well* that I am *going* to university, and I *need* Higher to get there. If you want to change me, instead why don't you change this *silly* school, and its *silly* rules, and leave me alone! We're *not kids*, you know.' The word *silly* so powerful there, that his anger was purged by risking it, and he'd look at me again, softly. Till next time . . . .

In the last of these interviews, Kamau drew a deep breath and seized his resolve. 'Here!' he said, reaching into the pockets of his uniform khaki shirt for cigarettes and money, and thrusting them towards my hands. 'Take these bloody things!'

'Good!' I said. 'I'll keep them for you till the end of the term.'

'No. Keep them till I am finished, till I *finish* Higher and *leave* the school.' As he got up to go, he added: 'Thank you,' and pursing his lips, 'Suh!' Then he executed an elaborate Jacobean bow that I had taught him for his part in *Much Ado*.

I told the weekly Staff Meeting that Kamau had decided to shape up, and would cause no more trouble.

Over the next few days, the bow became language between us. He rose and performed it before answering my questions in class, and I waved it back to him when his answers were brilliant. On the hockey field, he lounged chatting to the goalie, his back to the game; when I whacked him lightly with my stick, he swung around in a flash of hot surprise, then began running at the same time as he commenced a bow. He fell in a tangle of cracking knee joints. I laughed: 'Your Grace is not hurt, I trust?'

'A trifle, my Lord, a mere trifle.' He ran back into the game, tears filling his eyes.

One morning, a knock on my front door woke me. 'Kamau, sir,' said the house prefect. 'This time, he's gone crazy. He's got some bottles of beer under his bed, and this morning he got up and refused to do work. He just sat on the bed, smoking. When I ordered him to get to work, he took the panga and began sharpening. He won't speak, sir. The other boys say he's going to kill me. He just sits there filing the panga. I'm afraid, sir.'

I told Lang'at to keep out of his way, and I would see Kamau at Parade in a few minutes. But he was announced absent. After chapel, I walked home. I was troubled. I hoped in a way that he had made his decision, packed up and gone.

Spooning egg into my son's mouth, I looked up and saw Kamau through the panes of my front door. 'Come in,' I yelled, motioning.

He opened the door and stood stiffly at the threshold. 'I would like to see you outside please,' he said.

'No, come in and have a cup of coffee with us, and I'll walk down with you.'

'No. I am sorry to interrupt you, please come outside.'

He stood under a large cork tree, a few yards from the house, and I walked towards him, saying: 'Now, what is all this, Kamau?'

He was moving as I spoke, the bright edge of the panga above his head like a dancer's prop. He was floating towards me in swift, athletic motion and there wasn't time for fear. I kept walking towards him as he came, surprised at the sight of the panga, noticing how bright and even he had filed the blade, and saying irritably, 'Put that down, Kamau,' my hand out to take it.

As he reached me, his tall, thin body rolled against my right arm and shoulder, and I saw the panga falling onto the grass on my left. I caught the faint smell of his body, and a streak of anguished eyes passing mine. I still could feel the warmth of touch along my arm, as he regained his balance behind me and ran around the back of the house.

I began to shake, and automatically reached down for the panga, fumbled it, gripped it, and stood there in tremors, with the panga dangling from my hand. Kamau emerged on the far side of the house, and ran unevenly through the woods towards the school.

I walked straight to the principal's house and told him what had happened. The Old Man stood ponderously, wiping his lip, half risen from the breakfast table. 'Well,' he said, 'Kamau is expelled from this moment. He's to be off the compound by nine o'clock. I'll arrange about your classes, and you drive him to Nairobi. Put him at the Akamba bus stop and let him have bus fare to his home village. You can tell him I never want to see or hear from him again.'

In the car, I scowled ferociously, and hoped he would not speak. He sat thin and erect, sucking breath in through his nose in long, emotional drags, like a man about to cry. He stank of sweat and beer and cigarettes. His eyes bulged white and crazy against his dark skin. I drove as fast as I could down the dirt road to town.

When we came out onto the smooth tar highway at Dagoretti, Kamau suddenly yawned and relaxed into the seat. 'You have something of mine,' he said.

I pointed to the glove compartment, and he reached in and took out the envelopes with his cigarettes and money. 'Do you mind if I smoke?' he asked. I shook my head. He rolled down the window and lit up. He gave a short laugh: 'At least it's better that I'm going in with you. Thought I was going to have to go in the Old Man's Volkswagen.' Then, tightening out his lips, he began to imitate the Old Man's deep voice: '*Kamau, I'm going to ask you to try and pray. Remember, Jesus is with us always, if we let him into our hearts!*' He sat remembering, and amused. Softly, he sang: '*Who would true valour see / Let him come hither / One here will constant be / Come wind come weather / There's no discouragement / Shall make him once relent / His first avowed intent / To be a Pilgrim / Who so beset him round / With dismal stories / Do but themselves con-found / His strength the more is*—aagh!' He threw his butt out the window and looked at me.

'So, you are going to Canada?'

I frowned and gave a brisk nod.

'For how long?'

I swallowed and said quickly, 'Two years.'

'Two years, huh? And will get a Master's degree? Very good.' He yawned, gazing out the window. 'Well,' he said, 'I'll come and visit you there.'

Driving back to the school, I remembered the time we had fought on stage with metal swords. I wanted sparks, the real clash of weapons, not that silly clack-clack of wooden stage props. The blacksmith in the village made the swords in time for the dress rehearsal, but the actors were shy to use them. 'Come on!' I yelled, leaping up over the apron. 'Make it a bit more *real*, will you!' And seizing a sword, I turned where

Kamau stood with his weapon up, stiff like a sentry. I slid blade against blade, and he sprang back at the ready. I could always rely on him to respond. After five minutes, we both had bloody knuckles, and Kamau's sword was bent. The stage smelled of burnt metal from the sparks. 'There,' I said, 'like *that*!' And behind me, I heard Kamau parodying: 'Yah, like *that*! See the blood? On opening night, we are going to kill a few Form Ones!'

He was an actor all right. I remember the time he had told me about his father's death, acting out before my horrified eyes how he had stood in the doorway of the hut, a six-year-old child, and watched his mother, the notorious Mau Mau terrorist, chop his father's head in two with an axe. 'Split in half,' he said, 'and dashed the brains out.' Later, when he introduced me to his father and I said, 'Oh, but—' he smiled and said blandly: 'Resurrected.'

A month after the expulsion, I got a letter asking about Kamau, from the manager of the Industrial Branch of Barclay's Bank (Dominion, Colonial, and Overseas). He'd applied for a job as a teller and had given my name as a reference. I thought for a long time and decided at last to write the letter. I told the manager that Kamau was an intelligent man who worked well in a mature environment.

Then, the day before leaving for Canada, I got a letter from Kamau himself. There was no mention of the bank job. The tone of the writing was comfortable and relaxed: 'You are quite an interesting man to me. In school, I always watched you while you were teaching us. You explain this point of view and then that point of view. One never knows exactly what is your own point of view. There is something strange about the way you look at people. One eye is looking on the left side, and one eye is to the right. So, when something is directly in front of you, you don't even see it. You called me *nyangau*, and I call you chameleon. Consider it a term of endearment.'

FRED WAH

(b. 1939)

The author of seventeen volumes of poetry including *Selected Poems: Loki is Buried at Smoky Creek* (1980), Wah was one of the founding editors of the avant-garde poetry newsletter *Tish* while a student at the University of British Columbia in the 1960s. Since then he has been at the forefront of poetic innovation in Canada, a poet writing out of a profound sense of place and, under the influence of Charles Olson's projective verse theory, of breath and movement.

Wah was born in Swift Current, Saskatchewan, but grew up in the West Kootenay region of British Columbia. Following his studies in music and English literature at the University of British Columbia, he pursued graduate studies in literature and linguistics at the University of New Mexico in Albuquerque, where he was editor of *Sum* magazine. He received an M.A. (1967) from the State University of New York at Buffalo, where he was co-editor of *The Niagara Frontier Review* and *The Magazine of Further Studies*. He returned to the Kootenays in the late 1960s and from there he edited *Scree*. The founding coordinator of the writing program at David Thompson University Centre, he taught at Selkirk College until moving to Calgary, where he is professor of creative writing and poetics at the University of Calgary.

'Much of the impetus of my writing,' Fred Way says, 'comes from the hyphen in "half-bred" poetics—Half-bred poetics as a game of reaction from within the egg-yolk of my own cultural ambivalence (white on the outside, yellow on the inside).' The self-reflexiveness and the complex texture of his writing make for demanding reading. As Wah remarks, 'I've tried to make language operate as a non-aligned and unpredictable material, not so much intentionally difficult as simply needing a little complication—A little complication for me has always been how to create enough camouflage so that the grand intentions of meaning don't get to name me before I do—Before I do any writing I always stop whatever I'm doing—Whatever I'm doing might make a difference—Make a difference.'

Some of his early publications include *Lardeau* (1965), *Mountain* (1967), *Pictograms from the Interior of B.C.* (1975) and *Breathin' My Name With a Sigh* (1981), which includes 'waiting for saskatchewan', the first poem in the selection that follows. His book, *Waiting for Saskatchewan* (1985), won the Governor General's Award in 1986, and includes 'Father/ Mother Haibun #4.' Wah explains *haibun* as 'short prose written from a haiku sensibility and, in this case, concluded by an informal haiku line'. More recently, Wah has published *Music at the Heart of Thinking* (1987), selections from which also appear here, *So Far* (1991), which was awarded the Stephan G. Stephanson Prize in 1992, *Alley Alley Home Free* (1992), and *Snap* (1993). Wah is presently working on a collection of essays on ethno-poetics and has finished what he calls a 'biotext', a prose narrative that deals with racial anger and traces, through many detours and elliptical movements, his personal history.

Waiting for saskatchewan
and the origins grandparents countries places converged
europe asia railroads carpenters nailed grain elevators
Swift Current my grandmother in her house
he built on the street
and him his cafés namely the 'Elite' on Centre
looked straight ahead Saskatchewan points to it
Erickson Wah Trimble houses train station tracks
arrowed into downtown fine clay dirt prairies wind waiting

for Saskatchewan to appear for me again over the edge
horses led to the huge sky the weight and colour of it
over the mountains as if the mass owed me such appearance
against the hard edge of it sits on my forehead
as the most political place I know these places these strips
laid beyond horizon for eyesight the city so I won't have to go
near it as origin town flatness appears later in my stomach why
why on earth would they land in such a place
mass of pleistocene
sediment plate wedge
arrow sky beak horizon still waiting for that
I want it back, wait in this snowblown winter night
for that latitude of itself its own largeness
my body to get complete
it still owes me, it does

FATHER/MOTHER HAIBUN #4

Your pen wrote Chinese and your name in a smooth swoop
with flourish and style, I can hardly read my own tight
scrawl, could you write anything else, I know you could
read, nose in the air and lick your finger to turn the large
newspaper page pensively in the last seat of those half-
circle arborite counters in the Diamond Grill, your glass
case bulging your shirt pocket with that expensive pen,
always a favourite thing to handle the way you treated it
like jewellery, actually it was a matched pen and pencil set,
Shaeffer maybe (something to do with Calgary here), heavy,
silver, black, gold nib, the precision I wanted also in things,
that time I conned you into paying for a fountain pen I
had my eye on in Benwell's stationery store four dollars
and twenty cents Mom was mad but you understood such
desires in your cheeks relaxed when you worked signing
checks and doing the books in the back room of the café
late at night or how the pen worked perfectly with your
quick body as you'd flourish off a check during a busy
noon-hour rush the sun and noise of the town and the café
flashing.

**High muck-a-muck's gold-toothed clicks ink mark red green
on lottery blotting paper, 8-spot (click, click)**

FROM *MUSIC AT THE HEART OF THINKING*

2

PREACT THE MIND AHEAD OF THE WRITING BUT STOP TO
think notation of the mind ahead of the writing
pretell the 'hunt' message doesn't run like the
wind simile makes it the belief of the wild
imagination or trees or animals too to preface up
the head ahead but notice the body as a drum-
mer preacts the hands to do to do insistent so it
can come out tah dah at every point simply the
mind at work won't do or the body minding
itself thinking (which is why the drum's cedar)
get it right or get it wrong just strike from the
body falling back thoughts felt behind to the
notes sometimes gives it shape or thought as
body too my drum tah dum

10

NOW I GET TO HEAR THE LANGUAGE RATHER THAN
only see it in French over my head fingers want
to touch the sight of the letter oral tactile
fragment hunger in another language the wolf's
ear to make it up before it happens to hear it
somewhere inside my body before the lips
touch the mouthpiece or fingertip valves as soft
as silk intelligence like that gets carried in the
language by itself the cow simply eats the
whole field I have to practise to get it right and
blow away anyway

50

Going through the language of time.
Chronometrics. Horologicals. A book of years.

I like the water in it. And the footprints.
That movement. As you look for words
'sans intermission'.

Of course it's the heart. Pictograph—
                     pictogram.
Epigram—epigraph. Cardiogram. Histograph.
The paw again.

Cellular. Un instant. Je vais voir si je la trouve
dans ce livre.
It's that 'yelping pack of possibilities'
the hour as the order.

The predication, the pre-form of foot
in snow, log
on truck, finding out it never was lost,
                          fooling.

51

Everywhere I go here, here I go again.
But even if I worked it out ahead of time
I'd do it.

I know me. This train
crosses all the Chinese rivers in Canada.
Each one the same world water, the same
trestle, same deep gulley.

In Japan Mt Fuji no more
than a quiet, black Shinkansen tunnel,
out of sight, out of mind.

When Dorn said
the stranger in town
is the only one who knows
where he's been and where he's going
I could see Pocatello's tracks.

Your symbol as 'accent
to the basic drum of consciousness' lurks.
St Am stutters and stumbles.
These rails are only half continuous.

52

> tongue mist lip boat brown gull hill town bed
> stone shadow crow tooth rain boat flood ham-
> mer star gill shadow skin hammer mouth town
> mist hill rock brown bed bird tongue snow creek
> lip crow circle brown lip wave boat shadow city
> light hill sky mouth talk snow gull hammer fog
> moon wet grey stone boat bed mist skin gill
> word flood crow tongue river mouth star brown
> lip night flood sail wave sky tooth rock red bird
> shadow stone snow city blue hammer bed hill
> crow tongue

55

Map of streets stream of dreams
map of creeks street of cream, fragments
and imago imprint, geomance a glyph,
a place on earth, under, or from it.

Name's broken letters maybe
words your body made.
Idiot bridges to parts of our selfs still lost
in the palindrome.

A found chain on the coffeetable,
Some Scapes as a bookmark
to automobile between 3 and 6;
flex, flux, flooding, fl-

(ə Creekscape: Looking Upstream)

Fred Was. Fred War. Fred Wan. Fred Way.
Fred Wash. Fred Wag. Fred Roy. Fred What.

Creek water hits rock with hollow sound.

DAVID ARNASON

(b. 1940)

'Because of the nature of our country and the way it came into being,' David Arnason says, 'a very real and heightened physical, spiritual, and cultural isolation has been and continues to be a fact of Canadian existence. This isolation and the alienation that sometimes accompanies it has meant that Canadian writers and artists, reflecting their own cultural situation, have turned again and again to isolation as the central focus of their work.' Arnason's writing registers this kind of isolation and alienation, but it does so with wit and irony that reflect the author's postmodern sensibility. His fiction plays with and against the limits of realism, showing him to be a writer who self-consciously constructs narratives of great formal versatility.

Arnason has written often about the background of his great-grandparents who emigrated from Iceland, and much of his fiction is set in Gimli, on Lake Winnipeg, the main Icelandic settlement in Canada, where he was born. He received his B.A. (certificate in Education) and his M.A. (English) from the University of Manitoba, and his Ph.D. (English) from the University of New Bruns-

wick. He was a founder and editor of the *Journal of Canadian Fiction* and the General Editor of the Macmillan 'Themes in Canadian Literature' series. The co-founder and co-editor of Turnstone Press in Winnipeg, Arnason is also a member of the editorial advisory board of the House of Anansi, and a professor of Canadian literature at the University of Manitoba. He has published four collections of short fiction, *Fifty Stories and a Piece of Advice* (1982), *The Circus Performers' Bar* (1984), *The Happiest Man in the World* (1989), and *If Pigs Could Fly . . .* (1995); two poetry collections, *Marsh Burning* (1980) and *Skrag* (1987); and a novel, *The Pagan Wall* (1992). As a playwright, and radio and television script writer, Arnason has had many of his plays produced on stage and on CBC radio.

'All writing is writing,' David Arnason has said, 'but you can code it in a voice that sounds like it's a storytelling oral voice, and that's the voice I prefer.' This is indeed the case with the story that follows, a tale that belongs to the oral storytelling tradition but whose tight structure reflects Arnason's self-reflexiveness about the act of writing.

THE SUNFISH

Dawn was just spreading its red glow across Lake Winnipeg when Gusti Oddson reached for the buoy to pull in the first of his seven nets. And what was he thinking, that second cousin once removed of my great-grandmother, on a June morning in 1878? Perhaps he was thinking of the smallpox epidemic that had recently taken his wife and three children, or perhaps he was thinking about nets and why they sometimes caught fish and sometimes didn't. He wasn't thinking about talking fish, or at least the scattered diaries he left behind give no indication that he was thinking about talking fish, and why, after all, should he have been? That's why he was startled when the sunfish he had just pulled into his boat, the first sunfish of the day, spoke to him.

'Gusti,' the sunfish said, its silver scales bright in the first rays of the rising sun, 'listen to me. I have much to tell you.'

Gusti did not answer right away. He was a man of common sense, and he knew that fish do not speak. Still, in the past three years, his faith in common sense had been somewhat shaken. Common sense worked perfectly well in Iceland, but it seemed to be of less value in this new country. Common sense had told him that when water is covered with ice, you do not bother to fish. Here though, you fished underneath the ice, and when you pulled fish up through the ice, they gasped and froze solid in the winter air. Common sense told you that land which could grow trees fifty feet high could also grow potatoes, but that was apparently not necessarily so.

He had come to the Republic of New Iceland three years ago. The first year, he had nearly starved. The second year, his family had died in the smallpox epidemic. The third year, religious argument had split New Iceland into two warring camps. Seri Bjarni argued that the struggle between God and the devil was being fought out for the final time on the shores of Lake Winnipeg. Seri Jon argued that there was no devil, that Jesus was not the Son of God, but only a religious leader, and that God was a spirit that was in everything in the world, but was not a person.

So, when the sunfish spoke to him, Gusti asked it, 'Are you of the devil's party?'

'Don't talk nonsense,' replied the sunfish, 'there is no devil, or God either, for that matter.'

Gusti pondered for a moment, then asked, 'Are you then a Unitarian?'

'I am a sunfish,' said the sunfish, 'and I'm not here to give you any selfish wishes. Greed and lust,' he went on sadly, 'that's all you find nowadays.'

'Then you are one of the Huldafolk,' Gusti said, 'or maybe a Mori raised by enemies to bring me bad luck.'

'More nonsense,' the fish replied. 'Ignorant superstition. How could your luck be any worse than it is? Everybody you love is dead. You haven't got a penny to your name. You hardly catch enough fish to eat, much less to sell. Everybody in New Iceland calls you Gusti Foulfart because you live on dried beans and never wash your clothes. No woman will look at you.'

'There is no need,' Gusti told the fish, 'to be rude. Things have not gone well for me in the last while, it is true, but that is not to say that they will not soon improve.'

'Progress,' sneered the fish, if indeed his opening and closing his mouth could be counted a sneer, 'delusion, a snare and a trap, the vast enslaving device of the western world. Only peasants and fishermen and fools believe in progress. Things never get better, they only get different.'

'How is it that you speak Icelandic?' Gusti asked the fish, who seemed to be having some trouble with his breathing.

'A better question might be, "How is it that you come to speak Sunfish?"' the fish replied, flopping around on the bottom of the skiff, as if to get a better view of Gusti. 'Or indeed, it might be more to the point to ask, "What is the nature of language?"'

'There are plenty of preachers on land,' Gusti told the fish. 'Already the sun is well above the horizon, and I have seven nets to lift. In New Iceland they have taken to calling me Gusti Madman because my wife sometimes comes to me in dreams and I cry out for her. I have no time to argue religion with a fish.'

'Wait,' cried the fish, with what might have been real fear, 'I am speaking to you. Is this not remarkable? Do you not want to know what I have come to tell you?'

'I believe the evidence of my senses,' Gusti replied, 'when my senses give me evidence I can trust. I know that fish do not speak. Perhaps there is a voice-thrower on the shore, or perhaps I am still in my bed dreaming of fish. The least likely thing is that I am actually in my skiff talking with a fish. So, I am going to hit you on the head with my oar, and I will take you in and boil you and eat you with potatoes and butter. You are not a large fish, but you will do.'

'Wait,' the fish almost shouted, alarmed that Gusti had picked up an oar and seemed to mean business. Gusti had let go of the line and they were drifting away from the net toward the southeast. 'I'll give you a wish. Not three wishes, but just one, and try to be reasonable.'

Gusti put the oar down. 'I'll have my wife back.'

The fish groaned, or made a sound that was close to a groan. 'I asked you to be reasonable. Your wife has been dead two years. How could you explain her return? Bringing people back from the dead destroys the natural order of things. Besides, you fought like cats and dogs when she was alive. Let me give you a new boat instead.'

Gusti reached for the oar again.

'No, wait,' the fish continued. 'I can give you Valdi Thorson's wife, Vigdis Thorarinsdottir, instead. She's the most beautiful woman in New Iceland and you know you've lusted for her for years, even when your wife was alive.'

Gusti pondered for a moment then replied, 'No. She is a fine woman, but a man shall cleave to his wife. It is either my wife that you give me, or I eat you for supper this very night.'

'OK,' the fish grumbled, 'but it's not the way you think. She won't be there waiting for you when you get back. She'll arrive in two weeks as a young woman, the cousin of your wife. Her name will be Freya Gudmundsdottir and she'll claim kin and come to live with you. But you'll have to woo her. And you'll have to shape up or else she'll marry Ketil Hallgrimsson, and then you'll have neither wife nor supper.'

'Good,' said Gusti, 'that's fair. Now what have you come to tell me?'

The fish appeared to be sulking. 'It's ridiculous,' he complained. 'I appear at great personal risk to offer mankind wisdom, and I get petty arguments, greed and lust. It's always the same. And I don't suppose you'll pay any attention to what I tell you anyway. Do you think I like to breathe air? Do you think it's comfortable here on the bottom of this boat? I don't know why I do it.'

The sunfish fell silent. Gusti felt a little sorry for it and he asked gently, 'What is it I should know? I will listen carefully, and if things work out as you say and my wife returns, I will try to carry out your instructions.'

The fish seemed a little mollified at this. 'OK,' he said, 'listen carefully.'

Gusti leaned forward, attentive. 'It's over,' the fish told him. 'Done. Finished. Kaput. They're closing down the whole show. Moving on to bigger and better things. Cutting their losses.'

'What do you mean?' Gusti asked the fish, who by now was slowly opening and closing his mouth.

'All of it. Everything. Sun, moon, stars, trees, birds, animals, men, dogs, cats, the whole shooting works.'

'You are telling me then,' said Gusti, 'that the world is going to end.'

'You got it,' said the fish, 'go to the head of the class.' He flopped once and continued, 'And not a moment too soon. Nothing but greed, lust, dishonesty and pride. And self-righteousness. If it weren't for self-righteousness, they might give it another go. If you knew how often I've flopped around the bottom of boats trying to explain things, talking to selfish louts with no more in their minds than their own little comforts, it'd make you sick.'

'And when is this to happen?' Gusti asked.

'I don't know. Maybe tomorrow, maybe a couple of millennia. They're busy, they've got things to do. Anyway, I've done my part. I've delivered the message. Now if you just heave me over the side, I'll be on my way.'

Gusti ignored the fish. 'This,' he said, 'is no great news. Everyone knows that the world will end some day. What matters is to live a proper life while you are here.'

'Makes no difference,' said the fish. 'Proper or improper. What one man does is of no concern. If the whole world changed then maybe they'd reconsider. But it's far too late now for that. Go ahead, rob, murder, steal, it isn't going to make any difference. And if you don't get me in the water soon, you're going to have my death on your conscience as well.'

The fish's eyes had started to cloud over. 'Just one last question,' Gusti went on. 'What day will my wife arrive?'

'You see,' said the fish, as if addressing someone not in the boat but in the blue sky overhead, 'you see what I have to put up with. I bring the most important message in the history of the universe and I have to answer foolish questions. Friday. Or Wednesday, or maybe Saturday. A week or a month. I've given you your wish. I'm not in charge of travel arrangements.'

The fish had ceased to gasp, and lay in the bottom of the boat like a dead fish. Gusti picked it up gently, and slipped it into the water. The fish lay on its side, drifting slowly away from the boat. Gusti watched it for a long time, until finally, with a flick of its tail, it disappeared under the shining surface of the lake.

The next morning Gusti did not go out to his nets. Instead, he hauled water from the lake and heated it over an open fire. He took every article out of his shack and washed it. Then he washed the entire shack, inside and out, including the roof. He rechinked every crack he could find with clay, and then he whitewashed the shack inside and out. The entire community came out to watch him with wonder. The children began by singing the song they always sang when he came near, 'Gusti Foulfart, Gusti Foulfart, smells like rotten meat. Stinky beans and stinky fish is all that he will eat.' Their parents hushed them and threatened to send them home unless they stopped.

Vigdis Thorarinsdottir was the only one brave enough to speak to him. She knew she was the most beautiful woman in New Iceland and she had seen Gusti look at her out of the corner of his eye.

'Gusti,' she asked, 'what happened? Are you expecting someone?'

'There has been a change,' he replied. 'The world will end soon and so a man cannot mourn forever. I will fish no longer. From now on I will be Gusti Carpenter. If you will make two blankets of the finest wool, I will repair the leaking roof on your shack which your husband will not repair because he prefers to sit on the dock repairing nets and telling stories. And, Alda Baldvinsdottir,' he went on, 'you have a cow. If you will give me a jug of milk each day for a year, I will put another room on your shack so that the twins will not have to sleep in the same bed with you and your husband, and you will not have to worry that he will roll over and smother them.'

In this way, Gusti conducted business with the entire community. Halli Valgardson exchanged a year's supply of firewood for a new boat. Inga Gislasdottir agreed to make him a new suit in exchange for a brick chimney. The fishermen agreed to provide him with all the fish he could eat if he kept the dock in good repair. When the sun went down that day, Gusti was the richest man in New Iceland, and everyone had forgotten to call him Gusti Foulfart or even Gusti Madman.

One month later, twenty new settlers arrived on Hannes Kristjanson's boat. They told frightening stories of the trip, how their ship had nearly foundered on the rocks on the coast of Scotland, and how a marvellous silver fish had appeared and led the boat to safety; how, coming up the St Lawrence, they would surely have crashed into another ship had not a marvellous silver fish come to the captain in a dream and warned him in time. Just that morning, coming down the Red River, they had run aground in the delta, but a school of silver fishes had bumped into the boat until it floated free.

Among the passengers was Freya Gudmundsdottir. She was eighteen years old, with blonde hair that hung down to her waist and eyes so blue that from that day on, no one in New Iceland called anything blue without explaining that it was not as blue as Freya's eyes. She looked like Gusti's wife had looked when she was young, but Gusti's wife had only looked pretty, and Freya was beautiful.

Ketil Hallgrimsson was the first to meet her when she got off the boat. He asked her to marry him then and there, and he vowed to devote his life to making her happy. Ketil was a handsome young man, only twenty-three years old, with hair that hung in curls and muscles that rippled when he moved. The smile with which Freya answered him made Gusti's blood freeze. Still, she said she had not come to marry the first man she met, and she asked for Gusti. She told him she was the orphaned cousin of his wife, and asked if she might live with him until she could support herself. Gusti's tongue was so tied in knots that he could barely stammer yes.

She gave him her trunk to carry and followed him down the street to his newly whitewashed shack. The first thing she said when she got into the shack was, 'I can see there hasn't been a woman's hand around here for a while.' Then she scrubbed the table that Gusti had scrubbed until the top was thin. She sniffed the blankets that Vigdis Thorarinsdottir had just made and which had never been used. She screwed up her nose and hung them out on a tree to air. Then she swept the cleanest floor in New Iceland, threw out the fish that had been caught that morning, saying they had gone bad, and she started to make bread. Gusti sighed and thought, 'Yes, this is my wife all right. The fish has delivered his part of the bargain.'

And that was pretty much the way things went until the following spring. Gusti found himself occupying a smaller and smaller part of the house. He left early in the morning to do the jobs he had promised the others, and he came back late at night to find the house getting cleaner and cleaner. Freya made him new clothes. She cut his hair and clipped his fingernails and toenails. He had almost no time to write in his diary, but what he wrote pretty well describes his life. 'Thursday, January 11. More snow, the weather very cold. Freya is cleaning again. Worked all day repairing Helgi's roof. I may no more chew tobacco.' Any entry reads like any other.

Then that spring, Freya was chosen to be protector of the god in the wagon. Gusti should have expected it. Each year the prettiest young woman in the community was chosen, and Freya was certainly the prettiest of the young women.

Things changed very quickly. One morning Gusti awoke to find that his breakfast had not been made and Freya was not in her bed. He thought, because it was spring, that she might have gone for a walk, but she was not on the beach, nor was she in the garden behind the house. He walked to the dock and asked the fishermen if she had gone by. They laughed and said it would be some time before he saw her. He asked the children on the road, but they only laughed and ran away. Finally, he knocked on the door of Vigdis Thorarinsdottir, and she told him not to be a fool. 'When the god in the wagon comes you will see her,' Vigdis said, 'now go away and act like a man.'

Gusti knew then that he was in trouble. The protector of the god must marry that spring, and Gusti had not begun his wooing. Though they had shared the house for eight months, they were no closer than the day she had arrived. Gusti had been silenced by her wonderful beauty and even more silenced by her terrible temper. Still, he had changed for her. He was clean, obedient, sober and hard-working, an ideal husband. Ketil Hallgrimsson, on the other hand, had given up all work, and did nothing but sulk on the dock and wait till Freya came by, when he would leap to his feet and do tricks of strength until she had passed.

It was time, Gusti thought, to consult the fish. He walked all the way out to the south point and around to the channel, where the water was deep and he knew that fish liked to sun themselves. He stopped near a large white rock and shouted to the gentle waves that lapped at the shore. 'Sunfish, come out of the water, I have to talk to you.' The only reply was the splash of a tern diving for minnows. He shouted again but still there was nothing but the quarrelling of gulls. He was about to leave, when he decided, 'No, I have walked all this way, I will try once more. Sunfish,' he cried, 'come out.' With a splash, the sunfish landed at his feet.

'If you would read something besides the newspaper,' the sunfish said, 'you would know that you have to call three times. Now what's wrong? Is the wife I brought you not good enough?'

'Oh, she's fine,' Gusti replied, 'even more beautiful than I remembered, though her temper is strong.'

'You just forget,' the fish said. 'She is exactly as she was. You were just younger and didn't pay as much attention to her.'

'Well,' said Gusti, 'she has now been chosen as protector of the god in the wagon, and so must marry this spring. What shall I do?'

'Marry her.'

'I am not so sure she will marry me.'

'Well, that's your problem, isn't it?' said the sunfish. 'I've fulfilled my part of the bargain. Face it, you're getting on, you're not a young man anymore. And besides, you've become incredibly dull. You've given up tobacco, you don't drink, you work hard all the time, you've even shaved off your beard. What woman would give you a second glance?'

'There is no need to be insulting,' said Gusti. 'I have only asked you politely for advice.'

'I'm busy,' said the fish. 'The world is coming to an end. I've got things to do. I have no time to give advice to the lovelorn.' With a flick of his tail, he flipped himself back into the lake. Then his head appeared, silver in the sunlight, and he added, 'Give her a philtre,' and disappeared.

'What kind of philtre?' Gusti shouted at the waves, but the sunfish was gone and the waves didn't answer.

For the rest of the week, Gusti stayed in his house, watching the dishes go dirty, the dust begin to gather on the table and the floor. He stopped shaving and began to chew tobacco, spitting the juice into a basin on the floor. Freya did not appear. She was gone wherever the women had taken her to prepare, and he knew there was no reason to expect her. Once, Ketil Hallgrimsson came over and they shared a bottle, but neither had anything to say. In the community, women were frantically baking, and the men were decorating the doors with willow boughs. The first green leaves were starting to sprout on the poplars and maples, and already in some yards, the poppies were starting to bloom, white and yellow and red.

On Friday at dawn, she arrived. The whole community, men, women and children, had gathered in the street to await her. She came down the road from the south, dressed in a flowing white robe, her long golden hair ruffling in a slight breeze, her blue eyes flashing. Gusti thought he had never seen anything so beautiful. She was leading Helgi Gudmundson's white ox. The ox had a garland of flowers around its neck and was pulling the wagon with the god. The god was the largest Gusti had ever seen. He towered above the wagon and swayed with every step of the ox. His heavy hands, palms upturned for rain, rested on the front of the wagon. His shirt was a brilliant patchwork of colour and his great painted face beamed at the whole community. The wagon was filled with flowers, and there were flowers and branches with green leaves sticking out of every crevice in the enormous body. Gusti noticed that one of the legs was draped in the blanket that Vigdis Thorarinsdottir had made for him. 'Where,' he wondered, 'where do the women find so many flowers, so early in the season?'

The ox stopped right at the foot of the dock, and Freya climbed into the wagon and seated herself in the lap of the god. She began the oration, and all the community sat down on the ground to listen. Gusti was so entranced by her beauty and her frailty, there in the lap of the god, that he hardly heard what she said. She spoke of rain. She spoke of sunlight and crops. She spoke of trees bursting out of the earth, of animals in the fields, of nets dripping with fish. She spoke of love and of little children. Her voice mingled with the voices of birds and the lapping of waves. And then she was gone.

Then the women brought out the steaming vats of coffee and plates full of pönnukökur. They brought out turkeys glazed with honey and chokecherries, chickens and pigeons and ducks. They brought out roasts of venison and roasts of beef, plates of boiled sunfish and fried pickerel and broiled whitefish. They brought out hangikjot and rullupylsa, lifrapylsa and slàtur. They carried out bowls of skyr and ram's heads pickled in buttermilk. They brought out vinarterta and kleinur and àstarbolur.

The men pulled corks out of bottles and threw away the corks. They said, 'It is never too early for good whiskey,' and they aimed the bottoms of the bottles at the sun. The children were into everything, laughing and crying and squealing, but no one paid any attention to them. Husbands and wives who had hardly spoken for months kissed like young lovers, so it is no surprise that no one noticed that Gusti had slipped away and returned to his house.

Freya was there. She had changed from her white robe into an old blue house-dress. She was staring out the window and hardly noticed Gusti's arrival. She seemed not even to have noticed the mess in the house. 'You were wonderful,' Gusti began. 'Never has there been such a beautiful protector nor so clever an oration.'

Freya glanced at him, then looked out the window once more. 'I shall marry,' she said. 'In nine days, I shall marry.'

'And who shall you marry?' Gusti asked, his heart wrenching inside him.

'There are many I might marry,' Freya responded, though without enthusiasm. 'In the meanwhile, it is not seemly that I should live longer with you. I will go to stay with Vigdis Thorarinsdottir until my wedding day.' Then she packed her trunk, and Gusti carried it down the road to Vigdis's house.

The next day was quiet as the community rested from the celebration, but by Monday the town was buzzing with rumours. Who had Freya chosen? Would it be Ketil Hallgrimsson, or one of the other young men of the community? Or had she perhaps betrothed herself to an outsider who would arrive on the wedding day? There was even a rumour that the priest was angry because they had received the god in the wagon, and that he would refuse to perform the wedding ceremony. Ketil Hallgrimsson was dressed in his best clothes, and stood in the road before Vigdis Thorarinsdottir's house, doing feats of strength.

That week, Gusti had plenty of time to write in his diary. He pondered over what he might put in the philtre to gain Freya's love, and he wondered who might help him. He considered whether it was right to use a philtre at all. Could love that was gained by a trick be real? In the end, he decided that the philtre should contain pure water. What else, he thought, is so close to love? It may be taken cold or hot, it is clear and insubstantial, it refreshes, but when it is consumed it is gone. And most important, there is more of it in the world than anything else.

Here you must bear with me, because the diaries end, and so I have had to recon-struct what actually happened. My aunt Thora, whose mother was there, says that Gusti went to Vigdis Thorarinsdottir and told her of his trouble. She led him to a clearing in the bush where she comforted him in her own way and promised to slip the contents of the philtre into Freya's coffee on the morning of the wedding day. That morning, Freya chose Gusti and they were married and had thirteen children. Ketil Hallgrimsson was so sad that he drowned himself in the lake the same day.

My aunt Lara, Thora's sister, agrees with the story, but claims that Vigdis drank the water herself. That morning, Freya chose Ketil Hallgrimsson and he did not drown for twenty years. By that time, he had fathered all the children whose descendants now live in Arborg. Vigdis left her husband and went to live with Gusti and they had thirteen children, though they never married. All their descendants now live in Riverton.

The people from Arnes tell a story very much like the story of Gusti, but in their version, a marvellous stranger dressed all in silver appeared on a magnificent boat and claimed Freya for his bride. They moved to Wynyard and had thirteen children and all the Icelanders in Saskatchewan are descended from them.

My cousin Villi, who is only six years older than me, but who speaks better Icelandic, says that the family is trying to hide something. He has overheard whispers, and he believes that Freya chose both Gusti and Ketil, that the three of them raised thirteen children and no one ever knew who was the father. He says the whole thing about the fish is just made up so people will think it is only a fairy tale and not enquire any further. After all, our uncle is the mayor, and any scandal might go bad for him in the next election.

I have my own ideas. If I were making up this story, I would tell you that, yes, Gusti did go to see Vigdis and tell her his troubles, and yes, she did comfort him in her own way, telling him of the secret love she had always felt for him and begging him to forget Freya. If it were my story, I could tell you that Gusti was not a flexible man, that he had made the faithful Vigdis pour the water into Freya's coffee, that she had chosen Gusti and they had married. Then, because I would want a happy ending, I would show you how Freya's bad temper and wicked tongue drove Gusti away, so that he married the faithful Vigdis, while Freya chose the hapless Ketil, who, for all his feats of strength, could never get the better of her. I would say they each had thirteen children, and all the people of Gimli are descended from them.

But I would go even further, because a story needs a proper ending, and I would do something about the fish. I would let Gusti catch him once more in a net and when the fish began all that nonsense about the end of the world, I would have Gusti take him home to Vigdis, who would boil him and feed him to the thirteen children. So there you are.

JAMILA ISMAIL

(b. 1940)

In her 'afterword' to her self-published pamphlet *from the DICTION AIR* (no date), Jamila Ismail annotates 'serendipity', one of the words she redefines in her 'dictionary': 'when serendipity was coined in the 1750s it meant "the faculty of making happy & unexpected discoveries by accident". a brutish example, from the 1750s, might be, the takeover of bengal; which financed the english "industrial revolution", & so england went on to Empaaah. no of course i hadn't it figured this way when the word first buzzed me, testily, in the 1960s in hong kong. herstory comes & history goes and sensor's always here. it bothered me that the word was plucked from native tongues i did not speak. i dint want to ape the brits, stopped passing it, it went in bardo with other words i couldn't use until , well untilled.'

Exposing the layers of hidden meanings and histories behind language, writing prose and poetic narratives whose plot lines can only be traced in a serendipitous way, is typical of Ismail's work. Her writing is political and playful at the same time.

Born in 1940 in Hong Kong, Ismail moved to Canada in 1963 after living in India and completing her B.A. in English at the University of Hong Kong. During her first years in Canada, she pursued doctoral studies at the University of Alberta (1963-66). She moved to Vancouver in 1966, where she taught in the Department of English, Simon Fraser University. During the last few years, she has divided her time between Hong Kong and Vancouver.

Her work has appeared in many literary journals, and has been anthologized in *Many-Mouthed Birds: Contemporary Writing by Chinese Canadians* (1991). Ismail prefers to publish her own work. *sexions* (1984), including poetry, prose, essays, photographs and found poems, challenges not only the traditional assumptions about what constitutes a book or a literary genre, but also the ways in which gender and ethnic origins are constructed. This is apparent in the way in which Ismail parodies the conventional method of classifying books according to the Canadian Cataloguing in Publication Data; she defines her book as 'paltry, pose. friction & 2 kinds of dreamer, strategy & comely. nitwitwoo'.

FROM *SCARED TEXTS*

a.
1. at dinner they sit facing the tall windows. hillside's pulsing
        & billowing trees.
    i like that so much   (one thinks).
    there must be much life there, & families   (two
        murmurs).
    of course there is   (three chimes),   what d'you think,
        only families have trees?

2. flora was kettling water for herbal tea & assembling caps of
        greenstuff & earths of several colour.
    elder said: each morning, when i wake up, i consider
        how i should feed myself today, i think of what i've eaten
        yesterday & other days.

3.   hibiscus mentioned that mushrooms are good for
          cholesterol.
      jaggery scoffed: what d'you mean, good for!
      chestnut dehisced: she means good against, good against
          cholesterol.
      flame-o'-the-forest said to jaggery: we know you speak
      better english & that you know what we mean.

4.   . mean pause   .
              said :   menopause   .
                    said :   hm .   men pause.
                          said :   me no pause!

5.   visiting a married couple, ivy got all wisteria about couples.
      cypress observed: you seem to think that married people
      practise marriage.

     . . .

b
2.   in chinatown whenever bosan said (in cantonese):   can't
      read chinese,   chinatown storekeepers would scold.
      in cheung chau* they would say: oh another (denatured
      returnee from overseas).
      in hongkong marie-claire said: you should say you don't
      know how to read, not, you don't know how to read
      chinese.

      oh, sorry!   the waitress apologized, rushed back with the
      english-language menu, & waited on bosan most
      sympathetically.

      *long island, an hour by ferry from hongkong

4.   hah?   bosan crossing georgia street said, to the driver
      who'd muttered something.
      the light turned amber.
      he stuck his head out the window, yelled: hey ricie!
      grinned, & zoomed off.
      bosan cracked up: ricie! it's pretty-funny!
      sum wan said: hey, you just got insulted.
      ginger smiled: we've always had to tell bosan how
      oppressed she is.

5.　　| jianada |　'canada' seems well liked in this part of china.
　　　　　　　hun how (very good)!　　said the pork-pie hat
　　in the muslim eatery in dali, thumb up.

　　canada hah?　　nods the uniform in kunming.　　china
　　　likes canada number one!　　he says.

　　on the street the money changer hustles:　　you from
　　　where?
　　bosan said:　　jianada.
　　jianada?　　she points to bosan's hair & lifts her own in
　　　rhyme rhyme.
　　katib translates:　　she didn't know there is black hair in
　　　canada.

6.　　| *we've* |　　during a break at the gathering of first nations
　　　　　　　　in vancouver, they say to bosan,　　　come
　　along, we're going to the sub (student union building) for
　　lunch.

　　jeanette orders rice with her bacon & eggs. stories are
　　　swapped of food combos that boggle middle-class anglo-
　　　cans. robt is seen wandering, plate in hand, & | waved |
　　　over. to make space, chairs snug up, it happens, all to the right.

　　is this how the | wheel | was invented,　　bosan flashed.
　　round table laughs.

　　. . .

c.
1.　　| ratio quality |　　young ban yen had been thought
　　　　　　　　　　italian in kathmandu, filipina in hong
　　kong, erasian in kyoto, japanese in anchorage, dismal in
　　london england, hindu in edmonton, generic oriental in
　　calgary, western canadian in ottawa, anglophone in
　　montreal, metis in jasper, eskimo at hudson's bay
　　department store, vietnamese in chinatown, tibetan in
　　vancouver, commie at the u.s. border.

　　on the whole very asian.

　　. . .

3.   remarks had been exchanged about the irish epicist james
       jokes.
     in between turns at pingpong, the talk turned to local
       (canada) poetry.
     a transplant from hunan asked: what's happening in the
       united sates?
     xylem twigged: i like your name for the government!

5.   cockleburr hooked up with this word 'autonomy':   *autoe,*
       that's greek for . . . self. *self* in north american means . . .
       me. does *auto*nomy mean . . . *me*tonymy?

     the dictionary slipped, as if its heaviest corner wanted to
       thump toesie, but burr grabbed the small print: *me* is
       a . . . pronoun,   nagged burr.   so, is the question:
       autonomy, what am i *pro*?

7.   cabbage said: the students were unreasonable. of course,
       that's not how newspapers sell, but many folks in chinese
       street think so. the gummint had already been so patient,
       letting them mess up the capitol so many weeks without
       punishing them. really, what did they expect!

     sorghum laughed: ya, the radicals certainly succeeded in
       forcing the gummint to show a bad hand. you think
       people now wanna shake that hand?

d.
1.   what,   déjà sighed,   do you have against the word
       'consciousness'?
     bonsai frowned: anglomerican cultural imperialism.
       mediacrity! i prefer the word 'awareness.' i like the where
       in awareness, i like the space & nothing of it. 'conscious-
       ness' is too visible, positivist, also i don't like the sound
       of it, *shush,* it's sticky!
     doji said: i like it because that sound is like where one
       has to go, deep, inside. to me it has the same meaning as
       'awareness,' it's everything!
     binosa said: going into the whirlpool may be why i
       don't like the word. 'awareness' seems cleaner, airier,
       roomy.
     dai ji said: aware*shush*!
     you sniper!   biosan laughed, a bit wet.

3. | bassoon | a r d e nt   ,   f l o w
    | transmutes | er ,   of the mil k
    | *analects* | wh it e throa   t,   morning
    | 9. xxx | glo ry   bl oo
    | with the | m ,
    | help of a | sweet art ?
    | morning | smaller than the purple
    | glory in | how i've not . missed . you
    | kathmandu |

e.
1.   moby dyke turned sceptic around the harpoons of erudition.
      merlin said: what marlin said to me was,   you must
          learn to use the master otherwise he will kill you.

4.   this work is magic,   native said,   except for that part
          about 'shush' being sticky. how can you say such a thing,
          i'm really angry! shush is the wind in the trees, we have
          that sound a lot in our language! whereas 'awareness,' is,
          maybe the sound a   horse would make, but it's not
          ·one of our sounds!
      nomad winced. 'salish,' 'snohomish,' 'squamish,' came to
          mind.
      native smiled: just because you're scared doesn't mean
          this work isn't sacred.

6.   a master announced failure, disciples sluffed it off as senile
          depression.
      i have not conquered mount avarice,   the master said.
      drop-out hmmed: the up-&-coming should heed this,
          legacy.

8.   at cappuccino in joe's cafe gā je said: what is this
          iridology.
      bassoon said: various organs & functions have nerve
          endings in the iris, so it's possible to read the condition of
          the body right there in the eye.
      dai ji said: that's why, looking is a lot of work.

BETH BRANT

(b. 1941)

'I started writing when I turned forty,' Beth Brant has said. 'It was a gift brought to me by Eagle. In these ten years I have been writing, I am always conscious that I am writing for my own People. That is my audience. That is who the stories are about and for. And if non-Natives pick up a book of mine and learn about the effects of racism and colonialism on Native Peoples and then take that within themselves to make change, that is a good thing.'

Since 1981, the beginning of her writing career, Brant has edited *A Gathering of Spirit: Writing and Art by North American Indian Women* (1988), the first anthology of Native women writers, and published two collections of short fiction, *Mohawk Trail* (1990) and *Food and Spirits* (1991), which includes the story that follows. A frequent instructor of creative writing, Brant has also published widely in many literary magazines, including those focusing on lesbian and gay issues, and is one of the founders of Turtle Grandmothers, a group that facilitates the editing and publishing of manuscripts by Native women, and

gathers archival information about North American Native women writers.

Beth Brant (Degonwadonti), a Bay of Quinte Mohawk, was born on the Tyendinaga Reserve in Deseronto, Ontario, and has lived in Detroit, Michigan, for many years. In Penny Petrone's words, Brant's fiction 'ranges confidently in tone from the humorous to the poignant. Hers is a refreshingly down-to-earth literary voice' that speaks of working-class Native families, urban Natives, lesbian relationships, and the gift of spiritual re-empowerment that traditional Native stories offer to Native people. Behind the confident voice of her writing, there lies, however, the painful process that leads to it. As she says in her preface to *Food and Spirits*, 'This pen feels like a knife in my hand. / The paper should bleed, like my peoples' bodies. . . . How do I show the blood of them? The ink of our own palette? / Medicine. / Who will heal the writer who uses her ink and blood to tell? / Telling. / Who hears?' Brant's most recent book is *Writing As Witness: Essay and Talk* (1994).

THIS IS HISTORY

for Donna Goodleaf

Long before there was an earth and long before there were people called human, there was a Sky World.

On Sky World there were Sky People who were like us and not like us. And of the Sky People there was Sky Woman. Sky Woman had a peculiar trait: she had curiosity. She bothered the others with her questions, with wanting to know what lay beneath the clouds that supported her world. Sometimes she pushed the clouds aside and looked down through her world to the large expanse of blue that shimmered below. The others were tired of her peculiar trait and called her an aberration, a queer woman who asked questions, a woman who wasn't satisfied with what she had.

Sky Woman spent much of her time dreaming—dreaming about the blue expanse underneath the clouds, dreaming about floating through the clouds, dreaming about the blue color and how it would feel to her touch. One day she pushed the clouds away from her and leaned out of the opening. She fell. The others tried to catch her hands and pull her back, but she struggled free and began to float downward. The Sky People watched her descent and agreed that they were glad to see her go. She was a nuisance with her questions, an aberration, a queer woman who was not like them—content to walk the clouds undisturbed.

Sky Woman floated. The currents of wind played through her hair. She put out her arms and felt the sensations of air between her fingers. She kicked her legs, did somersaults, and was curious about the free, delightful feelings of flying. Faster, faster, she floated toward the blue shimmer that beckoned her.

She heard a noise and turned to see a beautiful creature with black wings and a white head flying close to her. The creature spoke. 'I am Eagle. I have been sent to carry you to your new home.' Sky Woman laughed and held out her hands for Eagle to brush his wings against. He swooped under her, and she settled on his back. They flew. They circled, they glided, they flew, Sky Woman clutching the feathers of the great creature.

Sky Woman looked down at the blue color. Rising from the expanse was a turtle. Turtle looked up at the flying pair and nodded her head. She dove into the waters and came up again with a muskrat clinging to her back. In Muskrat's paw was a clump of dark brown dirt scooped from the bottom of the sea. She laid it on Turtle's back and jumped back into the water. Sky Woman watched the creature swim away, her long tail skimming the top of the waves, her whiskers shining. Sky Woman watched as the dark brown dirt began to spread. All across Turtle's back the dirt was spreading, spreading, and in this dirt green things were growing. Small green things, tall green things, and in the middle of Turtle's back, the tallest thing grew. It grew branches and needles, more and more branches, until it reached where Eagle and Sky Woman were hovering.

Turtle raised her head and beckoned to the pair. Eagle flew down to Turtle's back and gently lay Sky Woman on the soft dirt. Then he flew to the very top of the White Pine tree and said, 'I will be here, watching over everything that is to be. You will look to me as the harbinger of what is to happen. You will be kind to me and my people. In return, I will keep this place safe.' Eagle folded his wings and looked away.

Sky Woman felt the soft dirt with her fingers. She brought the dirt to her mouth and tasted the color of it. She looked around at the green things. Some were flowering with fantastic shapes. She stood on her feet and felt the solid back of Turtle beneath her. She marveled at this wonderful place and wondered what she would do here.

Turtle swiveled her head and looked at Sky Woman with ancient eyes. 'You will live here and make this a new place. You will be kind, and you will call me Mother. I will make all manner of creatures and growing things to guide you on this new place. You will watch them carefully, and from them you will learn how to live. You will take care to be respectful and honorable to me. I am your Mother.' Sky Woman touched Turtle's back and promised to honor and respect her. She lay down on Turtle's back and fell asleep.

As she slept, Turtle grew. Her back became wider and longer. She slapped her tail and cracks appeared in her back. From these cracks came mountains, canyons were formed, rivers and lakes were made from the spit of Turtle's mouth. She shook her body and prairies sprang up, deserts settled, marshes and wetlands pushed their way through the cracks of Turtle's shell. Turtle opened her mouth and called. Creatures came crawling out of her back. Some had wings, some had four legs, six legs, or eight. Some had no legs but slithered on the ground, some had no legs and swam with fins. These creatures crawled out of Turtle's back and some were covered with fur, some with feathers, some with scales, some with skins of beautiful colors. Turtle called again, and the creatures found their voice. Some sang, some barked, some growled and roared, some had no voice but a hiss, some had no voice and rubbed their legs together to speak. Turtle called again. The creatures began to make homes. Some gathered twigs and leaves, others spun webs, some found caves, others dug holes in the ground. Some made the waters their home, and some of these came up for air to breathe. Turtle shuddered, and the new place was made a continent, a world.

Turtle gave a last look to the sleeping Sky Woman. 'Inside you is growing a being who is like you and not like you. This being will be your companion. Together you will give names to the creatures and growing things. You will be kind to these things. This companion growing inside you will be called First Woman, for she will be the first of these beings on this earth. Together you will respect me and call me Mother. Listen to the voices of the creatures and communicate with them. This will be called prayer, for prayer is the language of all my creations. Remember me.' Turtle rested from her long labor.

Sky Woman woke and touched herself. Inside her body she felt the stirrings of another. She stood on her feet and walked the earth. She climbed mountains, she walked in the desert, she slept in trees, she listened to the voices of the creatures and living things, she swam in the waters, she smelled the growing things that came from the earth. As she wandered and discovered, her body grew from the being inside her. She ate leaves, she picked fruit. An animal showed her how to bring fire, then threw himself in the flames that she might eat of him. She prayed her thanks, remembering Turtle's words. Sky Woman watched the creatures, learning how they lived in community with each other, learning how they hunted, how they stored food, how they prayed. Her body grew larger, and she felt her companion move inside her, waiting to be born. She watched the living things, seeing how they fed their young, how they taught their young, how they protected their young. She watched and learned and saw how things should be. She waited for the day when First Woman would come and together they would be companions, lovers of the earth, namers of all things, planters and harvesters, creators.

On a day when Sky Woman was listening to the animals, she felt a sharp pain inside of her. First Woman wanted to be born. Sky Woman walked the earth, looking for soft things to lay her companion on when she was born. She gathered all day, finding feathers of the winged-creatures, skins of the fur-bearers. She gathered these things and made a deep nest. She gathered other special things for medicine and magic. She ate leaves from a plant that eased her pain. She clutched her magic things in her hands to give her help. She prayed to the creatures to strengthen her. She squatted over the deep nest and began to push. She pushed and held tight to the magic medicine. She pushed, and First Woman slipped out of her and onto the soft nest. First Woman gave a cry. Sky Woman touched her companion, then gave another great push as her placenta fell from her. She cut the long cord with her teeth as she had learned from the animals. She ate the placenta as she had learned from the animals. She brought First Woman to her breast as she had learned, and First Woman began to suckle, drawing nourishment and medicine from Sky Woman.

Sky Woman prayed, thanking the creatures for teaching her how to give birth. She touched the earth, thanking Mother for giving her this gift of a companion. Turtle shuddered, acknowledging the prayer. That day, Sky Woman began a new thing. She opened her mouth and sounds came forth. Sounds of song. She sang and began a new thing—singing prayers. She fashioned a thing out of animal skin and wood. She touched the thing and it resonated. She touched it again and called it drum. She sang with the rhythm of her touching. First Woman suckled as her companion sang the prayers.

First Woman began to grow. In the beginning she lay in her nest dreaming, then crying out as she wanted to suckle. Then she opened her eyes and saw her companion and smiled. Then she sat up and made sounds. Then she crawled and was curious about everything. She wanted to touch and feel and taste all that was around her. Sky Woman carried her on her back when she walked the earth, listening to the living things and talking with them. First Woman saw all the things that Sky Woman pointed out to her. She listened to Sky Woman touch the drum and make singing prayers. First Woman stood on her feet and felt the solid shell of Turtle against her feet. The two companions began walking together. First Woman made a drum for herself, and together the companions made magic by touching their drums and singing their prayers. First Woman grew, and as she grew Sky Woman showed her the green things, the animal things, the living things, and told her they needed to name them. Together they began the naming. Heron, bear, snake, dolphin, spider, maple, oak, thistle, cricket, wolf, hawk, trout, goldenrod, firefly. They named together and in naming, the women became closer and truer companions. The living things that now had names moved closer to the women and taught them how to dance. Together, they all danced as the women touched their drums and made their singing prayers. Together they danced. Together. All together.

In time the women observed the changes that took place around them. They observed that sometimes the trees would shed their leaves and at other times would grow new ones. They observed that some creatures buried themselves in caves and burrows and slept for long times, reappearing when the trees began their new birth. They observed that some creatures flew away for long times, reappearing when the animals crawled from their caves and dens. Together, the companions decided they would sing special songs and different prayers when the earth was changing and the creatures were changing. They named these times seasons and made different drums, sewn with feathers and stones. The companions wore stones around their necks, feathers in their hair, and shells on their feet, and when they danced, the music was new and extraordinary. They prepared feasts at this time, asking the animals to accept their death. Some walked into their arrows, some ran away. The animals that gave their lives were thanked and their bones were buried in Turtle's back to feed her—the Mother of all things.

The women fashioned combs from animal teeth and claws. They spent long times combing and caressing each other's hair. They crushed berries and flowers and painted signs on their bodies to honor Mother and the living things who lived with them. They painted on rocks and stones to honor the creatures who taught them. They fixed food together, feeding each other herbs and roots and plants. They lit fires together and cooked the foods that gave them strength and medicine. They laughed together and made language between them. They touched each other and in the touching made a new word: love. They touched each other and made a language of touching: passion. They made medicine together. They made magic together.

And on a day when First Woman woke from her sleep, she bled from her body. Sky Woman marveled at this thing her companion could do because she was born on Turtle's back. Sky Woman built a special place for her companion to retreat at this time, for it was wondrous what her body could do. First Woman went to her bleeding-place and dreamed about her body and the magic it made. And at the end of this time, she emerged laughing and holding out her arms to Sky Woman.

Time went by, long times went by. Sky Woman felt her body changing. Her skin was wrinkling, her hands were not as strong. She could not hunt as she used to. Her eyes were becoming dim, her sight unclear. She walked the earth in this changed body and took longer to climb mountains and swim in the waters. She still enjoyed the touch of First Woman, the laughter and language they shared between them, the dancing, the singing prayers. But her body was changed. Sky Woman whispered to Mother, asking her what these changes meant. Mother whispered back that Sky Woman was aged and soon her body would stop living. Before this event happened, Sky Woman must give her companion instruction. Mother and Sky Woman whispered together as First Woman slept. They whispered together the long night through.

When First Woman woke from her sleep, Sky Woman told her of the event that was to happen. 'You must cut the heart from this body and bury it in the field by your bleeding-place. Then you must cut this body in small pieces and fling them into the sky. You will do this for me.'

And the day came that Sky Woman's body stopped living. First Woman touched her companion's face and promised to carry out her request. She carved the heart from Sky Woman's body and buried it in the open field near her bleeding-place. She put her ear to the ground and heard Sky Woman's voice, 'From this place will grow three plants. As long as they grow, you will never want for food or magic. Name these plants corn, beans, and squash. Call them the Three Sisters, for like us, they will never grow apart.'

First Woman watched as the green plant burst from the ground, growing stalks that bore ears of beautifully colored kernels. From beneath the corn rose another plant with small leaves, and it twined around the stalks carrying pods of green. Inside each pod were small, white beans. From under the beans came a sprawling vine with large leaves that tumbled and grew and shaded the beans' delicate roots. On this vine were large, green squash that grew and turned orange and yellow. Three Sisters, First Woman named them.

First Woman cut her companion's body in small pieces and flung them at the sky. The sky turned dark, and there, glittering and shining, were bright-colored stars and a round moon. The moon spoke. 'I will come to you every day when the sun is sleeping. You will make songs and prayers for me. Inside you are growing two beings. They are not like us. They are called Twin Sons. One of these is good and will honor us and our Mother. One of these is not good and will bring things that we have no names for. Teach these beings what we have learned together. Teach them that if the sons do not honor the women who made them, that will be the end of this earth. Keep well, my beloved First Woman. Eagle is watching out for you. Honor the living things. Be kind to them. Be strong. I am always with you. Remember our Mother. Be kind to her.'

First Woman touched her body, feeling the movements inside. She touched the back of Mother and waited for the beings who would change her world.

HIMANI BANNERJI

(b. 1942)

With the recent publications of *Thinking Through* (1995), *Returning the Gaze: Essays on Racism, Feminism and Politics* (1993), which she edited, *Writing on the Wall: Essays on Culture and Politics* (1993), and *Unsettling Relations: The University as a Site of Feminist Struggle* (1991), which she co-edited, Himani Bannerji has established herself as a major figure in cultural and anti-racist politics in Canada. Poet and fiction writer, and a professor of Sociology at York University, Toronto, since 1989, Bannerji thinks of her roles of creative writer and social critic as being unavoidable for a Canadian non-white woman writer like herself: the 'one-sided visibility as creative writers has actually put us in a double jeopardy. In the first instance, as non-white women, our experiences of "difference" need form and expression. For this reason, creative writings or oral histories are crucial, and make a fundamental demand for change. But this demand calls for a systematic analytical thinking, and this is what needs to be elaborated by us.'

The kind of elaboration that Bannerji is talking about is not a matter of 'transplanting' or 'reproducing' an ethnic culture. As she says, 'I don't think the issue is culture; the issue is politics,' an 'expressive act' that resists what she calls the 'multicultural ossificatory imperative', the tendency of official multiculturalism to fossilize the ethnic origins of Canadians. 'Multiculturalism to me,' she says, 'is a way of managing seepage of persistent subjectivity of people that come from other parts of the world, people that are seen as undesirable because they have once been colonized, now neo-colonized. So we are not talking about Germans or Finns and Swedes or the French, for that matter. We are talking about the undesirables. It is southern Europeans, sometimes, and Third World people who have to be ethnic. Now the fact that our children may not even feel like becoming ethnic is another problem for them. They may not want multiculturalism, one day set aside to eat yams and get dressed up.' Her poems included here clearly reflect the complexity of cultural politics that have been her major concern since she began writing.

Bannerji was born in Bangladesh when it was still part of pre-independent India. She began her education at the experimental university founded by Rabindranath Tagore, Visva Bharati University, Santiniketan, and subsequently received an M.A. in English (1965) from Jadavpur University, West Bengal, where she taught English until 1969, the year she arrived in Canada to pursue graduate studies at the University of Toronto. The mother of Kaushalya, also a poet, Bannerji has published two collections of poetry, *A Separate Sky* (1982) and *Doing Time* (1986), as well as a children's novel, *Coloured Pictures* (1991). Her poems, stories, and essays have appeared in many literary and academic journals.

'PAKI GO HOME'

1.

3 pm
sunless
winter sleeping in the womb of the afternoon
wondering how to say this
to reason or scream or cry or whisper
or write on the walls

reduced again
cut at the knees, hands chopped, eyes blinded
mouth stopped, voices lost.

fear anger contempt
think filaments of ice and fire
wire the bodies
my own, of hers, of his,
the young and the old.

And a grenade explodes
in the sunless afternoon
and words run down
like frothy white spit
down her bent head
down the serene parting of her dark hair
as she stands too visible
from home to bus stop to home
raucous, hyena laughter,
'Paki, Go home!'

2.

the moon covers her face
Pock-marked and anxious
in the withered fingers of the winter trees.
The light of her sadness runs like tears
down the concrete hills, tarmac rivers
and the gullies of the cities.
The wind still carries the secret chuckle
The rustle of canes
as black brown bodies flee into the night
blanched by the salt waters of the moon.
Strange dark fruits on tropical trees
swing in the breeze gently.

3.

Now, and then again
we must organize.
The woman wiping the slur spit
from her face, the child standing
at the edge of the playground silent, stopped.
The man twisted in despair,

disabled at the city gates.
Even the child in the womb
must find a voice
sound in unison
organize.
Like a song, like a roar
like a prophecy that changes the world.

To organize, to fight the slaver's dogs,
to find the hand, the foot, the tongue,
the body dismembered
organ by organ rejoined
organized.
Soul breathed in
until she, he
the young, the old is whole.
Until the hand acts moved by the mind
and the walls, the prisons, the chains of lead or gold
tear, crumble, wither into dust
and the dead bury the dead
until yesterdays never return.

DEATH BY TRIVIA

In these days there is no big living for us.
Grand emotions, curtains rising and falling with a
thunderous applause.
No ultimate moment of the last surrender, commitment
that permits
no going back up the stairs, when we could say, 'I will
not live without you'
'Loving means this or that', and when the moment
comes apply the aspic to
our breast. We can not turn to someone and pour out all
that knowledge
we got by ingesting so many deaths. We have chewed so
long on so many
deaths we have grown fat as maggots in the world's
coffin.

These are days that are small with fine steel teeth in
their edges.
They are grinding us down, they are filing away at us.

Our vows are tentative, shamefaced, murmured below
our breath,
often not heard, always at the fine point of retraction.
We have loosened our arms around eternity
which alone could have given our lives that fine sculpted
shape.
Looking into someone's endless eyes, tired lines around
the mouth,
looking at the lights across the river, the sad outline of
the bridge
that joins nothing with nowhere, we could have spoken
words to each other
with the sad solemn intonation of bells. We could have,
we could wish to have
spoken the ultimate, could have marked the moment in
the exquisite
calligraphy of a testament. All this could have been but
at another time
when time was marked by peaks not successions.

In this sterilized time
with nothing, no signs, the words we give are careful
and banal.
I did not tell you that I had eaten on death or that
forever was possible.
We covered ourselves in bed under the patchwork quilt.
We spoke trivia,
we smoked a few cigarettes, I drank a glass of water, you
fell asleep and
turned to me on your elbows knitted, your left hand
open you groped for
something. But I did not put my hand in yours, for what
you
sought lay elsewhere perhaps in childhood. I lay there in
the light
sleep of nomadic people. Time passed, one thought
melted into another,
no will for permanence, only a sudden impulse to pray to
a good that does
not exist, for me, for you, for all of us, to be forgiven for
our inability
to will, to make meanings beyond the moment, to love,
for our slow suicide,
for our death by trivia.

APART-HATE

In this white land
Where I wander with scape-goats
there are laws

Apart-hate

In this whiteland
rocks blackhands gold and diamond
blood oozes from the mouth

Apart-hate

In this whiteland
Chinese coolies, black slaves, indian indentures
immigration, head tax, virginity tests

Apart-hate

Sudden attacks in the dark
in the dawn with cops and dogs
White Cop plays with her mouth—resuscitates
London   Pretoria   Toronto

Apart-hate

Reagan extends his whitehand from the whitehouse
fingers cash sells arms
the shop smells of blood, vomit and gunpowder
'divestment hurts the blacks'

Apart-hate

In this white land
skin is fingered like pelt
skin is sold and the ivory of her eyes

the category human has no meaning
when spoken in white

Apart-hate

A LETTER FOR IRAQ

Dearest,

Sitting in cafes and museums of Europe,
Amsterdam to be precise, places where you
have not been, nor where the dark and the
green that is in you, in the delicate lines of
your face, in the curves of your eyes, are never
reflected, I carry you in the lines of my palms.

  Except perhaps in their Tropen, colonial museum,
where you lie fragmented in the objects
which they have torn apart from their history,
like limbs from the whole, live body, and put
on display. There my sweet, in clay, wood,
beads, pieces of bamboo, your humble body
is offered to my sight as artefacts. I cannot
touch you; this is Europe, you are a museum
piece, a million miles of distance by air, a
fantasy formed in airline posters and
shatterproof fibreglass which preserves the
death of our everyday lives, to create their
civilization.

  And now there is spring in Europe,
the sweetness of the purple crocuses, the
white of the hyacinths, the blue of the iris
melt you with their sun. Trees whisper their
green secrets and in the official museum
of the city they display their prizes, horrors,
visions of war and peace, in an exhibit
of photo journalism. For decades Europe nurses
its sores. When they heal they are
photographically provoked to bleed, to let
the pus of memory ooze out. Europe remembers—its nazi past. In slow rhythm
strikes chest, forehead, forces
tears and grimaces. But behind the collage of guilt,
memories and predations of the past,
Tropens, British museums, nazis later,
send bombs, cameras and transforms

a war into lightshows and videogames.
Your body—arab, indian, black,
vietnamese, chilean, panamanian,
nameless, dark, splinters, cracks into
a thousand pieces thrown up into the sky
by jets of oil: Every pore of your body
visible to the radar eye of the dark.
Wind of peace blowing in the operation
desert storm whistles through the pores of
your singed skin. A hundred thousand
sorties without blood!

Dearest, the soles of your singed feet, your
child's body charred—a charcoal graffiti of
history, your old man's unruly tears, swollen
veins in the hands, your young woman's defiant
curse, your old woman's hands raised to an
Allah who has fled the sky of starwars and
taken refuge with the dead Mesopotamian
gods. Ya Ali, Ya Hassan, Ya Hussein,
Karbala in flames a second time and a
horse runs wild, with hooves of fire through
the bombed streets. And the good King Haroun
al Rashid once upon a time in Baghdad
in a child's book flees with Duldul into an
ocean of blood. Your cry rips apart the
television screen—will no one stop this war
machine? My sweet, say nothing to them. Nothing
has stopped their march of civilization, while
their blind hearts whisper tales of our savagery
and their strategic adjustments. Let us hold
each other by the hand and walk together
through our myriad lives.

In this terror of a golden spring, where
the clay jar holding the ashes of our ancestors,
the gentle hand of time reaching out to be held,
is smashed, crushed, thrown into the grime
of betrayals, wars, cynicisms, let us my
love go together into that cave, where
others wait with a secret
sign, where darkness holds the key to
dawn where conspiracy sings in the

wind of the courage to create again a new
world—where your body, smile and
sweet reserve, breaking the glass of
the Tropen, will be re-membered in
the shapes of our good earth.

13/3/91 Amsterdam

SANDRA BIRDSELL

(b. 1942)

'I write with a sense of an invisible reader,' Sandra Birdsell says: 'I don't know who that reader is, but it's just a reader who keeps me honest in terms of ambiguities in the text.'

Of Cree-French and Russian-Mennonite background, Birdsell was born in Hamiota, Manitoba, and grew up in an environment without books—'except for The Bible': 'we weren't encouraged to read fiction or non-fiction. So I had to discover, as a writer, "What do I like to read?"' Influenced by writers ranging from Flannery O'Connor to Margaret Laurence and from Maxim Gorky to Milan Kundera, Birdsell published her first collection of short fiction when she turned forty. The stories in *Night Travellers* (1982), which won the Gerald Lampert Award, deal with characters belonging to the same family. Her second volume of stories, *Ladies of the House* (1984), is less tightly structured as a collection, and shows Birdsell making more conscious decisions about style and form. The two volumes have been collected together in one book, *Agassiz Stories* (1987), the title reflecting the fictional valley and town where her characters live.

Although tempted to write a third collection of stories—'sort of like a triptych', as she said—Birdsell's next book was *The Missing Child* (1989), a novel that won the W.H. Smith-*Books in Canada* First Novel Award. Described by the author as a 'great big sprawling, panoramic novel', it reflects, in its style and structure, her 'love with the form of film-making, and what the camera could do, and with the whole idea and desire to write a film'. Indeed, Birdsell has written dramas and film scripts, including one for television that was an adaptation of her second novel, *The Chrome Suite* (1992). This novel was nominated for the Governor General's Award for Fiction, and was the winner of the McNally Robinson Best Book of the Year in Manitoba. It was after the publication of this book that Birdsell felt compelled to go back, in her next novel, to her 'Menno roots, even to the extent of wanting to get some of the stories back in Ukraine', her maternal ancestral origins.

A resident of Winnipeg, Birdsell was one of the founding members of the Manitoba Writers' Guild, and served as its president. Her fiction has been translated into Italian, French, and Spanish. She won the Marian Engel Award for 'a woman writer in mid-career' as well as the Canadian Book Information Centre's 45 Below Award.

FLOWERS FOR WEDDINGS AND FUNERALS

My Omah supplies flowers for weddings and funerals. In winter, the flowers come from the greenhouse she keeps warm with a woodstove as long as she can; and then the potted begonias and asters are moved to the house and line the shelves in front of the large triple-pane window she had installed when Opah died so that she could carry on the tradition of flowers for weddings and for funerals. She has no telephone. Telephones are the devil's temptation to gossip and her God admonishes widows to beware of that exact thing.

And so I am the messenger. I bring requests to her, riding my bicycle along the dirt road to her cottage that stands water-marked beneath its whitewash because it so foolishly nestles too close to the Red River.

A dozen or two glads please, the note says. The bride has chosen coral for the colour of her wedding and Omah adds a few white ones because she says that white is important at a wedding. She does not charge for this service. It is unthinkable to her to ask for money to do this thing which she loves.

She has studied carefully the long rows of blossoms to find perfect ones with just the correct number of buds near the top, and laid them gently on newspaper. She straightens and absently brushes perspiration from her brow. She frowns at the plum tree in the corner of the garden where the flies hover in the heat waves. Their buzzing sounds and the thick humid air make me feel lazy. But she never seems to notice the heat, and works tirelessly.

'In Russia,' she says as she once more bends to her task, 'we made jam. Wild plum jam to put into fruit pockets and platz.' Her hands, brown and earth-stained, feel for the proper place to cut into the last gladiolus stalk.

She gathers the stalks into the crook of her arm, coral and white gladioli, large icy-looking petals that are beaded with tears. Babies' tears, she told me long ago. Each convex drop holds a perfectly shaped baby. The children of the world who cry out to be born are the dew of the earth.

For a long time afterward, I imagined I could hear the garden crying and when I told her this, she said it was true. All of creation cries and groans, you just cannot hear it. But God does.

Poor God. I squint at the sun because she has also said He is Light and I have grown accustomed to the thought that the sun is His eye. To have to face that every day. To have to look down and see a perpetually twisting, writhing, crying creation. The trees have arms uplifted, beseeching. Today I am not sure I can believe it, the way everything hangs limp and silent in the heat.

I follow her back to the house, thinking that perhaps tonight, after the wedding, there will be one less dewdrop in the morning.

'What now is a plum tree but a blessing to the red ants and flies only?' She mutters to herself and shakes dust from her feet before she enters the house. When she speaks her own language, her voice rises and falls like a butterfly on the wind as she smooths over the guttural sounds. Unlike my mother, who does not grow gladioli or speak the language of her youth freely, but with square, harsh sounds, Omah makes a sonatina.

While I wait for her to come from the house, I search the ground beneath the tree to try to find out what offends her so greatly. I can see red ants crawling over sticky, pink pulp, studying the dynamics of moving one rotting plum.

'In Russia, we ate gophers and some people ate babies.' I recall her words as I pedal back towards the town. The glads are in a pail of water inside my wire basket. Cool spikelets of flowers seemingly spread across my chest. Here I come. Here comes the bride, big, fat and wide. Where is the groom? Home washing diapers because the baby came too soon.

Laurence's version of that song reminds me that he is waiting for me at the river.

'Jesus Christ, wild plums, that's just what I need,' Laurence says and begins pacing up and down across the baked river bank. His feet lift clay tiles as he paces and I squat waiting, feeling the nylon filament between my fingers, waiting for something other than the river's current to tug there at the end of it.

I am intrigued by the patterns the sun has baked into the river bank. Octagonal shapes spread down to the willows. How this happens, I don't know. But it reminds me of a picture I have seen in Omah's Bible or geography book, something old and ancient like the tile floor in a pharaoh's garden. It is recreated here by the sun on the banks of the Red River.

'What do you need plums for?'

'Can't you see,' he says. 'Wild plums are perfect to make wine.'

I wonder at the tone of his voice when it is just the two of us fishing. He has told me two bobbers today instead of one and the depth of the stick must be screwed down into the muck just so. Only he can do it. And I never question as I would want to because I am grateful to him for the world he has opened up to me. If anyone should come and join us here, Laurence would silently gather his line in, wind it around the stick with precise movements that are meant to show his annoyance, but really are a cover for his sense of not belonging. He would move further down the bank or walk up the hill to the road and his bike. He would turn his back on me, the only friend he has.

I have loved you since grade three, my eyes keep telling him. You, with your lice crawling about your thickly matted hair. My father, being the town's barber, would know, Laurence. But I defied him and played with you anyway.

It is of no consequence to Laurence that daily our friendship drives wedges into my life. He stops pacing and stands in front of me, hands raised up like a preacher's hands.

'Wild plums make damned good wine. My old man has a recipe.'

I turn over a clay tile and watch an earthworm scramble to bury itself, so that my smile will not show and twist down inside him.

Laurence's father works up north cutting timber. He would know about wild plum wine. Laurence's mother cooks at the hotel because his father seldom sends money home. Laurence's brother is in the navy and has a tattoo on his arm. I envy Laurence for the way he can take his time rolling cigarettes, never having to worry about someone who might sneak up and look over his shoulder. I find it hard to understand his kind of freedom. He will have the space and time to make his wine at leisure.

'Come with me.' I give him my hand.

Omah bends over in the garden. Her only concession to the summer's heat has been to roll her nylon stockings to her ankles. They circle her legs in neat coils. Her instep is swollen, mottled blue with broken blood vessels. She gathers tomatoes in her apron.

Laurence hesitates. He stands away from us with his arms folded across his chest as though he were bracing himself against extreme cold.

'His mother could use the plums,' I tell Omah. Her eyes brighten and her tanned wrinkles spread outwards from her smile. She half-runs like a goose to her house with her apron bulging red fruit.

'See,' I say to Laurence, 'I told you she wouldn't mind.'

When Omah returns with pails for picking, Laurence's arms hang down by his sides.

'You tell your Mama,' she says to Laurence, 'that it takes one cup of sugar to one cup of juice for the jelly.' Her English is broken and she looks like any peasant standing in her bedroom slippers. She has hidden her beautiful white hair beneath a kerchief.

She's not what you think, I want to tell Laurence and erase that slight bit of derision from his mouth. Did you know that in their village they were once very wealthy? My grandfather was a teacher. Not just a teacher, but he could have been a professor here at a university.

But our heads are different. Laurence would not be impressed. He has never asked me about myself. We are friends on his territory only.

I beg Laurence silently not to swear in front of her. Her freckled hands pluck fruit joyfully.

'In the old country, we didn't waste fruit. Not like here where people let it fall to the ground and then go to the store and buy what they could have made for themselves. And much better too.'

Laurence has sniffed out my uneasiness. 'I like homemade jelly,' he says. 'My mother makes good crabapple jelly.'

She studies him with renewed interest. When we each have a pail full of the dust-covered fruit, she tops it with a cabbage and several of the largest unblemished tomatoes I have ever seen.

'Give my regards to your Mama,' she says, as though some bond has been established because this woman makes her own jelly.

We leave her standing at the edge of the road shielding her eyes against the setting sun. She waves and I am so proud that I want to tell Laurence about the apple that is named for her. She had experimented with crabapple trees for years and in recognition of her work, the experimental farm has given a new apple tree her name.

'What does she mean, give her regards?' Laurence asks and my intentions are lost in the explanation.

When we are well down the road and the pails begin to get heavy, we stop to rest. I sit beside the road and chew the tender end of a foxtail.

Laurence chooses the largest of the tomatoes carefully, and then, his arm a wide arc, he smashes it against a telephone pole.

I watch red juice dripping against the splintered grey wood. The sun is dying. It paints the water tower shades of gold. The killdeers call to each other as they pass as silhouettes above the road. The crickets in the ditch speak to me of Omah's greenhouse where they hide behind earthenware pots.

What does Laurence know of hauling pails of water from the river, bending and trailing moisture, row upon row? What does he know of coaxing seedlings to grow or babies crying from dewdrops beneath the eye of God?

I turn from him and walk with my face reflecting the fired sky and my dust-coated bare feet raising puffs of anger in the fine warm silt.

'Hey, where are you going?' Laurence calls to my retreating back. 'Wait a minute. What did I do?'

The fleeing birds fill the silence with their cries and the night breezes begin to swoop down onto our heads.

She sits across from me, Bible opened to the grey arborite, cleaning her wire-framed glasses with a tiny linen handkerchief that she has prettied with blue cross-stitch flowers. She places them back on her nose and continues to read while I dunk pastry in tea and suck noisily to keep from concentrating.

'And so,' she concludes, 'God called His people to be separated from the heathen.'

I can see children from the window, three of them, scooting down the hill to the river and I try not to think of Laurence. I haven't been with him since the day on the road, but I've seen him. He is not alone anymore. He has friends now, kids who are strange to me. They are the same ones who make me feel stupid about the way I run at recess so that I can be pitcher when we play scrub. I envy the easy way they can laugh at everything.

'Well, if it isn't Sparky,' he said, giving me a new name and I like it. Then he also gave me a showy kiss for them to see and laugh. I pushed against his chest and smelled something sticky like jam, but faintly sour at the same time. He was wearing a new jacket and had hammered silver studs into the back of it that spelled his name out across his shoulders. Gone is the mousey step of my Laurence.

Omah closes the book. The sun reflects off her glasses into my eyes. 'And so,' she says, 'it is very clear. When God calls us to be separate, we must respond. With adulthood comes a responsibility.'

There is so much blood and death in what she says that I feel as though I am choking. I can smell sulphur from smoking mountains and dust rising from feet that circle a golden calf.

With the teaching of these stories, changing from pleasant fairy tales of far away lands to this joyless search for meaning, her house has become a snare.

She pushes sugar cubes into my pocket. 'You are a fine child,' she says, 'to visit your Omah. God will reward you in heaven.'

The following Saturday, I walk a different way to her house, the way that brings me past the hotel, and I can see them as I pass by the window, pressed together all in one booth. They greet me as though they knew I would come. I squeeze in beside Laurence and listen with amazement to their fast-moving conversation. The jukebox swells with forbidden music. I can feel its beat in Laurence's thigh.

I laugh at things I don't understand and try not to think of my Omah who will have weak tea and sugar cookies set out on her white cloth. Her stained fingers will turn pages, contemplating what lesson to point out.

'I'm glad you're here,' Laurence says, his lips speaking the old way to me. When he joins the conversation that leaps and jumps without direction from one person to another, his voice is changed. But he has taken my hand in his and covered it beneath the table. He laughs and spreads his plum breath across my face.

I can see Omah bending in the garden cutting flowers for weddings and funerals. I can see her rising to search the way I take and she will not find me there.

ARNOLD ITWARU

(b. 1942)

'It is said that a person who adopts a country is simultaneously adopted by it. In Canada this is a mythology of rather high currency. But what does this mutual adoption entail?' This is the question with which Arnold Itwaru deals in his study *The Invention of Canada: Literary Text and the Immigrant Imaginary* (1990). 'The stranger categorized in the name and label "immigrant" is already invented as "immigrant",' Itwaru argues, a 'term of depersonalization which will brand her and him for the rest of their lives in the country of their adoption.' For Itwaru, born in Guyana and a resident of Toronto since 1969, '[e]thnic identity cannot exist in severance from . . . its members' history, their social memory, their fundamental historical consciousness.' *Shattered Songs* (1982), *Entombed Survivals* (1987), and *body rites (beyond the darkening)* (1991), all poetry collections, are certainly the product of a consciousness deeply rooted in this kind of social and cultural remembering.

Itwaru studied at York University, where he received an M.A. in literary and critical theory, and a Ph.D. in critical and cultural theory. His literary work has been widely anthologized, and his journalism and critical essays have been published in many magazines. He has worked as teacher, therapist, and as a university lecturer in sociology. His concern with the immigrant experience and the function of power systems informs his critical studies, including *Mass Communication and Mass Deception* (1989), as well as his first novel, *Shanti* (1990). Shanti, meaning peace in Hindi, is the novel's child protagonist whose life on a plantation in colonial Guyana, like the lives of her parents and those of the other despondent members of their community, is constantly victimized. The excerpt that follows presents the superindentent's male and imperialist power in all its brutality. Itwaru's most recent book, co-authored with Natasha Ksozek, is *Closed Entrances: Canadian Culture and Imperialism* (1994).

FROM *SHANTI*

Shanti had never known this pall of silence, this growing stone, this uncertainty in her. Her hands were fearful of the surfaces and objects here—the new dishes, the new sink, the new stove, the new refrigerator, the cold porcelain kitchen counter, the cold arborite kitchen table, the cold solarium floor, the mop, the plastic bucket, the woodless walls.

It was difficult for her to be enthused about this house, their very own as Latch, her husband, would remind her. It was for her an unaccustomed structure. It was called a house. She supposed it was a house, but it was unlike any house in which she had ever lived. Made of concrete instead of wood, attached like an extension to the rooms on the other side of the wall called another house, where strangers lived—she found this disconcerting. It was a place where, regardless that she did things unviolated by public view, she felt violated by the rejecting silence of strangers with whom she shared the same wall. She felt both walled in and walled out in this roof over carpeted floors, carpeted corridors, carpeted stairs, a building over a windowless hole in the ground called a basement. It was an address, a domicile, not home.

In here she walled herself in, needing to hide again, to be freed from the outside, to be invisible. For the first time she had begun to shut the door when she was in during the day. She had begun to lock herself in, to try to shut out an amorphous, lurking menace out there.

Keeping the door closed like this was something she had learned only since she came here. In the villages of her life doors were closed when no one was at home, when someone died, and at night. Wooden, open to the sun, the wind, the neighbours, friends, relatives—even the mosquitoes and sandflies when they were in season—life inside embraced life outside. But here, this side of her long flight from all she had known and loved and hated, here doors were always closed, always wall to wall of unfamiliarities, opaque glances, unknowing privacies on the other side of curtained windows, here where, unseen, she looked, locked in, away from the alien grass on the narrow green of her alien yard, her alien fence, the alien sidewalk, all engulfed in an alien silence.

There was another silence once, nights of dew on footpaths and windows heavy with jasmine and stars, nights when she could hear the village women singing before the occasion of certain Hindu weddings, the village women's plaintive unrehearsed labouring wail and chant within the thwacking clap and boom of ancient drums in the ancient darkness, that broken unmusical music which told of the loss of a paradisal idyll called India, a place Shanti had never known.

India was a name whose image was her enigmatic legacy. No one whom she had known had ever been to that magical place though they declared themselves Indian, followed customs said to be Indian, some even spoke snatches of Hindi punctured by broken English.

The singers did not know India. The people did not know India. Shanti did not know India. But this was of little consequence. Their ancestors were born in India. Civilizations and dim centuries had intervened since then, but they were nonetheless Indian. They held on to this, for in it there was at least some dignity.

But for Shanti, named after and within the OM, indivisible syllable of the self in tranquillity, the speech of peace, Shanti, peace, daughter of peace—there was shame. Shame wore her in the tattered dresses of her childhood—the two dresses, always the ones which were too torn and ragged to be worn to school, and thus became her 'house dress', one of which was worn while the other was drying on the line. These dresses made of her a painful and indecent display. The men would stare in open lust at her exposed thighs, her back, her buttocks, her belly, wherever the torn fabric of her tatters exposed her innocent and personal flesh. Not only was she ashamed of this: she was also ashamed of herself.

In her shame she was afraid to leave the thatched *cabbage-board* mud floor two-room shack that was her home, where the continuing illness of her father, an old consumptive bow-legged emaciated caricature of a man, was another source of pain for her. He moaned in agony nearly all night every night of her life. His limbs trembled when he walked, and sometimes he would stumble and fall, unable to make it to the latrine behind the starapple tree backyard. Shanti's mother would have to clean him and help him up, and it would hurt to see how humiliated he felt at these times.

This man, her mother would remind her, this man had worked all his life before he came to this. He was one of the best cane-cutters in the sugar estate. Yet, like the others, there was never enough to improve his condition. It was impossible for him to build a better life. He had given his youth, his manhood, his health to the sugar plantation, and now, in his illness, there was no money to pay the doctors or to purchase medicine. There was barely enough to eat, and had it not been for the meagre sale of vegetables and fruit which her mother was able to make at the roadside market, having rented a patch of land in the bush which she farmed, there would be no money even for this, and certainly none for clothing.

Shanti's mother's voice was a repressed wail, a choked lament, and upon exceptional occasions when, unbelievably, there was something to laugh about, she sounded as if she were sobbing, smitten by a brief hysteria.

Shanti did not dream of India. She wished she were invisible. It seemed the only way. It was easier to be alone, not looked at, not seen, hidden, Shanti did not dream of India.

In the eternal yesterday the village women's singing voices seemed to know and to not know this in their harmony and discord. Chaotic, contradictory, they merged nonetheless in shame and pain and hope in their long night of troubled joy.

'Shanti,' her mother would say, 'lemme tell you dis, me daughta. Yuh mus guh to school. You mus learn, me daughta. Learn. Dis nah life fi yuh. Dis nah life, me tell yuh.'

Shanti learned very quickly. She was driven by a fierce thirst for learning. With her school uniform neat and clean and well ironed, with no shameful rips or holes in it, she found school a precious world. She excelled. She was admired. Her teachers were certain she would go far and they paid special attention to her. She was going to get out of the shadow, the shame, the misery. She did not know how. But she was. Perhaps if she continued to pass all of her exams she might even be a school teacher. Teachers did not seem to suffer. They were not the poor.

But Shanti's pain was to be compounded. One afternoon when she returned home from school she found, to her alarm, Mr Booker, the yellow-haired blue-eyed heavy-browed big-nosed red-faced white overseer, standing on the earthen floor of the open gallery of her home. Her father sat, huddled in silence, staring unseeingly at a crack in the mud-daubed ground. He looked crushed. His legs trembled as though they had been severed. He coughed occasionally, unknowingly trying to smother it in the respected white man's presence. Her mother stood by the fireside, weeping silently.

'Hello, Shanti,' Mr Booker said, smiling below his huge nose, sweat trickling down his red face.

'Ma, what happened?'

Thunder rumbled in ominous menace in the collapsing distance.

Was the sugar estate threatening again to take away their land? They had lived here for over forty years, but from time to time the plantation manager would send them a letter, stating that the land, their land, was the plantation's, according to the plantation's survey, and should it be needed, they would be evicted.

Overseers did not visit with the local people. Overseers rode mules, horses, motor

bikes. They drove jeeps. They were aggressive, proud, indifferent, these minor func-
tionaries of the sugar empire. They ensured that the labourers worked without visible
unrest. To aid them, some of the 'locals' were employed as their agents, men who
knew each worker by name, whose supervision was thus considerably effective. The
plantation named these men 'drivers', in the unconscious remembrance of the empire
days of slavery and glory, when especially selected enslaved human beings were treated
slightly better than their fellows to lord the slavemaster's will over their own kind.
But no one said anything about this. These drivers were paid to protect the interests
of the plantation, often against their very neighbours. And, filled with the importance of their status, they lived proudly and distinctly apart from the folk of lesser
importance in the ranking and ordering of the empire. On remarkably exceptional
occasions an overseer would deign to visit, with some degree of imputed adventure,
one of these drivers at home.

But Shanti's father was never a driver. Her parents had long been removed from
the plantation's payroll. They were deemed too old to withstand the physical strain
and dangers of work in the sugar-cane fields. They would not be able to keep up with
the pace and output of the younger workers, and the plantation could not risk employ-
ing liabilities to cultivation, harvesting, production. In its economic wisdom it struck
Shanti's parents from the payroll. They were of no further use to the plantation. They
had to find subsistence elsewhere. It did not matter that there was no other source of
regular wages for them.

What did Mr Booker want? Why was he here? Why was Ma weeping? What happened to Pa?

The thunder rumbled.

Overseers were feared. They were disliked. And nearly everyone was afraid of the
overseer, Mr Booker. He was an impatient, fierce, arrogant man, a proud representative of Great Britain, that magnificent power, the British Empire which Shanti's
schooling spoke of in glowing terms.

Mr Booker once licked three cane-cutters who confronted him about not having
been paid for half a *punt* of sugar-cane which they had cut and loaded. Mr Booker
told them to go fuck their mothers and to keep their illiterate selves away from him.
Outraged, the men struck out at him, but he was quick, in excellent health, well
trained in the 'art' of self-defence, and when he was finished with them, one man had
a fractured rib, the other was bleeding from a broken nose, and the third lay buckled
up, vomiting on the red brick plantation road.

'Hello, Shanti,' Mr Booker said again. He stank of sweat and rum. He tried to
smile but his lips curled in a gross quiver.

And Shanti heard it then: the ominous roar which preceded the blackening sky, the
hot burning air. The strong sick sweet smell of acre upon acre of burning cane leaves,
the fields of leaping flame, had always horrified her. Over the seasons several of the
thatch-roofed houses in the village had been burnt to the ground, their dried cane-leaf
roofs ignited in the chaotic velocity of thunderous tongues of fire. Once a woman's
skirt was thus set ablaze and she was burnt to death. And this rage of fire rampaged in
the horror of Shanti's dreams in which she ran, kicking, screaming, engulfed, burning.

These cane fires always took her in their overwhelming suddenness.

'No money, me daughta, no mo money,' she heard her mother's lament and wail in the fire's rage in her father's feeble silence in the gargantuan overseer's menacing presence.

Mr Booker stretched out his thick, muscular arm. The sun had turned red.

Shanti did not know what to do. The thought of running came to her like an inner betrayal. She could not move. She could not lift her feet off the ground which was her home.

'No mo money,' her mother sobbed, her eyes fixed in the distant presence of the raging fire.

Shanti stiffened at the touch of Mr Booker's hand on her hair. She tried to push him off but her tearful resistance was of no use. His powerful hands drove up her skirt, her panties, her tender personal flesh, pinned her on the ground in colonising force and violation as the fire devoured her screams and horror. The earthen floor, the smoky eaves, her mother's wail, her father's urgent spasmodic coughing, drowned in blood in the battery and assault of Mr Booker's conquering empire lust. The skeletal figure of her father rose once and collapsed, and the smell of shit, stronger than the overseer's foul breath, filled the rage of the plantation night of her pain and darkness as she wept, vomited, wept, a wretched bundle of human nothingness on the earthen floor of the open gallery of that shack.

'O me daughta,' her mother wailed across the tides of horror. 'Me only daughta, me only chile, me flesh, me blood.' She tried to touch her child, but Shanti recoiled from her and squirmed away in a weeping foetal retreat.

'My daughter,' her mother had told her, 'your father is dying and I am too weak to earn anything anymore. We do not have any money left. All this work, this lifetime of work, and nothing to show for it, my child. No more health, no more money for food, nothing in this godforsaken world. Nothing, I tell you, nothing, nothing.'

*

Shanti's mother had always been afraid of the managers and overseers. They did not speak to people like her and she did not know how to speak to them. Her bits and pieces of broken English would founder in her throat, her speech reduced to splutters and bleats when she tried. She would become dizzy, her tongue twisting in unaccustomed, stupid ways. She was ashamed, and she was angry for being so inferior. But despite all this, there were certain things she did understand. Their gunfire accents were not completely beyond her. But how could she talk to them? She was a 'local', a 'creole', a work-soiled labourer babbling in a language *they* called a dialect.

She had waited in the shadow under the red brilliance of a giant immortelle in full bloom near the pay office one Saturday morning, and when Mr Connel, the plantation manager, drove up in his jeep she rushed toward him.

'Manja, Sah, Mista Connel, *Sahib*, me gat fi talk wid yuh, Sah! Please, Sah,' she pleaded. She did not want to offend. She was here to beg his mercy.

Mr Connel was unprepared for this intrusion in his path of power. No local was allowed to speak to him directly. If this woman had any concerns she should have talked to her driver. If he could not deal with it he would have taken it to his overseer.

The sun shuddered.

'Manja, Sah!' the woman insisted.

Connel brushed her aside and walked on but she held his arm. 'Please, Manja, Sah, mi gat fi talk wid yuh. Yuh *gat* fi lissen.'

Connel jerked his arm away from her, and she staggered with the vehemence of his gesture and threat, but she did not go away. He was the manager of this plantation. She and her husband had worked under his and other managers' regimes. She knew he was the supreme authority. He had to listen to her or all was lost.

'Mista Connel!'

Her plaintive voice grew louder. Its sharpness startled Connel. She was drawing attention to him. She was creating a scene. This could stir the other ignorant bastards, he thought in panic. They could mob him. These people were trouble. They were too stupid to follow simple rules. They did not know the meaning of order. She should have taken her case to her driver. That was what drivers were for. The driver would, according to the established rule, decide whether it was important enough to let one of the overseers deal with it. In exceptional circumstances the overseer would take concerns he could not handle to the manager. Connel was angry. Incompetence always bothered him, but impudence galled him. He was not here to listen to the petty complaints of the locals. He was here to administer the plantation. *Who was this woman?* What was her diatribe about?

Connel was rather uncomfortable whenever he was even physically close to one of these natives. He was the great personage of the plantation, but there was a fear which nibbled at him at these times. They made him feel unclean, irritable, angry. It was best to avoid them. He could not understand most of the nonsense their creole vernacular was all about. He had more important things to do than to try to learn more of it. He brushed the audacious woman aside and hurried to the pay office building.

But the little tar-black trembling emaciated creature followed him. 'Please, Sah, Manja Mista Connel Sahib, yuh gat to lissen to me. Me gat fi talk wid yuh, Sah, Manja, please!'

She was shouting. These bloody loud-mouthed coolies. This could easily start a riot. These bastards are always itching for a riot. They love to make trouble. These bloody ungrateful natives. So fucking stupid! You can never be sure about them. They could rush him. Some of them had their cutlasses, and he knew how razor sharp they were. These sweaty filthy coolie bastards! He had thought of making it a precondition to being paid that they washed and left their working tools at home before they came for their wages on Saturdays. Perhaps he should act on it. It would be safer.

'Please, Sah! Please, Sah! Manja Mista Connel!'

The little woman was becoming hysterical. This would not do. Connel hurried to the door, but with an agility which startled him the woman insinuated herself between him and the half-opened door. She was trembling like a leaf. She was weeping. But she would not leave. In all his days here no labourer had dared to demand his attention like this. What could she want?

Already there was unrest in the yard. The talk, the jabbering, as Connel called it, was growing louder. Cutlasses arched glittering forebodingly in the sun. Some of the men were gesticulating towards the door. Perhaps, Connel conceded, he should hear her out, but just to be safe he rang the police station. He could always rely on those taciturn niggers to enforce the law with the brutal efficiency required to teach these coolies a lesson.

'Baboolall!'

Connel liked this coolie book-keeper whose efficiency outstripped that of many of his highly paid English accountants. Baboolall, dressed in stiffly starched and ironed khakis, similar to an overseer's but considerably cleaner, a proud Indo-Guyanese, came into the room with such promptness and dispatch he seemed to be reporting for military duty. Connel was pleased. He should, one of these days, order a raise for Baboolall.

'What is this woman pestering me about, Baboolall?'

Baboolall was immediately angry with the woman. These were his people, these no-goods, they were a constant source of embarrassment for him. He knew her. She was no longer on the pay-list. She had no right to be here. And just look at her, dressed like a beggar crying like an old fool in front of Mr Connel, the manager of all persons! Was she out of her mind?

'Woman, get out of here!' Baboolall barked at her. 'Go home! The manager is a busy man. Stop this nonsense and go home!'

But the woman ignored him. She knew him. She expected him to behave like that. What could you expect from dogs?

'Manja, Sah, me an me husban wuk all we life in de sugar estate. Massa Manja, awee nuh gat money fi food, fi clothes, fi sickness, fi nutting! All me ask you, Sah, me *beg* you, Sah, awee gat to get dat penchan, give we de penchan or awee guh stahve to death! Please, Manja Mista Connel Sahib!'

'What is she saying, Baboolall?' Connel was sweating. He wanted her out. She was a misguided old fool. She was trouble.

Baboolall translated with an iron face.

'She is saying, Sir, that she and her husband worked for all their life on the estate and they now have no food or money for clothing and medicine, and she wants a pension. She feels she should be paid a pension by the estate, Sir.'

There was much more to what the woman had said, but for Connel it was enough. His face reddened. He gritted his teeth. He fought with the sudden urge he had to hit her. He hated the wizened face, the toothless mouth, the parched black lips.

'My dear woman,' Connel announced, enraged. 'It is not my fault that you and your husband have been stupid enough to fritter your money away.' He towered over her. He was in charge here. He was the manager. 'I am not running an alms-house. It is not the policy to give labourers who are no longer with us a pension. Why, it's preposterous! And now I would like you to leave. *Get out, woman. Get out!*'

'But Manja, Sah—' she began and faltered.

'Go on!' Baboolall barked. 'You heard what the manager said. Get out!'

A heavy hand grasped her shoulder from the back.

'Come wid me, Shanti *Mai.*'

It was Sergeant Detective Felix Reid, the policeman whose brutality towards the East Indians was matched by his hatred of them, and was common knowledge in the entire district. Sergeant Detective Felix Reid himself had answered Connel's call. In fact none of his officers dared answer the only telephone which the precinct had when he was there. Reid was a massive Afro-Guyanese who ruled the men under him, all of whom were fellow black policemen, with uncompromising authority. Behind his back they referred to him as 'Bully Reid', and 'Stink Reid'. Reid's sweat was as offensive as the scowl on his clean-shaven fat black face. He embodied force, order, power. It was the only way to have respect as far as he was concerned. No one 'played de ass wid him' and got away with it.

Reid was the law in the district. And god help anyone, Indian or black, who crossed him. He worshipped the white men. It was always an honour for him to be of service to them. They were the possessors of civilization. They knew how to do things. They got things done. They invented the law. They were no nigger-yard good-for-nothings nor were they backward dhall-an-rice miserly coolies who had nothing to boast about who yet thought themselves better than the black man. They were the agents of the British Empire, the Queen whose loyal subject he also was.

Sergeant Detective Felix Reid yanked the frail woman out of the doorway. He was not afraid of the shit-ass coolie bastards with cutlasses out there. He had ten armed men with him. He had called for reinforcements from the town. He was prepared. One move and he would slam their backsides in jail so quickly they wouldn't know what had hit them.

'What kinda kiss-me-ass behaviour yuh getting on wid, woman? You got no shame? Yuh makin yuhself such a nuisance to de manager! Like yuh really want to bring shame pon yuh lovely daughta, Shanti or wah? Ah tell yuh, people like you don't gat no pride, yuh know. Is jail yuh askin for and dat is right where Ah takin yuh to. Get in dat blasted jeep!'

It was at this point that Mr Booker, the overseer intervened. 'That won't be necessary, Sergeant,' he said. 'I'll talk to her. Your prompt response is appreciated, however. Thank you.'

Sergeant Detective Felix Reid clicked his heels. He was disappointed, but he did not let it show. Besides, the manager and the overseers knew he was reliable. But he wished he had had the opportunity to teach this trouble-making coolie woman a lesson.

'I've seen your daughter,' Booker said to the distraught woman. 'Quite an eyeful, to say the least. Yes, indeed. Shanti, I think is her name, isn't it?'

*

When Shanti's father collapsed he lost control of his bowels. He stopped talking. He refused to look at anyone. He stopped eating. He died a week later. Her mother deteriorated so rapidly that she was barely able to leave her bed to stagger to the latrine. But there was some money. Mr Booker had left fifty dollars for his victorious feat.

Shanti took her mother to the doctor ten miles away in the town. Dr Lall, the son of a wealthy Indo-Guyanese ricemill owner, was known as a good doctor. He had

had his medical training in England. He returned to live in a ten-room colonial mansion with an exaggeratedly rouged ugly unfriendly Englishwoman as his wife. Dr Lall had developed a peculiar accent, something somewhere between a bad imitation of the English and colonial Guyana. He had a soft voice which sounded as if he were on the verge of spluttering. He wore a white lab coat over his immaculately tailored striped suit and sober, tightly drawn neck tie, despite the heat. He charged Shanti ten dollars for his services but was afraid he could find no disease to treat. There was nothing he could do, he said. Her mother was exhausted. She needed a long rest.

Mr Kissoon, the village shopkeeper, refused Shanti any more credit. He told her he knew things were hard for her, but he had a business to run, and she should understand that money was needed to do this. She must find a way to pay him. Things were getting more expensive every day. She offered to wash his family's clothes, to clean their floors, to do some work to recompense for the debt, but Kissoon was sorry he could not oblige. He already had hired help. He was not a millionaire. She should understand.

There was death in the dark bedroom of Shanti's travail. Death had not departed at her father's funeral. Death haunted the silences here, the brooding morning, the foreboding night. What could she do? To whom could she turn? The neighbours kept their distance in their separate dwellings, bush patches and mud paths away. They felt death there, and they avoided Shanti and the house, as if to exorcise themselves of this unwanted presence, to postpone, despite their hardships, that final meeting.

Lloyd T. Booker downed his flask of gin, smacked his lips, belched, farted, swayed in his elevated position on his mule from where he felt he was the monarch of all he surveyed. This was his domain of power. He was overseer and lord here. His word was law. He dismounted, swayed, wiped sweat off his crimson forehead, and eyed the firm smoothness of the backs of the weeding gang women's dark brown thighs. Bent forward, their backsides in the air, their hands clearing the tall grass, thistles, thorns, wild shrubs with practised certainty, they seemed to Booker little more than self-conscious beasts, not worth a second look, except for certain strong, proud-bodied younger ones whom he found pressingly arousing.

Animals, Booker surmised, vigorous, fuckable female animals at his disposal and pleasure. The wind in a burst of cane-juice odour, molasses, burnt earth, sweat, urine, whipped up one of their discoloured tatters, revealing for a vertiginous moment her naked flesh. And Booker decided.

He followed the young woman into the canes when she went to urinate unseen by the others. He pounced, his superior strength quickly overpowering her, pinning her under, smothering her shock, her rage, her sobs, her humiliation as he raped her in his empire urgency.

'What's your name?'

'Gladys,' she wept.

'Gladys *what?*'

'Gladys, Sah,' she corrected, covering her face in shame.

Booker stood tall and proud and manly. He was irritated by this whimpering, sweaty, bundled up, hairy Indian bitch. He held back the urge to kick her. 'You married, Gladys?'

'No, Sah.'

'Good!'

The pleasure of power charged through him.

'Stop whimpering, you fuckable bitch! You won't die. It'll do you good to have a white man. You should be happy!'

He noticed with growing curiosity the vulnerable deep pink through which his rejected discharge was seeping out. Goodness, he thought, these Indian bitches have pink cunts too! And he attacked Gladys again.

DAPHNE MARLATT

(b. 1942)

From *Frames of a Story* (1968), her first publication, to her novel, *Taken* (1996), Daphne Marlatt's work deals with the representation of otherness and with the desire to question, and write over, formal and social boundaries. Difference—in her own words, 'a high-intensity beam'—characterizes both her treatment of language and her subject matter.

Her continuous engagement with various aspects of displacement can be traced to her cultural background. Born in Melbourne, Australia, to British parents, she lived in Penang, Malaysia, until her family emigrated to Vancouver in 1951. She often writes out of the 'common wealth of memories' of her childhood years. 'In the Month of Hungry Ghosts' (1979), a text comprised of letters, poems, and diary entries, records her first visit back to Malaysia. As a Canadian now, but also through memory that 'seems to operate . . . like a murmur in the flesh one suddenly hears years later', Marlatt responds to the complex impact of colonialism on class, race, and gender differences.

Marlatt studied English and creative writing at the University of British Columbia (B.A. 1964), where she was a contributing editor to *Tish* (1963-65). Her attention to language as a living thing, as what constructs the world, can be traced back to those days, as well as to the influence of the Black Mountain poets. She studied comparative literature at the University of Indiana (M.A. 1968). She returned to Vancouver in 1970, where, as an oral historian, she edited *Steveston Recollected: Japanese-Canadian History* (1975), and co-edited *Opening Doors: Vancouver's East End* (1979). As an active editor she co-founded and co-edited *Periodics* (a magazine of innovative prose) and *Tessera* (a bilingual journal of feminist theory). She was the Programme Coordinator for the 'Women and Words/Les femmes et les mots' conference held at the University of British Columbia in 1983, and the Ruth Wynn Woodward Professor in the Women's Studies Program at Simon Fraser University (1988-89).

Her early poetry books, including *leaf leaf/s* (1969), *Rings* (1971), and *Vancouver Poems* (1972), demonstrate her attentiveness to images and speech patterns as the means of registering the pulse of a place. They point the way to her much anthologized long poem, *Steveston* (1974). In a more recent text that includes poetry and a novella, *Salvage* (1991), Marlatt revisits that same territory and works through her earlier 'blocked' perceptions in the light of her feminist consciousness.

Zocalo (1977), a prose narrative set in Mexico that is often seen by critics as a novel, announces Marlatt's ongoing interest in autobiography. As she says, 'remembering is a fiction . . . we have this funny thing . . . remembering is real, and inventing is not—inventing is purely imaginary or fictional. What interests me is where those two cross.' More apparently autobiographical is *What Matters: Writing 1968-1970* (1980), which shows Marlatt's continuous attempt to understand the relationship between body and language. Exploration of her mothering experience and the act of writing reappears in *How Hug a Stone* (1983), a prose text of poems and journal entries recording her visit, with her son Kit, to England in an attempt to trace her mother's origins.

Her concern with the construction of motherhood—'the mother's so strong,' she says, 'and we all have this in common'—is the driving force in the novel *Ana Historic* (1988): 'a woman's version of history, that being a difficult area for women because they don't inhabit history in the same way that men do.' Women's desire has already been dealt with by Marlatt in many of her other works, including her prose poetry volume *Touch to My Tongue* (1984), a representation of lesbian eroticism, and *Double Negative* (1988), a poetic collaboration with Betsy Warland. 'Woman's body,' as Marlatt says, 'is never present in its own desire, so if you start writing about it, you have to combat a kind of fear that you feel because you know you're breaking a taboo.'

Influenced by some of the feminist writers of Quebec, Marlatt has collaborated with Nicole Brossard in *Mauve* (1985) and *charac-ter / jeu de lettres* (1986). One of the editors of *Telling It: Women and Language Across Cultures* (1990), Marlatt is interested in 'the ways in which we are connected to other forms of life, to other races, other classes' in order to 'work against the domination of one over all the others.' Her most recent publication is *Two Women in a Birth* (1994), which collects her poetic collaborations with Betsy Warland. Marlatt lives in Victoria, British Columbia.

FROM *MONTH OF HUNGRY GHOSTS*

22nd July
Penang 11:30 PM
A cheecha running along the ceiling above makes a funny chirping noise—light brown almost pink legs, one beady eye upon me writing at this glasstopped desk. Waves of cricket & treefrog sounds continuously breaking outside around the house. Barking dogs in the distance. Hot. Dark.

Once out on the road by myself, walking down it—vague memories of walking down it as a child, knew where the golf course was where we used to pick mushrooms in the early morning—once out in that humming dark, the trees—one I did seem to know, spreading its great umbrella arms (sam-cha? the same?) writhing in the light (streetlamp), it's the *vivid*ness of everything here—I was afraid, had to force myself to walk—afraid of this life & what the night hides, bats? cobras? At the last house on the road (such huge gardens around each mansion) a tall frangipani tree dropping white blossoms on the grass (which isn't grass but a kind of low growing broadleafed plant). I came back to find Mr Y in his pyjamas & Dad outside looking for me. Locking up. Then a to-do about locking the ironwork gate in the upper hall that separates the bedrooms from the rest of the house ('we've had a spot of trouble') . . .

Mr Y moves like water in a conversation, either rushing forward with endless talk of company affairs or receding into not hearing much else. A habit of not directly answering questions, the servants do that too. Very kind. The old world courtesy, the constant talking about a thing to be done while doing it, the concern over little things like leaving a door open or closed—Yeat's lapis lazuli old man with a touch of the absurd. His passion is business, he's full of gossip about all the people whose lives have been involved with the company to any extent—& all the internal dissensions, inner politics—absorbing, the game business is, played with utter seriousness. He hints at many things yet overstates, 'it was cruel' etc., which makes for a curious style of conversation.

Eng Kim: recognized her as soon as I saw her, but curiously didn't want to show my recognition immediately. She's hardly changed at all—so amazingly similar in appearance after 25 years. Still that almost shy, perfectly naïve sweetness—how can she have lived these years so apparently untouched? She's 'worked for the bank' (i.e. looked after the bank manager & family) most of the time. The perfect servant, neat & unassuming, quiet as a shadow—yet I catch a glint of humour in her smile. Will it be possible to know her better? It's so strange to be, now 25 years later, someone she serves, instead of the child she chivvied along.

O the disparities—how can I ever relate the two parts of myself? This life would have killed me—purdah, a woman in—the restrictions on movement, the confined reality. I can't stand it. I feel imprisoned in my class—my? This is what I came out of. & how else can I be here?

July 28th

Dear Cille,

. . . It's not so much a holiday as a curious psychic re-dipping in the old font, & most of the time I'm kicking against it. Because it's so insidious, the English habits of speech & perception, English patterns of behaviour. (Suppose I got the longest conditioning anyhow, of the 3 of us kids.) But what's amazing is that it still exists, much as it has done, tho obviously it's the end of an era. It ain't *my* era, or Pam's, tho everyone we meet seems to want to suggest it is, implicate us in it. I've never before understood what a big move it was for them, to come to Canada.

Sometimes I panic—I want to rush home, as if I might get trapped here, this honeyed land. Mrs J. Saying how she didn't want to leave Penang, 'it's such a beautiful place.' It is, & yet it all feels unreal to me—there's no authentic ground here for 'Europeans'. I want to rip out of myself all the colonialisms, the taint of colonial sets of mind. That's why as kids we hated everything 'English'—not because it was English but because we equated what was English with a colonialist attitude, that defensive set against what immediately surrounds as real on its own terms—because to take it on as real would mean to 'go native' & that was unthinkable to them.

July 29th

Dad speculates, as we peer over the bridge into the rushing darkness of the brook, cicadas trilling all around us, that in some previous life he must have been a rich Chinese in Malacca with a fleet of junks trading spices to China. Says he always feels at home here, loves the smell of camphorwood chests, the songs of birds, the plants. I ask him has he never felt alien, never felt there were places he couldn't enter, wasn't welcome in? He says only recently, with the political situation the way it is, but that before, the only animosity he remembers encountering was in the Indian temple where he filmed the Typoosum rites & he could understand that. That leads to the further comment that he's never liked Indian temples anyhow.

What we make our own—or separate from us. The interests of the Chinese middle class here as commercial as the British, & the same sense of formality, & pragmatism.

Earlier, as we rode a trisha down to the Chartered Bank Chambers, Pam wondered how people on the street regard white women (she herself thinks English women look 'dumpy') & whether they found us sexual or not, commented on the looks various people gave us as we passed. We both felt separate & visible in our hired trisha pedalled by someone else (an incredibly skinny man)—uncomfortable parodies of the leisured class. Is this the only way to be a white woman here? Or is this the condition of being a member of an exploitive & foreign moneyed class?

& yet the sun shines on all of us alike—everywhere the flare of colour, glint of metallic thread running thru a sari, shining flesh, oil gleaming off black hair—we feel pale by comparison, & immaterial (living always in our heads?) It's the same feeling I had coming home from Mexico, that people walk the streets of Vancouver mostly as if they are invisible. Here people sleep on the sidewalks, piss in the gutters, women nurse their babies by the roadside, everyone selling food & eating it, or fingering goods, or eyeing each other (likewise tactile)—but not separate. The press in the streets is almost amniotic, it contains & carries everyone.

Today I've heard both an Indian (the cloth salesman in the market whose son is training to be a doctor in England) & a Chinese (Catholic convert, committed to both Christianity & the English language, living in a nation devoted to advancing Islam & teaching Malay) protest against the unfairness of the Malayanization policy of the govt (e.g. how 65% of all university entrants must be Malays, the other races compete for what's left). & yet this *is* Malaysia & the largely rural & labouring Malays have a lot to catch up on, fast. I can't believe the stereotype passed on to us that they're 'lazy', don't want to work, don't have a head for business, etc. & yet how long, how many generations these Chinese & Indian families have lived here, feel they belong, & then are separated off on the basis of race. All the separations.

Penang

July 23/76

Love,

Frangipani fading on the desk, Eng Kim just ran by in bare feet, so quiet in pajamas, it's 6 p.m., post-tea, post evening rain like a monsoon, mosquitoes out in the fading light (dark here by 7) & what i've tracked in the birdbook as the black-naped oriole (a yellow as brilliant as the saffron robes of the yellow men monks) trilling from the trees, flame of the forest just outside my window . . .

(dusky pink cheecha playing peekaboo behind a gilt frame, me not at all sure i want to feel those pale pink lizard feet suddenly land here, just shot up the wall to nab a midge then leap six inches onto a post & disappear to a ledge four feet above me) so much life here not even the walls are still . . .

It's strange being a princess again, the sheer luxury of this house, its spaciousness, its accoutrements (every bedroom has its own bathroom), everything kept spacious, uncluttered, unlittered & clean by servants who pick up after you, wash your clothes, cook your food, do your dishes, ad nauseum (a little work would make me feel at home). & Eng Kim herself, oh Roy that is the strangest. I recognized her as soon as she came down the steps to greet us (old baronial family style), she's hardly changed in 25 years, still climbs the stairs with all that girlish quickness & like any good servant, utterly silent. But more her smile—it's as if i'd never gone away i know that smile so completely & love it, yes it's the love that astonishes me. That face told me as much as my mother's, by its changing weather, how the world was with me, or against, what i, as any rebellious child, was up against. I must have spent hours of accumulated moments watching it. & yet her face is not maternal in any way, at age 45 or whatever it's still utterly girlish & in our smiles i catch a little of the old mischief we shared, playing our own peekaboo with all the rules.

& my god, the rules of the house & how it's been explained to Pam & me several times that we mustn't 'upset the routine', how difficult it is to finally 'get things done the way you want them' (breakfast at such & such an hour, for instance, & how the toast or coffee should be etc.),—how 'they' get confused if you alter things, so that the routine becomes itself a prison. As the women of the house, Pam & I are supposed to 'look after things', give the orders, make sure the system functions smoothly. Both of us dislike the role & like children, rebel by acting dumb. What we want is to break down the wall that separates us from Eng Kim in the very fact of our roles & yet we haven't quite figured out how.

Except that tonight we began by earlier expressing an interest in the terrible durian fruit whose stench has been much mythified since we were little (& the old durian tree in the garden where our dog was buried is gone, cut down). One of the Chinese men in the office said he'd be happy to bring some durians round for us to try tonight & kindly did so. Mr Y., when told, requested that they not be brought into the house (haven't i learned the dialect well?) so our benefactor & Pam & I regaled ourselves at an old wooden table on the walkway from kitchen to servants quarters, as he chopped them open with a cleaver (they look like wooden pineapple bombs) & split the meat to reveal the butterycovered seeds: an incredible flavour, not fruitlike, something like coffee & bitter spices compounded with onions, really strong. Eng Kim & Ah Yow (the cook) love them & when we brought Dad down to try some a little while later, they were perched on the table happily eating away & watched with amusement Dad's valiant but obviously ginger chewing & swallowing—Eng Kim's amusement in her eyes tho she'd never speak it to 'the tuan'.

I'm going to stop this, being haunted by echoes of earlier (age 12 etc) letters & journals, that so stilted proper English. 'To the manner born.' How completely i learned to talk Canadian (how badly i wanted to). & how fast it drops away here. Wonder how it sounds to you?

July 25th

Sunday & the frangipani blossoms on the desk have gone all brown. Hot today, hottest yet, tho it clouded over as usual (haven't seen a sunset, been mostly cool for here, & cloudy—waterfalls of rain the other morning, woke up to its wet descent all round the open verandahs of the house, the open windows—no glass on some, for breeze).

We drove up to Ayer Itam, the Buddhist hill shrine—driving is such a trip. I love winding thru throngs of brilliant sarong & sari dressed women, children, sellers of ramibitans & chinese noodles, cyclists of all sorts, young chinese youths zooming by on Honda bikes, cars trucks hundreds of buses all dodging the cyclists & the goats.

Went up to the reservoir above the temple & walked a path thru jungle, o the smell came back so vivid, that deep sandloam fern palm dank smell. Everybody drives on the left here so the whole car is reversed, i keep reaching for an invisible gear shift & frightening Dad & Pam by turning into oncoming traffic. But i think i'm the only one who enjoys driving. Unfortunately it's a fancy Ford Cortina the company owns so i can't just take off in it whenever i want to.

My (hardwon) independence as a Western woman is being eroded every day & of course i'm seduced by my senses into just giving in—to the heat as much as to everything else. Finally let myself have an afternoon nap today, but the swimming—every afternoon the sea takes me in, old mother sea, sand dusky (no clarity like the Caribbean), & warm.

Mostly it's a struggle, an old old resistance against the colonial empire of the mind. For all the years that Mr Y's been here he knows almost nothing about what surrounds him, what the trees or birds are, what the fruits are—he doesn't like native food, exists on a kind of dilute European diet that includes lots of canned food. Private hedges of the mind as complete as the locked & bolted doors, the iron schedule of the house. Living in armed defensiveness against even the earth (don't go barefoot, nevah, nevah, for fear of hookworm etc.) I remember it all from my childhood, the same. Everything tells me this is not where i belong (including the odd intense look from Malays, boomiputras, 'sons of the soil'): the tourist experience compounded with colonial history. Europeans don't live here: they camp out in a kind of defensive splendour that's corrosive to the soul.

Aug 1st

Amah, age 74, in her sarong & shirtwaist, light gauze scarf hung round her neck, hair grey underneath the black, Amah, with her deep voice, expressive ways, 'yah yah', enthusiastic confirmation when Pam turned into the right road, driving her home— home to the house she works in, still housekeeping. 'Daphne mari, Pamela mari,' exclaiming over & over on the fact that we'd come. A lovely resilience, living in the present, genuine affection for the 'tuan', being herself a complete person with physical grace, even at 74, & dignity, not heavily insistent on it, only sufficient to herself. Her grace has to do with accepting what life brings & marvelling at it, laughing much, a deepthroated chuckle, & laying claim to nothing.

Buddhism says it is want that chains us to the world, us 'hungry ghosts'. & I see (just as I stands for the dominant ego in the world when you is not capitalized), that i want too much, just as, a child, i wanted affection. Growing sense of myself as a Westerner wanting, wanting—experience mostly. Anxiety arises from the discrepancy between my wants & my actual condition. Why plans so chain me—wanting too much from the day, wanting too much from others who can never be more than they are. In want: in fear. The 'liberated' woman in me insisting on her freedom & in terror of its being taken away. Passive resistance a better stance. Say 'yes' to restraints & simply do what you need to: act in silence.

ROY MIKI

(b. 1942)

'As a Japanese-Canadian school kid growing up in the 1950s, I can remember wondering about the absence of writers who told stories that mirrored my community's turbulent history in BC. The literature studied was always from "over there" in England and Europe. One exception was the prairie poem of the Depression years, Ann Marriott's "The Wind Our Enemy". Though it was supposed to be a representation of "our" local place, for me all the tension focussed on one line: "Japs Bomb China". Sure enough, on the day the class read it out loud, my turn came at that line, and I had no choice but to speak the word that was anathema in my home. I'm sure the other students weren't aware of my anguish—many simply chuckled at the match between the word and the "me" speaking.'

A sansei (third-generation) Japanese-Canadian, the child of parents forced to evacuate their home in Haney, British Columbia, Roy Miki was born in Winnipeg only months after his family relocated there in 1942. His experiences as a child and the racist policies that affected the entire Japanese-Canadian community in the 1940s have had a lasting effect on him. From the late 1960s to the present, Miki has undertaken personal and academic research into the uprooting and internment of Japanese-Canadians. In the 1980s he rose to prominence as a leader and spokesperson for the Japanese-Canadian redress movement. A community leader, researcher, strategist and negotiator, and writer, Miki worked both locally, for the Greater Vancouver Japanese Canadian Citizens Association, and nationally, for the National Association of Japanese Canadians (NAJC). As a member of the NAJC Strategy Committee, he was one of the Japanese-Canadians who negotiated the historic redress settlement with the Canadian government in September of 1988. *Justice in Our Time: The Japanese Canadian Redress Settlement* (1991), which Miki co-authored with Cassandra Kobayashi, documents that process. In recognition of his work, Miki received the Dr William Black Award from the Vancouver Multicultural Society (1985), The President's Award for outstanding contribution to Simon Fraser University and Canadian society (1989), and the Renata

Shearer Human Rights Award from the United Nations Association and the BC Human Rights Coalition (1990).

Miki's reputation does not rest on his political activities alone. Since moving to Vancouver in 1967, where he received his M.A. (English) at Simon Fraser University and his Ph.D. from the University of British Columbia (1980), he has been an active editor, poet, and critic. He is the founder and editor of the literary journal *Line*, recently renamed *West Coast Line*. As a poet, he has published three collections of poetry: *Saving Face: Poems Selected 1976-1988* (1991), *Market Rinse* (1993), and *Random Access File* (1995). His critical studies include *Tracing the Paths: Reading & Writing The Martyrology* (by bp Nichol) (1987), and *A Record of Writing: An Annotated and Illustrated Bibliography of George Bowering* (1990), which won the Gabrielle Roy Prize for Canadian Criticism (1991).

As the Chair of the Racial Minority Writers' Committee of the Writers' Union of Canada, Miki co-ordinated 'Writing Thru Race: A Conference for First Nations Writers and Writers of Colour' (Vancouver, 30 June-3 July 1994). The first conference of its kind in Canada, 'Writing Thru Race' was designed 'to provide a safe space for writers to talk about the impact of racism on their lives'. A month before the conference took place, under pressure from a Reform Party member of parliament who 'had attacked the conference as "racist"' because it was intended only for First Nations writers and writers of colour, the Department of Canadian Heritage decided to withdraw its promised financial support. This led to a nation-wide media controversy. Many individual artists and artist-run organizations as well as cultural and labour organizations 'rallied to save the conference'. 'Writing Thru Race' ended up being a resounding success. As Miki says, in his 1994 article 'From Exclusion to Inclusion', an account and analysis of the events that surrounded the conference, 'Writing Thru Race' created a forum where 180 First Nations writers and writers of colour came together 'to share histories, cultural contexts, issues and strategies, to build networks and coalitions, and to find ways of making contact to intervent the otherwise in/visible lines of "race" that separate and isolate.'

A resident of Vancouver, and a professor of Canadian and American literature in the Department of English, Simon Fraser University, Miki is currently working on an in-depth, documentary study of the Japanese-Canadian redress movement that blends archival sources, interviews, and commentary. He continues to write poetry.

THE RESCUE

                    bleed on

            the me

        of it all

feigned sites

        of nomenclature
derived in stride

uneven handfuls
of sounds drift by

            hold it now
        what's the scathing
in the dawn snow?

dine on burnt syllables
interrogate the blithe
seams of grammatique

so blame it   on the weather
the easterly   casting of doubt

basement rummage sale
of costumes from another
seraglio proposition

            the silenced ones
        impassive by mirror
refractions

aberrant
            (not abhorrent

or torrent of terraced stories
estranged by raw definition

the trade route   at intersection
of the commodified   nouns

                        (verbs

of glaring fisheyes
itching to lasso the dormant view

⤳

love in the astructured ozone of forensic practice

all aboard this transit of body palpitations

riotous participles lined on the market shelves

i'm in it for its value
its parcelled accounts
& the unwinding airwaves

                        the poem!
                only the made poem!

watch it, eh?

striated harmony trespasses on privacy

lukewarm water for like inspiration

hanging on the clothesline
in the backyard almost
serene between two posts

              don't lie to me
          don't give up the ghost
              don't underline

              or italic me
              or bold
          or enhance my typeface

broadness mellows the fruit of the loom

telling 'me' to dig up

puns in the garden
waiting to be eaten

waiting to be
eaten

SEPTEMBER 22

–up–or—
—i—us
as–o—din–
holy smoke
'—can't——it,
how——be?'

——

the panic button's off
the sky's clear
the crash alert's
gone

home
free the fruits
of labour

——

three years later
still rubbing eyes
in the tangled glaze
of rear view mirrors

in mutual need friendship's
dream of receding mountains
rivers of baggage so many
voices caught in the rapids

'signs up on all highways—
japs keep out!'
words by muriel k
to wrestle down
still nestling

where was it
this persistence?

the personal wavering
the trace of community

the erased road
took 'us' home

⟶

'i you she he
they too
yes they do remember'

lit up stories interned
in barbed wire tongues

words on words on track
in the dusk of departure
'don't forget to write'

'but——did you——?
—was——baby
—hastings——?'

'is——so?————
—angler?——time
————taken—'

⟶

the body
eases

'what's done's done'
the line's drawn

is this complacency?
rest on laurels
settle to old habits
undo birth commotion?

clerical stabs at monetary
bureaucracy and ledger sheets
the debits and credits alone
get the groceries home?

while 'he' rises again
the hollow chamber
'e says the pulling
apart the scattering

⟿

'we' say what's left
until all's said

for the sake of story
in our telling times

IN FLIGHT, 1/4

> *in memory of april 1/49*
> *when jcs were freed to*
> *return to the coast*

one day i'd like to write
(in the summit of reason)

a straight poem
with all the no answers

busy signals attuned
to crescendos of disquietude

not the kind that passively waits
no not the ones that warn you

to fasten your seat belt
there's heady turbulence ahead

i mean the gratuitous nihilism
of gratitude for a job well done

glad to be of servitude etc
you know the language

communicational bridge of
communal 'blessings in disguise'

i'm prepared for that onslaught
believe me the focused

is trained to be alert to
disruption of services

intaglios of deregulation
the buddha of carry-on-baggage

⤙

forty-three years to
day the air

tangible again
the law unmade

in mind's trap tease
door chambers white

wash of propaganda's
paw in the ledger machine

innocent indigenous pulp
like 'see you there'

in celebration but
cerebral cerebrations in

home's stead for those
who never left fielded

in folded imaginations
their line of meanderings

rings through to me at least
in this compression chamber

coated with ottawa's verbiage
the power lines buzz buzzing

wily truism that one antidote
a bureaucrat's bliss on parole

with dusk's birth on my own
lid's visor so close down the era

this arrear this roar
this 'up up & away'

MEMBRANE TRANSLATE

japanese should realize
they are their own
best 'salesmen' in the east

    (why dont you
turn the stiles

that they will win friends
& dissolve prejudice most
successfully & quickly by

    (engineer the values
in the wine-cellars
of deepest taste

hard work good manners
unselfish conduct &
pleasant cooperation

    (the ethnic is
yearned for

: get acquainted with your white
fellow workers & neighbours

    (blind trust or
itinerary of winds
blow eastern currents

: go out of your way to help
them when they need help

    (dints in the armour
so amour they say
adios to retrieval systems

when suspicions dissolve
away you will find them
much like yourself

    (analogies or logistics
of amber halos

: normal human beings
grateful for cooperation
& assistance & willing
to repay you in kind

    (you'd be crazy
not to bury truth
by the tall oak

by your own words &
actions you can do more
to solve 'the japanese
problem' in canada
than any other group

    (the itinerant scribes
scribble by the wayside
with heartaches of intent

: your most
important task
at present

    (the by-product of waste
management you say

signed ht hammett
department of labour
february 22/43

    (couldn't help the words
ords in the elbow's bend
toward the market's bite

ANDREW SUKNASKI

(b. 1942)

Although Andrew Suknaski has not published a new book of poetry in ten years, he remains one of the most important poets to have come out of Saskatchewan. Of Ukrainian and Polish ancestry, Suknaski was born in the farming community of Wood Mountain, Saskatchewan, whose history, both Native and immigrant, has had a profound impact on his writing. As he says, 'the first things connected with the far EAST are my UKRAINIAN father (once a european wanderer/labourer—a man who still has difficulty with twelve languages) and JIMMY HOY who came from HONG KONG to build a small café in the first hamlet of WOOD MTN near the old NWMP POST OF WOOD MOUNTAIN. . . . HOY built the first cafe/HOTEL where he began to hang his calendars from HONG KONG. my word/picture vision began there. . . . a few years before i left WOOD MTN, HOY went to HONG KONG (JIMMY was 80 then) and brought home a beautiful young bride. for me she compared to the picture of the VIRGIN i saw on my mother's POLISH calendars.' The writing style and imaginative associations here are typical of his many poetry collections. *Wood Mountain Poems* (1973; a revised and enlarged edition was edited by Al Purdy in 1976), like many of his other titles, celebrates the layers of Saskatchewan's past but also laments the bitter legacies of history, especially in relation to Native culture.

Suknaski began learning English only after he entered grade one, and did not finish high school until years later, having wandered in the meantime in Canada and around the world as an itinerant worker and aspiring artist. He studied at the University of Victoria (1964-65), the School of Fine Art and Design at the Montreal Museum of Fine Arts (1965), the Kootenay School of Art, where he received his only Diploma (1967), the University of British Columbia (1967-68), and Simon Fraser University (1968-69). During his stay in Vancouver in the 1960s he was introduced to the new poetry movement there, influenced by the Black Mountain school of poets, but Suknaski's art had already found forms of expression that went beyond the conventional venues of writing.

Interested in found and concrete poetry, he constructed poetry books out of, among other things, brown paper bags and, as Douglas Barbour records, made 'poems to be dropped from an airplane, and one issue of [his underground *Elfin Plot*] magazine which was floated down the North Saskatchewan River in Al Purdy's empty cigar tubes'. *Writing on Stone: Poem Drawings 1966-76* (1976), a collection of his poem-drawings, shows how his concrete poetry has its roots in Jimmy Hoy's Chinese calendars and in Suknaski's desire to escape 'from a neurosis generated from a CHRISTIAN background'. These early influences, however, keep surfacing in many of his works, for example *Four Parts Sand* (1972) and *Old Mill* (1972). The formal and cultural hybridity of these books results from his use of Chinese ideograms and Eastern Orthodox iconography. As a concrete poet, he was one of several artists to represent Canada at the Expo/International de Proposiciones a Realizar exhibition held in Buenos Aires in 1971.

Whether written in a romantic, humorous, or despairing voice, all of Suknaski's poetry reveals his deep concern with disenfranchised peoples and with displacement. *Octomi* (1976), whose title refers to the spider as trickster figure, gathers together Teton Sioux stories for children. *The Ghosts Call You Poor* (1978) casts the poet's preoccupation with Native and immigrant cultures within a wider range to embody material about the Métis, Chinese 'coolies', and Ukrainian immigrants in British Columbia. *East of Myloona* (1979) incorporates some of his best drawings. *In the Name of Narid: New Poems* (1981) reflects his growing despair about political suffering in places like the former Soviet Union, whereas *Montage for an Interstellar Cry* (1982) is a book written in a prophetic kind of voice that continues to explore the history of such troubled places as Chile, Hiroshima, and Dresden. In 1982, Stephen Scobie edited a selection by Suknaski, *The Land They Gave Away: New & Selected Poems*. The most recent book by Suknaski, who won the Canadian Authors Association prize for poetry (1978), is *Silk Trail* (1985).

PHILIP WELL

prairie spring
and i stand here before a tire crimper
two huge vices held by a single bolt
(men of the prairies were grateful to a skilled man
who could use it and fix wooden wheels
when the craft flourished)

i stand here
and think of philip well found in his musty woodshed
this morning
by dunc mcpherson on edge of wood mountain—
philip well lying silent by his rusty .22

and i ask my village: *who was this man?*
this man who left us

in 1914
well and my father walked south from moose jaw
to find their homesteads
they slept in haystacks along the way
and once nearly burned to death
waking in the belly of hell they were saved by mewling mice
and their song of agony—
a homesteader had struck a match and thought he
would teach them a lesson

well and father lived in a hillside and built fires
to heat stones each day in winter
they hunted and skinned animals to make fur blankets
threw redhot stones into their cellars
overlaid the stones with willows
and slept between hides

father once showed me a picture
nine black horses pulling a gang plough
philip well proudly riding behind (breaking
the homestead to make a home)

well quiet and softspoken
loved horses and trees and planted poplars around his shack
when the land began to drift away
in tough times well brought a tire crimper

and fixed wheels tanned hides and mended harnesses
for people

and later (having grown older and often not feeling well)
moved to wood mountain village
to be near people who could drive him to a doctor
if necessary

today in wood mountain
men's faces are altered by well's passing
while they drink coffee in jimmy hoy's cafe
no one remembers if well had a sweetheart
though someone remembers a school dance near
the montana border one christmas—
well drunk and sleeping on a bench in the corner
while the people danced
well lonelier than judas after the kiss
(the heart's sorrow like a wheel's iron ring
tightening around the brain till
the centre cannot hold and
the body breaks)

WEST TO TOLSTOI, MANITOBA (CIRCA 1900)

the story of the young ukrainian immigrant
imprisoned   in his language and ghetto
his name no longer remembered
but an aging woman in assiniboia
tells the rest about him
spending those lonely winters in montreal with nothing
but a friend's letters from tolstoi
ukrainian hamlet in rural manitoba
whitewashed   straw and mud shacks
with thatched roofs
the way it was done   in the homeland

others who relate the story   are not certain
how many times he left montreal on foot
each spring
with never more than a couple dollars change in his pocket
and how he always followed   the railway tracks west
stopping at some station   to check a map
to see where he was

occasionally helped   by some station agent
who offered food   and a bed
hassled by railway officials
who always failed to understand his talk
and sent him   back on an eastbound train
free

no one knows   how far he got each time
until one year   he met some ukrainian immigrants
at a station   in central ontario
where he embraced one of them   and told his story
'please   take me with you
i never   want to speak
to another englishman
for the rest of my life'

VASYLYNA'S RETREAT

vasylyna
      retreating into wilderness
                had it
   po vukha!
   'to the ears'
        with people
vasylyna
    perfectly able
        building herself
    adobe house
        with straw roof
vasylyna
    constructing
        a simple shelter
  of shakes
      and scrap lumber
            for a goat
     one milk cow
         and a few chickens
  arrive alone
      on the margins
            of vasylyna's
     poplars
       and the ghostly

flatbreasted
        figure
                with a doublebarrel shotgun
delicately
           angled
               across the right shoulder
will call

KHTO TAM?
'WHO GOES THERE'
and failing to answer
              in vasylyna's language
                        or going
any further
          can only end
in feet
       e x p l o d i n g
              beneath one

though vasylyna's gun
              has never been fired
                    in fifty years
but go there
       with mykola
              if you ever find him
and vasylyna
          will make tea
              and reveal
unspeakable things
           in translation

'. . . do you know
the englishmen
they are snakes!
sometimes   i fry them
in my frying pan! yes!

. . . and the frenchmen
they are   dogs! yes!
i keep them tied
in the poplar! yes!

. . . do you know   last night
there was a mist

Jesus Christ   and i
we flew high above vita!

children   would you care
for some more tea?

IN THE BEGINNING WAS THE
after barry mckinnon's the inquiry

lady coyote
        in the beginning was *the*
                    whole *world*
   swelling
       a single cock
             inside
                her mouth

  in the beginning was
              the sea
      around
         her small
             mountain
      his tongue
          like *the*
             fabled ark
        ploughing
            through damp
               earth

lady coyote
      that was
        the ascent
  the cat from
        nazareth
           fled
  stipple it in memory
         forever
            lady coyote
that
  was the beginning
         and millennia later
             the word is
       doled out
          like fucking
      sunday
        mints

LETTER TO BIG BEAR

World's Best Coffee
Broadway / W 158th Street
Uptown Manhattan
NYC
April 24, 1979

Big Bear
c/o *NeWest Review*
10123-112 Street
Edmonton, Alberta
Canada

Dear Big Bear,

Here at THE MUSEUM OF THE AMERICAN INDIAN your medicine bundle lies in some dusty drawer. And I must confess, I came here wanting to look into your sacred bundle; however, having arrived here now in Washington Heights on the edge of the Hudson River, it now seems more important not to do that. After all, Big Bear, some things are sacred. Your people kept talismans and sometimes certain remains of ancestors in such bundles. And they say before a long journey, or for many other reasons, you would carefully open your medicine bundle. And pray for strength.

I donno, Big Bear, it seems wiser to understand clearly what lured me here. It seems best to let these things be—part of those private things on earth. For the truth is, there were always only two places where the medicine bundle ever went: one being where the possessor, and all of us, must someday finally go; the other, remaining in the caring hands of one's lineage. This place is neither of those. Making it sad.

Best to you,
Mahzahkahzah

THE FACELESS GOODBYES

what little is
           remembered
                           the borgesian problem
           memory's
                   betrayal
                       each image

the nebulous
        vestige
            witnessed
in distortion
        of things serving
as amazing
        mirrors

what little
      endures
          clear enough
  suknatskyj
        traitor
          of spirit
  acquiescing
        to cruelty
          never facing
    women
        when things
           got tough
      portents
        of unrequited
            love

what little
    traces that
        faceless parting
following the
      razed church
        suknatskyj's
      mother
        a profile
          mirrored
      by a window
        beneath
          an ikon
      where she
        feigned
      a fainthearted
        . . . goodbye

RENATO TRUJILLO

(b. 1942)

Renato Trujillo's work comes, in his own words, from 'looking at the world through the cultural eyes of someone who—not knowing better at the time—was born in Chile'. Trujillo was widely published in Chile before he arrived in Montreal in 1968. While there, he participated in such ventures as the collective production of 'The Main' at Centaur Theatre (1988) and the 1985 Montreal Sound Exhibition. As founder of the musical group, Los Quinchamalas, he has performed in Canada and the United States.

Trujillo, who writes in Spanish, French, and English, has written scripts for television and radio, and his short stories and poetry have appeared in many literary magazines and anthologies in Canada. His first poetry book in English was *Behind the Orchestra* (1987). It was followed by *Rooms: Milongas for Prince Arthur Street* (1989), whose lyrics have been described as 'unpretentious . . . at times achingly sad, and at other times filled with intense purity and joy'. *The Price of Fish* (1990) is his most recent poetry collection.

Since 1993, Trujillo has been living in Pittsburgh, Pensylvania, where he is a college teacher.

RAIN

In Chile
children die with clouds of sadness
embroidered in their eyes. That's all.
Aside from this,
one gets old
and the thought of Rancagua
nonchalantly seizes us.
We think of Toltén
in the autumn
evening
where we never were.
We saunter down a road
stepping on dry leaves
in Temuco
or
we remember an embrace
in Arica.

Far away from Chile,
the humus of the forests
grows in our memory,
the smell of *humitas*
swells up in the air

and the skin of a brunette
transposes itself
into our dreams.
And then it comes,
like a nightly visitor,
shy and light, the soft rain
of our pueblo,
running down our cheeks
when we least
expect it.

HUNGER

to Club 'La Piedad,' Sn. Vte.

The hunger of the people in Chile
makes it nearly impossible
for me to fix the ribbon
of this typewriter so I can write
these words. The hunger of millions
of Chileans makes my spine shiver
when I sit down to write a poem.
Outside my rooming-house
some son-of-a-bitch
is making money
selling Solidarnozc posters,
Che Guevara t-shirts and other
paraphernalia. But that
doesn't bother me so much.
It's the hunger of those in Chile
that makes me despair.
Their hunger makes it nearly impossible
for this man to eat the steak
in front of him: a piece of meat
he bought with the money
he received from the first poem
he sold
talking about the hunger
down
in
Chile.

UNSOLICITED MAIL

Dear, dear Rosita,
I have reached Amerika.
I have begun to speak its language.
I am writing these poems for you, to show you
how much I've grown, how much
I love you, in a new language.
In the process, I have lost
two front teeth, a
disc from my spine
and my kidneys need repair.
Mopping floors doesn't help.
But otherwise, I'm fine.
I can talk like Marlon Brando.
I can even imitate Bogie
and also W.C. Fields. You wouldn't
know who these are.
You are much too young for that.
But, all in all, it's not
so bad. I've got a car,
expensive shoes, and know
the capitals of all the
provinces of Canada by heart.
Furthermore, I've been
to Washington, D.C.,
New York City and Boston.
I spent a week in Philadelphia
which, for some reason,
felt like three. But
I heard Freddy King and Albert King
live, performing in Chicago—
but you're too far away to know them.
I've grown a bit thinner
since the last picture I sent you.
And a bit more cynical, too. You can't
help it.

Amerika is great. In every respect.
But for some reason
I have trouble with that word 'respect' . . .
I don't think I conjugate that verb
often enough. I don't think
they do, either. And this whole thing

is falling on me like a private
Niagara Falls in my soul.
I'm not trying to dissuade you
from coming up here, Rosita, no.
I'm only trying to tell you about
the pleasure one can find here and
also tell you that everything
has an end. (For some peculiar reason
these two seem to go together;
it's hard to distinguish
between them.) But most importantly,
I am trying to tell you about
all those things we leave behind.

Only yesterday, Ali, my neighbour,
asked me if by any chance
I had a flask of pills
or a gun of some kind.
I guess he hasn't got
someone like you in his hometown
he could write about
the wonders of
this land that grows
more foreign as time goes by.
Forever yours,

Ramon Rascacielos (Ramon Skyscraper)

THOMAS KING ◈

(b. 1943)

Although the question of 'what it means to be Indian' is not one that concerns Thomas King 'all that much personally', as he says in an interview, 'it is an important question in my fiction. Because it's a question that other people always ask. . . . it's part of that demand for authenticity within the world in which we live. It's the question that Native people have to put up with. And it's a whip that we get beaten with—"Are you a good enough Indian to speak as an Indian?"'

King's treatment of these questions relies formally on both the Native oral storytelling and the Western narrative traditions, thus reflecting his life and personal heritage. The son of a mother of Greek and German origins, and a Cherokee father, King was born in Oklahoma, but doesn't 'think of Oklahoma as home. If I think of any place as home, it's the Alberta prairies, where I spent ten years with the Blackfoot people.' Although he is both a Canadian and an American citizen, King 'think[s] of [him]self as a Canadian writer because that's all [he] write[s] about.' If anything, his double citizenship and mixed heritage—'With my looks,' he admits, 'I could have gone either way'—have made him all the more aware of borders—between countries, between Native and white people, between men and women, between urban Natives and Natives living on reserves. As he says, for 'Native people, identity comes from community, and it varies from community to community. I wouldn't define myself as an Indian in the same way that someone living on a reserve would. That whole idea of "Indian" becomes, in part, a construct. It's fluid. We make it up as we go along.'

King, who holds a Ph.D. in English and American Studies from the University of Utah, was professor of Native Studies at the University of Lethbridge, Alberta, for ten years, where he had an enormous impact on young Native writers and began writing creatively himself. Subsequently, he was professor of American Indian Studies at the University of Minnesota in Minneapolis, where he also served as Chair of the Department. Before joining the Department of English at Guelph University, King lived in Toronto (1993-94) where he was Story Editor for *The Four Directions*, a CBC-TV dramatic production about Native people. King, whose short stories and poems have appeared in many literary magazines in Canada, was the editor of the special issue of *Canadian Fiction Magazine* (1987) on Native writers, and of *All My Relations: An Anthology of Contemporary Canadian Native Writing* (1990).

King's first book was the novel *Medicine River* (1990), which has been dramatized by CBC-TV. It was followed by a children's book, *A Coyote Columbus Story* (1992), which won him his first Governor General's Award nomination. His second nomination came with the publication of his second novel, *Green Grass, Running Water* (1993). His short stories have been collected in *One Good Story, That One* (1993).

King's fiction, as is the case with the story that follows, illustrates that 'the range of "Indian" is not as narrow as many people try to make it.' Through the Coyote trickster figure, which he often uses as a 'sacred clown', through puns, which he has learned from '[t]alking to storytellers and to Native people', and through humour—'Comedy,' he says, 'is simply my strategy'—King has proven himself to be one of the most innovative and popular Canadian Native writers.

THE ONE ABOUT COYOTE GOING WEST

This one is about Coyote. She was going west. Visiting her relations. That's what she said. You got to watch that one. Tricky one. Full of bad business. No, no, no, no, that one says. I'm just visiting. Going to see Raven.

Boy, I says. That's another tricky one.

Coyote comes by my place. She wag her tail. Make them happy noises. Sit on my porch. Look around. With them teeth. With that smile. Coyote put her nose in my tea. My good tea.

Get that nose out of my tea, I says.

I'm going to see my friends, she says. Tell those stories. Fix this world. Straighten it up.

Oh boy, pretty scary that, Coyote fix the world, again.

Sit down, I says. Eat some food. Hard work that, fix up the world. Maybe you have a song. Maybe you have a good joke.

Sure, says Coyote. That one wink her ears. Lick her whiskers.

I tuck my feet under that chair. Got to hide my toes. Sometimes that tricky one leave her skin sit in that chair. Coyote skin. No Coyote. Sneak around. Bite them toes. Make you jump.

I been reading those books, she says.

You must be one smart Coyote, I says.

You bet, she says.

Maybe you got a good story for me, I says.

I been reading about that history, says Coyote. She sticks that nose back in my tea. All about who found us Indians.

Ho, I says. I like those old ones. Them ones are the best. You tell me your story, I says. Maybe some biscuits will visit us. Maybe some moose-meat stew come along, listen to your story.

Okay, she says and she sings her story song.

Snow's on the ground the snakes are asleep.
Snow's on the ground my voice is strong.
Snow's on the ground the snakes are asleep.
Snow's on the ground my voice is strong.

She sings like that. With that tail, wagging. With that smile. Sitting there.

Maybe I tell you the one about Eric the Lucky and the Vikings play hockey for the Oldtimers, find us Indians in Newfoundland, she says. Maybe I tell you the one about Christopher Cartier looking for something good to eat. Find us Indians in a restaurant in Montreal. Maybe I tell you the one about Jacques Columbus come along that river. Indians waiting for him. We all wave and say, here we are, here we are.

Everyone knows those stories, I says. Whiteman stories. Baby stories you got in your mouth.

No, no, no, no, says that Coyote. I read these ones in that old book.

Ho, I says. You are trying to bite my toes. Everyone knows who found us Indians. Eric the Lucky and that Christopher Cartier and that Jacques Columbus come along later. Those ones get lost. Float about. Walk around. Get mixed up. Ho, ho, ho, ho, those ones cry, we are lost. So we got to find them. Help them out. Feed them. Show them around. Boy, I says. Bad mistake that one.

You are very wise grandmother, says Coyote, bring her eyes down, like she is sleepy. Maybe you know who discovered Indians.

Sure, I says. Everyone knows that. It was Coyote. She was the one.

Oh, grandfather, that Coyote says. Tell me that story. I love those stories about that sneaky one. I don't think I know that story, she says.

All right, I says. Pay attention.

Coyote was heading west. That's how I always start this story. There was nothing else in this world. Just Coyote. She could see all the way, too. No mountains then. No rivers then. No forests then. Pretty flat then. So she starts to make things. So she starts to fix this world.

This is exciting, says Coyote, and she takes her nose out of my tea.

Yes, I says. Just the beginning, too. Coyote got a lot of things to make.

Tell me, grandmother, says Coyote. What does the clever one make first?

Well, I says. Maybe she makes that tree grows by the river. Maybe she makes that buffalo. Maybe she makes that mountain. Maybe she makes them clouds.

Maybe she makes that beautiful rainbow, says Coyote.

No, I says. She don't make that thing. Mink makes that.

Maybe she makes that beautiful moon, says Coyote.

No, I says. She don't do that either. Otter finds that moon in a pond later on.

Maybe she make the oceans with that blue water, says Coyote.

No, I says. Oceans are already here. She don't do any of that. The first thing Coyote makes, I tell Coyote, is a mistake.

Boy, Coyote sit up straight. Them eyes pop open. That tail stop wagging. That one swallow that smile.

Big one, too, I says. Coyote is going west thinking of things to make. That one is trying to think of everything to make at once. So she don't see that hole. So she falls in that hole. Then those thoughts bump around. They run into each other. Those ones fall out of Coyote's ears. In that hole.

Ho, that Coyote cries. I have fallen into a hole, I must have made a mistake. And she did.

So, there is that hole. And there is that Coyote in that hole. And there is that big mistake in that hole with Coyote. Ho, says that mistake. You must be Coyote.

That mistake is real big and that hole is small. Not much room. I don't want to tell you what that mistake looks like. First mistake in the world. Pretty scary. Boy, I can't look, I got to close my eyes. You better close your eyes, too, I tell Coyote.

Okay, I'll do that, she says, and she puts her hands over her eyes. But she don't fool me. I can see she's peeking.

Don't peek, I says.

Okay, she says. I won't do that.

Well, you know, that Coyote thinks about the hole. And she thinks about how she's going to get out of that hole. She thinks how she's going to get that big mistake back in her head.

Say, says that mistake. What is that you're thinking about?

I'm thinking of a song, says Coyote. I'm thinking of a song to make this hole bigger.

That's a good idea, says that mistake. Let me hear your hole song.

But that's not what Coyote sings. She sings a song to make the mistake smaller. But that mistake hears her. And that mistake grabs Coyote's nose. And that one pulls off her mouth so she can't sing. And that one jumps up and down on Coyote until she is flat. Then that one leaps out of that hole, wanders around looking for things to do.

Well, Coyote is feeling pretty bad, all flat her nice fur coat full of stomp holes. So she thinks hard, and she thinks about a healing song. And she tries to sing a healing song, but her mouth is in other places. So she thinks harder and tries to sing that song through her nose. But that nose don't make any sound, just drip a lot. She tries to sing that song out her ears, but those ears don't hear anything.

So, that silly one thinks real hard and tries to sing out her butt hole. Pssst! Pssst! That is what that butt hole says, and right away things don't smell so good in that hole. Pssst.

Boy, Coyote thinks. Something smells.

That Coyote lies there flat and practise and practise. Pretty soon, maybe two days, maybe one year, she teach that butt hole to sing. That song. That healing song. So that butt hole sings that song. And Coyote begins to feel better. And Coyote don't feel so flat anymore. Pssst! Pssst! Things smell pretty bad, but Coyote is okay.

That one look around in that hole. Find her mouth. Put that mouth back. So, she says to that butt hole. Okay, you can stop singing now. You can stop making them smells now. But, you know, that butt hole is liking all that singing, and so that butt hole keeps on singing.

Stop that, says Coyote. You are going to stink up the whole world. But it don't. So Coyote jumps out of that hole and runs across the prairies real fast. But that butt hole follows her. Pssst. Pssst. Coyote jumps into a lake, but that butt hole don't drown. It just keeps on singing.

Hey, who is doing all that singing, someone says.

Yes, and who is making that bad smell, says another voice.

It must be Coyote, says a third voice.

Yes, says a fourth voice. I believe it is Coyote.

That Coyote sit in my chair, put her nose in my tea, say, I know who that voice is. It is that big mistake playing a trick. Nothing else is made yet.

No, I says. That mistake is doing other things.

Then those voices are spirits, says Coyote.

No, I says. Them voices belong to them ducks.

Coyote stand up on my chair. Hey, she says, where did them ducks come from?

Calm down, I says. This story is going to be okay. This story is doing just fine. This story knows where it is going. Sit down. Keep your skin on.

So.

Coyote look around, and she see them four ducks. In that lake. Ho, she says. Where did you ducks come from? I didn't make you yet.

Yes, says them ducks. We were waiting around, but you didn't come. So we got tired of waiting. So we did it ourselves.

I was in a hole, says Coyote.

Pssst. Pssst.

What's that noise, says them ducks. What's that bad smell?

Never mind, says Coyote. Maybe you've seen something go by. Maybe you can help me find something I lost. Maybe you can help me get it back.

Those ducks swim around and talk to themselves. Was it something awful to look at?
Yes, says Coyote, it certainly was.
Was it something with ugly fur?
Yes, says Coyote. I think it had that, too.
Was it something that made a lot of noise, ask them ducks.
Yes, it was pretty noisy, says Coyote.
Did it smell bad, them ducks want to know.
Yes, says Coyote. I guess you ducks have seen my something.
Yes, says them ducks. It is right there behind you.
So that Coyote turn around, and there is nothing there.
It's still behind you, says those ducks.
So Coyote turn around again but she don't see anything.
Pssst! Pssst!
Boy, says those ducks. What a noise! What a smell! They say that, too. What an ugly thing with all that fur!
Never mind, says that Coyote again. That is not what I'm looking for. I'm looking for something else.
Maybe you're looking for Indians, says those ducks.
Well, that Coyote is real surprised because she hasn't created Indians, either. Boy, says that one, mischief is everywhere. This world is getting bent.
All right.
So Coyote and those ducks are talking, and pretty soon they hear a noise. And pretty soon there is something coming. And those ducks says, oh, oh, oh, oh. They say that like they see trouble, but it is not trouble. What comes along is a river.
Hello, says that river. Nice day. Maybe you want to take a swim. But Coyote don't want to swim, and she looks at that river and she looks at that river again. Something's not right here, she says. Where are those rocks? Where are those rapids? What did you do with them waterfalls? How come you're so straight?
And Coyote is right. That river is nice and straight and smooth without any bumps or twists. It runs both ways, too, not like a modern river.
We got to fix this, says Coyote, and she does. She puts some rocks in that river, and she fixes it so it only runs one way. She puts a couple of waterfalls in and makes a bunch of rapids where things get shallow fast.
Coyote is tired with all this work, and those ducks are tired just watching. So that Coyote sits down. So she closes her eyes. So she puts her nose in her tail. So those ducks shout, wake up, wake up! Something big is heading this way! And they are right.
Mountain come sliding along, whistling. Real happy mountain. Nice and round. This mountain is full of grapes an other good things to eat. Apples, peaches, cherries. Howdy-do, says that polite mountain, nice day for whistling.
Coyote looks at that mountain, and that one shakes her head. Oh, no, she says, this mountain is all wrong. How come you're so nice and round? Where are those craggy peaks? Where are all them cliffs? What happened to all that snow? Boy, we got to fix this thing, too. So she does.
Grandfather, grandfather, says that Coyote, sit in my chair put her nose in my tea.

Why is that Coyote changing all those good things?

That is a real sly one, ask me that question. I look at those eyes. Grab them ears. Squeeze that nose. Hey, let go my nose, that Coyote says.

Okay I says. Coyote still in Coyote skin. I bet you know why Coyote change that happy river. Why she change that mountain sliding along whistling.

No, says that Coyote, look around my house, lick her lips, make them baby noises.

Maybe it's because she is mean, I says.

Oh, no, says Coyote. That one is sweet and kind.

Maybe it's because that one is not too smart.

Oh, no, says Coyote. That Coyote is very wise.

Maybe it's because she made a mistake.

Oh, no, says Coyote. She made one of those already.

All right, I says. Then Coyote must be doing the right thing. She must be fixing up the world so it is perfect.

Yes, says Coyote. That must be it. What does that brilliant one do next?

Everyone knows what Coyote does next, I says. Little babies know what Coyote does next.

Oh no, says Coyote. I have never heard this story. You are a wonderful storyteller. You tell me your good Coyote story.

Boy, you got to watch that one all the time. Hide them toes.

Well, I says. Coyote thinks about that river. And she thinks about that mountain. And she thinks somebody is fooling around. So she goes looking around. She goes looking for that one who is messing up the world.

She goes to the north, and there is nothing. She goes to the south, and there is nothing there either. She goes to the east, and there is still nothing there. She goes to the west, and there is a pile of snow tires.

And there is some televisions. And there is some vacuum cleaners. And there is a bunch of pastel sheets. And there is an air humidifier. And there is a big mistake sitting on a portable gas barbecue reading a book. Big book. Department store catalogue.

Hello, says that mistake. Maybe you want a hydraulic jack.

No, says that Coyote. I don't want one of them. But she don't tell that mistake what she wants because she don't want to miss her mouth again. But when she thinks about being flat and full of stomp holes, that butt hole wakes up and begins to sing. Pssst. Pssst.

What's that noise? says that big mistake.

I'm looking for Indians, says that Coyote, real quick. Have you seen any?

What's that bad smell?

Never mind, says Coyote. Maybe you have some Indians around here.

I got some toaster ovens, says that mistake.

We don't need that stuff, says Coyote. You got to stop making all those things. You're going to fill up this world.

Maybe you want a computer with a colour monitor. That mistake keeps looking through that book and those things keep landing in piles all around Coyote.

Stop, stop, cries Coyote. Golf cart lands on her foot. Golf balls bounce off her head. You got to give me that book before the world gets lopsided.

These are good things, says that mistake. We need these things to make up the world. Indians are going to need this stuff.

We don't have any Indians, says Coyote.

And that mistake can see that that's right. Maybe we better make some Indians, says that mistake. So that one looks in that catalogue, but it don't have any Indians. And Coyote don't know how to do that either. She has already made four things.

I've made four things already, she says. I got to have help.

We can help, says some voices and it is those ducks come swimming along. We can help you make Indians, says that white duck. Yes, we can do that, says that green duck. We have been thinking about this, says that blue duck. We have a plan, says that red duck.

Well, that Coyote don't know what to do. So she tells them ducks to go ahead because this story is pretty long and it's getting late and everyone wants to go home.

You still awake, I says to Coyote. You still here?

Oh yes, grandmother, says Coyote. What do those clever ducks do?

So I tell Coyote that those ducks lay some eggs. Ducks do that, you know. That white duck lay an egg, and it is blue. That red duck lay an egg, and it is green. That blue duck lay an egg, and it is red. That green duck lay an egg, and it is white.

Come on, says those ducks. We got to sing a song. We got to do a dance. So they do. Coyote and that big mistake and those four ducks dance around the eggs. So they dance and sing for a long time, and pretty soon Coyote gets hungry.

I know this dance, she says, but you got to close your eyes when you do it or nothing will happen. You got to close your eyes tight. Okay, says those ducks. We can do that. And they do. And that big mistake closes its eyes, too.

But Coyote, she don't close her eyes, and all of them start dancing again, and Coyote dances up close to that white duck, and she grabs that white duck by her neck.

When Coyote grabs that duck, that duck flaps her wings, and that bit mistake hears the noise and opens them eyes. Say, says that big mistake, that's not the way the dance goes.

By golly, you're right, says Coyote, and she lets that duck go. I am getting it mixed up with another dance.

So they start to dance again. And Coyote is very hungry, and she grabs that blue duck, and she grabs his wings, too. But Coyote's stomach starts to make hungry noises, and that mistake opens them eyes and sees Coyote with the blue duck. Hey, says that mistake, you got yourself mixed up again.

That's right, says Coyote, and she drops that duck and straightens out that neck. It sure is good you're around to help me with this dance.

They all start that dance again, and, this time, Coyote grabs the green duck real quick and tries to stuff it down that greedy throat, and there is nothing hanging out but them yellow duck feet. But those feet are flapping in Coyote's eyes, and she can't see where she is going, and she bumps into the big mistake and the big mistake turns around to see what has happened.

Ho, says that big mistake, you can't see where you're going with them yellow duck feet flapping in your eyes, and that mistake pulls that green duck out of Coyote's throat. You could hurt yourself dancing like that.

You are one good friend, look after me like that, says Coyote.

Those ducks start to dance again, and Coyote dances with them, but that red duck says, we better dance with one eye open, so we can help Coyote with this dance. So they dance some more, and, then, those eggs begin to move around, and those eggs crack open. And if you look hard, you can see something inside those eggs.

I know, I know, says that Coyote, jump up and down on my chair, shake up my good tea. Indians come out of those eggs. I remember this story, now. Inside those eggs are the Indians Coyote's been looking for.

No, I says. You are one crazy Coyote. What comes out of those duck eggs are baby ducks. You better sit down, I says. You may fall and hurt yourself. You may spill my tea. You may fall on top of this story and make it flat.

Where are the Indians? says that Coyote. This story was about how Coyote found the Indians. Maybe the Indians are in the eggs with the baby ducks.

No, I says, nothing in those eggs but little baby ducks. Indians will be along in a while. Don't lose your skin.

So.

When those ducks see what has come out of the eggs, they says, boy, we didn't get that quite right. We better try that again. So they do. They lay them eggs. They dance that dance. They sing that song. Those eggs crack open and out comes some more baby ducks. They do this seven times and each time, they get more ducks.

By golly, says those four ducks. We got more ducks than we need. I guess we got to be the Indians. And so they do that. Before Coyote or that big mistake can mess things up, those four ducks turn into Indians, two women and two men. Good-looking Indians, too. They don't look at all like ducks any more.

But those duck-Indians aren't too happy. They look at each other and they begin to cry. This is pretty disgusting, they says. All this ugly skin. All these bumpy bones. All this awful black hair. Where are our nice soft feathers? Where are our beautiful feet? What happened to our wonderful wings? It's probably all that Coyote's fault because she didn't do the dance right, and those four duck-Indians come over and stomp all over Coyote until she is flat like before. Then they leave. That big mistake leave, too. And that Coyote, she starts to think about a healing song.

Pssst. Pssst.

That's it, I says. It is done.

But what happens to Coyote, says Coyote. That wonderful one is still flat.

Some of these stories are flat, I says. That's what happens when you try to fix this world. This world is pretty good all by itself. Best to leave it alone. Stop messing around with it.

I better get going, says Coyote. I will tell Raven your good story. We going to fix this world for sure. We know how to do it now. We know how to do it right.

So, Coyote drinks my tea and that one leave. And I can't talk anymore because I got to watch the sky. Got to watch out for falling things that land in piles. When that Coyote's wandering around looking to fix things, nobody in this world is safe.

MICHAEL ONDAATJE

(b. 1943)

Michael Ondaatje was nine years old when in 1952 he left his birthplace, Colombo, Ceylon (now Sri Lanka), to attend Dulwich College in England. As he says, 'I was part of that colonial tradition of sending your kids off to school in England, and then you were supposed to go to Oxford or Cambridge and get a blue in tennis and return. But I never went to Oxford or Cambridge, I didn't get a blue, and I didn't return.' Instead, Ondaatje moved to Canada in 1962 to attend Bishop's University, and subsequently the University of Toronto where he received his B.A. in English (1965). Immediately after he received his M.A. (1967) from Queen's University, he began teaching in the English Department, University of Western Ontario, and in 1971 he joined the faculty of Glendon College, York University, with which he is still affiliated as a professor.

As a poet, novelist, critic, and documentary filmmaker, Ondaatje sees himself as belonging to the generation of writers that 'was the first of the real migrant tradition . . . of writers of our time—Rushdie, Ishiguro, Ben Okri, Rohinton Mistry—writers leaving and not going back, but taking their country with them to a new place.' Still, not until *Running in the Family* (1982), a book about his parents which defies generic definition in that it employs novelistic, autobiographical, poetic, and documentary elements, did Ondaatje's country find its way into his work in an extended form. His poetry books, *The Dainty Monsters* (1967), *Rat Jelly* (1973), *There's a Trick with a Knife I'm Learning to Do* (1979), and *Secular Love* (1984), are collections of lyrics. Through an intensely private, if somewhat exotic and violent, imagery they reflect, in his own words, 'my landscape here in Canada, my family here, certain rural landscapes here'.

In contrast, his other books seem to 'have begun with . . . the germ of document, with the rumour or incident that one reads about in the newspaper, or some paragraph in a biography.' His fascination with documents, and the way they tease the boundaries of truth and history, began with his second poetry book, *the man with seven toes* (1969), a long poem in which Ondaatje reinvents a Mrs Fraser's historical encounter with a convict in Australia. It was,

however, with the publication of his second long poem, *The Collected Works of Billy the Kid* (1970), the winner of a Governor General's Award, that Ondaatje's characteristic mode of writing took flight. Its collage of poetry, prose, and illustrations and its imaginative and deliberate distortion of facts about the famous American outlaw figure announce Ondaatje's preoccupation with characters that occupy extreme positions, with the romantic possibilities of life-in-art, with the limits of literary forms. 'I am not really interested in inventing a form, as such,' says Ondaatje; 'I want my form to reflect as fully as possible how we think and imagine. And these keep changing, of course. With each book I try to do something I think I can't do.'

Coming Through Slaughter (1976), which won the *Books in Canada* First Novel Award, is about yet another legendary American figure, this time jazz musician Buddy Bolden, and is set in New Orleans. It resonates with jazz rhythms against 'a kind of mental landscape' that is, as Ondaatje says, 'believable, tactile', a poetic narrative in prose of a 'personal story' that 'wrestle[s] against the documentary'. *In the Skin of a Lion* (1987), which Ondaatje has called his first novel, is indeed more direct in its treatment of setting and characters, but still reflects Ondaatje's attention to language and his inclination to aestheticize experience. Set in the Toronto of the late twenties and thirties, the narrative casts its central character, Patrick Lewis, among immigrants, especially Macedonians. As the excerpt that follows demonstrates, the novel attempts to 'represent', as Ondaatje says, 'the unofficial story' of Toronto's history, particularly about the events concerning the construction of the Bloor Street Viaduct and the water filtration plant by immigrants. '[R]eclaiming untold stories,' Ondaatje remarks, 'is an essential role for the writer. Especially in this country, where one can no longer trust the media.' His most recent novel, *The English Patient* (1992), which won, among other prizes, the Booker Prize, takes place at the end of the Second World War, and is set in Italy.

Ondaatje, who has also written criticism and worked as an editor with Coach House Press and *Brick* magazine, lives in Toronto.

FROM *IN THE SKIN OF A LION*

A truck carries fire at five A.M. through central Toronto, along Dundas Street and up Parliament Street, moving north. Aboard the flatbed three men stare into passing darkness—their muscles relaxed in this last half-hour before work—as if they don't own the legs or the arms jostling against their bodies and the backboard of the Ford.

Written in yellow over the green door is DOMINION BRIDGE COMPANY. But for now all that is visible is the fire on the flatbed burning over the three-foot by three-foot metal dish, cooking the tar in a cauldron, leaving this odour on the streets for anyone who would step out into the early morning and swallow the air.

The truck rolls burly under the arching trees, pauses at certain intersections where more workers jump onto the flatbed, and soon there are eight men, the fire crackling, hot tar now and then spitting onto the back of a neck or an ear. Soon there are twenty, crowded and silent.

The light begins to come out of the earth. They see their hands, the textures on a coat, the trees they had known were there. At the top of Parliament Street the truck turns east, passes the Rosedale fill, and moves towards the half-built viaduct.

The men jump off. The unfinished road is full of ruts and the fire and the lights of the truck bounce, the suspension wheezing. The truck travels so slowly the men are walking faster, in the cold dawn air, even though it is summer.

Later they will remove coats and sweaters, then by eleven their shirts, bending over the black rivers of tar in just their trousers, boots, and caps. But now the thin layer of frost is everywhere, coating the machines and cables, brittle on the rain puddles they step through. The fast evaporation of darkness. As light emerges they see their breath, the clarity of the air being breathed out of them. The truck finally stops at the edge of the viaduct, and its lights are turned off.

The bridge goes up in a dream. It will link the east end with the centre of the city. It will carry traffic, water, and electricity across the Don Valley. It will carry trains that have not even been invented yet.

Night and day. Fall light. Snow light. They are always working—horses and wagons and men arriving for work on the Danforth side at the far end of the valley.

There are over 4,000 photographs from various angles of the bridge in its time-lapse evolution. The piers sink into bedrock fifty feet below the surface through clay and shale and quicksand—45,000 cubic yards of earth are excavated. The network of scaffolding stretches up.

Men in a maze of wooden planks climb deep into the shattered light of blond wood. A man is an extension of hammer, drill, flame. Drill smoke in his hair. A cap falls into the valley, gloves are buried in stone dust.

Then the new men arrive, the 'electricals', laying grids of wire across the five arches, carrying the exotic three-bowl lights, and on October 18, 1918 it is completed. Lounging in mid-air.

The bridge. The bridge. Christened 'Prince Edward'. The Bloor Street Viaduct.

During the political ceremonies a figure escaped by bicycle through the police barriers. The first member of the public. Not the expected show car containing officials, but this one anonymous and cycling like hell to the east end of the city. In the photographs he is a blur of intent. He wants the virginity of it, the luxury of such space. He circles twice, the string of onions that he carries on his shoulder splaying out, and continues.

But he was not the first. The previous midnight the workers had arrived and brushed away officials who guarded the bridge in preparation for the ceremonies the next day, moved with their own flickering lights—their candles for the bridge dead— like a wave of civilization, a net of summer insects over the valley.

And the cyclist too on his flight claimed the bridge in that blurred movement, alone and illegal. Thunderous applause greeted him at the far end.

On the west side of the bridge is Bloor Street, on the east side is Danforth Avenue. Originally cart roads, mud roads, planked in 1910, they are now being tarred. Bricks are banged into the earth and narrow creeks of sand are poured in between them. The tar is spread. *Bitumiers, bitumatori,* tarrers, get onto their knees and lean their weight over the wooden block irons, which arc and sweep. The smell of tar seeps through the porous body of their clothes. The black of it is permanent under the nails. They can feel the bricks under their kneecaps as they crawl backwards towards the bridge, their bodies almost horizontal over the viscous black river, their heads drunk within the fumes.

Hey, Caravaggio!

The young man gets up off his knees and looks back into the sun. He walks to the foreman, lets go of the two wooden blocks he is holding so they hang by the leather thongs from his belt, bouncing against his knees as he walks. Each man carries the necessities of his trade with him. When Caravaggio quits a year later he will cut the thongs with a fish knife and fling the blocks into the half-dry tar. Now he walks back in a temper and gets down on his knees again. Another fight with the foreman.

All day they lean over tar, over the twenty yards of black river that has been spread since morning. It glistens and eases in sunlight. Schoolkids grab bits of tar and chew them, first cooling the pieces in their hands then popping them into their mouths. It concentrates the saliva for spitting contests. The men plunk cans of beans into the blackness to heat them up for their lunch.

In winter, snow removes the scent of tar, the scent of pitched cut wood. The Don River floods below the unfinished bridge, is banging at the feet of the recently built piers. On winter mornings men fan out nervous over the whiteness. Where does the earth end? There are flares along the edge of the bridge on winter nights—worst shift of all—where they hammer the nails in through snow. The bridge builders balance on a strut, the flares wavering behind them, aiming their hammers towards the noise of a nail they cannot see.

* * *

The last thing Rowland Harris, Commissioner of Public Works, would do in the evening during its construction was have himself driven to the edge of the viaduct, to sit for a while. At midnight the half-built bridge over the valley seemed deserted—just lanterns tracing its outlines. But there was always a night shift of thirty or forty men. After a while Harris removed himself from the car, lit a cigar, and walked onto the bridge. He loved this viaduct. It was his first child as head of Public Works, much of it planned before he took over but he had bullied it through. It was Harris who envisioned that it could carry not just cars but trains on a lower trestle. It could also transport water from the east-end plants to the centre of the city. Water was Harris' great passion. He wanted giant water mains travelling across the valley as part of the viaduct.

He slipped past the barrier and walked towards the working men. Few of them spoke English but they knew who he was. Sometimes he was accompanied by Pomphrey, an architect, the strange one from England who was later to design for Commissioner Harris one of the city's grandest buildings—the water filtration plant in the east end.

For Harris the night allowed scope. Night removed the limitations of detail and concentrated on form. Harris would bring Pomphrey with him, past the barrier, onto the first stage of the bridge that ended sixty yards out in the air. The wind moved like something ancient against them. All men on the bridge had to buckle on halter ropes. Harris spoke of his plans to this five-foot-tall Englishman, struggling his way into Pomphrey's brain. Before the real city could be seen it had to be imagined, the way rumours and tall tales were a kind of charting.

One night they had driven there at eleven o'clock, crossed the barrier, and attached themselves once again to the rope harnesses. This allowed them to stand near the edge to study the progress of the piers and the steel arches. There was a fire on the bridge where the night workers congregated, flinging logs and other remnants onto it every so often, warming themselves before they walked back and climbed over the edge of the bridge into the night.

They were working on a wood-facing for the next pier so the concrete could be poured in. As they sawed and hammered, wind shook the light from the flares attached to the side of the abutment. Above them, on the deck of the bridge, builders were carrying huge Ingersoll-Rand air compressors and cables.

An April night in 1917. Harris and Pomphrey were on the bridge, in the dark wind. Pomphrey had turned west and was suddenly stilled. His hand reached out to touch Harris on the shoulder, a gesture he had never made before.

—*Look!*

Walking on the bridge were five nuns.

Past the Dominion Steel castings wind attacked the body directly. The nuns were walking past the first group of workers at the fire. The bus, Harris thought, must have dropped them off near Castle Frank and the nuns had, with some confusion at that hour, walked the wrong way in the darkness.

They had passed the black car under the trees and talking cheerfully stepped past the barrier into a landscape they did not know existed—onto a tentative carpet over the piers, among the night labourers. They saw the fire and the men. A few tried to wave them back. There was a mule attached to a wagon. The hiss and jump of machines made the ground under them lurch. A smell of creosote. One man was washing his face in a barrel of water.

The nuns were moving towards a thirty-yard point on the bridge when the wind began to scatter them. They were thrown against the cement mixers and steam shovels, careering from side to side, in danger of going over the edge.

Some of the men grabbed and enclosed them, pulling leather straps over their shoulders, but two were still loose. Harris and Pomphrey at the far end looked on helplessly as one nun was lifted up and flung against the compressors. She stood up shakily and then the wind jerked her sideways, scraping her along the concrete and right off the edge of the bridge. She disappeared into the night by the third abutment, into the long depth of air which held nothing, only sometimes a rivet or a dropped hammer during the day.

Then there was no longer any fear on the bridge. The worst, the incredible, had happened. A nun had fallen off the Prince Edward Viaduct before it was even finished. The men covered in wood shavings or granite dust held the women against them. And Commissioner Harris at the far end stared along the mad pathway. This was his first child and it had already become a murderer.

The man in mid-air under the central arch saw the shape fall towards him, in that second knowing his rope would not hold them both. He reached to catch the figure while his other hand grabbed the metal pipe edge above him to lessen the sudden jerk on the rope. The new weight ripped the arm that held the pipe out of its socket and he screamed, so whoever might have heard him up there would have thought the scream was from the falling figure. The halter thulked, jerking his chest up to his throat. The right arm was all agony now—but his hand's timing had been immaculate, the grace of the habit, and he found himself a moment later holding the figure against him dearly.

He saw it was a black-garbed bird, a girl's white face. He saw this in the light that sprayed down inconstantly from a flare fifteen yards above them. They hung in the halter, pivoting over the valley, his broken arm loose on one side of him, holding the woman with the other. Her body was in shock, her huge eyes staring into the face of Nicholas Temelcoff.

Scream, please, Lady, he whispered, the pain terrible. He asked her to hold him by the shoulders, to take the weight off his one good arm. A sway in the wind. She could not speak though her eyes glared at him bright, just staring at him. *Scream, please.* But she could not.

During the night, the long chutes through which wet concrete slid were unused and hung loose so the open spouts wavered a few feet from the valley floor. The tops of these were about ten feet from him now. He knew this without seeing them, even though they fell outside the scope of light. If they attempted to slide the chute their weight would make it vertical and dangerous. They would have to go further—to reach the lower-deck level of the bridge where there were structures built for possible water mains.

We have to swing. She had her hands around his shoulders now, the wind assaulting them. The two strangers were in each other's arms, beginning to swing wilder, once more, past the lip of the chute which had tempted them, till they were almost at the lower level of the rafters. He had his one good arm free. Saving her now would be her responsibility.

She was in shock, her face bright when they reached the lower level, like a woman with a fever. She was in no shape to be witnessed, her veil loose, her cropped hair open to the long wind down the valley. Once they reached the catwalk she saved him from falling back into space. He was exhausted. She held and walked with him like a lover along the unlit lower parapet towards the west end of the bridge.

Above them the others stood around the one fire, talking agitatedly. The women were still tethered to the men and not looking towards the stone edge where she had gone over, falling in darkness. The one with that small scar against her nose . . . she was always falling into windows, against chairs. She was always unlucky.

The Commissioner's chauffeur slept in his car as Temelcoff and the nun walked past, back on real earth away from the bridge. Before they reached Parliament Street they cut south through the cemetery. He seemed about to faint and she held him against a gravestone. She forced him to hold his arm rigid, his fist clenched. She put her hands underneath it like a stirrup and jerked upwards so he screamed out again, her whole body pushing up with all of her strength, groaning as if about to lift him and then holding him, clutching him tight. She had seen the sweat jump out of his face. *Get me a shot. Get me . . . .* She removed her veil and wrapped the arm tight against his side. *Parliament and Dundas . . . few more blocks.* So she went down Parliament Street with him. Where she was going she didn't know. On Eastern Avenue she knocked at the door he pointed to. All these abrupt requests—scream, swing, knock, get me. Then a man opened the door and let them into the Ohrida Lake Restaurant. *Thank you, Kosta. Go back to bed, I'll lock it.* And the man, the friend, walked back upstairs.

She stood in the middle of the restaurant in darkness. The chairs and tables were pushed back to the edge of the room. Temelcoff brought out a bottle of brandy from under the counter and picked up two small glasses in the fingers of the same hand. He guided her to a small table, then walked back and, with a switch behind the zinc counter, turned on a light near her table. There were crests on the wall.

She still hadn't said a word. He remembered she had not even screamed when she fell. That had been him.

* * *

Nicholas Temelcoff is famous on the bridge, a daredevil. He is given all the difficult jobs and he takes them. He descends into the air with no fear. He is a solitary. He assembles ropes, brushes the tackle and pulley at his waist, and falls off the bridge like a diver over the edge of a boat. The rope roars alongside him, slowing with the pressure of his half-gloved hands. He is burly on the ground and then falls with terrific speedy grace, using the wind to push himself into corners of abutments so he can check driven rivets, sheering valves, the drying of the concrete under bearing plates and padstones. He stands in the air banging the crown pin into the upper cord and then shepherds the lower cord's slip-joint into position. Even in archive photographs it is difficult to find him. Again and again you see vista before you and the eye must search along the wall of sky to the speck of burned paper across the valley that is him, an exclamation mark, somewhere in the distance between bridge and river. He floats at the three hinges of the crescent-shaped steel arches. These knit the bridge together. The moment of cubism.

He is happiest at daily chores—ferrying tools from pier down to trestle, or lumber that he pushes in the air before him as if swimming in a river. He is a spinner. He links everyone. He meets them as they cling—braced by wind against the metal they are riveting or the wood sheeting they hammer into—but he has none of their fear. Always he carries his own tackle, hunched under his ropes and dragging the shining pitons behind him. He sits on a coiled seat of rope while he eats his lunch on the bridge. If he finishes early he cycles down Parliament Street to the Ohrida Lake Restaurant and sits in the darkness of the room as if he has had enough of light. Enough of space.

His work is so exceptional and time-saving he earns one dollar an hour while the other bridge workers receive forty cents. There is no jealousy towards him. No one dreams of doing half the things he does. For night work he is paid $1.25, swinging up into the rafters of a trestle holding a flare, free-falling like a dead star. He does not really need to see things, he has charted all that space, knows the pier footings, the width of the crosswalks in terms of seconds of movement—281 feet and 6 inches make up the central span of the bridge. Two flanking spans of 240 feet, two end spans of 158 feet. He slips into openings on the lower deck, tackles himself up to bridge level. He knows the precise height he is over the river, how long his ropes are, how many seconds he can free-fall to the pulley. It does not matter if it is day or night, he could be blindfolded. Black space is time. After swinging for three seconds he puts his feet up to link with the concrete edge of the next pier. He knows his position in the air as if he is mercury slipping across a map.

CYRIL DABYDEEN

(b. 1945)

'I express the "other" in the Canadian milieu and spirit,' says Cyril Dabydeen; 'all that I am, where I've come from, those narratives and the metaphor of the hinterland place, mind and consciousness. Caves of memory, too.' Many of those memories evoke Dabydeen's East Indian, South Asian, and Caribbean origins.

Born in Berbicé, Guyana, Dabydeen was already an award-winning poet before he emigrated to Canada in 1970. He studied English at Lakehead University, where he received a B.A. with Honours (1973), and at Queen's University, where he received an M.A. (1974). A resident of Ottawa for many years, Dabydeen taught at Algonquin College and at the University of Ottawa, and has worked with community groups, municipalities, and the federal government as a race relations professional. His commitment to community relations is strongly inscribed in his writing.

Widely anthologized and published in numerous literary magazines both in Canada and overseas, Dabydeen has edited *A Shapely Fire: Changing the Literary Landscape* (1987), one of the first anthologies of black and Caribbean writing in Canada, and *Another Way to Dance: An Anthology of Canadian Asian Poets* (1989). Poet Laureate of Ottawa during the period 1984-87, he has published eight collections of poetry, including *Goatsong* (1978), *This Planet Earth* (1979), *Islands Lovelier Than a Vision* (1988) and, most recently, *Stoning the Wind* (1994). His poetry records, in his own words, 'the changing landscape of the imagination, or the life in Canada as "I quarry silence and talk / In riddles so that the maple leaf / Itself will understand."' Although he bemoans the fact that, in Canada, some immigrants remain forever immigrants, as the title of one of his poems suggests, Dabydeen's writing reveals at once a commitment to Canada and a concern with the alienating impact of Canadian society on immigrants and people of colour.

This creative process, which mirrors, as he says, 'the extent to which I try to illuminate experience . . . [and] to understand myself as I come to grips with all others', also informs his fiction. His short story collections, *Still Close to the Island* (1980), *To Monkey Jungle* (1988), and *Jogging in Havana* (1992), address in different settings—including his native Guyana—the various configurations of otherness, while avoiding stereotypes. His characters' unease both about where they come from and to where they find themselves displaced is similarly present in his novels, *Dark Swirl* and *The Wizard Swami*, both published in England in 1989. Dabydeen has won the Sandback Parker Gold Medal (1964), the Louise Plumb Poetry Prize (1978), the Okanagan Fiction Prize, and the Canadian Author and Bookman Award (1982).

LADY ICARUS
'ordered deported—for the 5th time'

You fell, you
fell from seven
stories high
tempting gravity
from the Strathcona
hotel

not skyward
only landward

like a recalcitrant
angel, Maria,
all the way
      from Ecuador

you came, wanting
desperately to stay
in Canada

        so glorious
and free—defying
another deportation
order when suddenly
your rope

of sheets and blankets
broke
no sun now melting wax
your hold snaps

        as you plunge
to sudden death
we stand on guard for thee
oh so glorious and free

O Canada O Canada

MULTICULTURALISM

I continue to sing of other loves,
Places . . . moments when I am furious;
When you are pale and I am strong—
As we come one to another.

The ethnics at our door
Malingering with heritage,
My solid breath—like stones breaking;
At a railway station making much ado about much,
This boulder and Rocky Mountain,

CPR heaving with a head tax
As I am Chinese in a crowd,
Japanese at the camps,
It is also World War II.
Panting, I am out of breath.

So I keep on talking
With blood coursing through my veins,
The heart's call for employment equity,
The rhapsody of police shootings in Toronto,
This gathering of the stars one by one, codifying them
And calling them planets, one country, really . . .

Or galaxies of province after province,
A distinct society too:
Québec or Newfoundland; the Territories . . .
How far we make a map out of our solitudes
As we are still Europe, Asia,
Africa; and the Aborigine in me
Suggests love above all else—
The bear's configuration in the sky;
Other places, events; a turbanned RCMP,
These miracles—

My heritage and quest, heart throbbing;
Voices telling me how much I love you.
YOU LOVE ME; and we're always springing surprises,
Like vandalism at a Jewish cemetery
Or Nelson Mandela's visit to Ottawa
As I raise a banner high on Parliament Hill
Crying 'Welcome!' we are, you are—
OH CANADA!

I AM NOT

1

i am not West Indian
i am not—
let me tell you again and again
let Lamming and Selvon talk of places
        too distant from me;
let me also recover and seethe
& shout with a false tongue

if I must—
that i am here
nowhere else

let me also conjure up other places
as i cry out that all cities are the same,
rivers, seas, oceans—
how they swell or surrender
  at the same source

2

i breathe in the new soil
engorging myself with wind,
yet flaccid—

i inhale the odour
of rice paddy
cane leaves in the sun
& birds blacker than the familiar vulture
circling my father's house
with a vague promise
  amidst other voices
i come together with you,
crying out
that there are hinterlands,
other terrain

3

we fashion new boundaries
  and still i do not know,
i do not know,
in the cold, this heat
of the insides—
wetness at the corners of the mouth

skin grown lighter,
& once the giant lake,
foamy whiteness of my Ottawa river—
  now Mohawk or Algonquin . . .
whither Carib or Arawak?

i breathe harder
with my many selves,
  turning back

HAROLD SONNY LADOO

(1945-73)

Although he never achieved popular recognition during his lifetime, Harold Sonny Ladoo was acknowledged by his peers in Canada as a writer of great talent. Dennis Lee, whose elegy 'On the Death of Harold Ladoo' laments Ladoo's premature passing, was one of his supporters, and it was in fact the House of Anansi, Lee's press at the time, that published Ladoo's two novels, the second one posthumously. Ladoo saw *No Pain Like This Body* (1972), excerpts from which are included here, and *Yesterdays* (1974) as being part of a highly ambitious project, a cycle of about 100 novels that would have incorporated his personal history as well the histories of Canada and the Caribbean. Fragments of that projected work remain in his literary estate.

Born in Couva, Trinidad, and the descendent of East Indian indentured workers, he grew up on a plantation. An avid reader of Victorian literature, he received his first education in a Canadian Church Mission School. He arrived in Toronto in 1968. While studying towards his B.A. in English, which he received from Erindale College, University of Toronto, he supported himself with an assortment of odd jobs.

He died (some suspect he was murdered) while on a visit to Trinidad.

His novels, whose style has been compared to that of Faulkner and Hemingway, is concerned with the day-to-day demoralizing experiences of characters whose lives seem to be fatally sealed as much by their Hindu faith as by the colonial and social forces that surround them. At once tragical and fabulistic, *No Pain Like This Body*, set in 1905 and narrated from the perspective of a child, focuses on characters who attempt to maintain their human dignity against all odds, in a landscape that allegorically evokes both the beauty and chaos of their lives. *Yesterdays*, set fifty years later and described as 'scatological comedy', employs irony and satire to explore a Hindu man's plan to fight religious and colonial oppression: in the fashion of Canadian missionaries in Trinidad, he wants to come to Canada with the sole intent of converting Christian Canadians to Hinduism. Part of the power of Ladoo's fiction lies in his use of Indo-Caribbean dialect and the ways in which it documents and dramatizes the particularities of his characters.

FROM *NO PAIN LIKE THIS BODY*

Pa came home. He didn't talk to Ma. He came home just like a snake. Quiet.

The rain was drizzling. Streaks of lightning like long green snakes wriggled against the black face of the sky. Balraj, Sunaree, Rama and Panday were in the riceland, not far from where Ma was washing clothes. The riceland began about ten feet away from the tub. Balraj was trying hard to catch the tadpoles; they were black black, black like rain clouds, and they were moving like spots of tar in the water. Balraj was the oldest. He was twelve. He tried hard like hell to catch the tadpoles and put them in the ricebag. But the tadpoles were smart, smarter than Balraj. They behaved like drunk people in the water; they were giving a lot of trouble; they kept running and running in the water; they had no legs, but they were running in the muddy water; just running and running away from Balraj. Balraj wanted to catch the tadpoles so he kept on running behind them; and they knew that Balraj wanted to put them inside the ricebag, so they ran all the time away from him.

Sunaree was ten years old. She was dragging the ricebag in the water, just behind Balraj. But Balraj was getting fed up. The tadpoles were hiding away from him.

Rama and Panday were eight years old. Twins. They were naked. Both of them were running behind Sunaree. As they ran they kicked up water and soiled Sunaree's dress. Sunaree turned around. She was vexed and her face looked like a rain cloud. Then she said, 'Now Rama and Panday behave all you self!'

While she was talking to Rama and Panday, Balraj dragged his hands in the water to catch the tadpoles. He lifted his hands out. There were about ten tadpoles inside them. They were trying to jump out of his hands and go back into the water. Balraj turned around to put the tadpoles in the ricebag. Sunaree was not paying attention; she had the bag in the water, and she was talking to Rama and Panday. Balraj got mad; he bawled out, 'Sunaree I goin to kick you! Where de bag is?'

'De bag in de wadder bredder.'

'Wot it doin in de wadder?'

'It not doin notten.'

'Well pick up dat bag and open it.'

'Oright.'

Sunaree had a great love for the tadpoles also, so she opened the ricebag. Balraj dropped the crappo fish inside the ricebag, and bent down in the water again.

Rama and Panday walked up to Sunaree. They were not walking easy as a fly walks; they were walking like mules; their feet went *splunk splunk splunk* in the water.

'Rama and Panday all you walk easier dan dat,' Balraj told them. 'Dese crappo fish smart like hell. Wen dey hear all you walkin hard hard dey go run away.'

Rama and Panday didn't listen to Balraj. They held on to the ricebag. They opened it and peeped inside the bag. Their eyes were bulging like ripe guavas; they were trying hard to see the tadpoles that were in the bag, but they could not see anything. Rama sucked his teeth and said, 'I want to go in dat bag.'

Sunaree told him he couldn't go inside the ricebag, because he was going to kill the tadpoles.

'I want to go in dat bag too,' Panday declared.

'But I say all you cant go in dat bag. All you goin to kill de fish.'

Rama and Panday tried to pull the ricebag away from Sunaree. She was talking and begging them not to pull the bag; crying and begging them not to pull it away; crying not for her sake but for the tadpoles' sake, because she wanted the crappo fish to live. But Rama and Panday pulled the bag away from her.

Balraj walked in the water. His back was bent as if he was an old man. He knew that the tadpoles were smart, so he watched them carefully. There were some crappo fish near the bamboo grass; there were hundreds of them; they were dancing and moving like a patch of blackness. Balraj walked quietly. He moved closer to them; they did not see him, because they were dancing in a group. He bent down. Slowly. He stretched his hands. Then *wash wash* his hands swept through the water. He turned around to put the tadpoles in the ricebag. Balraj just turned around and dropped them inside the bag. But there was no bag; the tadpoles fell back into the water. Balraj just stood and looked and looked at the tadpoles that were free again in the water, then he got mad like a bull. He looked. Rama and Panday were dragging the bag in the water.

'Wot de hell all you doin wid dat bag?'

'We just playin bredder,' Panday said.

'Now all you drop dat bag!'

Balraj couldn't control himself. He ran up to them just like a horse. Rama and Panday dropped the bag in the water and started running towards the cashew tree.

Sunaree saw Balraj coming like a jackspaniard. She did not know what to do, so she just stood there and stared at Balraj.

'Why you give dem two son of a bitches dat bag?'

'I not give dem it.'

'Den who give dem it?'

'I tell you dey take it deyself.'

Sunaree had long black hair; it was thick like grass. Balraj grabbed her hair and started kicking her in the water. She pushed Balraj, and he fell *splash* in the water. Sunaree wanted to run away, but she couldn't run away; Balraj grabbed her hair again; he was pulling her hair as if he was going to pull out her head. Then he started dragging her in the muddy water.

Balraj couldn't see Pa at all. Pa just stood in the banana patch like a big snake and watched all the time. Ma was busy washing the clothes; she couldn't see Pa either. Pa was just hiding and watching with poison in his eyes. Ma was just washing the clothes under the plum tree. Her back was bent low over the tub, and she was washing as if the clothes were rottening with dirt; she just bent over the tub and scrubbed like a crazy woman. Then she heard Sunaree bawling. Ma lifted her head. Balraj was still dragging Sunaree in the water. Ma shouted, 'Leggo dat chile Balraj!'

'I not lettin she go!'

'Boy I is you modder. I make you. You just lissen to me. Leggo she.'

'I not lettin she go!'

'I comin in dat wadder for you right now Balraj!'

Ma was fed up. She washed out her hands in the soapy water. Then she walked to the edge of the riceland. Ma was quarrelling and pointing at Balraj. Suddenly she stood up. She saw Pa. Ma turned around and walked back to the tub.

Pa came out of the banana patch.

'Now all you chirens come outa dat wadder!' he shouted.

Pa had a voice like thunder. When he spoke the riceland shook as if God was shaking up Tola.

Rama and Panday were near the cashew tree. They were trying to hold the mamzels, but they moved like the wind.

'Let we catch dem crabs,' Rama suggested.

'And do wot wid dem?' Panday asked.

'Kill dem.'

'It not good to kill notten.'

They had to be careful in the riceland. There were deep holes all over the place, especially near the cashew and barahar trees. The holes were not deep like a well or a river, but they were deep enough to drown Rama and Panday.

'It have crabs near dat barahar tree,' Rama said.

'It too deep by de barahar tree,' Panday told him.

'It not too deep. Dem red crabs livin in dem holes.'

'But dem holes deep deep.'

'I still goin to walk to de barahar tree,' Rama declared.

Rama began walking eastward across the riceland. Panday was begging him not to go, but Rama was not listening; he was harden like a goat. But Rama couldn't go. He and Panday heard when Pa shouted at Balraj and Sunaree. Panday and Rama ran out of the riceland, passed through the banana patch and went by the rainwater barrel. The rainwater barrel was almost touching the tapia wall at the eastern side of the house.

When Pa shouted, Balraj released Sunaree. She ran out of the riceland, passed Ma by the tub, and went and joined Rama and Panday by the rainwater barrel, but Balraj remained inside the riceland. He stood up and looked at Pa; he was watching as if he was going to eat Pa; he was really playing man for Pa. Pa made an attempt to go in the water. Balraj was afraid; he ran to the eastern side of the riceland. He ran as fast as a cloud moves in the sky. Then he stood up on a meri on the other side of the riceland and looked at Pa.

'Now Balraj come outa dat wadder!'

'I fraid you beat me.'

'I not goin to do you notten boy.'

'Oright.'

Pa was smarter than a snake; he began to talk soft as if a child was talking. He said that he was not going to beat Balraj, because he was a child. He thought that Pa was talking the truth; he began to walk to meet him. Pa just stood there and looked at him; just stood on the edge of the riceland and waited as a snake.

Balraj walked slowly. His feet didn't go *splash splash* in the water; they went *splunk* and *splunk* and then *splunk* as if a little child was walking in the water. He watched Pa with fear in his eyes as he came closer to the western edge of the riceland. Pa wasn't backward; he was watching Balraj with snaky eyes. The wind was blowing cold cold. Balraj was trembling. His teeth went *clax clax clax*. The wind was blowing from the north. It was cold as ice cream, and Balraj was trembling and watching Pa. The sky was black as Sunaree's hair, and Pa was watching Balraj. Balraj was almost out of the water. Pa leaned over the edge of the riceland and tried to hold his hand. Balraj ran *splash splash*. Pa ran eastwards along the riceland bank; his feet went *tats tats tats*. There were many snakes in the riceland; they lived inside the deep holes near the barahar tree. Balraj was trying to keep away from the holes, because he was afraid of the snakes. Balraj was tired running. He just stood in the water and looked at Pa. Pa was mad. He jumped up and down on the riceland bank.

'Balraj come outa dat wadder!' Pa shouted.

'I fraid you beat me.'

'Boy come outa dat wadder!'

Balraj was afraid. He knew Pa was going to beat him real bad. *Crax crax cratax doom doommm doomed!* the thunder rolled. Balraj looked at the sky; it was blacker than a dream of snakes and evil spirits. Pa bent down and picked up dirt from the riceland bank. He started to pelt Balraj. Balraj was moving from side to side trying hard to get away from the dirt. Pa couldn't hit him. Pa was in a rage; he was pelting as a madman. Then Pa shouted, 'Now come outa dat wadder boy! I goin to pelt inside dem snake holes.'

Balraj made no effort to come out of the riceland. Pa kept pelting dirt into the deep holes. The water was bubbling and bubbling and bubbling; bubbling and bubbling as if it was boiling over with rage; it was boiling and bubbling as when a ricepot bubbles over a fireside, but Balraj just stood there and looked at Pa.

'You feel you is a big man?' Pa asked him.

'No.'

'Den come outa dat wadder!'

'I fraid you beat me.'

'Den you is a big man?'

'No. I is a little little chile. Little little.'

'Well I goin to make a snake bite you ass!'

It was August, the middle of the rainy season. The rain was falling and falling and falling as if the sky was leaking or something. Sunaree, Rama and Panday were still by the rainwater barrel. Sunaree was holding the enamel dipper, but it slipped from her hand and fell in the yard. The dipper was dirty; full of mud all over. Rama and Panday were still naked. Trembling.

'I feelin cold.'

'Hush else Pa go bust you liver wid a kick,' Rama said.

'Pa stupid,' Panday declared.

'Pa stupid like God.'

'Now God have big eyes and he seein wot all you doin,' Sunaree said.

'Somebody shouda hit God one kick and bust he eye!' Rama shouted.

Sunaree told Rama that God had great big eyes; God never winked; even if dirt or flies or smoke went into his eyes, he never winked; God never slept or drank or ate; he never sheltered with a leaf from the wind and the rain; he just lived in heaven and stared at the earth all the time.

And Rama: 'Den God like a stone. He just like a stone I tell you.'

'You mean dat God does see wen Rama pee on me in de night?' Panday asked.

'Yeh,' Sunaree said.

Sunaree picked up the enamel dipper, rinsed it inside the rainwater barrel, and said, 'Now Rama and Panday come on inside dat house.' She walked in front, and they followed her.

Balraj was still watching Pa; he was trembling like a banana leaf, but he was watching Pa. Pa was strong like a mango tree, so his teeth were not going *clax clax clax*, because he was not feeling cold.

Ma finished washing the clothes. She put them in the old bucket. She looked. Balraj was still inside the riceland. Ma said to Pa, 'Dat chile fraid you. I bleed blood to make dat chile. Dat chile come from my belly after I carry him for nine monts. Now you let dat chile come outa dat wadder. I bleed blood to make dat chile!'

Pa spoke like a stone rolling down from a hill, 'Now you just shut you kiss me ass mout woman! Shut it!'

Ma talked back as water falling from a house roof. She complained that Pa was not acting as a father at all. Pa had no heart because he was running Balraj in the riceland. She threatened that if anything happened to Balraj in the water, she was going to walk the three miles to Tolaville; walk the three miles just to get a policeman to lock up Pa.

'Kiss me ass!' Pa shouted.

And Ma talked again; she talked as a spider that is full of poison. Pa hated the way she talked. He began to pelt more dirt into the water. The water was still bubbling. Pa aimed carefully. He threw the dirt. It fell *plunk* inside one of the deep holes. A huge water snake came to the surface of the muddy water.

Balraj started to run in the water. The snake moved *clips clips clips*. Fast. Faster. The snake moved as oil on the water. Balraj knew that the snake was chasing him, so he didn't look back. The snake went just a little way and turned back. But Balraj thought that the snake was following him; he ran out of the riceland and went by Ma. It was only when he reached by Ma that he looked back. There was no snake.

Pa was serious. He ran by the tub. There was not a laugh or a smile on his face; he just came by the tub to beat Balraj.

'Behave youself and leff me son alone!' Ma shouted.

'Shut you kiss me ass mout woman!'

Pa held Ma real hard beside the tub; he was pulling her; just pulling and pulling as if he was uprooting a sapodilla tree. Ma held on to Balraj, and he was holding on to the hog plum tree. Pa tried his best to kick Balraj, but Ma was in his way. Pa was sweating and blowing. 'I goin to drownd you in dat tub woman!'

'Balraj is a little chile. You is a big man. You have no right to make a snake run him in dat wadder. But it have a God and he watchin from dat sky.'

'God could kiss me ass!'

'Well wen a man coud cuss God he deserve to dead!'

Pa hated Ma and he hated Balraj, so he picked up Ma as if he was picking up a little child and he held her in the air. Ma bawled like a cow hard hard hard. She tried to hold the hog plum tree, but she couldn't meet it. Ma didn't want to go inside the tub; she was turning and twisting as a worm; just turning and twisting and bawling; just bawling and trying to get away. The water in the tub was full of soap suds. Pa held her high, and he held her tight as a tree holds another tree. Ma was bawling and getting on; getting on and calling God, but the sky was black and God was only watching with his big eyes from heaven; he was not even trying to help Ma a little. Pa turned her over and pushed her face inside the tub; trying hard to drown her like. Her feet were high in the air, and her whole body was shaking as a banana leaf shakes when the wind blows.

Balraj got his chance. He ran by the rainwater barrel. But Balraj was confused. He didn't know where to run. He just stood by the rainwater barrel behind the house, and stared at Pa.

Then Pa changed his mind. He took Ma out of the tub. She coughed and coughed and coughed. She could not stand. She fell, got up, then she fell again. She rolled on the ground and vomited the soapy water.

Pa left Ma alone. He ran about twenty feet and came by the rainwater barrel. Balraj saw Pa coming but he couldn't move. Pa grabbed him by the barrel and struck him with his right hand. Balraj was not a man; he was not strong like a carat tree; he was just a boy, so the blow flattened him. Pa held his feet and dragged him away from the rainwater barrel. Balraj was bawling and rolling like a pig. Pa stood on his chest and told him to shut up.

Ma was still vomiting, but when she saw Pa standing on his chest, she got up. And Pa was not standing on Balraj's chest alone; he was standing on his chest and saying, 'I go bust you liver today!' Pa was squeezing his chest real hard, and Balraj was bawling and bawling.

Ma ran up to Pa like a rat. Pa couldn't see her coming, his back was turned. She gave a good push; he almost fell over. Still standing on Balraj's chest, Pa threw a blow at her head. It sounded *biff!* as when a dry coconut falls. Then Pa picked up Balraj as a wet bundle of grass and threw him *splash* inside the drain. Pa turned around. He was looking for Ma. She ran past the rainwater barrel and went by the outhouse. Pa ran through the banana patch, but before he reached the outhouse she ran westward, crossed Tola Trace and went inside the sugarcane field.

Balraj got up from the canal. He looked. Pa was still by the outhouse. He ran to the front of the house. He looked. Pa was coming through the banana patch again. Balraj dashed across Tola Trace and hid in the sugarcane field.

Sunaree, Rama and Panday were inside the house. Trembling. They peeped through the wide creases in the earthen wall. They saw Ma running and bawling; they saw her cross Tola Trace; they saw Balraj too; they saw him as he ran as a mad-man inside the sugarcane field. They wanted to run out of the house too, but they were afraid. Pa was walking up and down in the backyard as a crazy man. They were quiet in the house, just looking at him; looking and praying to God to keep Pa away from the house. Pa fished out a bottle of rum from his pocket and took a good drink. He drank out all and threw the flask away; it broke *splinks!* Sunaree, Rama and Panday were joined together in a living heap. They peeped through the creases again; Pa was walking towards the riceland. A streak of lightning danced inside the house.

'Hide de dipper Panday!' Sunaree screamed.

'I fraid like hell to move from where I standin up.'

'Hide dat dipper befo de lightnin cut out you tongue.'

'I fraid I tell you!'

Sunaree took the dipper and flung it under the settee.

'Why God not kill dat lightnin ass?' Rama asked.

'Quiet befo dat lightnin hear you and cut out you tongue!' Sunaree told him.

They peeped through the creases again. Pa was standing under the barahar tree.

'God go care for we,' Panday said.

'Dat is true bredder.'

But Rama: 'God does only eat and drink in dat sky.'

'God go give you sin. Wen you dead de Devil go ride you like a horse in de night,' Sunaree said.

They peeped through the creases again. Pa was walking back to the house.

'Let we run outa dis house fast!' Sunaree shouted.

They were ready; Rama and Panday were ready; they were naked and they were ready to run out of the house. Sunaree held their hands as they dashed out of the house. They ran across the yard into Tola Trace. They faced south, because they were running to meet the house of Nanna and Nanny in Rajput Road; they ran fast, because Nanna and Nanny lived half a mile away at the corner of Tola Trace and Rajput Road. Lightning jumped out of the clouds as green snakes and gold fishes, and the thunder shook up the whole of Tola, yet they didn't stop running. Dark clouds were coming closer to the earth like a black spider with a huge body, yet they kept on running. They ran, because they were sure that God was watching them with his big big eyes.

Glossary

Crappo: frog.
Crappo fish: tadpoles.
Meri: a low straight bank in the riceland, usually built to control the water in the *cola* (or *kola*). The meris meet at right angles, forming plots, the colas.
Tola: village, settlement.
Trace: unpaved road, dirt path.

PATRICK FRIESEN

(b. 1946)

'Writing to me is medicine,' Patrick Friesen has said. 'It's a life and death issue. . . . It's better yet than medicine, yes.' But Friesen, who spent the first nineteen years of his life in the Mennonite community of Steinbach, Manitoba, has also had to fight against the Mennonite notion that writing is 'immodest', a 'presumptuous act'. 'There was a time in my youth,' he says, 'when preachers didn't preach sermons. All you were allowed to do was read the Bible. You couldn't comment on it . . . that is the whole truth and that's the received truth and to do anything more is to be pretentious or unnecessary or maybe to admit failure of that book.' 'Making yourself go public', that is, publishing, was for Friesen 'a wrenching act'—an act whose complex consequences and significance are made apparent in the opening stanzas of his first poetry book, *the lands i am* (1976): 'I'll be staunch / subdue the rabble / and be aristocrat again / be king / for a moment.'

Still, Friesen 'discovered that I couldn't reject the background which I was shying away from. . . . I realized that there was something to be redeemed and one of the main things was the language I grew up with . . . which was biblical, which was sermons and that kind of rhetoric . . . So I began exploring that language, going back to it and saying, "Look, I can still like the language even though I don't like what was done with it. I can redeem it for myself, I can use it in different ways."' Much of the rhythm and imagery of his poems go back to his roots, but the energy of his writing also comes from the ways in which his body registers the physical world around him. From the short lines characteristic of his first book and his second publication, *bluebottle* (1978), Friesen has moved to the undulating rhythms of longer lines in *Unearthly Horses* (1984) and *Flicker and Hawk*

(1987). Obsession with death and a desire to find 'the intangible, finding god through the world'—not 'the "capital g" god. . . . That's a God that doesn't understand. Small g, I understand. Big g is a "daddy", something else. That's outside of me. Small g is inside'—are two of the major themes that run through his work.

The Shunning (1980), a long documentary poem that consists of poetry, prose, and photographs, marks his shift from the lyricism of his early work to more dramatic tensions. Adapted by Friesen for the stage in 1985, and later for CBC Radio (1990), it marks the beginning of his involvement with theatre and performance. Friesen, who received a B.A. (1969) in English from the University of Manitoba, had already produced and directed a number of documentary films, including *Spy in the House: Esther Warkov* (1982) and *The Spirit of Assessippi: Don Proch* (1983). *The raft*, staged in Winnipeg in 1992, is his second play.

Friesen's other stage work includes the multidisciplinary performances *Anna* (1987), with choreographer Stephanie Ballard and guest artist Margie Gillis, and *Handful of Rain* (1991), with choreographers Ruth Cansfield and Gaile Petursson-Hiley. The poems he wrote for the latter work are included in *You Don't Get to Be a Saint* (1992), a book nominated for the McNally-Robinson Book of the Year and the winner of the Manitoba Book Design of the Year Award.

Friesen, a resident of Winnipeg, was the founding president of the Manitoba Writers' Guild (1981-83). In collaboration with Per Brask, he has translated *God's Blue Morris* (1993), selected poems by Danish poet Niels Hav, and *Stealing Lines From A Dance, An Anthology of 21 Danish Poets*. Friesen's most recent publication is *Blasphemer's Wheel: Selected and New Poems* (1994).

SUNDAY AFTERNOON

on sunday afternoons all the fathers in town slept
I think they dreamed of old days and death
sometimes you could hear them cry
the summer air was still at the window
flies on the screen and the radio playing softly in the kitchen

mother slid a fresh matrimonial cake onto potholders on the stove
picked up a book a true book of someone else's life
sunglasses a pitcher of lemonade and a straw hat
spread a blue blanket in the backyard near the lilac shrubs for shade
lay down one ear hearing children in the garden
she never escaped all the way nor did she want to not quite
this much on a sunday afternoon went a long way

downtown boys rode main street toward fiery crashes they imagined
twisted wrecks with radios playing
rock 'n' roll insulting the highway
townspeople gathered on the shoulder
standing as near as they could to the impossible moment between
    what's here and not

a girl's body sprawled in the ditch no one knew at first whose
    daughter she was
though someone pulled her skirt down for decency
the smell of alcohol and fuel everywhere
her lipstick so so red beneath the headlights
they couldn't take their eyes from her lips
what was she doing in a wild car like that? who was she?

at night I shivered in bed wondering how to get out of town
side-stepping wrecks they were everywhere on all the roads heading
    out toward the lights and laughter
a dented hubcap an amazing shoe with its laces still done up
    made you wonder how someone could step right out of a shoe
    like that like the flesh was willing or surprised or not there to
    begin with

in nightmares angry lords walked through my room
it took my breath away how ferocious love could be
sometimes jesus hung on the wall or was it the shadow of an elm?

in the morning at the kitchen table green tomatoes on the window
    sill we held devotions with careful hands
father's eyes focused hard on me so he wouldn't remember but of
    course he did
listening often to mother's sunny childhood dreams
I thought I was free I was a child with a dancing mother
and my town was filled with children and my town had backstreets
    and sheds and black dogs and sugar trees but she disappeared
    and he died and I got out I'm getting out I'm getting out
what I left there the child gathering raspberries in an enamel bowl
he's not dead he went back to where you are before you're born again
waiting for the next time and another town

BIBLE

the bible was a telephone book
of levites canaanites and reubenites
it was a television set
my favourite program being revelation
until someone told me what it meant

the bible whispered to itself at night
I thought I heard the song of solomon and lamentations
maybe job   and later second thessalonians
in the morning there were always new underlinings

it was a vacuum cleaner once
a week later it was a close shave

the bible was a cockroach
scuttling its dark way through the house
would it survive the holocaust?

it was a black dog behind the couch
I could see its muzzle from where I sat at the piano

the bible took me aside
and taught me how to squint
it grasped my hand
and showed me how to shake

once
I remember it was fall
the bible took me to a show
of time-lapse photography

EVISCERATION

lord I'm coming apart this is the time of my evisceration this is
    when my singing ceases and something almost silent begins
I'm not safe in the night turning in my sleep I'm not safe throughout
    the day
in all weather in my walking or my talk in my room or when my
    heart is open there is no safety
I have danced and slipped I have fallen I have been cruel and I
    have lain in the arms of betrayal
everything has happened and I've gone nowhere I'm spinning
    you're not here you're not there
I'm bereft of love and sense I'm stupid in my collapse no one
    hears me I'm not saying the words that could make anyone
    see or know my descent
I'm bereft of words but not the need to find them

you may hear or not you may walk away still I will speak my fears
    I will admit the shoes and hats I wear
I'll be your fool take my foolishness and hold it up for me to know
I would drown for love because that's love it is hard and unrelenting
there is no return there is only the wall I walk toward

yesterday I threw my hat in the air today I wear it again gravity
    is not always a friend
I'm falling it's not this I fear it's falling forever
it's not love's refusal to forgive I fear I fear its absence
I fear my love will not reveal its true face I fear what I am in the
    night and what I conceal all day
lord I fear each breath I fear this paradise I do not fear death it will
    catch my fall

what do I ask where are you to hear there is emptiness everywhere
when I come to the end of myself when I stand at the basin and
    look through the window of the mirror what will I see?
give me ropes and water I will place them in my shrine
I will learn the love that tears me open
give me celestial burial my body spread-eagled and dispersed
    throughout the world

I will be your fool in the talons of an iron bird I will be free in the
    horrible sky

BREAKING FOR LIGHT

I just stepped out of the cold dream that's it I won't be in
    dreams anymore
no more walls or webs it's not me in your cards I'm swimming
    upstream heading out of the dream
I'm no one's goat anymore I'm no dreaming joseph I'm thrashing
    through water half the time I'm drowning the rest of the way
    I'm breaking for light

I am myself when I write I know I've got the glory it spreads
    like heat from the heart sometimes I'm standing on my chair
    downstairs singing harmony or slow-shuffling around the room
    with smooth rhythm
it happens the lord's there no question and I take the words
    I'm hungry for the words there's love there someplace between
    the words
and I say them and sing them you can see the red and blue in
    the room
and I know where I am it feels clean no clothes no dreams I
    feel you my heart's open come on come on whoever you are

I know somewhere outside the room it's warm it's a place to find
    seems to me love is warm when it's not cold
froze my feet long ago it's not every day you thaw and come out
    smiling not every day love's born and grows old but it happens
you never called me lover you strung me along but I'm catching
    on to you I'm not in your dream I'm a lover and you're
    smiling in spite of yourself it's what you said you wanted
    all along can you take it?

you pull away just when I'm drawing near it's an old trick lord
    and I'm fooled again
there's no going back it's been too hard I've earned my touch
    I'm not going where it's cold
lord I've found earth and feet I'm out of dreams you're here by
    a thread

could be love we'll finally come out clear it's time and we're
    worn out

things falling around us the tricks the knife all the rage the night
it feels like last chance to bless our wounds and let them blossom

I'm asking can you take me straight on? I'm a lion some days a
    rabbit I'm not anyone else
can you take my kisses and my juice? I want you all the way
    sometimes at close quarters and at length I want to be everyone
    I am with you
when I'm lewd or unruly can you laugh? when I'm tender what then?
when the streetlight's in the window and the children asleep
    can you know my absence?

 could be we'll come out clear I've fallen out of dreams there are
    no arms to hold me this is where I swim
you want to know where I am this is my hand this is how we
    touch is there anything else we could want?
I'm breaking for light I don't know what's next but I keep
    finding out

THE FORGE
(the man who licked stones)

the man in the long coat licked stones memorizing the world's first
    fire on his tongue
he didn't have time to speak though he had nothing else he didn't
    speak because he hadn't come to words
his slow hands hung from the stillness of his torn sleeves reaching
    only to touch what he might remember
with his hands how carefully he brushed dust from stones with his
    tongue revealed their rose or cobalt blue
he walked outside town on gravel roads he walked outside love too
    close to worship to say
around him earth's rubble and striations sign and witness of the
    forge he longed to find
his mouth craving volcanoes the taste of ash and rain his mouth
    ground stones in his sleep
I thought he would vanish one day spellbound in his cellar among
    the roots
I thought in the end he might walk into the river with his heavy
    pockets but there was no such privilege for him
with the years I forgot him or he became a shape I couldn't see
    wandering around town
I don't know if he took form again or if it was time for me to see I

saw him emerge like a photograph in its bath
he was walking past the church he reeled suddenly with a stiff-
    legged pivot and fell straight on his back
no one falls like that the body in surrender to gravity no one falls as
    if nothing matters and nothing did
his eyes glistening like wet sapphires in snow his dead eyes looked
    through us seeing their way into stone

J.J. STEINFELD

(b. 1946)

Although his imagination, as J.J. Steinfeld says, 'is attracted to many themes, . . . the effect of the Holocaust on subsequent generations is the theme that is most personal and dominant' in his work. *The Apostate's Tattoo* (1983), *Forms of Captivity and Escape* (1988), *Unmapped Dreams* (1989), and *The Miraculous Hand and Other Stories* (1991), all collections of short stories, evolve out of Steinfeld's fictional dialogue with the past, and dramatize 'how the turmoil and struggle of existence stir some people to rage and action while paralyzing others'.

Steinfeld was born in a Displaced Persons camp in Munich, Germany, of Polish parents, and moved to Canada in 1972. Prior to his arrival in Canada, he received a B.A. in English (1968) from Case Western Reserve University in Cleveland, Ohio, and began graduate studies at Ohio State University. He resumed his studies at Trent University, where he received an M.A. in History (1978).

Since 1980, Steinfeld has been a full-time fiction writer and playwright. His short stories, which have appeared in numerous literary magazines, have won him many awards, including the 1990 Creative Writing Award from the Toronto Jewish Congress Book Committee. *Our Hero is the Cradle of Confederation* (1987) was the winner of the Great Canadian Novella Competition in 1986. He has written two full-length plays, and five one-act plays that have each won the Theatre Prince Edward Island's Playwriting Competition. Steinfeld, whose most recent book is *Dancing at the Club Holocaust* (1993), is a resident of Charlottetown, Prince Edward Island.

IDA SOLOMON'S PLAY

After a performance of my one-woman play, such as tonight, it takes me a long time to calm down, to escape the character I play. Sometimes I get frightened that I'll never become myself again, but I always do. I have my restorative ritual: several cups of strong tea, and then a long walk. Some nights I only need an hour or two, other nights all night, before I can go home to sleep, later awaking as myself. Lately, it's been all night.

On stage, performance after performance, I am Ida Solomon, born Radom, Poland, 1921, died Toronto, Ontario, Canada, 1977, through the eight stages of her life I selected as the most dramatically important to tell Ida's story. I go from sixteen in 1937 through age fifty-six in 1977, forty years of a woman's life, the transformation from the dancing, joyous teenager to the wailing, sad woman seeking a solitary death. My makeup and costumes create an incredible sense of realism; I have Sally and Heather to thank for that. I've learned to dissolve my own forty-one years and become sixteen or twenty-three or fifty-six, whatever I need to be.

This play means everything to me, but who would have ever thought that it would become a success, after the setbacks and bad luck associated with its production. Yet those very nerve-racking problems gave us what got the public interested in the play: priceless publicity, some of it more than a little concerned with the morbid. Fortunately, I'm not a superstitious person. My director Estelle is, but she has her good-luck charms and protective medallions. I wrote the play to keep from jumping off my balcony. Every time I stood too long on the balcony and that familiar dizziness started to take over, I went to my desk and wrote. Thank God for the play! For the years I knew my mother, I relied on memory; for the years before I was born, I talked to her two older sisters, the surviving ones.

The first time I left the theatre in costume I wasn't going to speak, just walk until I felt myself returning. I walked to a part of the city I ordinarily would never go near, and went into a bar that seemed to be out of a third-rate play about dead dreams and babbling drunks. I intended to sit in the bar silently, and drink myself into recovery. But I had to speak, in my mother's voice. Too much silence and I would have had to scream.

'I was in a concentration camp,' I heard myself tell the bartender. He was young, at least ten years younger than me. 'Too bad about that,' he said. Maybe if I had told him my house had burned down or I needed to have a tooth pulled, I would have received more of a reaction. The man sitting two stools away heard me. Through his drunkenness he said, 'Poor lady.'

'The Nazis raped me,' I told him when he moved to the stool next to mine. He groaned in sympathy and put his hands on my clenched fists. As he patted my fists, he kept repeating, 'Poor lady, poor lady. . . .' Then I gave him, word for word, my mother's speech to the unseen psychiatrist during the sixth scene, when she was forty-five and more than ever encased in her painful past. I saw that the man wanted to leave but I held him with my performance. Even that first night out in costume, I wasn't scared and didn't feel unnatural. My mother was an exceptional woman.

Another man who had been listening bought us both drinks. We moved to a table and talked about World War II and the old Nazis that he heard were living in the city, two around the corner from the very bar we were in. For a moment I suspected he was a Nazi in disguise. I drank until I was drunk, and started to cry. My tears are better on stage, but the barroom flow was convincing all the same. My mood changed for the better when I thought that I probably could get a lifetime of free drinks by going from bar to bar, city to city.

Before leaving I performed for the men the entire third scene, Ida twenty-three and in a concentration camp. When I awoke the next afternoon I wasn't certain if I had really done what I had remembered doing. My costume was folded neatly on a chair in the bedroom, but I didn't recall taking it off. The creative process exacts a large price, I told myself, both seriously and foolishly, the way I console myself whenever I do something troublesome or painful or excessive. The next performance was only a few hours away—had I slept *that* long, I remember thinking—and began to become my mother again. I need no less than an hour of mental preparation, even before setting foot in the theatre, to become my character.

I don't know how much longer the play will run or how much longer I want or need to play my mother. I'd like to see the play last as long as possible, but I don't know if I can trust another actress with the role. Perhaps as long as I have my outlets, the dismal bars and all-night eating places and dark streets, I can continue. I never considered myself much of an actress, but I knew Ida Solomon. Estelle thought that

I was crazy even to attempt the role, but I won her over. I changed my walk and posture and voice; not knowing exactly how, but I transformed my entire being to resemble my mother. And on Sundays I would go to the cemetery and perform before my parents' graves. Then I would beg my parents for forgiveness. After a while, I no longer needed to be forgiven. I wanted to know their secrets, the ones I couldn't find out from relatives or books. What had they thought about during those days and hours and minutes of hell? How had they survived the concentration camps? I wanted to know if I could have survived. Every night on stage I tried to find out.

On occasion I consider going out as Ida at sixteen or thirty-five or forty-nine, but I never do; always in the costume I wear in the last scene, at fifty-six, when Ida releases her hold, allows the past to triumph. In a strange way, I feel safest at fifty-six, despite what happened to my mother and despite what sometimes happens to me in costume.

If not for the cut on my hand, I would have thought that it had been a dream. He seemed to be so sympathetic at first, a bright-eyed, sensitive night wanderer with a lovely face. He drank coffee, and I tea, strong tea like my mother drank. He told me that he had once lived with a Jewish woman, but she had left him two years ago. He pointed to his heart and said that he still had the scars. I told him about Ida's sexual experiences, the tender ones like the night I was conceived, and the horrid, damaging ones in concentration camp. I would never have gone back with the stranger to his apartment, but my mother did. Not to be alone another night, not after seven years of nights alone since her husband had died. I didn't know my mother as well as I had thought.

Almost from the first moment in his apartment my new acquaintance became aggressive. Pushing me about his living room, he said that he would make love to me the way a dirty old Jew deserved. I fought back, hitting the guard hard, and I couldn't believe the Nazis weren't going to kill me for resisting. He was surprised by my strength. That's when he picked up the knife. I smashed a flowerpot into his lovely face just as he cut me. After he fell, I ran from the apartment, from the concentration camp. So few were able to escape successfully. I think I got into a taxi. I never saw the man with the lovely face again, if he ever existed. The cut on my hand was real, but I could have gotten it anywhere that night.

After only two or three performances of the play about Ida Solomon, I became totally unaware of the audience, even when the play ended and applause filled the theatre. There was no audience when my mother died; her years in concentration camps were unscripted. Because of my need to prepare before the play, and calm down afterwards, the distinction between on stage and off stage grew vaguer and vaguer for me.

I don't know if I could have done this play if my mother were still alive. She died in 1977, when I was thirty, and it took me years to come to terms with her death. As long as I could remember, my father had his heart condition and that illness was real, graspable; his death, for me, was comprehensible. My mother appeared to be whole. Growing up, I thought that she was the strongest woman anywhere; her breakdown was not real for me, until I wrote the play. It frightens me knowing that what my mother had to endure is enabling me finally to make a living as a playwright and actress. When my mother was alive I went through the worst financial struggles and wrote the most abominable rubbish. I thought I was a writer in those days, but it was nothing but self-delusion and vanity. Now I am a writer, and an actress to boot.

None of the women who auditioned for the part could get it right. There were plenty of good actresses who wanted to play Ida Solomon but something was always missing. Maybe I was too critical, but it was my play . . . more than a play: a way to confront the past. The past is a tangible character in the play. The first actress Estelle and I decided on was adequate. At least she could handle the forty-year range. She was best as a sixteen-year-old; her fifty-six-year-old, however, was not an inspired performance. It made me somewhat uneasy that she wasn't Jewish; not that she need-ed to be a Jew—she was an actress, after all. The direction, makeup and costumes are superb; the women I have working with me on this play are dedicated and brilliant, especially Estelle, Sally and Heather.

But for relaxation our first Ida liked to ski a little too fast and managed to break both a collarbone and a leg. That was our first setback, after three weeks of rehearsals. The next actress to play Ida Solomon was also not Jewish. To her credit, she impressed me with her improvement as rehearsals progressed, becoming more 'Jewish' each day. She had been my fifth choice and Estelle's second, but I relied on my director's instincts. The second Ida neglected to tell us that she was undergoing chemotherapy for cancer. I assume in her mind she was determined to be the undaunted, show-must-go-on trouper, but she became weaker and weaker and finally backed out—doctor's orders—telling us that she wanted to spend the remainder of her life in London, England, going to plays.

The third actress's previous stage experience had been mainly in comedies and musicals, and I questioned her ability to handle the depth of emotion required for Ida Solomon's life. She did happen to be Jewish and that gave me hope if nothing else. But she was the mistake to end all mistakes. I should be thankful the little junkie didn't kill herself on stage. I think that was her intention. Estelle doesn't agree with me, but it's my theory that the third actress to play Ida got so disoriented she thought the dressing room was centre stage. She was dressed as the sixteen-year-old; it would have made more sense to me, of course, if she was the fifty-six-year-old; but then she would have been following the script and that I'm sure was no longer of interest to her. In the dead actress's dressing room, waiting for the police, is when I first thought that I might be able to play Ida Solomon—*had* to play her. The transition from ten-tative notion to fixed idea was swift, an explosive inner communication. No one knew the character better than I did. Estelle cried for the corpse, for the play she was direct-ing; I thought about what my mother had endured in concentration camp.

'We'll put it on. I don't care how long it takes . . . I promise we'll do it,' I told Estelle, but she was convinced the play was both cursed and doomed.

'There won't be a sane actress in town who will touch the role now,' my director said.

'So, who needs to be sane,' I told her.

We barely needed two weeks of preparation before the play was ready to open again. The publicity we were getting was unbelievable. I refused to tell anyone that the play was about my mother, almost literally so. My standard reply became that my play was based on a composite of the mothers of two of my childhood friends. When a swastika was painted on the outside of the theatre, the publicity increased. We had a full house on opening night, and for most of the nights after that.

I can't remember exactly when I started to leave the theatre in costume, but it might have been the very first night. When I sat in the dressing room in front of the mirror, I swear I saw my mother. She needed some fresh air. I was going to take only a short walk, around the block at most. Soon I was unable not to take my after-show excursions.

As far as I know, I have been recognized only a few times on the street. I was startled the first time I was noticed by someone who had seen the play. I didn't understand right away what the person was saying to Ida. My mind was elsewhere, in Poland, worrying about getting through another dreadful, imprisoned day. The second time, an excited couple told me how wonderful my performance had been, and that they planned to see the play once more. I began to talk to them in Yiddish, and they walked away, smiling, as if I had been trying to entertain them. Usually it creates no great difficulty for a fifty-six-year-old Jewish woman to walk the streets; it is not an occasion for disbelief. Yet the streets I choose, the bars and dingy eating places I go to, and above all, my words, that is a different matter altogether.

There are so many people that Ida meets, but some stick in memory more than others. I'll never forget the guy who liked to rip up his money in the most wretched bar in the city. After I delivered the first part of Ida's pre-suicide soliloquy to my audience of one, the man began to tell me that this was going to be *his* last night on earth. He had had enough. I demanded justification: What was causing his suffering? What horrors had he seen? When had God betrayed him? The man told me that he failed at everything he had ever tried; he had no desire to try again. No purpose, no will, no sense, he babbled way. His desire to die seemed to be an offence against my mother's death, her need to die after surviving concentration camp and living with her European memories for thirty North American years. I belittled each reason for dying the man mentioned, perhaps attempting to bully him back to life, perhaps merely loathing him. I didn't know for certain.

'Have you ever tried acting on stage?' I asked the suicidal man. I'm sure he thought I was a lunatic. He took out money from his wallet and ripped up five ten-dollar bills, as if to confirm his resolution to die. 'I have money. Money is nothing, the Devil's toilet paper,' he shouted. I could hear protests from other parts of the bar against his sacrilege. I knew that his suffering was genuine, even if I couldn't accept it; what I didn't know was whether he was sincere in his desire to kill himself or just letting out a pitiful call for help. We sat in the bar together for what must have been an hour, debating the substance and validity and worth of his proposed act.

'You must go on living, no matter what the pain. No matter how great the adversity, there is always reason to live,' Ida told the man. I didn't believe in what Ida was telling him; I knew what *she* had been compelled to do. But Ida, for some reason, felt an obligation to attempt to keep this pathetic creature alive.

'What method are you going to use?' I asked. He smiled, or what looked like a smile brought on by a jolt of electricity. He left twenty-five dollars on the bar to cover his tab, and ripped two more tens before leaving. For a confused instant, I thought of following the man, of taking my costume off in front of him, of suggesting that making love was better than dying, but even the prospect of the pursuit sickened me. Several patrons in the bar came over to where I was sitting and gathered up the pieces of ripped money, and then went back to their tables for the attempt at restoration. I never returned to that bar or inquired if the man had followed through on his threat to kill himself. Maybe he had been acting too. I didn't care about him; Ida, bless her tormented heart, cared about that whimpering fool.

I want to write a new play—something about the old, lonely street women I have been observing on some of my walks—but I can't sustain anything new. Ida Solomon isn't interested in writing a play. She is sad because she was able to have only one child, and that child is grown and doesn't seem to need her.

Tonight another dismal bar and performing my play to another numbed soul. It's the numbed who draw me, seem to be the only adequate nighttime audience. I don't know why I want to inhabit their empty, deadening worlds. This man looked about Ida's age, perhaps five or six years older. He listened politely to Ida's recollections of Poland and her life during the war. Only his eyes indicated any interest. After I got good and drunk, I put two complimentary tickets to my play about Ida Solomon down on the bar. 'Good for thawing out your frozen soul,' I told the old man when he didn't touch the tickets. 'An evening at the theatre is better than this goddamn place.'

His expression remained fixed, indissoluble. 'So what do you think about the life I've lived?' I asked the old man, becoming annoyed that he wasn't saying anything. His eyes had a curious vitality to them, but I couldn't understand the messages they were sending. Improvising a new scene, I showed him my concentration camp number, the one Sally puts on for me with such care every night. The old man grabbed my left wrist and held it down against the wooden counter of the bar. He began to hurt me, but Ida could stand the pain, at least this kind of physical pain. The bartender came by and pulled the old man's hands away, slamming them down hard on the wooden counter. He kept slamming the old man's hands down again and again. 'Stop!' Ida screamed. With her own hands she forced the bartender to release his hold, told him to leave her and the old man alone.

Before I could deliver any more of Ida's lines, the old man had pushed up the left sleeves of his suit coat and shirt. His eyes closed as he showed me his concentration camp number. 'I'm so sorry,' I said; Ida had disappeared. I embraced the old man and searched for Ida.

I no longer want to be my mother in the play, to go through the eight stages of her life that I selected in some madly punishing and creative attempt to make sense of the past, to counteract my guilt, to justify remaining alive. I want the play to end, but I cannot under any circumstances allow my mother to die and remain lost to me, not again, never again.

MARLENE NOURBESE PHILIP

(b. 1947)

'How does one write poetry from the twin realities of being Black and female in the last quarter of the twentieth century? How does one write poetry from a place such as Canada, whose reality for poets such as myself is, more often than not, structured by its absence? How does one write from the perspective of one who has "mastered" a foreign language, yet has never had a mother tongue; one whose father tongue is an English fashioned to exclude, deride and deny the essence of one's be-ing? . . . How does the poet work a language engorged on her many silences? How does she break that silence that is one yet many? Should she? Can she fashion a language that uses silences as a first principle?'

These questions formed the opening paragraph of Marlene Nourbese Philip's letter covering her manuscripts *She Tries Her Tongue, Her Silence Softly Breaks* and *Looking for Livingstone: An Odyssey of Silence* sent to publishers in 1987. They are also the questions that form the core of all her writing. After twenty-five rejections, these manuscripts were published, in 1989 and 1991 respectively, and established Nourbese Philip as one of the most evocative literary voices in Canadian literature writing from a space of cultural and political differences, a voice that has forced many readers, as well as cultural agencies, to listen, if not to agree with its message.

An African Caribbean, Nourbese Philip was born in Moriah, Tobago. Upon completing a degree in Economics at the University of West Indies, she moved to Canada in 1968. She received an M.A. (1970) in Political Science and an L.L.B. (1973) from the University of Western Ontario, and successfully practised immigration and family law in Toronto until she decided to become a full-time writer. For her, writing is an integral part of culture, a culture that she sees 'as a site of contestation'. As a poet, a novelist, and a cultural critic, Nourbese Philip's task has always

been, on the one hand, to examine language—not only as her instrument of writing, but also as the carrier of colonialist and racist attitudes—and, on the other, to go beyond the fact that, as she writes, 'we Africans in the New World have been weaned forever on the milk of otherness.'

Widely published in such cultural journals as *Fuse Magazine*, Nourbese Philip's first books were the poetry collections *Thorns* (1980), from which 'Blackman Dead' below comes, and *Salmon Courage* (1983). Her novel for young people, *Harriet's Daughter* (1988), was originally published in England because rejected by Canadian publishers, but it subsequently appeared as a Canadian publication, and was a finalist for the Canadian Library Association Book of the Year Award for Chirdren's Literature, The City of Toronto Book Awards, and the Max and Greta Ebel Memorial Award. Nourbese Philip won the prestigious Casa de las Americas Prize for *She Tries Her Tongue, Her Silence Softly Breaks*, the first anglophone woman and the second Canadian to win the prize. The poem 'Discourse on the Logic of Language' that follows appears there. Nourbese Philip was also the recipient of a Guggenheim Award for poetry (1990-91), during which time she moved back to Tobago to finish *Looking for Livingstone: An Odyssey of Silence*, a novel that, focusing on Dr David Livingstone 'as a concept' that presents the female traveller searching for him with 'an alternative view of history', declares that 'history is not dead'.

Nourbese Philip's cultural statements, critiques, and essays have been collected in *Frontiers: Essays and Writings on Racism and Culture* (1992). Her most recent book is *Showing Grit: Showboating North of the 44th Parallel* (1993), a critical look at the cultural and political sources as well as conditions that have produced the musical play *Show Boat*.

BLACKMAN DEAD

The magnum pistol barked
its last command
broke his chest—
red words of silence erupt
silken ribbons of death
wreathe the sullen Sunday morning madness.

A magnum pistol broke the secret
Sunday morning pact,
red roads of silence
lead us
nowhere

but to bury him
bury him
in a plain pine coffin
and repeat after me
how bad he was because,
because he was
just another immigrant
I say repeat
after me
how he deserved to die

because he didn't learn our ways
the ways of death
repeat
after me blackman dead, blackman dead
blackman dead.

as we dress dong
in we tree piece suit
we disco dress
an' we fancy wheels—
dere is a magnum fe each one a we.

Listen me, listen me,
dey say every man palace is 'is 'ome
dat no man is
one hisland honto 'imself
dat if yuh mark one crass
pon yuh door

in blood
all we fus born is safe,

I say repeat
after me
how he deserved to die
because he didn't learn our ways
the ways of death
repeat
after me
blackman dead, blackman dead
blackman dead.

Toronto has no silk cotton trees
strong enough to bear
one blackman's neck
the only crosses that burn
are those upon our souls
and the lynch mobs meet
at Winstons. . . .

Blackman dead, blackman dead,
blood seeps beneath
the subterfuged lie
living as men
how can we die as niggers,
red roads of silence
lead us where
no birds sing
blackman dead
blackman dead
black roses for blackman dead.

DISCOURSE ON THE LOGIC OF LANGUAGE

WHEN IT WAS BORN, THE MOTHER HELD HER NEWBORN CHILD CLOSE: SHE BEGAN THEN TO LICK IT ALL OVER. THE CHILD WHIMPERED A LITTLE, BUT AS THE MOTHER'S TONGUE MOVED FASTER AND STRONGER OVER ITS BODY, IT GREW SILENT—THE MOTHER TURNING IT THIS WAY AND THAT UNDER HER TONGUE, UNTIL SHE HAD TONGUED IT CLEAN OF THE CREAMY WHITE SUBSTANCE COVERING ITS BODY.

English
is my mother tongue.
A mother tongue is not
not a foreign lan lan lang
language
l/anguish
 anguish
—a foreign anguish.

English is
my father tongue.
A father tongue is
a foreign language,
therefore English is
a foreign language
not a mother tongue.

What is my mother
tongue
my mammy tongue
my mummy tongue
my momsy tongue
my modder tongue
my ma tongue?

I have no mother
tongue
no mother to tongue
no tongue to mother
to mother
tongue
me

I must therefore be tongue
dumb
dumb-tongued
dub-tongued
damn dumb
tongue

EDICT I

*Every owner of slaves
shall, wherever possible,
ensure that his slaves
belong to as many ethno-
linguistic groups as
possible. If they can-
not speak to each other, they
cannot then foment
rebellion and revolution.*

Those parts of the brain chiefly responsible for speech are named after two learned nineteenth century doctors, the eponymous Doctors Wernicke and Broca respectively.

Dr Broca believed the size of the brain determined intelligence; he devoted much of his time to 'proving' that white males of the Caucasian race had larger brains than, and were therefore superior to, women, Blacks and other peoples of colour.

Understanding and recognition of the spoken word takes place in Wernicke's area—the left temporal lobe, situated next to the auditory cortex; from there relevant information passes to Broca's area—situated in the left frontal cortex—which then forms the response and passes it on to the motor cortex. The motor cortex controls the muscles of speech.

THE MOTHER THEN PUT HER FINGERS INTO HER CHILD'S MOUTH—GENTLY FORCING IT OPEN; SHE TOUCHES HER TONGUE TO THE CHILD'S TONGUE, AND HOLDING THE TINY MOUTH OPEN, SHE BLOWS INTO IT—HARD. SHE WAS BLOWING WORDS—HER WORDS, HER MOTHER'S WORDS, THOSE OF HER MOTHER'S MOTHER, AND ALL THEIR MOTHERS BEFORE—INTO HER DAUGHTER'S MOUTH.

but I have
a dumb tongue
tongue dumb
father tongue
and english is
my mother tongue
is
my father tongue
is a foreign lan lan lang
language/
l/anguish
  anguish
a foreign anguish
is english—
another tongue
my mother
  mammy

    mummy

    moder

    mater

    macer

    moder
tongue
mothertongue

tongue mother
tongue me
mothertongue me
mother me
touch me
with the tongue of your
lan lan lang
language
l/anguish
  anguish
english
is a foreign anguish

EDICT II

*Every slave caught
speaking his native
language shall be severely
punished. Where
necessary, removal of the
tongue is recommended.
The offending organ, when
removed, should be hung
on high in a central place,
so that all may see and tremble.*

A tapering, blunt-tipped, muscular, soft and fleshy organ describes
(a)   the penis.
(b)   the tongue.
(c)   neither of the above.
(d)   both of the above.

In man the tongue is
(a)   the principal organ of taste.
(b)   the principal organ of articulate speech.
(c)   the principal organ of oppression and exploitation.
(d)   all of the above.

The tongue
(a)   is an interwoven bundle of striated muscle running in three
      planes.
(b)   is fixed to the jawbone.
(c)   has an outer covering of a mucous membrane covered with
      papillae.
(d)   contains ten thousand taste buds, none of which is sensitive
      to the taste of foreign words.

Air is forced out of the lungs up the throat to the larynx where it
causes the vocal cords to vibrate and create sound. The metamorphosis from sound to intelligible word requires
(a)   the lip, tongue and jaw all working together.
(b)   a mother tongue.
(c)   the overseer's whip.
(d)   all of the above or none.

JEANNETTE ARMSTRONG

(b. 1948)

'It took a long time for me,' says Jeannette Armstrong, 'to realize the value of having a grandmother who could speak to me in the total purity of our language, the total purity of the words which have been handed down through thousands of years from mind to mind, from mouth to mouth, encompassing actions generated for I don't know how long—thousands and thousands of years. I was given an understanding of how a culture is determined, how culture is passed on. It *is* through words, it *is* through the ability to communicate to another person, to communicate to your children the thinking of your people in the past, their history, that you *are* a people.' The people Armstrong comes from are the Okanagan people of the Penticton Indian Reserve where she was born 'into a traditional family . . . with a long history' that it has passed down 'to other people in the Okanagan'. Armstrong considers herself 'one of the lucky people' on her reserve for coming from such a family, but also for having grown up speaking her mother tongue. Her family started learning English from her older sister who began attending school at twelve. Armstrong was almost bilingual by the time she started grade one.

Her first education followed the traditional ways of Okanagan elders. She credits her love for storytelling and language partly to her mother's aunt, Mourning Dove, an Okanagan living on the American side of the border, and one of the first published Native authors in the United States, whose stories about Coyote were read to her as a child. After receiving a Diploma in Fine Arts from Okanagan College, Armstrong moved to Victoria, British Columbia, where she received a BFA (1978) from the University of Victoria. She returned to Penticton, to work as an educator, writer, researcher, and cultural and political activist for En'owkin Centre, a cultural and educational association directed by six bands of the Okanagan Nation. As Penny Petrone

has said, '[n]o one has portrayed the native dilemma more energetically or with more emotional intensity.'

Armstrong's first books, *Enwhisteetkwa* (*'Walk in Water'*) (1982) and *Neekna and Chemai* (1983), both told from the point of view of young girls, were written for children. Her novel *Slash* (1985) is one of the best known novels by a Canadian Native writer. It follows the life of Tommy Kelasket ('Slash') on his reserve and in Vancouver to retell the history of Native people in British Columbia and their participation in the American Indian Movement (AIM) in the 1960s and 1970s. Although Armstrong has said that 'I do write for my people. I do at all times speak to my people when I'm writing,' this novel, blending traditional oral stortelling with the conventions of writing, has played an important role in educating white readers as well.

Armstrong, who has also produced video scripts and 'Rattle-Bag', a storytelling mini-series televised in 1989, is one of the founders, and Director since 1989, of En'owkin International School of Writing in Penticton, the first credit-giving school designed by and for Native writers. As a Native educator, Armstrong believes 'that First Nations cultures, in their various contemporary forms, whether an urban-modern, pan-Indian experience or clearly a tribal specific (traditional or contemporary) . . . have unique sensibilities which shape the voices coming forward into written English Literature' (*Looking at the Words of our People: First Nations Analysis of Literature*, 1993). This is the reason she, like other Native authors, wants to see First Nations literature 'defined by First Nations Writers, readers, academics and critics'.

Armstrong's more recent books include *The Native Creative Process: A Collaborative Discourse Between Douglas Cardinal and Jeannette Armstrong* (1991), with Métis architect Douglas Cardinal, and *Breathtracks* (1991), which contains the poems that follow.

HISTORY LESSON

Out of the belly of Christopher's ship
a mob bursts
Running in all directions
Pulling furs off animals
Shooting buffalo
Shooting each other
left and right

Father mean well
waves his makeshift wand
forgives saucer-eyed Indians

Red coated knights
gallop across the prairie
to get their men
and to build a new world

Pioneers and traders
bring gifts
Smallpox, Seagrams
and rice krispies

Civilization has reached
the promised land

Between the snap crackle pop
of smoke stacks
and multicolored rivers
swelling with flower powered zee
and farmers sowing skulls and bones
and miners
pulling from gaping holes
green paper faces
of a smiling English lady

The colossi
in which they trust
while burying
breathing forests and fields
beneath concrete and steel
stand shaking fists
waiting to mutilate

whole civilizations
ten generations at a blow

Somewhere among the remains
of skinless animals
is the termination
to a long journey
and unholy search
for the power
glimpsed in a garden
forever closed
forever lost

MAGIC WOMAN

in broad daylight
she can turn
a man
with the flick of an eyelid
into
a warm bungalow
a nice honda beside it
anything she wants
magic woman
don't close your eyes
for a moment
magic has its price
bungalow windows
have bars
barely visible
in the light
the doors
click shut
lock
ever so quietly
as the sun goes down
where is the magic
when you find that some things
in the dark
have more power
than you
and the bungalow turns back
into the man

don't sleep now
magic woman
you will have to crack walls
to get out

WIND WOMAN

Maggie at night sometimes I hear you laugh

when I was ten we rode to huckleberry mountain
carrying ragged quilts and pots and pans
packed on an old roan mare called jeep
given to Maggie to help fill her baskets
I followed her
picking berries her failing eyes had missed
I listened as she talked in our language
half singing sometimes
for all the pickers to hear
her voice high and clear in the crisp mountain air
telling about coyote

I know how the trees talk
I said to Maggie
I heard their moaning in the night
while we lie so tiny in our tents
with those tall black pines swaying over us

she told me a story then
of how the woman of the wind
banished by coyote
carried her eternally howling child
tied to her back
as they moved forever through the tree tops
mother crooning to the child
how sometimes she would swoop down in anger
scattering berries off bushes

Maggie told me I had heard
the wind woman sing
she told me that I would remember that song always
because the trees were my teacher

I remember the song clearly
but it is always Maggie's voice singing
her songs
filling my world
with the moan of old dark pines
as the wind woman
that sings to me
follows
with her hungry child
wherever I go

INDIAN WOMAN

I am a squaw
a heathen
a savage
basically a mammal

I am female
only in the ability
to breed
and bear papooses
to be carried
quaintly
on a board
or lost
to welfare

I have no feelings

The sinuous planes
of my brown body
carries no hint
of the need
to be caressed
desired
loved
Its only use
to be raped
beaten and bludgeoned
in some
B-grade western

I have no beauty

The lines
cut deep
into my aged face
are not from bitterness
or despair
at seeing my clan destroyed
one by one
they are here
to be painted or photographed
sold
and hung on lawyers walls

I have no emotions

The husky laughter
a brush of wings
behind eyes
soft and searching
lightly touching others
is not from caring
but from the ravaged
beat of black wings
rattling against the bars
of an insanity
that tells me
something is wrong here.

Some one is lying.

I am an Indian Woman

Where I walk
beauty surrounds me
grasses bend and blossom
over valleys and hills
vast and multicolored
in starquilt glory

I am the keeper
of generations

I caress the lover gently
croon as I wrap the baby
with quietness I talk
to the old ones
and carefully lay to rest
loved ones

I am the strength
of nations

I sing to the whispering
autumn winds
in the snow
I dance
slowly
filling my body
with power
feeling it
knowing it

I am the giver of life
to whole tribes

I carry the seeds
carefully through dangerous
wastelands
give them life
scattered
among cold and towering
concrete
watch them grow
battered and crippled
under all the lies
I teach them the songs
I help them to hear
I give them truth

I am a sacred trust
I am Indian woman.

KRISTJANA GUNNARS

(b. 1948)

As her first books of poetry, *Settlement Poems, I and II* (1980-81) suggest, Kristjana Gunnars was, as a child, 'sandpapered with Nordic mythology', with Icelandic history and folklore. Her interest in her Icelandic origins continues to permeate her work, and she lives periodically in Iceland. Yet, as she says, 'I have tried to move away from the "ethnic" stuff. I didn't like always having to pose as an Icelander, rather than just as a writer. And I didn't like the marginalization of my work, so I tried just to participate in some sort of international setting. It's a hard skin to shed, because once people identify you as a member of a certain ethnic group, they won't drop it. They just won't let it go.' Influenced by such writers as Sheila Watson, Colette, and Marguerite Duras, and loving literary theory while avoiding incorporating its 'dogmas' into what she calls 'the frail openness of a work of poetry or fiction', Gunnars writes in a way that deliberately resists easy labels.

Born in Reykjavik, Iceland, of an Icelandic father and a Danish mother, she immigrated with her family to Oregon in 1964 when she began learning English. She moved to Canada in 1969, and since then she has lived in many Canadian cities, including Vancouver, Regina, Winnipeg, and more recently Edmonton, where she is a professor of Creative Writing at the University of Alberta. Gunnars studied at Oregon State University where she received a B.A. in English (1974), at the University of Regina where she earned an M.A. in English (1977), and pursued doctoral studies at the University of Manitoba.

The official translator of Stephan G. Stephanson's selected poetry, Gunnars is the editor of *Unexpected Fictions: New Icelandic Canadian Writing* (1989), and *Crossing the River: Essays in Honour of Margaret Laurence* (1988). Her collections of poetry include *One-Eyed Moon Maps* (1981), *Wake-Pick Poems* (1982), *The Night Workers of Ragnarök* (1985), and *Carnival of Longing* (1989).

Widely anthologized, Gunnars has published two collections of short fiction, *The Axe's Edge* (1983) and *The Guest House* (1992). With the publication of *The Prowler* (1989), which won the McNally Robinson Award for Manitoba Book of the Year, she moved into a self-reflexive writing mode that goes beyond the conventional boundaries of literary forms. Although called a novel by its publisher, *The Prowler*, as is shown in the excerpts that follow, is composed of numbered sections that do not follow a specific chronological order or story line. It is as much about its writing process as it is about the experiences of a young girl growing up in Iceland during the Second World War. Her more recent publications are *Zero Hour* (1991), a memoir of her father's death, which was nominated for the Governor General's Award for non-fiction, and *The Substance of Forgetting* (1992), which, like *The Prowler*, crosses the borders of genre.

FROM *THE PROWLER*

3

It is a relief not to be writing a story. Not to be imprisoned by character and setting. By plot, development, nineteenth century mannerisms. A relief not to be writing a poem, scanning lines, insisting on imagery, handicapped by tone. A relief just to be writing.

4

I do not want to be clever. To make myself laugh. I do not feel clever. If I laugh at myself, it is because I have nothing to say and I am full of love. Because nothing I can say says anything. There will be mere words.

It is because I am full of love that my words have no meaning.

5

It is a book marked by its ordinariness. That knows there can be nothing extra-ordinary in a life, in a language.

6

Yet the story intrudes. Where did it begin? How far back can you take cause and effect until your story starts? I could go back to the day of my birth, but that is too far. Or back to the day my father came out of the airplane that took him far away. He brought in his suitcase Toblerone chocolates and stories of gypsies.

But my father was always going far away in airplanes and bringing home Toblerone chocolates. He did not tell stories of gypsies. My sister and I made up the stories. The gypsies were out on the Hungarian plains, and our father went to see them. He was in love with a gypsy. He stole our mother and brought her back, for she was a gypsy as well.

7

We had visits from Dr Patel. Dr Patel was a short East Indian man with a dark complexion, something like cocoa. He smiled a great deal. When he came to dinner, my mother did not know what to cook. Dr Patel did not eat meat, and there were no vegetables in our country.

My sister and I sat in anticipation at the table and worried about Dr Patel. He would die of starvation. But he was laughing.

Dr Patel did not speak our language, and my sister and I did not speak English. But if he asked about the vegetables, what do you then eat? we would say: we are the white Inuit. We eat fish. And in summers we graze like sheep among the mountain grasses.

8

It is true we grazed like sheep in the mountains. I cannot deny it. In the spring it was a preoccupation to hunt for those sour dark green leaves that grew among the grasses in the hills. The ones we called sour-dogs. And I ate daisies, carefully picking out the yellow disks. On the shore we gathered wild rhubarb, nibbling as we went.

During the war it was said people scraped up those unappetizing strings of sea-weed that lay on the rocks by the water. I thought about it.

In the fall everyone took to the hills, sometimes to the remote interior, to pick berries. It was important. Families took time from work and spent days filling buckets with currant berries and blueberries.

On rare occasions a lemon would appear in our house. It would have come in the cargo of some fishing boat that stopped in Bremerhaven or Hull. I was like a prospector eyeing gold. I was stuck to the lemon, thirstily devouring the juice, the meat, the rind, everything but the seeds.

9

I do not think this is the story of a starving nation. During the Cuban crisis and the Korean war, the decade after World War II, we did have cod roe and cod liver, whale meat and sheep heads. On holidays and Sundays we always had legs of lamb.

My sister was so thin her bones stuck out of her sweater. She had sores on her hands. It was some form of malnutrition. I thought the boats should bring more vegetables, surely.

At school we received CARE packages from the United States. Small boxes were distributed to each child sitting patiently at his desk while the woman went from one to the other. I opened my box. It contained some tiny used toys donated by some American family. I rummaged among these useless objects, looking for a lemon.

10

Since there was no fruit, and there were no vegetables, there were no trees either. If there were trees once on these mountains, they had all been cut away. There was a great campaign to plant trees. At bus stops, in shop windows, on postage stamps, there was the slogan: *Let us clothe the land.*

We had very few clothes. I was always cold, and when it rained I was always wet. It was a thought so selfish I hardly dared think it: *I* need clothes. My body needs clothes.

At night I fell asleep shivering. It often took many hours to warm up, curled in a ball under the quilt, and finally sleep came to the exhausted, still shivering.

It was not a country where children spoke to the adults. Only the adults spoke to the children. I could not say: father, I am cold and need more clothes.

Later, much later, when I had been in America for a long time, my timidity finally collapsed. I had money in my wallet. I went into one of the thousands of stores filled to the brim with clothes and began to buy them. I bought clothes for all kinds of weather and shoes for all kinds of ground. Especially for rain. Never again would I be wet and cold. I bought a carload full of clothes and felt like a criminal.

11

Somewhere in all this, the story begins. It is not *my* story. If there is a God, it is God's story.

12

Sometimes I saw my mother would stop her weaving and look out the window. Perhaps she was remembering a better place than this.

There would be snowflakes coming down.

If it had been a country where children spoke to adults, I would have said: you are lucky that family of yours came up from the Hungarian plains to the Danish peninsula. And you are lucky that my father, the white Inuit, found you there and brought you to this island where there are many seals and where occasionally a polar bear drifts over on the Greenland ice.

I knew this was true because we had a radio. On the radio the woman said there was a revolution in Hungary, and then there was an invasion. Russian tanks went into Budapest.

13

On the bus I met the beautiful black-haired young woman who once lived in my village. She had gone to America, where there were more flowers and trees than could be counted. I said to her: why on earth are you here? It is raining and cold. She told me the president, President Kennedy, ordered everybody to go home where they came from. Why? I asked. There is a missile crisis in Cuba, you fool, she said. Is there no radio in your house?

I did not know what a missile crisis was, but I knew what a cold war was.

On the street my girlfriend and I met two American soldiers. We must have been fourteen. They wanted us to come into the hotel and smoke cigarettes. That is how I knew about the cold war.

Later I was told the American soldiers had been cordoned off at the American Base. There was a fence around the Base, and the men were not allowed to go out. Even then it was not time to speak, but I would have said: that is the right thing to do. Because American soldiers are interested in children.

14

In the following decade I came to know those American soldiers, as people, in their own country. Some were my friends. They played music, sang ballads, wrote poetry like other people. I knew them before they went to war, naïve and happy, and after they came back from war, not so naïve and much more cruel. It was no longer a cold war. It was the time when the television showed many pictures of maimed Asian children.

15

Who are the people looking over my shoulder, writing stories in my name? Is it my great-great-grandfather from the remote north of Thingeyjarsýsla, who had so much to do with the liberation of my father's people from the clutches of my mother's people? Of is it my great-grandfather from the Danish island of Fyn, who gambled away his entire estate? If that man ever wrote a will, there could have been nothing in it.

16

In my father's country I was known as the dog-day girl, a monarchist, a Dane. Other kids shouted after me: King-rag! Bean!

In my mother's country other kids circled me haughtily on their bicycles. They whispered among each other on the street corners that I was a white Inuit, a shark-eater. The Icelander. My sister did not care for this injustice. She went on a hunger strike against God.

24

For a story it is enough to find the beginning. Because the end is contained in the beginning. The fulfilment is contained in the desire.

The answer is also contained in the question.

I imagine a story that has no direction. That is like a seed. Once planted, the seed goes nowhere. It stays in one place, yet it grows in itself. It blossoms from inside, imperceptibly. If it is a vegetable, it nourishes.

25

I have read treatises on male writing. The male line. The masculine story. That men have to be going somewhere. Men are always shooting something somewhere. And that women do not. That women can grow all things in one place. That the female story is an unfolding of layers.

I do not know if this is true. It is incidental.

47

The story is always somewhere else. I imagine a book that pretends to tell an official story. In the margins there is another story. It is incidental, it has little bearing on the official story, but that is where the real book is.

The ideal reader, James Joyce said, *who suffers from an ideal insomnia.* The reader is unable to sleep because in the other story there is something wrong. It is a detective story. The reader thinks the enemy must be found. There are clues. They must be pieced together.

The solution is contained in the clue.

Has anyone been murdered?

48

It was not a country where murders took place.

There was development. Geothermal energy had been tapped. Greenhouses were built in the village of Hveragerdi. Fruits and vegetables were cultivated in the greenhouses. Tomatoes, cucumbers, oranges, bananas. There were not enough to go around, and the produce was expensive, but it was a beginning.

I went with my mother and her friend in a jeep to Hveragerdi. She had saved enough money for a bag of tomatoes. We drove for what I thought was a long time, perhaps an hour or two, and went into the greenhouse. There was a sulphuric smell in the air. The scent of the plants was strong and spicy. It was a jungle of plants I had never seen, never known existed.

My mother bought her tomatoes and we drove back. She let me hold the bag as we drove. I sat in the back seat alone while the two women talked in front. I opened the bag and smelled the small dark red tomatoes. It was an overwhelming sweet smell that went into my head and down my throat. Gripped by an irresistible urge to eat one tomato, I surreptitiously swallowed the bites soundlessly. There were many, so I ate another. And another.

When we got home my mother discovered the empty bag. I stole out of the car shamefully. I was afraid she would scold me. Instead she started to cry.

49

Perhaps she thought her life was taking on a hopeless air. It had happened before.

She told me, sometime later, about the strawberries. When she was a young girl, she picked strawberries one summer to earn money. Her family was not wealthy, and she wanted to have a record of some beloved music. It was strenuous work, bending down for many hours, day after day, filling baskets with red berries. In the end she bought her record. On the way home she fell and the record broke.

Many years later I wrote a poem about that pathetic incident. It happened in Denmark, where new strawberries grow every summer.

118

My great-aunt Sirrí, in my father's country, imitated those Danish ways. She was, or so it was rumoured, upper crust, so she had househelp in the kitchen as well. But that was an elderly Icelandic woman with large breasts and a warm smile. I spent my time on a stool in the kitchen, listening to her talk, watching her wash dishes. She was laughing.

I noticed my father's people could not play the game they were supposed to play without laughing. They made fun of themselves.

119

It was a time when the pattern was not yet clear. Stories had only begun. There had been no development of plots, no interweaving of incidents, no coincidences had meshed. There were no endings in sight.

I could afford a view of the world that was constructed out of simple chance. There was no order to history. Fate took random turns.

The longer you live, I thought much later in life, the more deliberate the pattern that emerges seems to be. If it is God's story, I considered, then it must be waited for. It is a story that is read in time. It is not my story. The author is unknown. I am the reader.

120

The writer is a prowler in a given story that emerges in time. The writer reports on incidents. There are no protagonists in the given story. Any subject is a contrived subject. The point of view is uncertain. The writer is necessarily part of the story.

The writer cannot report on everything. It is not necessary to tell the whole story. There will be just enough to provide a faint sketch of the pattern.

In any case the writer expects rough seas. The entire work may find itself on the floor in the end, again in shambles.

121

There was an imprint in those early years. I was looking for that imprint already in childhood. It was a face. I did not know whose it was, but someone looked at me and left an imprint.

FRANK PACI

(b. 1948)

Talking about the fact that all his novels centre on Italian-Canadians, Frank Paci says that 'I wasn't so much writing novels on immigrant themes as novels about certain families who happened to be of Italian descent. The family was the major focus.'

It was after his first journey back to Italy in 1972, twenty years after his parents emigrated to Canada when he was four, that Paci became 'dramatically . . . aware that I had to come to terms with my background and the tangle of emotions it had engendered.' Discovering first-hand the differences between Italian and Canadian cultures made him 'appreciate' for the first time what his parents, and their generation of Italian immigrants living in Northern Ontario, experienced. Hence Paci's realization that his task as a writer was 'to preserve the accomplishments of my parents, with the accent on "serve".'

Still, Paci does not 'think in terms of Italo-Canadian literature, or exile, or native literature. . . . I think in terms . . . of certain characters in certain contexts. . . . Conceptualizations like "Italo-Canadian" literature are all right as handy terms to use after the fact, and I may have used it myself in certain contexts, but I've never seen myself as an Italo-Canadian writer.'

Born in Pesaro, Italy, he emigrated with his family to Canada in 1952. He grew up in Sault Ste Marie, Ontario, where he worked, like his father, in a steel plant. His working-class neighbourhood in Sault Ste Marie forms the settings of most of his fiction.

He began writing while an undergraduate at the University of Toronto, where he took a Creative Writing course from David Godfrey, and was encouraged to pursue his writing by Margaret Laurence who was there as writer-in-residence. He earned his undergraduate degree at the University of Toronto and his graduate degrees at the Universities of Toronto and Carleton.

His fiction deals with the kind of 'ethnic duality or ambiguity' that 'starts as an external conflict in the clash of cultures and languages', a conflict 'internalized' by some of his characters while rejected by others. His first novel was *The Italians* (1978), which appeared in Quebec in French translation, followed by *Black Madonna* (1982) and *The Father* (1984). His most recently published novels, *Black Blood* (1991), *Under the Bridge* (1992), and *Sex and Character* (1993), form a series that he expects will continue.

The fiction included here is a section from *Black Madonna*. Perhaps Paci's best known novel, it dramatizes, in his own words, 'the painful clash between *la via vecchia* (the old way) and *la via nuova* (the new way)' as represented by characters who are, respectively, immigrants and Canadian-born. Assunta, the title's mother figure dressed in black mourning clothes, remains painfully attached to her native Italy. In contrast, her daughter Marie rejects the past that she sees ossified in, among other things, her mother's hope chest, and moves away from the steeltown where the family lives; the anorexia nervosa that she suffers from is a sign of the internal and external conflicts she experiences in her attempt to negotiate, as her brother does, a past culture she does not initially appreciate and the present world she inhabits in Toronto.

A full-time teacher in Toronto, Paci held the Mariano Elia Chair in Italian-Canadian Studies at York University, 1988-89.

FROM *BLACK MADONNA*

It was late in February when she finally received the letter. Her mother had left it with the rest of the mail on the kitchen table. It had been conspicuously placed to the side, as if it had been studied for a while and then haphazardly tossed back.

Marie's heart started to beat furiously. Without removing her coat or boots she stared at it for a minute, trying to prepare herself for the worst. After all, it wasn't as if her whole life depended on it.

She tore open the letter.

Dear Miss Barone,
We are pleased to inform you that you have been unconditionally accepted by the University. . . .

For a while she couldn't quite believe what the words were saying. Then a warm delicious glow started to collect in her stomach, sprang up suddenly, and burst in her head, causing her scalp to tingle.

At that moment, however, she heard the sounds of her mother making dinner downstairs. Instead of bringing her boots and coat to the basement closet, she left them just inside the back door, took her books, and quickly went up to her room.

She sat on the bed and for the next fifteen minutes read and reread the letter, savouring every last morsel of triumph. Presently, tears sprang to her eyes. Marie watched them plop onto the paper, interested in seeing which of the words would be hit.

It was utterly quiet in her room. She raised her head and looked at what had virtually been her home the past four years. There was space for only a dresser, a bed, and a desk. It was a refuge she could call her own, yes, but it was also the last corner she had been backed into. It seemed so small at times that she was afraid to breathe too hard lest she suffocate.

Ever since Adamo had built the second bathroom in the basement, her parents rarely came upstairs to the second floor. She had the duty of keeping her room and Joey's tidy and of making the beds. Some days the only time she'd see them was at dinner—or if she relaxed in front of the TV.

Marie thought of herself as a foreigner in her own house. Usually it was home from school, rest for a while before doing the beds, the sullen dinner, dishes, homework, and perhaps a little TV before going to bed. If neighbourhood friends arrived to see her parents, she'd immediately go up to her room and close the door, not even bothering to say hello. Her radio, if turned on loud enough, just managed to drown out the exuberant and sickening Italian voices.

As for the neighbourhood, it was crumbling all around her. At least she could say she had prevailed there. People were moving out steadily, either because of expropriation or to avoid further depreciation on their property. Since the erection of the International bridge, the future of James Street had long been determined. Most of the stores were vacant now and ready for demolition. She had heard her father speaking to his friends occasionally of how business owners were losing money. Adamo knew Pee-Pee quite well, and he had done some masonry work for Spina, the owner of the hardware store.

'The kids, they move out first,' Adamo said. 'As soon as they get enough money to buy a house in the East End. They move away from their parents. They don't want to do with their parents anymore, hey. They become *English*,' and he'd make an insulting Italian gesture with his hands. 'And Spina told me—he said people stopped coming from the old country. *Porca miseria*, what're you going to do? It's all finished. Things that you build, they have to be torn down. Look how many years I work on this house. I ask for a good price, let me tell you. They don't take *my* house so easy.'

Ghost town or not, however, she couldn't stand it any more. As she walked home from school, the very sight of the familiar buildings and the derelict houses was repugnant. It was as if she were walking back in time, while she was so anxious to burst out of her old skin and emerge totally new. She had something of a chance to spread out her wings at school, but when she went back home it was the same old thing. She crept around like a bug.

The only feasible way to salvage some measure of self-respect in all this was to stay in her room as much as possible—stay there and wait.

Now the waiting had paid off. She could almost taste her freedom. Giving out a whoop of joy, she raised her arms in triumph and fell back onto the bed, unable to control a fit of delirious laughter.

Later she went downstairs and phoned Rita from the TV room. Rita's parents had long since moved from the West End to a fashionable house in a new development in the expanding north end of the city. She had just been accepted by the new local university. It was a single brick building that once was the Christian church on the Indian reservation. Rita was quite content to stay in the city. She had a steady boyfriend and was thinking of settling down in the near future. When Marie spoke to her about the more ambitious possibilities that life had to offer, Rita merely crinkled her face in exaggerated helplessness and said, 'For me a home and kids. That's all I want. You can have the rest.'

Rita asked her if she had told her parents yet.

'My mother knows I got the letter, but she doesn't know what's inside. I can't wait till I break the news. First her, tonight. Then my father.'

'Be careful with them, Marie,' Rita warned.

As it turned out, maybe from her experience in having to serve them at Guzzo's, Rita had developed an easy manner with older people. It was interpreted by Assunta as the exemplary behaviour of a good Italian daughter. Her friend had the knack of indulging them in their customs, and at the same time of being above it all. She'd often walk arm-in-arm with her mother downtown. Or she'd talk endlessly of children and recipes with the neighbourhood women on their front steps. Later she could easily laugh about it.

'What's the harm,' she'd say. 'People are funny. They just want to feel a little comfortable with you. They don't want to feel that you threaten them. Is that so hard? Let me tell you, Marie, it hasn't been too easy for our people.'

Marie couldn't say she envied Rita her easy-going manner. It was probably the one ingredient that had extended their friendship so long. Rita was very accommodating and good-natured. She was able to offset her moodiness and aloofness.

'I will,' Marie said. 'But they can't stop me now.'

'Marie, why do you fight so much? You always fight. Has it ever occurred to you that maybe no one's fighting back?'

Marie laughed it off. They agreed to meet later in the evening for coffee. When Joey came in, Marie followed him down to dinner.

The table was set for three. Adamo was working afternoons. Assunta was at the stove, her back to them. The way she was sullenly absorbed in her work indicated that something was amiss. Marie looked at her closely, observing how she avoided her eyes. And when she spoke she only said a few words to Joey.

It was virtually impossible to speak to her mother these days. Marie had found that her Italian had deteriorated to the point where she got stuck fairly often. It was so frustrating at times that she had to avoid saying anything but the most habitual phrases. If she used English equivalents Assunta would get annoyed and refuse to understand. Marie found herself speaking like a child, regressing ever more into the only infantile expressions that came to mind.

Complaining about this to her father once, she was surprised by the vehemence of his reply.

'Why don't you learn Italian at your high school, *stupida*!'

It hadn't even occurred to her to take Italian. She needed all the math and science courses in order to enter a math program at university. She had, surprisingly, found herself to be very adept in mathematics, often scoring perfect marks on tests and exams. She liked the step-by-step method of solving problems and the indisputable nature of the results. She was one of the few girls in the city who had done well in the provincial math aptitude tests.

'But Babbo,' she said, shaken by the reply, 'it's up to her to learn English. This is an English-speaking country.'

Her father looked at her in such a knowing, sad way that she entertained the possibility that he might know more than she thought.

'And this is an Italian-speaking house,' he said.

She and Joey started eating while her mother was still preparing the salad. The silence stretched. Joey kept his face close to the huge plate of gnocchi, obviously sensing something was wrong.

'*Per la Madonna di Dio, Giuseppino*, lift your face,' her mother said in dialect. 'You eat like a horse, you be a horse.'

Joey made a face, as if he had heard the adage hundreds of times. He had a voracious appetite. His two preoccupations, sports and watching TV, pretty well kept him out of her hair, but he could be a pest at times. Marie at one time had felt it incumbent upon her to try to counteract the influence of their parents by attempting to rear him according to certain principles she had picked up away from home. But Joey had become obstinate as he grew older and had ended up doing the exact opposite of what she told him.

'He is a horse,' Marie said playfully.

'What a farmer!' Joey made a face at her.

'My dear, what rudeness at the dinner table.'

Her mother looked sternly at him. 'Joey, you eat slower. You make yourself sick. Then I have to take care of you.'

'Ah, we have a game at seven. I gotta go.'

'*Basta*, Joey.'

'Ah, Ma. . . . '

'You eat slower,' she raised her voice.

He made a feeble effort to eat like a regular human being, but once she wasn't looking he started wolfing down his food again. His bag and stick were at the bottom of the stairs, ready to go.

Marie looked at her mother. 'Ma, the letter—you see it?'

'Joey, eat some vegetables now,' Assunta disregarded her. 'You never eat enough vegetables.'

'Ma, you see the letter?'

'I see it.'

Her mother looked anxiously at her for a moment, in an expression of such doleful consequence that Marie had to lower her eyes from embarrassment.

Later, when Joey was finished, Assunta put another piece of chicken onto his plate. 'You eat that, Joey. *Non hai mangiato 'bastanza.*'

'Ma,' Marie tried to intercede for him, 'already he eat three . . . ' and she couldn't find the word for 'pieces'.

'He didn't eat enough,' her mother looked at him, as if it were a personal insult against her. 'Joey, eat that. I don't want you to eat in front of the TV tonight.'

'Ma, can I have some pop?' Joey said.

'Maria, get some pop in the cantina.'

Joey left shortly after. Marie started piling the dishes. Assunta was still eating. She always started late and lingered over her food. It was a source of continuous puzzlement that while her mother forced the food down their throats she herself ate sparingly and remained amazingly thin.

'Ma, I'm going to Toronto,' Marie said abruptly. 'They . . . ' She couldn't find the Italian word for 'accepted'. 'They took me.'

There was a pause.

'Ma?'

'Speak to your father,' Assunta snapped back. 'Why do you bother me?'

'Ma, I have to go. More times I go to school, better job.'

'You tell to your father.'

Marie was burning to explain. There were so many things to say, such exciting possibilities to share—and here she was unable to render them in their simplicity to her own mother. She could just as well have been speaking to a stone.

'Ma, I wanna tell you,' she pleaded.

'These things, I don't understand,' Assunta said, as if it were an acknowledgement of defeat. And then in a more irritable tone: 'You go to school—good. You smart—good. But you crazy. Your head in the clouds. The older you get, the crazier you get. I don't understand you. To *Toronto* you want to go?'

'Most people, the parents, they would be happy for this. But you . . . you . . . ' and she couldn't find any Italian words whatsoever. She stopped. She could feel herself breathing heavily. Her hands were soaked in dishwater.

'You go to school here like Rita. What's the matter with that?'

'This place here, Ma, it's not such a good school. I wanna go to one of the best schools. Understand? It's important to me.'

'Yeah, you become doctor,' she said sarcastically.

Marie raised her voice. 'Maybe I will.'

'*Ma*, yeah.'

'Yes! What do you know, ah, Ma? You speak to my teachers? You read the books I read? You do the things I do? You don't even know me.'

Assunta gave a short biting laugh. 'I don't know you? Why, *carina*, I wash the shit from your pants all the time.'

Her mother's earthy vulgarity never ceased to sting her. She would always manage to find something to use against her, something that would strike at the bone and belittle her beyond measure. As a girl, whenever she was particularly naughty or Assunta found fault with her, her mother would maliciously bring up the fact that she wet her bed well past the acceptable age. '*Che stupida ragazza*, you pissed your pants like a fountain,' she'd say. Or, 'I had to wash your sheets every day, you little pisser.' Even when other people were present: 'Look at her, the little piss-pants of the street.' It seemed her mother took delight in turning the knife brutally and humiliating her.

In the silence Marie could feel her indignation rising into a sharp, searing hatred.

'I'll do my own clothes,' she said in English, glancing over her shoulder at her mother's implacable shape.

Assunta turned slightly. Marie caught the blank questioning face. It seemed to waver momentarily, as if unsure of how to proceed. Or as if it had gone too far.

Marie continued in English, her tone as icy and vindictive as she could make it.

'What's the difference if I speak English or Italian to you? You don't understand either way. I don't care any more. If you want to know me learn my language. That's all there is to it. And I'm going as far from here as I can get. You can go back to where you came from, for all I care.'

Marie wasn't sure how much her mother had picked up. Sometimes she pretended she understood less than she actually did.

'Speak Italian, *pazza*.'

'If I want to speak English I'll speak English.'

Assunta shrugged her shoulders wearily and turned back to her food.

Finishing the dishes Marie wiped her hands. She stood at the head of the table, looking down on her mother.

'Ma, I *have* to go away,' she said in Italian, trying to make her understand.

'I do the best for you, Marietta.'

There seemed no answer to that. She turned her head away, trying to control the emotion that was damming up her thoughts.

But Assunta's tone became sour again: 'I cook your food. I wash your clothes. I clean up your mess. And then what do you want to do? You want to leave. You can't even take care of yourself. Is this gratitude?'

'Gratitude!' she said, shaking her head incredulously. '*È mia vita*, Ma. It's my life you're speaking about.'

'*Ma*, sure. . . .'

'You can't stop me,' Marie said coldly.

'Do what you want. You don't listen anymore. You read your books. They teach you how to act? You too good for this family?'

'There's more in the world, Ma, than cooking and keeping house for a man. You don't understand. A girl has to make a life for herself. There are no dowry trunks here. You still live in the old country. You don't understand anything about this place.'

'*Ma*, sure. . . .' she turned her head away disgustedly.

'Many of the students, they go away to school.'

'But not Rita, ah. She's a good daughter.'

She couldn't understand her mother's reasoning. She pulled out a chair and sat down at the table, wanting to understand what she was saying. It seemed that Assunta wasn't telling her everything.

'Is it because you think I won't come back? Or is it because I'm a girl, Ma? Is that why you don't want me to go?'

Her mother looked blankly at her, as if she had missed the point entirely.

'Can't you tell me?' Marie said.

Assunta merely made a wry face. She got up and brought her plate to the sink, obviously annoyed.

'I don't want to speak anymore. You speak to your father.'

'But, Ma, you don't talk anything. I don't know about you. You don't tell me things. I can't tell you things.'

Marie was choked with emotion, ready to cry at any second.

But Assunta reacted angrily. 'You go away then! I don't care!'

She stiffened instantly. 'I will! I will! See if I don't!'

'And see if I care if you never come back!'

'I won't! I hate this place. I won't come back, don't worry about that.'

Marie's whole body was bristling with anger.

Her mother shouted: 'You're nothing but an *ingrata* who can't even wipe herself clean in the ass. See what you do!'

'And you, Ma—what about you?' Marie yelled back, wanting to hurt. 'You couldn't even get married by yourself. Did Babbo choose you from a book? Did your parents sell you like a sack of potatoes?'

Assunta slapped her hard across the face. Stepping back, Marie was absolutely thunderstruck. It was the first time she had been hit since she was a girl. Putting her hand to her cheek, she felt such a tide of emotion rising up in her throat that she was rendered speechless. One instant she felt the urge to break down and sob. To hug her mother fiercely and ask for her forgiveness. The next she was loathing her with an unrestrained passion.

They stared at one another, both as surprised and helpless as they could be. Her mother's face then assumed such a terribly pained expression that Marie again felt an overwhelming desire to go into her arms. But, somehow, a more powerful force kept her back. Neither of them made a move toward the other.

The next moment Marie found herself running upstairs, unable to control her tears. She quickly put on her coat and boots and left the house. Walking down the street, the cold freezing her tears, she was overtaken by a blinding hatred of her mother. Of her ignorant peasant ways and her stupid dialect. Of her screaming. And her abominable eating habits. Her cheap hairspray and the way she had her hair done. Her stupid obsession with food. The way she made them all eat until they were bursting. And the way she repeated things so often, not even listening to what was said to her. She was so stuck in her ways. So unchangeable. And so cold. Like a stone.

So help her, she'd never speak to her again. She'd show her she could do things on her own. Go away to school and never see her again. She'd show her.

Later that evening she met Rita downtown at a coffee shop and told her everything that happened.

'Maybe you shouldn't have said those things,' Rita said.

'You don't know how much I hate her.'

'But Marie . . . '

'She's never loved me. She hasn't shown me the slightest bit of affection even. Only finding fault with me. Telling me this and that all the time. Treating me like a little girl all the time. Never encouraging me. She knows nothing about me. She's never even tried, Rita. She deserves it. It's as if I've been entirely alone in that house. I'll never speak to her again, so help me.'

Luckily, when she got home that night Assunta wasn't there. Joey was watching TV.

For some reason Marie went straight to her parents' bedroom and sat on the bed. Staring at herself in the dresser mirror, she noticed her eyes were still a little discoloured. Even though her acne had not completely cleared, she had to conclude her face wasn't that bad to look at. She had tried to experiment with makeup on a few occasions, according to the information she received from women's magazines. It hadn't turned out all that bad, actually, but it all seemed futile as long as her body remained plump and unattractive. It had been her experience that male eyes never stayed fixed to a girl's face too long.

It sometimes seemed to her that her high-school years had gone by in one long embittering nightmare. In all that time only one boy had taken an interest in her. And it was another Renzo Lepera experience. He was a thin boy with thick glasses and a pinkish face whom the others called Booby—a nickname that was more than deserved. Unlike Renzo, however, he hadn't been transformed, and she had to persistently repel his bungling advances through a whole school year. The boys she had really been interested in had never given her a second glance. It was as if it had been a test and they had failed to discern her other body underneath the cocoon. She had given them no hints either. They had to find out for themselves. And it was humiliating to be so clearly snubbed. She took it as a personal affront.

Who needed boys anyway, she thought, if they expected you to be a giggling Kewpie doll? She was too serious about maintaining her high grades and getting out of the West End to fool around like some of the other girls.

'But it's not only because you're studious,' Rita had once told her. 'You're so glum all the time. Who wants to go out with a stick-in-the-mud? Why can't you smile and enjoy life a little?'

How could she, though, when it was all such a vicious circle? Surely someone had to love her first, she thought. Someone had to see through the surface and open her up.

Marie couldn't help thinking of her body as gross and indecent. Its urges caused her constant embarrassment and revulsion. Every so often it was overcome by a sort of befuddling daze that seemed to paralyze her mind. All sensation was focused in between her legs. Her blood felt viscous and heavy. She had vivid disquieting dreams of faceless men breathing down on her, causing goose bumps all over her body. A while back she had seen a movie of a couple of men, unwashed and unkempt in Cinemascope, contemptuously manhandling a rather arrogant woman before raping her. The scene had such a disarming effect on her that she had orgasmed in her seat. It was so unexpected and so scary that she didn't go to films for a few months afterward. But variations of the scene had crept into her dreams. She'd wake up wet between the legs the next morning.

It seemed if she wasn't wetting the bed one way she was doing it another. It was so debasing. She couldn't talk about these things even to Rita.

There was absolutely no one to talk to.

Sometimes she just couldn't help it and did the unpardonable—touched herself to relieve that intense befuddlement that consumed her body like a fever. And these things just couldn't be related to Father Sarlo in the confessional. She'd be shamed beyond measure if he ever recognized her voice. It also stopped her from going to church altogether. She felt too unclean to be in the presence of statues with beatific expressions on their faces. Or with holy water and incense. And Father Sarlo's admonishing wrath for all the sinful.

She had long ago stopped fooling herself that she could control the urges of her body. It had wiped out her religion altogether and therefore the last thing she had in common with her mother. Her refusal to go to church any more had caused so much friction between them that this day's open breach was long in coming.

It was enough to make her obliterate the past five years. Put them away in some dark compartment of her memory where they'd never be opened. And start fresh somewhere else. Away from a dead neighbourhood in a narrow-minded provincial city. Away from a family that had nothing in common with her—and a mother who lived in another world.

Out of habit Marie searched for the key to the Hope Chest. The overcoat pockets in the closet. Under the bed. The dresser where her mother kept all sorts of things like an inveterate hoarder. Old bank books and furniture bills. Sales slips. Broken watches and jewellery. Commemorative photos of deceased people. A few of herself and Joey at their first communion and confirmation. Old stamps from Italy. And all manner of small trinkets and odd bric-a-brac she had collected in the past fifteen years. But nothing before Assunta had come over from Italy.

The good jewellery was kept in an opened shoebox in the top drawer. Pearls and necklaces. Earrings. A couple of old rings. All revoltingly cheap stuff her mother had bought from the five-and-dime stores. When Marie was a kid she used to go with Assunta to Kresge's and Woolworth's and see her be absolutely fascinated by all the bright displays of merchandise.

On the other side of the top drawer were the handkerchiefs and smaller apparel like scarves and gloves. She pressed her hands over everything quickly to make sure nothing was hidden inside. The sight of her mother's personal things was vaguely repulsive, as if they brought her presence closer than she cared to have it. Indeed, every so often she looked up to make sure Assunta had not come upon her unawares. She thought she'd die if she ever caught her.

The next drawer had lingerie and *mutande*, which was the only name Marie used for panties. She went through the drawer very quickly. She was becoming increasingly revolted by the whole exercise. The mere sight of her mother's handmade *mutande*, made of plain coarse cotton, made her stomach queasy. They were the same kind Assunta had made for her till she absolutely refused to wear them when she was fourteen.

Marie went through everything else too quickly to care any more. Her interest had evaporated. She thought of the possibility of breaking the trunk open with a crowbar. But the whole point, upon closer deliberation, was that she wanted to see what was inside without her mother knowing.

But it was getting late. Her mother was sure to return at any minute. Fear of being caught completely snuffed out any remaining curiosity.

All the lights were out and she was in bed later that night when she heard the slow footsteps of her mother ascending the stairs. Assunta used to check up on them when they were younger, but she had stopped a while back.

It occurred to her that Assunta might have discovered something askew in her bedroom and was coming up to question her. Or perhaps she was sorry for having struck her and was coming to ask her forgiveness. Either way, however, Marie dreaded seeing her. Assunta was the last person in the world she wanted comfort from at this moment.

She'd show her.

Assunta seemed to tiptoe to the door. Marie closed her eyes and pretended to be asleep. The door opened slightly. She felt the light from the hallway. She determined to pretend to be asleep no matter what.

There was a long pause. Marie hoped with all her might that her mother would go away and leave her alone. She wanted no part of her. She would show her soon enough that she could do things alone. Go to Toronto. Become a doctor even. There were endless possibilities once she got away. She would be so glad to be rid of them all. She'd show them that she didn't need them.

Six more months of torture and she'd be gone forever.

The door closed quietly. Marie breathed a sigh of relief. She clutched the acceptance letter and felt the exultant joy at all that it meant.

ARMIN WIEBE

(b. 1948)

'I lived the first 18 years of my life in southern Manitoba between the Red River and the Pembina Hills, after the war and before the hippies,' says Armin Wiebe. 'Most of my published fiction to date is set in that time and place when we still spoke Low German a lot in the way that the kids following us did not. This time and place is now largely an unreliable region of my memory where my characters stumble through their lives. Conscious attempts to write "Mennonite" tend to result in writer's block.'

Born in Altona, Manitoba, Wiebe taught school for many years before he began writing. His first novel, *The Salvation of Yasch Siemens* (1984), was nominated for the *Books in Canada* First Novel Award as well as the Stephen Leacock Medal for Humour. As Magdalene Redekop says, it is a novel that creates 'a peculiarly Mennonite carnival' that revolves around the grotesque body of Oata, its female central character. It is narrated from the point of view of Yasch, who speaks in Flat German that 'is related to the Low German of southern Manitoba, and . . . uses many of the actual words found in that dialect. But in essence,' Wiebe points out, 'the language of Yasch is a buggering up of both English and Low German. And this buggering up of the language is at least a conscious pose on Yasch's part. He knows better. After all, he took Grade 10 correspondence and passed everything, except algebra not.'

Widely published in literary magazines, Wiebe taught school for a number of years in Lac La Martre, Northwest Territories, and now lives and teaches in Winnipeg. His most recent books are *Murder in Gutenthal: A Schneppa Kjanls Mystery* (1991), which was a finalist in the McNally Robinson Manitoba Book of the Year competition, and *The Second Coming of Yeeat Shpanst* (1995), which continues the story of Oata's life.

OATA, OATA

Oata, Oata
Ossentoata
Pesst em Woata
Truff ein Koata
Truck sich dann dei Becksi oot
Funk doa einen brunen Kloot
Howd sich dann ne grote Frei
Docht dowt veah ein Ouster Ei
Schmeickt seh eesht ein kleenet Beet
Yowma me dowt ess blous Sheet

Penzel Panna made it up one day at recess time behind the girl's beckhouse while Oata was inside. By dinner the whole school had learned it off by heart, even Pug Peters who couldn't learn the shortest Bible verse, 'Jesus wept'. The grade oners on the horse swings said it as they pumped and pulled. The girls with their braided binder twine ropes said it while they were skipping. Some, that hide-and-go-seek played, said it instead of telling numbers to a hundred.

Everywhere Oata went on the school yard we called out the Flat German verse to her. At first she tried some of the smaller ones to chase but she was then already 180 pounds so it was easy to run from her away. So Oata gave up and sat herself down by the big climbing sugar tree and looked to the church over the road. Her back was to us and she made like she didn't listen but every once in a while her shoulders would hop up and down and we could see she was onioning her eyes out.

Oata's eyes were not onions now as she reaches out a two-back bun to me full with mustard pickles and *Pannash Worscht*. I take it without looking in those eyes, one brown and one blue, and lean myself back against the big wheel of the 4010. She has at least one button on her shirt closed now, not open and flying back in the wind like when she came bouncing the field over on the Ford Tractor.

But with Oata Needarp you never know what she will do. I found that out last year when I worked for her Foda, Nobah Naze. Muttachi was tired from me already lying the house around all winter and she made me to get a job at saddle-time with Nobah Naze Needarp. All the summer through Oata was after me to take her to ball games and Sunday Night Christian Endeavours so I was the laughing stockade of the ball team. At one game somebody wrote 'Oata, Oata' with lipstick all over the window of my half-ton truck. So I was for sure happy this year I got a job with Ha Ha Nickel and his skinny daughter, Sadie, only yesterday she left me by the ball game in Panzenfeld and went to the 'Town Without Pity' show with Pug Peters. And it sure didn't put any jam on my bread this morning when Ha Ha sent me to work by Nobah Naze Needarp's because the old man a heart attack had and that's why I'm here eating faspa with Oata in the shade from the 4010.

I try to quietly chew the sandwich so that Oata can't nerk me for chewing loud and I don't say nothing, just look over the ripples of earth to the end of the field. I don't want to look at the three-cornered patch of creamfat ripples showing where Oata's shirt hangs down from the one button she has closed by her tits. I hear Oata chewing, then the tin scrapes on the glass when she screws off the lid from the jar of Freshie.

'Oata, Oata, Ossentoata,' she says and I feel the bottom of the jar press into my hand. I have to look at her to take the jar.

'Pissed in the water
Hit a catter'
I get some Freshie into my Sunday throat and start to cough.

'Pulled herself the panties down
Found a lump there nice and brown
Thought it was an Easter egg
Rolled it up and down her leg
Tasted first a tiny bit
Holy cow it is just shit'
Oata's finger touches the flesh of my thumb and she takes the jar out from my hand.

'Nobody ever made up a verse about you, eh?' she says, then she laughers herself so that her whole front bobbers up and down. I say nothing, only look at the weeds on the part of the field that isn't diskered yet. A klunk of earth digs into my narsch and I wonder why I always get into such a pit. Then Oata says, 'You made up the English one, didn't you?' I don't look at her but I can feel that brown eye mixing with the blue one and boring me through. Salt water leaks down the side of my ribs. 'But then you are a Reimer on your mother's side, aren't you, Yasch?'

I look at my clock and see that it is time to get on with the seeding or I won't get back to Ha Ha Nickel's in time to play catch with Sadie before fire evening.

'I phoned to Ha Ha Nickel,' Oata says just before I press the starter button. My hand freezes. 'I said to him that you would stay here for supper so you can me to the hospital take to visit Futtachi. Ha Ha said it was okay, and said you should stay for night already. I . . . '

I press the button to drown her out and rev the engine up so that the diesel coming from the stack is so black that it matches the words from my mouth. And they don't rhyme, neither, as I make the 4010 pull that disker through the field, make it struggle because that tractor is the only thing I can boss around. Everything else in the world bosses me around. It matters nothing what I want to do, there is always something to make me do what I don't want. The wind pushes a empty fertilizer sack over the summerfallow, shoves it from one klunk to another, waiting for a chance to chase it into a thorn bush or a barbed-wire fence.

I try to look my way around going to town with Oata but nothing for sure falls me by and when it is half seven already my stomach is hanging crooked and the fuel gauge is showing empty. So I finish the round and hook loose the disker and drive to the yard and hold still by the diesel tank. Oata hurries herself out of the house as soon as the motor stops and I almost trip myself over the gearshift.

That such things one can see here on Nobah Naze Needarp's farm would I me not have thought even if the bull had farrowed. From a white elephant I had heard but here coming the yard across is Oata in a pink dress like a tent that would hold almost the Brunk Tent Crusade. She has her yellow brown grey hair tied up with a pink scarf and when she closer comes I can see her mouth is smeared with pink, too. Her pink in between the toes shoes with high heels yet dig in the ground, but when she stops and leans herself with her hand against the back tire of the 4010 all I can see is the little plastic pink butterflies screwed on her ears.

'Yasch, Yasch, hurry yourself up! The visiting hours start already at seven o'clock and you must yet eat and wash the summerfallow from yourself. Go behind the house. I put fresh water in the washcumb.'

My ears still ring from the tractor motor and the words from those pink-smeared lips fly me by and then, even through the stink of the diesel and the grease, my nose sucks in a sinus full of *Evening in Schanzenfeld* perfume and proost so hard that one gob of mucus membrane sizzles on the muffler.

Half-warm water in the white washcumb with the red stripe around the rim. And lye soap with *Evening in Schanzenfeld* spritzed on it. I can't gribble it out if Oata is nerking me or trying too hard with 'limited resources' like the ag rep said at a 4H meeting one time.

Oata sticks out her head from the green screen door of the ovenside and says she has made something hartsoft special for my supper, and I mutter to my chin that I hope it's not porridge with lots of salt like she used to make last year all the time. And it isn't. My faspa almost climbs up from my panz when she says, 'It is today so hot that I thought you would like some *Schmauntzup*.' I can hardly look at the big bowl of thick sour milk mixed up with green onions and cucumbers. Muttachi used to make it for Futtachi and he would just shovel it down like it was the best treat in the world but I could never make myself eat it. I mean I don't even like to eat glumms, except when they are in verenichi.

So I look at the white clock with the red numbers that hangs by the chimney and say, 'It's feadel to seven already so we have to go or you'll for the visiting hours be late.' I hurry the screen door out and Oata comes me after.

Nobah Naze's half-ton is still on the field with the seed so I flitz around the barn to the Ford tractor and hump spreadlegged on to the seat. I push on the starter and there's only a click and when I reach for the key there's nothing in the key hole.

'Yasch, Yasch, not the tractor! We will the car take!'

The car? For sure, the car. Nobah Naze has a car. Only it is hard to remember it because he never drives it if he thinks there will be mud or dust. When I worked for him last year I saw it once just, in the ovenside of the chicken barn when we spent three hours in the middle of the best combining day of the harvest looking for the Jack-All. That was the one time I saw the dark green '51 Ford four door, with white walls and radio yet, and one scratch just, so small you wouldn't see it except if Nobah Naze showed it to you, there by the 'R' in FORD on the trunk. Nobah Naze said to me that the bengels at church had scratched it the first Sunday when the car was new and so that's why he only the half-ton to church drives because the dow-nixes like the preacher's son and the deacon's nephew play hookey from the church and fool around with people's cars while the elders are preaching and praying and holding the collect for wayward children's homes like Ailsa Craig. 'Dose studs of the church,' he spits at me, 'can see de flyshit in Ontario but dey can't see de snudder which from dere own nose leaks.'

Oata is jingling the keys to the car by the ovenside door and I walk over trying to gribble out the 'consequentlies' of taking Nobah Naze's pet car, knowing for sure that Nobah Naze will blame me even if it Oata's fault is. Oata has her door already open and throws me the keys over the roof before she squeezes herself into the woman's side and closes the door on her pink dress.

So sticks the fork in the handle, I think to myself, then I open the man's side and slide in behind the steer. For a moment I get a noseful of new car smell, then the *Evening in Schanzenfeld* drives out any other smells that might have been brave enough to even try to reek.

The car starts up like new and the gas gauge shows three-fourths full and I figure I'll fill some gas up from the tank when we get back. I slowly back out from the ovenside and as soon as I turn the door to the road Oata switches the radio on loud and CFAM sings into our ears but Oata cuts that out quick when she pushes the button to bring in Portage. The western music makes me to feel good, even if I had started to listen to the rock and roll because that is what Sadie Nickel likes. Somehow the guitars and banjos, fiddles and steel guitars touch me in the heart and make me feel amost churchy in a funny way, like when I was just a *Jungchi* with a brushcut and I used to go to Sunday Night Christian Endeavours because that's where the action was, and the girls would sit on the choir loft benches and their skirts would pull up a little over the knees and a guy could feel right happy to be in the church even if the children's story was just a little bit young and the gospel message was always too long. But the best part of it all was when the people in the choir who could guitar play would put those coloured cords with the fuzzy tassels around their necks and put the picks on their thumbs or hold them between the fingers and line up behind the choir leader who had a hand plaything, and they would play old songs from the *Evangeliums* book and it would sound just like angels and the girls' fingers would scratch the picks over the strings and for days afterward I would make the sounds they made with my tongue—DUNG

DANG DANG, DUNG DANG

DANG, DUNG

DUNG

DUNG

DUNG DANG DANG, DUNG DANG DANG

and sometimes Schallemboych Pete's bride from Somerfield would play her mandolin and go DWEET, DWEET, DWEET. But then they put up a wine-coloured curtain fence in front of the choir loft so the girls' legs didn't show any more and the leader started to go to choir leading schools in Winkler or some place and learned such things as to have the choir people stand one behind the other and hit the person in the front with the edge of your hand on the back at choir practice. And they stopped the guitars to play and only tried to sing such high music like Contatas and so I stayed home on Sunday nights if Muttachi would let me and listened to a States station which good country music had on Sunday nights.

And so now the radio has on good country songs all the way to the hospital except for one Ray Price song that I don't like the fiddle for and I guess even Oata doesn't like it because that's when she starts to talk with me and tells me not to be so shittery and drive a little faster. That makes me mad and when we reach the highway I figure, let's see if this thing can squeal on pavement. I shift into low gear, rev up the motor and pop the clutch. The loose gravel squirts from the spinning tires and the rear end from the car swings to the side and when the rubber hits the pavement there is just a bit of a squeal and then the Ford hots up to sixty real fast. I check the mirrors for a green '58 Ford that the Mounties use, then I floor the thing and the needle shoots up to eighty-five and the wind blows in through the vents and lifts up that pink dress like a tarp in a tornado and I can't help myself I have to look at the creamfat white between the tops of the pink nylons and the pink elastic stuff that schneers into the soft skin under the garter. Oata doesn't bother herself to put the dress down and she just leans back in the seat with her elbow on the door handle that is like a little shelf. I had thought that maybe the speed would make her scared a little bit but she seems to like this going fast and she bounces one big round knee along with the guitars from an instrumental 'Golden Wildwood Flower' and her big pink lips have half a smile on them and I start to feel like she is maybe laughering herself over me and I make that Ford go even faster and when we get to the CFAM towers the needle is showing almost a hundred and Oata's lips are smiling so that her teeth are showing and her tent dress is blowing up in her face. Then she leans over and closes the window and the vent and the pink stuff falls down like a parachute and I take my foot off the footfeed and let the car coast till we go just sixty and it's a good thing, too, because I am only going sixty for about half a minute when the green '58 Ford meets us on the curve that leads into town.

'The stripey gophers almost got you for showing off to a girl,' she says and so I slow the car down to fifteen miles an hour and go slow like that till we to the hospital get.

Oata wobbles the hospital steps up on her spikes and I hunch myself down in the seat and hope that nobody will see me in Nobah Naze's car. Then I feel my stomach hanging crooked and so I go to the little store there beside the hospital and buy myself some Oh Henry bars and two bottles of Wynola. Just when I'm going to walk out the little bell klingers on the door and in comes Tiedig Wien's Mumchi who onetime best friends with Muttachi was and she talks me on and I have to talk her back. Tiedig Wienses used to be neighbours with us but now they live in town close to the hospital and the olden home so the Mumchi can better visit all those that are going dead. That's what she says me now, except that I know that Tiedig Wiens had his driving licence taken away and now he lives close enough to the parlour so that he can walk. Anyways, Tiedig Wiens' Mumchi tells me all about her boy Melvin who in Regina is learning to be an RCMP and that he likes it very much and it's easy for him because he's so smart, especially the taking care of the horses part. And I think about the time Melvin Wiens went to visit by Hingst Heinrich's place on a Sunday after dinner and the boys decided to ride the old shrug that Heinrich keeps for pulling the manure sled in winter. Now it took the shrug a little while to get the idea about what she was to do but by the time it was Melvin's turn she had it in her head that when something sat on her back she should run. The shrug took off as soon as Melvin climbed on and galloped him around the fence three times going faster and faster and Melvin is holding the mane on with both hands and yelling: 'Help! Help!' so loud that Hingst Heinrich's sister (that Melvin really wanted to visit but didn't have the nerve for) comes running to the barn just in time to see the shrug dump Melvin into the pig pen beside the fence and it had rained an inch the night before. Melvin Wiens was wearing his Sunday pants yet, too. Anyways, Tiedig Wiens' Mumchi says me again how happy she is to have such a nice boy who doesn't smoke and drink and who even to RCMP church goes on Sundays. Just then the storeman's cuckoo clock goes off and the old lady lets me get away without saying her anything myself or Muttachi.

I go back to the car and eat my stuff while the sun glances off the hospital windows and the shadows get longer. The Wynola bottles get empty and I feel still thirsty and I gribble in my head if I should quickly drive to the hotel and pick up a six. But then Oata comes out the door where the sun isn't glancing off the glass any more and I watch her come down the big steps with her pink dress.

'Take me to the Dairy Dell for soft ice cream,' says Oata when she has sat herself back in the car.

Now the Dairy Dell was where I wanted to take Sadie Nickel after the ball game against Panzenfeld last Sunday only she left me before the game over was because that snuddernose Pug Peters was taking her to the 'Town Without Pity' show in Neche. The Dairy Dell is the place where everybody goes in the summer time after anything is over and there is always somebody there that knows you and will come to talk you on, for sure if you have a woman along. I mean it's always that way on Sunday nights if you are lucky enough or brave enough when you are driving through all the darps or up and down the main street to hold still by some girls that are walking the road along and you find enough nerves to talk them on in a nice way and sometimes you get full of luck and they will get in the car and you can go driving the sunflower fields through on the middle roads but you always go to the Dairy Dell before the night is over. And at the Dairy Dell all those that didn't pick up some girls crowd the cars around where the girls are in and so I sure don't feel like going there with Oata in Nobah Naze's car.

But it is Monday evening and when we get to the Dairy Dell there just is one big truck and it doesn't look like it matters so I park the car close to the shack so that Oata can see the food list that's painted on the side. Besides, I didn't eat any supper. I ask Oata what she wants and she says, 'Just soft ice cream' and so I go to the window and tell Trudy Teichroeb's mom that I want a soft ice cream and a nip and a milkshake. Then I lean myself on the shelf that they have by the window and look at the truck and see one beard, one polka dotted kerchief, and two little boys with suspenders. Just some Huttatolas eating soft ice cream.

My food is ready and I pay for it and I think I will be lucky enough to get from the Dairy Dell away before somebody sees me but no such luck. I am just passing Oata's ice cream through the window to her when Pug Peters and Hingst Heinrichs come skidding into the yard and throw dust over everything. I hurry myself into the car and shove the milkshake and nip to Oata and say 'Hold this!' and I let loose the car and peel out of the yard with as much dust as those other guys brought in.

But it is already too late. Those dipsticks make a U-ball and come us after down the 14A. Oata hollers '*HOLEM DE GRUEL*' and rutches herself over the middle of the seat so that her side is leaning me against. Just what I yet need when I want to go fast as the Ford can and I have to steer with both hands and Oata is leaning me against so that my arm is clamped in between my ribs and her lard but I floor that thing anyway and Oata counts along with the red needle: 65 70 75 80 85 90 95 100 and I look in the mirror behind and I can see Hingst's car is getting closer and I step harder even if the pedal is flat on the floor already but the needle stays there just by hundred. And then I see it.

'LOOK, YASCH!'

The grey Vauxhall creeps the white line along, five 'n twenty miles an hour just like always and I know that Happy Heppner's grandfather is driving his Mumchi around again. But then I see in the other lane coming us on from the front a big yellow combine, and another one behind and another and another and another. Five new Cockshutt combines creeping us towards and I know for sure that Nobah Naze's '51 Ford better have good brakes or me and Oata will have to make a detour through the ditch.

Oata just leans herself closer to me and licks her ice cream when the rubber starts to squeal and the car wags its tail a little but I manage to make the Ford stop the Vauxhall five feet behind, just when the first combine is even with it. Happy Heppner's grandfather keeps just on driving and I don't think he noticed us or the combines. Burned rubber smell drowns out the *Evening in Schanzenfeld* perfume and at the same time there is loud honking behind and I know that Hingst and Pug have caught up.

I put the car back in gear and creep after the grey Vauxhall and those penzels behind us keep blowing their horn and Oata leans her head on my shoulder yet and bites off the side of the cone, but then I see my chance because the last combine is farther behind than the other ones so I floor that Ford and whip it around the Vauxhall and shoot away.

'Yippee Doodles!' yells Oata and she turns herself around to look out the back and she shteepas herself with her hand on my leg a little bit too close to the intersection for me right now because I have the footfeed flat on the floor again trying to get as far as I can before Pug gets by those combines. Well, I'm going 95 again when Oata pinches me on the leg and her chin is leaning on my shoulder and her hair is making my ear itchy and she yells: 'They made it around!' So I jerk myself frontward to make that car go faster and then for sure her hand is in the wrong place and I see some lights coming from the front but I am going 100 now and then I think that I don't have my lights on but it is already too late—the car that is coming on is blinking a red light already. For a few seconds my foot stays flat on the floor, then I take it off the gas and shove Oata out of the way a little and shitts the lights on. I let the car coast till it's just going 50 then I hold it there but the blinking red light is already turning around behind us and I can hear the siren.

Oata doesn't say nothing while we wait for the police to come to the car. Then the police is there and I can see from his thin shnuitsboat that it is the same police that held me up one other time and he looked all through the half-ton cab with his flashlight but he couldn't find nothing and I got away with having a 24 of States beer under the hood.

'You were driving without your lights on,' he says to me.

'Well, it wasn't yet altogether dark.'

'You were travelling pretty fast too.' I don't say nothing but I know now that he doesn't know for sure how fast I was going. Then he wants to see my driver's and the car registration. He looks at them for a minute then he leans his head in the window as far as his hat will let him and he says to Oata: 'This your father's car?'

'Yeah,' says Oata.

'Do you have a driver's licence?'

'Yeah, sure,' she says, and she starts to stir around in her purse and she pulls out a driver's licence and I wonder me what the hund I am doing here when Oata could have driven herself to the hospital and I could have gone back to Ha Ha's and played catch with Sadie Nickel at fire evening. Just then a car drives slowly past and I hear Hingst Heinrichs yell: 'PAUSS UP WITH NOBAH NAZE'S CAR!' My ears are sure hot and they get hotter yet when the police reaches Oata's driver's and the registration through the window to her and he says: 'Why don't you drive your father's car home before show off here has an accident?'

'Okay,' she says, and the police opens my door. What can a guy do? I get out and Oata rutches herself behind the steer. The police looks my driver's on a little bit more.

'Aren't you getting a bit old for these tricks?' He lets his eyes bore at me from under the hat, then he gives me back my driver's and stands there watching while I creep into Nobah Naze's car on the woman's side.

Oata starts up the car and grinds it into low gear. Then she gives it gas before she lets the clutch out and the tires spin in the dirt beside the pavement and she stalls the motor. I look back and see the police standing there and I can see he is laughering himself. Oata tries again and this time she gets the car going except she doesn't shift out from low gear and the car is making lots of noise so I say: 'Shift gears already.' Oata steps on the clutch but she keeps her foot on the throttle and the motor revs like crazy but she gets it into second and we go like that till we get to the turn off corner. This time she remembers to shift gears and then she even goes fast enough to need high gear so I tell her to shift again.

'Eat your nip already,' she says. 'Soon it will be cold.'

The nip is cold, but I eat it. Oata doesn't say nothing else, she just drives and all of a sudden I'm thinking about the time when I was 10 years old and we had just moved to Gutenthal from Yanzeed, where my Futtachi was working out for a farmer by Chortitz. Handy as in Chortitz the people always said but it wasn't handy for us even if you could back up with the harrow. So Futtachi moved us to Gutenthal and for a whole year in school the other guys always ran from me away. Every time I came close they would run and hide and then say things to nerk me from behind the trees. It didn't feel so good to always be run away from and when Oata quietly says I shouldn't forget to drink the milkshake I don't feel so good about the things we used to do to her in school.

It is dark already when we get to Nobah Naze's place and it suddenly falls me by that Oata hasn't said nothing about her Futtachi, if he is very sick or not. So I ask her and she just says 'Not so good' and she turns the radio louder because the song is about the old log cabin for sale.

The yard is very still and the moon is coming up over the willow trees by the waterhole where the frogs are having choir practice and I think about the time when it was forty degrees cold and Shacht Schulz brought his tape recording machine to school and played us some frog singing that he had taped by Buffalo Creek and he thought it would warm us up to hear frogs on such a cold day. And while we were listening Irene Olfert was looking back to me with her little mirror and I got this tickling feeling in my bones and I thought it would be nice to sit on a waterhole hump with her and listen to real frogs in the summertime but when summertime came the Olferts had moved to Ontario to pick tomatoes.

Now Oata makes the door open to the house and I start to wonder me what I am doing following her to the house when I should be walking to my Muttachi's place for the night. It would be only a mile and a half across the field. Or I could even the tractor take and then come back in the morning to finish the seeding.

'Make the door closed. The mosquitoes are coming in.'

So I do it and I stand there in the kitchen and the lights aren't switched on and it falls me by that Nobah Naze hardly ever used the hydro at night in the summertime because he said too many flies come to the house when the lights are on. Now it doesn't seem such a silly idea after all, even if by Ha Ha Nickel's they have a yellow bulb outside by the porch door that is supposed to keep the bugs away. And anyway if the mosquitos get bad Ha Ha just lights on some do do coils, which is like having mosquito smoke, only it is handier, and stinks a little like perfume.

But here now in Nobah Naze's kitchen it is dark except for one slice of moonshine that through the little window over the cook oven shines on the Elephant Brand fertilizer calendar, and the *Evening in Schanzenfeld* is still strong enough so we don't need any do do coils. Oata steps into the streak of moonshine and her eyes blitz a little and the rhinestones on her butterfly earrings glance the light off like snow on a Christmas card. The pink dress fuschels as she goes to the cupboard and reaches the oil lamp and puts it on the table. Then she sticks her hand inside her dress by the shoulder and pulls a strap straight. 'Light on the lamp, and I'll get us something to drink,' Oata says and she turns on her high heels so that the dress swings around and she takes two steps then she bends over and lifts the ring in the floor and opens the lid to the cellar. The pink tent sinks down the steps and I take the chimney off the oil lamp and turn the little wheel so the wick comes up. Then I take a farmer match from the little tin holder on the wall by the stove and I light on the lamp. The lamplight makes the room darker because the flame chases the moonshine away and all the shadows are big from everything that is away from the table. I sit myself down on one of the chairs without thinking and feel right away that it is the chair with the crack in it and when I move my ham I get a pinch. So I take a different chair and sit there looking at the lamp and listen to a cricket that is fiddling away somewhere in the house. Everything is still. Even from the cellar I can't hear Oata, and I think a little bit that it would be nice if it was Sadie in the cellar, but then I remember that Sadie went to the 'Town Without Pity' show with Pug Peters on Sunday, and it doesn't seem so nice if Sadie was in the cellar.

Some glass clinks down there and then creak the steps and I watch past the lamp as Oata rises from the hole in the floor. The flame from the oil lamp makes shadows on the pink dress and in her hands she holds a big catsup bottle but it sure isn't catsup that is in it. Oata sets the catsup bottle on the table beside the lamp and she goes over to the cupboard and gets out two glasses with handles, the kind you can buy peanut butter in, and she puts them down beside the lamp. Then she tries to pull the cork out from the catsup bottle but it won't come loose so she reaches it to me and I try to wiggle it but it is real tight so I put the bottle between my knees to get a better grip and then the cork starts to move and out it comes with a pop.

I reach the bottle back to Oata and she pours one glass half full and then the other one and it looks real pretty there with the flame from the lamp showing through. Oata pushes one glass over the table to me, then she sits down and lifts the other glass with the handle. I lift my glass, too, and she reaches over her glass so it clinks with mine. Then she pulls the glass to her pink lips and takes a sip. Some of the pink stays on the glass when she puts it back on the table beside the lamp. I take a sip, too, and the chokecherry wines taste a little shtroof on my tongue but it's good and I take another sip, too.

'Pretty good, huh, Yasch?' I wobble my head up and down and take another sip. 'I made it myself.'

Everything is still, except one cricket is playing the fiddle some place. And the white clock with the red numbers is ticking with that sound that always makes me think about a rocking chair. Every sip from the wine is better than the one before and mixed with the chokecherry smell the *Evening in Schanzenfeld* is quite nice and Oata's pink fingernails sparkle when they reach around the catsup bottle to pour us some more wine and the rhinestones in her butterfly earrings glitter when she laughs. I say, 'It's good that your Foda buys catsup in such big bottles.' Oata smiles and sips a little more wine and then she licks the spitz of her tongue around those pink lips and the lamplight funkles in her brown eye and then in her blue eye and I start to think some place in my head that it is maybe something special to have a blue eye and a brown eye and I wonder if the world looks better with a blue eye or a brown eye and then Oata says:

'Yasch, you have pink eyes!'

And I know for sure that I have a pink face because the stubble on my chin feels hot and Oata rutches her chair closer to me so she can pour the last wine from the catsup bottle into our glasses and as she holds the bottle so that the last drops of the chokecherry wine can leak into my glass she is leaning close by me and at first the *Evening in Schanzenfeld* is real strong again but then the nose starts to pick up something else, like if the wine and the perfume and Oata got mixed up together into one sweet blooming garden of strickroses, tea blooms, butterflowers, and sweet clover in a hay loft. And Oata clinks her glass to mine again and we both take just a little sip to make it last longer and a drop runs over her pink bottom lip and I think for sure that it shouldn't go to waste and I lean over and stick my tongue out to catch it and Oata rutches her chair closer and we share the last drops from the glasses and Oata says, 'I forgot the lid to close' and she starts to stand up and I say 'I will for you it close' and we are standing both beside the cellar lid and I bend over and make it closed. Then Oata leans on me and I have to shteepa myself against the door frame that leads into the *Grotestove* and the next thing we are in the moonshine on the wine-coloured sofa with the big flowers all over it and I am driving the double dike along in a big rain with the big ditch between the dike and Nobah Naze's half section and the half-ton is schwaecksing from side to side on the slippery mud and the canal is half full with water and I am turning the steer from one side to the other as fast as I can and the truck plows through a deep mud puddle and the windshield is smattered full and I can't see nothing and the wipers only schmaus it fuller and I can say for sure that looks matter nothing and the tires feel the slippery road over a hump and I try the brakes to use but the truck is going already down and it is too late to be afraid of anything there could be to see and I just let myself feel what there is to know. Then the truck stops and the motor sputters and dies and I can hear my heart hammering away like an old John Deere two-cylinder driving along in road gear. I feel the water seepering in through the floor of the truck. But I just sit there till the water starts to leak into my boots and I turn and look out the window on the woman's side of the cab and I see the wild mustard blooming on Nobah Naze's field.

Then there is ringing in my ears like a saw blade hitting a nail in an old fence pole and Oata pushes me away and schluffs off to the phone with her pink stockings on her feet just. I hear her say 'Hello,' and 'Yes' and 'Oh' and then 'Oh' again. Oata comes slowly back into the moonshine by the sofa. She steps on a pink shoe and she falls me beside on the bench. I take her around with my arms and she leans her head on my chest. I stroke her hair a little and she starts to shudder. Then the tears let go and I feel them when they run off from her cheek into the hairs on my belly. And there is nothing to say. Nothing to see. Just to feel. Nobah Naze Needarp is dead.

JIM WONG-CHU

(b. 1948)

Jim Wong-Chu felt compelled to write when he was about twenty-five because, as he says, 'I had so many stories about so many people that the stories would die with me. I felt I had to write them, I had to put them down.' The stories he wanted to put down, but could not because he 'didn't feel that I could write' English properly, were about the old Chinese-Canadian people he met while doing volunteer work at the Pender YWCA in Vancouver's Chinatown. It was his interaction with these people that helped him come to terms with his own Chinese-Canadian experience.

Wong-Chu, born in Hong Kong, arrived in Canada as a 'paper son' when he was four-and-a-half years old. Because between 1923 and 1947 the Chinese Immigration Act prohibited the Chinese (except for diplomats, children born in Canada, students, and merchants) from entering Canada, many people 'would create a son on paper', which paper was then given 'to a nephew, and this poor guy will have to assume an identity. It was,' as Wong-Chu says, 'like living a borrowed life.' This was how Wong-Chu himself came to Canada—as the nephew-son of an aunt. It was years after he was shipped at age eight back to his real family and then again to Canada that he added Chu, the name of his biological father, to Wong, the name of his adoptive parents. While growing up in Vancouver and during his four years in Hong Kong, he 'always felt as an outsider' both because of his alienation from his Canadian and Hong Kong families and because of language problems: his Cantonese dialect was not the Chinese dialect spoken in Hong Kong, and by the time he returned to Canada his English 'was getting very rusty'.

Wong-Chu worked as dishwasher, potato-peeler and delivery boy in relatives' and friends' restaurants in Merritt and Prince George, British Columbia, and in Chicago before he settled in Vancouver's Chinatown. He was one of the 68 individuals who formed the media-based collective Pender Guy that produced weekly broadcasts on Co-op Radio, Vancouver, from 1976 to 1981. After studying at the Vancouver Art School for four years, Wong-Chu produced *Pender Street East*, a major photographic essay. A founding member of the Asian Canadian Writers Workshop, he began writing poetry in his late twenties. The poems of *Chinatown Ghosts* (1987), which include those that follow, evoke, as Wong-Chu says, 'paintings': 'Very simple, very stark and with very austere words, but fully packed', they mirror the concise and economical way of his Cantonese language as well as his intimate knowledge of life in Vancouver's Chinatown.

Wong-Chu continues to live and write in Vancouver. His poetry has appeared in many literary magazines and been translated into Portuguese, German, and Chinese. He is the co-editor of *Many-Mouthed Birds: Contemporary Writing by Chinese Canadians* (1991). He works as a letter-carrier for Canada Post.

TRADITION

I grasp
in my hand
a bundle of rice
wrapped in leaves
forming triangles

I pull the string
unlocking the tiny knot
releasing the long thin strand
which binds

I tug at the dry green leaves
holding the sweet rice within

peeling it back
I begin to open

BAPTISM 1909

god
an easier word than
christian . . . kisjin

his tongue grinds
like dry bread
bumping against each syllable

k-k-kkkrrrrrrrrrrrrr

missus murray
reverend murray's wife
corrects him
for the ninth time

krrrrrriiiisttiiiiaaannnnn

he stares
at this woman giant
then
timidly
offers her an O

kooooooooooisjin

CURTAIN OF RAIN
(*from Paul Yee*)

curtain of rain
another act unfolds

chinatown
forever changing
you and I
actors audience
watching being watched

pender street east
nothing dampens its spirit

quiet yet dignified
unassuming yet proud
hidden under umbrellas
steady as raindrops

EQUAL OPPORTUNITY

in early canada
when railways were highways

each stop brought new opportunities

there was a rule

    the chinese could only ride
    the last two cars
    of the trains

that is

until a train derailed
killing all those
in front

(the chinese erected an altar and thanked buddha)

a new rule was made

    the chinese must ride
    the front two cars
    of the trains

that is

until another accident
claimed everyone
in the back

(the chinese erected an altar and thanked buddha)

after much debate
common sense prevailed

the chinese are now allowed
to sit anywhere
on any train

PIER GIORGIO DI CICCO

(b. 1949)

'I've been labelled a surrealist, a romantic, a social-reformer, an ethnic writer, a moralist,' says Pier Giorgio di Cicco. 'In any case, most of my work has been fuelled by a discomfiture with dualism.' Di Cicco, even as the editor of one of the earliest ethnic anthologies, *Roman Candles: The Discovery of Canada by Seventeen Italo-Canadian Poets* (1978), expresses his scepticism about the dualities that might inform identity, especially those that might define one as an ethnic Canadian. As he says in his introduction, 'I'd been a man without a country for most of my life.'

Di Cicco, born in Arezzo, Italy, arrived in Montreal with his parents in 1952. In 1958 they moved to Baltimore, Maryland, after a short period in Toronto, but di Cicco moved back to Canada in 1968 to attend high school. He studied at the University of Toronto, where he received a B.Ed., and years later a Masters in Divinity (1990). He was actively involved with various literary journals, and his poetry has appeared widely in many magazines.

With his first collection of poetry, *We Are the Light Turning* (1976), di Cicco began a prolific poetic career, publishing a total of fourteen books in twelve years, among them *The Circular Dark* (1977), *Dolce-Amaro* (1979), *The Tough Romance* (1979, 1990), which was translated into French, *Flying Deeper into the Century* (1982), and *Women We Never See Again* (1984).

In the 1980s, with the help of a Canada Council grant, he began reading widely in philosophy and quantum physics, 'looking for new cosmogonic paradigms, rather less interpersonal and more cosmic, paradigms that would embrace ultra-social ecologies as well as the human.' The various routes he pursued during this search are apparent in *Virgin Science* (1986), the collection that includes the poems that follow. The figure of the poet in this volume functions, in di Cicco's words, as a 'true meta-physician [who] alchemizes dualities with a sense of humour; experiential duality, that is, paradox.' Using metaphors that come from the language of science, these poems offer at once an ironic critique of Protestant attitudes in Canadian society and a Christian perspective; about the latter, as di Cicco says, 'There's no alternative to sacralizing what you humanly make in order to elevate it to the realm of human value. In that sense alone, to be poetic, you can redeem matter, or the inert. . . . It is through human love that the world is animated and knowledge released.'

Di Cicco, who received the Italo-Canadian Literary Award from Carleton University in 1979, became a Brother in the Order of St Augustine, and is now a priest in Ontario.

WAKING UP AMONG WRITERS

I am so lucky, so ridiculously
lucky; luck oozes from my palm tree,
my fashionable view, sony tv,
lucky in luckiness, lucky in the hands
of the clock, I wheeze luckiness,
lucky in talent, lucky in friends,
lucky in Toronto, lucky to be in Canada, not
Zimbabwe, lucky in health, contacts,
money, I am so lucky—never did an honest

day's work in my life, never wept, never
depressed; I was born chipper, a happy-go-lucky
son of a bitch, never battered, always touched,
spoiled, lucky from the right side of the bed—
and of course absurdly lucky in love—
everything a gift horse. Things are exactly the
way they seem; I was born to the fashion, genes
programmed for sitting in the Courtyard Café, all my
books as good as printed as soon as I think of them, poems
coming trippingly off the tongue, my fingers can
barely keep up. What is it to be alone? People appear
magically. What is immigration? What is feminism?
How do you spell rent cheque, suicide, debt. I know
you think I will live forever, so I will. I always
seemed less out at sea than you, because I was born
lucky, to show you up at parties; when you resist me
you will always know there were scores who couldn't.
I will dog you all the days of your life; when you get
close to the top you will always suspect I'll have
gotten there first. You will try to sleep with the
women I have loved. I will publish the story you thought
of writing just as you think you've caught up with
the lucky bugger. What can I do wrong, feeling this
lucky, for you. I can't hate you—it's part of my luck
and even that bothers you. I will always remain a
mystery to you. It sells books, and you will buy them
and understand nothing, and you will feel unlucky.

Ladies and Gentlemen, I present to you a lucky
bastard. If you go to sleep, I will be there when
you wake up, precisely as I was before—lucky.
I of course will have slept less, if at all. I will
have been up writing the poems you wanted to write, loving
the women you wanted, pulling off incredible stunts that
will bring me money, security, romance.

If only I could put my hands around your throat and
squeeze you like a lover. This poem can afford to be
cocky. It will appear blank to you. It is the way
you are—you see what you need to see.
Are you asleep now?
Is anybody there? Please wake up, so I can get
your goat first thing in the morning.
We go back a long way.

Lord, how lucky can anyone be.
You will wake up and you will have missed me.
Another perfect day.
It must be hell for somebody.
Me? I slept fine. I have been around the world
for a long time
and I have landed in your heart, like a vulture,
sad, like a friend, like a lonely hunger
for the hours when you love me.

LATIN ONTARIO

I am a coward, always thinking
of the other guy, never trusting my
words without thought; my insincerities have
banished a thousand lines into a
composite weeping figure, an idiot of
a man I take in and feed periodically
because I disown no one.
But I will get rid of this self-pity one day
and have no patience for others with self-love
and we'll spit sacred days like seeds at the sun,
unparsimonious at last.

I have been a protestant too long. I have had
to confess instead of sing,
and when you confess to other protestants
you get suggestions for editing;

and I pray for the day when I shall not even preach
to feminists out of misguided love—

what have I to do with Utopian gods, I who
knew how to waste time on street-corners
praising the sun by whistling at it—I who

can still remember that, who, for want of
company tried to teach nonchalance.

Like my friend Luciano who wants to play among
Calvinists, I have grown hateful with waiting.
He wears black among them. He is like the angel
of death among the crippled.

What he really wants to do is wear white
at the wedding of the world,
but this is the only job he could get
in a protestant country.

SYMMETRIES OF EXCLUSION: DUO-GENESIS

'Teach us to care and not to care'
—T.S. Eliot

Heisenberg's uncertainty principle has been a thorn in my heart for years. It is a physical justification for all symmetries of exclusion. I can still hear my mother saying I can't have everything—that I have to choose. Subtler phoenicians of the real world said I couldn't be in two places at once, that I couldn't have a modern woman and a traditional woman. Things seem to slip from between your fingers unless you pay no attention to what you're doing. Art is the science of duplicating accidents. That is why artists exhaust themselves at cause and effect, drugging their bodies or burning themselves out. What is left over is nonchalance. It's what you fool matter with to make it act natural.

Heisenberg was a twit. His marital situation should have alerted him to the either/or behaviour of particles. The obvious escaped him, not unlike the knowledge of either position or momentum.

The choice of the world 'complementary' is poignant. The word palliates the dogged acceptance of polarities. It's as if his love-making had crept into his scientific-linguistic underwear. That's mean. But why be patient with Calvinists? Let them get to heaven on their own time, without sacrificing the superluminal potential of the race.

MARY DI MICHELE

(b. 1949)

'My status as an ethnic writer is conferred, right?' was Mary di Michele's ironic response to an interviewer questioning her feelings about her 'status as an ethnic writer'. She finds ethnic labelling and the hyphens that come along with it to be limiting and discriminatory. 'That hyphen,' she says, 'is the rift in us all, perhaps. One which is typographically evident in the language. . . . You run into me in Italian-Canadian writers' conferences because I know how important it was to me as a writer to find in literature an imaginative construct that contained and reflected some of my own kinds of experience.' This involvement, together with the encouragement she received from novelist Joyce Carol Oates, has facilitated her shift from 'the negative aspect of [her] academic training . . . [that] concentrate[d] primarily on intellectual information' to her own experiences and background.

Born in Lanciano, Italy, she received her B.A. in English from the University of Toronto (1972) and her M.A. in English and Creative Writing from the University of Windsor (1974). She has held the position of writer-in-residence in many places, including the Universities of Toronto (1985-86) and Rome (1991). Her poetry won the First Prize in the CBC Literary Competition and the Air Canada Award for Writing. A professor of Creative Writing in the English Department, Concordia University, Montreal, since 1990,

di Michele has published many collections of poetry, including *Tree of August* (1978), *Bread and Chocolate* (1980), *Mimosa and Other Poems* (1981), and *Necessary Sugar* (1984).

'All my poetry,' she says, 'is meant to be heard as well as read. The voice, the music and rhythm of the human voice, is the animator, is the anima, of the poem.' Much of her earlier work addresses, in her own words, 'a sort of Houdini-like wrestling with' the values of her traditional immigrant background, with 'bonds which are sometimes restrictive, sometimes repressive . . . but which are also bonds of love, like family ties and sexual relations.' In her more recent poetry, di Michele writes out of a strong sense that 'gender is the stronger factor in identity for me over ethnicity. The body,' she says, 'is the more powerful sign.' The poems in *Immune to Gravity* (1986) and *Luminous Emergencies* (1990) reflect 'how our bodies write our lives. . . . This is central to me,' she says, 'a desire always to incorporate, to make part of the whole body, not to amputate, but to find, through a process which is not either-or, but more like yes-and-no.'

Di Michele's poetry has been widely anthologized and translated into Spanish. She is the editor of *Anything is Possible: A Collection of Eleven Women Poets* (1984). Her most recent books are *Under My Skin* (1994), a novel, and *Stranger in You: Selected Poems and New* (1995).

LIFE IS THEATRE
OR
O TO BE AN ITALIAN IN TORONTO DRINKING CAPPUCCINO ON BLOOR STREET AT BERSANI & CARLEVALE'S

Back then you couldn't have imagined yourself
openly savouring a cappuccino,
you were too ashamed that your dinners
were in a language you couldn't share

with your friends: their pot roasts,
their turnips, their recipes for Kraft
dinners you glimpsed in TV commercials—
the mysteries of macaroni with marshmallows.
You needed an illustrated dictionary
to translate your meals,
looking to the glossy pages of vegetables
melanzane became eggplant,
African, with the dark sensuality of liver.
But for them even eggplants were exotic or unknown,
their purple skins from outer space.

Through the glass oven door
you would watch it bubbling in pyrex,
layered with tomato sauce and cheese,
melanzane alla parmigiana,
the other-worldliness viewed as if
through a microscope
like photosynthesis in a leaf.

*

Educated in a largely Jewish highschool
you were Catholic.
Among doctors' daughters,
the child of a fruit vendor.
You became known as Miraculous Mary,
announced with jokes about virgin mothers.

You were as popular as pork on Passover.

You discovered insomnia, migraine headaches,
menstruation, that betrayal of the self
to the species. You discovered despair.
Only children and the middle aged are consolable.
You were afraid of that millionth part difference
in yourself which might just be character.
What you had was rare
and seemed to weigh you down
as if it were made of plutonium.
What you wanted was to be like everybody else.
What you wanted was to be liked.
You were in love with that Polish boy
with yellow hair everybody thought
looked like Paul Newman.

All the girls wanted to marry him.
There was not much hope
for a fat girl with good grades.

*

But tonight you are sitting in an Italian café
with a man you dated a few times,
fucked, then passed into the less doubtful
relationship of coffee and conversation.

He insists he remembers you as vividly
as Joan Crawford upstaging Garbo in *Grand Hotel.*
You're so melodramatic, he said.
Marriage to you would be like
living in an Italian opera!

Being in love with someone who doesn't love you
is like being nominated for an Oscar and losing,
a truly great performance gone to waste.
Still you balanced your espresso expertly
throughout a heated speech,
and then left without drinking it.
For you Italians, after all, he shouted after you,
life is theatre.

AFTERWORD: TRADING IN ON THE AMERICAN DREAM

Listen, whatever I write here, what you read, is safe. It's between us. In North America writers don't disappear. They are not tortured. They are ignored. People are not arrested. They are illiterate.

Entertainment has become an industry, hybrid of boardroom and circus. How can we be touched by what the video screen dissolves into snow? It's a cold country.

Sitting on the floor, writing in my notebook, I can see under the table the network of spiderwebs holding up my printer. Displacement

is vision. How can we be touched?

Two NASA planes from Punta Arenas, Chile, measure the damage to the ozone over Antarctica. There is a growing rent in the sky. The blue we will view as through O'Keeffe skulls. But not bovine, our own. Our skin and our children's will burn and fester. On the network the voice-over, with the gravity of an anchorman, urges the nation on. 'To survive is not success!' it proclaims. Images of executives, Wall Street grey suits, Rolex watches, leather portfolios, men scrambling to work: 'So America has been made GREAT!'

Over the planet the ozone is thinning, over the earth where to succeed is not to survive.

WHAT IS DESIRE?

('Language allows men to reckon with each other as with themselves.'
John Berger from *Why Look At Animals*)

Why have women been taught to feel so ashamed
that desire must be dis
owned, dis
eased as an agency of some
body else, like a mirror
reflecting us without containing us?

Women who only know their bodies through men,
know them in bits, in the way the man appraises,
his eyes fastening on a leg (needs to be shaved),
a breast (smaller than the other),
the hips (she hates)
and the curve of a buttock (too big).

It's almost as if men were always
looking through rearview mirrors (all ass men)
not to be aware
of oncoming cars but to check out
the traffic in bodies, the hitchhiker
at the side of the road, does she want
to ride along or bitch about his journey?

When the male poet echoes Plato
crying that each of us were born only half
a body, after his searching, in the coupling,
is there one body? or is it *his* body
forming the whole?

When men come
(together) with women, we do not
meld, but like a more primitive life form,
the amoeba, the larger engulfs the smaller.

Must it be the privilege of gay men and lesbians
to truly look at each other? I envy
such recognition. While men regard women
as if they were animals, as field,

not being, and acquire them as they do pets,

perhaps to address a species loneliness,
certainly not for this reckoning in their own
language. No, even the poorest bloke
when he looks at a woman is seated in a limousine
with the windows blacked out
so that he can observe her but she
can only see her own image and to freshen
up her lipstick. It seems as if all women are *prisoners*
of sex and the male guards
wear reflector glasses.

    What women have you heard sing
deeply of desire? of desire for men?
I want to thank Bessie Smith
who makes me feel proud
her blues in the body
know what the woman want
put a little jelly in my roll,
slip that hot dog. . .

                thus,
I perceive some use for the male poet's
hapless sausage. Do not
                         beat it alone.

Is desire escape
from the self or rest
lessly to re
           invent it?

    Perhaps it is right to be sick
of men wanting women's bodies,
of women wanting them to,
seeing themselves only desired in the snatch
ing of the pie they have baked, men
eating their fill and then going
on to another course, their main business
themselves, not call
girls. The trouble is women are
too sweet for men to shun
the pastry is

             healthier. When I sit beside my lover
at dinner and glance down at his thigh

where the fabric forms a loose pocket and the
muscle tenses and I touch him
and he turns to me and this is familiar
and I know him with my mouth and my cheek where
it rested the night before and with any language
which must refer to the body,
thigh, buttocks, penis, hand,
and mouth, la bouche, la bocca,
or ear, l'oreille, l'orecchio

                        where I enter

him and he listens, with my tongue.

   This alone is completion
desire meeting desire,
oh for that tangle of fabric and flesh
marked his and hers.

   But when the woman in the male
poem looks back, she disappears (remember Eurydice),
she becomes a little cave
she cannot be full
                 filled except by him, except by

music from his flute. Even new men fear
the feminist censor, the censure, the politically
correct marks Dick with an X-rating,
he suffers the guilt, the recriminations
for what should be joyous and free, his
desire. But that is white
out compared to what he brands on every woman,
for those who will remain nameless

                     except for his own.

We must postulate a self
to have relief from it.
So what men want to abandon briefly
through sex women want to assume.

Beware females are pod people
duplicating your body as you sleep.
And He has planted the seeds.

The moment I learned that my lover's desire
was not for my *self* I did nothing:
when he helped me move into my new apart
ment, to motivate himself he played
a game where with each glass he unwrapped
he undressed another woman.
He dropped one,
        me,

and then there was no

           one to sweep up the splinters,
          the bro
         ken
           b
              i t
               s

MARWAN HASSAN

(b. 1950)

'It would be totally false for me to say,' comments Marwan Hassan, 'that one surface of my being is not bound up with being Canadian or Arab or, on a regional basis, a southwestern Ontarian. All of these are significant parts of my self, of my make-up.' Yet, as a writer, Hassan does not see himself as being 'affiliated with a national culture in any immediate way. My first levels of identification have to do with class, and class resists.' His comments reflect his background, specifically his family's migration from Lebanon that 'extends over a hundred years', which was both 'a physical migration, but, at the same time, a migration through classes'.

Hassan was born in London, Ontario. He began his education at the University of Waterloo in 1969, and then moved to the University of Windsor where he received his Honours B.A. in English (1974), and subsequently his M.A. in English (1976). After various jobs, including cook and mail sorter, he began writing in 1974. Now a resident of Ottawa, Hassan was a member of the collective (1986-93) that ran Octopus Books, a store that contributed to 'an activist oppositional politics' in Ottawa. His continuing involvement with the booktrade business has

led to his writing essays on the subject, and a work-in-progress on the 'political economy of book publishing'.

'I am an Anglophone Canadian,' says Hassan; 'I can't write very fluently in Arabic. It would be pretentious of me to pretend that I could go back and recreate an Arabic identity as a writer.' Still, as he remarks, '[m]y status as a writer is somewhat contradictory because I am an Anglophone, but not of Anglo-Saxon culture, yet feel thoroughly knowledgeable about the details of Anglo-Saxon literature and its history. What's more,' he adds, 'I have a deep and detailed . . . even intimate, emotional and profound knowledge of a particular region and geography of Canada, that is southwestern Ontario . . . This will cause howls of laughter, but if there is a physical place I miss, it is not so much Asia or the Mediterranean, but southwestern Ontario.'

The fiction that follows is an excerpt from the first novella in Hassan's *A Confusion of Stones: Two Novellas* (1989). His most recent book is the novel, *The Memory Garden of Miguel Carranza* (1991). Another novel, *Nobody Knows Bloor-Yonge Station*, is forthcoming.

FROM *THE CONFUSION OF STONES*

The night always begins this way: the guard in the drab olive green uniform appears with a bronze key to lock the door and to bid him goodnight.

'See you Nick. I'll be back at two-thirty.'

'Yes, good evening.' The guard closes the door and turns the key in the lock.

He is anxious but he starts to work. Walking to the centre of the space, he begins to lift wooden chairs onto the imitation marble tops of the cast iron tables. He works steadily and rhythmically knowing that by two-thirty in the morning the entire plaza must be clean. He is conscientious at first, invaded by the sensation that someone may be watching but at nine o'clock he pauses, stares up at the vaulted glass ceiling and, oppressed by the pervading sterility, realizes that the atmosphere is not pregnant with silence but rather permeated by humming from the heating ducts.

The janitor bends over the bucket and presses the mop dry, leans it against the wall and proceeds to the white wrought iron staircase. Climbing these steps, he ascends others . . . the double stairs in the hotel in Homs . . . the marble flight in the hotel off Marj Square in Damascus . . . the stone steps leading up to the communal fountain in his native village in the southern Latani valley . . . the series to the restaurants in Zahle where the waters flow down the rocky cliffs . . . and the steps winding up from the souk to the road where the sheep and goats graze on the domes in Aleppo . . . vertigo . . . as he ascends into the heights, confronted at every step by the angled sheets of glass which surround him, he struggles with the fear of tumbling backwards into the panes. The white noise becomes concrete in the glass and twisted metal. The chameleon nature of the sand and iron shimmers in the surfaces of the stairwell blended with replicas of himself which he is obliged to encounter. Halfway up, he trembles at the possibility of colliding with one of these other selves, and his eyelids squeeze shut. His left hand gropes along the railing guiding the way up the stairs, like a child's groping in water for a tadpole.

At the top, he runs hands over his body expecting it to be covered with scales of silver fish. It is not the labour with the mop that has enervated him but this climb. He goes down the hallway to the washroom. An image of hands appears in the mirror, above the sink. The janitor washes his face. The left hand appears strong and tenacious with a massiveness that belies the essentially fine bones. The knuckles, sinews and veins protrude. The right, with a scar across the back and palm, is pale and delicate. Pressed palm to palm as if in prayer, the contradiction is obscured because in outline they are unequivocally congruent. Only in movement do they appear paradoxical. The janitor dangles his left limb before the mirror and a smile appears on his face. His features are irregular but distinct and a faint scar runs diagonally from below the left nostril to the edge of the upper lip. A pale scar mars the right eyebrow. He turns away from the image, leaves the washroom, and descends the staircase. In the janitorial closet, he sits down on a carton of towels and leans against the wall. A sliver of light filters in from the crack at the bottom of the door. The contours of objects: enamel sink, mop poles leaning against the wall, buckets upside down on the floor. He holds the hand up in the dim light before his eyes. The tip of his tongue traces the scar on the palm. Daffodils in a green clay vase appear. He smiles and calls out softly:

'Falah, the flower won't die.'

The words circle seven times around the solar face of the blossom, counting the petals as the corona with stamens and pistils explode. He covers his skull as the Israeli Phantoms appear in the turquoise heaven over the stone village.

The peasant, stretched out beneath a fig tree in the orchard is eating a pomegranate. He drops the lush fruit and watches the scatter bombs tumbling down. The earth begins to tremble, the sky lights up as he is hurled onto his face. An ant crawls across his cheek into the corner of his right eye.

After a brief time, his eyes open. He stares at a rock, and tries to reach out for it with his right hand. But the hand is scarlet and the attempt is futile. The hand weighs more than a boulder and is rooted to the earth more tenaciously than an olive tree. With a little effort he is able to sit up. He inspects the injured hand which has been severed clean across the palm along the heartline just below the Mounts of Jupiter, Saturn, Apollo and Mercury and above the line of the head, by a hunk of metal implanted in the soil like a cleaver delivered from the heavens. The severed half lies in a bed of blue grass, fingers reaching out for the half consumed pomegranate.

Weeping and ululation from the village. The peasant picks up the amputated segment and holds it against the edge of the stump as if this action in itself will wed the four fingers to the limb. The hand appears miraculously healed. He smiles, releases it: the fingers point towards the clouds for an instant, then waver and collapse into his lap. The peasant unwinds his *kafiya*, sets the bloody fingers in the white headcloth and wraps the cloth about the stump, holding it in place with the left hand.

He walks the orchard road towards home, left hand holding the stump in the cotton cloth, while blood drips into the dust.

In the heart of the village, peasants are trying to enter buildings where blocks of stone are strewn everywhere, donkeys' heads and sheep's limbs are scattered about the earth like broken chess pieces. A woman in a black dress squats against a wall, her nose long, her thick, pink tongue hanging out between bucked teeth as she smiles. He nudges her softly on the shoulder with his elbow and the head rolls off and splatters blood on his shoes. He recoils from the staring eyes. 'I'm sorry . . . I'm sorry. . . . '

A donkey appears in the middle of the road saddled on a peasant dressed in baggy black pants while the leaves of an Islamic calendar flutter in the smoke and flames, a lamb is a circus contortionist and holds a set of silver prayer beads in its jaws, counting the names of god.

A hand seizes the peasant's neck from behind and twists his head around.

'Falah, by the hand of god, Falah help me save my family. Don't just stand there. For god's sake help me. They're trapped in the house.'

He tries to release his head but the woman's hold is like a vise. He pulls back the white cloth, revealing the wound.

'Help me. Please help me,' he moans as blood drips down the woman's breasts.

She releases her grip, staggers back and clambers among the boulders of her home.

'O god! Where are you? Aziza. Ya Aziza. Where are you Najeeb? Ali? Ya Hussein? Hassan? Where are you?'

He stumbles down his own laneway by habit, passes the usual distance to where the house is located. There is nothing but rubble.

'Baba. Immie. Sitty. Where are you?' His voice calls out like the littlest kid hidden beneath the bed crying for the nanny goat. He collapses in the stone wreckage.

Women in black abayas press their lips to the gold and silver screen of the martyr's tomb. They stuff *qur' anic suras* wrapped in coloured ribbons into the crevices. An afrit appears, white faced with a long nose, large eyes, green hair and beard. Three pronged horns protrude from his forehead. Gilled thorax. Clawed feet. Spurred heels, gold and green ribbons twisted round the ankles. Green wreaths about his head, a pleated kilt tied at the waist with a green silk sash. His clawed hands hold a dagger with which he stabs Falah in the carotid vein: blood gushes out and flows across the hems of *abayas*, but no one says a word as Falah staggers back from the coffin and the afrit, and gazes up at the crystal ceiling where he sees the dagger plunged in his throat a thousand times. He stumbles out of the mosque, sword in either hand, walking a line of fire like an acrobat, until he loses his balance and falls into the sand. The sun is large and red in the western sky, three figures approach on camels. He feels his neck and finds the dagger still implanted in the vein but there is no blood. His throat is parched. He tries to call to the figures in the wavering heat but his voice does not go out into the air. A green banner with black script flutters down onto his body. The men draw nearer but they appear to have no faces. He moans but they say nothing, until they make their camels kneel down and climb off the animals' backs. Their faces are covered with white veils. The one man carries a two-pronged scimitar. He approaches the peasant, pulls back the green banner.

'You're not hurt. Come now, rise up.' And with these words the man plunges the two bladed sword into Falah's chest. 'Come Hassan. Come Hussein. Wash his heart . . . '

The others plunge their hands into his breast as blood flows out and smears their white veils and gowns. They roll the heart around in the sand like a boulder and then stuff it back into the cavity.

'Rise up boy! Awake!'

Opening his eyes, he sensed the hand embedded in his abdomen, crawling up through the belly like a spider crab between the lungs, through the throat and manipulating the movements of his brain until, so busy at its task of exploration, it was finally protruding from the orifices of his skull: a thumb from an ear, a finger between the gently curving lips, another finger from an eyesocket. He screamed. A nurse and doctor appeared and constrained him.

'Give me my hand. Where's my hand? What have you done with it? I want my hand back.'

'Please be calm. Tell us your name.'

'Give me my hand.'

'Please tell us your name. You're from the village of B*****?'

'Yes . . . '

'Tell us your name.'

'My name . . . My name is Falah Azlam.'

'It's all right, Falah. We're trying to save your hand.'

'Where's my true hand? What have you done with it?'

'Here. Here, everything is going to be all right.'

'You've hidden it.'

'No. It's all right. You still have it.' The doctor lifted the sheets and slipped back the night gown to reveal the hand grafted to the abdomen. 'See. We're saving your hand. We're doing all we can to make you whole again. This is how we do it.'

'It's impossible. Where's my hand? I beg of you, please give me back my hand. Don't hide it among the rocks. I'll do anything, I beg of you to please show me my real hand.'

'Nurse, give him a sedative.'

He stared at the hand joined skin to skin to the abdomen, as the nurse took a syringe, swabbed and pressed it into his arm.

'I beg of you . . . I beg of you . . . I only want my hand back. I won't slaughter any more goats.'

After the sedation wore off, Azlam's composure returned, marked by a brooding over the location of the hand. He was unsure whether the hand was moulding and giving birth to his body by a perverse act of creativity or whether, as the Palestinian doctor claimed, the abdomen was protecting, regenerating and healing the tissue. Each time he focused on the process, he could not escape the sensation that the fingers were manipulating his mind. He lay in bed, doing nothing, hesitating to draw back the sheets and nightgown and see the hand wedded to his belly.

As days passed, he grew more obsessed with this mutilation, which had flown into the *Ka'ba* of his heart. Secretly, he reproached the doctors for their skill, believing it better to sustain the loss of the hand than endure the bizarre act of healing. Azlam looked to the time when the hand would be separated from the abdomen, he told himself that his sanity would crumble.

After a time, a nurse working with the Red Crescent approached the bed and inquired if he wanted anything.

'Where's my family? How long have I been here?'

'Eight days.'

'Why does no one come to see me? Don't they know I'm here?'

'I'm not certain,' replied the nurse.

'What's happened to them?'

'I don't know. I can only tell you there were many injured and killed in the bombing. It was a very heavy raid. They not only hit the village but the refugee camp. Hundreds have died or are injured. And after nightfall, after you were removed, the Israelis and Haddad's men entered the village. There was heavy fighting with the PLO and the *Harakat*. So you see, Falah, it's difficult to say. Some of the injured were taken to Jezin, others are in Saida, others in Beirut. Just now it's a little early to know what became of your family . . . '

'But I saw our house, it was bombed . . . '

'Have some hope. I promise you, I'll try to find out.'

His once lithe, muscular frame grew increasingly gaunt and tense. And yet, under the encouragement of the doctor he took up a pencil and paper and began to practise the letters of the alphabet with his left hand.

After some days, he confronted the nurse and doctor on their rounds.

'Did you find out what happened to my family?'

'Falah, how do you feel?'

'I'm all right. What of my family?'

'Where's your hand, Falah?'

The young peasant flung back the sheets and pulled up the white gown.

'Here, where it belongs.'

'Do you feel any pain?'

'I feel nothing. You are making my hand better. What of my family?'

'Well . . . '

'Well?'

'They died in the bombing.'

'Who? My father? My mother? Who?'

'It was a bad raid.' The nurse sat on the edge of the bed, straightened the sheets and patted his left arm. 'As I told you. They were all trapped in the house. And the house was bombed as you said. Your mother died in the hospital in Jezin. The others died in the house or were shot by Haddad's forces. It was a very heavy attack.'

He did not weep, but recalled the vision of the smashed, mud roof as he had stood before the rubble with the hand wrapped in the bloody *kafiya*. He tried to wiggle his fingers in the fold of the belly skin as his face turned pale.

'It's not possible . . .'

'Falah, do you desire anything?'

He gazed up at the nurse's face. For the first time he noticed that she had blue eyes that were very clear. Her hand was still gently rubbing his forearm.

'I want my *kafiya*.'

The doctor looked at the nurse and discreetly touched her shoulder with the tips of his fingers.

'Don't worry, we'll get it.'

'Do you want anything else?'

'No. What could I possibly desire? You've given me back my hand.'

'Do you want a Qur'an to read, Falah?'

'No. Go away. Bring me my *kafiya*.'

'Give him a mild sedative,' whispered the doctor.

That night he awoke and wept until the dawn, when the nurse arrived with a snow white headcloth.

'Falah, here's your *kafiya*.'

'No.' He brushed her arm away. 'That's not mine. Mine has blood on it.'

'We washed it.'

'No. I tell you that's not mine. Take it away. I can't bear to look at it.'

'Please Falah . . .'

His head fell back on the pillow.

'Please take it away. I'm sorry. But that's not mine. Mine is from Kerbala. My mother brought it for me from the holy city.'

'Forgive me. I didn't mean to deceive you.' She turned away.

In the afternoon, the nurse returned with a book of fables which he accepted but tossed on the floor the moment she left. The following day he picked it up, began to read carelessly and to look at the pictures.

'It's for kids. She's stupid, you'd think she couldn't read.'

He had not read much since leaving school, but he had always liked the stories which the old people in the village told and had enjoyed the tales and fables his mother had recited. He took up the book and glanced through the pages. Each tale revolved around a fabulous creature: a sphinx, a mermaid, a centaur, a phoenix . . . as he flipped the pages, he spoke: 'For children. I'm not a child.' Until he arrived at the fable of the minotaur, which disturbed him. Never before had he seen such a creature. He turned the page rapidly to escape the bullman, telling himself that he was confronting a stupidity. He feigned disgust, threw the book on the floor by the bed and began to brood over his hand, while the image of the minotaur lingered on.

He did not touch the book until the nurse re-appeared.

She observed the book on the floor.

'Didn't you care for the fables, Falah?'

'It's for boys. I'm a man.'

'I didn't mean to insult you. I'll get another . . . '

'Don't you read?'

'Of course.'

'Well, why bring a man a boy's book?'

'I meant it only for a small pleasure. These last days have been difficult.' She paused, then with clear eyes and a firm voice added, 'Listen, Falah, you must stop brooding if your hand is to heal. I don't want to sound harsh but look around Falah, you can see many people injured. Not you alone suffer, but your hand can't heal if you are always depressed. I thought this book would cheer you up a little. You told me, you didn't desire the Qur'an. I hoped this might please you . . . Would you prefer another?'

'Leave the book. Thank you.'

The following week, the hand was separated from the belly while a second surgery was performed in which the tendons and nerves were examined for damage, the bones rebroken and reset. Falah had continued to practise writing with the left in case he did not regain full use of the right. He had progressed from the alphabet—in awkward and inordinately large letters that amused him—to a slow but steady copying out of the fables. He had grown to empathize with the minotaur and believed that the beast, rather than the Greek youths, was the victim. The creature's death was a brutal murder delivered by a relentless justice. Falah repeatedly copied them out until they were engraved on the shield of his memory like tattoos on the skin of a bedouin.

Azlam had worked assiduously at developing the left hand so that by the time of his release from the hospital he wrote well enough, and yet the skills of the surgeons had been so fine that it appeared that he might regain some dexterity in the right hand.

Azlam thought to return to B***** for it was all the life he had known but this was an impossibility. Major Haddad's forces, backed by the Israelis, had occupied his village. Many of the peasants were dead, those who had survived were either injured or destitute, scattered about the Beka'a countryside or trapped in the bombed slums of the northern cities seeking aid from relatives in Lebanon or abroad.

During his stay in the hospital, he made contact with a relative in Canada from whom he had received a letter. This paternal uncle had for some years been forwarding funds to assist the Azlam family during the years of war. The uncle, being notified of the destruction and occupation of the village, and the nephew's straitened circumstances, wrote prevailing on Falah to proceed to the Canadian embassy in Beirut and to file an application to immigrate. The uncle would do everything in his power to bring Falah to Canada.

The peasant had dismissed this suggestion until it was apparent that the notion to return to B***** was nothing but a delusion, and that Lebanon, torn by discord from within and aggression from without, was plunging deep into a Sargasso Sea. Under these circumstances, he arrived in the city of Beirut and squatted in a bombed-out building with fellow villagers. His own injury appeared minor amongst the multitude of mutilated refugees of the South and the Palestinians of the camps while the Beirutis continued their daily lives amid the Israeli bombings, explosions in booby-trapped cars and endless sniper fire. He had visited the city several times in the past but now it was so divided and damaged as hardly to be recognizable.

For days, he huddled in the wrecked building, eating little, growing thinner, waiting for the Lebanese government to issue the necessary passport which he was only able to secure after giving *baksheesh* from the money which his uncle had forwarded to him via a fellow Lebanese returning from Canada.

Each morning for several weeks, he set out for the Canadian embassy located on the Rue Hamra, only to be discouraged by the long lines of unhappy people and the early closure. When he finally reached the clerk behind the bullet proof counter, the man grudgingly gave him the forms and information and told him to return them. Upon returning, Azlam was confronted by queues. However, he patiently arose shortly before dawn and stood in line to submit the application. When he reached the counter after some days, he was confronted by an overbearing official.

'You're Muslim, eh?' noted the man.

'That's right.'

'Canada's a Christian country. Surely you're aware of that.'

'My uncle is there.'

'Possibly.' He inspected the form. 'So you say. However, you have no reason to go there. You don't have any skills.'

'But . . . '

'They don't need more people who won't work.'

'But I can work.'

'Listen hick, they don't need your kind over there to make more trouble and a bad reputation for Lebanon. What skills do you have? None. I can see here you didn't even finish high school. You don't know English or French. It's useless to send this application to the ambassador, he'll only laugh. Go. Go. It will take some time to process this application but I can tell you, don't hope for too much. Next.'

'But my uncle said they take each application on its own.'

'Does your uncle—if you have one at all in Canada—does he work for the department of immigration in Ottawa?'

'No. He works in a butcher factory.'

'Then I'm not interested in what your uncle thinks or says. What would a butcher know? Nothing. Go now. Next.'

'But when will I know? When can I return?'

'Only god knows. These things take time. Maybe four or five months, maybe a year. Now go before I get the guard to throw you out.'

Azlam turned away, telling himself that he did not want to go to Canada anyway. Lebanon was good enough if the war would only end and he could return to the village, plow the land, grow olives, grapes and figs, but then he stared at the mutilated limb and cursed: 'Not fit for a day's work. I'm no longer a man.'

Jets hammered through the heavens. Azlam glanced up at the sky of smooth, grey, opaque slabs of rock with asymmetrical fissures, each slab set to the next like blocks in a wall without a trace of mortar. Soon it would crumble.

'Go to Canada!' called out the peasant at the jets. 'What an absurd notion! Damn my uncle for putting the idea in my skull in the first place.' He spat on the pavement and then gazed again at the jets. 'You go to America.'

CORINNE ALLYSON LEE

(b. 1950)

'By virtue of the shape of my eyes and the colour of my hair,' says Corinne Allyson Lee, 'I am considered by Canadian society to have membership in a "visible" minority, and am also called a "woman of colour".' These attitudes often result in 'internalized racism' that Lee describes 'as fear or hatred of one's own ethnic heritage or prejudice against one's own race. For myself,' she says, 'it has taken decades to get to the point of claiming ownership of such feelings.'

Born in Calgary in 1950, Lee was fluent in both Chinese and English by the time she started school. It was after she left the prairies to settle in Vancouver that she began to come to terms with her ethnic heritage and overcome her 'sinophobia'—what she calls 'fear or hatred of anything or anyone Chinese'—a process greatly facilitated by her becoming involved in various groups of Asian lesbians. Lee has worked as an instructor and counsellor for street-entrenched and Native youth, as a dental auxiliary in prison, and as a medical research technician. One of the organizers of the 'Writing Thru Race' conference (Vancouver 1994), Lee is 'committed to striving to make accessible an opportunity and safe space for writers and would-be writers'. 'I will not be censored,' she says, 'minimized, misrepresented, dismissed or silenced without consequence.'

A poet and prose writer, Lee had her poem 'Sinophobia' nominated by *The Capilano Review* for the Western Magazines Awards; another poem, 'Owed to Grandmother', won first prize in the poetry competition of *Possibilities*. The co-editor, with Makeda Silvera, of *Pearls of Passion: A Treasury of Lesbian Erotica* (1994), Lee has been published in literary journals, and is a contributor to the anthologies *Out Rage: Dykes and Bis Resist Homophobia* (1993) and *Piece of my Heart: A Lesbian of Colour Anthology* (1991).

RECIPE

Separate carefully the following ingredients (with the help of family, friends, co-workers and the general public):

Why do they always hang around in groups or gangs?

Why don't you stick to your own kind?

*

So how come they let them into this country if they caint speak English?

No, I don't speak Chinese.

*

They **all** look alike.

No, we aren't sisters.

*

They **all** do that.

They give the rest of us a bad name.

*

They talk so loud and get so pushy.

Why are they always so wimpy and reserved?

*

If I could be born all over again, I'd be born white.

If you marry a white boy, we'll cut you out of our will.

*

You'll have to try three times harder in order to be half as good as a white person.

Those Chinese work such long hours without complaining. They do what they're told and they never ask questions.

*

They're driving up all the housing prices and they're taking away all our jobs.

Why can't you get a decent, respectable job like everyone else? Something like business, accounting or pharmacy?

*

They're everywhere, taking over the world.

We didn't get the vote until 1949.

*

See how dorky they look, with those thick glasses and flat noses?

> Attractive Straight White Male, middle-aged business executive looking for that special little China Doll, preferably short, petite and obedient. Object: to fulfill typical fantasies of the stereotype of Oriental ladies anxious to marry a Canadian in order to get out of Hong Kong or the Philippines and willing to do anything to pamper and please her man. Photo required.

*

Do **you people** celebrate Christmas?

That Lo Faan looks ridiculous in that Chinese silk dress.

*

Tch, tch . . . another Chinese driver. Those people are such lousy drivers.

Oh no! Not another Chinese Volvo fender bender. How embarrassing!

*

You know, I just read a really interesting book on China the other day . . .

What's the use of studying drama if there is never going to be a Chinese actor allowed to play Lady Macbeth? (Take MY milk for gall!)

*

You know, I went to a really good Chinese restaurant the other day.

Look at all these Lo Faan in this restaurant. They're ordering exactly what **we're** having! Bunch of 'Wanna Bees.'

*

More crime! Violence! Must be Asian gangs again.

Look at all those whites wanting to do martial arts, trying to be like Bruce Lee.

*

Do you cook Chinese food at home?

Do **you**?

*

Do you speak Chinese?

Do **you**?

*

I didn't know **you people** could sing jazz!

We all have vocal cords, too.

*

Where do you come from, originally?

My mother's womb—how about you?

*

Have you ever been back to Hong Kong?

How can you go back to some place you've never been? I'm not Shirley MacLaine.

*

Wow—lookit that beautiful Chinese girl. Such nice, almond-shaped eyes and lovely black hair!

Just because the person who passes me on the street is Chinese doesn't mean that I have to look him/her in the eye and acknowledge him/her.

*

Hey, some of my best friends are Chinese.

You should be playing with more Chinese kids!

*

Why don't they go back to where they come from?

Why don't **they** go back to where they come from?

*

Exclusion Act.

A dollar a day on the C.P.R.

*

Mix in a blender the following ingredients (in any home, school, workplace or public place):

> Chink
> Chinaman
> Gook
> V.C.
> Slant-eye
> Rice Gobbler
> Gwai Lo
> Lo Faan

Throw in a dash of guilt, shame and embarrassment, and a pinch of intimidation, resentment, jealousy and fear. Reinforce solidly with threats, condescension and a patronizing tone.

Subtly fold all ingredients together in a large, liberal multicultural bowl.

Place in a large pressure cooker and seethe at the following temperatures (NOTE: the temperatures may be altered depending on attitude):

1950	Colourblind, Invisible
1960	Don't Wanna Be
1970	Third Generation Canadian-born Chinese
1980	Woman of Colour, Visible Minority
1990	Asian Canadian
	Asian Pacific Lesbian
	Asian Lesbian of Vancouver

Cook patiently for one generation and release pressure briefly no more than once a year.

Stir up frequently, to taste.

Do not clean out the pot after any explosions.

Season with Japanese soy sauce; no one will know the difference.

Guaranteed to stay in the stomach for a lifetime; you won't be hungry again, even after a couple of hours.

> *Serves millions.*

LEE MARACLE

(b. 1950)

'Raven, why aren't you sleeping? You are disrupting some important business with your pitiful "broken wing again" dance. . . . It's a bad joke Raven . . . to remind me that these white men re-stirred dreams of you in me when I was so young. Go to sleep, while I wrestle with truth and conscience.'

Wrestling with truth and conscience is precisely what characterizes Lee Maracle's work. And she does so from within her Native tradition and through a constant dialogue between history and the present, as is evident in these opening words of an essay she published in 1989.

Born in North Vancouver of a Métis mother and a Salish father, Maracle did not finish high school. As she says, 'The difficulty for myself has been mastering a language different from my own, without having my own. Most of us learned English from parents who spoke English in translation. Many of our parents had been to residential school and thus did not speak the old language any better than the average five-year-old speaks English.' An avid reader since her young years, Maracle has read widely in the areas of history, especially that of her own people, politics, and social issues, and studied Creative Writing and sociology at Simon Fraser University in 1987. Education, be it an instrument of control as it was used by the Canadian system with regard to Native children, or a form of empowerment and self-knowledge, is one of the central themes in her writing.

Beginning with *I Am Woman* (1988), which was published by her husband's Write-on Press in North Vancouver, Maracle established her writing style as that of 'oratory'. 'That's my political discursive style,' she says: 'As orators, we are not short on vocabulary . . . Our best orators, in English or their own language, are those who have struggled with the language unencumbered by the tedious commas and colons of the English language.' Written as a collage of autobiographical and testimonial statements, poetry, and illustrations, *I Am Woman* offers an anatomy of colonialism examined through Maracle's own experiences as a Métis, woman, writer, mother, and lover.

Similar themes are explored in *Bobbi Lee: Indian Rebel* (1990). Initially presented orally in the 1970s, this book is a first-person narrative account of Bobbi, a Métis woman writer. Bobbi's writing journey, in its thematic range and stylistic immediacy, reflects what Maracle says in yet another essay/oratory that appeared in 1992: 'Part of our colonial condition is that we are still too busy struggling in the whirl of it, paddling through the rapids of it, to be able to enter the dreamspace at the edge of it. Few of us have had the time to study our remembered story. Some have no memories to ponder. But those of us who have pondered our memorized stories know we have a criteria for story.'

The same impetus characterizes *Oratory: Coming to Theory* (1990). Practising what its title announces, it offers a meditation on storytelling and theory as two of the most important elements of Maracle's creative process, a process she sharply contrasts to the European intellectual traditions.

Sojourner's Truth and Other Stories (1990), which opens with 'Bertha', the story that follows, is Maracle's attempt 'to integrate two mediums: oratory and European story': the stories 'don't have orthodox "conclusions"' and they try 'very hard to draw the reader into' their centres 'in just the same way the listener of our oral stories is drawn in.'

Sundogs (1992), a novel, is about the lives of a Vancouver Native family in 1990, the year that the Native Manitoba MLA Elijah Harper blocked the Meech Lake Accord and the summer of the Oka crisis. Her second novel, *Ravensong* (1993), set in the early 1950s, revolves around the lives of two sisters who, in their different ways, try to keep their Native community together during a flu epidemic. Raven, as the trickster figure that she is, inspires, admonishes, and teases the characters all at the same time.

Maracle, who has lived both in Toronto and in Vancouver, has also published a poetry book, *Seeds*, and has contributed to the *Renga* poetry project, *Linked Lives* (1991), which has appeared in both English and French. One of the contributors to and the co-editor of *Telling It: Women and Language Across Cultures* (1990), Maracle has also acted in plays, most recently in the Vancouver 1995 production of Drew Hayden Taylor's *Someday*.

BERTHA

The accumulation of four days of rain reflected against the street lamps and the eternal night-time neon signs, bathing the pavement in a rainbow of crystal splashes. In places on the road it pooled itself into thin sheets of blue-black glass from which little rivulets slipped away, gutter bound. From eaves and awnings the rain fell in a steady flow; even the signposts and telephone poles chattered out the sounds of the rain before the drops split themselves on the concrete sidewalks. Everywhere the city resounded with the heavy rhythm of pelting rain. It cut through the distorted bulk of the staggering woman.

The woman did not notice the rain. Instead, the bulk that was Bertha summoned all her strength, repeatedly trying to correctly determine the distance between herself and the undulating terra beneath her feet to prevent falling. Too late. She fell again. She crawled the rest of the way to the row of shacks. Cannery row, where the very fortunate employees of the very harassed and worried businessmen reside, is not what one might call imaginatively designed. The row consists of one hundred shacks, identical in structure, sitting attached by common walls in a single row. The row begins on dry land and ends over the inlet. Each shack is one storey high and about eighteen by twenty feet in floor space.

They are not insulated. The company had more important sources of squander for its profits: new machines had to be bought, larger executive salaries had to be paid— all of which severely limited the company's ability to extend luxuries to the producers of its canned fish. The unadorned planks which make up the common walls at the back and front of each shack and at the end of each row are all that separate people from nature. A gable roof begins about seven feet from the floor and comes to a peak some eight feet later. Each roof by this time enjoyed the same number of unrepaired holes as its neighbour, enabling even the gentlest of drizzles in. The holes, not being part of the company's construction plan, are more a fringe benefit or a curse of natural unrepaired wear, depending on your humour.

None of the buildings are situated on the ground. All were built of only the sturdiest wood and were well creosoted at the base to fend off rot for at least two decades. Immersed in salt water and raw sewage as they have been this past half century, they are beginning to show a little wear. In fact, once during the usual Saturday night rough-housing which takes place on a pay night, X pitched his brother over the side. They had been arguing about whether the foreman was a pig or a dog. X maintained dogs did not stink and what is more, could be put to work, while his brother held he would not eat a dog, and food being a much higher use-value, the foreman was a dog. He then let go with a string of curses at X, which brought X to grievous violence. On the way to the salt chuck X's brother knocked out one of the pilings. It was never replaced. The hut remains precariously perched on three stilts and is none the worse for that. Unfortunately, the water that filled X's brother's lungs settled the argument forever. The accused foreman has since been known as a pig.

Not to discredit the company. In the days before modern machinery, when the company had to employ a larger number of workers to process less fish, it used cheaper paint—whitewash to be honest. One day all the workers who had congregated in the town at the season's opening beheld a fine sight at the end of Main Street: exterior house paint of the most durable quality. These stains come in a variety of colours but the company, not wishing to spoil its workers with excessive finery, stuck with the colour which by then had achieved historical value.

The paint did not really impress anyone save the foreman. So delighted was he with the new paint that he mentioned it time and again, casually. The best response he got was one low grunt from one of the older, more polite workers. Most simply stared at their superior with a profoundly empty look. *Thankless ingrates*, he told himself, though he dared not utter any such thing aloud.

Although the opinion of the foreman about his workers had stood the test of time over the decade that had lapsed, the paint job had not been so lucky. The weather had been cruel to the virgin stain, ripping the white in ugly gashes from the row's simple walls. The rigorous climate of the North West Coast destroyed the paint in a most consistent way, exactly with the run of the wood grain. Where the grain grooved, the stain remained; where the grain ridged, the salt sea wind and icy rain tore the stain off.

At the front of the dwellings some of the doors are missing. Not a lot of them, mind you, certainly not the majority have gone astray. The plank boardwalk in front of cannery row completes the picture of the outside. Over the years, at uncannily even intervals, each sixth board has disappeared, some by very bizarre happenstances.

Inside, the huts are furnished with tasteless simplicity. A sturdy, four-legged cedar table of no design occupies the middle of the room. Four wooden, high-backed chairs built with unsteamed two-by-twos and a square piece of good-one-side plywood surround the table. The floors are shiplap planks. Squatted in the centre of the back wall is a pot-bellied cast-iron stove, though those workers who still cook use a Coleman. Shelving above the pot-bellied stove keeps the kitchenware and food supplies immodestly in view. Two bunks to the right and two to the left complete the furnishings. It was not the sort of place in which any of the workers felt inspired to add a touch of their personal self. No photos, no knick-knacks. What the company did not provide, the workers did not have.

The residence, taken as a whole, was not so bad but for one occasional nuisance. At high-tide each dwelling, except the few nearest shore, was partially submerged in water. It wasn't really such a great bother. After all, the workers spent most of their waking time at the cannery—upwards of ten hours a day, sometimes this included Sunday, but not always—and the bunks were sufficiently far from the floor such that sleeping, etc., carried on unencumbered. A good pair of Kingcome slippers[1] was all that was needed to prevent any discomfort the tide caused. The women who used to complain violently to the company that their cooking was made impossible by such intrusions have long since stopped. After the strike of '53 cooking was rendered redundant as the higher wage afforded the women restaurant fare at the local town's greasy spoon. Besides which, the sort of tides that crept into the residence occurred but twice or thrice a season. Indeed, the nuisance created was trifling.

Bertha is on the 'sidewalk' crawling. The trek across Main Street to the boardwalk had taken everything out of Bertha.

---

[1] Hip waders

'F.ck.ng btstsh' dribbles from her numb lips.

She glances furtively from side to side. The indignity of her position does not escape her. Being older than most of her co-workers, she is much more vulnerable to the elements. Bertha donned all the sweaters she brought to cannery row and her coat to keep warm. She spent the whole night drinking in the rain on the hill behind the city and now all of her winter gear is water-logged. The fifteen extra pounds make it impossible for her to move. She curses and prays no one sees her.

Her short pudgy fingers clutch at the side of residence No. 13 in an effort to rise above her circumstances. She is gaining the upper hand when a mocking giggle slaps her about the head and ears.

'F.ck.ng btstsh'

Trapped. Emiserated. Resigned. What the hell? She is no different from anyone else. Her memory reproaches her with the treasure of a different childhood. A childhood filled with the richness of every season, when not a snowflake fell unnoticed. Her memory retreats to another time.

* * *

The early autumn sunlight danced across lush green hillsides. Diamond dew drops glistened from each leaf. Crisp air and still warm sun excited the youth. Chatter and bantering laughter filled the air. Bertha in her glory punched out one-liners and smiled at the approval of the old ladies who chuckled behind their aging hands. Things were different then. Each girl was born in the comfort of knowing how she would grow, bear children and age with dignity to become a respected matriarch.

On the hills, basket on her back, Bertha was not called Bertha. She wanted to hear her name again, but something inside her fought against its articulation. In her new state of shame she could not whisper, even to herself, the name she had taken as woman. Old Melly staggered into view, eyes twinkling. Bertha didn't really want to see her now.

'Hey Bertie,' the giggle hollered out her nickname, unmindful of the woman's age and her own youth. 'I got some wine.'

'Khyeh, hyeh, yeh' and the circle of memory that crept out at her from the fog dimmed, but refused to recede. You had another upbringing before all this, the memory chided her. The efforts of the village women to nurture her as keeper of her clan, mother of all youth, had gone to naught. Tears swole from behind her eyes. 'Damn wine,' she muttered to herself. In the autumn hills of her youth the dream of motherhood had already begun to fade. Motherhood, the re-creation of ancient stories that would instruct the young in the laws of her people and encourage good citizenship from even the babies, had eluded her.

In the moment of her self-recrimination, Bertie contemplated going home. Home? Home was a young girl rushing through a meadow, a cedar basket swishing lightly against dew-laden leaves, her nimble fingers plucking ripe fat berries from their branches, the wind playfully teasing and tangling the loose, waist-length black hair that glistened in the autumnal dawn while her mind enjoyed the prospect of becoming . . . becoming, and the words in English would not come. She remembered the girl, the endless stories told to her, the meanings behind each story, the careful coaching in the truth that lay behind each one, the reasons for their telling, but she could not, after fifty years of speaking crippled English, define where it was all supposed to lead. Now all that remained was the happiness of her childhood memories against the stark emptiness of the years that stretched behind them.

Her education had been cut short when her great-grandfather took a christian name. She remembered a ripple of bewildered tension for which her language had no words to describe or understand what had gone through the village. The stories changed and so did the language. No one explained the intimacies of the new feeling in either language. Confusion, a splitting within her, grew alongside the murmur that beset the village. Uncertainty closed over the children. Now, even the stories she had kept tucked away in her memory escaped her. She stared hard down the narrow boardwalk trying to mark the moment when her memories had changed.

The priest had christened the most important man in the village. Slowly, christians appeared in their ranks. The priest left no stone unturned. Stories, empowering ceremonies, became pagan rituals, pagan rituals full of horrific shame. Even the way in which grooms were chosen changed. The old women lost their counsel seats at the fires of their men. Bighouses were left to die and tiny homes isolated from the great families were constructed. Little houses that separated each sister from the other, harbouring loneliness and isolation. Laughter died within the walls of these little homes. No one connected the stripping of woman-power and its transfer to the priest as the basis for the sudden uselessness all the people felt. Disempowered, the old ladies ceased to tell stories and lived out their lives without taking the children to the hills again.

For a short time, life was easier for everyone. No more shaking cedar, collecting goat hair or carefully raising dogs to spin the wool for their clothing. Trade—cash and the securing of furs by the village men—replaced the work of women. Bertha could not see that the feelings of anxiety among the youth were rooted in the futureless existence that this transfer of power created. A wild and painful need for a brief escape from their new life drove youth to the arms of whiskey traders.

An endless stream of accommodating traders paddled upriver to fleece the hapless converts. Those who lacked trap lines began disappearing each spring to the canneries where cash could be gotten. Young women followed on their heels. The police, too, gained from this new state of affairs. As the number of converts increased so did the number of drinkers. Interdiction caught up with those unfortunates not skilled at dodging the police. Short stays as guests in the queen's hotel[2] became the basis for a new run of stories, empty of old meaning. The rupture of the old and the rift created was swift and unrelenting. Things could be bought with money, and wages purchased the things of life much more swiftly and in greater quantities than did their pagan practices. Only great-grandmother, much ridiculed for her stubbornness, remained sober and pagan to her death. Her face lingered in the fog while Bertha wondered why the old woman had stopped talking to her. The process was complete before Bertha was out of her teens. Then she, too, joined the flow of youth to cannery row.

Bertha had come to cannery row full of plans. Blankets could be purchased with

[2]Jail

the cash she earned. How could she have known the blankets they sold were riddled with sickness? She paid the trader who delivered the blankets, as had some of the other youth. She experienced the same wild abandon that life outside the watchful eye of grannies and mothers gave rise to. They learned to party away the days of closure when there were not enough fish to work a whole shift. At season's end they all got into their boats and headed home. A lone canoe bobbed in the water just feet from the shore of their village; a solitary old man paddled out to greet them.

'Go back, death haunts the village, go back.' Confused, they went back. The story of the blankets did not catch up to them until years later. In their zeal to gift their loved ones they had become their killers. In their confusion and great guilt, wine consoled them.

* * *

Bertha stared blankly at her swollen hands. With blurred vision she peered unsteadily towards hut number nine. It wasn't home. She had no home. Home was fifty years ago and gone. Home was her education forever cut short by christian well-meaning. Home was the impossibility of her ever becoming the intellectual she should have been; it was the silence of not knowing how it all came to pass. Slowly her face found the young girl leaning out of the doorway.

'Ssr.'

She lumbered reluctantly to where the giggle sat, her mouth gaping in a wide grin exposing prematurely rotten teeth. Bertha could hardly look at her. No one as young as this girl should have rotten teeth. It marred her flawlessly even features. The large, thickly-lashed black eyes only sharpened the vileness of bad teeth. What a cruel twist of fate that this girl, whose frame had not yet acquired the bulk that bearing children and rearing them on a steady diet of winter rice and summer wine creates, should be burdened with a toothless grin before her youth was over.

The consumption of wine was still rational in the girl's maiden state, though not for long. Already the regularity of her trips to the bootlegger was beginning to spoil her eyes with occasional shadows. Her delicately shaped face sometimes hinted of a telling puffiness. On days like that it was hard for the girl to pose as a carefree and reckless youth. Today was not such a day.

Bertha hesitated before sitting, staring hard at the jug on the table. Unable to leave, but not quite up to sitting down, she remained rooted to the spot. She struggled with how it came to be that this girl from her village was so foreign to her. The moment threatened the comfort of shallow oblivion the girl needed. A momentary softness came over her face as she beckoned Bertha to sit. 'Relax, Bertha, have a drink.' Bertha sighed and sat down. The girl shucked the tenderness and resumed her gala self.

By day's end the jug was wasted and so were the women. There had been conversations and moments of silence, sentimental tears had been shed, laughter, even rage and indignation at the liberties white-male-bottom-pinchers took with Native women had been expressed. In all, the drunk had been relatively ordinary, except for a feeling that kept sinking into the room. It seemed to the girl to come from the ceiling and hang over their heads. The feeling was not identifiable and its presence was inexplicable. Nothing in particular brought it on. Only the wine chased the feeling from the windowless room. For the giggle, these moments were sobering, but Bertha seemed unruffled by it. If she was bothered, she betrayed no sign. At such moments, the giggle snatched the bottle and furiously poured the liquid into her throat. The wine instantly returned the young girl's world to its swaying, bleary, much more bearable state.

Bertha rarely left anything started unfinished, even as concerns a jug of wine. But the more she drank the more she realized she did not know this woman, this daughter who was not nurtured by her village grandmothers, but who had left as a small child and never returned to her home. She was so like all the youth who joined the march to cannery row of late. Foreign and mis-educated. Callous? Was that what made them so hard to understand? The brutal realization that she, Bertha, once destined to have been this young woman's teacher, had nothing to give but stories—dim, only half-remembered and barely understood—brought her up short. Guilt drove her from her chair before the bottle was empty. The feeling again sank from the ceiling, shrouding the girl in terror. Foreboding feelings raced through her body, but her addled consciousness could not catch any one of them and hold them long enough for her mind to contemplate their meaning.

Bertha stopped at the door, turned and stumbled back to the shaking girl. She touched her so gently on the cheek that the girl would hardly have been sure it happened except the touch made her eye twitch and the muscles in her face burn. The realization that the gulf between them was too great, their difference entrenched by Bertha's own lack of knowledge, saddened Bertha. Bertha wanted to tell her about her own unspoiled youth, her hills, the berries, the old women, the stories and a host of things she could not find the words for in the English she inherited. It was all so paralyzing and mean. Instead Bertha whispered her sorrow in the gentle words of their ancestors. They were foreign to the girl. The touch, the words, inspired only fear in her. The girl tried to relieve herself by screaming—no sound found its way out of her throat. She couldn't move. The queerly gentle and wistful look on Bertha's face imprinted itself permanently on the memory of the girl. Then Bertha left.

Bertha's departure broke the chains that locked the girl's body to the chair. Her throat broke its silence and a rush of sobs filled her ears. 'Damn wine, damn Bertie. Damn,' and she grabbed the jug. As the warm liquid jerked to her stomach the feeling floated passively to the ceiling and disappeared. Not convinced that Bertha's departure was final, she flopped the length of her body onto the bunk and prayed for the ill-lit, rat-filled cannery come morning to be upon her soon. Her body grew heavy and her mind dulled. Sleep was near. Before she passed out, her mind caught hold of the notion that she ought to have said goodbye to Bertha. Still, she slept.

* * *

Bertie's absence at the cannery went unnoticed by all but the foreman. The young girl had blocked the memory of the disturbing evening from her mind. They had been drunk. Probably Bertie's still drunk, ran her reasoning. The foreman, however, being a prudent and loyal company man, thought of nothing else but Bertie's absence. By day's end, he decided by the following reasoning to let her go: Now, one can withstand the not infrequent absences of the younger, swifter and defter of the Native workers. But Bertie is getting old, past her prime, so much so that even her half century of experience compensates little for the disruption of operational smoothness and lost time that her absence gives rise to. Smoothness is essential to any enterprise wishing to realize a profit, and time is money.

This decision was not easily arrived at. He was not totally insensitive to human suffering. He had been kept up all night weighing the blow to Bertie and the reaction of the other workers that firing her might cause, against the company's interest in profits, before finally resolving to fire her. Firing her could produce no results other than her continuing to be a souse. As for the workers, they would be angry but he was sure they wouldn't do anything. In any case, he was the foreman and if he didn't put his foot down these Natives were sure to walk all over him. Her absence again this morning convinced him that he had made the right decision. Still, he could not bring himself to say anything until the end of the day, in case the others decided to walk off the job. No sense screwing up the whole day over one old woman.

In a very loud voice, the foreman informed Bertie's nephew that his auntie Bertie was fired and could he tell her to kindly collect her pay and remove herself by week's end to whence she came.

'Can't be done.'

'I beg your pardon and why not? I have every authority to fire every one of you here.'

His voice rose and all became quiet but for the hum of machinery. The blood of the workers boiled with shame at the tone of this white man. No one raised their eyes from their fixed position on their work and no one moved.

'Can't be done is all,' the nephew flatly replied without looking at the foreman. His hands resumed work, carefully removing the fins from the fish.

'I asked you why not, boy.' Angry as he was, he couldn't fire Bertie's nephew. Had he been a shirker, he would have, but Bertie's nephew was one of the more reliable and able of his workers, so he could not fire him. All he could do was sneer 'boy' at him and hope that this, the soberest and most regular worker, did not storm out in defiance of the foreman's humiliating remark.

'She's dead.'

An agonized scream split the silence and the knife that so deftly beheaded the fish slipped and deprived the lovely young girl of her left thumb and giggle forever.

GERRY SHIKATANI

(b. 1950)

'I approach writing as a practice of attention, the possibilities of my openness to the quotidian particulars,' says Gerry (Osamu) Shikatani. 'It's a kind of attending to that place where one can be stopped by presence and enables a return.' This 'practice of attention'—a 'practice of process', he also calls it—is rooted in Shikatani's upbringing. 'My parents had little material wealth,' he says, 'but attended to their work and children in an extraordinary generosity. It's this nurturing wealth, an unquestioned devotion and honouring which instructs me to writing as a devotion. Their names—Masajiro and Mitsuko (Mukai) Shikatani. Language offers the wondrous act of gently holding the luminous, the lasting shimmer of parents, in the process of descendance.'

His poetry, be it traditional, visual, minimalist, or otherwise experimental, reflects his meticulous attention to craft, his careful listening to the cadences of language and, above all, his intention to construct, through writing, what he calls the 'tenuous thread in "ecological being"'.

Born in Toronto, Shikatani is a Nisei, a second generation Japanese-Canadian. His parents were evacuated from Port Essington, a small fishing community in northern British Columbia, and relocated at the camp in Slocan during the Second World War. 'The sounds, the silences I first felt and heard,' he says, 'were of [his parents'] Japanese and this first language . . . remains the starting point.' As he points out, 'the mothertongue with its dialects, its accents is for us all a place of art-making.' These early experiences account for the critical and formal approach he has taken in his poetry: 'because of my own broken, Canadian's Japanese,' he remarks, 'I ended up among writers,' like bp Nichol and Roy Kiyooka, 'who've pushed at and from margins.'

Shikatani, who studied religion at the University of Toronto, has worked as a creative and media writing instructor, and as a researcher-consultant specializing in gastronomy. Active for many years in Toronto's poetry scene, he has published many chapbooks, including *The Book of Tree: a cottage journal* (1987), *Our Nights in Perugia* (1984), *Ship Sands Island* (1978), and *Barking of Dog* (1973). The poems that follow are from his major collection, *A Sparrow's Food* (1984). *1988: Poems 1973-1988* (1989) was the second major gathering of his work. His writing, which has received an Honourable Mention of the bp Nichol Chapbook Award (1987), has been represented in many English Canadian, Quebecois, and French anthologies, including the *International Anthology of Concrete Poetry* (1977), *Haiku Anthologie Canadienne / Canadian Anthology* (1985), and *Performance Au / In Canada 1970-90* (1991).

A workshop leader at the 'Writing Thru Race' conference (Vancouver 1994), Shikatani is presently working, with filmmaker Jesse Nishihata, on a film that documents his recent explorations into language and writing through his personal history. A resident of Montreal, he has been a professor of Creative Writing at Concordia University (1993-95). Shikatani is also the co-editor of *Paper Doors: An Anthology of Japanese-Canadian Poetry* (1981).

AFTER A READING OF ISAN

laughing so hard, mind's
eternal focus.
then, a rim of silence.
steam rises
from a kettle of boiling water.

but I'm dogged
at the heels
by every kind of shit.

I try to look
for the end
of such self-made fire,
still must I
look, lust every opposite,
every manner of change
    to penetration?

perhaps, when cooking.
Buddha / God. whatever
    I call you,
it's never there,
Buddha, God
both shit.

the tree stands,
makes me a farce.

driving me crazy,
tree laughs
in my very face.

Isan (1795-1864), a Zen poet

BIRD OF TWO FORMS

1 hut in the mountain
   mount   hut

   Mount Eyes:
   Mount Mouth:
   Mount Third Finger:
           Mount If you are hungry: Eat!

2 hut in the mountain
   mount   hut

   all grown over, hidden
   cover of thick branches

   or, a single fishing-boat

   bell, drifting
   stiff hands dry with salt.

THE THREE COINS

three coins shock
me. in the night
I am in the pocket
of it. footsteps clack
and ring
scattering across the hard
stones of the plaza.
in the pocket in
it darkness, currency
I count
three stallions of light,
shock. shock.
clash of cold coins
footsteps ring a plaza.
hard stones.

HAIKU
for Chris Cheek

o.k. pigeons.
looking out my window.
hmm.
what's this?
distracted like
that.

     how can I define
     a haiku?

       well, haiku's on this page
/maybe cut out this word
a rectangular box
with some scissors.
then what?
stick it in the refrigerator?
            on the shelf?

hmm. o.k. pigeons
time to get out
of my window,
yer time's up.

M.G. VASSANJI

(b. 1950)

M. (Moyez) G. Vassanji sees his generation of writers as being '[u]niquely placed because we're just between independence and colonialism, and between cultures, and between religions, and between countries. And even in the West, many of us move from one country to another.' Vassanji finds the mobility of his diasporic generation to be an 'exhilarating' experience: 'I like that rawness; it's very exciting to have so many different experiences in one life.'

Vassanji sees himself as an 'Afro-Asian', an identity that reflects the complexity of his background. Born in Nairobi, Kenya, from parents who were second- and third-generation Indians in Africa, he moved with his family, after his father's death, to Dar es Salaam, Tanzania. '[A]lthough we were Africans, we were also Indians,' he says. 'We were brought up as Indians. We grew up speaking two Indian languages—Cutchi and Gujarati—and we also understood Hindi from the movies we watched. And then we were also brought up speaking Swahili and English. We had all of this within us.' All of 'this Indianness . . . transformed by the Africanness', Vassanji has made the central focus of his first novel, The Gunny Sack (1989), which won the Commonwealth Prize for First Novel in the region of Africa.

With the assistance of a scholarship, Vassanji moved to the United States in 1970 to study at the Massachusetts Institute of Technology where he received a B.Sc. (1974). After receiving his Ph.D. in nuclear physics (1978) from the University of Pennsylvania, he moved to Canada for a job at the University of Toronto. After ten years and thirty published papers in nuclear physics, Vassanji, who had begun writing seriously in 1986,

decided to become a full-time writer. The co-founder and editor of The Toronto South Asian Review (1982-), he is also the publisher of TSAR.

No New Land (1991), his second novel, reflects Vassanji's move to Canada. Set in the Toronto suburb of Don Mills, it deals with what Vassanji has called 'the predicament of "in-between" societies—in this case East and West', dramatized by characters who have to negotiate their past with their Canadian reality, or, as Vassanji puts it, 'acknowledge the past and . . . move forward'. But if Vassanji's characters' hard adaptation experiences represent the acculturation process of most immigrants, it is a process that Vassanji sees the process as paralleling the changes that the dominant culture must undergo: 'Anything that is already old and is established needs new infusions; otherwise, it dies. So the mainstream society has no choice but to accept us. However,' he adds, 'if I felt completely oppressed, then I wouldn't live here.' And 'here', Toronto, is where he 'feel[s] most at home'.

In Uhuru Street (1992), a collection of short fiction that includes the story that follows, Vassanji returns to his African settings, but he continues to write about characters who are marked by their diasporic movements. His most recent novel, The Book of Secrets (1994), winner of the Giller Prize for fiction, focuses again on Vassanji's Asian community of East Africa that unfolds through various generations of characters shaped by colonialism and the First World War as well as by their own passions and intrigues.

Vassanji is presently at work on a travelogue about India, which he visited for the first time during the period of the communalist riots there.

THE LONDON-RETURNED

We still went back for our holidays then and we formed a rambunctious group whose presence was hard to miss about town. We were the London-returned. For two or three joyously carefree months the city became a stage for us and we would strut up and down its dusty pavements parading overseas fashions, our newly acquired ways. Bare feet and Beatle-style haircuts were in then, drawing conservative wrath and doomsday prophecies. We sported flashy bell-bottoms, Oxford shirts and bright summer dresses. And fat pinkish-brown thighs below the colourful mini-skirts of our female companions teased the famished adolescent eyes of our hometown. Come Saturday morning, we would gather at a prearranged rendezvous and conscious of every eye upon us, set off in one large and rowdy group towards Independence Avenue. There to stroll along its pavements a few times over, amidst fun and laughter, exchanging jokes and relating incidences in clipped, finished accents.

The acacia-lined avenue cut a thin margin at the edge of town. It looked out at the ocean a short block away, black and rust red steamers just visible plying in and out of the harbour. Behind it was crammed the old town, a maze of short dirty sidestreets feeding into the long and busy Uhuru Street, which then opened like a funnel back into the avenue. From here Uhuru Street went down, past downtown and the Mnazi Moja grounds into the interior: the hinterland of squat African settlements, the mainroad Indian stores, the Arab corner stores—in which direction we contemptuously sniffed, suppressing a vague knowledge of our recent roots there.

On Saturday morning you came to Independence Avenue to watch and to be seen. You showed off your friends, your breeding, your money. It was here that imported goods were displayed in all their glory and European-looking mannequins threw temptation from store windows. And yes, hearts too were on sale on these pavements. Eyes could meet and the memory of a fleeting instant live to fuel one's wildest dreams . . .

We walked among tourists and expatriate shoppers, civil servants and messengers in khaki. And we passed other fugitive groups like ours, senior boys and girls (always separate) from the high schools, who somehow had managed to walk away this Saturday. Our former classmates, many of these. With some I had managed to keep up a brief correspondence. Now some exchanged short greetings, others pretended not to see, and a few turned up their noses with the moral superiority of the uncontaminated. Yet they stoked our merriment no end—these innocents—by their sidelong glances at our miniskirted companions, or their self-conscious attempts at English accents and foreign manners while sipping iced capuccinos in the European surroundings of Benson's.

It was at Benson's where it began.

She was sitting with a group of friends sipping iced capuccino. They were all in uniform, of course. How can I forget, the green and white, the skirt and blouse? For a brief instant, between two intervening sandy-haired tourist heads, our eyes met. And lowered. And then again a fleeting, fugitive appointment. She had me then.

I think of her as she was then. A small figure, not too thin, with a heart-shaped face: a small pointed chin, high cheekbones, a large forehead. Her hair was tightly combed back and tied into a plain pony tail. She sat sipping through a straw, stirring the frothy contents in the tall frosted glass to turn them more liquid. I hadn't heard her voice and I didn't know her. Yet I sat there a few tables away, flustered, self-conscious, saying silly things, laughing uncertainly.

At her table an animated conversation was underway. They talked in Cutchi, not too loudly nor timidly. How self-contained they looked, how comfortable with each other! I felt a little envious, looking in from outside. My subject never looked up again although she must have known I was watching. Presently they waved at the uniformed waiter and went out through the frosted glass door.

We had a word for the kind of state I was in in the few days that followed. Pani-pani: liquid. It means, perhaps, melted. With stylish and refined company—at least as I saw it then—beside me, what made me turn pani-pani at the sight of so plain a figure? The mating instinct, I tell myself a little cynically many years later; how surely it singles out and binds! Kismet, our elders called it. You could walk to the end of the world and not find the right partner, they told you, until your kismet opened up for you. And when it did, as surely and beautifully as a flower, no amount of reason could dissuade you from your choice. In our case it sought to bridge our two worlds. And where else should it strike but on Independence Avenue where these two worlds met.

* * *

She lived in what I called the hinterland; not in a squat mud and limestone dwelling but a modern two-storey affair that had replaced it. They were newly rich and moving up; they owned the building and ran the bustling store on the street floor. It had a perpetual sale on, announced by huge signs painted on the walls, pillars, and display windows. And periodically leaflets would be distributed in the area, announcing 'Sale! Sale! Sale!' This much I knew as soon as I came home and gave her description to my sister; it was common knowledge. I learned that she was the daughter of Amina Store. Four times a day an elegant blue hydraulic-suspensioned Citroën sailed smoothly over the potholes and gravel of our backroads, carrying the daughter of the house and her neighbourhood friends to school and back.

* * *

On Saturday nights, after a rest from our frolics of the day, we partied. We met on the rooftop of a modern residential building called Noor-e-Salaam in our new suburb of Upanga well away from the bustle of the downtown shops and streets. The latest from the London hit parade wafted down from here. We swung to the rhythms of the Mersey beat while our former friends still drooled over the lyrics of Elvis and Jim Reeves. And to friendly locals we dispensed some of the trendier scraps from our new lifestyles. We talked about nights out in London and trips to the Continent. We introduced new words and naughty drinks.

The Saturday night following my first sight of her I managed to get Amina invited, and also her gang just to keep talk from spreading that I had been stricken. Yet how long can one hide the truth where even the slightest conjecture or suspicion could become truth merely by the force of suggestion? The blue Citroën dutifully unloaded its passengers outside the garden of Noor-e-Salaam and sailed away. They had all come. But I paid attention only to her and what pleased me was that she let me. I had come prepared for the kill, to sweep her off her feet before anyone else realized that she was available. With these unspoilt maidens who haven't left home, I told myself, you can't go wrong with books. And so on the dance floor under a modestly bright series of coloured lightbulbs, while the Rolling Stones sang 'Satisfaction', while we sipped Coke and looked down over the sidewall at the rustling trees and the few people walking on the dark street below, we talked in soft tones about nothing but books. Books!

But it was by her books that my sister swore, a few days later, when she came back from school. Two years younger, she knew I was stricken and had me on the rack, torturing me with bits of information about Amina.

'Look! I swear by holy knowledge!' Brown-papered exercise books held up solemnly as if they meant that much to her.

'Don't lie, or I'll . . .'

'Okay, then.' A mock sullenness. The books are thrown on the sofa. She sits with a long face and draws her knees up close, looks from the corners of her eyes.

'So? What was she asking?'

'But you said I was lying! So I was lying.'

'Come on now, *what?*'

'What will you give me if I tell you?'

'You'll get a slap if you don't!'

'She was asking about you. They are teasing her about you, you know. The news has got around!'

'They are stupid.'

'Well, what do you expect? You danced with no one else. And to talk of studies all the time!' She chuckles.

'I don't know her, silly! What if she is the pious type?'

It didn't hurt, being laughed at like that in the Girls' School. To be studious was still a virtue in those days. No small matter. It was the way out. And it tickled my vanity no end to learn that I had been talked about in a conversation among girls. But perhaps she had found out about me only to reject me?

Because she never came to those parties again. That was the last time, for the entire group. It indicated a certain rejection on her part: of my lifestyle and my friends. She's chosen against me I thought. Perhaps she thinks I'm a loafer. Doesn't she know I go to school, I don't go around London cutting people's hair? I go to school. To have come this close to victory—and to lose out without explanation. Maybe she was teasing, testing me; to show how vulnerable even we could be, the sophisticates who seemed to have the world in the palms of our hands.

What agonizing days I spent, keeping a lookout for her up and down Independence Avenue, entering Benson's on impulse and coming out pretending to have forgotten something, a ridiculous figure altogether. There was no way of contacting her; you needed an excuse for that. I could not think of any that would not have seemed a direct proposition. But she could, and she did.

* * *

I stand on our balcony looking down on the street. It's five-thirty in the evening or thereabouts. There's not a moving car on the road but some pedestrians are about. Except around noon this sidestreet is shielded from the sun by buildings and it always feels like five-thirty in the evening. A gloomy street. The sun always shines on Uhuru Street a block away. There the heat roasts you and you seek the shelter of the shadier streets.

Below me two boys play marbles on the pavement. Some distance away a figure walks towards them. A circle with a diameter is drawn in charcoal, two marbles placed on the straight line. A game of 'pyu' beginning. I look away to the figure that is closer now and I see it's a girl. Below me a marble gets projected by a forefinger pulled back, lands on the ground, rolls for a while, then takes a sudden turn and sweeps away towards the road—Oh God, it's her! as she walks around them—'Aaaaaaah!' Rage and disappointment, fists clenched. What did he expect, on such a surface? It's the other one's turn now. My heart leaps: she's entered the doorway of our building. I picture her walking through the courtyard past the boys playing cricket against the wall and taking the stairs. I keep looking down at the road, chest pounding away, face flushed to a fever. Who could she be visiting?—four possibilities . . . no, three . . .

A knock on the door.

'Yes,' says my sister behind me in a voice obviously spilling over with glee, 'he's right here!' I turn away from the balcony and greet her.

She is in a hurry. 'Can I borrow Tranter's book from you? I need it for my revision.'

I bring the book, careful to avoid the mischief in my sister's eyes.

'You can keep it as long as you want—I'll tell you when I want it back.'

'Only for a few days. I have to rush now. Our driver's waiting. Thanks!'

So it was Tranter's *Pure Mathematics* to begin with. She kept it for two months. Meanwhile I borrowed Cooke's *Organic Chemistry* from her, and so it went on. Other books, other excuses, the books untouched. Anything for a chance to meet and talk under plausible cover. Education was not to be tampered with. I would on occasion miss my stroll on Independence Avenue and walk two miles down Uhuru Street with a book in my hand, past the barren grounds, the small dingy shops packed close together, to the flat above Amina Store where she lived. How delicious, luxurious, the anxieties of those days; how joyful the illusion of their pain! They consumed my existence. Her mother fed me hot bhajias when she was there, inviting me in with: 'Come on in, babu, don't stand there in the doorway!' The servant would bring in the delights. At other times her young brother would sit at the dining table doing sums in an old exercise book while we sat on the sofa. I tried sending him downstairs to buy a Coke or something, but he wouldn't budge. And the two of us would smile, embarrassed.

People noticed—and they talked, made up their minds. But for us nothing was decided—it could not be—the future was open. This was a chance to be together, to explore the bounds of possibility; and if it lasted long enough, it would lead to an eventuality that was acceptable. But of course, meanwhile, I had to leave. At the end of the holidays, when it was time for me to go back, I asked her: 'Can I write to you?' 'You may, if you want to,' she said. And so we corresponded.

* * *

All this is eighteen years ago, and dead: but surely, the dead deserve their due? Or, as our elders said, they come to haunt your dreams.

I sit here in the cosy embrace of a north Scarborough living room in winter, looking out through glass doors, mulling over the last years of our marriage. An intimacy that turned insipid, dried up. Not for us the dregs of relationships, the last days of alternating care and hatred. 'I need a life of my own,' she said. 'I can change; we both can change. You can quit work and go back to college. Is that it?' 'Alone,' she said, 'we've moved apart.' 'And she?—I'll want to keep her.' 'You may, if you want to.'

The open field before me stretches northwards—a vast desert of snow. There are towns out there, I tell myself, cities full of people. Yet I see only endless stretches, a bleak landscape with a few brambles blown by a light wind. And way beyond, beyond which I cannot see a thing, there is a point marked by a pennant strangely still on a short pole. The North Pole as I've always imagined it. In that landscape I see a figure from the past, a former hero . . . Captain Scott from my Standard Six reader, cowering from biting winds . . . Why Captain Scott, out of the blue, as it were and at the wrong Pole? I cannot say for sure . . .

I tell myself I walked too far, too north, and left too much behind. We inhabited a thin and marginal world in Toronto, the two of us. Barely within a community whose approval we craved, by whose standards we judged ourselves the élite; the chic and educated. Our friends we counted on our fingers—and we proudly numbered Europeans, Asians, North Americans. Friends to talk about, not to bring together; points on our social achievement score. Not for us the dull weekend nights of nothing to do. We loved to entertain. And we clamoured for invitations; when we missed one we would pretend not to care and treat ourselves to an expensive dinner instead. We had things to do.

This marginal life she roundly rejected now—just as she did once many years ago. But then she sought me out in spite of it. She came to borrow Tranter's blue and red book though I don't believe she ever needed it . . . and now? She's back in the bosom of Uhuru Street. Or rather the companionship that's moved up Uhuru Street and into the suburban developments of Toronto. Her friends gradually came, one by one, and set themselves up with their families long after we ourselves had moved from London. And it bloomed once more, that old comradeship of Uhuru Street with Amina at the centre—first helping them to settle and then being with them just like old times. Slowly, Toronto, their Toronto became like Dar, and I was out of it.

She came to London exactly a year after the summer in which we had exchanged books and shy but satiated looks in her sitting room, while her little brother pretended to do sums in his warped exercise book on the dining table. This was a time of political change in our country: Asian students from all backgrounds were now desperately trying to go abroad. Her arrival was therefore a surprise; a cousin went to pick her up. A week later, on a Sunday morning, she telephoned me and with heart beating wildly I went to see her. It had been a long wait, a year in which we exchanged letters which delicately hinted at increasing affection. At least I did, and she did not object. I told her I missed her, she reminded me of a funny thing I'd said. I graduated from signing 'Sincerely' to 'Affectionately' and finally 'With love'. She stuck to 'Affectionately'.

She had put up in a hostel on Gloucester Road not far from High Street Kensington run by a Mr Toto, our townsman and reputedly a former valet to an oriental prince. It was a dismal place, this hostel, and I had been through it too. It was your first stop in London when you hardly knew a soul there. It picked you up and prepared you, sometimes for the worst.

Here you could see what might become of you in a week, a month, a year. Previously it had been more pleasant, a hangout for rich kids, when Mr Toto let you have parties on Saturdays. Now, in the sixties, the faces were more desperate, lonely and white from the cold since they all flew in in September and October. Boys who left early in the morning in home-made Teteron suits carrying attaché cases full of certificates, returning late, hopeless, to a night of exchanging notes on the old, sunken mattresses Mr Toto provided for his iron bedsteads. English pop songs mingled with tear-drenched Hindi film songs, the atmosphere was darkly nostalgic supported by a hollow boisterousness in the corridors. I knew the place so well, its mildew-smelling interior, the migrant Spanish maids in black, landings full of clutter to be picked up, bathrooms stained, taps leaking. I had come here many times, to meet relatives, pick up parcels from home, give advice. Over the years how many must have wept on those soiled, striped mattresses of Mr Toto, prayed on them or indulged themselves in the cold, lonely nights of London!

I entered through the black door with the brass knocker that opened directly onto the street and went straight up to the first floor and knocked on Number One as instructed. There was a shuffle of feet behind the door, which was then opened by a girl in a faded pink home-style nightie with a laced neckline. Behind her, sitting on a bed already made, was my Amina, writing letters. On Sunday you write home I said to myself.

It was still breakfast time and we went down three flights of creaky stairs into the basement. There a narrow pathway through junk and clutter led into a medium-sized brightly lit room laid with blue linoleum, long tables and some benches. There was a steady trickle of traffic in and out of this room and up and down the stairs. Here you could get onion omelettes, cornflakes, and black tea and milk ('English style') from waiters with strangely familiar faces who added advice and humour to the morning's fare.

Later we went out sightseeing. She made her pilgrimage to Trafalgar Square and with her Instamatic I took a picture of her feeding the pigeons to send back home. Then Buckingham Palace and finally Parliament with Big Ben, which for ages had chimed out the nine o'clock hour to us over the radio. 'Eighteen hours, Greenwich Mean Time,' she echoed with amusement in a mock BBC accent.

That night we had dinner at my flat. Rice and curry from a take-away Indian store in Earls Court. After dinner we sat side by side on the sofa to watch television. From the floor below came the sounds of female laughter and hilarity. I knew them well, a group of Asian girls from back home who in their inimitable way mothered the boys they knew. I often stopped at their place and had dinner there. Later I was to introduce Amina to them, but meanwhile I hoped they wouldn't come up to fetch me this night. They didn't and we sat quietly holding hands. Then we went to bed. I slept on my box spring and she on my mattress on the floor. She would not have it otherwise. 'I have to learn to be tough,' she said. For a while we talked in the dark, holding hands. We caressed, touched, our hands trembling, groping for each other in the space between us. Finally the tension reached a breaking point and I looked down in the darkness at the figure below me. 'Can I come down?' I asked, my voice straining. 'Yes,' she said.

How frail our defences, how easily cast aside when the time comes. Nothing could have been more natural. Yet nothing could have shocked more, caused greater pain, in a different setting. How easy it was to judge and condemn from there. Yet no sooner were you here than a layer of righteousness peeled down from your being.

* * *

Last night we took a drive down Yonge Street, my daughter Zahra and I. We drove among the Saturday night traffic, among the Camarros and Thunderbirds swooping down south for the evening, or just a zoom past downtown, as we'd done before. This time we parked the car and started walking with the crowd, caught by the summer-like festive mood. People waited outside restaurants and cinemas; vendors of popcorn and nuts called out; cars hooted; stores were open and display windows lighted. At Bloor Street we exchanged salaams with a Sikh vendor, then stopped and I bought the little lady some flowers from him. We walked along Bloor Street for some time, arm in arm, talking about our joint future. Fortunately loneliness is not a word in her vocabulary yet. We reached the end of a queue outside an ice cream shop and joined it. We were happy, the two of us. We kept walking on Bloor Street. Somewhere nearby was her mother's apartment; she knew where, but I didn't ask. We reached a repertory cinema where another crowd was queueing and I picked up a schedule. Then, at a whim, I turned on her and asked, 'How would you like to see *Wuthering Heights*?'

Tugging my arm playfully she pulled me along. 'How about seeing *Star Wars*? Finally?'

LILLIAN ALLEN

(b. 1951)

Lillian Allen has been called the 'birth mother of dub' poetry in Canada. Born in Spanish Town, Jamaica, she was early 'dazzled by the sheer festivity of the Jamaican language'. The rigid separation between proper English and the 'natural, joyous, and feisty way' of talking outside of school made her all the more aware of the important role language plays in questions of identity.

She began writing plays and short stories in the 1970s, after her moves to the United States in 1969, where she studied at the City University of New York, and to Toronto in 1974 where she received a B.A. in English from York University. Discouraged by difficulties in getting her work published and produced at the time, she switched to poetry. 'It was like art to go. Take-out art,' she says; 'Me, my poetry and the public.' A dynamic performer, she had no difficulty finding an appreciative audience. She has since become the prime mover of dub poetry in Canada.

Dub poetry, a term coined by Oku Onuora in the late 1970s, as Allen explains, has its roots in reggae music, a Jamaican grassroots musical tradition. '[Reggae music's] birth was an undeclared act of subversion . . . an authentic people's voice with a rhythm of resistance and hope.' When 'Bob Marley appeared on the heels of Louise Bennett' (a Jamaican writer now living in Toronto whose books and performances since the early 1940s marked the beginning of dub poetry), the popular cultural scene in Kingston, Jamaica, was immediately responsive. As Allen puts it, 'In the early seventies in the dance halls of Jamaica, competing sound systems with highly skilled DJs and refrigerator-size speakers vied for the biggest crowds. This was the indigenous pop culture of the people and this music did not find acceptance on the island's radio stations until much later on. . . . DJs were so totally marginalized from mainstream or official Jamaican culture that no subject matter and no individual, no matter how powerful, was sacred. These DJs talked about anything and everything in the society, from the private and personal to social and political taboos.'

Dub poetry, which, says Allen, 'developed simultaneously in and outside of Jamaica,' is traced back to this popular movement. '[N]ot just an art form,' Allen points out, dub poetry 'is a declaration that the voice of a people, once unmuzzled, will not submit to censorship of form.' It will also not translate as effectively onto the page. This is the reason Allen has 'been reluctant to commit my poetry to the page over the years because, for the most part, these poems are not meant to lay still.' Yet, she is the first dub poet in Canada to challenge the dub poets' apprehension of the printed word. *Rhythm an' Hardtimes* (1983), 'self-published and distributed,' as Allen says, 'demystified the publishing process for many who had not considered publishing as an option before.' It sold over 8,000 copies. Although the printed page cannot possibly carry the dynamism of voice and body in Allen's performances, it still conveys her strong rhythms and love of language, as these from her poem 'Tribute to Miss Lou,' indicate: 'Heartbeat / Pred out yuself Miss Lou / Lawd, yu mek wi heart pound soh / yu mek wi just love up wiself / an talk wi talk soh / spirit words / on a riddim fire / word flame beat / pumps de heart / pulses history's heat.'

Allen has performed her poetry in Canada, the United States, and England. She also attempted what for a long time was an experiment of mixed results, combining dub poetry with its musical roots. Her collaboration with a grassroots reggae group and the Canadian group Parachute Club was a resounding success. Her album *Revolutionary Tea Party* (1986) won the 1987 Juno Award for best reggae/calypso album. This was followed by another album, *Conditions Critical* (1988), also the winner of a Juno Award. Recordings of her work also include the record *De dub poets* (1984) and the cassettes *Curfew Inna B.C.* (1985) and *Let the Heart See* (1987). A participant in 1993 in Toronto's first International Dub Poetry Festival, Allen has also published *Women Do This Every Day: Selected Poetry of Lillian Allen* (1993).

NOTHING BUT A HERO

Harriet Tubman
you're nothing but a hero
a real cool
super duper visionary
revolutionary shero

you didn't just sit there on your bum bum bum
waiting for freedom to come come come
you got up and kicked some butt butt butt

said 'It's time to let my people go
          let 'em go, let 'em go'
so you planned the escape routes
your underground railroad

they coulda charged you with treason
but freedom and justice your reasons
nothing was gonna hold you down
nothing coulda hold you down
(When you mean business Harriet
you sure mean business)

Harriet Tubman
you're nothing but a hero
a real cool super duper
visionary revolutionary shero

You said
'Since equality under the law does not exist
. . . all this slavery business
slave masters . . . whips
and all that shhhhhhhhh . . . stuff!
I'm outta here . . .
my mind is set on freedom!
freedom for my people!!!!'

so you planned the escape routes
your underground railroad

they coulda charged you with treason
but freedom and justice your reasons

nothing was gonna hold you down
nothing coulda hold you down

Harriet we thank you
your skill your dedication
your lifelong determination
your love of Black people
a mind so strong and free

Harriet Tubman
you're nothing but a hero
a real cool super duper visionary
revolutionary shero

With Criminal Intent

They wrapped their hatred around him
a hollow tip dum de dum dum dum
blow his black head to pieces
since he was just a blackity black black blackkk
wohoose tight minds into blackout
into thinking that everytime they see we
one of us
they have to account to a soul
brutality deception crunched into centuries
the horror the horror the horror

If we could just dance
and disappear
blunt instruments that plowed the fields
served the plantations
this house of capitalist plenty
that jack and every jack one a we build
no Jackman want to say it was built
by plunder, exploitation, murder, bondage and rape
making the Black print blue
and even losing that too

They carried their hatred, psychic scar
cocked on a trigger
set to blow away forever
a black boy's right to exist, to justice, to imperfection

On a dowdy Mississauga street in December '88
just after Christmas
and you know what Christmas is like
all that good cheer and so much greed
the Kangaroos struck
black blackity black black black blackkk blackout

A cowardly aim
a decidedly, deliberate, privately purchased
banned, illegal bullet
and you don't have to join the ku klux klan anymore

They wrapped their hatred around him
heaped up bursting out
they had to let it off somewhere
and since you and you and you and you were out of sight
they hurled spite on this young son
and blow his blackity black black blakkk head to pieces
black blackity blackity blackity blackity blackkk
blackout

I tell you
justice is swift
with a fullness of criminal intent
at the end of an illegal bullet
when you face your serve and protectors
your jury, your executioner and judge

JANICE KULYK KEEFER

(b. 1952)

'No writer, no matter how passionately she identifies with a particular community, ethnic or otherwise, can transparently and comprehensively project the views and voices of that community in her writing. . . . It is the task of the writer to situate herself off-centre from her own community in order to be able to critique as well as communicate what she knows of it,' says Janice Kulyk Keefer. And this is the position from which she writes, a position of ambivalence and, partly, the result of her upbringing 'as a hyphenated Canadian, the child of immigrants'.

Born in Toronto, she 'grew up with the fact that [her] mother's experience as an immigrant', whose family had emigrated from a village in Poland that is now part of Ukraine, 'was a very painful one, for psychological as well as economic reasons.' As a young woman, Kulyk Keefer was 'convinced that only people with names like Smith or MacPherson could be published and read in this country—a belief that led me,' as she says, 'to think and write, for the most part, in what I understood to be the manner of a Smith or MacPherson.' The webs of 'otherness' within which she moved as a child continue to 'haunt' her.

Talking in 1990 about those early years, she attributes part of the reason she wanted to study and live outside of Canada to her ambivalent feelings of being seen as 'ethnic'. With a B.A. in English from the University of Toronto, and a postgraduate fellowship, she moved to England in 1974 to study at the University of Sussex, where she earned an M.A. and a Ph.D. in English. When she returned to Canada after an absence of six years, during which time she lived in France as well as in England, she was determined to become a writer, a decision that made her aware of the kind of 'foreigner' she had become to her own literary tradition: 'I was discouraged at the university [in Canada] from reading Canadian writing, and encouraged to read American or British. And so I was really quite patronizing in my attitude toward my own culture.'

Kulyk Keefer launched her career as writer with the publication of a collection of poetry, *White of the Lesser Angels* (1986), and a collection of short stories, *The Paris-Napoli Express*

(1986), having already won the CBC Radio Literary Competition First Prize in 1985 and 1986. Her stories, about expatriate Canadians in Europe and Europeans living in Canada, reflect the critical distance she believes a writer ought to keep from her background. Conversely, *Transfigurations* (1987), a collection of short fiction, and *Constellations* (1988), a novel, are both set in Nova Scotia, where Kulyk Keefer lived with her family for ten years after 1980, and where she taught English at the Université Sainte-Anne. Her critical studies, *Under Eastern Eyes: A Critical Reading of Canadian Maritime Fiction* (1987), nominated for the Governor General's Award for non-fiction, and *Reading Mavis Gallant* (1989), show her critical sensibility to be, like her fictive imagination, focused on figures and issues of ambivalence. A Professor of English at the University of Guelph, Ontario, since 1990, Kulyk Keefer displays in her writing a concern with indeterminacy, a condition that characterizes many of her journeying characters in the short story collection, *Travelling Ladies* (1990).

Despite her resistance to the marginalizing effect of the label of ethnicity—'it's the unfortunate tendency still to marginalize the ethnic, to see it as something colourful and peripheral'—or rather because of it, Kulyk Keefer has participated in the debates that have taken place about multiculturalism in the early 1990s. In an article she published in *Books in Canada* (1991), she laments the use of the term multicultural in 'speak[ing] of a group of people, or of a writer'. We need, she says, a new term 'to denote those literary works in which a writer's ancestral country or culture seems as important as the country in which he or she actually resides.' The term she proposes, which she borrows from other writers, including Ven Begamudré, is 'transculturalism': transculturalism 'brings out the dynamic potential of cultural diversity, the possibility of exchange and change among and with different ethnocultural groups.'

Widely anthologized and published in literary magazines, Kulyk Keefer is currently finishing a collection of poetry and a novel, *The Green Library*. Her most recent book is her novel, *Rest Harrow* (1992).

Nach Unten

I am on the Bloor Street bus with Annie—she is taking me home with her to the bungalow she and her husband bought after they sold the huge brick house downtown. We have long since exhausted her store of questions about the health of my parents and my sister and my brother, and so we ride side by side in silence. This is not just a matter of my being young enough to be Annie's granddaughter, and yet knowing no more about her than that I've always known her. Perhaps the truest reason for our silence is that the only language we have between us is still foreign ground to Annie, though she's lived in Canada for over half her life. Sometimes I hear English people saying things like, 'Fifty years since they got off the boat and they still can't speak a proper sentence—can't pronounce even the simplest words.' English people, you understand, are not necessarily from Britain: they are simply those who are born with the language like a silver spoon inside their mouths, who say Winnipeg instead of Veenipeg, Thunder and not Toonder Bay. They are the ones who have never been anywhere but home; who are disobliged when people who have lost everything but their lives go on carrying the one thing that will never abandon them.

The silence between Annie and myself is camouflaged by the fact that so many other people are talking. Across from us is an old, old woman with a face that could have been made out of flour, water and a rake. What is left of her hair has been dyed the colour of the liver spots on her hands. The woman is talking in a high, precise voice to a man with a cast on his leg. They are speaking of their parents, of aunts and uncles a long time dead. 'Epsom salts,' she is saying. 'Every morning they drank a mixture of Epsom salts and lemon juice, and they never knew a day's sickness. No arthritis, and not a wrinkle on their faces.'

I smile at Annie but there's no response—she is staring at a child sitting further down the aisle. The girl is no older than five or six—her red socks and bright black shoes stick out over the edge of the seat, where an adult's knees would be. In her long, straight hair are barrettes shaped like flowers; her hair has the sheen of snow, and perhaps it's this that makes her eyes so blue, like blocks of azure or cerulean in a brand new paint box. Annie is smiling at the child, who has been warned, no doubt, never to speak to strangers, never to let them speak to her, even this silent kind of speech in which all the bones of Annie's face seem to lift and tilt. For a moment it's as if everything this woman has been burdened with—the years and years of labour in a foreign land and foreign tongue—slides off the shelf of her bones and is gone, leaving her as light as something still unborn.

The child folds her hands and begins to sing, first under her breath, then loud enough that I catch a few words: *nach unten geh'n, nach unten, nach unten.* It is a refrain of some kind, perhaps to a nursery rhyme or folk song. The child's mother looks at us uncertainly—this is not, she feels, correct behaviour for the bus. She whispers something to the child, who stops singing and stares into the windows of her bright, black shoes. Annie tugs my sleeve: this is our stop. She doesn't look after the bus as it pulls away, but points to her house, three doors down. It seems to be a point of pride with her that the stop is so close to her house, as though the Toronto Transit Commission had arranged this for her private convenience. Perhaps she feels this makes up for the noise and rush of the street; for the small brick box in which she has to spend her days.

It looks, in fact, no bigger than a gingerbread house. As we walk inside I keep thinking of the other house, the one Mike and Annie bought for a song when people like my parents were moving from old, dark, three-storey houses downtown into sub-urban split-levels with picture windows and prodigious lawns. Annie always kept as lush a garden as she could: summer after summer her narrow city yard would bear bushels of rhubarb and runner beans, onion and garlic, strawberries and cherries. '*Berih*'; she'd say to my mother: '*Yeest*. There's just the two of us—you have a family to feed.' And so we'd take and eat the food from Annie's garden, until even strawberries lost their savour, and there was no room on our cellar shelves for all her jars of pick-les and preserves.

Mike is watching television; Annie simply turns down the volume, letting the colours blare instead of the voices: sports or soap opera or an endless succession of commercials, I can't tell which. The set is as diminutive as the house itself—every-thing is miniature and yet there is hardly room to move: I seem to have entered an overstocked ark, bearing icons instead of animals. Cross-stitched antimacassars, that same reproduction of Khmelnitsky's *Triumphant Entrance into Kiev* which my par-ents have exiled to the garage, egg-sized busts of the great patriotic poets: Shevchenko, Ukrainka, Franko; brandy snifters crammed with painted easter eggs.

Mike gets up to greet me: he shakes my hand and won't let go until Annie gently disengages us, asking Mike to go to the kitchen and bring us something to drink. I have made it clear that I cannot stay for very long—I've only a week before I leave, there are still a hundred things to pack, and besides, my parents are expecting me for dinner. But the gift I've brought stays locked in my purse, for it is ginger ale, not whiskey Mike is offering. I'd forgotten that he doesn't drink any more; the chocolates I chose are shaped like small casks filled with cognac and Cointreau and Courvoisier. And so I sit, hands clasped around my glass, my purse tucked well behind my feet, smiling and saying nothing as Mike and Annie, equally silent, smile back at me.

Mike and Annie. Their English names seem as familiar to them now as the shape of their hands or the shoes on their feet. But were I to call out *Miháhsh, Hányu*, who would answer me? I want us to talk to one another, I want to hear their stories, but we sit in a silence loud as any shouting. If only they could speak to me in their own language and not in an English that breaks in their mouths, falling in awkward pieces that I gather stealthily, so as not to embarrass them. If only I could feel at home in their language, if to speak it were not to feel a stump instead of a tongue in my mouth. And I feel before them the shame I knew as a child who could not understand more than a smattering of what my Ukrainian school teachers, who in Kiev and Lvov had been doctors and professors and who, in Toronto, were janitors and factory workers, called *móva réedna*, my true and native tongue.

As my mother says, I am going away for a long time, and who knows what may happen before I return. I have grown up under the eyes of these people. I have been told that they have had a hard life, and I, with my easy one, feel that edge of guilt which presses into everything that has to do with who and how I am. I am sitting here in Mike and Annie's living room because of a voyage made on a lucky hunch some forty years ago. Had my grandmother put off leaving Poland in 1936, and she stayed in the house where my mother was born, on land bought with the money my grandfather sent each month from Canada, then everything I am would be nothing. For my grandmother's house has disappeared, along with her village; the land she never sold belongs to a different country now, her only proof of ownership an envelope of brittle papers inscribed in a forbidden language: *moyèh pòleh*—my fields.

Mike and Annie have been lucky in a different sort of way. I know that they came to Canada after the war; that, like my Ukrainian school teachers, they were what we children called Dee-Pees, not knowing the grander terms on which they were with history: Displaced Persons. They survived the war, they made a new life for themselves—witness this house and all the belongings which make it look like a passport stamped on every page, with hardly a free space showing. Canada has been good to us, their silence seems to say—how can you leave, why are you going away? It's the same rebuke I seem to hear everywhere these days, and I counter it by talking too much and too fast. I don't know how much of what I say they understand—that I'm going by ship, that we dock first at Le Havre and then Tilbury, and that the boat goes onto Bremerhaven, Leningrad. I am studying English literature, I need to work with people in England, English is my mother tongue: English, not Ukrainian—.

There is silence then. I am reaching for my purse, signalling that it is time for me to go, when Mike begins to speak. He tells me that he and Annie went to England after the war.

'We be living in Leeds'—he pronounces it 'Lyeedz'. 'Five year. Annie, me, two both working in cloth factory. Five year until we coming to Toronto.' He is cradling the glass of ginger ale in his large, rough hands, but he does not drink.

'I be go to store one day. Five year I live in Lyeedz, and I be go to store, for buying'—he stops for a moment—*'bèelyee pahpèer.* "Paper white," I say, and shopkeeper, he look at me like I be dog or rat'—*rrrat,* he rolls his r's—*'Bèelyee pahpèer* behind him, on shelf, I point and he be shake his head, "I no know what you want, go on, get out, *gerrrroutta heeerrrr*".'

Annie gets up from her chair and, touching Mike's hand, takes the glass away from him. Then she asks if I would like to see round the house. I nod my head too brightly, too quickly, as if to say, 'Yes, please, show me everything.' And so we go in procession, Annie letting her husband explain about the cupboards he has made for the kitchen, the new doors he has put onto the bedroom closet, the shower installed from a kit he picked up at the hardware. And that is the house: sitting room, kitchen, bathroom, bedroom. Doll-sized, and looking curiously exposed, the way in a doll's house the rooms are always missing a wall, so that you can look in and rearrange the furniture.

This is all there is of the house, but Annie says there's a surprise I must see. She takes my hand as if I were a child who must be protected from my own excitement; she opens a wooden door and leads me into a glassed-in porch filled with potted plants, their small green hands pressed against the windows, beseeching whatever light can fall through the narrow glass. Between the leaves I make out something blue, impossibly blue, like a billboard image of tropical seas. But as Annie pushes open the last door it is clear that what I took to be a mirage is really there: a swimming pool that takes up the whole of the cemented-over yard.

Were Annie and Mike to get into the pool together they would scarcely have room to turn. But I know without asking that no one swims here, any more than angels float suspended in the blue above us. A leaf from the neighbour's poplar drifts into the water: it floats, a golden coin, a small, eye-shaped fish, until Annie gets down on her knees and leans over the edge to pluck it out. As she folds the leaf into her pocket I realize that it is not the leaf but the pool's blue absolute that she is rescuing. I remember the child singing on the Bloor Street bus, her eyes the blue of ice melting, of streams running under snow: I remember Annie looking, longing. And for no reason, and because it seems, suddenly, needful, I find some words to say. I repeat what I remember of the child's song: *nach unten, nach unten.*

'Nach unten geh'n.'

It is Annie speaking now, not me. She pulls herself up from her knees: I can hear her bones speak: hoarse, straining for breath. *Nach unten geh'n*—that was how, she says, they asked permission of the guards to go down to use the latrines. 'In the camp,' she explains. 'Work camp, labour camp.' And that is all she says, either because she has run out of words, or because the words themselves have run out of any meaning they could give.

Mike has come to join us: Annie unfolds the leaf from her pocket and shows it to him; he nods his head. They do not touch one another, yet they seem joined in a way I had never recognized. Perhaps it is the narrowness of the cement strip on which they stand, or a trick of the light, like the illusion of blue with which the pool's painted floor infuses the water.

When I tell them it is late, now, that if I do not hurry I will miss my bus, they step apart. Annie asks Mike to walk me to the bus stop; I insist that it isn't necessary. Annie leads the way inside and then the two of them stand at the window, waving goodbye to me as I walk away from their house. I walk past the first and then the second stop; finally I flag down a cab and ride all the way downtown.

That night I phone my mother—for I have not gone home to dinner, I have met with friends and spent the evening taking leave. When I phone it is nearly midnight, but my mother goes to bed late, and always needs to talk, she says, before she can fall asleep. I say I have seen Annie and Mike in their new house. It is she who mentions the swimming pool, saying how crazy it is for them to have taken on a burden like that; how, with their love of gardening, they ought to have bought a house with a bit of land attached. My mother points out how dangerous it is for two people who have never learned to swim to have a pool in their backyard. Supposing a small child hopped the fence and fell in and needed rescuing? They could be sued, stripped of everything they own. And then she says something that shocks me, though of course I might have expected it. 'Annie's my age, you know.'

After I hang up I think of everything I didn't tell her: that I have been told a story about a shopkeeper in Leeds, and have discovered the one phrase in German that

Annie can, or will remember. And I think of that curious expression on Annie's face, half longing, half delight, when she smiled at the child singing in the Bloor Street bus, and knelt to look into the clear and perfect eyes of the water.

I am far away now, from Annie's and my parents' houses; from the country in which I was born and the country I have known only through other people's memories and stories. Living so far away, I have gone to books and films and photographs to find out things that I could never ask of anyone at home, that no one could ever have told me, no matter how much they knew.

In one of the books which I have read since leaving home, I learned of how, after the Nazi occupation of Ukraine, many of the country's people were shipped to Germany: slave labour for camps and arms and factories. It often happened, the book said, that doctors would round up the young women before they were boarded onto the trains and, as if they were so many sturdy glass beakers, would sterilize them, to ensure the right kind of productive capacity and, more importantly, the purity of their future owner's race. I believe that this is what happened to Annie—I believe this because, of course, I could never ask her, and because I saw her once on the Bloor Street bus, looking longingly at a small German child as she may have looked through barbed-wire fences at the children who lived in the town beside the labour camp: as beings not so much apart as immune. Immune just as angels, with all the buoyancy of their beauty, are immune from dirt and suffering and death.

My mother has stopped mentioning Mike and Annie in her letters, and I have never inquired after them, as if the act of asking, directly, whether they are still alive, would make their deaths a certainty. But now and again, on that blurred, shifting border between sleep and waking, I have caught a glimpse of Annie. She is not, as I have so often seen her, bent over the earth of her garden. She no longer feels the need to grow flowers and fruit, to fill glass jars with beets and cucumbers and peaches. Instead, she is walking down into the blue, painted waters of her swimming pool, stretching out and gently floating, her face tilted up to the night. There are lights like fallen stars, shining from the bottom of the water: they show the body of a young girl, bathed clean of all stains and wounds, of all loss and longing. She is singing to herself, though I can't make out the words; in the cool, blue water she is singing.

DI BRANDT

(b. 1952)

'i came to writing as a powerfully transgressive act,' says Di Brandt. 'there was so much silence in me, so much that had been silenced over the years, by my strict religious Mennonite farm upbringing, my experience as *other* at the university, as immigrant from a separatist culture & as a woman (i tried so hard to learn how to think like Modern WASP Man at the university), trying to be a hippie, becoming a mother.' These contradictions, located in her background and in her consciousness of gender differences, are at the heart of Brandt's poetry.

She was born in Reinland, a separatist Mennonite farming community in southern Manitoba. 'In contrast to a lot of other ethnic groups who are trying to become assimilated into Canadian culture, the Mennonite community worked very hard to stay separate from a Canadian identity and define itself against the rest of the world around it . . . in that sense they wanted to be treated with discrimination and in fact they have been.' Trying to write from within and against that background has involved coming to terms with 'three different languages, which referred to different codes of behaviour as well as consciousness. We used Low German at home for everyday life . . . High German was the public language we used in church. That was God's language. And then there was English, the worldly language we used in school that referred to the rest of the world.' Along with that, Brandt had to overcome feeling 'mute' as a woman, in that 'there was no language for' women.

Although she left her community at 17, it has taken her 'the rest of my life to begin to make sense of the huge cultural differences that exist between that community and modern Winnipeg.' After receiving a B.Th. (1972) at the Canadian Mennonite Bible College, Brandt studied at the University of Manitoba, where she received a B.A. in Honours English (1975), at the University of Toronto, where she received an M.A. in English (1976), and then again at the University of Manitoba, where she received her Ph.D. (1993). Nominated for the McNally Robinson Award for Manitoba Book of the Year, her revised dissertation, *Wild Mother Dancing* (1993) is a critical study dealing with one of the pervasive themes in her work, the role of mothers. Brandt, a professor of English and Creative Writing at the University of Winnipeg, has been actively involved as poetry editor with *Prairie Fire* and *Contemporary Verse 2*.

Her first poetry book, *questions i asked my mother* (1987), won the Gerald Lampert Award, and was nominated for the Governor General's Award as well as the Commonwealth Poetry Prize. Although its publication caused a scandal in her community, it has also found an 'intense and warm' response in many Mennonite women who are 'scared to say' aloud what Brandt articulates in her poetry. A dialogue of many voices, it challenges the authority structures of her heritage in her attempt to invent a separate identity for herself. *Agnes in the sky* (1990), the winner of the McNally Robinson Award for Manitoba Book of the Year, is, as Brandt says, 'about what do you do after you've exploded your family story'. About 'specific abuses' in her culture, it is written in the rhythm and language that characterize all of Brandt's poetry. In fact, as Brandt says, 'what turns me on in writing most of all is rhythm, trying to capture "orality" in writing, making the text disappear by lifting the sound off the page, running words together to subvert proper syntax and punctuation, playing with breath and spacing, making the body present on the page.' *mother, not mother* (1992), nominated for the Pat Lowther Award, and her most recent book, *Jerusalem, Beloved* (1995), nominated for the Governor General's Award, are written in a similar style.

FOREWORD

learning to speak *in public*   to write love poems
for all the world to read   meant betraying once &
for all the good Mennonite daughter i tried so
unsuccessfully to become   acknowledging in myself
the rebel traitor thief   the one who asked too
many questions   who argued with the father & with
God   who always took things always went too far
who questioned every thing   the one who talked too
often too loud   the questionable one   shouting
from rooftops what should only be thought guiltily
in secret   squandering stealing the family words
the one out of line   recognizing finding myself
in exile   where i had always been   trying as
always to be true   whispering in pain the old
words   trying to speak the truth as it was given
listening in so many languages & hearing in this one
translating   remembering   claiming my past
living my inheritance on this black earth   among
strangers   prodigally   making love in a foreign
country   writing coming home

WHEN I WAS FIVE

when i was five i thought heaven was located
in the hayloft of our barn the ladder to get
up there was straight & narrow like the Bible
said if you fell off you might land on the
horns of a cow or be smashed on cement the men
in the family could leap up in seconds wielding
pitchforks my mother never even tried for us
children it was hard labour i was the scaredy
i couldn't reach the first rung so i stood at
the bottom & imagined what heaven was like there
was my grandfather with his Santa Claus beard
sitting on a wooden throne among straw bales
never saying a word but smiling & patting us
on the head & handing out bubble gum to those
who were good even though his eyes were half
closed he could see right inside your head so
i squirmed my way to the back of the line &
unwished the little white lie i had told which

i could feel growing grimy up there & tried
not to look at the dark gaping hole where they
shoved out black sinners like me but the best
part was the smell of new pitched hay wafting
about some of it fell to where i stood under
the ladder there were tiny blue flowerets pressed
on dry stems i held them to my nose & breathed
deep sky & sun it was enough heaven for me for
one day

BUT WHAT DO YOU THINK

but what do you think my father says this verse means if it's not
about the end of the world look that's obviously a misreading i say
the verb grammatically speaking doesn't have an object in this
instance so it can't possibly be made to that's exactly what i mean
he says waving the book in mid air if my father ever shouted he
would be shouting now you don't really care about the meaning all
you ever think about is grammar & fancy words i never even heard of
where i come from the reason you learn to read is to understand God's
Holy Word i only went to school 7 year & it's done me okay what are
you going to do with all this hifalutin education anyway don't you
think it's time you got a job & did some honest work for a change
the meaning i say through clenched teeth is related to the structure
of the sentence for godsake anybody can see that you can't just take
some old crackpot idea & say you found it in these words even the
Bible has to make some sense the Bible my father says the veins in
his neck turning a slow purple is revealed to those gathered together
in His name you don't even go to church how can you know anything of
the truth you're no better than the heathen on the street the way
you live around here if i'd aknown my own daughter would end up like
this you're the one i say who started this conversation what did you
ask me for if i'm not entitled to an opinion please my mother says
crying as usual why don't we go for a walk or something you think
i'll weep i'll not weep we glare at each other with bright fierce
eyes my father & i she still tries after all these years to end this
argument between us arrest deflect its bitter motion does she know
this is all there is for us these words dancing painfully across the
sharp etched lines of his God ridden book & does she does he do we
really want this crazy cakewalk to stop

MISSIONARY POSITION (1)

let me tell you what it's like
having God for a father & jesus
for a lover on this old mother
earth you who no longer know
the old story the part about the
Virgin being of course a myth
made up by Catholics for an easy
way out it's not that easy i can
tell you right off the old man
in his room demands bloody hard
work he with his rod & his hard
crooked staff well jesus he's
different he's a good enough lay
it's just that he prefers miracles
to fishing & sometimes i get tired
waiting all day for his bit of
magic though late at night i burn
with his fire & the old mother
shudders & quakes under us when
God's not looking

MISSIONARY POSITION (2)

there was a great crashing in my
ears the day God became man & the
last heavy link of the great command
came tumbling to earth i became my
own mother that sunlit morning on
the rose faded carpet i swallowed
her bird cries her deep granite
frown i took the great godman into
my belly unchained we savoured each
hot whispered word made flesh we
mouthed our slow pleasure in long
grass dizzied along the blood earth's
singing

SKY LEE

(b. 1952)

'I want all our community art and writing to become part of mainstream culture,' says Sky (short for Sharon Kwan Ying) Lee. 'But we shouldn't have to *goy* (change). Canadian attitudes should change. . . . "Canadian" is not just hockey and apple pie. It means all kinds of things—anything from any immigrant, new or old—because we're all immigrants here. None of us have been in Canada long enough to set cultural standards for other people. . . . We've all been sucked in by these colonial in-group versus out-group values.' Lee's sense of Chinese-Canadian identity is synonymous with her political consciousness as an artist.

She was born in Port Alberni, a mill town on Vancouver Island, British Columbia, to parents who did not participate in the community's life both because of their poverty and because of the racism that surrounded them. Lee's father, born and grown up in Victoria, married her mother in 1936 on one of his trips back to China. It was not, however, until 1951 that his wife and three children arrived in Canada. Born about a year after her mother's immigration, Lee says that her 'parents' stubborn refusal to accept Canadian culture ironically boosted [her] identity.' As one of the few Chinese-Canadian children in town, she 'learned basic survival techniques', and had her 'own tough neighborhood group': 'We were the clique of poor ethnics—Italians, Japanese, East Indians. There were enough of us from the wrong side of the tracks that I didn't suffer too much from not being invited to parties.'

She began developing a different sense of her identity when her family moved to Vancouver in 1967. She discovered not only that her Hong Kong friends did not speak Toisanese, but that there were also 'prejudiced against Canadian-born'. It was after her trip to China in 1972 that she saw her 'identity as definitely Canadian', and realized that the 'only *real* Chinese left in this world are the Chinese in China.'

In Vancouver, Lee became a member of the Asian-Canadian Writers Workshop, founded by Jim Wong-Chu, a writer who was instrumental in encouraging Lee to publish. While studying toward her B.F.A. at the University of British Columbia, Lee, discouraged by the lack of support she encountered as a woman of colour, joined the Makara Women's Art Collective (1976-77). Her visual work has appeared, among other places, in the children's book *Teach Me How to Fly*, *Skyfighter* (by Paul Yee) and in *Makara* magazine. Lee, who also holds a Diploma in Nursing from Douglas College, British Columbia, works as a registered nurse to support herself and her son, Nathan Wong. She is also one of the co-editors of, and contributor to, *Telling It: Women and Language Across Cultures* (1990).

Her novel, *Disappearing Moon Café* (1990), which was nominated for the Governor General's Award and was the winner of the City of Vancouver Book Award, chronicles the lives of four generations of Chinese-Canadians. Told from the point of view of Kae, it is in effect the novel she sets out to write by way of understanding the secrets of her family and her own needs as a woman who has just become a mother. Lee's second book, *Bellydancer* (1994), a collection of stories that includes the one that follows, is written in a voice that she says is 'far more self-conscious' than that of her novel. Her characters, be they bag ladies, bellydancers, or lesbians, move in and out of situations that challenge the cultural barriers that have constructed the conventional notions of race, gender, and sexuality.

'I'm politicized enough,' Lee says, 'to know that I want to look into cultural alternatives, and one of the most wonderful things about the '90s is that so many people are doing it. . . . Everybody's coming out with fantastic, inspiring ideas. So that kind of leaves me free as an artist to just fly off on my own tangent. I don't have to worry about being a representative of the community or whatever any more, I'm just like an artist on my own.'

BELLYDANCER: LEVEL ONE

When I still lived among them, my people always told me that I was born into a box. Every time they said that, I always thought the same nasty thing—out of one box and into another. I know all about boxes. I make boxes, I live out of boxes, and I mostly feel safe in them. With them all around me, I'm not a bag lady, I'm a box lady.

My father was murdered two months and two weeks before I was born, you see. My mother was only twenty-one at the time, with a baby still in diapers, and another still wetting the bed. After the murder she tried to keep things together, but five days before I dropped, it came to light that it was my uncle, my father's only brother, her own favourite brother-in-law, who had stabbed her husband to death. She just went to pieces, or, she went 'partying' (as my granny euphemistically called her binge-ing, until her own death in the snow, some twenty years later). You see, in her grief, and in one moment of weakness, she let this same man find his unscrupulous way between her legs a bit too easily. A pretty mean feat, I would add, with all her little children around and in the way.

Anyway, Mom was so drunk she didn't realize she was cramping real bad. People tell me that at a house party during an early-morning brawl, she suddenly felt an urge to squat, and I shot out like a bloodied projectile, my little head smacking the linoleum floor like a slap on the bum. People blew that party scene screaming in horror. Apparently I didn't so much as twitch an eyelid; I was so limp and purple they thought I was stillborn. Well, you can imagine me, poor little thing, thoroughly pickled in alcohol, and such an irreverent entry to this world as well!

Then there was that unholy gash where my cute little suckling mouth should have been. Even I have to admit that I would have hurriedly wrapped me in a blanket and put me in a pine box too. I don't know if I would have thrown me on top of the wood-pile in the shed, though, but who knows what whoever was the ad-lib undertaker was thinking at the time.

Anyway, that's where my grandma found me two days later, wailing at the top of my little lungs, in the middle of a northern Alberta winter. She figured that big ol' cat named Henry had been glad to have a warm if squirmy blanket in a wooden box to sleep on.

Granny bundled me and my two brothers, Ernest and Edgar, into the cab of her and Granddad's pickup. It was so crowded she had to put me on Granddad's lap as he drove. Together they trundled us over treacherous icy backroads back to their ranch high in the mountains. When Mom sobered up that time, she just followed.

I don't know if this early encounter with a pine box is the reason I make boxes today with such a passion; those guys with white coats would have a heyday with such origins. But what do doctors know of hillbillies, eh? At least I was smart enough not to give them this story to chew on. Yeah, yeah, I've been through their mean sterilizing machine. In one fast hurry too.

So what, I always say. Mom's been dead these past seventeen years. And I figure that if one of my carved boxes is good enough for the Royal Winnipeg Museum of Art—permanent collection, no less—then I say, Hey, eh! Mom, you're OK; I'm OK;

everything's OK. Granny has always said that Mom was a good woman. I can see that; I saw otherwise too. She tried the best she could, I guess. I can still hear Granny repeating like a treadmill, 'Your mom did what she could, I guess.' So did I, I guess.

When it came time for me to leave their brown leathery faces, toothy grins and generous hugs, Grandpa stomped his worn cowboy boots, spat into his juice harp and sang:

'Pretty as a filly,
Brighter than a bee.
Send her to the city,
To see what she can be . . .'

Maybe Mom went out there trying to find out what she could be. Myself, I ventured out to see what I could see. I saw plenty, I guess. Enough to know now that I shouldn't have been in such a darn hurry to leave those hills, because I never saw my grandma and grandpa again. They never did know that I became famous, that the new owners had to name the restaurant where I once danced Seni's, after me, that Ernie, Edgar and I still keep the ranch, that there's hardtop almost to the gate now.

In my heart, I have always imagined Grandma telling Granddad, because she could read my letters, and he could not, 'Seni says she's learning bellydancing, Paw.'

'Bellydancin'!' A bear paw harumph. 'Bellydancin'? What for, learnin' bellydancin'?' Then I betcha he'd half joke and cajole at her for days after that. Time was different for them in those hills.

'Because, Grandma'—and I would have told her because she might have understood a ways, whereas he wouldn't have at all—'when I drape that silk veil over my mouth, I feel like a real queen. The rest of my body suddenly becomes gorgeous, and gorgeous loves to dance. Gorgeous loves to be adorned and adored. I become someone else, Gran. Not Scarface, Gran.'

And then of course my grandmother would have said what any grandmother would say: 'Now, Seni Biln, you're the prettiest girl we've ever seen. Isn't she, Paw? You'll always be a very special girl to us.'

Unless she had had a few too many herself, then another story about my scarred past always got a few snorts.

''Member, Paw, that time when Ernest and Edgar had to go and hide out in them Ghostkeeper Hills for three months, after Ern made such a mess out of ol' Mrs Oddy's boy? Damn, was that ol' shit *upp*set. Christ, you boys must have been cold up there! 'Member, Paw, even we were melting that brown-coloured ice on the stove for something to drink. Jesus, I fussed and worried and cried for days. With them big ferocious redcoats stomping and tearin' the place up lookin' for you two.'

In exasperation my brother Ernie would then have to say, 'Man, how many times do I hafta tell you, Gran? Ed and me, we just kept going and thumbed our way clear through to Calgary.'

But there was no way that she would believe him. So Ed would have to throw in his two bits: 'You know, I still think about that white guy who picked us up. He was kinda decent. Even offered us a job in Phoenix, Arixona, eh? Damn, should have gone and sent our gran a postcard with a cactus on it. Mebbe then she'd believe us, eh?'

A good-natured smile always perking, always warm, always ready. Back then, the only time my twisted mouth relaxed enough to laugh was when I was at home with my grannies, close to the woodstove and listening to them inside stories—this one about the Shoemakers. Tom Shoemaker was nicknamed Mrs Oddy after a teacher he bit a chunk of flesh off during a scuffle and swallowed in the desperation of the moment. He had been an abused kid who grew into an ornery man who begat Herman, who reduced me to tears when he painted bright red nail polish onto bobby pins, pinned them all over his upper lip and went around the high school imitating my petrified lisp. My big brother Ernie, then too hulkingly shy to string two words together, took the bobby pins off along with his lip with just one swipe. Blood all over the halls. End of Ernest ejacayshun too.

'I make my own costumes, Gran'—I used to talk to her by long-distance telephone—'with beads and sequins, and feathers, and, oh, Granny, you should see, the sheerest of gossamer chiffon.'

'Isn't that nice.'

'I dye the fabric myself, with a special ancient formula from a real old book. My bellydancing teacher—she got too old to dance any more—says that it's hundreds of years old, Gran. It was the only thing she brought with her. She's a refugee. She says my costumes are real works of art.'

'Ain't that wonderful, Paw?' she'd yell off into the background.

'Oh, Granny, I sure wish you could have met her. She was so good to me, picked me up where you left off. I sure do miss you and Grandpaw, Granny.'

'You bring her home. Home to visit. What's her name, Seni?'

'Lulu, Gran. But she's long gone too.'

My voice to the past fades as I watch the idea of a home to visit swirl down the drain of a sleek hotel bathtub. When I look into the bathroom mirror, I'm surprised to see how much of the misty reflection is still my small face pressed up against the frosty windowpane of their snug log house. It's almost flawless now, but that's something else my grannies never saw.

Two plastic surgeries later, one thin vague line, shaped like an upside-down check mark, remains. They were done by a miracle worker in San Francisco named Dr Hamazaki. He left my—he called them 'exotic'—lips with a heart-shaped courtesan pout, exactly as he drew on his one-of-a-kind colour-graphics computer screen to impress me. Before, after. Watch again. Before, after.

I was greatly impressed, because he was truly an artist. And with an income seven digits long, he had reached sainthood, I'm sure. Furthermore, as his receptionist piously pointed out, I should have been more grovelling grateful, 'Because Dr Hamazaki doesn't usually do show people any more. He's busy enough.' By then the filipina actresses and caribbean beauties he had picked up in the early part of his career had all married rich tyrants and were desperately trying on one mask after another to keep up appearances. Apparently there was a more altruistic part to his career; he does slash-and-burn patients for free if he gets written up as a human-interest story in a major magazine. Of course the receptionist didn't use those exact words. I did. I just think it's a slash-and-burn world.

Oh, I was dreadfully grateful for his charity. Of course I was. I remember how I first came to him with a quivering handshake, malnourished, days on a Greyhound, still underaged then—clutching a pitiful bundle of the same twenty-dollar bills that had been stuffed down my sequined bra by countless mauling hands. I didn't even have enough. But to him I was another dirtied brown baby like those from the war-torn places he used to touch down in, with his heroics and golden touch, with his international team of god doctors flying . . . flying. He took pity on me.

Aah, maybe bellydancers get too canny to think of a good enough reason to leave home. I just hate the fragmented being from another time and place that I become when I travel, so I don't any more, except in my head. Yet here I am. I come out of the bathroom and gaze at the four-star-hotel suite. There is a basket of fruit and champagne with a card I cannot bring myself to read. A massage table is already set up. I have a few minutes before my masseuse comes back, so I don't bother getting dressed. I climb naked onto the white sheets and immediately fall asleep.

I awake to the sound of Susie Wong's key in the lock, to the vertigo one feels when being dragged around and about unconsciousness.

Susie looks just as frazzled as I feel, but she hauls up the heavily laden ritual kit and picks out the lemon-grass toner first, exactly as she does before every live performance. And I don't mean only the ones up on stage. She's been with me for six solid years. I'm so grateful that she has come on this expedition that I would have gladly grovelled, except she won't hear of it.

'You'll pay for it.' Susie derided my feelings the way mothers do to harden daughters who have to go out there and expose themselves. I have paid for a first-class flight for her, but I know she has endured a ten-hour standby and pocketed the difference—her excuse being homely, married to a bum, with three 'hongry kids'. I don't care. Every slave needs a slave, I always say. The important thing is that she knows every inch of me. She does her unadorned work of slapping me around, rubbing on the scent of crushed cloves and saffron, helping me slip into fifteen pounds of jingle-jangle. She gets me into the mood.

'What's it going to be today?' She stands there, staring holes through me, already sensing my anxiety. I am quivering with anticipation. At a time like this, I feel I need pain to block the shame. And the rougher, the more familiar. 'Deluxe. Super Special or a Real Lulu?'

I pretend I don't need it. Yet I roll over on my back and expose myself completely. 'I don't care,' I say. 'As long as you do tits and ass and do it hard.'

'I don't do cunts,' she mocks as she starts. Light insinuations at first, but I know how deep and profound she can get. And I am dying for it and dreading it at the same time.

'I figure a smart lady like you can get that done proper,' she adds.

Don't I always swear this is going to be the very last time that I sabotage myself. Scarcely forty hours ago, Susie patiently held the flashlight as I arranged my packed cedar boxes and layers of foam on the floor of my Chrysler van and commented dryly, 'You won't fly. You can't decide. You never gonna make it in time.'

'Never you mind.' I was all wound up, because I knew she was right: I had designed it so that I would make it only at the expense of sleep or, worse, injury to the sacred body.

'You just make sure you show up.' My parting words to her were brusque to protect my fear, then I averted my face from her thin beam of light. As I swung away from the curb, my terrified headlights swept past Susie, her hands lingering on the door handle of her rusty Nissan. And I had to carry the crisis of confidence I created for myself, snivelling, for another hundred miles, perspiring the sour smell of public-phobic stress the rest of the way. Having to face strangers alone is a recurring nightmare of mine. I recoiled at the way they recoil from my nigger-bitch skin, thin scornful nostrils sniffing out my low creeping herbal scents.

Irrational fear. Masked rage. My van, my locked box. I hid from human contact as much as I could, fasting as I went, brewing tea on a camp stove, listening to taped music. Hermit on the I-5 of life, I purged my body daily of toxins, burning incense, euphoric dreams, portable potty, giddy with hunger for I don't know what. I got lost, the second night frozen; high in the interior mountains, teeth chattering, shampooing my hair on plush towels in the idling van, I climbed out to shower under a hillside waterfall, then fell into a fitful sleep. In my dreams, I played a dancer, all right, but a dancer who couldn't perform for the sad life of her.

'But I have made it, haven't I? Here I am.' I grin at Lulu, who is close by.

'And I'm done,' Susie decides with a slap on my butt. 'You look good. You ready for Al?'

'I don't know.' I catch my breath.

'Hey, you're breathing too high in your belly. Lower!' she orders. 'Relax, will ya!'

I cringe.

'OK, OK, refocus, then.'

'I can't.' Before I know it, I am shaking uncontrollably; goose bumps all over my naked arms and torso; her work undone. 'Susie, help me, please,' I cry. 'I was wrong to come. I still can't face this.'

Susie moves towards me and gathers me into her arms; I shut my eyes and breathe in the warm scent of her hair; she doesn't let go, and I cling and cling.

'Hey, hey, easy now. Yes, you can. Breathe. Look inside. Tell me—what do you see?'

I tell her that I see escape like this: I am going back to see the women at the trailer park. They are my family in the desert. I am cruising down the highway, blinded by sun, hot dry air blasting against my face, dragging through my hair, sucking up every salty grain of moisture. I am sipping lemonade sweetened with maple syrup and heated with cayenne pepper. My little peepot right beside me. On my own again, I am wonderful. I tell her I can dance among friends. I can't dance with the enemy. The donning of veils is too flimsy a cover.

'Honey, go for it, then.' She makes it sound so simple.

I dial boss Al on the hotel phone. I sing out, 'Al. Seni here. I can't stay. I gotta head into the desert tonight. Be a sport and cancel my engagements, will ya?' I hang up because I figure he wouldn't care. Small time, I tell myself, small potatoes.

Minutes later, there is knocking at the door as Susie and I are hopping around like mad, stealing hotel towels, giddy with relief.

'Don't forget the fruit basket,' I tell her. 'The girls at the trailer park will love—'

By the time she opens the door, I am ready to outperform. I make as if I am wallowing in pleasure in the desert heat out on a nineteenth-floor balcony, still as naked and as untamed as the day I was born. Entertained that I am lit up, fluorescent, flashing, wired to my ultra-neon surroundings; always the rasping din of trafficking and the twitching of electricity.

A gross, exhausted man, heaving about on painfully stout legs, steps out into the evening sky and glances not at me but at the last pink glow on a faraway horizon. Leaning against the railings, he asks very patiently, very softly, 'What's going on, Seni?'

I haven't seen Al in eight, maybe ten, years. And I am truly dismayed by this miserable version of his former self. I thought I had it bad. This was the wizard who made me famous? Who pushed and bullied and shoved me further than I ever wanted to go. I want to blurt out loud, Never mind me, what the hell happened to you?

Twenty years ago, Al was a hotshot, dynamite—he like to call himself compere for the lesser-known club acts in Las Vegas. Then, he was full of expressive energy, had an ambitious smile and loved the fun and games of being big daddy—a chunky, jolly kind of daddy-o. He and his lover, Mike, scoffing at Lulu's wheedling, at her french foreign legion accents and theatrical gestures, until that ludicrous moment when she drew the satin veil off me like a magic show. Then their faces fell, awed by my enticing innocence. After my dance, Al gathered me to his thick chest like the scared stiff cardboard doll I was and spoke the traditional line, 'Come to Papa.'

Today, when he doesn't turn to face me or whatever he has lost, I know: Al got squashed. So who the hell didn't? I rise from the chaise longue, hold out my arms and wait for his eyes to return from their embarrassed retreat. When they finally do, glancing somewhere near my lips, then stumbling down my breasts and along my outstretched arms, he allow himself to come into my embrace. We press against each other, my lightness against his heaviness. My exposure, his balls in chains. I can feel his pudgy hands slide over the silky freedom of my skin.

'Come to Mama!' I whisper into his fleshy ear and feel him tense.

There's either vanity or void. That's something I quietly contemplate all the time. Myself, I prefer void. Less cramped. But I suspect Al is into the vanity of power. Tsk, tsk, Al, what a surefire way to fall short of the big times. I used to hate Al's guts, feared him with a livid passion. He'd crack his big ol' whip, and I'd be made to dance. But isn't that just about the most tired worn-out old story in this whole wide world?

Vanity or void? At first glance one can just as easily jumble us up, because I'm the one floundering about in vain. I mean, look at me. As hard as I try, I still haven't lost one ounce of my hatred of what he represents to me. All needles and pinpricks around him. And what for? Look at him! At first glance, some wheezy old fart about to go belly up at any moment. Vanity or void, eh? Pitiful either way?

That's why I've learned to stay cocooned in the emptiness of those boxes I carve so passionately. These many winters long, in my warm little cabin, after the dishes, after the snowfall, after the watering, hay and feed, I'd shave and scallop, scoop and tunnel through sweet scented blond wood to my heart's delight. You'd think that I was god carving out a whole new world or something, because by the time I looked up, it'd be springtime, and the river thawing out.

Cedar, walnut, pine, oak, cherry boxes, all with gorgeous wood grain. Hand built, bent and fitted by my brothers. I made them swarm with thick twisting snakes—one pert woman at an art opening referred to them as cosmic serpents, looked at me with amazement, and there I was, trying to hold my wineglass just right.

As a final touch I'd put a japanese paperfold doll inside. One time a series of ten boxes came out of me. I birthed them like children. Then I sold them all. Couldn't keep them anyway, a bag lady like me. They all toddled off rather quickly, though. Hear one got married to a rich art dealer in New York. Vanity or void? I always end up asking myself that.

So here I am, dressed at least, and squealing at Al as he takes me into his office; it is full of flowers, which shocks me because he said they were mine. Eek! Eeek! I hear me, like a plastic squeak toy. Childlike because the older I get, the less I want to know, and being a child is as good a way as any to hold the whole goddamn world in check, if I want. But then I realize.

Al reminds me, 'Your dance is still very important to some people. Surely you haven't forgotten them.'

But I recall only the years and years of dancing, or was it squirming, in front of guys who couldn't tell the difference. Suddenly I want to change the subject. I say, 'I'm threatening to walk out on you, and you're plying me with flowers. Who the hell gets flowers any more?'

'I don't know. They came from all over. Nobody has faithfuls like you do, Sen. A bunch of them have been raising hell at the front desk all week.' He watches me the way I feel—an edgy, hungry hummingbird hovering over each bloom, plucking out sappy well-wishes. 'A lot of them are little old women pushing little old men around—in wheelchairs, I mean.'

'Lulu's refugee crowd,' I muse. 'At least I'm not the only haunt from the past. They want to see Lulu alive, not me.'

'They want to see Lulu's art alive and well.' He's still trying to hold Lulu over my head.

'Al,' I say, 'Let's leave her in peace. You and I both know extinct when we see it.'

'Maybe they want to see a little faith in Lulu's girl. You know Lulu was the best, but she used to tell people that the way you dance couldn't have been taught. She said it was a spiritual gift—'

'It's true, then,' I interrupt, 'those rumours of you retiring?'

'Yeah, so?'

'Yeah, well, I can tell.' My punch line timed to perfection. I don't want to stick around to hear some fat white guy tell me that dark goddesses are in again, and I should trust what he says because he makes all the rules anyway.

'Listen, Al,' I finally say, 'I'm sorry. No hard feeling, OK? I don't dance cabaret any more. You've gotten together the best collection of dancers I've ever seen. You've really outdone yourself. Lulu'd've been proud. But nobody's going to miss an over-aged bellydancer—' Oops, I think, slightly overdone; I didn't mean to overdo it, but I did, and do again, '—except other over-aged bellydancers, I guess.' Damn, Al does that to me. I look at him.

There's Al gloating for all he weighs now. He's having fun. He doesn't have to say it; he's a sensitive guy, so his slitty eyes say it: Aww, Seni, here I thought you'd have transcended such small peevish things. Al and I go back a long way along a rocky road of you hurt me, so I hold out on you. Old friends, so to speak.

'I'm disappointed to hear that. I didn't think you were the type to hold a grudge or to pull a prima-donna pout on me. You used to be a hell of an artist. Don't forget to take your flowers, though. I was just saving them for you onstage. It would have been a nice touch, don't you think?'

Oh, don't I just grit my teeth. I hate having my nose rubbed in what I want so badly to forget, because it's over, dead and gone. Lulu, Al and I used to swim in the beauty we so lovingly created for each other. Together we wove a fabulous dream, but we blinked our eyes, didn't we, Al? The mirage dried up. And since then I've slapped and rubbed and pinched, but this cultural wasteland is not going to go away. Dying roses, gushy sentimental gestures won't do it. Sorry if Papa can't stage meaning and romance back into our crumbling lives, no matter how much he wants it back. No matter how much I pretend that I don't want it back.

'I don't suppose we got you to sign a contract—' Al tries a hard poke of reality, after he couldn't say it with flowers.

I laugh and laugh at him, but my laughter is hard eggshell; inside a wet, ugly duckling still cringes from him. Too many years of him paddling my butt. I want to tell him off so much. OK, Al, it turns out there are lots of hard feelings 'kay! No matter what, you'll always be the white-slave trader and I'll always be the black pair of tits. That doesn't give either of us much credibility. But I don't say any of that. Neither do I say, So sue me! Just you try suing an indian, see how far you get. Al, you son of a turtle, you paid me to show up. I showed up, and now my mind flits off. When I get to some deserted canyon somewhere, tell you what, I'll fete fire and dance my little heart out in honour of your retirement. Al, sweetheart, you've always gotten away cheap.

I am silent. Maybe the trouble is that I don't ever say enough to Al. Maybe that's been our one saving grace.

'You going by the trailer park?' he asks.

'You betcha.' I gather up my overcompensated pride, make gestures to leave.

'No one's there, Seni. The girls are all on their way here to see you.' He takes me by my arm and puts me out of his office. Before he closes his door in my duped face, he says, 'I understand that you need to rest tonight, sweetie. That's OK. We can do without. But tomorrow I need you for some crowd teasers. I still have to fill up the amphitheatre. Seni, darling, if you want for anything at all, feel free to talk to my girl.'

I am truly touched. Al's one smart bitch. I guess he knows it. So here I am. I know I am loved. And I am walking along the edge of the crowded casino. I am shimmering satin, flowing show, tripping on tiptoes. I get lots of attention. And I give a lot back. Crowd teasers, said the man. In this way, I'm a professional right down to my choice of lady luck emerald green, wild desert blooms clipped onto dense black wavy hair. I move through the crowds of tourists milling around, smoking, looking. Slot-machine cycles are up, yeasty housewives swarming. They're looking for something too; their laundered househusbands in cheap, crisp hawaiian shirts look at me. It's nice to be appreciated, and Al sure has taken a lot of trouble to get me here and to keep me here.

Oh, look, I spy cowboys. Ohh. And they're cowboys and indians too. Love those cowboy and indian colours. These ones tall and slim and dark and cowboy chic. I see a silver-and-turquoise bracelet clipped over an embroidered cuff, bolo ties, the spit and pearly polish of skin-tight black boa boots, and I can't help smiling my approval. These ones traditional; they wear their wealth unabashedly. They pause in frank surprise, then flash their teeth in delight. And they are absolutely delightful. Sky-blue teardrops weigh down an old-fashioned blackbrimmed reservation hat. They all tip theirs. Duster coats sweep the floor. Life is a feast, and I pass through, my tongue moist, ready to taste.

ROHINTON MISTRY

(b. 1952)

'One must write for the sake of writing, to create good literature,' says Rohinton Mistry. 'The other things follow in a very natural way. I grew up in Bombay. Now I am here. I'm a writer. I am determined to write good literature. . . . But to write well, I must write about what I know best. In that way, I automatically speak for my "tribe".' Mistry's 'tribe' is the Parsi community in Bombay, India, where he was born. The Parsi characters in his stories and novel, and 'their dreams, ambitions, and fears, are as accessible to the Western reader as the Indian reader. The universalities of the story are sufficient.' Mistry believes that many of the themes taken to be the recurring motifs in immigrant literature are not just that: 'I don't think this looking forward and yearning backward is restricted to an immigrant. It's a universal phenomenon.'

Mistry received a B.Sc. in Mathematics and Economics from the University of Bombay before immigrating to Toronto in 1975. He worked for ten years in a bank, and studied English and philosophy part-time at the University of Toronto (B.A. 1984). He began writing in 1983 when, encouraged by winning two Hart House Prizes for his first two short stories, he decided to become a full-time writer. Describing himself as 'a traditional writer. I am not trying to break new ground or pioneer new techniques,' Mistry published his first book to high acclaim. *Tales from Firozsha Baag* (1987), which was shortlisted for a Governor General's Award, is a collection of interlinked stories about Kensi, a young man and an aspiring writer, his childhood years in Bombay and his later life in Canada. 'Swimming Lessons', the story included here, in which Kensi sends his first manuscript of stories to his parents in Bombay, concludes the collection.

Such a Long Journey (1991), Mistry's first novel, received the Governor General's Award, the Commonwealth Writers Prize for Best Book, and the W.H. Smith-*Books in Canada* First Novel Award; it was also a finalist for the Booker Prize. Set in Bombay in 1971, the action takes place, as Mistry says, 'more than a thousand miles away' from the war between India and Pakistan that resulted in the creation of what is now Bangladesh. His third novel, *A Fine Balance* (1995), won the Giller Prize. Set in both urban and rural India, it spans the years between 1975 and 1984 in the lives of an uncle and nephew, two tanners who are Untouchables, whose destinies converge with those of numerous other characters.

Mistry, who lives in Brampton, Ontario, does not try to write by way of moulding himself as a writer to what he says are the expectations 'in the establishment': 'I think they feel that when a person arrives here from a different culture, if that person is a writer, he must have some profound observations about the meeting of the two cultures. And he must write about racism. He must write about multiculturalism. He has an area of expertise foisted on him which he may not necessarily want, or which may not really interest him. He may not want to be an expert in race relations.' Mistry's impetus as a writer lies in his desire to be a story-teller.

SWIMMING LESSONS

The old man's wheelchair is audible today as he creaks by in the hallway: on some days it's just a smooth whirr. Maybe the way he slumps in it, or the way his weight rests has something to do with it. Down to the lobby he goes, and sits there most of the time, talking to people on their way out or in. That's where he first spoke to me a few days ago. I was waiting for the elevator, back from Eaton's with my new pair of swimming-trunks.

'Hullo,' he said. I nodded, smiled.

'Beautiful summer day we've got.'

'Yes,' I said, 'it's lovely outside.'

He shifted the wheelchair to face me squarely. 'How old do you think I am?'

I looked at him blankly, and he said, 'Go on, take a guess.'

I understood the game; he seemed about seventy-five although the hair was still black, so I said, 'Sixty-five?' He made a sound between a chuckle and a wheeze: 'I'll be seventy-seven next month.' Close enough.

I've heard him ask that question several times since, and everyone plays by the rules. Their faked guesses range from sixty to seventy. They pick a lower number when he's more depressed than usual. He reminds me of Grandpa as he sits on the sofa in the lobby, staring out vacantly at the parking lot. Only difference is, he sits with the stillness of stroke victims, while Grandpa's Parkinson's disease would bounce his thighs and legs and arms all over the place. When he could no longer hold the *Bombay Samachar* steady enough to read, Grandpa took to sitting on the veranda and staring emptily at the traffic passing outside Firozsha Baag. Or waving to anyone who went by in the compound: Rustomji, Nariman Hansotia in his 1932 Mercedes-Benz, the fat ayah Jaakaylee with her shopping-bag, the *kuchrawalli* with her basket and long bamboo broom.

The Portuguese woman across the hall has told me a little about the old man. She is the communicator for the apartment building. To gather and disseminate information, she takes the liberty of unabashedly throwing open her door when newsworthy events transpire. Not for Portuguese Woman the furtive peerings from thin cracks or spyholes. She reminds me of a character in a movie, *Barefoot In The Park* I think it was, who left empty beer cans by the landing for anyone passing to stumble and give her the signal. But PW does not need beer cans. The gutang-khutang of the elevator opening and closing is enough.

The old man's daughter looks after him. He was living alone till his stroke, which coincided with his youngest daughter's divorce in Vancouver. She returned to him and they moved into this low-rise in Don Mills. PW says the daughter talks to no one in the building but takes good care of her father.

Mummy used to take good care of Grandpa, too, till things became complicated and he was moved to the Parsi General Hospital. Parkinsonism and osteoporosis laid him low. The doctor explained that Grandpa's hip did not break because he fell, but he fell because the hip, gradually growing brittle, snapped on that fatal day. That's what osteoporosis does, hollows out the bones and turns effect into cause. It has an unusually high incidence in the Parsi community, he said, but did not say why. Just one of those mysterious things. We are the chosen people where osteoporosis is concerned. And divorce. The Parsi community has the highest divorce rate in India. It also claims to be the most westernized community in India. Which is the result of the other? Confusion again, of cause and effect.

The hip was put in traction. Single-handed, Mummy struggled valiantly with bedpans and dressings for bedsores which soon appeared like grim spectres on his back. *Mamaiji*, bent double with her weak back, could give no assistance. My help would be enlisted to roll him over on his side while Mummy changed the dressing. But after three months, the doctor pronounced a patch upon Grandpa's lungs, and the male ward of Parsi General swallowed him up. There was no money for a private nursing home. I went to see him once, at Mummy's insistence. She used to say that the blessings of an old person were the most valuable and potent of all, they would last my whole life long. The ward had rows and rows of beds; the din was enormous, the smells nauseating, and it was just as well that Grandpa passed most of his time in a less than conscious state.

But I should have gone to see him more often. Whenever Grandpa went out, while he still could in the days before parkinsonism, he would bring back pink and white sugar-coated almonds for Percy and me. Every time I remember Grandpa, I remember that; and then I think: I should have gone to see him more often. That's what I also thought when our telephone-owning neighbour, esteemed by all for that reason, sent his son to tell us the hospital had phoned that Grandpa died an hour ago.

The postman rang the doorbell the way he always did, long and continuous; Mother went to open it, wanting to give him a piece of her mind but thought better of it, she did not want to risk the vengeance of postmen, it was so easy for them to destroy letters; workers nowadays thought no end of themselves, strutting around like peacocks, ever since all this Shiv Sena agitation about Maharashtra or Maharashtrians, threatening strikes and Bombay bundh all the time, with no respect for the public; bus drivers and conductors were the worst, behaving as if they owned the buses and were doing favours to commuters, pulling the bell before you were in the bus, the driver purposely braking and moving with big jerks to make the standees lose their balance, the conductor so rude if you did not have the right change.

But when she saw the airmail envelope with a Canadian stamp her face lit up, she said wait to the postman, and went in for a fifty paisa piece, a little baksheesh *for you, she told him, then shut the door and kissed the envelope, went in running, saying my son has written, my son has sent a letter, and Father looked up from the newspaper and said, don't get too excited, first read it, you know what kind of letters he writes, a few lines of empty words, I'm fine, hope you are all right, your loving son—that kind of writing I don't call letter-writing.*

Then Mother opened the envelope and took out one small page and began to read silently, and the joy brought to her face by the letter's arrival began to ebb; Father saw it happening and knew he was right, he said read aloud, let me also hear what our son is writing this time, so Mother read: My dear Mummy and Daddy, Last winter was terrible, we had record-breaking low temperatures all through February and March, and the first official day of spring was colder than the first official day of winter had been, but it's getting warmer now. Looks like it will be a nice warm summer. You asked about my new apartment. It's small, but not bad at all. This is just a quick note to let you know I'm fine, so you won't worry about me. Hope everything is okay at home.

After Mother put it back in the envelope, Father said everything about his life is locked in silence and secrecy, I still don't understand why he bothered to visit us last year if he had nothing to say; every letter of his has been a quick note so we won't worry—what does he think we worry about, his health, in that country everyone eats well whether they work or not, he should be worrying about us with all the black market and rationing, has he forgotten already how he used to go to the ration-shop and wait in line every week; and what kind of apartment description is that, not bad at all; and if it is a Canadian weather report I need from him, I can go with Nariman Hansotia from A Block to the Cawasji Framji Memorial Library and read all about it, there they get newspapers from all over the world.

The sun is hot today. Two women are sunbathing on the stretch of patchy lawn at the periphery of the parking lot. I can see them clearly from my kitchen. They're wearing bikinis and I'd love to take a closer look. But I have no binoculars. Nor do I have a car to saunter out to and pretend to look under the hood. They're both luscious and gleaming. From time to time they smear lotion over their skin, on the bellies, on the inside of the thighs, on the shoulders. Then one of them gets the other to undo the string of her top and spread some there. She lies on her stomach with the straps undone. I wait. I pray that the heat and haze make her forget, when it's time to turn over, that the straps are undone.

But the sun is not hot enough to work this magic for me. When it's time to come in, she flips over, deftly holding up the cups, and reties the top. They arise, pick up towels, lotions and magazines, and return to the building.

This is my chance to see them closer. I race down the stairs to the lobby. The old man says hullo. 'Down again?'

'My mailbox,' I mumble.

'It's Saturday,' he chortles. For some reason he finds it extremely funny. My eye is on the door leading in from the parking lot.

Through the glass panel I see them approaching. I hurry to the elevator and wait. In the dimly lit lobby I can see their eyes are having trouble adjusting after the bright sun. They don't seem as attractive as they did from the kitchen window. The elevator arrives and I hold it open, inviting them in with what I think is a gallant flourish. Under the fluorescent glare in the elevator I see their wrinkled skin, aging hands, sagging bottoms, varicose veins. The lustrous trick of sun and lotion and distance has ended.

I step out and they continue to the third floor. I have Monday night to look forward to, my first swimming lesson. The high school behind the apartment building is offering, among its usual assortment of macramé and ceramics and pottery classes, a class for non-swimming adults.

The woman at the registration desk is quite friendly. She even gives me the opening to satisfy the compulsion I have about explaining my non-swimming status.

'Are you from India?' she asks. I nod. 'I hope you don't mind my asking, but I was curious because an Indian couple, husband and wife, also registered a few minutes ago. Is swimming not encouraged in India?'

'On the contrary,' I say. 'Most Indians swim like fish. I'm an exception to the rule.

My house was five minutes walking distance from Chaupatty beach in Bombay. It's one of the most beautiful beaches in Bombay, or was, before the filth took over. Anyway, even though we lived so close to it, I never learned to swim. It's just one of those things.'

'Well,' says the woman, 'that happens sometimes. Take me, for instance. I never learned to ride a bicycle. It was the mounting that used to scare me, I was afraid of falling.' People have lined up behind me. 'It's been very nice talking to you,' she says, 'hope you enjoy the course.'

The art of swimming had been trapped between the devil and the deep blue sea. The devil was money, always scarce, and kept the private swimming clubs out of reach; the deep blue sea of Chaupatty beach was grey and murky with garbage, too filthy to swim in. Every so often we would muster our courage and Mummy would take me there to try and teach me. But a few minutes of paddling was all we could endure. Sooner or later something would float up against our legs or thighs or waists, depending on how deep we'd gone in, and we'd be revulsed and stride out to the sand.

Water imagery in my life is recurring. Chaupatty beach, now the high-school swimming pool. The universal symbol of life and regeneration did nothing but frustrate me. Perhaps the swimming pool will overturn that failure.

When images and symbols abound in this manner, sprawling or rolling across the page without guile or artifice, one is prone to say, how obvious, how skilless; symbols, after all, should be still and gentle as dewdrops, tiny, yet shining with a world of meaning. But what happens when, on the page of life itself, one encounters the ever-moving, all-engirdling sprawl of the filthy sea? Dewdrops and oceans both have their rightful places; Nariman Hansotia certainly knew that when he told his stories to the boys of Firozsha Baag.

The sea of Chaupatty was fated to endure the finales of life's everyday functions. It seemed that the dirtier it became, the more crowds it attracted: street urchins and beggars and beachcombers, looking through the junk that washed up. (Or was it the crowds that made it dirtier?—another instance of cause and effect blurring and evading identification.)

Too many religious festivals also used the sea as repository for their finales. Its use should have been rationed, like rice and kerosene. On Ganesh Chaturthi, clay idols of the god Ganesh, adorned with garlands and all manner of finery, were carried in processions to the accompaniment of drums and a variety of wind instruments. The music got more frenzied the closer the procession got to Chaupatty and to the moment of immersion.

Then there was Coconut Day, which was never as popular as Ganesh Chaturthi. From a bystander's viewpoint, coconuts chucked into the sea do not provide as much of a spectacle. We used the sea, too, to deposit the leftovers from Parsi religious ceremonies, things such as flowers, or the ashes of the sacred sandalwood fire, which just could not be dumped with the regular garbage but had to be entrusted to the care of Avan Yazad, the guardian of the sea. And things which were of no use but which no one had the heart to destroy were also given to Avan Yazad. Such as old photographs.

After Grandpa died, some of his things were flung out to sea. It was high tide; we always checked the newspaper when going to perform these disposals; an ebb would mean a long walk in squelchy sand before finding water. Most of the things were probably washed up on shore. But we tried to throw them as far out as possible, then waited a few minutes; if they did not float back right away we would pretend they were in the permanent safekeeping of Avan Yazad, which was a comforting thought. I can't remember everything we sent out to sea, but his brush and comb were in the parcel, his *kusti*, and some Kemadrin pills, which he used to take to keep the parkinsonism under control.

Our paddling session stopped for lack of enthusiasm on my part. Mummy wasn't too keen either, because of the filth. But my main concern was the little guttersnipes, like naked fish with little buoyant penises, taunting me with their skills, swimming underwater and emerging unexpectedly all around me, or pretending to masturbate—I think they were too young to achieve ejaculation. It was embarrassing. When I look back, I'm surprised that Mummy and I kept going as long we did.

I examine the swimming-trunks I bought last week. Surf King, says the label, Made in Canada-Fabriqué Au Canada. I've been learning bits and pieces of French from bilingual labels at the supermarket too. These trunks are extremely sleek and stream-lined hipsters, the distance from waistband to pouch tip the barest minimum. I wonder how everything will stay in place, not that I'm boastful about my endowments. I try them on, and feel that the tip of my member lingers perilously close to the exit. Too close, in fact, to conceal the exigencies of my swimming lesson fantasy: a gorgeous woman in the class for non-swimmers, at whose sight I will be instantly aroused, and she, spying the shape of my desire, will look me straight in the eye with her intentions; she will come home with me, to taste the pleasures of my delectable Asian brown body whose strangeness has intrigued her and unleashed uncontrollable surges of passion inside her throughout the duration of the swimming lesson.

I drop the Eaton's bag and wrapper in the garbage can. The swimming-trunks cost fifteen dollars, same as the fee for the ten weekly lessons. The garbage bag is almost full. I tie it up and take it outside. There is a medicinal smell in the hallway; the old man must have just returned to his apartment.

PW opens her door and says, 'Two ladies from the third floor were lying in the sun this morning. In bikinis.'

'That's nice,' I say, and walk to the incinerator chute. She reminds me of Najamai in Firozsha Baag, except that Najamai employed a bit more subtlety while going about her life's chosen work.

PW withdraws and shuts her door.

Mother had to reply because Father said he did not want to write to his son till his son had something sensible to write to him, his questions had been ignored long enough, and if he wanted to keep his life a secret, fine, he would get no letters from his father.

But after Mother started the letter he went and looked over her shoulder, telling her what to ask him, because if they kept on writing the same questions, maybe he would understand how interested they were in knowing about things over there; Father said go on, ask him what his work is at the insurance company, tell him to take some courses at night school, that's how everyone moves ahead over there, tell him not to be discouraged if his job is just clerical right now, hard work will get him ahead, remind him he is a Zoroastrian: manashni, gavashni, kunashni, *better write the translation also: good thoughts, good words good deeds—he must have forgotten what it means, and tell him to say prayers and do* kusti *at least twice a day.*

Writing it all down sadly, Mother did not believe he wore his sudra *and* kusti *any more, she would be very surprised if he remembered any of the prayers; when she had asked him if he needed new sudras he said not to take any trouble because the Zoroastrian Society of Ontario imported them from Bombay for their members, and this sounded like a story he was making up, but she was leaving it in the hands of God, ten thousand miles away there was nothing she could do but write a letter and hope for the best.*

Then she sealed it, and Father wrote the address on it as usual because his writing was much neater than hers, handwriting was important in the address and she did not want the postman in Canada to make any mistake; she took it to the post office herself, it was impossible to trust anyone to mail it ever since the postage rates went up because people just tore off the stamps for their own use and threw away the letter, the only safe way was to hand it over the counter and make the clerk cancel the stamps before your own eyes.

Berthe, the building superintendent, is yelling at her son in the parking lot. He tinkers away with his van. This happens every fine-weathered Sunday. It must be the van that Berthe dislikes because I've seen mother and son together in other quite amicable situations.

Berthe is a big Yugoslavian with high cheekbones. Her nationality was disclosed to me by PW. Berthe speaks a very rough-hewn English, I've overheard her in the lobby scolding tenants for late rents and leaving dirty lint screens in the dryers. It's exciting to listen to her, her words fall like rocks and boulders, and one can never tell where or how the next few will drop. But her Slavic yells at her son are a different matter, the words fly swift and true, well-aimed missiles that never miss. Finally, the son slams down the hood in disgust, wipes his hands on a rag, accompanies mother Berthe inside.

Berthe's husband has a job in a factory. But he loses several days of work every month when he succumbs to the booze, a word Berthe uses often in her Slavic tirades on those days, the only one I can understand, as it clunks down heavily out of the tight-flying formation of Yugoslavian sentences. He lolls around in the lobby, submitting passively to his wife's tongue-lashings. The bags under his bloodshot eyes, his stringy moustache, stubbled chin, dirty hair are so vulnerable to the poison-laden barbs (poison works the same way in any language) emanating from deep within the powerful watermelon bosom. No one's presence can embarrass or dignify her into silence.

No one except the old man who arrives now. 'Good morning,' he says, and Berthe turns, stops yelling, and smiles. Her husband rises, positions the wheelchair at the favourite angle. The lobby will be peaceful as long as the old man is there.

*

It was hopeless. My first swimming lesson. The water terrified me. When did that happen, I wonder, I used to love splashing at Chaupatty, carried about by the waves.

And this was only a swimming pool. Where did all that terror come from? I'm trying to remember.

Armed with my Surf King I enter the high school and go to the pool area. A sheet with instructions for the new class is pinned to the bulletin board. All students must shower and then assemble at eight by the shallow end. As I enter the showers three young boys, probably from a previous class, emerge. One of them holds his nose. The second begins to hum, under his breath: Paki Paki, smell like curry. The third says to the first two: pretty soon all the water's going to taste of curry. They leave.

It's a mixed class, but the gorgeous woman of my fantasy is missing. I have to settle for another, in a pink one-piece suit, with brown hair and a bit of a stomach. She must be about thirty-five. Plain-looking.

The instructor is called Ron. He gives us a pep talk, sensing some nervousness in the group. We're finally all in the water, in the shallow end. He demonstrates floating on the back, then asks for a volunteer. The pink one-piece suit wades forward. He supports her, tells her to lean back and let her head drop in the water.

She does very well. And as we all regard her floating body, I see what was not visible outside the pool: her bush, curly bits of it, straying out at the pink Spandex V. Tongues of water lapping against her delta, as if caressing it teasingly, make the brown hair come alive in a most tantalizing manner. The crests and troughs of little waves, set off by the movement of our bodies in a circle around her, dutifully irrigate her; the curls alternately wave free inside the crest, then adhere to her wet thighs, beached by the inevitable trough. I could watch this forever, and I wish the floating demonstration would never end.

Next we are shown how to grasp the rail and paddle, face down in the water. Between practising floating and paddling, the hour is almost gone. I have been trying to observe the pink one-piece suit, getting glimpses of her straying pubic hair from various angles. Finally, Ron wants a volunteer for the last demonstration, and I go forward. To my horror he leads the class to the deep end. Fifteen feet of water. It is so blue, and I can see the bottom. He picks up a metal hoop attached to a long wooden stick. He wants me to grasp the hoop, jump in the water, and paddle, while he guides me by the stick. Perfectly safe, he tells me. A demonstration of how paddling propels the body.

It's too late to back out; besides, I'm so terrified I couldn't find the words to do so even if I wanted to. Everything he says I do as if in a trance. I don't remember the moment of jumping. The next thing I know is, I'm swallowing water and floundering, hanging on to the hoop for dear life. Ron draws me to the rails and helps me out. The class applauds.

We disperse and one thought is on my mind: what if I'd lost my grip? Fifteen feet of water under me. I shudder and take deep breaths. This is it. I'm not coming next week. This instructor is an irresponsible person. Or he does not value the lives of non-white immigrants. I remember the three teenagers. Maybe the swimming pool is the hangout of some racist group, bent on eliminating all non-white swimmers, to keep their waters pure and their white sisters unogled.

The elevator takes me upstairs. Then gutang-khutang. PW opens her door as I turn the corridor of medicinal smells. 'Berthe was screaming loudly at her husband tonight,' she tells me.

'Good for her,' I say, and she frowns indignantly at me.

The old man is in the lobby. He's wearing thick wool gloves. He wants to know how the swimming was, must have seen me leaving with my towel yesterday. Not bad, I say.

'I used to swim a lot. Very good for the circulation.' He wheezes. 'My feet are cold all the time. Cold as ice. Hands too.'

Summer is winding down, so I say stupidly, 'Yes, it's not so warm any more.'

The thought of the next swimming lesson sickens me. But as I comb through the memories of that terrifying Monday, I come upon the straying curls of brown pubic hair. Inexorably drawn by them, I decide to go.

It's a mistake, of course. This time I'm scared even to venture in the shallow end. When everyone has entered the water and I'm the only one outside, I feel a little foolish and slide in.

Instructor Ron says we should start by reviewing the floating technique. I'm in no hurry. I watch the pink one-piece pull the swim-suit down around her cheeks and flip back to achieve perfect flotation. And then reap disappointment. The pink Spandex triangle is perfectly streamlined today, nothing strays, not a trace of fuzz, not one filament, not even a sign of post-depilation irritation. Like the airbrushed parts of glamour magazine models. The barrenness of her impeccably packaged apex is a betrayal. Now she is shorn like the other women in the class. Why did she have to do it?

The weight of this disappointment makes the water less manageable, more lung-penetrating. With trepidation, I float and paddle my way through the remainder of the hour, jerking my head out every two seconds and breathing deeply, to continually shore up a supply of precious, precious air without, at the same time, seeming too anxious and losing my dignity.

I don't attend the remaining classes. After I've missed three, Ron the instructor telephones. I tell him I've had the flu and am still feeling poorly, but I'll try to be there the following week.

He does not call again. My Surf King is relegated to an unused drawer. Total losses: one fantasy plus thirty dollars. And no watery rebirth. The swimming pool, like Chaupatty beach, has produced a stillbirth. But there is a difference. Water means regeneration only if it is pure and cleansing. Chaupatty was filthy, the pool was not. Failure to swim through filth must mean something other than failure of rebirth—failure of symbolic death? Does that equal success of symbolic life? death of a symbolic failure? death of a symbol? What is the equation?

The postman did not bring a letter but a parcel, he was smiling because he knew that every time something came from Canada his baksheesh was guaranteed, and this time because it was a parcel Mother gave him a whole rupee, she was quite excited, there were so many stickers on it besides the stamps, one for Small Parcel, another Printed Papers, a red sticker saying Insured; she showed it to Father, and opened it, then put both hands on her cheeks, not able to speak because the surprise and happiness was so great, tears came to her eyes and she could not stop smiling, till Father became impatient to know and finally got up and came to the table.

When he saw it he was surprised and happy too, he began to grin, then hugged Mother saying our son is a writer, and we didn't even know it, he never told us a thing, here we are thinking he is still clerking away at the insurance company, and he has written a book of stories, all these years in school and college he kept his talent hidden, making us think he was just like one of the boys in the Baag, shouting and playing the fool in the compound, and now what a surprise; then Father opened the book and began reading it, heading back to the easy chair, and Mother so excited, still holding his arm, walked with him, saying it was not fair him reading it first, she wanted to read it too, and they agreed that he would read the first story, then give it to her so she could also read it, and they would take turns in that manner.

Mother removed the staples from the padded envelope in which he had mailed the book, and threw them away, then straightened the folded edges of the envelope and put it away safely with the other envelopes and letters she had collected since he left.

The leaves are beginning to fall. The only ones I can identify are maple. The days are dwindling like the leaves. I've started a habit of taking long walks every evening. The old man is in the lobby when I leave, he waves as I go by. By the time I'm back, the lobby is usually empty.

Today I was woken up by a grating sound outside that made my flesh crawl. I went to the window and saw Berthe raking the leaves in the parking lot. Not in the expanse of patchy lawn on the periphery, but in the parking lot proper. She was raking the black tarred surface. I went back to bed and dragged a pillow over my head, not releasing it till noon.

When I return from my walk in the evening, PW, summoned by the elevator's gutang-khutang, says, 'Berthe filled six big black garbage bags with leaves today.'

'Six bags!' I say. 'Wow!'

Since the weather turned cold, Berthe's son does not tinker with his van on Sundays under my window. I'm able to sleep late.

Around eleven, there's a commotion outside. I reach out and switch on the clock radio. It's a sunny day, the window curtains are bright. I get up, curious, and see a black Olds Ninety-Eight in the parking lot, by the entrance to the building. The old man is in his wheelchair, bundled up, with a scarf wound several times round his neck as though to immobilize it, like a surgical collar. His daughter and another man, the car-owner, are helping him from the wheelchair into the front seat, encouraging him with words like: that's it, easy does it, attaboy. From the open door of the lobby, Berthe is shouting encouragement too, but hers is confined to one word: yah, repeated at different levels of pitch and volume, with variations on vowel-length. The stranger could be the old man's son, he has the same jet black hair and piercing eyes.

Maybe the old man is not well, it's an emergency. But I quickly scrap that thought—this isn't Bombay, an ambulance would have arrived. They're probably taking him out for a ride. If he is his son, where has he been all this time, I wonder.

The old man finally settles in the front seat, the wheelchair goes in the trunk, and they're off. The one I think is the son looks up and catches me at the window before I can move away, so I wave, and he waves back.

In the afternoon I take down a load of clothes to the laundry room. Both machines have completed their cycles, the clothes inside are waiting to be transferred to dryers. Should I remove them and place them on top of a dryer, or wait? I decide to wait. After a few minutes, two women arrive, they are in bathrobes, and smoking. It takes me a while to realize that these are the two disappointments who were sunbathing in bikinis last summer.

'You didn't have to wait, you could have removed the clothes and carried on, dear,' says one. She has a Scottish accent. It's one of the few I've learned to identify. Like maple leaves.

'Well,' I say, 'some people might not like strangers touching their clothes.'

'You're not a stranger, dear,' she says, 'you live in this building, we've seen you before.'

'Besides, your hands are clean,' the other one pipes in. 'You can touch my things any time you like.'

Horny old cow. I wonder what they've got on under their bathrobes. Not much, I find, as they bend over to place their clothes in the dryers.

'See you soon,' they say, and exit, leaving me behind in an erotic wake of smoke and perfume and deep images of cleavages. I start the washers and depart, and when I come back later, the dryers are empty.

PW tells me, 'The old man's son took him out for a drive today. He has a big beautiful black car.'

I see my chance, and shoot back: 'Olds Ninety-Eight.'

'What?'

'The car,' I explain, 'it's an Oldsmobile Ninety-Eight.'

She does not like this at all, my giving her information. She is visibly nettled, and retreats with a sour face.

Mother and Father read the first five stories, and she was very sad after reading some of them, she said he must be so unhappy there, all his stories are about Bombay, he remembers every little thing about his childhood, he is thinking about it all the time even though he is ten thousand miles away, my poor son, I think he misses his home and us and everything he left behind, because if he likes it over there why would he not write stories about that, there must be so many new ideas that his new life could give him.

But Father did not agree with this, he said it did not mean that he was unhappy, all writers worked in the same way, they used their memories and experiences and made stories out of them, changing some things, adding some, imagining some, all writers were very good at remembering details of their lives.

Mother said, how can you be sure that he is remembering because he is a writer, or whether he started to write because he is unhappy and thinks of his past, and wants to save it all by making stories of it; and Father said that is not a sensible question, anyway, it is now my turn to read the next story.

The first snow has fallen, and the air is crisp. It's not very deep, about two inches, just right to go for a walk in. I've been told that immigrants from hot countries always enjoy the snow the first year, maybe for a couple of years more, then inevitably the dread sets in, and the approach of winter gets them fretting and moping. On the other hand, if it hadn't been for my conversation with the woman at the swimming registration desk, they might now be saying that India is a nation of non-swimmers.

Berthe is outside, shovelling the snow off the walkway in the parking lot. She has a heavy, wide pusher which she wields expertly.

The old radiators in the apartment alarm me incessantly. They continue to broadcast a series of variations on death throes, and go from hot to cold and cold to hot at will, there's no controlling their temperature. I speak to Berthe about it in the lobby. The old man is there too, his chin seems to have sunk deeper into his chest, and his face is a yellowish grey.

'Nothing, not to worry about anything,' says Berthe, dropping rough-hewn chunks of language around me. 'Radiator no work, you tell me. You feel cold, you come to me, I keep you warm,' and she opens her arms wide, laughing. I step back, and she advances, her breasts preceding her like the gallant prows of two ice-breakers. She looks at the old man to see if he is appreciating the act: 'You no feel scared, I keep you safe and warm.'

But the old man is staring outside, at the flakes of falling snow. What thoughts is he thinking as he watches them? Of childhood days, perhaps, and snowmen with hats and pipes, and snowball fights, and white Christmases, and Christmas trees? What will I think of, old in this country, when I sit and watch the snow come down? For me, it is already too late for snowmen and snowball fights, and all I will have is thoughts about childhood thoughts and dreams, built around snowscapes and winter-wonderlands on the Christmas cards so popular in Bombay; my snowmen and snowball fights and Christmas trees are in the pages of Enid Blyton's books, dispersed amidst the adventures of the Famous Five, and the Five Find-Outers, and the Secret Seven. My snowflakes are even less forgettable than the old man's, for they never melt.

It finally happened. The heat went. Not the usual intermittent coming and going, but out completely. Stone cold. The radiators are like ice. And so is everything else. There's no hot water. Naturally. It's the hot water that goes through the rads and heats them. Or is it the other way around? Is there no hot water because the rads have stopped circulating it? I don't care, I'm too cold to sort out the cause and effect relationship. Maybe there is no connection at all.

I dress quickly, put on my winter jacket, and go down to the lobby. The elevator is not working because the power is out, so I take the stairs. Several people are gathered, and Berthe has announced that she has telephoned the office, they are sending a man. I go back up the stairs. It's only one floor, the elevator is just a bad habit. Back in Firozsha Baag they were broken most of the time. The stairway enters the corridor outside the old man's apartment, and I think of his cold feet and hands. Poor man, it must be horrible for him without heat.

As I walk down the long hallway, I feel there's something different but can't pin it down. I look at the carpet, the ceiling, the wallpaper: it all seems the same. Maybe it's the freezing cold that imparts a feeling of difference.

PW opens her door: 'The old man had another stroke yesterday. They took him to the hospital.'

The medicinal smell. That's it. It's not in the hallway any more.

In the stories that he'd read so far Father said that all the Parsi families were poor or middle-class, but that was okay; nor did he mind that the seeds for the stories were picked from the sufferings of their own lives; but there should also have been something positive about Parsis, there was so much to be proud of: the great Tatas and their contribution to the steel industry, or Sir Dinshaw Petit in the textile industry who made Bombay the Manchester of the East, or Dadabhai Naoroji in the freedom movement, where he was the first to use the word swaraj, *and the first to be elected to the British Parliament where he carried on his campaign; he should have found some way to bring some of these wonderful facts into his stories, what would people reading these stories think, those who did not know about Parsis—that the whole community was full of cranky, bigoted people; and in reality it was the richest, most advanced and philanthropic community in India, and he did not need to tell his own son that Parsis had a reputation for being generous and family-oriented. And he could have written something also about the historic background, how Parsis came to India from Persia because of Islamic persecution in the seventh century, and were the descendants of Cyrus the Great and the magnificent Persian Empire. He could have made a story of all this, couldn't he?*

Mother said what she liked best was his remembering everything so well, how beautiful-ly he wrote about it all, even the sad things, and though he changed some of it, and used his imagination, there was truth in it.

My hope is, Father said, that there will be some story based on his Canadian experience, that way we will know something about our son's life there, if not through his letters then in his stories; so far they are all about Parsis and Bombay, and the one with a little bit about Toronto, where a man perches on top of the toilet, is shameful and disgusting, although it is funny at times and did make me laugh, I have to admit, but where does he get such an imag-ination from, what is the point of such a fantasy; and Mother said that she would also enjoy some stories about Toronto and the people there; it puzzles me, she said, why he writes noth-ing about it, especially since you say that writers use their own experience to make stories out of.

Then Father said this is true, but he is probably not using his Toronto experience because it is too early; what do you mean, too early, asked Mother and Father explained it takes a writer about ten years time after an experience before he is able to use it in his writing, it takes that long to be absorbed internally and understood, thought out and thought about, over and over again, he haunts it and it haunts him if it is valuable enough, till the writer is comfortable with it to be able to use it as he wants; but this is only one theory I read some-where, it may or may not be true.

That means, said Mother that his childhood in Bombay and our home here is the most valuable thing in his life just now, because he is able to remember it all to write about it, and you were so bitterly saying he is forgetting where he came from; and that may be true, said Father, but that is not what the theory means, according to the theory he is writing of these things because they are far enough in the past for him to deal with objectively, he is able to achieve what critics call artistic distance, without emotions interfering; and what do you mean emotions, said Mother, you are saying he does not feel anything for his characters, how can he write so beautifully about so many sad things without any feelings in his heart?

But before Father could explain more, about beauty and emotion and inspiration and imagination, Mother took the book and said it was her turn now and too much theory she did not want to listen to, it was confusing and did not make as much sense as reading the stories, she would read them her way and Father could read them his.

My books on the windowsill have been damaged. Ice has been forming on the inside ledge, which I did not notice, and melting when the sun shines in. I spread them in a corner of the living-room to dry out.

The winter drags on. Berthe wields her snow pusher as expertly as ever, but there are signs of weariness in her performance. Neither husband nor son is ever seen outside with a shovel. Or anywhere else, for that matter. It occurs to me that the son's van is missing, too.

The medicinal smell is in the hall again, I sniff happily and look forward to seeing the old man in the lobby. I go downstairs and peer into the mailbox, see the blue and magenta of an Indian aerogramme with Don Mills, Ontario, Canada in Father's flawless hand through the slot.

I pocket the letter and enter the main lobby. The old man is there, but not in his usual place. He is not looking out through the glass door. His wheelchair is facing a bare wall where the wallpaper is torn in places. As though he is not interested in the outside world any more, having finished with all that, and now it's time to see inside. What does he see inside, I wonder? I go up to him and say hullo. He says hullo without raising his sunken chin. After a few seconds his grey countenance faces me. 'How old do you think I am?' His eyes are dull and glazed; he is looking even further inside than I first presumed.

'Well, let's see, you're probably close to sixty-four.'

'I'll be seventy-eight next August.' But he does not chuckle or wheeze. Instead, he continues softly, 'I wish my feet did not feel so cold all the time. And my hands.' He lets his chin fall again.

In the elevator I start opening the aerogramme, a tricky business because a crooked tear means lost words. Absorbed in this while emerging, I don't notice PW occupying the centre of the hallway, arms folded across her chest: 'They had a big fight. Both of them have left.'

I don't immediately understand her agitation. 'What . . . who?'

'Berthe. Husband and son both left her. Now she is all alone.'

Her tone and stance suggest that we should not be standing here talking but do something to bring Berthe's family back. 'That's very sad,' I say, and go in. I picture father and son in the van, driving away, driving across the snow-covered country, in the dead of winter, away from wife and mother; away to where? how far will they go? Not son's van nor father's booze can take them far enough. And the further they go, the more they'll remember, they can take it from me.

All the stories were read by Father and Mother, and they were sorry when the book was fin-ished, they felt they had come to know their son better now, yet there was much more to know, they wished there were many more stories; and this is what they mean, said Father, when they say that the whole story can never be told, the whole truth can never be known; what do you mean, they say, asked Mother, who they, and Father said writers, poets, philoso-phers. I don't care what they say, said Mother, my son will write as much or as little as he wants to, and if I can read it I will be happy.

The last story they liked the best of all because it had the most in it about Canada, and now they felt they knew at least a little bit, even if it was a very little bit, about his day-to-day life in his apartment; and Father said if he continues to write about such things he will become popular because I am sure they are interested there in reading about life through the eyes of an immigrant, it provides a different viewpoint; the only danger is if he changes and becomes so much like them that he will write like one of them and lose the important difference.

The bathroom needs cleaning. I open a new can of Ajax and scour the tub. Sloshing with mug from bucket was standard bathing procedure in the bathrooms of Firozsha Baag, so my preference now is always for a shower. I've never used the tub as yet; besides, it would be too much like Chaupatty or the swimming pool, wallowing in my own dirt. Still, it must be cleaned.

When I've finished, I prepare for a shower. But the clean gleaming tub and the nearness of the vernal equinox give me the urge to do something different today. I find the drain plug in the bathroom cabinet, and run the bath.

I've spoken so often to the old man, but I don't know his name. I should have asked him the last time I saw him, when his wheelchair was facing the bare wall because he had seen all there was to see outside and it was time to see what was inside. Well, tomorrow. Or better yet, I can look it up in the directory in the lobby. Why didn't I think of that before? It will only have an initial and a last name, but then I can surprise him with: hullo Mr Wilson, or whatever it is.

The bath is full. Water imagery is recurring in my life: Chaupatty beach, swim-ming pool, bathtub. I step in and immerse myself up to the neck. It feels good. The hot water loses its opacity when the chlorine, or whatever it is, has cleared. My hair is still dry. I close my eyes, hold my breath, and dunk my head. Fighting the panic, I stay under and count to thirty. I come out, clear my lungs and breathe deeply.

I do it again. This time I open my eyes under water, and stare blindly without see-ing, it takes all my will to keep the lids from closing. Then I am slowly able to dis-cern the underwater objects. The drain plug looks different, slightly distorted; there is a hair trapped between the hole and the plug, it waves and dances with the move-ment of the water. I come up, refresh my lungs, examine quickly the overwater world of the washroom, and go in again. I do it several times, over and over. The world out-side the water I have seen a lot of, it is now time to see what is inside.

The spring session for adult non-swimmers will begin in a few days at the high school. I must not forget the registration date.

The dwindled days of winter are now all but forgotten; they have grown and attained a respectable span. I resume my evening walks, it's spring, and a vigorous thaw is on. The snowbanks are melting, the sound of water on its gushing, gurgling journey to the drains is beautiful. I plan to buy a book of trees, so I can identify more than the maple as they begin to bloom.

When I return to the building, I wipe my feet energetically on the mat because some people are entering behind me, and I want to set a good example. Then I go to the board with its little plastic letters and numbers. The old man's apartment is the one on the corner by the stairway, that makes it number 201. I run down the list, come to 201, but there are no little white plastic letters beside it. Just the empty black rectangle with holes where the letters would be squeezed in. That's strange. Well, I can introduce myself to him, then ask his name.

However, the lobby is empty. I take the elevator, exit at the second floor, wait for the gutang-khutang. It does not come: the door closes noiselessly, smoothly. Berthe has been at work, or has made sure someone else has. PW's cue has been lubricated out of existence.

But she must have the ears of a cockroach. She is waiting for me. I whistle my way down the corridor. She fixes me with an accusing look. She waits till I stop whistling, then says: 'You know the old man died last night.'

I cease groping for my key. She turns to go and I take a step towards her, my hand still in my trouser pocket. 'Did you know his name?' I ask, but she leaves without answering.

DANIEL DAVID MOSES

(b. 1952)

'Sometimes I feel so esoteric because I do think my basic impulse is that spiritual one of looking for meaning, and the fact that it gets turned into writing is a lucky bonus,' says Daniel David Moses. 'People should take that into account when listening to anything I say.' For Moses, spirituality—'the sense of knowing the meaning of your life, what you are doing and why you are doing it'—is juxtaposed to mainstream culture. 'The mainstream god,' he says, 'got killed a while back and a lot of people are desperately holding on to the corpse. Meanwhile Native peoples' traditions, the meanings of their life, are intimately connected to the actual physical world they live in, so they don't have to hold on desperately to their sense of who they are. Unless, of course, they come to the city and believe what's going on here but then they are just partaking of the mainstream dilemma.'

This tension between the city and the natural world represents Moses's background. A Delaware from the Six Nations lands along the Grand River near Brantford in southern Ontario, he grew up on a farm, 'nominally Anglican in a community of various Christian sects and of the Longhouse, the Iroquoian traditional religious and political system'. A 'city person' who has lived in Toronto for many years, beginning with part-time jobs that allowed him to pursue his writing of poetry and drama, Moses calls himself 'a loner' but also stresses the importance of community for his work, 'that broader sense of community that doesn't exist here in the city. It's something that . . . really energizes my work, even though I keep to myself and don't spend a lot of time with any of the communities I could connect with here in town.'

Intent on becoming a writer since his high school years—'I was the one in the class who was pushing things, directing things. If I wasn't writing I was getting someone else to write them. If they wouldn't perform I would have to do it myself'—Moses studied at York University where he received an Honours B.A. in General Fine Arts, and at the University of British Columbia where he received an M.F.A. and where he was the winner of the Creative Writing Department's play-wrighting competition in 1977. He returned to Toronto in 1979 where, along with part-time jobs, he began writing full-time and became involved in many of the cultural organizations of Native artists.

His first book, *Delicate Bodies* (1980), is a collection of poetry that conveys his careful attention to the natural world, a world, however, that holds the balance of human consciousness and spirituality: '. . . Forget all dreams of / perfect fruit. Look to the pruned sticks, search for / hieroglyphs, though you'll find no lyrics for the odd, sharp / tune. . . .' *The White Line* (1990), his second poetry collection, is similarly characterized by the ironic humour and elegance with which Moses responds to his immediate world. Not overtly engaged with historical issues but subtly rooted in the reality of his Native heritage, his poetry reflects a great command of the versatility of the lyric form and of textured imagery.

With Tomson Highway and Lenore Keeshig-Tobias, Moses was a founder of the Committee to Re-establish the Trickster (1986). Partly an ironic move as its title suggests—'the very name "Trickster" we took from anthropologists; it has nothing to do particularly with native communities'—it was intended to create a supportive environment for Native artists in Toronto. As Moses says, 'I got the idea that maybe if we promoted ourselves as Native writers and just thought about what it was that we were doing that was different, that might be useful.' Moses sees the 'trickster' figure as 'the embodiment of our sense of humour about the way we live our lives. It's a very central part of our attitude that things are funny even though horrible things happen.' This is dramatized in his play *Big Buck City* (produced by Tarragon Theatre, Toronto, 1991), which also reflects the way Moses sums up the impetus behind his writing: 'my program is to write about the dilemma of cities. This is civilization but it's also the cancer on the planet.'

Moses, who says 'my imagination is theatrical', has published three plays, including *Almighty Voice and His Wife: A Play in Two Acts* (1992), *Coyote City: A Play in Two Acts* (1990), which was a finalist for the Governor General's Award, and *The Dreaming Beauty* (1989), which received the first prize in the One-Act category of the Theatre Canada's National Playwrighting Competition. In addition to these, Moses has had other plays produced, including *The Moon and the Dead Indians* (Cahoots Theatre Projects / Theatre Passe Muraille, Toronto, 1993), and *Belle Fille de l'Aurore* (Theatre de Jour, Saskatoon, 1991).

ADMONITION TO AN ICE-SKATING CHILD

When the mercury sun sinks below zero,
pretend you're blind so you won't be afraid
you can't see. Listen for your mother and
don't tap too loudly. The river's lonely
under its white sky. With fish eyes frozen
it sees only bubbles of dark. It twists
around searching for a deep place it passed
too quickly to know. It's sure someone's there.
If the river hears you, its wings will lift
and flicker through its clouds saying, *Sh*!
Now you're not lost. Its tongues will unfold
and wash your face and wrap your hands in muffs
of frost. You'll slide off its smile into black
kisses, forgetting you need to grow old.

PAPER

We are so well-mannered we never move
without sending a letter of intent
months in advance. Always we sign it *Love*
though we know little of hearts or rose scent.
We wouldn't recognize red if it fell
out of our mouths. Its very existence
depends on rumours and it's possible
to believe only so much that's nonsense.
It's too bad if anyone imagines
that words have ever bled when the blackness
of letters on this paper should imply
that it's easy to live. You can't deny
the truth of salutation or address—
that there's nothing but white between the lines.

THE END OF THE NIGHT

Here in the black dream you're small once again
against the tall back of your grandfather's
rocking chair. And you're following a crack
between two boards of the veranda, towards

and over its brink. And there the lawn and
the garden are dark and still as a dried
spill of ink. And only along what should
be the dawn horizon is there any

illumination. There it comes, a grey
flicker showing through the line of thunder
clouds. And it comes quicker now, the closer
together those clouds get, the more lightning

they exchange. Now they let an electric
white rising sun erase the dark. The land's
too bright to read in the glare, paper no
longer marked by trees or fences. Your eyes

start burning and there's no turning away
from the solar wind. Your grandfather's chair
is carrying you into ashes. You're
in the white dream going blind once again.

BEARWALK

At night I stroll behind my eyes,
trying to avoid the bears.
Now they're invisible in the snow,

I've got to take care not to sweat,
not to let them know I know they're there,
what they are, dangerous.

If I'm ambushed I pretend
the bear's an igloo, walk up and push
my head into its maw

and comment on the reek.
Make a bear question the repute
of its jaw and it's spiritless.

Point at its mouth and say
A star! Is it Christmas?
and it's done with. I've tripped on

bones of bears who'd bitten
their own hearts out. Once they're extinct
I'll never wake up dead.

DIONNE BRAND

(b. 1953)

'Every word turns on itself, every word falls after it is said,' writes Dionne Brand. 'None of the answers that I've given over the years is the truth. Those answers have all been given like a guerrilla with her face in a handkerchief, her eyes still. She is still, poised for quick movement, but still. . . . And I've answered like the captive giving answers in an interrogation, telling just enough to appease the interrogator and just enough to trace the story so she could repeat it without giving anything away and without contradiction the next time she has to tell it.' This self-portrait of Brand as a writer indicates the energy and tensions in her work as well as the cultural and political conditions under which she, as a black lesbian writer, creates.

Born in Guayguayare, Trinidad, Brand moved to Toronto in 1970, after graduating from a private school. 'I really didn't think of myself as an immigrant *per se*,' she says. 'I could escape being an immigrant, but along with the black people who have lived in this country for three centuries, I would not escape my race at any point.' She studied at the University of Toronto, where she received a B.A. in English and Philosophy (1975), and at the Ontario Institute for Studies in Education, where she received an M.A. in History and Philosophy (1989). She works with such community organizations as the Black Education Project and the Immigrant Women's Centre and agencies like the Caribbean Peoples' Development Agency. *Rivers Have Sources, Trees Have Roots: Speaking of Racism* (1986), co-authored with Krisantha Sri Bhaggiyadatta, recording people's experiences with racism, and *No Burden to Carry: Narratives of Black Working Women in Ontario 1920s to 1950s* (1991), with the assistance of Lois De Shield, containing the life narratives of 16 black women, demonstrate Brand's ongoing commitment to combating racism. 'I don't see Marxism and feminism as theories I need to graft onto people,' she says, 'I see them as living things. Analysis is supposed to work, to be living, growing.'

Widely published in literary magazines and anthologies, and a contributing editor of such journals as *Spear* and *Fuse Magazine*, Brand is also a documentary film maker. She worked with the National Film Board, Studio D, to produce *Older, Stronger, Wiser* (1989), *Sisters in the Struggle* (1991), and *Long Time Comin'* (1993), documenting the art and politics of various black women in Canada. Her most recent book, *Bread Out of Stone: recollections sex recognitions race dreaming politics* (1994) is an impassioned and eloquent record of her life as an artist, intellectual, and activist. 'We're now battered by multicultural bureaucracy,' she says, 'co-opted by mainstream party politics, morassed in everyday boring racism.' As she says elsewhere, only by addressing '[r]eal power—which is economic power and political power' can we begin to deal with racism. What multiculturalism 'does essentially is to compartmentalize us into little cultural groups who have dances and different foods and Caribana. But it doesn't address real power.'

Brand's writing, beginning with her first books of poetry, *'Fore Day Morning* (1978), *Primitive Offences* (1982), and *Winter Epigrams: Epigrams to Ernesto Cardenal in Defense of Claudia* (1983), is directly engaged in questioning power and the traditional constructs of femininity. In *Chronicles of the Hostile Sun* (1984), through lyrics that are at once elegiac and militant, Brand documents her ten-month sojourn in Grenada after the US invasion. *No Language is Neutral* (1990), her most recent poetry collection, nominated for the Governor General's Award, '[m]ixes the lyricism with the documentary'. Composed in longer lines, and often forming long sequences, these poems are written 'in the language that I grew up in,' she says. In this book, Brand explores the genealogy of her persona by delving into layers of history in order to undo the hold of the dominant gaze, be it imperialistic or masculine. Brand's other collection of poetry, *Earth Magic* (1979, 1990), with drawings by Veronica Sullivan, is for young people.

Of her short stories, collected in *Sans Souci and Other Stories* (1994), Brand says that 'I never begin from what might be universal. In fact, I'm wary of appeals to universality. It seems to me that only works written by writers who are not white are called upon to prove or provide universality.' Although, as she states, 'I am not trying to "show cultural differences",' Brand's 'writing is directed against stereotypes'.

Brand, who has taught English and Creative Writing at the University of Guelph, is now a full-time writer living in Toronto.

FROM *NO LANGUAGE IS NEUTRAL*

No language is neutral. I used to haunt the beach at
Guaya, two rivers sentinel the country sand, not
backra white but nigger brown sand, one river dead
and teeming from waste and alligators, the other
rumbling to the ocean in a tumult, the swift undertow
blocking the crossing of little girls except on the tied
up dress hips of big women, then, the taste of leaving
was already on my tongue and cut deep into my
skinny pigeon toed way, language here was strict
description and teeth edging truth. Here was beauty
and here was nowhere. The smell of hurrying passed
my nostrils with the smell of sea water and fresh fish
wind, there was history which had taught my eyes to
look for escape even beneath the almond leaves fat
as women, the conch shell tiny as sand, the rock
stone old like water. I learned to read this from a
woman whose hand trembled at the past, then even
being born to her was temporary, wet and thrown half
dressed among the dozens of brown legs itching to
run. It was as if a signal burning like a fer de lance's
sting turned my eyes against the water even as love
for this nigger beach became resolute.

There it was anyway, some damn memory half-eaten
and half hungry. To hate this, they must have been
dragged through the Manzinilla spitting out the last
spun syllables for cruelty, new sound forming,
pushing toward lips made to bubble blood. This road
could match that. Hard-bitten on mangrove and wild
bush, the sea wind heaving any remnants of
consonant curses into choking aspirate. No
language is neutral seared in the spine's unravelling.
Here is history too. A backbone bending and
unbending without a word, heat, bellowing these
lungs spongy, exhaled in humming, the ocean, a

way out and not anything of beauty, tipping turquoise
and scandalous. The malicious horizon made us the
essential thinkers of technology. How to fly gravity,
how to balance basket and prose reaching for
murder. Silence done curse god and beauty here,
people does hear things in this heliconia peace
a morphology of rolling chain and copper gong
now shape this twang, falsettos of whip and air
rudiment this grammar. Take what I tell you. When
these barracks held slaves between their stone
halters, talking was left for night and hush was idiom
and hot core.

. . .

Leaving this standing, heart and eyes fixed to a
skyscraper and a concrete eternity not knowing then
only running away from something that breaks the
heart open and nowhere to live. Five hundred dollars
and a passport full of sand and winking water, is how
I reach here, a girl's face shimmering from a little
photograph, her hair between hot comb and afro, feet
posing in high heel shoes, never to pass her eyes on
the red-green threads of a humming bird's twitching
back, the blood warm quickened water colours of a
sea bed, not the rain forest tangled in smoke-wet,
well there it was. I did read a book once about a
prairie in Alberta since my waving canefield wasn't
enough, too much cutlass and too much cut foot, but
romance only happen in romance novel, the concrete
building just overpower me, block my eyesight and
send the sky back, back where it more redolent.

Is steady trembling I trembling when they ask me my
name and say I too black for it. Is steady hurt I feeling
when old talk bleed, the sea don't have branch you
know darling. Nothing is a joke no more and I right
there with them, running for the train until I get to find
out my big sister just like to run and nobody wouldn't
vex if you miss the train, calling Spadina *Spadeena*
until I listen good for what white people call it, saying I
coming just to holiday to the immigration officer when
me and the son-of-a-bitch know I have labourer mark
all over my face. It don't have nothing call beauty

here but this is a place, a gasp of water from a
hundred lakes, fierce bright windows screaming with
goods, a constant drizzle of brown brick cutting
dolorous prisons into every green uprising of bush.
No wilderness self, is shards, shards, shards,
shards of raw glass, a debris of people you pick your way
through returning to your worse self, you the thin
mixture of just come and don't exist.

. . .

HARD AGAINST THE SOUL

II
I want to wrap myself around you here in this line so
that you will know something, not just that I am dying
in some way but that I did this for some reason. This
grace, you see, come as a surprise and nothing till
now knock on my teeming skull, then, these warm
watery syllables, a woman's tongue so like a culture,
plunging toward stones not yet formed into flesh,
language not yet made . . . I want to kiss you deeply,
smell, taste the warm water of your mouth as warm as
your hands. I lucky is grace that gather me up and
forgive my plainness.

III
She was a woman whose eyes came fresh, saying, I
trust you, you will not be the woman who walks out
into the Atlantic at Santa Maria and never returns.
You cannot dream this turquoise ocean enveloping
you in its murmuring thrall, your hands will not arrest
in the middle of gazing, you will not happen on an
easy thought like this in a hotel room in Guanabo, not
on a morning as you watch alone from this beach, the
sun dripping orange, or sitting on a marble bench in
Old Havana, vacantly. You will not look at your watch
on a night in early June and think this gentle sea as
good as any for a walk beyond the reflexes of your
flesh.

. . .

X
Then it is this simple. I felt the unordinary romance of
women who love women for the first time. It burst in
my mouth. Someone said this is your first lover, you
will never want to leave her. I had it in mind that I
would be an old woman with you. But perhaps I
always had it in mind simply to be an old woman,
darkening, somewhere with another old woman,
then, I decided it was you when you found me in that
apartment drinking whisky for breakfast. When I came
back from Grenada and went crazy for two years, that
time when I could hear anything and my skin was
flaming like a nerve and the walls were like paper
and my eyes could not close. I suddenly sensed you
at the end of my room waiting. I saw your back arched
against this city we inhabit like guerrillas, I brushed my
hand, conscious, against your soft belly, waking up.

. . .

ANTONIO D'ALFONSO

(b. 1953)

'1977 was an important year for me,' says Antonio D'Alfonso. 'It was the year I became an Italian. One is not born an Italian; one becomes an Italian. Especially when you come from the *campagna*, the country; especially when you are not born in Italy.' D'Alfonso was born in Montreal, three years after his parents' emigration from Italy to Quebec. He grew up trilingual, and studied at Loyola College where he received his B.A. in Communication Arts (1975), and at the Université de Montréal, where he received his M.Sc. in Communication Studies, specializing in semiology.

The year he 'became' an Italian was also the year he discovered the poetry of Pier Giorgio di Cicco and other Italian-Canadian writers. It was at this point that he began not only questioning what it means being Italian in Canada—'To be a Wop, a worker without a permit, a poet without a language of his own, without a tradition to work in, or to fight against?'—but also constructing his own identity as writer and becoming a major force in creating the very tradition he felt he lacked as an Italian poet in Canada.

In 1978 he founded Guernica Editions and has since published numerous books of literature and criticism by authors from Canada and around the world, many of them focusing on issues of hyphenated identities. D'Alfonso moved his press to Toronto in 1991, where he continues to be an active publisher, editor, translator, and writer. *In Italics: In Defense of Ethnicity*, a volume that collects his many essays on writing, publishing, and cultural politics, is forthcoming.

'Being an Italian,' writes D'Alfonso, 'is nothing to be frightened of or arrogant about. It is a fact of life, and one must live with it, like one's gender. . . . In many ways, coming to terms with one's *Italianity* is very much like coming out of the closet. Nevertheless you cannot shed overnight the layers of skin you have wrapped yourself in. . . . The transformation is slow and often painful. You have to *become* yourself. And this is what interests me

most: the process of becoming. Struggle is the force behind the process of identity which manifests itself in different ways. Not all struggle, however, need be expressed in stammers or with violence.' D'Alfonso's poetics and politics, the transformation and struggle he talks about, are clearly reflected in his writing.

Beginning with his first books of poetry, *La chanson du shaman à Sedna* (1973), *Queror* (1979) and *Black Tongue* (1983), D'Alfonso explores, through sensuous and often surreal imagery, the layers of identity, while inhabiting a space of discordances—'Dissimilar we coalesce. / We are hybrid.' With his later titles, D'Alfonso begins to 're-invent' himself in forms that allow his lyrical voice to speak from a position of both innocence and experience. *The Other Shore* (1986), translated into French as *L'autre rivage* (1987), *Panick Love* (1988), also available in French as *L'Amour panique* (1992), and *Julia* (1992) show D'Alfonso to be the kind of 'essential poet' that he sees emerging from the Italian-Canadian literary tradition: 'an *essential* poet is one who not only finds a point of intersection, no matter how durable or ephemeral, for all the contradictory forces working within and without him, but also a new language or a new way of using the language he chooses. A poet who finds himself in such a *situation* cannot be expected to vacuously adhere to the norms prescribed by the tradition imposed by the language he chooses.'

D'Alfonso's novel, *Avril ou L'anti-passion* (1990), has just been translated into English, under the title *Fabrizio's Passion* (1995). As a film maker, he has produced three 16mm black-and-white films, *L'Ampoule brûlée* (1973), *La Coupe de Circé* (1974), and *Pour t'aimer* (1982-87), and has collaborated either as scriptwriter, cameraperson, or as editor on other films. He is the editor of *Voix-off: dix poètes anglophones au Québec* (1985), and, with Fulvio Caccia, he has edited *Quêtes: textes d'auteurs italo-québécois* (1983). His most recent book is *In Italics* (1995), a collection of essays.

IM SACHSENHAUSEN

*La mia lingua / mi isolava /
l'ho abbandonata / con la tua /
imputridiscono / in me / i sensi.*
                                    Gino Chiellino

The language of one country in another country. Listen to the music coming in from the other room. Workers speak about the land in which they planted seeds of children and wives. Who knows what *father* and *mother* mean to them?

Not a question of nativeland. Our nativeland, a plane bringing us from point A to point B. Place, country: what do these mean to you, my love? Foreigner in a foreign land . . .

What do we desire from the soil of our bodies? Country without borders, country of our love. The language we speak is the language of our bodies, divided, united, poetry, poetry, why do you make love like this? Always telling me what I am not. Why do you come to me this way? Unexpectedly.

THE LOSS OF A CULTURE

Not the trip to a land where words are pronounced as you were taught to pronounce them. Not the adage your grandmother serves you at dinner. The language you speak as a child, flushed down the toilet bowl. Your mother-tongue sounds as foreign to you as any language you do not understand. Forgotten as the life-style you once had. Latin engraved on darkened school desks. What do you tell yourself when you find yourself alone at night? The uneaten bread becomes stale. The avoided meeting of a one-night stand, dreadful. Squashed tomato on the floor sinks into the tiles of your perfection. You forget the past but the past will not forget you. You sit on broken chairs and get cramps when you are about to say something intelligent. If you collapse and smash your head on the floor, it will not be from lack of proper diet, it will be your ancestors who will shoot you from behind.

THE FAMILY

Images one does not want to see. Images of sterility, images of life. Miraculous progenity. Unrolling, a homemovie, a scroll. Every father a daughter, every mother a son. A family rejuvenating itself without hardening into a fossil. Bones prove that death does not sign with an X: the only son with only a son and no son. 'I want to be modern. Drink down those images and forget them.' Images one refuses to look at, images one has been taught are vulgar, stilted, trite. O miraculous progenity. O imaginative life. Who gives you power to put marble on quicksand, build cities on water? What stubbornness of creation. You give birth, enhance the chances of change. Inventor of possibilities.

ON BEING A WOP

Per Patrizia Di Pardo

Who can say what national pride means? The feel for people living here, though they need not necessarily care? Not to come back to this place. What is my excuse if not the fear of what this country would do to me? Born abroad, this is how the world wants it. But national pride? This place, this city, this territory: almost twenty-seven centuries old. O Italia, nation beyond nation, where will we take you now? You are not nervous when you walk among your citizens in Rome, Montreal or Frankfurt. You drink a few beers and are beyond the grasp of people who wish to talk to you. *Foro Romano*. You, fired for having demonstrated on Via Nazionale. Protesting against the Mafia and the Heroin Plague. You want this march to be more than just a testimony, you want to express your people's desire to change. People without boundaries, people with homes in every country. The meaning of being Italian? The meaning of being European? American? To reconcile yourself to the world you belong to. What reconciliation is possible in what makes up the contradictions of being? To be one thing, to be another: what choice have you today? (Cold Frascati wine against your teeth . . .) What does struggle stand for, if not the people who gave you birth? Peasants without lands who have voices not for singing but rumours blowing in the wind. The cultures of being what being can never again be. Here or there: cultureless identity. The Italian culture: what does it mean to be Italian today if you live outside Italy? 'If you don't live in Italy, you're not Italian.' What does such a phrase mean? What does it stand for? To be anywhere just as long as you live your culture. To keep your batteries in full charge in order to become what you essentially are.

Roma, 30 ottobre 1984

MAKEDA SILVERA

(b. 1954)

'Fascinated' with 'process'—the process of writing, of fighting for a space for herself and other women writers of colour, of becoming an active participant in the making and unmaking of history about black women's lives—Makeda Silvera has been an energetic member of the tradition of black women writers in Canada since the early eighties. Born in Kingston, Jamaica, and brought up in a household of 'strong' and 'loving' women, she moved to Canada with her parents when she was thirteen.

Silvera began writing in the early 1970s as a reporter and freelance journalist, and later as an editorial assistant for Toronto's newspaper *Share*. Her journalism and community activism made her aware, among other things, of the problems Caribbean-born domestic workers faced in Canada. The result was *Silenced* (1983), Silvera's first book, a history of those women's lives where they speak in first person, not through the voices of 'academics who presumed to speak for them'. *Growing up Black* (1989), a resource guide for black youth, also reflects Silvera's involvement with her community.

A co-founder and publisher of Sister Vision Press, a Toronto press that publishes women of colour, Silvera has been instrumental not only in the publication of books by women of colour which were for a long time systematically rejected by mainstream publishers, but also in fostering younger women writers. The editor of *Piece of My Heart: A Lesbian of Colour Anthology* (1991), a groundbreaking collection in that it is 'the first such liaison of North American lesbians of colour,' Silvera has contributed to it 'Man Royals and Sodomites: Some Thoughts on the Invisibility of Afro-Caribbean Lesbians'. This essay/memoir, perhaps the first attempt in writing to explore Caribbean lesbian sexuality within a historical and social context, has played a key role in reestablishing Silvera's links with her heritage. 'It was important for me,' she says, 'to summon memory. . . . Again, I had to fall back on oral narratives to make sense of pieces of conversation from my mother, grandmother and women of their generation.' This essay/memoir, which 'was not written as a personal confession but as a family/community coming out', became, as Silvera notes, 'the basis for many of my stories. It became an opportunity to exercise that memory.'

Silvera has published two collections of short fiction, *Remembering G* (1991) and *Her Head a Village* (1994). The former includes stories that come out of the 'ordinariness' of her roots—'I wrote about the things I knew as a child. I wrote about eating cornmeal pudding. . . . I could make magic and laughter out of the ordinariness.' The latter, written in the rhythms of Jamaican language, still remains rooted in past memories, but also includes stories that deal with the present conditions of the African-Caribbean communities in Canada. Silvera is also the editor of *The Other Woman: Women of Colour in Contemporary Canadian Literature* (1995), a collection of essays and interviews that documents the writing lives of over twenty women of colour.

HER HEAD A VILLAGE

(for Nan)

Her head was a noisy village, one filled with people, active and full of life, with many concerns and opinions. Children, including her own, ran about. Cousins twice removed bickered. A distant aunt, Maddie, decked out in two printed cotton dresses, a patched-up pair of pants and an old fuzzy sweater marched up and down the right side of her forehead. Soon she would have a migraine. On the other side, a pack of idlers lounged around a heated domino game, slapping the pieces hard against her left forehead. Close to her neck sat the gossiping crew, passing around bad news and samples of malicious and scandalous tales. The top of her head was quiet. Come evening this would change, with the arrival of schoolchildren; when the workers left their factories and offices, the pots, banging dishes and televisions blaring would add to the noisy village.

The Black woman writer had been trying all month to write an essay for presentation at an international forum for Third World women. She was to address the topic 'Writing as a Dangerous Profession'. This was proving to be more difficult as the weeks passed. She pleaded for quiet, but could silence only the children.

The villagers did not like her style of writing, her focus and the new name she called herself—feminist. They did not like her choice of lovers, her spending too many hours behind her desk or propped up in her bed with paper and pen or book. The workers complained that she should be in the factories and offices with them; the idlers said she didn't spend much time playing with them and the gossiping crew told so many tales that the woman writer had trouble keeping her essay separate from their stories. Some of the villagers kept quiet, going about their business, but they were too few to shut out the noise. Maddie did not often side with the writer, but neither did she poke at her. She listened and sometimes smiled at the various expressions that surfaced on the woman writer's face. Maddie stood six feet tall with a long, stern face and eyes like well-used marbles. The villagers said Maddie was a woman of the spirits, a mystic woman who carried a sharpened pencil behind her ear. She walked about the village all day, sometimes marching loudly, and other times quietly. Some days she was seen talking to herself.

'When I first come to this country, I use to wear one dress at a time. But times too hard, now you don't know if you coming or going, so I wear all my clothes. You can't be too sure of anything but yourself. So I sure of me, and I wear all my clothes on my back. And I talk to meself, for you have to know yourself in this time.'

The villagers didn't know what to make of her. Some feared her, others respected her. The gossipers jeered behind her back.

Plugging her ears against spirit-woman Maddie, the Black woman writer sat in the different places she thought would be good to her. She first sat behind her desk, but no words came. It was not so much that there were no words to write down— there were many—but the villagers were talking all at once and in so many tongues that it was hard for her to hold onto their words. Each group wanted her to feature it in the essay.

Early in the morning, after her own children left for school, she tried to write in her bed. It was a large queen-size pine bed with five pillows in a small room on the second floor. The room was a pale green and the ceilings a darker shade of green— her favourite colour. She was comfortable there and had produced many essays and poems from that bed. Its double mattress almost reached the ceiling. She felt at peace under the patchwork blanket. It took her back to her grandparents' wooden house a mile from the sea, in another village, the tropical one where she was born. Easter lilies, powder-puff trees, dandelions and other wild flowers circled the house. She saw a red-billed Streamertail, then a yellow-crowned night heron and a white bellied Caribbean dove. Their familiar voices filled her head: 'Quaart, Tleeoo-ee, cruuuuuuu-uuuu,' and other short repeated calls.

She wrote only lists of 'To do's.'

washing
cleaning
cooking
laundry
telephone calls
appointments.

At the edge of the paper birds took flight.

Nothing to do with writing, she thought. On days like these, convinced that she would get no writing done, she left the village and lunched with friends. She did not tell her friends about the village in her head. They would think her crazy, like Maddie. When she was alone, after lunch, scores of questions flooded her head.

What conditions are necessary for one to write?

What role do children play in a writer's creativity?

Is seclusion a necessary ingredient?

Questions she had no answers for.

Sometimes, she holed up in the garden shed at the edge of the backyard. She had cleared out a space and brought in a kerosene heater. The shed faced south. Old dirty windows ran the length of it and the ceiling's cracked blue paint threatened to fall. There she worked on an oversize ill-kept antique desk, a gift from a former lover. She had furnished the space with two chairs, a wooden crate stacked with a dictionary and a few books, a big armchair dragged from the neighbour's garbage, postcards pasted on the walls to remind her of Africa. There were a few things from her village: coconut husks, ackee seeds, photographs of birds, flowers and her grandparents' house near the sea.

One afternoon, however, the villagers discovered the shed and moved in. The idlers set up their gambling table. Gossip-mongers sat in a large area and Maddie walked around quietly and read everything written on every piece of paper. Soon they all wanted to read her essay. The idlers made fun of her words. The gossip-mongers said they had known all along what she would write. Offices and factories closed early, as the others hurried into the shed to hear what all the shouting was about.

They were all talking at once, with varying opinions.

'Writing is not a dangerous profession, writing is a luxury!' shouted one of the workers.

'Many of us would like to write but can't. We have to work, find food to support our families. Put that in your essay.'

'Look here, read here, something about woman as a lover and the danger of writing about that.'

The Black woman writer's head tore in half as the villagers snatched at the paper. She shouted as loud as she could that there was more to the paper than that.

'See for yourselves—here, read it, I am also writing about the economics of writing, problems of women writers who have families.' Almost out of breath, she continued, 'See I also wrote about cultural biases.'

'Cultural biases,' snarled a cold, grating voice. 'Why not just plain old racism? What's wrong with that word?' Before she could answer, another villager who was jumping up and down silenced the rest of them. 'This woman thing can't go into the paper. It wouldn't look right to talk about that at a Third World conference.' They all shouted in agreement.

She felt dizzy. Her ears ached. Her mouth and tongue were heavy. But she would not give in. She tried to block them out by calling up faces of the women she had loved. But she saw only the faces of the villagers and heard only the sounds of their loud chatter.

'No one will write about women lovers. These are not national concerns in Third World countries. These issues are not relevant. These,' they shouted, 'are white bourgeois concerns!'

Exhausted, the Black woman writer tried again. 'All I want to do is to write something about being a Black lesbian in a North American city. One where white racism is cloaked in liberalism and where Black homophobia . . .' They were not listening. They bombarded her with more questions.

'What about the danger of your writing being the definitive word for all Black women? What about the danger of writing in a liberal white bourgeois society and of selling out? Why don't you write about these things?'

She screamed at them to shut up and give her a voice, but they ignored her and talked even louder.

'Make it clear that you, as a Black woman writer, are privileged to be speaking on a panel like this.'

'And what about the danger of singular achievement?' asked a worker.

'Woman lover,' sniggered another. 'What about the danger of writing about racism? Police harassment? Murders of our villagers?'

Many times during the month the Black woman writer would scream at them to shut up. And when she succeeded in muting their voices she was tired because they refused to speak one at a time.

On days like these the Black woman writer escaped from the garden shed to play songs by her favourite blues singer, drink bottles of warm beer and curl up in her queen-size pine bed. She held onto the faces of her lovers and tried to forget the great difficulty in writing the essay.

The writer spent many days and nights staring at the blank white paper in front of her. The villagers did not ease up. They criticized the blank white paper. It was only a few days before the conference. 'You have to start writing,' they pressured her. 'Who is going to represent us?'

Words swarmed around her head like wasps. There was so much she wanted to say about 'Writing as a Dangerous Profession', about dangers to *her* as a Black woman, writer, lesbian. At times she felt that writing the paper was hopeless. Once she broke down and cried in front of the villagers. On this particular day, as the hour grew close, she felt desperate—suicidal, in fact. The villagers had no sympathy for her.

'Suicide? You madder than Maddie!' they jeered. 'Give Maddie the paper and let her use her pencil,' they heckled.

'I'm not mad,' she protested with anger. 'Get out of my head. Here'—she threw the blank paper on the ground—'write, write, you all write.'

'But you are the writer,' they pestered her. They were becoming hostile and vicious. The woman writer felt as if her head would burst.

She thought of Virginia Woolf's *A Room of One's Own*. She wondered if Woolf had had a village in her head.

She took to spending more time in bed with a crate of warm beer at the side. Her eyes were red from worry, not enough sleep and too much drink. She studied her face in a small hand-mirror, examining the lines on her forehead. They were deep and pronounced, lines she had not earned, even with the raising of children, writing several essays and poetry books, cleaning, cooking and caring for lovers. She gazed at all the books around her and became even more depressed.

Interrupted by the angry voices of the villagers, overwhelmed by the force of their voices, she surrendered her thoughts to them.

'Well, what are you going to write? We have ideas to give you.' The Black woman writer knew their ideas. They were not new, but she listened.

'Write about women in houses without electricity.'

'Write about the dangers of living in a police state.'

'Write about Third World issues.'

'Write about . . . about . . .'

'Stick to the real issues that face Black women writers.'

'Your sexuality is your personal business. We don't want to hear about it, and the forum doesn't want to know.'

They accused her of enjoying the luxury of being a lesbian in a decaying society, of forgetting about their problems.

She tried to negotiate with them. 'Listen, all I want is a clear head. I promise to write about your concerns.' But they disagreed. 'We gave you more than enough time, and you've produced nothing.' They insisted that they all write the paper. She was disturbed by their criticism. She would never complete the paper with so many demands. The Black woman writer was full of despair; she wanted to explain to the villagers, once again, that what made writing dangerous for her was who she was—Black/woman/lesbian/mother/worker. . . . But they would not let her continue. In angry, harsh voices they pounded her head. 'You want to talk about sexuality as a political issue? Villagers are murdered every time they go out, our young people jailed and thrown out of schools.' Without success, she explained that she wanted to talk about all the dangers of writing. 'Have you ever heard of, read about lesbians in the Third World? They don't have the luxury of sitting down at an international forum and discussing this issue, so why should you?'

Her head blazed; her tiny, tight braids were like coals on fire. The villagers stayed in her head, shouting and laughing. She tried closing her eyes and massaging her forehead. With her eyes still closed, she eased her body onto the couch. Familiar footsteps sounded at the side of her head. Maddie appeared. 'All this shouting and hollering won't solve anything—it will only make us tired and enemies. We all have to live together in this village.' Not one villager joked about her two dresses, pants and sweater. Not one villager had anything to say about the pencil stuck in her hair, a pencil she never used. Maddie spoke for a long time, putting the villagers to sleep.

The Black woman writer slept late, dreaming first of her grandparents' village and then of her lovers. Now Maddie's face came. She took Maddie's hand and they set out down the village streets, through the fields of wild flowers, dandelions, Easter lilies. Maddie took the pencil from her head and began to write. With Maddie beside her, she awoke in a bed of wild flowers, refreshed.

ARITHA VAN HERK

(b. 1954)

'The writer is a mute in disguise,' says Aritha van Herk, 'knowing the deceptions of shaping words with mouth or on the page. Words are themselves trickery, only too often mockery, and their sounding, the displacement of tongue and lips to effect oral language, gestures a double danger. Once spoken, once written, words are not easily recalled/renounced/disavowed/rescinded/recovered: they hover over our lives in ghostly shapes and suggestions meddling with a mythology better left unstated/inart/iculate.' These words from the title text in her book *A Frozen Tongue* (1992) are an instance of what van Herk calls 'ficto-criticism', writing as reading, as a self-reflexive act. A style also characteristic of *In Visible Ink: crypto-frictions* (1991), and of *Places Far From Ellesmere: Explorations on Site* (1990), which she calls a 'geografictione', a coming together of geography and fiction, it reflects van Herk's relentless testing of the boundaries of fiction and criticism, her inclination to locate herself in places where there is friction between reality and imagination, objectivity and subjectivity, present and past.

Born in Wetaskiwin, Alberta, the first Canadian child of Dutch parents who arrived in Canada in 1949, van Herk grew up on her family's farm. She studied at the University of Alberta, where she received a B.A. Honours (1976) and an M.A. (1978) in English. A professor of English at the University of Calgary since 1983, van Herk has read and lectured widely, both in Canada and overseas, and is the editor of many anthologies of western Canadian fiction, including *Alberta Re/Bound* (1990) and *Boundless Alberta* (1993), as well as the editor, together with Rudy Wiebe, of 'Nunatak Fiction', a series of first novels published by NeWest Press.

Her novel, *Judith* (1978), was the first recipient of the Seal First Novel Award. It deals with the only woman farmer in a community set in the region where van Herk grew up. '[F]estive and mournful,' in van Herk's words, it reveals her 'injunction to write the familiar and [her] fascination with the rural grotesque'. It also announces her preoccupation with female characters who rise above the normative behaviour expected of them. Ja-el,

the central character of her second novel, *The Tent Peg* (1981), disguises herself as a man in order to get a job in the Yukon; Arachne is the picara protagonist in her most recent novel, *No Fixed Address: an Amorous Journey* (1986), which won the Howard O'Hagan Prize for Best Novel in Alberta and was nominated for the Governor General's Award. In all her fiction, as van Herk says, she is 'concerned with the unexplored geographies of landscape and person and with the recovery of mythical voice and identification in contemporary time and place'.

'Resistant to and yet complicit with my invented ethnicity,' as van Herk says, she seeks 'to read and write through the palimpsest of class, gender, and multiple personality'. The ambivalence of her relationship to ethnicity is apparent as she talks, in the third person, about 'the novel she has been trying to write for years'. Nearing completion, it is an immigrant novel 'not so much about her own parents' particular experience but about emigration from the Netherlands and immigration to Canada as profound acts of displacement.' She 'has learned that the two problems are not similar, are never the same.'

At once a regional writer and a writer who keeps redefining the borders of regions, van Herk approaches the question of origins by spelling out the hyphen that marks ethnicity ('I am a Dutch hyphen Canadian,' she says), by rereading what Canadian means. 'Canadian: a global immigrant dreaming the future, not conqueror but supplicant, outcast, exile, artist; creator of both past and point of arrival. The *act* of immigration has been omitted, deliberately excluded as an embarrassing part of our lack of definition. After all, it is journey, travel, movement, no *place* to it, maybe no purpose either, only longing and a continuous coming. The ethnic fixation, because it is an easy one, ignores immigration, would rather that decisive and displacing act had never occurred. Pretends it was only a temporary condition, a movement rather than a state of mind.'

Van Herk's novels have been translated into many languages. She was the 1986 recipient of the 45 Below Award as one of the ten best young Canadian fiction writers.

OF DYKES AND BOERS AND DROWNING

And oh, the mouth so full of words that never say themselves, bundled up in a back-wash of that other language, forbidden, choking, the one that everyone laughs at: Dutch, Dutch, Dutch, as ugly as its sound and the throaty gutturals of its pronunciation. Full of connotations of lowness, levelity; Netherlandish the bottom, like the bottom of a throat where words fathomage, clogged, choking, thick with *drakestijn* and drunkenness, their derogatory dungeons clanking in chains around the duplicities of Dutch concerts and Dutch courage, Dutch treats and Dutch cousins, Dutch collars and Dutch flight. Such yawning language is a sham, a cover-up, the language itself insists, compared to English and the derogation of the seventeenth-century Anglo-Dutch wars. Ah, to be a Dutchman; I'm a Dutchman if I do. Synonymous with all despicabilities, and as a term of refusal, the strongest possible term of refusal. And Dutch nightingales may be frogs, yes, lovely in their deep swamps, and yes, in Dutch is prison, terrible trouble, and this reputed fondness for heavy drinking as a substitute for courage, not to mention the constant mention of meanness, going Dutch going Dutch going Dutch going going gone, no generosity, and where shall we find such courage if not in *jenever* (yes, gin) with the *Engels* (yes, English) pursuingly there on the high seas. And in an endlessly Anglo alloy, where can another metal be discerned or alchemized, why not merely take issue with issue and be damned to this Dutchness, this thick-tongued accusation of the floundering sea against dykes and dykes and dykes. And although the claim may be that dyke is a twentieth-century slang word, a neutral ground from which to name against heterosexist declension, or Rita May Brown's, 'Are you really a dyke, Harriet?' 'I rather thought of myself as the Hoover dam' (*Sudden Death*, 1983). Those famous little boys and their famous fingers in the famous story of the famous dyke are really the plug of language grown thick in the back of the throat, grown mossy and sticky with twigs, holding back a flood of sea/she, the articulate water, a breach.

Tied to this tongue is a cartage of humiliation, enumerated and cavilled uncivilization, the *gauwigheid* (yes, quickness, immediacy, a jump to the gun) of affiliation with all that Dutch NOT, or nothing, or absence. A Dutch uncle isn't there, Dutch courage is cowardice shored by alcohol, and Dutchness, oh the sheer thickheaded, cleanser-coated blue serge milkcowedness of it, so boorish, it is better to be not.

Boer.

Another accent, classness classified on top of Dutchness, and yes, there to be defined as well: 'A Dutch colonist or person of Dutch descent in South Africa; of or pertaining to the Boers.' And of course, all their fault, *apartheid* is Dutch, its segregation not only Afrikaans but certainly inscribed by that Dutch origin, its heavy glottal speaking of decision and division. But the division goes deeper, into every corner of a languaged judgment, from *boer* to *boor*, an awkward and always ill-mannered person, a clownish rustic, he's the guy who doesn't know enough to wipe his wooden shoes, let alone take them off at the door, and he is always a peasant, irreversibly a Dutch peasant. Carrying with him his own associations of servitude and boorishness, not to mention rascality and baseness, rusticity, uncouthness, and yes, certainly, simple simple-mindedness. Always, of course from the Dutch *boer*. Strictly, a farmer.

A Dutch farmer, mind you, a farmer who will toil in muck and swamp to recover an inch of land from the north sea, and then will insist on grassing it and ferrying his cows across a canal and leaving them stranded on those soggy islands with nothing to do but eat that grass, in order to produce thick holstein milk from which will be churned butter, and renneted cheese, and both will be spread on renneted *roggebrood* (yes, tough brown bread) and stuffed between the teeth of the same *boer* who doesn't know enough to chew with his mouth shut. The *boer's* circle, endless, unforgiving, inarticulate, indefensible in all that churlish, loutish, clownish uncouthedness, from his blue serge coat with its row of horny buttons to his clodhopping feet.

And the *boerin* (yes, recognizably the feminine form) is no better, with her ersatz apron riding over a hefty chest beside a set of upper arm muscles like hams, she will give birth in the upper bedroom of her farmhouse at seven in the morning and be up to milk those same heavy holsteins that evening, maybe even slapping their flanks just as energetically, while the barely day-old baby in the *kram* (yes, the crib, the baby basket) is already learning to squall without answer, will certainly learn to wait her turn.

Ah yes, *boer*, tied to jacks and knaves and their belches, the way they turn the cards the other way, like the Dutch and their auctions, every possible order reversed to a contrary of what everyone else knows is good sense. And where's the melody in any Dutch concert, its uproar, its quarrelsome speechifying? While the *Boer* enjoys himself and the *boerin* shugs her shoulders, willing to tussle or lunge. And the *boerderij* (the farm, of course) continues on its merry and impossibly productive way, the animals bearing and breathing and switching their tails over great splats of cowshit, and the hens pecking the eyes out of the garden.

It is clear they have no sense of place or location, culture be damned, *de boer opgaan* (yes, it's the road) there they go, peddling round the countryside, selling whatever they can, and stopping often for flagons of beer, so that they can (albeit happily) *een boer laten*, let go a boer, or belch. And yes, there's a strange acceptance of adversity, *lachen als een boer die kiespijn heft*, laughing like a boer who has toothache, oh yes, laughing on the wrong side of one's face, out of the wrong side of one's face, bittersweet, *zuurzoet*, contrary again, and who cares if the teeth are rotten, or the boer can't bear the snotty dentist with his eternally clean and manicured hands, that has nothing to do with anything, at least not with making a living or putting up with the tribulations that persist.

And neither *boer* nor *boerin* minds their cousinal *boerenbedrieger* (yes, the one who takes the money and runs), trickster incarnate, pissing behind the *bomen* (yes, trees, ordinary trees), and even the trees have more culture and nature, more history than that ugly lot, celebrating its eternal country wedding, *boerenbruiloft*, with noisy noise, amplified glee and yodelling. For the *boerendochter* (yes, the farmer's daughter), that country girl, doesn't know the difference, does she, that you don't lick the jam from your knife, or scratch your inner thigh without thinking too hard about the itch or its need. And even the *boerenjongens*, who might be her brothers, or the country lads, their ruddy faces and their ill-cut thatched hair, enjoy slurping up their namesakes, *boerenjongens* (yes, raisins in brandy), the cheap stuff of course, strong enough to make the eyes water and the palms tingle. The more elegant, effete, the more christmassy and fussed over *boerenmeisjes*, and the *je* diminutive is a given for those peasant daughters (yes, peasant girls), love to fish finger them out of the crockery crocks with their nails never quite clean, *boerinmeisjes*, (yes, apricots in gin). Such excess calls for a celebration, doesn't it, loud and unruly? *Boerinkermis* (yes, a country fair), and every one of those clodhoppers can roam from kiosk to kiosk with their mouths open, jocular noise filling their over-large ears, *boerenkool* (yes, curly kale), but cabbages are delicate and refined next to those great handles, jug ears.

Ah, easy to want to believe that this rusticity is overdone, overstated, there must be a redemptive strain under such a language act, such judgment in the usage. No, there's more. The (yes, the stupid ones) *boerenkinkels* and *boerenkaffirs*—and of course, *kaffir* (yes, the Afrikaner designation for black, or useless, depending on the occasion) has been shifted onto the shoulders of the other, again South African parlance, but the *boer* still hears, carries, and weighs. Dull, beneath contempt. The knowledge of being and the essence of *boer*. Quite simply, calmly, without mitigation, stupid, in manners, in habit, in knowledge. Accepted parlance, and in an English-speaking enclave of superiority, my students can make fun of boors—the mannerless—in every pejorative way, and never even conceive of the hurt they inflict. The quick flash of pain in my father's eyes, he who has always been a *boer*, a genuine, quiet, and simple man who believed and still believes in working hard with his hands, who believes that raising food is a good thing to do for other people, for the world, and although he has never gotten rich, and although he is not a sophisticated thinker, he knows that *boer* is a word that degrades him, although his actions have never come out of a desire to degrade others. And as for the farmer's daughter, with the cumulative associations of both boorishness and déclassé availability, she who will sleep with every trickster in every hayloft, whose foreground is ignorance, how then to translate that 'delevated' role to the one I am trapped in now, where language is a high-strung, well-bred instrument that my clumsy hands and manners are supposed to manage well? If oblivion is no excuse for racism, does it pass for classism?

Boer.

And why not *agrariër*, the wider more politic arm of agrarian, agriculturalist; or *iemand die een agrarisch bedriff leidt* (yes, someone who runs an agricultural business)? No fun there, the appropriations of manners and mores get effaced in such technicalities and *wat een boer!* (yes, what a boor!) is of no use if it doesn't attribute superiority. *Iemand zonder manieren, lomperd, kinkel*; someone without manners, a clodhopper, a yokel; *boerenpummel*, a lout. And annexed to those attributions, the parking garage of staticity, refusal to change, such loutishness implies the luddite too, unable to adjust, accept progress. *Wat de boer niet kent, dat eet hij niet*; if the food is unfamiliar, the farmer won't eat it, meat and potatoes better be what they pretend to be. *Ter aanduiding van een conservatieve houding*; the mark of a resistant conservative, and all its baggage, conservatism. Easy to rest that attribution on the shoulders of a *boer*, those shoulders are broad, drafthorses to pull the heavy load of cultural distinctions and intolerances.

And the permissions of paternalism, the generous condescension of those who know better, who can afford to practise the cultural superiority of imitation. *De boer opgaan* (going out), said with a lilt, a note of humour, indulgence; *naar buiten gaan om te wandelen*, a leisured attendance of the outdoors for a stroll, imagining that leafy country lanes and glorious ponds are the life-realm of farmers, those lucky folks who never have to endure the heft of the silver fish knife, the lozenge of *neetjes voorgebeeld* (yes, nicely turned out, polite). And this imperial gesture will go so far as to bestow a patrician nod of recognition—*soms* (only sometimes, mind)—*als aanduiding van zuivere kwaliteit*, an indication of genuine quality! What a pinnacle to achieve, but the subtext here too, the class beyond and above using the mark of *boer* to anoint authenticity.

Examining these connotative figurations now, under the glass of *Inglish*, I begin to see and to understand why, in the powerfully Anglo world that my parents (Dutch *boers*) chose to emigrate to, displacing themselves from the comfort and safety of their known context, Dutch as place and language, I have tried and remarkably succeeded in effacing as much as possible of both my Dutch and my *boer*.

Passing, bell hooks calls it, and her analysis of passing as a cultural camouflage is one that I understand more clearly recognizing my own abrogation of both Dutch and *boer*. And it might seem easy enough, given my skin, visibility invisible, my only marker my name and sometimes a tinge of pronunciative oddness left over from the language I first spoke, before I so assiduously attached myself to English, determined to pass. Although there are certainly those who will smilingly and patronizingly insist there's an indelible mark of the boer in my vernacular enthusiasms, my often *common* language. So be it. I must, I suppose *Inglish* them too.

Back to the ubiquitous Dutch fable of the famous little boy with his famous finger in the famous *dyke*, the imploded metaphor of holding back a flood, an inundation, a wash of sea/she. More than anyone and with good cause, for a people who wrested land, inch by inch, from the sea, the Dutch fear of drowning, the landperson's (yes, *boer*) dread.

It was with a shock of recognition, my own terror of water, having once almost drowned because I stepped into a sudden and ear-filling hole in Buffalo Lake, Alberta, that I read in Simon Schama's *The Embarrassment of Riches: An Interpretation of Dutch Culture in the Golden Age*, his research on the Amsterdam *Tugthuis*, or house of correction (yes, jail), where one of the sentences or '"correctives". . . was the drowning cell or "water house"' (Schama, 22). Jan de Parival refers to it in 1662:

> If they do not want to work [the incorrigibly idle] they are tethered like asses
> and are put in a cellar that is filled with water so that they must partly empty
> it by pumping if they do not wish to drown. (Schama, 22)

Tourists went to watch. And many accounts there apparently are, describing this punishment cell as a cistern where delinquents or lawbreakers were set to work, 'placing only a pump by them for relief whereby they are forced to labour for their lives' (Schama, 22). One observant observer bothered to note that it took only a quarter of an hour for the cell to fill, were the pump not energetically employed. This drowning, a submersion. But most important, a punishment especially reserved for the incorrigibly idle, those unwilling to work with their hands, to use the *boer's* instrument.

Each time I hear the word *boer* I imagine myself in such a cell, *vochtig* (yes, damp) and tight. There is a pump in there with me, the old-fashioned kind with a long handle and a gushing mouth, the kind we actually had in our farm kitchen when I was a child. Crazily, it is the wrong kind of pump, the kind that pours water into a space rather than pumping it out. But that is the uncontrollable nature of the imagination when it is coupled with our meagre experience.

For there is water, rising, full of voices, upper class, condescending. I am not sure if the pump is Dutch and the water is English; or if the water is Dutch and the pump is English. Or if the pump is what I pass for and the water is my inevitably lower class background. All I know is that I must work the handle (with my solidly Dutch peasant body), because the water is rising and I cannot swim. Right now, it is inching past my knees.

NEIL BISSOONDATH

(b. 1955)

'[T]he only label that I am happy with,' says Neil Bissoondath, is that of "Canadian writer" ... because it means everything and it means nothing, because it includes Rohinton Mistry, Margaret Atwood, Robertson Davies, Timothy Findley, Neil Bissoondath and M.G. Vassanji. It is such an open concept ... There is no label, there is no stereotype to be attached to it any more. ... And that makes that label comfortable.' Bissoondath's acceptance of the label 'Canadian' marks in a way the point of departure of his controversial book *Selling Illusions: The Cult of Multiculturalism in Canada* (1994).

A 'book of a somewhat pugnacious kind', as he says in an interview, it begins by declaring Bissoondath's 'complete independence of all political parties', or, as he puts it elsewhere, that he is 'an enemy of ideology of any kind, political, racial, religious. All ideology depends on stereotypes, and human life is not so simple.' He acknowledges, and traces, his origins—'I was born a Trinidadian. I was brought up a Trinidadian. But that was a long time ago. I am no longer Trinidadian. ... I do not share the hopes, fears, joys and views of Trinidadians'—but, at the same time, he privileges his present: 'Nowhere [in Canada] have I felt myself a stranger. Alienation, expatriation, exile: they are just words to me now, not personal issues; they are intellectual concepts that fascinate me precisely because they are so distant.' Presenting his book as one that 'does not claim to be an objective examination of multiculturalism', Bissoondath attacks the Canadian federal policy and its various forms of implementation because they 'manipulate the ethnic communities'. As he says, 'multiculturalism constantly throws your ethnicity at you, thereby putting you at arm's length from society at large.' Multiculturalism, Bissoondath argues, and cultural events such as the 'Writing Thru Race' conference do not help eliminate discrimination. It is 'through effort, through work, through education' that 'Italians, or the Jews, or the Irish, or the Japanese ... [who] suffered through a period of discrimination, sometimes very serious discrimination ... made their way into the mainstream.' His vision of Canadian society, as he says in an interview, is one 'that

from the beginning makes an attempt to be colour-blind'.

The descendent of indentured labourers from India, Bissoondath was born in Arima, Trinidad, and grew up in Sangre Grande before arriving in Toronto in 1973 to study at York University. After he graduated with a B.A. in French (1977), Bissoondath taught French and English as second languages while pursuing his writing. With the assistance of a Banff School of Fine Arts scholarship, he completed his first book, *Digging Up the Mountains* (1986), a collection of short fiction about immigrant characters from various ethnic backgrounds.

A Casual Brutality (1988), Bissoondath's highly acclaimed novel, was the winner of the W.H. Smith-*Books in Canada* First Novel Award and a finalist for the Trillium Award. Its protagonist, Raj, an East Indian who studied and lived in Toronto, narrates his life story while he is on a return flight from his Caribbean island to Canada. Having lost a Canadian wife and their son to the racial violence that has torn his Caribbean island apart, Raj shares Bissoondath's resistance to ethnicity and avoids any identification, including glances of recognition, with other Caribbeans in Toronto. This novel was followed by another collection of short fiction, *On the Eve of Uncertain Tomorrows* (1990), also about various immigrants who lean for support on each other in their encounters with the Canadian system.

Bissoondath believes that 'writers have no social function. Writers have one function, and that is to tell a good story.' Yet his fiction revolves around many of the social problems that afflict immigrants. His second novel, *The Innocence of Age* (1992), shifts its focus from immigrants, who now appear only as secondary characters, to deal with the relationship between a father and a son. Written after his father's death, it is, as Bissoondath has described it, about 'people very different from myself, who have appropriated white, WASP faces. ... It is a search of what unites them in all their differences.'

A resident of Montreal, Bissoondath was the writer and host of a documentary about fathers and sons broadcast on CBC television.

ON THE EVE OF UNCERTAIN TOMORROWS

It is the violence of beating wings that attracts Joaquin's attention.

Two pigeons, colour only hinted at in the half-light, press in fluttering desperation against the chickenwire enclosing the little wooden balcony. They are too engrossed in battle to notice him at the open door. The air—though soft with the underlying warmth of the spring Jeremy Windhook, the lawyer, says is coming—feels cold, and he folds his arms against its subtle bite.

The wings of the birds flare like pouncing condors, the male—Joaquin now understands—pinning the female beneath him. He sinks his beak into her neck feathers, inflicting submission; steadies himself and, avoiding the ineffectual battering of her wings, awkwardly mounts her.

In the distance, past the complex geometry of withered buildings—garages, storerooms, walls of tin and brick—pressing in on the rear of the rooming-house, the colourless towers of a few tall buildings of the city sit one-dimensional against the sky. They suggest an unknown life, a world of blood and flesh and everyday ambition, a life within his sight but not, still, yet, within his grasp.

The wings scratch and scrape at the wire, batter at it. Create, in their terrified clamour, a raucous plea for escape.

His heart races, temples engorge with blood. Lucidity slips, his mind an ungraspable swirl, as he steps out onto the balcony, knowing for the moment nothing but the noise of the birds.

Slaps at the wire with the back of his open hand.

To no sound, no effect.

They cannot—will not—take note of his protest.

He stands back. Horrified. Witness, in the quiet of the morning, to unwilling coupling, an avian rape. It is the way of nature, he tries telling himself. But they are unattractive birds, with panicky, red-rimmed eyes, and this lack of beauty denies them his sympathy: they call to mind infection, physical corruption.

It is all over in seconds. The male has answered the call of nature, the female has been violated. Then, unconcerned, their congress concluded, they wing away in separate directions, are quickly swallowed by the dark grey sky.

Only then does it occur to Joaquin that the wire netting wrapped around the balcony is there not to keep the pigeons in but to keep them out, its function reversed. And he is the one confined, by the chicken wire and by so much more.

'They say that the waiting is the worst thing.' Amin, who says he will one day take the name Thomson, carefully pours the boiled coffee into their cups. 'But it is not so, I believe.' Joaquin silently admires Amin's delicacy, the economy with which he speaks, moves, handles objects, as if he has an abhorrence of excess.

Amin, usually not an early riser, has been up for a while, fussing and puttering in the bathroom. His curly black hair glistens with a shampooed freshness. His every movement tosses off a perfume that conjures for Joaquin a sweet but sweaty armpit. Amin is wearing the outfit that Jeremy Windhook brought him last week: a simple white shirt, pleated trousers, dark socks. It is a specific look that Jeremy Windhook seeks, that of a genteel poverty, an effect he must labour over for people like Amin, who, in their hunger, can so easily look brigand-like. Amin has taken special care this morning. He has showered, he has shaved, he has even clipped his nose hairs—for today, Joaquin knows, is his tomorrow; today is the day that will determine whether tonight he celebrates, or whether tonight he cries.

'The waiting is simple, after what we have been through.' The words swish easily from between his barely parted lips, as if he speaks only with his tongue. 'The hard part is not knowing what tomorrow will bring for me. Where will I be? What will I do? Will I be happy, or will I be sad?' He lets the condensed milk flow long and thick into his coffee, stirs it without letting the spoon clink against the side of the cup. 'These are sad questions, my friend, to ask about tomorrow. No man should have to ask them, I believe.'

Joaquin takes his coffee cup in both hands, blinks rapidly at the steam as he raises it to his lips.

'You did not sleep last night,' Amin says.

Joaquin smiles minutely at him. The coffee is bitter, the boiled grounds gritty between his teeth.

'I see it in your eyes, my friend. It is not good, I believe.' He sips from his cup, adds, 'Eh?' Amin has an ear for language. The exclamation is one of his new acquisitions. Joaquin thinks he is having an affair with one of the secretaries in Jeremy Windhook's office, although Amin says she is only helping him with his English.

Joaquin gives him a thin smile, an acknowledgement of his concern. But he is not sure how he really feels about Amin; he's too self-confident, in the sly way of the street survivor. Joaquin worries when Amin claims a communality of experience with him. He has never spoken to Amin of his life, has listened with silent skepticism to Amin's eagerly offered autobiography of civil war, starvation, forced conscription. Joaquin wonders whether Jeremy Windhook has told Amin his story; but Jeremy Windhook has never mentioned any of his other clients to Joaquin, so he has no reason to believe this. He thinks instead that Amin is simply assuming the comradeship of those involved in the same enterprise. It is, he thinks, a sign of Amin's struggle with his isolation, the isolation they all share.

Amin reaches into the cupboard for a box of crackers, stuffs two into his mouth with one hand as the other digs into the box for more. He no longer bothers to offer them to Joaquin, knows he does not like their salty dryness.

In the silence disturbed only by Amin's crunching, Joaquin wonders whether he should tell him about the pigeons—it seems somehow important—but Amin's camouflaged nervousness reveals itself in the desperation of his jaw. Joaquin knows that his tale of the pigeons will force Amin's natural melancholia to the surface, will smother his summoned ebullience. So he says nothing.

This day has no dawn.

It is the sun, in any case, and not mechanical precision that marks Joaquin's sense of time. Midday or midnight on his illuminated alarm clock is meaningless. So it is only with the lightening of the sky, its dimming of the lights in the distant buildings, that the day after tomorrow truly becomes tomorrow.

Tomorrow: it is like a forbidden woman, enticing, creeping into his daydreams, invading his fantasies. It robs him of sleep, grates his nerves into a fearful impotence.

It was earlier, when he couldn't stir except with the greatest of effort, when the stillness that gripped his body threatened to harden into a conscious permanence, that he struggled from the clasp of the blankets and trudged the cool confines of his room. He was thankful, in those moments of struggle, for the nightlight—the glowing Mickey Mouse face Jeremy Windhook's little daughter no longer needs—that held the darkness at bay. Joaquin cannot abide darkness. He has had too much of it, has experienced too intimately the concrete and imagined terrors of it. So he stalked his room in the thin glow, three paces one way, three paces the other, the scuffed boards squeaking like mice underfoot.

Stalked through the figures and effigies of nighttime evocations: the slow tearing of nails from fingers, the cracking of bone, the bite of saw-toothed metal into nipple. Liquid coursed thick and warm across his stomach. The gurgle of strangulated breath caught his throat, a blindfolded darkness pressed in on his eyes. Pain came in vivid memory, flushing hot and cold through his belly and into his chest. His hands throbbed, nipples burned—

Space: he let himself quietly out of the room, padded through the darkened corridor to the kitchen. To the tyranny of shadowed things: the fridge, the stove, the sharp angles of cupboards. The tap dripped rhythmically, maddeningly, into the aluminum sink. He tried the light, but it wouldn't work—the bulb had blown the day before and no one had bothered to change it—and so he opened the door to the little balcony, for space, for air, for escape from the demons of his mind.

Amin, satisfied, belched contentedly into his cupped palm. In the webby light, the hairs on the back of his hands and fingers stand out like stiff, black bristles. He offers more coffee and Joaquin accepts with a nod of his head. Amin refills the cup, careful not to pour in too much of the sediment. He empties the grounds into the sink, rinses the pot, places it on the counter; turns on the stove and, hands clenching and unclenching in his pant-pockets, waits for the burner to redden.

From within the house float the distant stirrings of the awakening others: doors and floorboards creaking, the splash of water and the tremble of old pipes, throats discreetly cleared. They are seven in all, the Magnificent Seven, as Jeremy Windhook mumbles in moments of exasperation: Joaquin, Amin, a Vietnamese couple, a Haitian, a Sikh, a Sri Lankan. Except for the Vietnamese couple—the man restless, the woman watchful, the two hard-eyed in the way of the ravenous—who spend much time walking the streets of the city, the others keep to themselves, frittering time away in newspapers, television, comic books, or the solitary flipping of cards. Joaquin prefers it this way—life has taught him that the friendliest smile may conceal the sharpest teeth—but he is secretly grateful, too, for Amin's extroversion, the ease of his conversation, the way he will begin talking as if he has been asked a question when he has not been—or as if he is anticipating the questions he may be asked and is eager to provide the answers. Amin fills empty time, provides distraction, but not in the impersonal way of the television; this is what Joaquin appreciates about him, why Joaquin will sit and listen to him, watch the graceful and communicative gestures of his hands, watch his smoke turn the air a soft blue-grey.

Amin takes a cigarette from his shirt pocket, holds the unfiltered end to the glowing element until a thin curl of smoke rises from it. Flicking off the stove, he pulls carefully at the cigarette, encouraging the fire, sucking until the end glows healthily and smoke billows from his nostrils. Sitting on the chair with an uncommon energy, he crosses his legs, looks intently at Joaquin through narrowed eyes, says, 'I will tell you why Thomson.'

Joaquin already knows why Amin says he will one day change his name to Thomson, but he does not interrupt, for to do so would be to disrupt Amin's optimism, his insistent planning for tomorrow; and thus to disrupt his own. And what else do they have, people like him and Amin and the Vietnamese and the Haitian, but fantasies of tomorrow, how it will be, how they will be? Besides, he likes the deliberation Amin has brought to the enterprise. It shows an initiative he wishes he himself had.

'Because no other name will do, I believe.' He sucks at the cigarette held between thumb and index finger. 'Canadian people respect certain names, but sometimes they fear them, too. Names of men who are rich and who are bright—maybe too bright, eh? Rich, bright men must not expect popularity in this world.'

Joaquin nods in agreement. Amin speaks like a man of the world, a man who understands much beyond his circumscribed experience—and who is he, this Joaquin, electrician by profession, union organizer by necessity, to contradict him? So he listens to Amin, believes he is learning something useful.

'So Thomson it will be. Rich, and bright, no doubt. But not a name that makes simple people—what is the word?—thrimble?'

Joaquin nods again. He thinks of the word *temblar*, raises a quivering hand before him.

'Yes, it is thrimble, I believe. This, the name Thomson does not do to simple people. Respect, yes, and admiration. But thrimble, no. So this is who I will be, eh? Amin Thomson, Canadian.'

Joaquin smiles thinly at Amin, envies him his certainties.

Amin goes to his room to finish getting dressed. The Vietnamese couple—eyes of a hounded intelligence—come quietly in. With a challenging glare at Joaquin, they slam the balcony door shut and—an eye always on Joaquin—wolf down a couple of peanut-butter sandwiches. They are gone after only a few minutes.

The Sikh, his hair twisted into a knot on top of his head, comes in, makes coffee, and drinks it sitting across the table from Joaquin. They nod at each other, but neither speaks.

Outside, the day proceeds through heavy cloud. Pigeons, soaring in the distance, present swift silhouettes.

To Joaquin, the day already feels old.

He looks at his hands, as he does at least once every day. They continue to heal. Slowly. Very slowly. They will never be as they were before, although the doctors tell him greater flexibility will return in time. He will never again hold a screwdriver or a pen—it is how they put it, confirming the expertise of those responsible—but he may, with patience, be able to type.

Jeremy Windhook, a solemn young man intent on evidence, proof, *the full story*, tells him with no hint of irony to look on the bright side. Show them your hands at the hearing, he says, keep them in plain sight, *front and centre*. They have never seen hands like yours. Let them see the fleshy cavities where once there were fingernails, let them see the knotty lumps of crushed knuckles left untended, show them the scars on the back where once flesh was sliced through to the whiteness of bone. Throw the scars at them, he says, bring home to them the enthusiasm with which your hands have been redesigned. Evidence, yes. Dramatic and irrefutable. Jeremy Windhook cannot see his hands without blanching, but it is as if he is in love with them, he speaks of them like a teenager ruminating on imminent coitus: with fascination, with fear.

And what more do you want, Mr Lawyer? Joaquin thinks. Maybe that I sit there naked so they see the greater mutilation? The hardened welts on back, chest, buttocks?

Tell them about the whip of steel cable, he urges.

The tattoo of cigarette burns on my stomach?

Marlboros, weren't they?

The circle of ragged flesh that has replaced my left nipple?

Make them feel the bite of the sharpened pliers.

All the practised disfigurement to which I have been subjected, Jeremy Windhook?

But no, Jeremy Windhook has had pictures taken, from every angle. His briefcase is stuffed with medical reports—the language cool and factual, menus of distress that Joaquin has seen—detailing anal violation, organ disruption, bodily dysfunction. It is amazing, Jeremy Windhook says—with fear, with fascination—that he survived.

Joaquin is relieved when, as the Sikh leaves, Amin returns. He is wearing the sombre grey jacket that is the final touch to the outfit Jeremy Windhook has provided. He sits and laces up his shoes. They are of brown leather, do not match the rest of his clothes, but they are freshly shined. He has decided not to wear the tie. Ties, like nooses, make him nervous. 'Do you know, Hakim—' It is Amin's name for Joaquin, his closest approximation. '—that it takes thirty-five gallons of sap to make one gallon of maple syrup?'

'Sap' is not a word Joaquin knows.

'It is juice from a tree,' Amin explains. 'They take it the way doctors take blood. Then they boil it to make a sweet syrup. It is a Canadian delicacy, I believe.'

Joaquin knows where Amin gets all this information, from his friend the secretary and from the newspapers he is always reading. He hopes that one day he, too, will acquire such knowledge.

Amin suddenly stares at him. His eyes, of a glittery and undiluted black, are steady and imploring. 'You know, Hakim,' he says, his voice breaking, 'you know.'

Joaquin nods: he knows.

'It is not too much to ask, I believe. A simple life. Khappiness. We forget to enjoy it when we have it, we let it wash over us like water—and then it is gone. If only we knew how to record it, like a film, so that we can recall it and comfort ourselves with the memory. But our brain—it is not strong enough. Khorror will come back with all its power. Khorror will frighten us many months later. But khappiness? Khappiness many months later will make us sad. This is the thing, Hakim. We, you and me, have too many prisons—' He taps at his temples with a finger. '—here.' His breathing goes raucous. 'We must learn how to make the keys, Hakim, for when our tomorrow comes.'

If our tomorrow comes, Joaquin thinks but does not say, for he wants to believe Amin is right yet fears, too, to believe it.

The front door bell buzzes twice. Amin glances at his watch. 'Jeremy Windhook,' he says.

They hear the door being opened, the Haitian's gravelly voice greeting the lawyer.

Amin stands up tucking his shirt more neatly into his pants. He buttons the jacket, runs his hands through his hair. 'Well?' he says.

Joaquin examines him, finds him stiff-looking. He reaches out and undoes the jacket button.

Just before Amin leaves, he glances through the window at the sky. The clouds are thinning, beginning to break up. 'Look, Hakim,' he says, 'the sun! It is a good sign, I believe, eh?'

Joaquin stands up. He cannot speak. Instead, he offers his damaged hand and, for long seconds, they share a firm handshake.

The day advances steadily into the forecaster's prediction of bulky cloud rifting into periods of delicate sunlight. The streets are dry. Cars rumble by spouting music, tires gritty on the asphalt. A sheet of errant paper, whipped along in the wake of the traffic, rasps on the sidewalk. The air teems with sharp, clean sounds unfamiliar from his months of winter waiting.

Joaquin removes his mittens, unzips his parka, the perspiration that is like that of fever drying instantaneously under his clothes. His senses awaken then, nudged through the heaviness of his fatigue into a heightened mindfulness.

There are people all around, people hungry for the sun like prisoners emerging into a prison yard after a too-long, too-dark night. They lounge smoking on benches in snowbound parks, they haul chairs onto their tiny balconies to read or to day-dream. Coats are bundled, convertibles converted, sunglasses unfolded. A man and a woman walk by, arms around each other. The woman says, 'Spring's around the corner.' The man, with a laugh, replies, 'Yeah, but it's a big corner.'

Joaquin smiles at the little joke. He is enjoying the growing lightness in his legs. He has always been sensitive to weather and is pleased—it is like a sign of a returning normalcy—to find his body reacting with such vigour. For the first time, he feels the city to be a friendly place, an entity apart—so different from the sterile and hermetic offices of officialdom that he cannot imagine the immigration officers he has encountered leading normal lives, relaxing in sidewalk cafés or hugging loved ones. He knows that they must: knows that they watch television, read newspapers, make love. But the implications of their professional functions are, to him, too enormous. Surely they must be immigration officers all the time, as doctors must be doctors all the time, or policemen policemen all the time. So it is, he thinks, so it must be with all people who wield the powers of life and death.

Soon he has left behind the snappier streets, the expensive boutiques and neon-signed cafés and renovated condominiums giving way, as he approaches St-Laurent, to stretches of run-down housing, Korean supermarkets, Portuguese restaurants. The laneways, bordered by crumbling garages, are still dense with snow and dirty ice. Two men in bloodstained lab coats—like morgue attendants, he thinks, clearing the site of a vigorous massacre—unload slabs of fresh-cut meat from a delivery van, while a young boy, attention wandering, sprays a jet of water at the sidewalk.

He turns right at St-Laurent—which Jeremy Windhook calls Saint Lawrence—and walks hurriedly up its length, the crowds here denser, more intent on their business; past the cut-rate stores and dark restaurants, the specialty-food shops and the sex cinema, turning off at last into a quieter street of curtained windows and peeling doors and, quickly, in a movement that feels furtive, into the shadowed cocoon of *La Barricada*.

Miguel, ever watchful, spots him the moment he enters, nods to him, his eyes only slowly losing their suspicion. Satisfied, he puts the beer flute down on the counter and turns away, to prepare, Joaquin knows, two glasses of his spiced coffee.

Miguel keeps his eyes open; is owner, bartender, cook, and watchman all rolled into one. He has installed a bell that warns him when the door is opening; looks for grim men in jackets and ties with badges to flash. They have never come, but all the regulars know that, should Miguel break the beer flute, those who must are to use the door to the second floor in the common washroom while the others, feigning fear, create diversion by heading for the rear exit. It is not a perfect system, but it is a system; it offers a fighting chance—and that, Joaquin appreciates, is all that anyone truly wants.

It is a curious place, small, with whitewashed walls and fake beams overhead, bits and pieces of his country, his continent, scattered around. Baskets hang from the ceiling, shawls cling to the walls, drums and Pan flutes dangle from crooked nails. Travel posters show Andean heights, Machu Picchu, the modernistic sterility of Brasilia. Quietly, as if wafting in from a great distance, the sad music of the mountains lingers just out of reach, a fading memory even before you can seize it.

On one wall, someone has painted lace curtains framing an open window. Through it stretches a field of trimmed grass, trees, flowers, and, in the distance, stark against a perfect and unreal sky, a line of women colourfully dressed but strangely lifeless. Joaquin finds it a profoundly unsettling work, a vision of rural paradise in which humans are trespassers. A beautiful and angry work, a work of despair. He sits always with his back to it.

Miguel brings the coffees over, the empty beer flute balanced between them; sits in front of Joaquin with elbows on the table, chin resting on his interlaced fingers.

He is a handsome man, his curly black hair, infrequently cut, generously sprinkled with silver. He sleeps little, always looks tired; tends *La Barricada* until late at night, then works into the early hours of morning at the jewellery he fashions as a lucrative hobby. It is these bracelets and earrings and intricate necklaces of silver that keep *La Barricada* afloat; he wholesales them to jewellery shops on St-Denis, enters the profits into the café's books as dinners served and coffees consumed. He sips at the coffee, licks his lips. 'You heard about Flavio?' he says in a flat voice.

Joaquin thinks of the sad-eyed young man he's often seen sitting by himself in a corner of the café. Remembers his discomfort at Flavio's hermetic absorption.

The truth is that Joaquin would not come here if he felt he had a choice. The furniture, of worn wood, is too decrepit, lends the place a dismal air, emphasizes somehow its sense of spirit broken into timidity. It is like a closet for the soul, built for containing dusty memories of lives long lost, for perpetuating the resentments of politics long past. Here, he thinks, there is no tomorrow; here, yesterday becomes forever.

'They're sending him back.'

Back—a fearful word.

Yet where else is he to go? A chic café on St-Denis? A glitzy bar on Ste-Catherine? He's tried doing both, but in each everyone—or, at least, so it seemed—noticed his hands. Here, too, they are taken note of, but the response is not of questions or queasiness. No, here his hands are accepted as simply part of the universal damage; they evoke no shy curiosity, no willed sympathy, no embarrassed revulsion. Everyone either has endured more or knows of someone who has. And everyone has loved ones who have been, as Miguel says, 'thrown through the Devil's Doorway'. It is why he is drawn to *La Barricada*, why he feels safer here than anywhere else.

'They say he wasn't involved in enough union activity.'

Enough—what is enough?

'Not enough to endanger his life.'

Joaquin shivers, twice.

More reason for discomfort: in the corner where Flavio sat, a young woman, Teresa, whom everyone calls Tere, sits biting her nails, or rather not her nails—they are too eaten down for that—but the flesh around them. Joaquin has seen the blood on her fingertips. Miguel has told him Tere's story. They had their Canadian papers, Tere, her husband, their two children; but on the night before their departure, with their farewell party in full swing, the door burst open. There were scuffles and screams, a brief burst of machinegun fire; and her husband was gone. Embassy officials reacted quickly; saw Tere and the children safely on the plane north, lodged a protest with the government, and demanded that a search be launched for her husband. But they knew—Tere knew—that all the official steps were just a cruel bureaucratic joke.

So Tere arrived, distraught, with the bewildered children; was met by a social worker who took her to a furnished apartment, left her there with mimed instructions—Tere spoke no English, the social worker no Spanish—that she was to prepare dinner for the children. The social worker returned an hour later, to find the apartment thick with smoke and the legs from two of the dining-room chairs smouldering in a cooking fire in the middle of the living room. Someone thought of calling Miguel, and it was up to him to tell Tere, two days later, that her husband had been found shown through the Devil's Doorway. They had identified him by his ring and clothes; it was all they had to go on, considering the condition of his head and fingers.

Miguel made arrangements. A woman he knew in the community looks after the children while Tere attends English classes or, as she has taken more and more to doing, while she comes here to *La Barricada*. It has been six months, and Miguel doesn't have the heart to force her to do what he knows she should be doing. She is torn, Miguel has told him, between returning to her country, where she still has family, and staying here, where her children have a future. She is, Miguel feels, herself seeing the outlines of the Devil's Doorway through the writhing of her demons.

Miguel says, 'If Canada will not give Flavio a visa, then God will.' Miguel is, in a curious and personal way, a religious man. He can, for hours and with feeling, quote the poetry of the Nicaraguan Cardenal.

Three men huddle in another corner. Two of them are crouched over the hand of the third who sits bolt upright in the chair, eyes shut, lips grimly set. On the table beside them are a box of bandages, a roll of cotton wadding, a bottle of rubbing alcohol, a pair of scissors, and an open package of razor blades.

With a twist of his eyebrows, Joaquin asks Miguel what they are up to.

'Medical care.' Francisco, he explains, cut his hand badly at work a couple of weeks before. He was washing dishes, a glass broke. He had no choice but to go to the Emergency. When they asked him for his medical insurance card, he said he'd forgotten it at home. They sewed up the cut, and warned him to bring the card the next time, when he went to have the stitches removed. Francisco was already paying fifty dollars a week to use someone else's social insurance number, and the man wanted two hundred for use of the medical card. Francisco couldn't afford it, so his friends— one a hospital orderly—were removing the stitches for him. The nightmare, Miguel adds, is if an appendix bursts . . . .

In the corner, Francisco draws a sharp and lengthy breath.

Joaquin thinks: just another day at *La Barricada*. He knows, and appreciates, that he is among the least damaged, least desperate of Miguel's clients. It is maybe, in the end, why he continues to come here, not just for himself but for Miguel, too.

Miguel prepares lunch for everyone, cheese sandwiches with sticks of carrot. Tere remains at her table, nibbles at the food. Francisco's friends have to leave and Francisco, his right hand roughly bandaged, joins Joaquin and Miguel.

As they eat, Francisco complains about the man whose social insurance number he is using. He is a blackmailer, he says, this man who seemed so sympathetic at the beginning. Even though Francisco has not been able to work for two weeks, the man continues to demand his weekly money, is threatening to tip off Immigration if he is not paid in full.

'Who is this man?' Miguel asks.

'Just a man,' Francisco replies.

Joaquin, eating, listening, appreciates Francisco's reticence, understands it. He knows—from the moment his mother's phone call reached him too late at work;

through the hours? days? of darkness to the unexplained release, followed by the harrowing weeks of movement and concealment during the transit north—what it is to be an illegal, understands the fears that lead to continuous vagueness and, eventually, to an invented self. He wonders what Francisco's real name is and for several minutes, as Francisco and Miguel dissect the situation, he tries different names, looking for the one that best matches Francisco's face. It is a haggard face, older than its years, severely scarred by acne; a face that Joaquin could only learn to trust in time. He is neither a Juan nor an Antonio, Joaquin decides, nor a Raul nor an Andres. Luis is too soft, Carlos too round. Alberto, Federico, Mario, Manuel—none quite fits. And then, as he finishes the first half of his sandwich, it comes to him: Francisco has the face of a Jorge.

Jorge. The name echoes in his head, the consonants a harsh whisper. His hands begin to throb and he is forced to drop the carrot stick he has picked up. Francisco and Miguel glance quizzically at him, but return to their conversation after he forces a smile. He tries clenching his hands in his lap—their stiffness prevents the forming of a fist, he can squeeze only so far—but the pain he feels is not a physical one, will not go away so easily.

The pliers, Jorge. No, not those. The smaller ones.

It was his mother who came to him in those moments of searing pain, her teary face alternating with a darkness deeper than that of the blindfold.

You see how he clenches his fist, Jorge. He knows what we want to do, don't you, friend?

A face aging instantaneously at the news of a daughter's dismemberment. A darkness sparkling with comets and exploding stars.

Any sharp knife will do. You just pull it down, from the wrist towards the fingers. See? Everything opens up. Including the fist.

Dark hairs greying before his eyes. The darkness growing brittle.

You put the pliers just so, getting a tight grip. If he's a nail-biter you have to push it into the flesh, but we're lucky with this one, he's not the nervous type, are you my friend? So you work it as you wish, a quick tug—

Face dissolving. Darkness shattering.

—or a slow twist, ripping it away—

Colours, and a roaring in the head.

—either way is effective.

Then only the face, smiling a soothing smile.

Jorge.

A long silence. Then—

Miguel: 'Ten minutes?'

Francisco: 'At least.'

'Maybe a problem with the stomach—'

'Fifteen, even.'

'That long?'

'Maybe longer—'

'Joaquin?'

'Yes—'

'Well? Ten, fifteen, longer?'

'Yes, possibly.'

Miguel's eyes flicker at him—an annoyed, inquisitive look, a look that in an instant realizes, absorbs, questions Joaquin's distance—then focus on a point past him.

Joaquin turns: a plate with an untouched sandwich, an empty chair pushed back from its table. He realizes how distant he has been, he never noticed Tere leaving.

Miguel considers the chair, the nail of his little finger working at a piece of food stuck between his front teeth.

Francisco drains his beer, draws the back of his hand across his lips. He, too, but with less intensity, considers the empty chair. 'So,' he says.

'So,' Miguel echoes.

Joaquin looks from one to the other. His hands, forgotten, relax in his lap, the pain ebbing.

Miguel dislodges the piece of food, flicks it to the floor. Abruptly pushes himself from the table. The beer flute tips, teeters, crashes onto the table top. He frowns at the pieces of broken glass. And then he is running, knocking chairs out of his way.

Blows of his fist on echoing wood.

Joaquin turns, to look.

Miguel is kicking in the bathroom door.

The stickiness that will not wash away from his hands dries quickly in the cold air.

The sidewalks are less crowded now, the streets busy with home-bound traffic. The sky, in the glow of the setting sun, is a brittle, icy blue.

Joaquin walks slowly along with his hands secure in his coat pockets, the air washing cool and fresh through his lungs. He feels good, strong; he enjoys a physical self-possession too long absent.

On impulse, he stops in at a fruit and vegetable store, buys a couple of oranges. The woman smiles as she hands him his change, and he realizes with a gentle jolt that he feels less distant from these people now, strangers become a little less strange not through any act of their own but—in a twist he cannot understand—through an act of *his* own: in this city, he has helped save a life.

It was his fingers, useless for so much, that Miguel pressed to the cuts on Tere's wrists, his parka snatched from the back of his chair that Francisco threw around her shoulders. Miguel and Francisco, faces glistening with sweat, fingers nimble and efficient, worked quickly with the cotton wadding and bandages.

Tere didn't fight, sat flaccid on the toilet cover, glazed eyes passively watching them. She had rested her hands on the edge of the sink but, growing weaker, hadn't been able to hold them there. The tiled floor was slick with blood.

Francisco's bandage came loose. Joaquin saw the fragile blending of the wound, pinpricks of blood forming on the pulpy skin. Francisco ignored it in the greater urgency, and Joaquin thought with a prickling shame of his judgement of him. This intensity, this urge to heal: he was wrong: Francisco was not a Jorge, he just had a misleading face.

Afterwards, Tere begged them in a voice weakened and fearful not to abandon her to the hospital. Her verb struck them all, prompted among them glances of uncertainty. They had stanched the blood flow and Miguel, soothing, reassuring, murmured his assent. While Francisco disinfected and rebandaged his own wound, Joaquin and Miguel helped her upstairs, to the bare room in which those who had to could take refuge. She curled up on a mattress on the floor, one hand resting lightly in the other. Miguel gently checked her bandages and, glancing backwards at her, led Joaquin from the room back down the narrow stairs. He would keep her there, he said, would make the necessary arrangements for the children.

Miguel cleared away the broken glass, poured them each a beer. They drank in silence, absorbed. *La Barricada* seemed to have gone inert. The music was off, there was nothing to say.

Eventually, with nothing more than a nod, Francisco left. Joaquin put aside his unfinished glass of beer, offered to help Miguel clean up the bathroom. Miguel refused with a shake of his head; he seemed, in the aftermath, to have no defence against his fatigue; said he would close the place for a few hours, work at his jewellery.

Joaquin walks along, the oranges tucked into the belly of his half-zipped parka. He is not unhappy that Miguel refused his offer. He did not, in truth, relish the thought of returning to the washroom. Much prefers being out here on the sidewalk, in the grip of his sense of having taken a vital step, looking in on the bars and cafés and little restaurants moodily lit behind glass, at the warmth and suggested security of their growing animation.

He lengthens the way back to the house, following streets never before followed, turning left or right or retracing his steps on pure impulse. As the sky darkens into night, windows frame lamplit scenes of comfort and domesticity: a couple preparing salad; two children tugging at a toy; a man absentmindedly twirling a glass of red wine by candlelight; a woman shuffling through papers in her briefcase. Joaquin drinks them in, these little domestic spectacles; they are so trivial, so inconsequential, so attractive in their banality. And as he watches a cat prancing in pleasure at the opening of a food can, Amin's words come forcefully back to him: *A simple life. Khappiness.*

A faint throb in his hands: Is it too much to ask?

In the sitting room the radio is on low in the background. The Haitian and the Sri Lankan, both slight, shy men, are hunched over the coffee table playing cards. They glance up without interest as Joaquin comes in, watch without acknowledgement as he removes his parka.

He wonders whether Amin has returned yet, but thinks it best not to ask. It would be like prying, would be frowned upon.

In the kitchen, the Vietnamese couple stands guard over a vigorously bubbling pot. They do not take kindly to his looking in so he goes to his room, puts on the overhead light, and sits on the edge of the bed. His mood, seized in the peculiar tensions of the house, robbed of air by the confines of the room, begins to evaporate. A familiar unease reasserts itself, a vice tightening in his intestines. He takes an orange, nips off chunks of the rind, chews them, the tanginess puckering the fleshy insides of his mouth, invading his nasal passages. It is not a pleasant taste, but is one he has grown to appreciate: for a week during his journey north, fresh oranges were his only sustenance; there was no part he could afford not to consume. The flavour calms him and he closes his eyes, returning in imagination to the scenes witnessed long minutes before. The salad, the toy, the wine glass. The cat circling in hungry anticipation—

The buzz of the doorbell jars him back to his room. He listens: the front door is opened, voices murmur.

Careful footsteps approach his door. He thinks: Amin. Drops the orange onto the bed, stands up, opens the door at the first knock.

No, not Amin. Jeremy Windhook. A jacket is draped over his arm. 'For tomorrow,' Jeremy Windhook says, holding the jacket out to him. 'Eight a.m. sharp. Be ready.'

Joaquin takes the jacket, recognizes it. 'And Amin?' he says.

Jeremy Windhook hesitates. Then: 'Amin was refused.'

'Refused?'

'They've classified him an economic refugee.'

'*No entiendo.*' Joaquin thinks: Are you less a refugee, Jeremy Windhook, if you are in danger of dying from hunger rather than a bullet?

'He doesn't qualify under the UN definition. He'll be deported tomorrow.'

'To his country?'

'To Germany.'

'Germany? Why Germany?'

'Because he made his way here from there.'

'But if they say he is in no danger in his own country, why do they not send him back there?'

'Because—' He shakes his head. 'Because it's the rule.'

'Why, Jeremy Windhook? Tell me why.'

'I don't know why.'

'Is it so that another country will do the dirty work for them? The Germans will send him back to his own country, I believe.' As he says the last words, Joaquin hears Amin's voice. 'And he will die.'

Jeremy Windhook says nothing in reply, silently eyes Joaquin.

'You can do nothing?'

'Nothing.'

The word hangs hollow in the room.

Jeremy Windhook turns, leaves.

Joaquin tosses the jacket onto the bed. He sees Amin in a room he cannot imagine. He is sitting, his face in his hands, in despair: 'Amin Thomson,' he whispers. 'My name is Amin Thomson.' Joaquin swallows hard, wipes his eyes on his sleeve. Picks up the orange and makes his way to the kitchen.

The light is off. All that remains of the Vietnamese is the lingering odour of their dinner. He goes to the door, stands, looks out. His hands throb, and he watches for the pigeons, waits for the dawn, here on the eve of his uncertain tomorrows.

VEN BEGAMUDRÉ ◈

(b. 1956)

'I try to be as authentic as a fiction writer can be in my writing, which means using my memories, using photographs,' says Ven Begamudré. Besides achieving verisimilitude, this kind of authenticity also relates to what Begamudré defines as the process of 'transculturalism', a process reflecting the various steps Canadian writers born in or coming from another country have to go through in order to approach their material. 'Because I am not really a part of the Indian community and I don't want to deal with the Indian community where I live simply for material,' he says, 'I write about what I know, what I don't know I research, and what I can't research, I make up. As a result of that, sometimes a scene which I will make up can seem more real than the actual place.' Constructing a fictional world that relies partly on memories and dreams and partly on the imaginative loops of story telling is characteristic of Begamudré's writing process.

Born in Bangalore, India, he was a year old when his parents left him with his grandmother on the island of Mauritius while they pursued their graduate studies in North America. His mother returned to take him back to Bangalore when he was three, and the two of them moved to Canada in 1962 to reunite with his father in Vancouver. The plot of his first novel, *Van de Graaff Days* (1993), although not autobiographical, deals with a family 'that doesn't know how to be a family' because of separations that resemble those in Begamudré's early years. Set in both India and Canada, the novel depicts a couple that must reshape the power dynamics of their roles as husband and wife when they reunite in Canada; it also explores the impact of the Indian caste system on relationships. '[T]hose conflicts,' he says, referring to his novel, 'are much more insidious than the conflicts that occur in Canada based on race. It's not that I try to play down issues of racism or prejudice, but they have to be looked at in the context of the people involved.' This context, Begamudré stresses, is a matter of class background.

Coming from a Brahmin family where women had at least one university degree, Begamudré is very conscious of class differences and how they can shape one's experiences

in Canada, as is the case with the central character in the story that follows. 'There's a lot of agonizing going on about the role of the minority writer in this country,' he says. 'But you have to look at what kind of minority the writer is from, and what class they belong to. The kind of person who comes here from a Third World country and has to write when he's not mopping somebody else's floor is in a completely different position from someone whose parents were allowed into the country because Canada needed doctors or scientists.'

Begamudré, who holds a B.A. (1977) in public administration from Carleton University, worked as a civil servant in Saskatchewan for a number of years before becoming a full-time writer. He began writing during his student years in Ottawa—'three huge novels for mass-market publication' that were never published—but his writing took a different turn after his first visit back to India, to which his father had returned, and after he won a scholarship to the Saskatchewan School of the Arts where he studied creative writing and discovered Canadian literature. His first publication was *Sacrifice* (1986), a novella.

He is the editor of two anthologies, *Lodestone: Stories by Regina Writers* (1993) and, with Judith Krause, *Out of Place: Stories and Poems* (1991), the latter described by Begamudré as an anthology of prairie literature 'on transcultural and other forms of dislocations'. His short fiction has been published in many literary magazines and anthologies, including *The Journey Prize Anthology* (1989). His collection of short stories, *A Planet of Eccentrics* (1990), which includes the story that follows, was the recipient of the F.G. Bressani Literary Prize for prose and the winner of the Saskatchewan Book of the Year Award as well as the City of Regina Book Award. The collection deals, as its title suggests, with characters who occupy off-centre positions, whose understanding of who they are—as immigrants, as women, as old people—depends a lot on how they see themselves mirrored in their immediate world or the world of their memories. Begamudré's immigrant characters, however, never occupy a position that is inherently marginal.

The author of essays as well as of poetry, Begamudré has also published stories for children. A resident of Regina, he was the writer-in-residence at the University of Calgary Markin-Flanagan Distinguished Writers Program in 1994-95.

MOSAIC

(I) ELLEN WHITMORE

Who? Oh, you mean Mr Ramesh. Of course I remember him. He was the sweetest little man. If he'd been taller, he would have been quite the ladies' man, too. I don't see what that particular incident had to do with anything, but, yes, I saw it all. He walked in just after twelve, not the best time on a payday. Especially not before Labour Day weekend. He took one look at the line-up and turned to leave. Then he changed his mind and started making out his deposit slips. What did he call them now? Chits. He did the same thing every month. He deposited half his cheque and bought a rupee draft with the rest.

I don't know if I should say, but he cleared about fifteen hundred a month. He sent the draft home, to India, for about five thousand rupees depending on the exchange rate. I teased him once about having a wife hidden away back home, and he came right back with, 'A Muslim can have as many wives as he pleases. I send the money to a different one each month.' I thought he was serious until I remembered his telling me once he was an orthodox Hindu. When I asked if he ate meat. That's why I liked serving him. I learned something every time.

He was concentrating so hard, he didn't even hear the man. They made such a strange pair: the man with his pot belly hanging out over his cowboy belt buckle, and Mr Ramesh in his charcoal grey suit. That's one thing I could never get over. He had such fine clothes, but he never had that extra bit of sense about how to dress. He always wore cufflinks and a tie clip, though they went out of style years ago. At any rate, he didn't even hear the man say, 'Buddy, can you help me out?' Those were his exact words. The second time, the man spoke louder: 'I said, can you help me out here?' This time Mr Ramesh looked up and did something so totally out of character I thought, 'This can't be the sweet little man I know!' He picked up his things and turned his back on the man. Normally he was so polite he even held doors open for other men. It was all a misunderstanding. Still, there was no reason for the man to shout what he did.

Something like . . . no, I can't repeat what he said. It makes you wonder when you hear language like that in public. Half the people in line turned to look, and some of them had the gall to smirk. Now, it's one thing to laugh at ethnic jokes. I like Irish ones myself, my maiden name being O'Reilly. But racist slurs are a different matter. Mr Ramesh pretended he hadn't heard, but he had. He was facing me, and I saw his mouth go hard, and the tips of his ears turned red. It's strange, isn't it? You'd never think coloured people blush, but they do. You just have to know where to look. Let me tell you something about observing people. We take the train every Christmas to see our grandchildren in Vancouver, and I always insist on sitting near the washroom. Everyone has to go to the washroom, so that way I see everyone in the car at least once. I get to know a lot of people by the end of the trip. Elwood, my husband, says I'm just a snoop, but that's not snooping. That's taking an interest in your fellow man.

Anyway, I felt so sorry for Mr Ramesh, I called him over. Some of the people in line grumbled, but if anyone deserved a good deed just then, it was him. The slip was made out exactly the same as every month, but this time he wanted a hundred dollars in cash. Almost immediately, he said, 'Imagine that fellow begging in a bank! No one begs indoors in India, and certainly not in a bank.' He had such a cute accent, it always made me want to laugh, as if he were imitating Peter Sellers imitating an Indian. 'Oh, Mr Ramesh,' I said, '"help me out" doesn't mean "give me money." It means exactly what it says. Look, that lady is showing the gentleman how to make out his slip. He must be new with us.' Mr Ramesh's face fell after he looked, so I simply had to reassure him. 'I think you did the right thing, though,' I said. I handed him his cash and his passbook and started making out his draft. 'We have people like that in India,' he said. 'They are called scheduled castes. They used to be called outcastes, but one cannot call them that any more.' He raised his eyebrows, like this, only they joined in the middle. 'It would be discrimination,' he said. 'So now the government discriminates against good students by lowering pass marks in college so these people will get degrees. It results in mediocrity only, not equality.' I asked him did he mean they still have castes in India. 'What caste are you then?' I asked. 'Is it not obvious?' he said, almost proudly. 'We are brahmins. We are lighter skinned than most South Indians because, centuries ago, our ancestors intermarried with the Aryans, who came into India over the Hindu Kush. That fellow had no business calling me a black man!'

No, those weren't the man's exact words, but they were close enough. 'Don't you worry about him,' I said. 'He couldn't know a thing about East Indians. But just a second now. I thought brahmins were priests. I read that somewhere.' I simply had to keep him talking, he was so interesting. 'We used to be priests and teachers only,' he said. 'That is why most modern brahmins are well-educated. But now anyone can become a teacher. There is no future in India for brahmin boys, so I came away here.' I said, 'Well, you certainly are making a fine contribution to Canadian society.' I meant it. 'All your people do,' I said. He laughed then and said something I still don't understand: 'That is because the government lets only well-educated Indians into Canada.' Do you think he meant we keep the uneducated ones out? 'Well,' he said, putting his draft away, 'I must be getting back to my office. I am expecting good news this afternoon.' I asked him oh, what's that, but he simply grinned and waved as he walked away.

(II) KAREL LUCHINSKI

Gimme a break. I don't ask people their names. Ya can't reserve a table 'cause there aren't any, not for sittin', an' there's lotsa guys in suits come in. Used to be lot more 'fore that Corn-hole Centre open' up.

Oh him. I read papers too. You sure you're not a reporter, Sweetheart?

Okay, he came in three, maybe four times a week. Always bought a veggie sub. Come to think of it, he does stick out in my mind. First time he came in must've been, Christ, I don't know. Asked for ground chilli peppers on his sub. I told him, 'You want ground chillies, go find a pizza joint.' Yeah, he was in that day all right. I remember those two girls were in here. Do you believe it? Twelve-thirty on a Friday and I could swing a cat in here. Hey, know how to make a cat go woof? Use a bit of starter fluid, light a match and it goes, 'Whhooof!'

The girls that were in here same time as him. Came in just before and ate in. Didn't ask their names either. Made a real mess and didn't throw their garbage in the can. But they were whores, I know that much. You can smell them a mile away. This neighbourhood always smelled of whores and it's getting worse. Used to be they hung out at the hotel other side of Broad. Then people around there got all pious. Cops shut it down, made it respectable. So where do they hang out now? Half a block that way, past the bank. Maybe not such a bad idea. Deposits, withdrawals.

It's coming back to me now. What they looked like, I mean. I only noticed because the guy kept staring at them. One of them was about your, ah, his height. Couldn't've been more than fourteen. I don't care if it was hot that day, I'd blister my daughter's ass if she dressed like that. Problem is, she does. Now this first whore, she was dressed like she was open for business. Haw, haw! Get it? Used to be the government's motto. Had a yellow halter top on. Hell, her old man could've strained Sterno through it, that top was so skimpy. Plus she was wearing these shiny blue gym shorts and sandals. I've seen more cotton on a Barbie Doll. No wonder the little guy's eyes were popping out of his head. He pretended he was trying to make his mind up what to order. As if he ordered anything but a veggie and a milk, day in, day out. Now the other girl, she was older. More sensible, too. Didn't have a sign saying, 'Rape me,' across her chest. Wore a red tube top and real tight jeans. Bet nothing got between her and her Calvin Kleins! Only she wasn't the Brooke Shields type. Sort of dumpy, with boobs like sacks of flour. Bit on the dog side. Hey, know how to make a dog go meow? You freeze it, lay it on a table saw and it goes, 'Nnneeow!'

Funny thing but she was white, so I thought maybe she wasn't a whore after all till she starts coming on to him. Right here, in front of the cash. Smiles real nice and says, 'Hi, want to go somewhere?' That pisses me right off. I yell, 'Hey, I'm selling subs in here, I ain't selling ass!' She just shrugs and goes back to her friend, but the guy actually takes a step over. 'Go somewhere for what purpose?' he asks. Is he kidding or what? Thinks they're tour guides or something? The younger one, the native Barbie Doll looks him straight in the eye and says, 'To fuck.' They start laughing and so do I. Who wouldn't've? The guy had it coming. He was practically slobbering over Miss August there, checking her navel for staples maybe. But when he turned around, he didn't look pissed off at all. Sort of squared his shoulders and said, 'One vegetarian submarine and a white milk, please.' In that Poonjab voice of his. I had everything ready so I handed it over. He must've been pissed off, though, because he paid with a five and and walked out before I could make change. Maybe he was just embarrassed. Just the type who would be, all clean hands and genteel. Don't get me wrong. I keep these hands clean because they handle food, but these nails have seen their share of dirt.

No, I didn't go after him. Gimme a break. Christ, he must've had money to burn. Me, I have to work for a living, on my feet. Look, you want a coffee or what? It's on the house, but you don't have to drink it on the roof. Haw, haw! Get it?

(III) JONI LEWVAN

You know what gets me? Ramesh was the only guy I ever worked with who never made a pass at me. When he talked to me, he looked at my face, not my body. He had class. I'm not crying the blues about how tough it is to have looks, but the way some guys look at you sometimes, it's like you're a banana they're itching to peel. I can see if it happened to a guy like Joe Tschepurny (he's one of the other consultants), but why a nice guy like Ramesh? Getting fired, I mean, not. . . . You know what Joe does if I'm wearing a low-cut dress? He makes sure he's got a handful of paper clips, and when he walks past the word processor, he tries to toss one in here—two points if it slips down. Honestly. Ramesh told him off once, just after starting here, so Joe stopped. I was so proud of him. Ramesh, I mean.

That's when we had the going-away lunch for Mel Smith, at the Chelton. He's our old business manager. Ramesh said he couldn't make it on account of having a doctor's appointment, but I knew he was just making excuses. He came to a barbecue we had on Willow Island in June a couple of months after he started. A meet-the-clients do. You get good at saying, 'Now, now!' when they get you alone and hum, 'You Light Up My Life.' He was so tongue-tied, he just stared at the lake all afternoon. He was the only one who showed up without a date. Poor guy. He just didn't fit in. After four months he still called Mel, Melvin, and Joe, Joseph. Al and Yvan he always called Mr McKendrick and Mr Larouche. They're the ones the outfit's named after? McKendrick-Larouche Consulting. Mel said once Ramesh was too. . . .

Not just distant. Aloof. But that's what I liked about him. It's like being introduced to a guy at a cabaret, and every time he catches your eye, he sort of bows. You know if you even dance with him, you'll end up not liking him as much. That's what being married is like, I guess. If I had to do it all over again, I'd still marry Steve—it's just that before we got married I never thought I'd be hiding his hockey equipment. So he wouldn't sneak out of the house for a game with the boys. Honestly. I put my foot down last winter when he broke his nose again.

I left the lunch a couple of minutes early to drop by the hardware store and get Steve's cheque. Ramesh was in his office when I got in, just after one I guess. He was kind of down, but after I told him Al and Yvan asked about him at lunch, he brightened up for a sec. He'd been waiting to hear about this survey he was designing for one of our clients. Then he went sort of dull-eyed, so I figured I'd sit right down and try and cheer him up. When I asked what the matter was, he said, 'Oh, it is nothing.' He always talked like that—like he learned his English from a book coming over on the boat. Then he told me how he'd made a fool of himself at the bank. 'Oh Ramesh,' I said, 'that guy probably didn't even need the help. I remember this Indian pulled the same stunt at the credit union last week. Expected everyone to help him and tried to butt in ahead of me. The main problem with guys like that—I meant the guy at the bank, not the Indian; everyone knows they've got it rough—is they don't have enough pride.' Ramesh thought about that for a while and said, 'It is probably true what you say about pride. I suppose that is why I am still angry at the fellow. Why could he not have tried to fill a chit and taken it to a teller? She would have helped him.' Then he bursts out with, 'No one helps landed immigrants here! We have to work harder than white men, because we have no constitutional right to be mediocre!' I laughed at that part. 'Oh Ramesh,' I said, 'you don't have to work harder. You're smarter than us. All the Indians I've heard of are doctors or lawyers or big-shot professors.' That's true, you know. The doctor who operated on my mom's spine is East Indian. You won't find many of them running grocery stores like the Chinese people do. Though I hear there's one just opened up near the General. Ramesh used to buy pickles and stuff there. Not dill pickles, mango and lime. He liked his food hot, and I don't mean temperature-wise. He kept a jar of ground chillies in his filing cabinet to eat with his subs. He always had subs for lunch, or cheese sandwiches. That's where he kept those newspapers he read during lunch, flimsy ones that came rolled up in brown paper. First time I opened one, I thought it was an Indian skin mag or something. I wouldn't blame him for reading them, though. I don't know how anyone could live alone like that, but then he has this girl waiting for him back home. I still don't see why he didn't just bring her over here.

He told me once, but I'm lousy with long names. Can you imagine having someone arrange a marriage for you? No way for me, boy. Ramesh said when he finished his degree, he wrote home to his mom and asked her to find him a wife. She sent back a list of six girls with—would you believe it—their pictures. He picked out the three he liked best and went back to India to meet them. He got along really well with one of them, and they decided to get married after he saved up some from working here. Isn't that the craziest thing you ever heard? I wouldn't kiss a guy my mom picked for me, never mind . . . let him touch me. Ramesh never talked about her much, but he said once her name was really poetic and she could play the violin. Not that I know anything about classical music. I could listen to Waylon and Willie till kingdom come. Plus Anne Murray. It really gets me when they talk about that farmer who's always chasing her. They always say he's from Saskatchewan. They drag out 'Sas-katch-e-wan' like it's the boonies. Honestly.

The only thing you could call unusual was after Ramesh went into Al's office. After I got back to the word processor. The door was closed but you could hear them yelling. I even heard Al call Ramesh a wimp. Ramesh opened the door and said something foreign-sounding to Al. Then he slammed the door and walked into his office. He didn't look mad. He just looked . . . defeated if you know what I mean. Didn't even look at me when I asked, 'You okay?' Ten minutes later he left with a cardboard box. I went in his office and saw his degree wasn't on the wall, and the garbage can was full of those flimsy newspapers. He—Oh, shoot, there I go again. I'm sorry. I can't help it. It's just so unfair. I mean, why him of all people?

(IV) AL MCKENDRICK

Sorry about the mess. These are just temporary quarters till we move to the new location. Business is booming. So, let's kick this thing off. Now there's one thing I want to set straight from the start, so there's no misunderstanding. I didn't put Ramesh on waivers because he was Indian. Or because he was short or had an accent. The people we play ball with don't care about such things. They want results. Of course I knew what a blow losing the job would be to him, but it's happened to all of us. Ramesh was out of his league, and he fumbled it. We had good defence in the form of Joe Tschepurny, though. He's the one who suggested, when I first handed Ramesh the ball, we send a draft of the model to our client. To see if it was what they wanted. The answer came back pretty damn quick: n-o. Like a rebound. By the way, are you interested in sports?

Rowing, eh? I took one look at you when you walked in here and thought, 'Now there's a young woman who knows how to look after herself.'

Basically the contract was to study the fiscal health of volunteer organizations. Ramesh had to design a model to survey them and analyze the results. It wasn't a huge job, so I thought he could go it alone. Besides, he'd been treasurer of the international students' club at York. He had an MBA from there and a BSc in math from some Indian university. His qualifications in the statistical area were first class, and he did two years as a stat clerk in Queen's Park before coming to us. He wanted a private-sector challenge, he said, so we gave him one. Unfortunately, he knew as much about our provincial scene as I do about . . . gourmet cooking. I'm a meat and potatoes man myself. Are you hungry? There's a new steak house around the corner.

That's all right, and it's Al, remember? I won't pull any punches, even at myself. I used to shadow box until my knuckles got too bruised. Hah! Certainly I overestimated his ability to learn about the province, but there was more to it than that. We were up to our eyeballs in alligators. Joe never had time to go over Ramesh's model in detail before we sent it off.

I don't concern myself with details. Now Joe's in extra innings revising the model. Something about nominal variables being used instead of ordinal ones, and too many open-ended questions on the survey. You likely know more about those things than I do. I'll be the first to admit I wasn't easy on Ramesh, but he didn't exactly make it easy on me. If he'd been at Mel's lunch it might have been a different ballgame, but damn it all, he wasn't a team player. Never went for a drink with us after work. Didn't even enter Corporate Challenge. Yvan—Mr Larouche, my partner—wanted me to fire him to set an example, but I convinced him to let the rookie opt for free-agent status. It was the decent thing to do. After lunch, I went to his office, the one next to the word processing station. Great girl, that Joni. You should talk to her too. Ramesh was reading his *India-Canada Times*, as usual, waiting for Joe to assign him more work. He'd always drag out a copy at coffee break and lecture us about why the Tamils were massacred in Assam or the Moslems were massacred in Sir Lanka. Sorry, it's the other way around. Last Friday, I remember he was circling an article about Sikhs rioting over that Golden Temple business, something about Mrs Gandhi getting herself in too deep. He grinned and said, 'Good afternoon,' as he showed the paper to me. 'These Sikhs are such violent people, you know. They would make good ice hockey players.' I wasn't too amused, but I wasn't about to break the news with Joni listening. I asked him to step in here and close the door. When he saw me take the letter from our client out, he leaned forward and said, 'So, how do they like our model?' He grinned, he was so excited. 'They don't like your model,' I said calmly. I never raise my voice. The grin stayed on his face, but a twitch started pulling at his right eye. 'That's not possible,' he said. 'You are making a joke.' I told him to see for himself and held the letter up for him to read. Then we had an exchange about how everyone had approved the model before it went out. 'You've embarrassed both Yvan and myself,' I said. 'It practically says in here McKendrick-Larouche doesn't know anything about the volunteer sector. If I hadn't smoothed things over, we'd be out a twenty-thousand-dollar contract. I was late for lunch, but you wouldn't have noticed. How did your appointment go by the way?' He fumbled for an answer, and we both knew why. If he hadn't been so big on playing games, if he'd only admitted he wasn't God's gift to mankind—Womankind? Personkind. Under different circumstances, I might have gone to bat for him more. He said, 'Sir, there is no need for all this worry. I will revise the model.' You had to give him credit, he was cool. Even picked a piece of lint off his suit and put it in this ashtray. Nice, eh? It was a going-away present when I left Manitoba. Know what *Nil Illegitimi Carborundum* means? 'Don't let the bastards grind you down.'

Cute? I suppose so. At any rate, I told him, 'You won't revise anything except your CV. You don't know a thing about this province. We knew that when we hired you, but you're obviously not too quick on the uptake. I'm sorry but you'll have to submit your resignation.' I told him to make it effective the end of September, but not to bother coming in next month. Meaning this month. No one can say I'm not generous, but he read my signals all wrong and said something that riled me; 'You simply want to replace me with a Canadian. I shall report you to the Human Rights Commission. I shall even take you to the Supreme Court!' I didn't know whether to laugh or pick him up by the scruff of the neck and throw him out. If there's one thing I hate, it's minorities trading on their so-called disadvantages. It's all the rage now. Of course, it's different with women. 'You don't have a hope in Hades,' I told him. Then I remembered the day I received my notice in Winnipeg, after the last election, and put myself in his shoes. First comes the disbelief, then the shock, then the anger. You need someone to show you the bright side of things. 'Look,' I said, 'can't you see I'm trying to do you a favour? I convinced Yvan to let you resign even though UIC will penalize you for quitting. It'll look better on your CV.' He stood up with his fists clenched and his eyes simply wild. I didn't know what to expect. He looked as if he'd either throw a punch or break down in tears. Punches I can handle. Tears, no. Except from women. 'My people do not collect unemployment insurance,' he said. That's a laugh and a half. Then he opened the door without looking behind him and said, '*Nil Illegitimi Carborundum*, Mr McKendrick. At least I'm not being fired for being a well-known party hack as you were.'

If he hadn't slammed the door I would have gone for him right there, even with Joni in the outer office. So help me, I was furious. That was truly a low blow. I was a political appointee in Winnipeg, not a hack. I'll tell you the difference. A political appointee is competent. A hack isn't. I guess that would make Ramesh a hack, eh?

I do say so. And what happened to him after he left had nothing to do with our letting him go.

(V) MYSORE, 18TH AUGUST, 1984

My Dear Son,

I received your aerogramme dated the fourth this instant. I am glad to note your duties are proceeding satisfactorily and you expect a good reception of your study. Do not work too hard. You will strain your health, especially during the coming winter, which I have heard can be very cold in the west of Canada.

Your Putu Uncle says he does not know where we have failed. Instead of coming home directly when you became bored with your duties in Toronto, why then did you move to such a Godforsaken place as Saskatchewan? He is still concerned you should secure an appointment here well before your marriage, and he has finally found one for you as purchasing officer at the ISRO factory in Bangalore. It does satellite research and assembly, and your appointment could begin 1st January. He thinks you will be very happy there, and you will be very close to Mysore, so you can visit us often.

I know your late father would be extremely proud of you. The factory is not at all like his foundry. You will have a clerk to take dictation and another to type your letters. I very much hope you will give this opportunity serious consideration.

Shakuntala's parents are anxious you should accept this appointment and be married on an auspicious day convenient to the both of you. She is very dark, it is true, but she is very good-natured, and she has taken a first class in her MSc. Also your horoscopes match perfectly. Please do not think I am insisting. I simply want to see you happily settled before I move to the ashram at Pondicherry. There I can renounce the world, but I can do so more happily if I am assured you also are happy.

Your loving Amma

Postscript. I hesitate to write this, but I feel you are postponing your return to India without intimating the reason. Do you not remember how Shakuntala's namesake, the heroine of Kalidasa's play, pleaded with her husband after he returned to court and forgot her? I realize you are not King Dushyant and this Shakuntala is not a heroine living in a forest, but please consider these words for your future peace of mind. No matter how much you earn there, you will always be a stranger in Canada.

(VI) PRAKASH DAVID

You copied the letter?

You're welcome. Nothing but the odd bill since. His mother phoned again last night. I still don't see what good flying all the way here will do. She can't even leave for another week, what with all the red tape over there. Still, I suppose she could do some good. They became really close after his father died. Now that was bizarre.

It doesn't really have anything to do with what you're after. Not directly, anyway. Ramesh's father worked his way up to foreman in a foundry. Seems one day the overhead crane got stuck, and his father decided to climb up to the catwalk to take a look. A mechanic could have done it, but Ramesh said he thought his father was trying to prove something—maybe that he hadn't gone soft as foreman. He must have, though, because he had a stroke up on that catwalk. Not that they could prove anything afterwards. He clutched his right arm and doubled over. Fell right off the catwalk, but instead of landing on the ground and breaking his back, he fell into a vat of molten lead.

You can say that again. What really hurt Ramesh was there wasn't even a body left to cremate, never mind ashes to immerse. I didn't find out about this till after he moved here. We were at an Indian film night at a prof's house in March. He was showing a classic, *Three Daughters* by Satyajit Ray. Ramesh came right up to us and introduced himself. I didn't care for him at first—he shook hands like overdone broccoli—but he knew a lot about Satyajit Ray films. Told us things like why the fellow in the beginning had to be a postmaster and not, say, a teacher. It turned out Ramesh was in town for his interview with McKendrick-Larouche, so we gave him a standing invitation to stay here till he found a place. If he got the job. Turned out he did, and a month or so later he was back for good. That's when I regretted the invitation.

It's hard to explain without going into the story of my life. He had this habit of crying, 'Rama! Rama!' if he spilled something or the baby started crying when he made a funny face. My sister used to do that when she got depressed, and I still can't stand people like that, who call on God for every little thing. It's as though, well, as though I'll be contaminated by their weakness. Huh, I'm no saint. I'm no crusader, either. I'd be the last one to say that attack was racially motivated, the way they're claiming in the news. Neither was his being fired. Sure, he was brilliant, but he was out of it even after four years in Canada, and it wasn't his being an immigrant either. Guys like Ramesh would be meek and mild even if they were white. But they survive. That's what I liked about him. Like, I should say. We finally found him the place near the tracks. I'd never live in a place like that—not now, anyway—but I've lived in worse during my BFA days.

I guess he'd gone home to check the mail first, when he showed up last Friday. This was his second home. He even listed us as next of kin. That's why the police called here. He showed up around three. I remember I'd just put the baby down and plugged in the kettle. I could tell something was wrong, he looked so dejected. I unplugged the kettle and got him a beer. He could have used a good stiff Scotch, but he never drank, so a beer was a lot for him. I sat here, and he sat where you are. He liked that chair because he could see the Fafard better. Melissa's parents gave it to us last Christmas. We both think boxing is stupid, but he's sort of grown on us. We call him 'George' because he was apparently modelled on George Chuvalo.

Sure, I'm good at giving advice even if I'm not asked. 'The Good Doctor,' Melissa calls me, after the Chekhov play I think. I told him to accept the new job. It was a gift from heaven. His mother couldn't have timed the letter better, but after we talked for an hour or so, he dug in his heels. I don't know if it was the beer—he was on his third by then and proud he could hold it—or if it was staring at 'George,' or if it was pride. A bit of each, I'll bet. 'Prakash,' he said slowly, 'I cannot go back. People would laugh if they knew why.' I asked so who would know. 'Is that what you would do?' he asked, and I said we weren't talking about me. He let his feet fall off the coffee table. I remember the thump. It must have hurt, but he didn't seem to notice. 'Oh,' he said, 'you are somehow better than me? You would not be in this predicament?' He was talking slowly, compensating for the alcohol. I poured some more Scotch and said, 'I'm not better, just different.' He snorted at that and I got annoyed. 'I came over when I was five,' I told him. 'I grew up here but you, you grew up in India. You belong there with your family. Besides, do you think I could have got a marriage arranged like you? What would I do? Bring the woman over halfway around the world from her folks? You know damn well she'd want to go back for a visit every couple of years. What would I say? "Sorry, Sweetie, but I'm just another struggling photographer, so find yourself a doctor"? I never thought I'd meet someone like Melissa.' Then, right out of the blue, he said, 'Do you recall that fellow from Guyana? Sammy someone-or-other?'

Nobody we knew. Sammy Narayan, I think. Ramesh was talking about an incident he'd told me about once. I think it happened the year he started at York. 'Strange,' he said. 'All the bad things happen in Toronto. Those goondas pushed Sammy down on the subway train tracks, and he broke both his legs. He came to Canada to succeed and he ended up being a cripple only. Why were all those liberal-minded people so shocked when he hanged himself? Everything was in his note: "I cannot go back like this."' I asked if that was him talking or you, Sammy or Ramesh. 'What is the difference?' he said. 'For one thing, you're a professional,' I reminded him. 'You told me he was a worker. You'll be better off in India than he could ever have been in Guyana. Besides, you were going to go back and marry Shakuntala after you saved some money. You've been working for more than two years.' Then it occurred to me. I can be a bit slow at times. 'You don't want to go back, do you?' I said. 'As long as you stay here, you're a big shot to the folks back home. And what about that poor girl?' That's when he lost his temper. 'Go home and leave Canada to people like you?' he said. 'People who turn their backs on their ancestry? I will not go home!' I was sure he'd wake the baby. 'Look at your boxer,' he said. 'Sometimes I think he is wondering, "What am I doing here?" but sometimes I think he is wondering, "I will show them!" That is what he is thinking now, and I will show them also. If I go back, people will ask me how much I am making as a foreign-returned officer. You know how they talk. They are crazy for coming to Canada or the US, any place to get away from the corruption. But I will know I did not return to earn a higher salary than my classmates. I will know I fled this place. That is exactly what people like Mr McKendrick and you expect me to do. Such people think I am a coward. I will remain in Canada. I will remain in Saskatchewan. I will remain in Regina. But I will never walk on the same pavement as goondas like Joseph Tschepurny. He is at fault for losing my position!' Ramesh was just livid, but the baby started crying, so I got up. He started following me upstairs. When I reached the landing, I heard a thump. He'd passed out at the foot of the stairs and spilled his beer. I checked to see if he was all right. After I brought the baby downstairs, I carried Ramesh in here and laid him on the sofa. He was still sleeping when Melissa got home from work. The three of us ate out so we wouldn't wake him up. And, I guess, so he wouldn't feel embarrassed at waking up with Melissa around. He had his rules about what men did or didn't do around women. I left him a note saying he could stay the night if he wanted, but by the time we got back—after seven—he was gone.

Not so much uncomfortable around women as . . . Too chivalrous would be a better way to describe it.

There's no contradiction. A man doesn't always go to a hooker because he's, um, desperate for sex. Sometimes all you really want is companionship. He didn't know any women except Melissa. As far as he's concerned, we're married, and some Indians won't even talk to a married woman unless her husband's in the room. I remember once the three of us went to see *Gandhi* when it came back. After we found our seats, I went to get popcorn. The minute I turned to go, he got up and offered to help, because he couldn't even stay one seat over from Melissa without fidgeting. The only other woman he knew was his secretary, Joni Lewvan. He couldn't very well visit her, so he sat through two showings of some movie and had a drink—a Scotch, he told me—before he went looking for Irma la Douce. Fifty dollars isn't much, you know. You can spend more than that on an evening out. I don't think losing his virginity had anything to do with it either, though he probably was one. The farthest he'd got was kissing a girl once—in Toronto, after they'd gone out for coffee or something—and he thought that was daring. He was like a kid when it came to women. He'd tell me about the great articles he read in *Playboy* or *Penthouse* and say, 'Of course, I only buy them for the articles.'

Look, let's leave the magazines out of it. I shouldn't have mentioned it. As for the hooker, you're confusing exploitation with the real issue. Besides, a man who goes to a hooker isn't necessarily exploiting her any more than she's exploiting him. Companionship, that's the issue. Just being able to touch someone. For a guy like Ramesh, fifty dollars is a small price to pay if he can actually hold a woman in his arms for fifteen minutes. It would be the high point of his life. Something he could romanticize till the day he died. Obviously it didn't turn out to be such a bargain.

Tell me what you find out from her if the cops do let you in. Oh, there's one other thing I liked about Ramesh besides his knack for survival. Even if his idea of survival was keeping a low profile. He had a real sense of humour. One day he brought over a song he wrote, or at least the beginning of one. How did it go? He had a thing about Sikhs. Thought they gave Indians a bad name. In India they tell Sikh jokes the same way we tell Ukrainian jokes here. The verse he wrote went something like, um:

Most Sikhs you see have turbans and masculine physiques.

Carry knives and bangles, don't shave for weeks and weeks.

But don't forget this simple rule or they can get quite piqued:

Every Sikh's a Singh, but not all Singhs are Sikhs!

That last line is sort of a litany in India. You know how we remember how many days in a month, 'Thirty days hath September'? The song had a lot of potential. Has, I should say. I don't know why I think about him in the past tense. Knowing him, though, he'll wish he were. He's the sort of person who could die of shame. Promise me something.

Don't try to see him after he gets better. He couldn't tell you anything. He wouldn't. He won't need crutches, not like Sammy Narayan did, but he'll need whatever is left of his pride.

(VII) CHARMAINE DES RIVIÈRES

I never laid a hand on th' guy. You b'lieve me, don'tcha? I tol' the cops an' the jerk from Legal Aid an' they keep hasslin' me, 'fess up! 'fess up! like broken records, an' that son-'f-a-bitch Wayne's got somethin' comin' if he thinks I'm takin' a rap for excess'ry. Th' little oinkers're talkin' outa their assholes if they think they can keep me here till they find him, an' when I get out I'll find him first an' break his arms, th' son-'f-a-bitch!

Talk about a weird scene. This guy you're so keen on showed up around midnight, walking real slow with his hands in his pockets and his shoulders all hunched up like a tough guy. I'm just leaning against a sign, minding my own business, and he sort of slows down as he goes past. I know the type. Too scared to ask you out, but they keep licking their lips like you're a double fudge hold the cherry. So I ask him instead, 'Want to go out?' He sort of looks me over real slow, like he's checking out the ingredients. Instead of saying okay, he says, 'Why not?' in this prissy voice and I think, 'Shit, another refugee.' Place is crawling with them. Only he isn't dressed like one. Has this white shirt on, nice pants, and shoes with silver buckles. Fancy watch, too. So I tell him to follow me around back, then I'll go in, open the door for him. Ask what his name is, and he doesn't answer, so I ask him again, and he says, 'Um, Prakash. What's your name?' Real polite, so I laugh and tell him to call me anything he wants. Except smoked meat; I'm not. He says, 'Very well,' like he's teaching school, 'I will call you Joni.'

You heard me right: Joni, like in Mitchell. I stop and look at him then because, I don't know, the way he says it makes me feel cold all of a sudden, like he's playing games. Turns out he was, too. Wayne's in the bar and I get my key from him, and you know what? The guy's still waiting in the alley near the big red garbage can, still licking his lips. I was sure he'd chicken out. He's moving his hands in his pockets like he's checking it's still there or something, but he just stands there staring at my tits and I think, 'Shit, he needs an invitation.' Next thing I know, he comes running up the stairs like he's afraid he'll lose whatever he's got. Turns out he must have. After we get in the room, I go to the can and when I come out he's staring at the bed like he's never seen a double before. I sit down and say, 'Sixty dollars,' and he says, 'Of course,' so I shrug and undo my jeans. Pull everything down to the floor, but he's still staring at my tits. Gives me the creeps, the way he stares at everything. Then he says, 'You have such lovely breasts,' and I think, 'Shit, this guy's a loser or what?' You want to see tits, you go to Victoria Park and look at the office girls at lunch time. Suntan in those bikinis they wear under their working clothes like they're not really for sale, just us. I should have told him that, but he's looking real spaced and says, 'Your breasts

are like those of the ap-sa-ras.' Something like that. 'They are the daughters of pleasure carved from the unyielding stone of temples.' That's when I get scared for real
and think, 'Shit, the guy's a psycho. Gets off just looking.' But he puts his hand on
my shoulder and it's real soft, kind of nice, so I let him move it down. But when he
slides it under my top—I'm wearing my new red tube top—I tell him, 'The money
first. Then you can touch.' He just squeezes my tit, and I look up to see him staring
at me like I've hit him in the balls. He practically whines, 'It is so soft. It should be
firm.' So I tell him, 'You want melons, there's a Safeway other side of Broad,' but he
doesn't crack a smile. Yanks his hand out and takes a step back. Bangs into the dresser and doesn't even feel it. Says, 'This is all so wrong, so unfeeling. No, never mind. I
have shamed you enough.' Talk about straight or what? I just sit there and think,
'Shit, the guy's a fucking social worker.' That's when I recognize him. He was in the
Mr Submarine at lunch when I went with Pearl and she scared him off.

What do you mean so I'm the one? I never did anything to him. Not there, not
later on.

What happens is, he looks like he's going to have a fit, foaming at the mouth or
something, but he turns around and walks out with his head high like he doesn't like
the smell. I do just what Wayne told me long time ago. I holler for one of the girls to
get him, and before I've got my jeans done up, I hear Wayne flying down the hall and
out the back. I tell him the guy grabbed my tit and didn't pay, and he says to the guy,
'You trying to get a freebie? Fucking Pakis make more than us and try to get free-
bies!' The guy looks real insulted and says, 'I am not a Pakistani.' Looks down for a
sec and says, 'It was a mistake. I changed my mind.' Wayne just laughs and says, 'After
wasting her time like that? Sixty bucks, asshole. Let's see your wallet!' The guy looks
around, but Wayne's got him backed up against the wall real good, so he takes his
wallet out, and Wayne grabs it. There's a bunch of bills, so he takes them all and
hands it back to the guy. It's all real civilized up till now, but Wayne says, 'Eighty-five
bucks?' The guy starts to say, 'It is for a new battery for my car,' as if we care and
Wayne says, 'A lousy eighty-five bucks for all our time you're wasting? You're going to
pay. Take that watch off.' But the guy says, 'I cannot. My mother exchanged a thousand rupees for hard currency, and I bought this very wristwatch in the duty-free
shop at Heathrow Airport.' Then it all happens so fast. I should have known something was up because the guy's flattening himself against the wall like he's going to
climb it. I don't know who he thinks he is, Spiderman maybe. Wayne goes for the
watch. The guy screams and kicks him in the balls. Wayne doubles over, starts swear-
ing, but before the guy can make his break, he gets one in the stomach. Not hard, but
he probably never took a punch in his life. Talk about soft. Starts whimpering like a
kid, something about, 'Ra-ma, Ra-ma,' and Wayne gets a couple in to the face. That's
when the guy goes down. I just stand there, but when Wayne starts kicking the guy, I
try to pull him back. I tried. You believe me, don't you? I yell, 'Let it go!' and the
whimpering stops. He must be out cold now, but Wayne just keeps kicking, kicking,
and the guy's jerking like he's being shot. The way they do on TV? When some guy
puts a couple extra shots into make sure. In the end Wayne's so tired out he lets up,
and we go back in. That's when I freak out. What would you do, huh? For all I know,

the guy's dead. Wayne brings me down with some real good stuff, what he saves for when one of the freshies wants out. They always fall for it. Next thing I know, somebody's waking me up and the place is crawling with cops. They get the cuffs on before I can even get my jeans up and march me out the front with all these people staring. Saturday shoppers. The pigs throw a blanket on top and we're off, sirens going and the whole bit, like it was some celebrity Wayne dumped in that big red garbage can out back. The jerk from Legal Aid says he's going to get those motherfuckers for police brutality and some other stuff I can't remember.

Rights? Girls like us don't have rights. Only the customer's right. Say, do you know if the guy's okay? He won't die or anything?

Naw, nobody told me shit about him. Just his name. Nar-ay-an-dra Ku-mar Ramesh. I can even spell it now, paper's having a field day. Poor Pakis come over here looking for a better life and see what they get. What about us? If they've got it so rough here, why don't they just go back where they're from!

YESHIM TERNAR

(b. 1956)

'A writer should take nothing for granted about the culture that was "given to" her or that she has "inherited",' says Yeshim Ternar. 'She should leave no aspect of it unexamined. Otherwise, she will never be able to take off . . ., but remain stuck at the original perch, heavy-footed and hesitant, repeating the same stories over and over again.' Ternar declares herself 'committed to drawing [her] inspiration from international as well as Canadian sources and reaching a readership far beyond the borders of Canada. I believe,' she says, 'that, as an artist, I and my work ultimately belong to the world.'

Born in Istanbul, Turkey, Ternar went to the United States in 1975 to study at Bennington College, Vermont, where she received a B.A. (1979). A resident of Montreal since 1980, she holds a Ph.D. (1989) in cultural anthropology. While she acknowledges that 'the problem I find being an immigrant in Canada [is] that you're never accepted totally if your name isn't an identifiably Christian French or English name,' she does 'not expect compensation or special treatment because I am a woman, because I am a Turkish-Canadian, because I am not a Christian, because I live in Montreal, because English is not the first language that reached my ears.' Such differences she considers to be 'advantages rather than handicaps in' her writing career.

Ternar has published a collection of short fiction, *Orphaned by Halley's Comet* (1990). Translated into Dutch, it was selected as the best local book in the 1993 survey of *Montreal Mirror*, and was short-listed for the Qspell Fiction Prize. A second collection, whose title story is the one that follows, is forthcoming in 1996. Ternar's fiction reflects her conviction that 'a good story is meant to entertain and to encourage its readers to explore the world in ways they have not considered before. Because of its ability to transport,' she says, 'a good story is necessarily cross-cultur-al, cross-generational, and international, however steeped it may be in regional details.' Although she resists the tendency of Canadian editors and critics to label her as an 'ethnic author', she does not 'perceive the relationship between [herself] and writers or administrators of the majority culture as an unequal one', perhaps because she comes, as she states, 'from a country that was not a member of the British Commonwealth. . . . I believe in the present and future of Canada, unhampered by a memory of its colonial past.' These are the ideas that informed Ternar's response to the 'Writing Thru Race' conference as being yet another event that might 'ghettoize and further discredit writers like myself'. Although, as she said at a time before the conference took place, 'I suspect that I would be in agreement with many of the conference participants in Vancouver about the types of changes needed to ensure fair play and fair competition for all Canadian writers, regardless of their ethnic origins and affiliations, . . . I just don't believe that drafting guidelines behind closed doors will initiate meaningful change.' As Ternar says in an interview, 'I come to the Canadian multiculturalism . . . with a knowledge of what happened in the Ottoman Empire, which lasted until the 1920s. Their ethnic minorities were regulated in many ways, but they were also allowed their own religious and cultural practices. They were marked, but they were not harassed. . . . In some ways they were allowed to be very free as long as they accepted that they were now citizens of the Empire. I try to operate with the same understanding.'

The author of a non-fiction title, *The Book and the Veil: Escape from an Istanbul Harem* (1994), Ternar has also written a play, 'Looking for Leonard Cohen,' broadcast on CBC's Arts National program (1992), and is currently completing her first novel.

TRUE ROMANCE WITH A SAILOR

There are three pictures. He does not appear in the first two, although they are about him. Both were taken before I slept with him. Then there is a third picture of him beside his chief machinist, both of them blond, both of them sturdy men. Their eyes give them away: these men are drinkers. In his third picture, the two men pose in front of a bower of grape vines. The grapes are in season, ready to be plucked, fermented and bottled.

I plucked my sailor right out of that picture in Italy. Friends told me they had never thought I would go for a guy like him. They're right. But he was around and said he liked me. He wasn't bad-looking. I sort of floated towards him, and if he wasn't there when I floated by, he steered his boat to catch me on the rebound.

There is a legendary Barbary private named Barbarossa—red beard—who conquered most of the Mediterranean for the Ottoman Empire. Some European women are reputed to have arranged to travel along certain sea routes so that they would be captured by him. A better life for a European girl could be had through slavery especially if Barbarossa was one's master. I had heard of such stories from the time I was a little girl, but they had nothing to do with why I got entangled with this sailor.

When I completed my bachelor's degree at a certain college in New England where I had been a foreign student on a scholarship, I owned so many books on subjects such as Marxist economics and Latin American literature that I decided to take a freighter back home to Istanbul with my books rather than send them away separately and risk losing them. I was fortunate enough to find a Turkish freighter, the *Marmara*, which was leaving New York in late June with certain stops in Italy and Tunisia and various other possible stops. It seemed fine to me. I bought more books, intending to read them on the slow journey home.

He first saw me when I entered the captain's cabin on the twentieth of June in 1979, demanding to know where they intended to install me. The sailor who had accompanied me to my assigned cabin in a side corridor had suggested that since I was the only single female on board, the other two women being spouses of sailors, I might benefit from a cabin with a private toilet. Even then, taking showers would have been a problem, but I may have felt safer and never gotten involved with the sailor in question.

My ticket was in fact a cargo lading charges bill. In the section which indicated the amount of space taken up by the cargo, they put down my boarding expenses. Into the box which normally would have contained the name of the receiving agency at the port of destination went my father's business address. I knew very well that I wasn't the kind of order he had ever placed, but I didn't let this on to the captain.

Once I got all my trunks into my cabin, I explored the ship a bit. But there wasn't much visible activity. Most of the doors were closed. Although officially forbidden to entertain visitors on board, every sailor of every rank and every size, that is, everyone who wished, was holed up with a woman. Even in instances when two or three sailors were sharing a cabin, they either took turns for privacy or simply forgot about the existence of others.

I'll never forget the trio of girls from St John, New Brunswick. Two were regular-sized blondes, but the third one was a whale of a woman who wore, over her enormous chest, a tight T-shirt imprinted with the photograph of her lover. She was the most strident, demanding, and lively woman I have ever met. I wondered how she could have so much energy when she claimed she had cancer in the preliminary stages and a heart condition resulting from a heartbreak and overall long-term hard luck. She and her friends had first met the sailors when the ship had stopped in Canada, and seeing that they had the best time and the best sex in many years, had driven down to New York to meet the Romeos there. To this day, I don't know if they were working girls, or if their drive down the Atlantic coast was a labour of love.

I hung out with Barbarossa since he seemed to be lonely for some company as he was still suffering from breaking up with the love of his life. We took walks around the pier in the evenings, stepping over spilled coffee beans and loose paper. Everything was exciting to me about the port, but there wasn't much we could talk about. Anyways he was a busy man. He had to meet with the ship chandler and with agencies requesting cargo transportation almost every day. He had to enter figures into books, make phone calls, rearrange the space in the container hold, and do countless other things.

So I took off with the Canadian girls and their sailors. The first time we all packed into the girls' red Chrysler to venture out of the pier gates, we got stopped by the police. We all clambered down, all eight or nine of us. The police checked us girls' purses first, then they frisked the men whom they pushed against the car, ordering them to put their hands up. I couldn't believe it. What was a nice girl like me doing in Brooklyn, being frisked by the police? Old Hassids passed by, staring at the scene from the corner of their eyes.

After we passed that hurdle, we had a lot of fun. More fun than I could have imagined myself having in New York with total strangers. There were evenings on 42nd Street, shopping trips to Canal Street, excursions to the Empire State Building and the World Trade Center.

I still have the photograph taken on top of the Empire State Building showing myself, three sailors, and a woman whose thigh, thicker than a Roman temple column, is bared by the wind. I smile in the photograph. The sailors pose with indifference to the city; they have posed the same stances at so many ports. As for the woman, she contradicts herself blatantly; she could not be dying of cancer or love or loneliness; each ship she sights in the distance renews her.

Perhaps the captain desired that affair between us. Perhaps he was tired of hearing the same story of the same wretched affair Barbarossa had a habit of recounting teary-eyed, sighing, over bottles of wine.

'She still loves me, I know,' he'd say, trying to convince himself. He'd pull out a locket that contained her wrinkled photo, the only one he was able to save from a tragic fight during which she had tried to destroy all traces of herself. Doped and drunk, they had copulated for hours on the remainders of fabrics and leather left over from her sweatshop days when she took in work to make ends meet. Ends were met, but the floor had not yet been swept. They rolled around her apartment, their sweaty bodies gliding over each other, bringing down the curtains and posters as they tried to hang on to something solid while they took each other across the vast distances of the American continent.

When they finally stopped, she started crying hysterically, tearing her hair, banging her fists into the wall, trying to demolish herself on the spot. They fought when she attacked the photographs in the album, crumbling and tearing all the photos, not only of herself, but of her husband and son. Barbarossa managed to save some photos when he slapped her face, making her loosen her grip on the batch she held in her hands.

It was then that her son who had been keeping to himself in the next room had walked into the scene and run over to his mom who was sobbing in the corner, naked and hysterical. Barbarossa had tried to cover himself up but he couldn't find anything within arm's reach and therefore had to face this kid the way he was: drunk, naked, and angry. 'That's what eats me up most,' he'd say, and empty his glass with a single gulp.

He'd know now that they were willing to listen some more although they had heard it all before. 'Yes, we love each other, still,' he'd say, expecting and finding the captain's emphatic pat on his shoulder. This was a cue for him to open the next bottle and fill the glasses for another round. He'd blow his nose and go on.

'I first met her at a party where I was supposed to be introduced to an American girl who I was told wanted to have a fling with a seaman. I had nothing serious in my mind, just a sweet night. Then I saw her drinking alone in the corner of the room. She didn't notice me. When she bent down to fix her shoe strap, I walked over and stood in front of her so she saw me smiling at her when she looked up. I knew then that we were destined to love each other. She was immeasurably sad, having lost her husband to cancer. Imagine, left alone with a young son in New York and no working papers. At first I wanted to hug her just to comfort her, but when my hand touched her arm I felt an electric shock.'

He'd draw in his breath here and stare his drinking buddies in the eye. 'Before long we were making love in the back room. She took me totally by surprise. No woman has ever loved me like this, ever. It was as if she had known my body for years. She made me ache for her, she made me want her over and over again.'

His drinking buddies would nod and their eyes too would cloud over as they reached for another glass.

It is not my fault that I happened to walk into the captain's cabin at this point in the story. I walked in like the child in Barbarossa's story, like the woman, like the photos. I came in embarrassed, vulnerable, sexy, hysterical, abandoned, marriageable, child-like, and nubile, all at once. In reality, I was not a child, no, I was not even a virgin. I was not the little boy in the story. I was a woman, but when they saw me first, I was a lot of things to those sailors that I also wasn't because I walked in their story.

Finally, ten years later, this is what I choose to blame: another story.

He wanted to marry me. He was sure of this from the start. He wanted to marry me when the ship reached port, get me pregnant as soon as possible, certainly before his next trip, and repeat the pattern for the next few years until I had one in my belly, one at my breast, and one down by my knees.

Later, after we got involved, I said I'd run away if that was his plan. Then he said, 'No, you won't, I'll get one of my men to break your knees, I'll shatter your legs, I'll kill your lover.' Except that I wasn't necessarily thinking of running away with another man. When I was thinking of running away, I meant walking into the darkness, disappearing out of his sight, disappearing from the tumult of Istanbul, its fighting factions, its evenings that seemed to descend from its minarets with a sadness and a flutter of pigeon wings through clouds of car exhaust. It was from these evenings of captivity which gave me headaches and his persistent desire to get me pregnant that I wanted to run away. Into what I wasn't sure. I was young and I was disillusioned. I guess I was ready to walk away into anything different that came along.

I was at the stern deck when the ship pulled out of New York. Leaning against the railing with the headwind blowing straight into my back through my thin sweater, I thought of the countless immigrants who had come to this city. They had stood up in boats to watch its skyline greet them, not to take their leave like me. As the Statue of Liberty became smaller, I thought of how the same statue had welcomed millions to her land. No one in their right mind would be turning her back to the course of history. Why was I? People came to this city armed with determination, with a winner's attitude. New York was a place of arrival. As usual, it took a departure for me to realize this. I surprised myself when I tasted not the salt in the wind but my own tears.

Barbarossa's friend, the chief machinist, approached me to make small talk. Noticing my tears, he told me to take care of myself, maybe wear a windbreaker because the wind was strong. 'You'll come back,' he said. I nodded. Hadn't the customs officer at the port told me the same thing? Gently, as she stamped my passport, she had said, 'I hope you'll come back soon, honey.'

I took one long last look at the miniature-sized lady of liberty, and vowed to come back, hell or high water.

Barbarossa was certainly not the only man on the ship who took a fancy to me. He was the most manageable-looking one. That's why he won. Or maybe that's why I lost.

There was a hirsute machinist with so much black hair all over his body that even his long-sleeved shirts couldn't hide his condition. Long dark strands of hair emerged out of the slits in his cuffs. Some spurted past the top button of his collar despite his meticulous efforts to conceal them. His mates speculated that he even had hair under his feet which was why he always kept them hidden in socks.

This man occupied a relatively nice cabin due to his responsible position on the ship. He had furnished it with appliances that are precious at sea such as a toaster oven and a private fridge and ice-box. If the road to a man's heart passes through his stomach, it couldn't be that different for a young woman, he must have reasoned, when he decided to court me.

Past everyone's bed hour and when the sailors on the night shift were at their respective posts, he tiptoed up the stairs and down the side corridor and knocked cautiously on my door.

'Who is it?' I asked, meekly, behind the closed door. 'It's your faithful friend, Abdullah,' he answered. The hum of the engine had drowned his whispered response so that I only heard the words 'your faithful' which was enough to set off alarm bells in my head.

'How many are you?' I asked. There was a moment of silence behind the door during which I heard my own heart race across the Atlantic way ahead of the ship I was on.

'It's only I. I made pizza for you, darling. I'm holding it right here in my hands. My hands are burning because it's fresh out of the oven. Open the door so we can eat it together.'

I had been reading late into the night. I could have used a nice snack, but my self-preservation instincts urged me to negotiate.

'Abdullah,' I said coyly. 'Go wake up your best friend Hasan so that he can have some, too. And give me about fifteen minutes to dress up. Then I'll come over to your place.' On the way, I knocked on Barbarossa's door and told him about my whereabouts. Barbarossa lost sleep that night and not over the pizza he hadn't eaten.

Abdullah's efforts were foiled. He must have known I wasn't all that impressed by him when I stood in front of his prized possession and laughed till my sides split. Over his bed, Abdullah had a poster of two giraffes in love. The poor animals had their necks intertwined, but they were still kissing passionately, their pulpy lips laboriously extended toward each other. I managed to eat Abdullah's pizza in between convulsive fits of laughter. I don't think I gave him any hope for an affair but he must have figured a frozen pizza was all he had lost so far, so he could afford to go on.

All across the Atlantic he sat at the table across from me, staring intently as I ate the rotten food on board. He had ordered the sailor in charge of the mess hall to clear the two settings on both sides, so that only he remained in my direct line of vision. When I still didn't pay attention, he started exposing more and more of his body hair. He rolled up his shirt sleeves, he unbuttoned his collar button, he took off his hat. I still didn't look. But one day, in anger, oblivious to the pockets of green rot bulging out of its sides, Abdullah dug into a steak that was badly decomposed. When the green rot spurted up and hit him in the eye, I paid attention to him. I laughed so hard and so loud that everyone else joined in, ending Abdullah's week-long siege in the officer's mess hall.

There were only three of us passengers on board in addition to the two sailor's wives, one of whom had come on the trip for her honeymoon but had gotten pregnant during the first week after the ship left Istanbul and now could barely walk out of her cabin. The other woman was the quiet second wife of the second mate; she mostly walked around with her three-year-old son.

I was the only unattached woman on board. The other two passengers were both retirees; one, a retired merchant marine who jumped on every trip he could schedule in succession since his retirement package offered him an unlimited number of free round-trips. The other man was a retired actor who occasionally received short newsletters from home on the ship's wireless. The message that shook him up most was the news that his brother's parrot had escaped and was nowhere to be found.

Two unknowns about this event distressed him seriously: whether the parrot was alive and well taken care of by whomever found him and whether the parrot was divulging family secrets all around Istanbul, which according to him, was already swarming with too many gossip mongers.

The two men spent the majority of their time on board arranging rotating poker parties with teams of sailors who replaced one another depending on their shifts. I spent most of my time reading. I created a little spot for myself on top of the ship, a safe distance from the stack where I would try to sunbathe and read despite the constant rumble, the grease, and the stink of hot tar. I tried to imagine I was on a cruise holiday.

Sometimes I'd go up to the bridge when Barbarossa was on duty. All the equipment seemed to be so dated and in need of repair that I thought it was a wonder we were able to cross the Atlantic at all. A small framed blessing in Arabic script fastened to the wall behind the steering wheel and the compass seemed to be the real motor of the boat.

In Italy and Tunisia, Barbarossa took me out to dinner whenever he was off duty. We would explore the cities on sea legs, but we never found the same sights interesting. We had no trouble in restaurants, however. But even there, a predictable pattern to which he subscribed throughout our relationship emerged.

Inevitably, Barbarossa would order a fish dish, asking for it to be steamed in a huge boat-shaped platter. He'd ask for mushrooms to be cooked in the juice. So when the fish arrived with mushrooms bobbing alongside it like buoys, Barbarossa would throw in bits of bread to soak the juice and proceed to serve me the bread as well as the fish. He'd make me drink, hoping to break my will, my stubbornness in denying him the promise of a lifelong commitment and multiple pregnancies.

I had never seen Barbarossa exhibit such a sense of urgency as the day I met his parents in Istanbul. I had bought a new outfit for this occasion, a mustard-coloured skirt and top, but the top had fuschia flowers imprinted on it. I was ironing this outfit when he came in, already breathless. 'Hurry up or we'll be late,' he kept repeating. He was pacing back and forth in the narrow corridor while I tried to iron with an old iron on an old ironing board. I got nervous and the iron slipped. Like an unmanageable ship heading toward a visible shore, it slid over my skirt and beached on my left wrist, leaving a burn, shaped like a small boat, which I carry to this day.

I met his father, a retired sea captain, much more intelligent than his son. He was a trim and handsome man, somewhat of a philosopher. He knew his son well. He loved his son despite his flab, his drinking, and his obsession with someone like me. From the start he knew I'd leave his son soon.

He asked me about my plans. I told him I wanted to study more, travel the world, write books. 'You'll be a professor some day,' he said. His son gulped visibly. His palms were probably already sweaty. 'As for this one,' he said, pointing at his son with his chin, 'most he'll be is the captain of a bigger ship.' I admired him immediately. We had an understanding.

'I can work in New York, papa,' said his son. 'You could get me a posting at the Trade Commission.'

'It's quite possible,' said Barbarossa's father. 'But you're only a king in your own country.'

Had he really pointed at the dinner table heaving under the weight of excessive amounts of food when he said this? I have in mind especially an oval dish heaped with fried spinach and cheese rolls of which I ate and ate at the insistence of the quiet and kind woman, his mother, who no doubt would have been an experienced prison warden when his son went out to sea.

Plates heaped with fries, fish, rolls, vegetables; plates like pyramids; no, more like freighters sailed towards me on the starched table cloth. I remember eating till my mustard-coloured skirt and fuschia flowered blouse stretched at the seams, till I couldn't hear what anyone said any more but was content to smile and nod at anything. I was already a captive. Should I blame that evening for breaking my will? Was it a table of food that made me lose my grip on my own destiny, at least for a few months?

My own father's business was in the harbour district of Istanbul. My childhood memories of father are always associated with water, boats, drunk sailors, harbour whores, drugged back-alley men, and the band of gypsies my father said lived in the building behind his workshop.

It was always when night was falling that my mother would be pulling my arm as we sped through the dirty harbour district streets to meet my father at his workshop. It was from this vantage point of a child being dragged behind a nervous and frightened woman at sunset that I first observed the world of seamen.

One building at the waterfront was particularly fascinating within the blur of my surroundings as we sped by. It was an old yellow building, its paint peeled off in places revealing a paler yellow layer underneath. Its wooden door always remained open. As I was pulled ahead by mother, each time, I'd try to discern what was in the deep dark corridor that was empty save for an old bench and a bare table. The metal plaque beside the door stated that this was the 'Venusian Diseases Hospital'. I could understand the word, 'hospital', but what were 'Venusian diseases'?

I was too young to be explained the facts of life and the diseases that accompany them, so my mother brushed off my question with the response that Venusian diseases happened to very bad people. But why was this the only hospital in the waterfront? Because sailors often carry these diseases, she answered. So in my mind sailors were like lepers with a secret, men who carried undesirable cargo which had to be delivered to the Venusian Diseases Hospital where invisible nurses tended sores that festered for years.

How would I have known then that later, when I grew up, I would be asked to be such a nurse, such a home, such a welcoming but silent door for a sailor who might also find himself burdened with unbearable cargo?

Barbarossa gave me my only case of crabs. He was a Cancer, a crab himself. Not that this is relevant. But I remember how desperate I got trying to identify the bug that had attached itself to my tender parts. I consulted all the encyclopedias in the house to compare the specimen I had caught with the pictures of common household bugs. Centrefold spreads of bugs informed me that one had the same legs, and another, the same body. One matched in colouring, but had different eyes. Did my bug have legs with serrated edges? Were the pictures life-size? Was the bug I had caught in its adolescent stage as opposed to the mature bugs depicted in the encyclopedias? Somewhere I had read that there were millions of insects that were not yet catalogued. However, most of these were believed to live in the Amazon rain forest.

As I pored over the pictures of insects, my grandmother happened to drop in. In desperation, I described to her my symptoms. I may even have shown her the dead specimen I had been using as a reference. Immediately her face changed. Curling her severe lips in disgust, she ordered me to go to a pharmacy as far away from our neighbourhood as possible.

'Ask the pharmacist himself, discreetly, for a bottle of Kwellada shampoo. You are old enough to do the rest yourself. Read the instructions,' she emphasized.

I never went down to the harbour to wait for Barbarossa's ship. He was certainly no messiah who would be rowed down the Bosphorus disguised in rags, only to be recognized by his disciples by the fire in his eyes and a ring of multicoloured lights on the bony index finger of his left hand. He certainly was not the man I had been taught to wait for. He was not the right Albanian.

He was the kind of Albanian I was told to watch out for, the kind with a flat head. Either they are all laid down the same way in their cribs as babies, or it's a genetic characteristic, but this Barbarossa had the same flat head which I had been told make these men of Albanian origin a ferocious lot.

Barbarossa was ferociously in love with me. I am not proud to admit this because it defied all logic and bothered everyone. He lost thousands at secret gambling dens, gambling his seafaring dollars on bets waged to predict if he would marry me. He called my grandmother in the middle of the night, drunk, confessing his love for me in slurred syllables.

He hugged neighbourhood girls, begging them to tell me how much he adored me. Then the mothers of these girls got the wrong idea and encouraged their daughters to put on make-up, dress up and wait for Barbarossa so maybe they'd get hugged again. If I was stupid enough to kick fortune in the chest when it came my way, certainly they weren't. Here was a greasy gander, as some mothers would have called him. For what, I asked. To make their greasy geese lay golden eggs, I suppose.

What did he want from me, really? Who did he think I was? A harbour for his boat, a safe refuge for his manhood, someone to come back to in no matter what shape? What did he think I'd do while I waited for him? He must have assumed I'd become like the other sailors' wives and mothers. There were all strong women, on the manly side.

His best friend's mother—the mother of the red-headed electrician who is not the man in the third photograph—was a huge woman with bulging fish-eyes and fat fish-lips. Her face reflected disappointment and wonder at once, the expression of mature fish when they are caught. I had gone over to her house to ask when the ships were coming in; she would know, being officially linked to the sea routes. She may have had a short wave radio at home. You got those when you were a devoted sea wife or mother. I, too, would have liked a short wave radio, but without the trappings. The woman opened her door to me and eyed me curiously before she said anything.

One fat fish-eyed, another, a younger one, scrutinizing her for the necessary qualifications. Was I worthy of membership in the same school?

She eyed my hips for child-bearing capacity. She eyed my shoulders for burden-bearing capacity. Were my arms strong enough to bring home bags of groceries and bottles of wine all on my own? Were my hands strong enough to knead dough for pastries for a boatful of sailors? Were my legs strong enough to go up and down a ship's ramp even if the sea were choppy? Could I throw my weight around well? There would be days when I'd have to lock the door with my body so that my sailor would not go out into the street drunk to make a fool of himself. There would be days when I'd have to pick him off the floor. There would be many days when that same body would have to be strong enough to subdue pent-up passion and fierce male desire which had grown forgetful that a woman also needs, although by different signs.

She eyed all of me. My hair, my lips, my ears, my eyes, all the outward parts a woman needs to attract a man and keep him hooked with her charms and her cleverness; her ability to process and produce bits of information and gossip. One thing she couldn't see was my heart, how it was the most mobile organ I had although it was imbedded deeply in my chest, at the centre of my strong and able body.

Maybe she knew anyway. She didn't invite me in. I was nothing until I took my vows to belong to her tribe. No, they weren't coming in yet. 'Maybe in two weeks if they don't get a last-minute load.'

She excused herself by saying she had a lot of work to do. She was pickling. She did not shake my hands to greet me or send me off. In fact, she never took off her pink plastic gloves full of holes from the barrels of brine she must have dipped them into. She didn't seem to mind the salt water dripping on her doorway, right between us. She bid me goodbye with her disappointed lips. Kindly or with disdain, I couldn't tell.

One grey day when Barbarossa was gone on a short trip in the Mediterranean and I was recovering from a cold which I had caught due to a nation-wide fuel oil shortage, my doorbell rang. In that ragged and despondent state, I opened the door to find myself face to face with an elegant woman wearing a fur coat in those politically dangerous times when a fur coat could invite an attack on the street from either the far right or the far left. Her face was fashionably made up and she seemed nonplussed by the fuel shortage, nerve-wracking urban guerrilla and police raids, the hundred-and-twenty-percent inflation rate, or the dark mud that pervaded the streets.

'May I?' she asked, and before I could respond, she waltzed into my living room. She clicked open her black briefcase and lined up bottles filled with creamy green fluids on my dining room table. 'All especially for you,' she said.

'May I?' she asked again and before I could even say, 'What?' I was dragged to the window where she cupped my chin in her hand and turned my face to the light. 'I knew it,' she said. 'A case of enlarged pores. Extremely enlarged.' She reached into her briefcase without letting go of my chin and brought out a huge magnifying glass. She peered closer. Behind the magnifying glass her eyes were like two large bugs, her eyelashes, hundreds of feathery feet.

'What I don't understand is why they're clean. With pores this large you should have many more blackheads. May I ask you how you manage to keep them unclogged?'

I mumbled something about scrubbing my face often.

'No, no, no!' she exclaimed. 'From now on you will use these.' She pointed to her row of bottles. 'This is a specially formulated anti-pimple, pore-shrinking, black-head-preventing beauty ointment made from specially cultivated Swiss seaweed grown right here in our country, away from the big city smog, in the fresh air. Your face will improve dramatically once you follow this treatment.'

I was so appalled by the fact that a woman in a fur coat had come to my door to sell me bottled seaweed while I and the whole country was in the midst of such misery that I bought her wares. But before she left, I asked her who had sent her my way.

'Several of your neighbours,' she answered. 'Nice women. They all said their daughters had fine skin, but you could use my help.'

I was convinced my neighbours were crazy: discussing my pimples with strangers. Did they really want to help me out or was it their way of reminding me once more that I had been lucky enough to catch the sailor in my condition; that their daughters with pearl skin who were more deserving were downstairs?

The bottles yielded a pale green cream that spread like slime over my face. It was a soothing sensation at first, but soon, when the concoction dried, it caked up and highlighted every otherwise indiscernible wrinkle and fresh pimple.

The day I got pregnant must have been the day before Barbarossa's ship left port. I was so relieved he was leaving, yet at the same time a little sad, knowing full well he cared for me and that there wasn't anyone else for many miles and many years to come who would want me that desperately. So I succumbed to his passion. I resigned myself to his ardour. I closed my eyes as I lay on the honey-coloured carpet with my clothes strewn about and that's how I think I got pregnant.

I put him on the bus after I told him, 'That's it, Barbarossa, I aborted your child and slept with another man all in the same week and I am leaving this city and I am leaving this country.'

'How could you do this to me?' he kept asking, even at the bus terminal.

I could have stayed silent like he always did when I asked him things. I could have done a sentimental disappearing act, something he had perfected after practising it for years like a B-grade movie actor who knows his biggest impact is the close-up shot of his face before the departure scene which precedes the end. I could have given him what he was used to giving others. But I answered him instead.

How could I leave him? I only wanted to be free. I wasn't ready for the life he was offering me. I wasn't his harbour, his hope and protection. 'You met me on a boat when I was in between continents. What made you think I would stay on one of them just for you?'

He left then, his chubby body bent forward, his shoulders arched like the shell of a sea animal who has seen the waves come and go for a long time. As the bus took off, a song came on the air from the driver's radio. It was an Arabesque song about a cruel woman, a heartless lover, the desert that's her heart and the brine she made him drink when he was thirsty.

Sometimes I wonder, now, was this my chance at true love? Did I miss the real thing because I paid too much attention to details? Here was a man with a simple desire, to get married and have a family. All he wanted was a safe harbour to return to, calm seas on a sunny day and I didn't have the patience for it. To this day, it puzzles me, why so many women have the patience for it.

Anyway, chances for another chance are long gone. My timing is way off as I write this story, single, in another land. For I am back here, in that city whose harbour is guarded by a free woman, alone with her torch, a woman who is hollow inside, yet sturdy and spacious enough to withstand a multitude of well-meaning visitors for many years.

YASMIN LADHA

(b. 1956)

'I am a word-shaper, creating and shaping words that are very strange and, at the same time, natural,' says Yasmin Ladha. 'The purpose of crafting words newly is to spur, ignite something hidden, in both the reader and myself. In writing then, I want to evoke *rasa*: juice, dance, music, magic, startle, both for my reader and myself.' Ladha embraces the word *rasa*, a Hindi word, not only because of its fluid meanings, but also because 'its English counterpart, "essence", [has] become blunt with over-use,' and because 'it is an elitist word, used by clergy and scholars.'

In its rhythms, styles, and idiosyncratic use of words, Ladha's fiction demonstrates the delight with which she subverts literary conventions and the fondness with which she addresses her reader. Her writing, as she says, 'occurs in the proximity of an evoker, the reader, whom I call Reader*ji*'. Speaking to the reader directly is a deliberate strategy: 'One of the "tools" I implement in order to do away with a consumptive reader is to address my reader, personally. Her name is Reader*ji*. In Hindi and Urdu,' she explains, 'the suffix "*ji*" added to a name is a polite form of address. I also use "*ji*" as an endearment: "My Reader*ji*", "*Ooi* Reader*ji*", "Come back, Reader*ji*". In other words, I seek a connection with my Reader*ji*.'

This desire to address her reader makes the borderline between fiction and reality a fluid one, and also creates what Ladha calls 'a process of disclosure to myself'. Ladha sees herself as a 'nomad'. Born in Mwanza, Tanzania, two years before the independence of Tanzania, Ladha grew up knowing 'very, very early that Africa is for the Africans'. Arriving in Canada, with her mother and brother, when she was eighteen, she considers the word home to be 'a dictionary word. A hard word.' She strives, then, to create out of what she calls 'an inward geography'.

Her collection of short fiction, *Lion's Granddaughter and Other Stories* (1992), which includes the story that follows, clearly reflects the multiple positions from which she writes. 'Being woman, Muslim, immigrant, first-born, thirty-five, beloved, plaiting the prairie in my craft, sprouting multiple goddess arms in the grasslands, occupying feminist theory, abandoning theory, Hindu-ing Allah out of my Gujarati Hindu heritage, writing out of the landscapes of Janpath-Delhi and Kensington-Calgary, incorporating Urdu calligraphy in English, whamming imperial English in a racist policeman's face'—all this forms the core of her writing.

A resident of Calgary, Alberta, Ladha studied at the University of Calgary, where she received an M.A. in Creative Writing (1993). She has been a facilitator of creative writing workshops and a teacher of English as a Second Language. Ladha, who was the guest editor of *Rungh*'s special issue on food, has also published a chapbook, *Bridal Hands on the Maple* (1992).

BEENA

Readerji, you have never wanted me forever
But this time
Won't you come a little farther?

I shan't call you reader. One who reads, hah! That's so undeclared. Blank as a daft blue form: 'Resident of?' 'In the Dominion of?' 'Port of Embarkation/Disembarkation?' 'Destitute-Festitute?' Blue muscle of power. Generic.

Between you and me, there is no glint of a badge. Badges are razor sharp. Between you and me, the ink quivers. Beena exists declared (fetch the trumpet, fetch the *dholak: dha dhin dhinaka*) because of you and me.

'A reader,' you say? You correcting me? My Allah! You have joined the critic's English! May he forever be buried in the Sahara. *Readerji*, I command you, banish the critic from your eye, this instant, *fatafat!* Look at his beauty nose, wide as a camel's nostrils!

My *yaar-Readerji*, sometimes with my own, I forget this definite and not so definite article stuff. Allah! You are turning grey because I call you my own! *Readerji*, by bending, yes-Masta, yes-Masta, you follow the colonizer-critic to his bed!

You and me: Our relationship is declared and you are off to the Camel-*wallah's* bed. *La!* I am breaking my bangles, because of you, *you Readerji*. You have made me a widow. Wait, I will even wipe off my red-*bindi*, this moon-dot between my eyebrows, my *shakti*-power. And the vermilion from my hair parting. *Readerji*, you are turning a nastier grey. You frighten me. Oh, I frighten you? No need to be so vehement with your nod. This *maha* critic's sun never sets, not even a wheezy sound of setting. You, breaker of my bangles, salaaming with yes-Masta, yes-Masta deference. *Readerji*, I ask you, will the critic's privilege, his Brahmin privilege, will it never cease? You are content to drink the incantations from his *soma* drink? He works on formulas while I, my precious reader, create. Without you *Readerji*, my *shakti*-power is swollen but my text is a widow, *gumsum*/quiet-quiet/sawdust. So. So. So. Fill my arms with green, green bangles, *Readerji*. From you, my hefty fertility. And the critic/Brahmin/camel/colonizer is out, out of text! *Readerji*, Beena *soma*-wine, yours-mine, *salut!* That needly bone in my kabab is the critic. So I have the camel-nostril-*wallah* mincemeated in a yellow plastic bowl. Do you know *Readerji*, I make lovely kababs, full of garlic and wet coriander? You would lick your fingers dry. Now this is religion. Only the critic's nostrils put me off.

Come *Readerji*, sit on my bed where I write. Make cool circles on the sheet with the heel of your foot. I dream of a study with pipe smoke and wooden floor (so briskly polished you want to wear your hair up). No colonizing table with loopy gold handles and filched Koh-i-Noors. Just rosewood mailboxes one finds in old fashioned hotels. But *Readerji*, dreams aside, I write here, on this bed. Have some carrot *achar* on *chapatti*. No my precious Reader, these are not green chilies, just peppers. Beena loves carrot *achar*. Your eyes have grown large. Why can't you accept you are declared in Beena? Don't smell my ink in the critic's nostril. I have a heart beat too.

Such a hoard of treasure I lay before you, yet you read like a *fakir*. A critic's *fakir*. Living off his scraps. Hey, don't leave me to my new-found independence! What do you mean I am scaring the shit out of you? Even I am unaccustomed to popping in and out of pages with *achar* and *chai*.

Careful, the *chai* is hot. Sugar? Only half a teaspoon? No wonder you are so disciplined. I take one, two, and finally three teaspoons of sugar. I like syrup in my throat. *Readerji*, trust me. No, I should not say this. At least, not when I am with Satya.

How do you know that *satya* means truth? Oh, the Gandhi film. Well, my dear friend's lies would send firecrackers up Gandhiji's ass, may his soul rest in peace.

One day on the C-Train, this friendly man comes up to us, Satya and me. Asks if we are sisters? Satya tells him, 'We have the same mother but different fathers.' And when the friendly man, now red, turns to me, Satya adds, 'Oh, she's the bastard.'

Readerji, this frown of yours is breaking Satya's magic. Her tongue is lightning. Satya in Beena's story? Faintly, I guess. *Readerji*, hood your glaring eye. There is never only *a* story. That's why a story's collar bones are chubby (always) because she carries layers and layers of stories.

Satya is my *sakhi*, my dearest friend. We hang rainbow saris on rooftops and fetch water from the well. *Ooi Readerji*, will you now forget the C-Train? Stand clear of the doors. And imagine a century where women wear pleated *lenga* skirts with tiny *bindi*-shaped mirrors around the hem. The skirts blast with colour, violent pink on orange, and green on pollen yellow. Each doorway arch painted with tendril leaves and parrots and water pitchers. The outside walls stamped with the orange benevolent elephant God. At doorsteps, coloured rice powder in sprawling circular patterns.

From the discreet *jharoka*, two *sakhis* stare out into the town square. One is a writer, the *Pen-walli*. The other is Satya, the *zenana* law-breaker.

'In this slumbering afternoon, not even a crow in sight,' says *Pen-walli*.

'I want *paan*.'

'Satya, *Amma* will eat us raw.'

'Only if she finds out. Don't know how a timid rabbit like you is a writer. Ring for *Maharaj* of the Kitchen.'

'The *Maharaj*, here! In the *zenana*! But all the women are sleeping and he will look in on each one of them!'

'That's why *pronto, fatafat*, he will rush to the female quarters. *Maha* opportunity for *Maharaj* to let his eyes slip on slumbering beauties.'

Knock. Knock.

'*Bibijis*, you remembered me.'

'*Nahi Maharaj*, it is we who remembered you.'

'*Salaam*, Satyaji, friend of our *Pen-bibiji*.'

'*Maharaj*, there is not a just word for this afternoon's yogurt lamb sauce and your *halva* full of blanched almonds, *hai* Allah, all my words have lost elasticity.'

'Lady Satyaji, and my bow grows insufficient in light of such praise. Bestow a command, my way.'

'But I have not finished, *Maharaj*. I swear in the presence of my writer *sakhi*, if you are lifted one fine day and find your auspicious self in the humble kitchen of our *haveli*, you must relieve me of any blame. You are a Koh-i-Noor meant to be stolen.'

'Satyaji, your *haveli* is the Grand Palace of our city.'

'Then, dear *Maharaj*, I hope you will not refuse the request of the dweller of the Grand Palace.'

'Your wish is my command, daughter of the Grand Palace.'

'*Maharaj*, you are forwarding us your precious tongue.'

'Indeed, my treasured organ on which spices punch and dance.'

'Then *Maharaj*, the secret mariner of sauces, maintainer of heirloom secrets, I bid you to fetch us *paan*, and an attached favour, spittoons from the male quarters.'

Readerji, now our *Maharaj* is Shinto calm. Not a crack in his eye. He has given his word. But he is a professional tongue shaker in more than just the Bengali fish *pilaff* way:

'Hot or sweet, O *cleverest* daughter of the Grand Palace?'

'*Maharaj* of the Kitchen, if I were a lamb, my throat would be at your disposal—awaiting on your stone slab. But today, the *zenana* rules, made possible of course, by your lavish promise. *Sweet-ta paan* with fragrant red paste for my writer *sakhi*. In mine, a hefty pinch of tobacco. And I must reiterate I have the honour of your tongue.'

'O Grand Palace one, I have been groomed by *haveli* nobility. To consume an ocean of secrets without a burp is my *dharma*.'

'*Cookji*, and if you would indulge us further—a small *taklif*-imposition on our behalf. . . . '

'Clever one, my pound of flesh at your service.'

'Dear *Cookji*, then if you would *purdah* your eyes on your way out, how can I say? As an extension of your *dharma*-duty, if you please.'

Satya and *Pen-walli* sit on the balcony on this slumbering afternoon. They rest their henna-painted feet on ice-wrapped cushions, their spittoons close by. Actually, of the two, the writer is the smart spitter. From her lightly bulged cheeks, the betel juice forms a red-rusty arc and lands unsplit in the silver receiver engraved with a cheetah chasing a deer. (*Readerji*, engraved on a courtesan's spittoon is an arched woman holding a mirror.)

Readerji, now what's the matter? Even you should know that courtesans never do things plainly. Anyway, the most important event in the history of story-telling is about to occur. Out with the *dholak: dhum dhum dhaa aha, dhum dhum dhaa*. (Forget the dictionary tom-tom—drums of India and West Indies, hah! Then I can only think of Tom of peep holes who peep-peeping so fast becomes Tom-Tom.) Twirling fingers swift on the drum, and the palm-beat, *dhumaka dhumaka dhaa*. LISTEN ONE AND ALL: *Readerji* IS ABOUT TO ENTER THE STORY.

Ooi Readerji, where are you off to? If you run away, how will I continue with the story? You will come to no harm, I swear on the story. You don't trust the story. How can I coax you to step in? You want no knotted embrace with the courtesan? Agreed. *Readerji*, tell me, what if I plan her *haveli* by a lake? Not possible, you say? You figure that her brothel is most likely behind the *paan-wallah's* shop. Of course, *Readerji*! One lucrative trade massages another. You co-create very logically, *Readerji*, but this is no city planning course. I like the idea of a languorous boat ride. Okay, okay, I won't put you on a boat ride with her. Why do you get so worked up? But *ooi* my friend, in the story, you have such style.

Satya sees you first.

'What a walk! Allah, thank you for releasing him, our way!'

The *Pen-walli* is content spittoon spitting. Now she ogles at you. *Readerji*, this time, she forgets to let out the proper cheek pressure and the juice lands on her bodice.

As you are about to pass under their balcony, Satya and *Pen-walli* bend over.

Only Satya clutches her heart. '*Hai hai*, what a city walk! What a cut in this lurch of a walk!'

My proper *Readerji*, rub away that hairpin frown of yours, for you *would* look up, I swear. Because Satya has ropy power. It pulls you. Look up, look back, heck, look anywhere you please. In this story, you won't turn to stone. Ah! You too are drawn to her voice. I know, I know, there lies a pressed thickness in it. Ah yes, you do look up, definitely.

(*Readerji*, shshsh! Just between you and me, you have that certain walk. It is a walk that finishes one like Emma Bovary's eyes.)

Readerji, do you want to see your picture in words? Sleek silk pantaloons. Not those billowy village pyjamas. Pantaloons and the embroidered belt, just above the hips, have a language of their own. They slice forward with a hint of a buck, while your hair jolts back, like wings at a terrific speed.

Ooi, now I see that I have lost my reputation with you. *Nahi Readerji*, I have never observed your walk this minutely. Don't pull your collar any higher, for I am not a courtesan. My microscopic eye is words.

Readerji, for a change, let me ask you a question? Why *Beena* from all the other books choked with dust (but oh so patient) on the tenth floor of the Library Tower?

The name pulled you. I told you, I create magic, my precious. Certainly, Beena is not of the common Safeway variety. Do you know there was once a filmstar in the fifties and her name was Beena? No, no, our Beena doesn't become an actress. But you asked! I have not given away anything! Then what is a Safeway and a filmstar doing in an Indian village where women wash their clothes by the river? Hey *Readerji*, where did you get these details? Imagination! Good for you. (May the critic forever remain in a yellow plastic bowl.) But did I mention a river? Yes, I know I mention a boat which you don't want to share with a courtesan. Ah! this reminds you of *Kama Sutra*. Oh no, don't turn shy *Readerji*, please go on. You say that *Kama Sutra* brings forth positions which you allow yourself to conjure only with the condition that a chiropractor's office is in visible proximity. And figs and a river, of course. *Readerji*, co-create Beena with me but don't be disappointed. You see, there is no *Kama Sutran* gymnast in this story. No, no, I am not patronizing you. I want to set the story straight, on my part at least. Oh this mad hairpin frown of yours. I know what it means. Don't bang the book shut, you will chop off my nose, I swear.

Readerji, may I speak the truth? *Nahi* what I told you before is also the truth, but now truth at the balcony level. What nonsense! What do you mean I am doing transcendental hocus pocus on you? No, I am not transmitting you to the Himalayas. Of course, I know you are not a California reader. Reader, my Reader, slow-slow. Tell me, what does an image of a balcony convey to you?

Ooi Readerji, how could you? I see Him, The Only Mr Pen, Mr *Vilayat*—Great UK, Mr #1 name in the Canon, top-top English, zoomed on your forehead. He is in his famous tutu pantaloons laden with oval-nosed conceit. This famous Mr *Pen-wallah's* balcony hogs other balconies in literature. Rub Him off! *Pronto! Fatafat!* Away with the Romeo and Juliet blinkers. Give this lovers' balcony a deserved break, au revoir, heart-bye, foot-bye, bye-bye, for ever! *Yaar*, there are other balconies too and other love stories, like Heer and Ranjha. In the desert, Heer shrieked for her lost Ranjha. There are some shrieks which can't be described. Heer's was such a shriek that God in heaven shook and descended instead. And Heer said to the Almighty Bufferer, 'But you are not my Ranjha!'

Yaar-Reader, balconies remind me of the *balcony level truth*. It is difficult to explain. When it happens, you don't know if it happened or not because it is a scratch, an instant recognition, clutching, and then a black out. Finished. Balcony level truth 'pings'. It hits you privately, in the eye or stomach. (Yes, yes I acknowledge you are not a California reader.) Okay *Readerji*, let me explain. On television, I see a veiled woman hurrying down the street. For the first time, she is voting for a woman leader. At the ballot box, the woman extends her wrist, uncovering rose bangles. The 'ping' for me isn't her vote for Benezir Bhutto as much as her rose bangles excited, out of black *purdah* shroud, out of prison. This 'ping' and I write 'Muslim Woman Pictures'.

> My friend paints women
> rib-eyed
> excavation stiff.
> She strokes them patiently
> hardening black paint
> head to heel.
> Nostrils flicked shut.
> On top of their hood skulls
> she fastens
> wingy birds.

Readerji, you and me on the balcony. Eye-lash, heart-beat, itch-scratch, Be-eena. I am because you are. No, *Readerji*, no need to giddy up to the parasitic critic. There is no hidden hyphenated meaning in Be-eena, though I am sure the critic will suck the book dry and author-interpret Beena. Yes, yes, I have my reasons for choosing the name. Have patience. Your eyes crackle like hers. You have eyes like her, my Guruji, Green, and slashing like a machete. 'If you bring a gun into the story, in the end, it must go off,' she says. That's when I get mad at you, *Readerji*. I am no large-lapped goddess, churning out word after word, which you devour, chug, chug, left, right, until the book finishes. Can't you pull the trigger sometimes? And let me warn you there is no guru in the story either. I see, you want to co-create by including a police station in the story. How odd you want police in the story. Ah, because you don't trust my disorder. *Abra Kadabra Jadhu Manter Phoosh*, kiss a toad! And a one and two and a three sugars in my tea! Presto! There *is* an RCMP in this story but Indian *ishtyle*.

What do you mean, also a Petro-Canada gas station? *Readerji*, in a bullock village? Ah, you are only kidding! Ha! Ha! Ha! Finallly, *Readerji* my *yaar*, you are de-starching but don't lose all your solemnity, what will happen to Beena?

I am not allowing you to read? I am chaotic, an interrupter, untrustworthy, fibber. Whoa! Whoa! I will tell you two things, and then I will disappear, in a flick second.

Beena's village has a *panchayat*. *Panch* means five. Five fingers. Five wise men of the village who handle disputes and maintain law and order. Oh yes, *Readerji*, Beena's father, Pindi, is one of the *panchayat-wallahs*. Hey, you know Pindi! So, your critic thinks Pindi is a scholar? *Readerji*, forget the critic with the small 'c.' Come with me a little farther. There are many hearts in Beena, yes, Pindi's included.

And now finally, *Readerji*. Turn around, it is time. Your hand. This is the edge of Beena's village. No, I still cannot abandon you. First, pour some water in the bathing bucket. Beena's mother is fanatic about cleanliness. Once you are through, rub the bucket well with sand and rinse it thoroughly. It should gleam like Mr Sunlight's bulge. Yes, yes, I know this is in poor taste. But not the time to argue, my pet. It is hot *Readerji*, so why don't you bathe under the *pipal* tree?

. . . Tepid water. The water splashing on the baked sands sprouts peppery smells. There is a sudden gust of wind and the air is hued with the smell of mangoes. And then, thud, a mango falls.

'*Amma*, let me go, a mango's fallen.'

'It won't run away, let me finish your hair.'

'*Amma*, gently!' Beena's slender form is caught between her mother's strong legs.

Beena's mother grunts an acknowledgement. Under her rough fingers, the saucer of coconut oil clatters.

'Don't hunch child, how can I do your scalp properly?'

Beena has a heavy wave like a squirrel's tail and in sunlight, her black hair glints purple. When her mother is lost in thought, her fingers turn violent in her hair.

When Beena is a child, her mother makes a bony basin with her thin legs and sinks her into it. Hoarsely, she sings:

> Sleep child sleep!
> Harass not your mother
> who has
> yet to boil the *dal*
> and grind spices.
> Lie soft
> so I can fetch water.
> The floor is unswept
> and Baba's trousers unpatched.
> Child,
> I have forgotten about firewood
> yet yet yet
> Oh scuttle off to sleep!

Beena also remembers her mother's ringed finger. She no longer wears the ring. She asks her about the ring but her mother's eyes only fill up. Beena cannot bear when her mother cries. She can't remember the ring except for the rhythmic thick sounds it made on her forehead, when she lay in her mother's lap, as a child. Each time her mother's hand came down on her forehead, her face must have screwed up like now, two wiry slits with thorny lashes. A dreadful grey creeps over her crunched face.

'Beena!, why so you always jump like that? You make my heart fall out! Up! Your hair is done.'

I am Beena's mother. As a young bride, when I stand in the doorway of my husband's home, everyone gasps, even the village priest, who is supposed to be above such matters, for my colouring is that of limpid gold. Even now, with Beena shot up, the priest says it outright to our shopkeeper, '*Lalaji*, how can you say this clotty honey is pure? In this village we know that the clearest honey must measure up to Pindi's wife's colouring.' The market crowd laughs. *Lalaji* does not let the *pandit* get away. '*Panditji*, don't stick me with a wandering bowl in my prime. How can I explain to your milk-lined stomach that dirty juice oils commerce?'

I have left my ring in *Lalaji's* care. Until Beena's wedding. It is a powerful ring with three rubies and two sapphires. Will hold merit amidst her shoddy dowry. There is also a silver water pot. Beena's father—I cannot leave anything to him. My shoulders are heavy. So heavy.

Yes, I am Pindi's wife.

I fell in love with my husband's walk. Tight gait of hips and hair flying back. There is a song in my village, 'whenever the city-boy walks like this, the virgin's heart is fish out of water.' Even now he startles me. The blue sky falls back as he strides forward, diminishing the mango tree and the thatched huts. His bent hip swerves, just, just so. It rushes his beauty and my green bangles turn dark.

That hot sleepy afternoon by the well. Shabnam and I are eating raw mangoes. Our skirts hitched up for any breeze. Now I am called Beena's mother. Pindi's wife. But my name is Dhano.

'Dhano, look, a city goat released our way. *Ooi*, he is wearing gold eye glasses, like white *dipti afficer*.'

'Shabnam, pull down your skirt! His vision with four eyes must be sharp.'

'*Ooi Babuji*, you with four eyes, in our village, the well is woman-space. You walk over here informally. Why? Is my friend Dhano getting married to you?'

'*Babuji*, my friend is cocky. Are you lost?'

'Perhaps I am. *Bibiji*, you with the edged tongue, tell your friend that her colour is intoxicating as a dimple.'

'*Babuji*, so this is how city-men praise women, with a saki-wine tongue?'

'Forgive my indelicate comparison. Your Dhanoji's colouring is warm like butter and honey.'

'Easy city-*Babuji*, you may slip on your oily-tongue, and this would be a pity, because your city strut has knocked us senseless. But really *Babuji*, our Dhano isn't a Maharani of some bakery. Butter and honey, hah!'

'Don't you offer a visitor water, friend of Dhano?'

'In our village, to feed you water, stranger-*Babu* is half the ritual.'

'The other half?'

'Marriage *dholaks*, city-*Babu*.'

'*Babuji*, I apologise for Shabnam's insolence.'

'Dhanoji! Thank you for intervening. Your friend's tongue is nothing like shabnam-dew. It's lightning sharp. Will you pour water for me? I may receive some sweetness from your bounty.'

'*Ooi Babuji* with four eyes, careful you don't get cramps in your tongue.'

'Shabnamji, tell your friend I will seal the vacant half of the ritual with *dholaks* and feed her a tumbler of almond milk.'

He kneels by me and holds out cupped palms. I lift my silver water-pot in one big arc and pour out a waterfall. He catches my eyes in an eye-lock.

'My name is Pindi,' he says.

Readerji, Beena's father, Pindi. Yes, I am back. Pindi is a scholar. Actor. Actually, neither. His speech is slightly chilled at the top. Scholars and actors cultivate the brisk tone. Never fails to harness an audience. (Even your critic.) Pindi the village hero.

I can't resist to deviate, *Readerji*. 'Hero' is a 'ping' word for me. Oh no, in Beena's story, there are no heroes. But for a while, pretend there is a young widow. (Really, I can't resist this deviation.) It's like a *pucca*-ripe film script.

Story (and *Ooi Readerji*, see this through a lens): There is a young widow. Her husband is butchered on the train. It is 1947. Partition of India. The husband and wife have left everything and are fleeing to India on a ghost train from Lahore. But her husband is butchered on the train. The hero of our story is a *Teacherji*. The refugee widow makes her new home in his village, the village where the train drops off all the refugees from Pakistan. This *Teacherji* is a radical. He wants change after independence. With the British ousted, it is now the turn of the Brahmin rule-setters. Away with the practice of wife burning on her husband's pyre. Away with widow exile and her food without garlic. Shake life into her mummy existence. Let the red marriage vermilion seep into her bloodless hair parting. Let her wear passionate green bangles.

Of course not *Readerji*, this is not a teacher-student romance, leave that to the Harlequin caste. But it is a teacher and widow romance. *Yaar*, we are talking progress. Feminism.

(Action): The radical *Teacherji* blocks her path. She is returning from the river. He asks her for water from a widow's pot! In her confusion, the white-clad widow, with loose blowing hair tilts her pot and fills his cupped palms. *Fatafat* the Panchayat gathers under the banyan tree.

O the commotion *Readerji*!

Heaved dust, hooves, children thrown up their mothers' waists, clanking of padlocks on shops, men's voices thrown right across, only to be drowned by temple bells, and picnic food.

Oh yes, *Readerji*, picnic food is a must when stripping takes place. Who wrote that story, you know, after witnessing a violent beating, the heroine says she could eat a horse? This is no theft or shopkeeper fight-commotion. *Yaar*, a widow has stepped out of bounds. Hero-*Teacherji* will get a beating. But it is the widow's end. She should have known better.

Deftly, the hawkers form an unending line, with baskets full of roasted peanuts, spiced peas, fried cassava dipped in paprika, coconut cubes, and sweet creamy *burfi* spotted with purple flies, but no one cares. The widow has already created a juicy hunger. Food and picnic. Blaring loudspeaker churns out fast-fast songs.

Readerji, ping! I tell you, I can see this all on the screen. The middle part: their eye love story and how it all began (*Ooi* I've yet to work out the details). But right now, I want to run to the end. The Brahmin-Khomenis wait with *lathis* and stones to hurl at our avant-garde hero. His forehead gleams and the cool green veins mapping his temples burst with power. He turns toward the widow, his last look, deep as a tongue in the desert (rub that frown of yours! I think the image conjures urgency/passion. So what if it doesn't make sense. Don't be such a tight accountant). His last look is really a tongue kiss (you cannot kiss on the Indian screen but all professional cinema goers know that deep-deep look is *really a kiss*). The hero is about to open the door, ready to be kicked in the face and belly.

But the widow hurls him round (their first touch and in the background the *dholak* goes wild! *dha-dhin dhin dhin*). She picks a blade which he uses for sharpening pencils from his desk and makes a gash in his thumb. Clutching his bloody thumb, she paints her hair parting. Now she is married to him. Her hair parting a pumping red. She pushes him behind her and opens the door. She steps out. He follows. (Cut.)

I am Pindi, the tailor. Never wanted to be a tailor but somehow I have become one. I live for my newspaper from the United Kingdom. It is greatly revered by the villagers because it is from *Vilayat*, the land of my British sahibs, my mother and father. The villagers insist that all sahibs live in *Vilayat*, London country. I tell them about America but they are not interested. The postmaster treats the paper reverently. Before my house he stops at Shiva's temple. The *Vilayat* paper under his arm. No one will steal it from his government khaki letter carrier, but it is out of respect for the newspaper. That's why my paper arrives tied with marigolds, and a yellow speckle of food at the top. The Postman's offerings at the temple returned after being blessed by the priest. Yes, the villagers never tire of feeling the newspaper. When the postmaster arrives, Beena's mother brings my tea, never in a tumbler but a proper cup and saucer. I like to frown and let my chin sink into my chest as I scan the headlines. The postmaster withdraws silently. I have never been to *Vilayat*. I know I never will. I label all garments sewn by me: 'By Pindi of Jamuna Village, London Returned.'

Readerji, in the evenings, everyone gathers around the Banyan tree to listen to Pindi. He adjusts his gold glasses and relates to the villagers the real news. 'Real news is from *Vilayat*,' he tells them. His fringed shawl never slips off this shoulder. '"One step for Man and a giant step for Mankind" says Neil Armstrong, the first man to set foot on the moon.'

A village boy asks, 'Pindi *Baba*, the *Vilayat*-London sahibs have even reached up there! They are God's special chosen, no?'

'Child, how many times must I tell you that *Neil-Babuji* is from America.'

'But *Baba*, even Amrika is in London country, no?'

The village Granny who is a medicine mother and the keeper of stories pushes Pindi's shawled shoulder, '*Ooi* Pindi child, what fairy wonder have your white *Babus* done now?'

Pindi laughs. 'Granny of the village, first of all, they will give your story of *Mamaji* who lives on the moon an eternal holiday! Grannyji, such stories you make of a wife's brother living on the moon. And when the moon looks scratched, it means *Mamaji* is carrying sticks on his back, and when the moon is low and swift between puffy dark clouds, *Mamaji* is playing "shut your eyes" with the children.'

'O villagers, and when children want to hear stories, don't send them to me but to Pindi, the favourite child of sahib *Babus*. Hah, as if the children will be content with stories of stiff machines on *Mamaji's* moon!'

Everyone giggles but they look at Pindi widely. He knows so much. *Readerji*, Pindi even swayed your intelligent critic.

At one time Beena's mother had soft eyes. Now I could stitch up her taunting eyes and chop off Beena's curving hair. Shabnam's lightning would have matched my passion. But I fell in love with my wife's colouring. Like honey, like bread gathering gold in warmth.

Beena catches her mother's sharp glare at her father as soon as he steps into the court-yard. Beena rushes to her father to deviate his attention. 'Come *Baba*, wash your hands, I will set out the food.'

Beena's mother storms into the kitchen to join her daughter.

'Why is he home for lunch today? Is he unwell?'

'He had to go to post office to fill out a money order to send to the landlord. The landlord will remain in the city for another month.'

'Is he planning to open shop this afternoon? Or is he going to spend the afternoon with his *Vilayat* papers. Those papers are my husband's other wife, and my wretched enemy.'

'*Amma*, let *Baba* eat in peace.'

'Let him have peace. That's his male-tribe right. Worrying about my daughter's dowry is all my headache. What's it to this village if the *Vilayat* country catches fire? Can't your father stick his nose in his own kitchen for once?' She grabs the straw hand fan, sprinkles water on it, and goes into the courtyard. She fans her husband while he eats.

'When I prepared the tiffin for you this morning, you never mentioned that you were coming home in the peak of the afternoon.'

'To visit the Post Office was not an item in my plans. My good friend Mirza Rashid and I entered into a discussion, and in the midst of our discourse, the matter of rent occurred to me and so I repaired to the Post Office.'

Yes husband. Revel in philosophies. Sit with your cronies, you empty spoon of the white sahibs. You would even praise the white sahibs' drawstrings! Let Beena age unbrided. Even in this frightening burden, I cannot ask your shoulder.

'I made my way to Ram Lal, the book seller next door,' continues Pindi, 'and gave him the food. His wife, as you well know, is away at her parents.'

Why husband, why? In the tiffin, I had packed a large coconut biscuit, an offering from the temple. No, not for *you*! My Beena loves these biscuits. I packed it out of wifely duty. Always, husband first. My true *dharma*. Damn!

'Beena, take this fan and sprinkle more water on it so your *Baba* can eat in cool peace. And Beena's father, won't you have more carrot *achar*, your daughter's favourite.'

Nothing pleases my mother more than the arrival of the milk seller. She squats beside him in the courtyard, feet newly washed. She won't cook anything in milk. Fresh from the cow, a tumbler of milk is poured for my father and myself. She sings to me then:

> One day
> He will come
> The king of grooms
> Saffron turbaned, kohled eyes
> And lift my Beena
> Bathed in milk
> She will rise from his navel
> And encircle his shoulder
> under the hood of
> the unhurt Goddess
> My Goddess of Protection

'*Hai* Beena, this silver-pot is your dowry piece! How dare you open the trunk!'
    '*Anma*, I had nothing to do. It is such a heavy afternoon, not even a crow on the roof.'
    'Then come daughter, let me oil your scalp.'
    'And tell me the story of the silver water-pot.'
    'Once upon a time, by the well one day, on a hot, slumbering afternoon, two girls with hitched skirts laugh and eat raw mangoes. One of the girls has a honey-yellow skin, like the flesh of a chickpea. Her friend is bold, her tongue lightning. She sees the groom-prince first. I remember his stylish pyjamas and his brocade hip belt. His walk slicing the sluggish afternoon. . . .'
    Beena gently removes her mother's fist from her hair. The greased fist heavy on Beena's shoulder.
    'When he asked for water, he knelt by me and held out cupped hands. I lifted my silver pot in one big arc and poured out a waterfall. He said, "My name is Pindi."'

Beena is washing her hair. She takes a bunch of hair and throws it over, not caring when the wet strands smack her shoulder. Her back has flushed, spindly marks. She feels the clutch of coconut oil which sticks her hair together.

> *Amma*, drink from this waterfall pot. Throw back your head and let the water cool your ashed liver. Mother mine, you are a bride. Your thick ring glitters. You stand in the hushed doorway. And *Panditji* keeps staring at you. When you meet your husband's eye, he hues you pink. In his gaze, you stand under a pomegranate shower. Open your mouth wider, mother. I am your unhurt Goddess. Your Goddess of Protection.

No, not yet, she decides, and grabs more hair soap. She has her father's dreamy throat in her fingers. Her digging fingers tear into her scalp, and where the scratching is violent, the soap burns.

Beena's mouth waters.

Readerji, don't shout. All these stories knotted together are also giving me a headache. What? No *Readerji*, no one can be at our door. Listen, Beena is yours-mine. This is *our zenana*. Textbook stories of this equals that are a critic's formula. *Yaar-Readerji*, life isn't organized linearly because it is constantly piling. When I go to heat the milk or clean the fridge, other small things happen along the way: I pick up my mother's sock from the couch (which really needs to be cleaned), close the bathroom door, slam down the receiver when I realize it is a salesman, and finally, finally, I come to the milk. God, I hope the saucepan is clean. Similarly, a story is never linear. A story's collar bones are full of meat—by her very nature, she is massing constantly.

Indeed, what happens to Pindi? Both you and your critic are partial to him. *Yaar*, the satisfaction from this kind of fiction is you cannot compel a single intention or conclusion.

You are getting edgy *Readerji*, are you about to chop off my nose? Okay, let's talk about Pindi. Why are you staring at the door? What do you mean, Beena is outside?

Readerji, don't spook me. No, I don't hear her scraping her scalp. She does not exist outside the door. Of course I'm sure—I'm writing her! Because . . . enough! Look, I don't like your game. Come back! *Readerji*, NO!

NICE RODRIGUEZ

(b. 1958)

'The longer I stayed in Canada, the more I felt I was being turned inside out into a different person,' says Nice (Maria Nicia) Rodriguez. Born in Naga City, Camarines Sur, the Philippines, Rodriguez came to Canada in 1988. Although she says that a 'Filipino never grieved for another who managed to escape the political turmoil in our country', hers was neither an easy departure nor an easy arrival, as her memoir pieces published in anthologies indicate.

Rodriguez studied painting at the University of the Philippines, where she also received a B.Sc. in Commerce and Accounting. Before emigration she was an established professional writer, providing trade and stock market reports for Manila's most prestigious business newspapers. As Assistant Entertainment and Lifestyle Editor for the *Philippine Daily Globe* and the *Philippine Tribune*, she wrote many feature articles. Following the assassination of Benigno Aquino, Rodriguez created and drew the daily comic strip, *Marcial*, published in *Malaya* (meaning 'freedom') and later on in *The Tribune*. She also worked as a photojournalist in business and alternative newspapers and magazines during the People Power Revolution against Ferdinand Marcos. A resident of Toronto, Rodriguez is a production artist for *Now* magazine.

Her writing in Canada reflects her desire to record the range of feelings and changes she has experienced since her immigration. 'It became important for me to document, even in fiction form, my experiences as a lesbian in the Philippines and a Filipino lesbian immigrant in Canada before I forgot who I was,' she says. Although 'aware that someone from a different culture would find [her] stories [about butch Filipino lesbians] sexist or absurd', that did not stop her from writing. Her collection of short fiction, *Throw It To The River* (1993), which opens with the story that follows, records that world without sentimentality. 'This is basically a butch book,' she says. 'When I was back home, people would tell me, "go away, it's more liberal out there." . . . I'm comfortable with myself now.' Humorous and ironic, Rodriguez's stories are written in a variety of forms, ranging from realism to fairy tales to parodies.

BIG NIPPLE OF THE NORTH

Once upon a time in the tropical village of Muñoz, there lived a girl who didn't like dresses. Folks said that even as a baby, the girl had refused to wear any style of female clothing.

Once, when her mom dolled her up in a red polka dot dress, the baby cried all day and night. The infant ran no fever, but her swollen eyes expressed an untold agony and her voice was hoarse from days of ceaseless crying. Her parents felt helpless and finally took her to the village chiropractor.

The doctor quickly put the exhausted infant on the bamboo floor and undressed her for examination. The baby sighed with relief as though he had plucked a thorn from her heart, but as soon as he clothed her in the red dress, she resumed her wailing.

The chiropractor read the baby's pulse and aligned her supple spine. He tossed her front to back and checked her genitals for, indeed, she had female genitals. He found nothing wrong and certified her good health. The baby was wet so the doctor changed her diaper with his son's Pampers for boys. She giggled with delight and an aide rushed her out of the clinic wearing only a blue padded diaper.

The baby's face brightened as she recognized her parents, but when her mom appeared with the red polka dot dress, her hair stood on ends and her eyes widened with terror. She began to weep again as if begging for some intuitive understanding. She could only speak through tears.

Her parents showed her another dress, a yellow tube blouse, but the baby howled two decibels louder than before. Next, they tried to put the native dress on, a white *saya* adorned with stiff U-shaped sleeves. Not only did she scream, but she also threw her arms and legs about.

Then from out of a bag, her daddy took a blue athletic shirt and the baby stopped trembling.

'Goo, goo, goo, goo,' she babbled her first words. Her eyes twinkled with approval. The puzzled doctor watched all this unfold and prescribed boys' clothes and shoes for her. He said they were good for her spine, but as soon as the family left, he scribbled some notes and filed the case under Ghosts and Other Strange Phenomena.

Word about the sick child spread throughout the village. One breezy afternoon the elders met under the tamarind tree, concerned that the western settlers had brought the virus which caused the ailment. A hunter said he had seen similar deviations among adults in far-flung and unconquered tribal towns. He added that the baby was merely a young freak and that it was not an epidemic. Nevertheless, they put her on a watch list.

The child performed well in the arts and garnered honours from her school. She was bright and well-mannered, and got into fits of melancholia only when required to wear a dress during formal occasions. Nevertheless, people still saw her as a freak for now she was growing breasts, but looked and acted like a boy.

Every Wednesday, the girl offered a peso to the saint of despair and attended a novena, praying that the village god would make her breasts stop their growth. At last, they stopped swelling but she realized no prayer could flatten her chest again.

As she had with the pimples on her face, the girl learned to live with this pubescent burden. It seemed that her heart had swollen too for one night in the cold month of December, she disappeared with her female math teacher.

The whole village talked about the incident for weeks. The school administration, although shocked, said they broke no rule. They probably just went away to work on a statistical project. The teacher, known about town for her frigidity, arrived in town with an exotic aura of fulfilment. The girl, imbued with more confidence in life and algebra, headed on to a brighter path.

She attended the university. Yet when she graduated, she couldn't find any work. She passed all written tests but, because she did not wear a dress nor a bra, flunked all her job interviews. She found odd jobs in journalism where there were other freaks slaving like her. She also settled down with a nice city girl.

When she walked the alleys of Muñoz with her wife, men jeered at them. They scornfully asked what they did in bed for their own bored wives wondered why the two women looked radiant.

She grew tired of the villagers' meddling looks but had learned to ignore them. Her own small world sustained her, but she could not plan her future. She gained weight and grew depressed each day. One night in her sleep, a voice told her to go to the Big Nipple of the North.

At first she thought it was another wild dream again about her busty ex-lover from Ilocos. The village seer said no, for that Big Nipple of the North was a place called Canada. A land with rich resources, it was like a nipple that had nursed many settlers to lives of unimaginable prosperity. The people in Canada had survived the land's extreme winters.

'But beware,' the seer warned, 'many have perished in that cold land, for it is cursed with big taxes. Go find your destiny and be as resilient as the bamboo that thrives on the outskirts of Muñoz.'

Before she left, she asked the seer, 'If breasts come in pairs, where is the other nipple?' The seer said the Other Big Nipple of the North was a place called the United States.

'But don't go there,' he stressed, 'for it is infected with a malignant tumour which, if left unchecked, could quietly spread to the Canadian nipple.'

Thus enlightened, she went to the Canadian embassy and applied for immigration. On the day of her interview, she wore a tailored suit but she looked like a man and knew she did not stand a chance.

They did not want masculine women in that underpopulated land. They needed baby makers, for as much as Canadians loved to fuck they were not making enough babies. Her wife got a mascara and lipstick, and made her look like a baby maker. During her interview with the consul officer, she looked ovulating and fertile, so she passed it.

Canada had strict immigration laws, but even bugs could sift through a fine mosquito net. Some of her village's most notorious people were now refugees in Canada. Like the mayor's killer and the textile magnate who ran away with millions of debts, causing the fragile economy of Muñoz to crumble. Also, the witch who enslaved her own children became a nanny there.

When the freak girl of Muñoz arrived in Mississauga, she had fear in her heart, but a vision overcame her when she saw the bi-coloured Canadian flag at the airport.

As the bright and blinding northern sun shone its rays through the flag, the red bars and the maple leaf gradually merged with the white. The banner's colour changed to pink—the rallying colour of radical freaks! She smiled with relief, for she knew she had found a home. She sang and danced towards Church Street, Toronto's gay capital. And lived happily on welfare.

NINO RICCI

(b. 1959)

'[T]he artist,' says Nino Ricci, 'is someone who stands outside the community and therefore sees it in starker, perhaps more realistic terms than those who are inside it and don't question its rules.' This kind of isolation informs Ricci's life but also the lives of his fictional characters. 'In my life,' he says, 'it started out as a sense of being marginalized. I perceived it as being marked out for my ethnicity or for being an immigrant, but it quickly expanded into other areas: very soon I was marked out for many other reasons!' In a similar way, the 'outside status' of his characters, whether they are Italians living in Italy or immigrants in Canada, is often the impetus behind their actions, as is the case with his first novel, *Lives of the Saints* (1990).

Reflecting the fact that Ricci 'came to writing from a desire to tell stories rather than from a concern with style and technique', this novel is a realistic portrayal of the childhood of Vittorio, its child narrator. It is set in a village that resembles the Italian birthplace of Ricci's mother because, as he says, 'I wanted . . . to give readers a sense of people within a community where they are not marginalized as ethnic.' Ricci, who was born in Leamington, Ontario, visited his mother's village for the first time when he was twelve. His initial dislike of it—'it seemed backward and barbaric'—was changed in subsequent visits when he developed 'a much stronger sense of what it meant to be Italian'. His 'appreciation for' what it means to be Italian was also affected by interviews in preparation for his novel, which he conducted with about 150 Italian immigrants. *Lives of the Saints*, the first of a trilogy of novels, received many awards, including the Governor General's Award, the W.H. Smith-*Books in Canada* First Novel Award, and, in England, the Winifred Holtby Prize of the Royal Society of Literature for Best Regional Novel.

In a Glass House (1993), the second novel in the trilogy, relates Vittorio's upbringing in Canada and his relationship with his father. Its focus on ethnicity speaks of Ricci's intention to convey to his readers 'the strangeness of that label—ethnic—for someone who is living it from the inside'. As does his first novel, *In a Glass House* comes from Ricci's desire to examine the 'mythology attached to the experience of immigration'. Seeing it as forming a continuum with 'the whole history of Western mythology', he is interested in exploring what constitutes what he calls the 'myth of the "other place"'. As he says, and as his fiction illustrates, '[t]hat other world that appears to a lot of immigrants before they leave as "paradise" often becomes, upon arriving in that other place, "hell". . . . And over time the paradise they imagined they were coming to was replaced by the paradise they imagine they left behind.'

These tensions between the mother country and the host country, between the past and the present, are dramatized in the story that follows. 'Going to the Moon' also reflects Ricci's upbringing close to Detroit. 'We . . . rooted for the Detroit Tigers, and watched American television. We only watched our one Canadian station for the American sitcoms,' he says. 'So there was a palpable sense of the great empire to the south.' Still, as he stresses, 'one of the things I was trying to do in "Going to the Moon" was also to deal with the disillusionment with "America".'

Ricci, now a resident of Toronto, studied at York University where he received a B.A. Honours in English (1981), and at Concordia University where he received an M.A. in English (1987). He taught English in Nigeria, and Creative Writing at Concordia. His novels have been translated into many languages, and he has published his fiction in many literary magazines. Ricci is an active member of the Canadian Centre of International PEN.

GOING TO THE MOON

Windsor seemed a kind of purgatory to me, a temporary stop between whatever hell my parents had left behind in Italy and the vague promise of the skyline that opened up beyond the Detroit River. In winter that skyline's tall buildings stood unnaturally still and crisp in the cold air, on the verge, it seemed, of singing; in summer they shimmered and burned in the heat and smog. But always they had a strange, unreal quality, at once both toy-like and profound, as if my eyes could not believe their own power to hold so much in a glance.

My great-uncle Bert had come over before the war, smuggling himself into Canada after he'd been turned away at New York and then working his way on road crews up the St Lawrence and along the Great Lakes till he'd arrived finally in Windsor. 'I stopped here because it was so close to the border,' he said. 'In those days there were people who would take you across the river at night, in little boats. But by the time I had enough money to pay them, well, I got lazy.'

Uncle Bert had shown me a picture once of the tiny room at the back of his old shoe-repair shop on Erie Street where he'd lived alone for twenty years, a room as grey and bare and gloomy as a prison cell. It seemed astonishing to me that he'd done that, that in all his years in Windsor he'd never so much as set foot in America, though its image had loomed over him daily, close enough to throw a stone at; and astonishing that we had all ended up in Windsor on account of him, family after family, aunts and uncles and cousins, stuck there in our narrow brown brick houses out of sheer inertia, like Dorothy falling asleep on the road to Emerald City. When my parents told stories about Italy they always talked about *miseria*, a word that meant 'poverty' but that conjured up in my anglicized mind images of vague tortures and chastisements; though according to my mother we were poor in Canada as well, owed thousands of dollars to the bank for our house, which was why she and my father both worked their long odd hours, my father at the Chrysler plant or in his basement workshop, building cabinets and tables he sold for extra money, his face always puckered as he worked as if he had just swallowed something sour, and my mother at different places, sometimes at a butcher's shop and sometimes cleaning houses and sometimes picking beans or tobacco on the farms outside Windsor.

My father had built a second kitchen in our basement, our upstairs kitchen too small to eat in comfortably and our dining room, with its heavy polished wood table, reserved for when we had special company, a non-Italian or someone from out of town. Whenever my uncle Mike came in from Ohio my mother made it seem as if eating in the upstairs dining room was something we did every day, putting on a new, strange, friendly personality then, talking to Uncle Mike and his American wife in English and letting their kids call her Aunt Tony instead of Zia Antonia; but normally she guarded the dining room like an avenging angel, keeping the doors that led into it perpetually closed and forever warning my brother Joe and me never to set foot in it while she was away at work. A tall china cabinet stood in one corner, housing small arrangements of silverware and copper pots that emerged from behind their glass doors only for their monthly cleaning; and on the cabinet's top, underneath a clear glass dome, sat a golden pendulum clock which my mother wound every Sunday after church with a special key, bringing an old chair in from the kitchen to reach it and setting aside its dome with a tenderness that seemed oddly out of keeping with the work-swollen ruddiness of her hands, with the hard set of her shoulders and chin. Two copper mementos, of John Kennedy and Pope John XXIII, hung on the far wall, and velour curtains covered the window; but the room's gloomy elegance made it seem sad somehow, as if it knew that it didn't belong to the rest of the house, its only purpose to remind us of the things that were forbidden to us.

Joe and I attended school at Assumption Separate. Before I started there I had looked up to Joe, because he was six years older and had his own paper route; but at school he seemed diminished, some of the older English boys calling him Mustasho because of the dark hairs that had begun to sprout on his upper lip. When the boys began to pick on me as well, Joe muttered insults at them; but I saw from the dark look that crossed his face then, and from the unthinking grimace he made when he found me waiting for him at the school entranceway at the end of the day, that it humiliated him to have a younger brother, to be made more conspicuous by my presence beside him, and I had the sense that we were both of us merely interlopers at school, moving uncertainly through a world that refused to admit us, that we had to hide ourselves within like animals changing the colour of their fur to fit into a landscape.

But each morning when my class filed into the grade one classroom and I saw again the varnished desktops, the polished floors, the multicoloured alphabet that ran across the tops of the blackboards, I felt the small bright hope that my life could be different, that the things that marked me out could be erased, a hope made urgent, desperate, by the love that I felt for our teacher Miss Johnson. Miss Johnson was one of the few lay teachers at Assumption, and she stood out from the stiff formality of the priests and nuns like a burst of colour in a grey landscape, coming to school in lipstick and high heels, in dress suits with trim vests and jackets, in blouses of shimmering silk, and leaving behind a fragrance of herself when she passed our desks that lingered like a spirit; and we were all in love with her, proudly, self-importantly, all vied with barely masked vehemence to sit beside her during our reading circles, all hoped to be chosen by her to wipe the blackboards or fetch chalk from the storeroom. I felt protected in that common love, in the importance I gained in sharing it, as if I'd been included in a game that could have no losers, no chance for ridicule or shame. Once near the beginning of the year Miss Johnson picked me out to stay in at recess to help her with a bulletin board, and while she stood shoeless on the seat of a desk, reaching down a braceleted arm for the pictures and pins I was to hand to her, she began to hum some song softly to herself as if she had forgotten that I was standing there beneath her; and it made me feel oddly relieved to be taken for granted like that, to have been drawn unthinkingly into the small private sphere of Miss Johnson's aloneness as if there were nothing strange or remarkable about me.

During first term Miss Johnson taught us about stars and planets. Every day she set some new vision before us like a brightly wrapped gift, brought in pictures and models of our solar system, read us stories about space travel and distant life. When we

had learned to write she had us each compose in our careful inch-high letters a question to the astronauts at NASA, stuffing all of them afterwards into a large brown
envelope; and a few weeks later, as if we had sent out like Noah a messenger who
returned now with proof of a world that existed outside our own, a large packet arrived
for us from NASA filled with brochures and posters and satellite photographs, so that
while all the other classes in the school were doing up bulletin boards about Advent
or All Saints' Day or the next year's Centennial, our own boards were filled with
images of space, our prized centrepieces a foldout of an Apollo rocket and a poster-
sized photo of the moon's Sea of Tranquillity.

One afternoon for art Miss Johnson had us push all our desks to the sides of the
classroom and then covered the floor with two adjoining lengths of newsprint, shim-
mying along them in stockinged feet to join them together with long strips of mask-
ing tape . We spent the rest of that afternoon on hands and knees, paint trays and
brushes and jars full of tinted water spread out on the floor around us as each of us,
assigned to our own little squares of terrain on the newsprint, painted out our private
versions of a lunar landscape. We ended up with a great hodgepodge of strange forms,
green mountains vying with eerie yellow cities, four-armed monsters perched over
ocean-filled craters, and in one corner Miss Johnson's own contribution, two bubble-
headed astronauts looking out over the whole scene with expressions of alarm. When
the paint had dried we folded our landscape at the seams, rolled it up, and deposited
it at the back of our cloakroom; but thereafter, whenever rain kept us inside for recess
or we had been especially well behaved, Miss Johnson would ask us again to move
our desks into tight little rows at the sides of the classroom, and we would know that
we were going to the moon.

To get to the moon we had to strap ourselves firmly into our seats and close our
eyes. Miss Johnson would start the countdown, and on zero our spaceship would lift
off and begin to climb; and as the earth receded and our ship veered off into space,
Miss Johnson, to hide the crinkling of paper as she laid out our landscape, would lead
us in our moon song:

> *Zoom zoom, zoom,*
> *We're going to the moon.*
> *Zoom, zoom, zoom,*
> *We're going very soon.*
> *If you want to take a trip,*
> *Step into my rocket-ship.*
> *Zoom, zoom, zoom,*
> *We're going to the moon.*

Now stray comets and satellites were flashing past our windshield as the moon
balanced in the vastness of space, grew larger and larger, until with a bump and a
lurch we touched down and opened our eyes to see its surface unfurled beside us; and
when we had removed our safety straps and taken off our shoes and packed ourselves
carefully into our spacesuits, we stepped out into space, our bodies moving weirdly

because of the lack of gravity, and set off like tiny gods across the watercolour strangeness of the moon.

In the new year, Miss Johnson pinned to the centre of our largest bulletin board autographed photos of the three astronauts who would be flying *Apollo I* in February, the caption 'Bon Voyage' stapled beneath them in black cut-out letters. She promised us she'd bring a television into the classroom the day of the launch so that we could watch the liftoff together; and in a lower corner of the blackboard we kept a running countdown of the days remaining, all of us competing every day to change the number, anxious to show our excitement over an event that Miss Johnson had deemed worthy of our attention. But the liftoff never took place: with twenty-five days still left on our blackboard counter, the astronauts whose faces had become so familiar to our class were burnt to death when a fire broke out in their cockpit during a preflight test. I saw pictures of the fire at home on the television news, of the billowing smoke, of the burnt-out rocket, the charged solemnity of the reports stirring in me a vague memory of when John Kennedy had died; and it was strangely thrilling to see so much attention being paid to a thing that I had thought of as merely personal, as belonging only to Miss Johnson and our grade one class, as if suddenly something that had been a kind of fiction, a story that Miss Johnson had made up to indulge us, following its fixed course, had become pressingly, dangerously real, unpredictable, unknown.

At school the pictures came down, the blackboard counter was erased, Miss Johnson wheeling the school television into our classroom finally to watch not a liftoff but a long funeral procession; and for a few days we wore our sorrow for the astronauts as self-importantly as we had worn our love for Miss Johnson, wanting to be true to the grown-up sense of tragedy, of loss, which Miss Johnson tried to impart to us. But afterwards, when our bulletin boards were done up with Centennial themes like the boards in other classrooms, our lunar landscape forgotten now under the bench at the back of the cloakroom, and when the songs we sang were Centennial songs, as devoid of meaning as the hymns we sang in church, I felt cheated somehow, felt that I had touched for a moment some larger world that had receded again, that had remained as elusive finally as the promise of the tall buildings across the river or of the golden pendulum clock that sat in my mother's dining room.

All my life, it seemed suddenly, was merely waiting for the fulfilment of that promise, for a redemption from the narrowness and meanness of the world I came from; but it seemed possible finally that nothing would change, that I was stranded in my own small world as on some barren planet, with no way to bridge the gap between the promise and the hundred small humiliations that kept me from it, that refused simply to fall away from me like an old skin. When the chrome zipper on my winter coat split and my mother, instead of buying me a new coat as I hoped she would, as I thought other mothers would, merely sewed buttons down the coat's front and cut crude holes for them along the track of the broken zipper, I was certain that the kids at school, that Miss Johnson, would see in those makeshift repairs my mother's swollen hands, our poverty, our strangeness; and the next morning I left the house in only my sweater, my parents already at work and Joe merely shaking his head at my stubbornness as if he couldn't be bothered to fight with me, to pretend that he didn't understand. But at school one of the teachers saw me shivering outside the entranceway and sent me inside before the first bell had rung, and by then I had understood already how hopeless my situation was, how my humiliation was not something that other people did to me but something I carried inside me like a sin, that was there even if other people did not see it. I had begun to cry by the time I got to my classroom, and knowing that Miss Johnson would be there, making her silent mysterious preparations for the day, I slipped into the cloakroom and huddled onto the bench at the back, not wanting her to see me like that; but she must have heard the sound of my crying, for suddenly she was standing over me, with her silk blouse and her limpid eyes and her perfume smell, and she was so beautiful and soft and gently rounded, and her quick sad concern for me so misdirected, so much the promise of all the things I would not have, that I only cried harder, only thought, we'll never go to the moon again, we'll never go to the moon.

That summer Uncle Mike's son Benny was killed in the war in Vietnam. They had been to visit us at Easter, Benny in his uniform, seeming much older than I remembered him, and afterwards my mother and father had had an argument.

'He's an idiot,' my father had said. 'He thinks the war is a game.'

'He has to go, he doesn't have a choice.'

'He doesn't have to go, he volunteered, your brother told me himself.'

But when the news came that Benny had been killed there were no arguments, only an awkward, oppressive silence that seemed to carry some unexplained burden of guilt. My father could not get time off work for the funeral but my mother went down on the bus, dressed strangely in a dark dress and hat and in nylons and high heels. I thought that going to the States would change her in some way, or that she would return with some unexpected gift, something exciting and strange, that could not be found in the Woolco mall; but she came back a few days later empty-handed, changed only in that she was more short-tempered and curt than usual. I thought she was angry about the time she had missed from work; but one evening before bed I caught a glimpse of her through the kitchen doorway sitting at the table with her head in her hands as if she were crying, and I understood then that she had been carrying the shame of Benny's death inside her the whole time, that his death was not a special thing like the deaths of the Apollo astronauts but was merely private and grim, a blemish or failure that needed to be hidden away and forgotten like any other.

That was the summer, too, of the riots in Detroit, and for days the news was filled with images of fires and gunfights and broken windows. My mother forbade Joe and me to leave our neighbourhood while the riots were still going on, but when the two of us stole down to the riverfront one evening with two of our cousins we found that Windsor outside our own neighbourhood was still much what it had always been, people talking on street corners as if nothing had happened, traffic flowing unabated on the main streets, the river wrapped in its usual twilight gloom. But across the river, the streets, cloaked in the shadows of dusk, seemed almost deserted; it was only when I stared hard that I began to make out some movement along the riverfront, the dim outlines of Jeeps and cars, a few shadowy figures. Higher up, though, where the after-glow of sunset still held the sky in unearthly blue, great clouds of dark smoke had formed, and were leaning against the taller buildings as if to topple them into the river; and for a long time we sat at the water's edge staring silently at the skyline as if we were watching a movie, were waiting for it to draw to some inevitable conclusion. But then night settled in around us, leaving us stranded there at the river's edge as on an island; and finally we rose up together and began to make our way home.

GEORGE ELLIOTT CLARKE

(b. 1960)

'I seek to bear witness to the beauty, history, and life of my too-often neglected, my too-often vilified community,' says George Elliott Clarke. 'I want to give voice to what it means, feels, to be Black Nova Scotian or, to use my neologism, Africadian. I plan to centralize my marginal homeland, to observe and decipher Canada, North America, and the world from the vantage point of my East Coast asylum, to apply African Baptist philosophy to literature, politics, and religion. I wish to recast the world in Africadian terms, to use the imperial against itself. I pledge to sing in a black, blues-scoured, saltspray-and-rum-tinctured voice.'

The rhythm and 'orature' style of this statement, its emphasis on community, and its fusion of political and apocalyptic gestures mirror the major elements in Clarke's work as well as the ways in which he has defined the cultural and literal tradition to which he belongs. In *Fire on the Water: An Anthology of Black Nova Scotia Writing* (1991, 1992), the two-volume anthology he edited, Africadian is the word he uses to define that tradition: 'a word I have minted from "Africa" and "Acadia" (the old name for Nova Scotia and New Brunswick), to denote the Black populations of the Maritimes and especially of Nova Scotia'. Its origins go back to the Black Loyalists and Black Refugees who arrived in Nova Scotia in 1783 and 1815. This tradition, Clarke says, includes oral literature; it 'becomes a secular bible'; it speaks of a community that is simultaneoulsy 'spiritual *and* political'; it uses biblical imagery and rhetoric in abundance; and it focuses on the liberation or destruction of identity.

Clarke's first collection of poetry, *Saltwater Spirituals and Deeper Blues* (1983), a finalist for the Bliss Carman Award, comes directly from this tradition. Through a lyrical 'i', Clarke revisits the history and the ancestors of his community, as he does when he writes about 'Lydia Jackson, / slave madonna', a woman indentured to the household of a Dr Bulman who beat and raped her. After coming to Nova Scotia in 1783, she moved to Sierra Leone, West Africa, with a large group of Black Loyalists in 1792.

Whylah Falls (1990), which won the Archibald Lampman Award, is similarly indebted to that tradition, but here, as in his other writing, Clarke makes use of formal elements that reflect the influence of such writers as Michael Ondaatje. A long poem that combines various kinds of lyrics, prose, and photographs, it is spoken by different 'dramatis personae' who belong to the mythical community of the title. Clarke writes in a vernacular that echoes his Africadian tradition but which also allows him, through his use of humour and irony, to blend its spirituality with the ribald passions of his characters.

A seventh-generation Canadian of African-American and M'ikmaq origins (on his maternal side), Clarke was born in Windsor, Nova Scotia, but grew up in North End Halifax. Active culturally and politically, he contributed to the establishment of the now-defunct Black Youth Organization of Nova Scotia, and was the organizer of the Weymouth Falls Justice Committee in 1985 that protested racism in the Nova Scotian justice system.

After receiving an Honours B.A. (1984) from the University of Waterloo, he became a social worker in the Annapolis Valley of Nova Scotia (1985-86). He received his M.A. in English (1989) from Dalhousie University, and his Ph.D. (1993) from Queen's University, where he wrote a comparative study of the Africadian and the English Canadian poetry traditions. During this period, Clarke also worked as parliamentary assistant to Howard McCurdy, MP in Ottawa. He presently lives in Durham, North Carolina, where he is professor of English and Canadian Studies at Duke University.

Widely published in literary journals, Clarke is working on a verse play, 'Beatrice Chancy', and on a bibliography of African-Canadian literature. His most recent books are *Provençal Songs* (1993) and *Lush Dreams, Blue Exile* (1994).

LOOK HOMEWARD, EXILE

I can still see that soil crimsoned by butchered
Hog and imbrued with rye, lye, and homely
Spirituals everybody must know,
Still dream of folks who broke or cracked like shale:
Pushkin, who twisted his hands in boxing,
Marrocco, who ran girls like dogs and got stabbed,
Lavinia, her teeth decayed to black stumps,
Her lovemaking still in demand, spitting
Black phlegm—her pension after twenty towns,
And Toof, suckled on anger that no Baptist
Church could contain, who let wrinkled Eely
Seed her moist womb when she was just thirteen.
　　And the tyrant sun that reared from barbed-wire
Spewed flame that charred the idiot crops
To Depression, and hurt my granddaddy
To bottle after bottle of sweet death,
His dreams beaten to one, tremendous pulp,
Until his heart seized, choked; his love gave out.
　　But Beauty survived, secreted
In freight trains snorting in their pens, in babes
Whose faces were coal-black mirrors, in strange
Strummers who plucked Ghanaian banjos, hummed
Blind blues—precise, ornate, rich needlepoint,
In sermons scorched with sulphur and brimstone,
And in my love's dark, orient skin that smelled
Like orange peels and tasted like rum, good God!
　　I remember my Creator in the old ways:
I sit in taverns and stare at my fists;
I knead earth into bread, spell water into wine,
Still, nothing warms my wintry exile—neither
Prayers nor fine love, neither votes nor hard drink:
For nothing heals those saints felled in green beds,
Whose loves are smashed by just one word or glance
Or pain—a screw jammed in thick, straining wood.

BLANK SONNET

The air smells of rhubarb, occasional
Roses, or first birth of blossoms, a fresh,
Undulant hurt, so body snaps and curls
Like flower. I step through snow as thin as script,

Watch white stars spin dizzy as drunks, and yearn
To sleep beneath a patchwork quilt of rum.
I want the slow, sure collapse of language
Washed out by alcohol. Lovely Shelley,
I have no use for measured, cadenced verse
If you won't read. Icarus-like, I'll fall
Against this page of snow, tumble blackly
Across vision to drown in the white sea
That closes every poem—the white reverse
That cancels the blackness of each image.

THE SYMPOSIUM

Don't gimme nothin' to jaw about, Missy, and I won't have nothin' to holler for!
Just sit back, relax, and be black. I'm gonna learn you 'bout the mens so you can 'scape
the bitter foolishness I've suffered. A little thoughtful can save you trouble.

Missy, you gotta lie to get a good man. And after you gets him, you gotta be set to
hurt him to hold him, so help my Chucky! 'Cos if you don't or won't or can't, you're
gonna be stepped on, pushed 'round, walked out on, beat up on, cheated on, worked
like a black fool, and cast out your own house.

Don't suck your teeth and cut your eyes at me! I be finished in a hot second. But
you'll hear this gospel truth so long you, my oldest, eat and sleep in my house. Best
cut your sass!

Pack a spare suitcase, one for him. If he proves devilish, it be easier to toss him out
that way. Put one change of clothes into it so he can't beg and bug you for nothin'!

If he be too quiet, he'll ruminate and feel that bottle more than he will you. Rum'll
be his milk and meat for months. It'll spoil him for anything. Won't be fit to drive his
nail. So when he's sleepy drunk, smack the long-ass son of a gun in the head, tell him
to wake his black-ass body up, and drive him out. If the fair fool don't come back
sober, he don't come back. Am I lyin'?

And if he be sweet-lookin', a heavy-natured man, always pullin' on women, and he
takes up with some spinny woman all daddled up from the cash he's vowed to bring
you, just tell him right up and down that you ain't his monkey in a dress, and raise
particular devil. Don't give him no shakes. And if that don't work, don't waste another black word, grab yourself a second man.

Watch out for two-faced chroniclers. These women will grin in you face, lookin'
for news 'bout you and your man. And just when you trust their acid chat and make

your man groan and grump and get all upset these gold-dust whores creep behind your back, crawl right in your bed, and thief him away. That's how they act. I know: I've been gypped so bloody much. And they don't care if it's a used love, a second-hand love, a stolen love, 'cos it's love all the same. And if it's good to you, they'll try to trick some too. So don't put no business on the streets that's conducted 'tween your sheets. But if some big-mouth humbugs you, tell the black bitch not to mess 'cos she's terrible lookin' anyway; a knife gash 'cross her face would just be improvement.

Missy! Gimme some of that bottle! Preachin' parches the throat. Besides, my eyes feel kinda zigzaggy today.

If some woman is grinnin' at your man, tell her straight: 'If it was shit that I had, you'd want some of that too.' Make her skedaddle. If her fresh fool follows, take everything he got and don't give a single, black penny back!

Missy, life's nothin' but guts, muscle, nerve. All you gotta do is stay black and die.

KING BEE BLUES

I'm an ol' king bee, honey,
Buzzin' from flower to flower.
I'm an ol' king bee, sweets,
Hummin' from flower to flower.
Women got good pollen;
I get some every hour.

There's Lily in the valley
And sweet honeysuckle Rose too;
There's Lily in the valley
And sweet honeysuckle Rose too.
And there's pretty black-eyed Susan,
Perfect as the night is blue.

You don't have to trust
A single, black word I say.
You don't have to trust
A single, black word I say.
But don't be surprised
If I sting your flower today.

To Selah

The butter moon is white
Sorta like your eyes;
The butter moon is bright, sugah,
Kinda like your eyes.
And it melts like I melt for you
While it coasts 'cross the sky.

The black highway uncoils
Like your body do sometimes.
The long highway unwinds, mama,
Like your lovin' do sometimes.
I'm gonna swerve your curves
And ride your centre line.

Stars are drippin' like tears,
The highway moves like a hymn;
Stars are drippin' like tears, beau'ful,
The highway sways like a hymn.
And I reach for your love,
Like a burglar for a gem.

ASHOK MATHUR

(b. 1961)

'I focus on language as a site of resistance,' says Ashok Mathur. As a writer, cultural worker, editor, and publisher, he sees his work as 'challenging a status quo that is extremely conservative and resistant to effective change, particularly in terms of race, but including gender, class, and sexuality.'

Born in Bhopal, India, Mathur is a resident of Calgary, Alberta. He studied at the University of Calgary where he received a B.A. in English (1988) and an M.A. (1990). He is currently at work on his Ph.D. dissertation, a study of activism. An active cultural worker, he has initiated and organized many cultural events, including a summer school of writing at Crowsnest Pass (1993-94), and events centring on anti-racism. In collaboration with Aruna Srivastava, he has presented papers and performances on anti-racist pedagogy in conferences across the country. A member of the editorial collective of the literary magazine *absinthe*, Mathur has co-edited,with Hiromi Goto and Suzette Mayr, a special issue of writers of colour and aboriginal writers called *The Skin On Our Tongues* (1993), a project conceived at 'The Appropriate Voice' session that was part of the gathering of writers of colour and aboriginal writers at Geneva Park in Orillia, Ontario, in 1993.

He is the publisher and editor, together with Nicole Marcotic, of DisOrientation Chapbooks, an alternative poetry-publication series that has published such writers as Erin Mouré, Roy Miki, Robert Kroetsch, Ian Iqbal Rashid, and Hiromi Goto. 'Our books,' he says, 'are bound in radically unconventional formats, the intent being to disrupt the normative reading patterns which are culturally induced and restrictive.'

Mathur's writing reflects a desire at once to locate language in the cultural and social contexts that inform it and to resist the strictures of literary conventions, a resistance that he sees as being 'an actual discontinuance of a formal (read: normal) approach, an out and out desistance'. As he stresses, desistance is 'not a refusal to read the page but a desisting insistence to stop and remake the page. This is turning left on a red light, reading right to left, cutting off the impulse to orient myself by the north star, turning my back on the balcony and saying, "It is the West, and Juliet is . . . not there." This desistance is disOrientation. A stopping and restarting. Beginning again.'

Mathur, who has taught English at the Alberta College of Arts (1992-94), has published his poetry and prose in such literary magazines as *West Coast Line, The Capilano Review, Rungh,* and *Fuse*. His book *Loveruage* appeared in 1994, and he has just completed a novel, *Once Upon an Elephant.*

INTO SKIN

Ho and the story begin to here. No story to beginning there before. But cause this is the way it happened, and I can't make it up if I try. It was happening this sort long ago but cause ten years back least that and when I would have kill my own self if wasn't for the sing. Ready to go as was but cause for the sing and the sleep and the branch but but but cause. Happened so fast so ago so I'm here try to telling this story but the words caughting but cause up up in the high highing branches which did saving my life. And so that look. Yes yeahyes I've been see that looking before always always when I begin of talking but cause no one can see be seeing what I say oh say now. When I first begin to speaking so in this way this new way in this new place from far far from where I being child, I yes but cause be get looking from all you all you just as now. But cause but you sit and wait for me I be changing changing all the time and soon you hearing the language you wait but cause for so long oh yeah. When I look forward seeing, look forward my talk and talking all of this but cause, but, so I have to be shift-like and look back when it was now and all different and not so hard as then. When it was now, ten years after.

When it was now, after years of learning and speaking and writing.

When it was now, a full decade after.

When it was now, and here I am, ten years older and growing older still, thanks to what happened those long years ago. And words are so different for me now.

Standing. Stilling. Swaying. Breezing. Standstillswaybreeze. Leaves falling. Sap slowing. Air cooling. Leavesfall sapslow aircool. Rope burn cut slice. Standing. Still.

Back then, when I was new here, everything seemed new here. So much action and speed. What a picture I was, dowdy and dazed, standing on the bus platform like I'd just stepped out of a Unesco postcard. My cousin said she'd be there but she wasn't. This was the new world. My new world. Everything full of action and speed and I was dazzled by the whiteness of it all.

'Say man, you lost?'

'?'

'I mean, ma'am—?'

'Gnugh!?'

'Cuz if you're lost or somethin' . . . '

'*Ujana sudhana.*' River flowing river river current up against, this is what I mean, this is my voice, choose the path of resistance, up against the current, swimming hard, banging off the waves, bouncing off the rocks, and make the path my own.

'I'm sorry? Well, take it easy ma'am—or, I mean . . . '

The young man was only trying to be helpful. He was my introduction to a spotless, unscented world. It wasn't his fault that he didn't know whether I was man or woman. At home I was—but no, that was there, the past, the dead past, and this was the here and now and I was whatever this new world gave me. I was greeted on the platform with a man-ma'am and I took the first step, first stroke, *ujana sudhana*, against the current. At home I was—but here I was newnamed and I became Manam. My cousin never did come that day and I left the platform by myself.

You left the platform by yourself. And you were by yourself for so many years. You were oogyana sa-dana? is that right? fighting against the current, going against the flow. To have known you then, to have met you then. When you were coming off that platform. Before everything happened. It must have been awful. Feel for you, really do. You were so fresh, as you say, a photograph come to life from a third world postcard. You must have been so beautiful. Must have been, huh. You are, you are beautiful, see it in you, emanating from you. Knew it when first saw you. Standing there, you were alone again, and your eyes were full of sorrow and love and couldn't help but fall in love. Watching you standing there; said:

'Couldn't help noticing you, sorrysorry, don't mean to be rude, but areyou areyou waiting for somebody?'

And you said: 'Uh-uh. Jus' standin' here.' Just like that, you said that jus' standin' here, and couldn't help (couldanyone?) couldn't help but fall in love with that sorrow in your eyes. Had to be with you. Had to love you. You, such a beautiful . . . beautiful . . . beautiful Manam. . . .

I floated for a long time. Uglily. A spotted and darkened blot on a frothy white sea, pristine white sea, clean oh so clean that's what it was, the world I was in. And I was an aberration, an abomination on this frothy surface. And I floated uglily for a long time.

'Do you have any skills?'

'Scellz?'

'Skills. Abilities. What can you do?'

'Do? Do. I can doing anything all sorts. Work in all sorts all sorts, all have. All can doing but cause if any help help . . . '

'All sorts? Like a handy—person? Well, that would come in . . . handy. Sure. Uh, do you have any education?'

'?'

'EDuCAtion? Training. School?'

'Ah school, but cause no good teacher if to teach the small childs with speak speaking this very very hard.'

'No, have you *had* any training, formal training as a handy, or whatever, anything. Ms . . . ter? I'm sorry, it doesn't say here whether you're, well . . . '

'Manam.'

'Yes, well, M-anam, then. It's very difficult for us to place someone without knowing exactly what they can do.'

'Work hard but cause need knowing how to speak then all will be righting all will be.'

'Yes. It will be.'

'Yes.'

But no. It was hardly an easy road. I floated in and out of the froth, working where I could and playing the roles asked of me. I had come from a world where nothing was asked and I had chosen to come here. And here they asked me to cleanse myself, to cleanse myself and purify the world I had come into. They asked this of me.

They asked this of you. You have told of this. How you floated between jobs as a manthenawoman but always as Manam. They asked you to clean yourself, you said, clean yourself and the world you were in. You tell, laughing now, how you began cleaning toilets at the bus station, the same station you first came to. And you went from there to cleaning floors. Then you cleaned windows. Then you moved to an office building, and late at night, when all the office workers were safely sleeping, you told how you'd clean from floor to floor. And that's where you were written, wasn't it? that's where you said it happened and kept on happening and hearing that, you telling that, there were tears here so many tears. Nothing to do.

Whisperly rustle. Tenderly twirling. Autumnly waiting.
Desperately dormant.
Whisperhiss. Tendertensed. Autumnugly. Desperatedying.
Whispertenderautumndesperate. Ropely sweet sensation
undercutly into bark.

I would work there in the office tower, darkened but for the perpetual light from the tubing in the hall. Work hard. And in the days I'd read the books I'd find, a glutton for the words that would one day wash away the smell of vinegar and lye. And yes I learned. Learned to speak the way the new world wanted me to speak. Learned to forget that *ujana sudhana* was my mentor, and that my true learning came as I soaped and scrubbed the floors walls desks doors. And when I met Him who would teach me more than I ever wished to know. . . . He was tall and large and His eyes were a smoggy grey and when I looked at them I was looking through Him. My shift was nearly over that morning. I was on my last floor, emptying waste paper baskets and, as I always did, seizing wads of computer sheets to practise my writing. I had a box of paper in my hands when I felt His presence.

'Wht th hll r y'dng?'

'Nothing, sir no sir nothing but cause going throw 'way and all so put for using in.'

'Tht's cmpny prprty, ya stpd ful.'

'Sir, yesyes sorry nothing but cause . . .'

'Gdm thf, shd kc sm sns'n tayou.'

I couldn't protect myself against the butterfly quickness and unpredictability of His words. They flew at me, landed angrily, then before I could grasp them they were replaced by new, yet more unfamiliar sounds.

'Foreigner, gv nch tk mile, tch a lsn, tch ya gd.' His face was pink and hot and so close I could feel the sweat leech from his pores; and my face, brown and smooth, passively bore his exhaustive torrent of verbal violence. Acquiescing, I bowed my head, to show respect, to acknowledge defeat and wrongness. And that's when words grew louder and blastier and when they stopped the silence was worse, for there He stood, breathing hate and closeness into my flesh my mind my

He was there forever and when He left I eased my body to the floor. He was gone. I could still hear and fear his words in my head. Banging and insistent. Compared to those words inside my body, his silence was nothing. But it stayed with me, shrouded around me. I rose. There were bootmarks, his, on the computer paper. I took that with me and, later that afternoon, over the stained, warped surface, copied neat lines of verse from a damaged and discarded book of modernist verse I had found in the garbage of a second-hand bookstore. My letters were neat and perfectly formed that afternoon.

Your letters were perfectly formed that day. And you continued to copy lines of poetry and prose from thrown-out books you had found. And you got better at writing on thrown-out computer paper from the office tower where you still worked. And every night, or almost every night, he was there and he would attack you with his words and then his breath and awful silence, and then his mouth would ooze more spit and filth upon you. But you kept going to work. You kept going and he kept coming. You said he was enjoying it now, unleashing those words on you like he could do to no one else. You said the standing silent, the breathy quiet, was not so bad, would not have been so bad, if it hadn't been preceded, always, by those words. Words tongued into your skin, welted into your body. But you kept going back. Going back. Why did you keep going back?

Braided branded sucked stucked rope into limb into side into skin. Wrapped warped corpsed cutted. Into

I. I remember. I remember that night. I remember that night He came and He cut and He wrote.

'Thr y r s-hole, cm here so'i cn shw y smthng spshl.'

'But cause this is nevernever bad thing, I working so good and cannot bear very much reality but cause.'

He turned out the light so the office was dark and all I could see was the pinky glow from His face and a grey light from His eyes. In His hand was a letter opener with a grey blade and I knew this time there would be no standing there silence, no quiet after the words.

'Dm bch. Bch? r y mn or wmn? Hrd t tl wth those clothes on.' And in the pinkgrey light from His face the blade came toward me and His hand reached out ripping tearing and the knife ripping tearing dully pulling shredding and and and He stood above me laughing spitting words and letters incomprehensible unconnected and then the letter opener coming closer to my body naked body open body blank unwritten body. And in the dark, lit only by the pinkgrey of his face, he began to write upon my skin with that dull blade words full words no mistaking them now, words I remembered painfully writing myself on bootstamped sheets of stolen computer paper and I could hear these words well, I could read these words in my body well, the vowels and consonants and carefully scribed syllables, written into me, and me, stonestill, fascinated, the bloodly ink obscuring obfuscating then revealing letters in my skin. He wrote my death into my body.

He wrote your death into your body. But he did not write you into death. He did not write you to death. He left you alone, ashamed, writhing with the writing on your bloody skin. The morning light was pinkgrey, too, but brighter than his face, and horrified workers saw you written on the office floor. You stood and clothed yourself, covered the words, and forever left the building of your learning. You walked to your home and you filled a bag with doubly inscribed computer paper. You took a rope. You walked far far and through the day and no words came to you except what words were with you and then it was evening and the city was behind. You saw the grove and you saw the tree. You touched its bark its coarsely written skin. You began to climb.

Stroke and stride. Cleave and climb. Breathe and brush. Rush
and rope.
strokecleavebreatherush
strideclimbbrushrope

I ascended with the rope. I touched the hoary bark and clawed words into the cracks; written bark clawed back and overwrote upon my skin. I reached the topmost branch and sat with words in me and over me. I tied the rope around the limb, tied it tight, and let the rope hang loose below. In setting sun the rope was silhouetted, a hanging silent O. I touched the coarseness of the rope the roughness of the bark the toughness of my skin and lay my head to rest upon the tree.

Sleepdreamriserest wordless wondrous dream a dream of life
dream a dream of wordless wondrousity dream a dream of
dreams dream into a life dream away from death undeathed
dream

You lay your head to rest upon the tree and when you woke the sky was dark and words had come and gone and would not hurt you now. You say the tree began to sing, a wordless song, singing to you in your sleep, song and sing and soft inside your ear. You came down from the tree and looked up at the O and smiled your gratitude. You burned the words you had so carefully inscribed on computer paper and left the ashes as an offering for your life. And two days later you were standing there, saw you standing there and you were beautiful, full of sorrow, but beautiful, too beautiful for words and who could not love you?

The words inside my skin are softer now. They fade and fall away with every passing day. We go back to the tree now. I see her in the grove and know that she is taller now. Up up so high silhouetted by the sky I see the O, still there, speaking to me wordlessly. O. O. O. I touch her written skin and sing the song she sang to me and then begin to climb her slowly stilly. I have no words I have no sex I have no song but what she sang to me singing softly Manam Manam Manam

Manam ma'am, no man wo man curl unfurl me let me breathe
untie me sift me sing me touch and tinge me manam manam
manam

Singing softly Manam manam manam, you fall asleep upon the branch, the singing limb, and breathe and listen wordlessly and under watchful eye you wake and wonder touch the aged O.

The rope is old and weathered but hangs there still. The limb is written into by the loop, the rope writes words upon the branch and I say O. I try untie the rope but fast it holds, imprinted on the tree I work unwork pull push try hard but cause no way grows there inside no way is buried so so but cause not worked and words worded in the tree unsinged pull but never never but cause and I say yes this happening just so but cause you never gonna believe this when I tell you, but I can't never make it up if I try. Never.

IAN IQBAL RASHID

(b. 1965)

"'A Pass to India" was written about a trip I made to the Subcontinent in 1987,' says Ian Iqbal Rashid about the first of his poems included here. 'I am fourth generation Tanzanian-born and grew up in Canada, but I was convinced at the outset of that trip that I was going home to a country and a history that was waiting, somehow, to be reclaimed. Although the poem is set at the beginning of the journey, it has been filtered through feelings that I had afterward—feelings of personal failure and, I must admit, great sadness.' Claiming India as a 'home' does not suggest a nostalgic movement towards the past, for Rashid. What it speaks of, instead, is 'finding a way to live within' this and other, similar, journeys, a way that reflects a resistance to 'being among the *exiled*, of the *diaspora*, of always referring back to a mythical or real *homeland'*. As Rashid asks in *Beyond Destination*, the publication that accompanied a film, video, and installation exhibition by South Asian Artists at Icon Gallery, Birmingham, England, curated by him, 'Is South Asia a place? . . . Is South Asia a geographical category? Is it racial? Or linguistic? . . . [O]nce the definitions are set, there is always a danger of slipping into a narrow way of viewing—and indeed making—cultural work: a kind of nationalism emerges.'

Born in Dar es Salaam, Tanzania, Rashid was raised in Toronto, where he has been active in the South Asian community of artists. He is the founder of the Desh/Pardesh Arts Festival in Toronto, an annual event, and the first of its kind to identify and explore the diasporic South Asian cultural practices in the West. Also a founding member of both *Rungh* magazine and the Canadian Centre for Lesbian and Gay Studies, Rashid has had his poetry published widely both in Canada and in England. His first book of poetry, *Black Markets, White Boyfriends (and Other Acts of Elision)* (1991), which was nominated for the Gerald Lampert Award, is concerned with racial difference and sexuality, and how these constructs affect power within personal relationships.

The former managing editor of Between the Lines press in Toronto, Rashid has been working during the past few years as an independent film and video curator in, among other places, Sao Paulo, Brazil, Melbourne, Australia, and Victoria, British Columbia. In London, England, he has co-ordinated *Does it Come in Another Colour: Race and Desire in Film and Video* for The ICA; *Flaming: Queer Film and Video* for Screen-on-the-Screen; and *Can-Asian Perspectives* for Canada House. With Sarah Turner, he has programmed a touring package for the London Film-makers' Co-op called *Hygiene and Hysteria: Assaults on the Body in the Late-Twentieth Century*. His own script, *Bringing Up Babu*, is scheduled to be televised as part of the BBC 2 Black Screen project.

Rashid's second collection of poetry, *The Heat Yesterday* (1995), deals with issues of memory and mourning, especially mourning in the age of AIDS, and addresses, once again, the concept of belonging. With DisOrientation Chapbooks in Calgary, he has also published an image/text chapbook called *Song of Sabu* that is based on the life of the film star Sabu. Rashid, who since 1991 has divided his life between London, England, and Canada, has just completed a collection of short stories, called *Muscular Bridges*.

A PASS TO INDIA

I take it with me
along with my bundle of belongings
that soon will seem to float beside me constantly

an absence of metaphor that my parents live with/out
no dreams of snow
home is a place without light
the dark continent
prize won for a victor for whom they mediated
a prize which mediates my narrative
this place of my birth which after it was conquered
    conquered
so they had to leave as I leave now
carrying the papers of a man
whom I imagine might vanish
becoming a man
like the men
I've never known disappeared
trying to finish a story suggested by a gaze at history,
a story told by old photographs
and older women
trying to redress the damage of absence
of early acts of elision
a story whose open end holds me often
in a fist
snake-tight
God(dess)-like
serpent embrace
except to caress me now and again
    now
mocking my obsession
this open hand of a story
its teasing misshaped fingertip of a subcontinent.

And I leave reading one of two epic poems
governing a struggle that will not vanish
held in a line that zips open a sky of myth
exposing its soft little boy's belly
leaving stiff vestments behind, leaving an anger behind
with the buildings that we are tunnelling by with a roar
leaving for a place as impenetrable as a cell
    under attack
    from a virus.

ANOTHER COUNTRY

All this new love of my parents' country:
We have bought the videotapes together,
bought the magazines and books,
all the advertisements,
each others' responses.
We watch the slides of your visit.
Your handsome face tanned, surrounded by mango trees,
planted above the poverty,
the moist beauty,
(which you think of blowing up and then framing,
building into your walls)
majesty imposed upon majesty.

Now I watch you watch Sergeant Merrick watch poor Hari Kumar.
And follow as the white man's desire is twisted,
manipulated into a brutal beating.
You are affected by the actor's brown sweating
body supple under punishment. What moves you?
The pain within the geometry of the body bent?

The dignity willed in the motions of refusal?
A private fantasy promised, exploding
within every bead of sweat?
Or is it the knowledge of later:
how my body will become supple
for you, will curve and bow to your wishes
as yours can never quite bend to mine.
What moves you then?

My beauty is branded into the colour of my skin,
my strands of hair thick as snakes,
damp with the lushness of all the tropics,
My humble penis cheated by the imperial wealth of yours.
Hari's corporal punishment, mine corporeal:
Yet this is also part of my desire.
Even stroking myself against your absence
I must close my eyes and think of England.

COULD HAVE DANCED ALL NIGHT

I
I once used to dream of being held knowingly by a man
on whom I would not look.

Then this all came again, the embrace held
in the ease of a dance, held within your hands small
yet capable and roped with thick vein.
And when I tried, it didn't surprise me
to be able to look into your eyes like mine,
the rough colour of night, into your shy, pie face.

Standing together tonight I long for the anise
taste of Thai basil on your skin,
your ass and thighs resplendent
in strobes of evening's light.
Tonight I would dance with you across an alien landscape.
We could fly. ('I'm positive.')
But this night finds our legs rooted, knotted,
planted painfully like a flag. ('I've tested positive.')

II
Tonight, I watch you walking away,
wheeling your burden before you into the night.
Fists jab my thighs on either side.
Fists which mean to unclench hold
fingers which mean to interlock
with yours, like pieces of a puzzle
join into a picture of two men dancing.

Tonight movement is limited:
from hand to mouth to mind.
Tobacco, caustic laughter in the lungs,
the careful sipping of our herbal teas,
the careful sipping of our everything-will-be-all-rights.

HOSPITAL VISIT: THE HEAT YESTERDAY

The heat yesterday gets a hold of my head,
becomes an absent presence: the memory of a
crown. Heat aggravates everything, bullies you
into a little less alive. The inverse of an

echo, the man you are about to become. Heat
peels back the wild, gamey smell of boy, which
is always there, waiting like curtains.

Heat erodes the gravelly bits that complicate
your voice, that confuses the air—a constant
static sound. Sound that has scored the last
angry days with you, our horrible misstepped
dance out of synch: every expression a glare,
every touch a threat. And my two hands always
struggling, working a pocket-sized game.
Nothing I could do was right: the tiny silver
balls never never in their nooks all at once in
the heat yesterday.

In the heat yesterday I leave impoverished
embarrassed, feeling foolish, misspent. (As
time goes into one of its own long, toffee-like
stretches.) I am amazed that I can leave, as if
this was early emergence from an afternoon
film. To turn the corner chased by so much
runny yellow noise. So much that had been
allowed to go on and on now on for so long now
without me.

The heat yesterday slices through today like
cellophane. Today is an unused shellacked
smell. And I am back again still. Still touch
the complicated bones of knee that peek out
from under a sheet. 'The heat yesterday . . .' You
cannot hear me. A love song seeps out from the
headphones that cup your innermost face. . . .

SHYAM SELVADURAI

(b. 1965)

Shyam Selvadurai, born in Colombo, Sri Lanka, grew up, as he says, 'aware of the interaction between the personal and the political'. With his parents and three siblings, Selvadurai came to Canada in 1984, after the 1983 communal rioting between the Tamil and Sinhalese communities. 'Being in Canada has been good,' says Selvadurai, who is a Tamil; 'it has given me a creative perspective that I might not have had otherwise.'

Selvadurai holds a B.F.A. from York University where he studied creative writing as well as theatre directing and play writing. He has written for television, and his writing has been anthologized. His book *Funny Boy* (1994), the winner of the W.H. Smith-*Books in Canada* First Novel Award, is 'a novel in six stories' narrated from the point of view of Arjie, a young boy when the book opens. It offers a realistic portrayal of characters whose lives are shaped by the tensions holding together—and separating—collective and personal yearnings. Through Arjie's soon-to-be-lost innocence, we witness the violent and insidious confrontations between the Tamils and Sinhalese as they are dramatized through love relationships and familial ties. 'Funny', Arjie gradually learns, stands for what his society decides is queer—strange, unpredictable, unmanageable, ultimately threatening to the status quo. It also speaks of Arjie's growing sense of gay identity, an awareness that further complicates his responsibility toward his Tamil community and his family.

Although not an autobiographical novel, it is an evocation of Selvadurai's background. Currently at work on his second novel, he has returned to his birthplace many times. 'Sri Lanka is still vivid,' he says. 'For me, life there is just a daily thing'.

PIGS CAN'T FLY

Besides Christmas and other festive occasions, spend-the-days were the days most looked forward to by all of us, cousins, aunts, and uncles.

For the adults a spend-the-day was the one Sunday of the month they were free of their progeny. The eagerness with which they anticipated these days could be seen in the way Amma woke my brother, my sister, and me extra early when they came. Unlike on school days, when Amma allowed us to dawdle a little, we were hurried through our morning preparations. Then, after a quick breakfast, we would be driven to the house of our grandparents.

The first thing that met our eyes on entering our grandparents' house, after we carefully wiped our feet on the doormat, would be the dark corridor running the length of it, on one side of which were the bedrooms and on the other the drawing and dining rooms. This corridor, with its old photographs on both walls and its ceiling so high that our footsteps echoed, scared me a little. The drawing room into which we would be ushered to pay our respects to our grandparents was also dark and smelled like old clothes that had been locked away in a suitcase for a long time. There my grandparents Ammachi and Appachi sat, enthroned in big reclining chairs. Appachi usually looked up from his paper and said vaguely, 'Ah, hello, hello,' before going back behind it, but Ammachi always called us to her with the beckoning movement of her middle and index fingers. With our legs trembling slightly, we would go to her, the thought of the big canes she kept behind her tall clothes almariah strongly imprinted upon our minds. She would grip our faces in her plump hands, and one by one kiss us wetly on both cheeks and say, 'God has blessed me with fifteen grandchildren who will look after me in my old age.' She smelled of stale coconut oil, and the diamond mukkuthi in her nose always pressed painfully against my cheek.

When the aunts and uncles eventually drove away, waving gaily at us children from car windows, we waved back at the retreating cars, with not even a pretence of sorrow. For one glorious day a month we were free of parental control and the ever-watchful eyes and tale-bearing tongues of the house servants.

We were not, alas, completely abandoned, as we would have so liked to have been. Ammachi and Janaki were supposedly in charge. Janaki, cursed with the task of having to cook for fifteen extra people, had little time for supervision and actually preferred to have nothing to do with us at all. If called upon to come and settle a dispute, she would rush out, her hands red from grinding curry paste, and box the ears of the first person who happened to be in her path. We had learned that Janaki was to be appealed to only in the most dire emergencies. The one we understood, by tacit agreement, never to appeal to was Ammachi. Like the earth-goddess in the folktales, she was not to be disturbed from her tranquillity. To do so would have been the cause of a catastrophic earthquake.

In order to minimize interference by either Ammachi or Janaki, we had developed and refined a system of handling conflict and settling disputes ourselves. Two things formed the framework of this system: territoriality and leadership.

Territorially, the area around my grandparents' house was divided into two. The front garden, the road, and the field that lay in front of the house belonged to the boys, although included in their group was my female cousin Meena. In this territory, two factions struggled for power, one led by Meena, the other by my brother, Varuna, who, because of a prevailing habit, had been renamed Diggy-Nose and then simply Diggy.

The second territory was called 'the girls', included in which, however, was myself, a boy. It was to this territory of 'the girls', confined to the back garden and the kitchen porch, that I seemed to have gravitated naturally, my earliest memories of those spend-the-days always belonging in the back garden of my grandparents' home. The pleasure the boys had standing for hours on a cricket field under the sweltering sun, watching the batsmen run from crease to crease, was incomprehensible to me.

For me, the primary attraction of the girls' territory was the potential for the free play of fantasy. Because of the force of my imagination, I was selected as leader. Whatever the game, be it the imitation of adult domestic functions or the enactment of some well-loved fairy story, it was I who discovered some new way to enliven it, some new twist to the plot of a familiar tale. Led by me, the girl cousins would conduct a raid on my grandparents' dirty-clothes basket, discovering in this odorous treasure trove saris, blouses, sheets, curtains with which we invented costumes to complement our voyages of imagination.

The reward for my leadership was that I always got to play the main part in the fantasy. If it was cooking-cooking we were playing, I was the chef; if it was Cinderella or Thumbelina, I was the much-beleaguered heroine of these tales.

Of all our varied and fascinating games, bride-bride was my favourite. In it, I was able to combine many elements of the other games I loved, and with time bride-bride, which had taken a few hours to play initially, became an event that spread out over the whole day and was planned for weeks in advance. For me the culmination of this game, and my ultimate moment of joy, was when I put on the clothes of the bride. In the late afternoon, usually after tea, I, along with the older girl cousins, would enter Janaki's room. From my sling-bag I would bring out my most prized possession, an old white sari, lightly yellow with age, its border torn and missing most of its sequins. The dressing of the bride would now begin, and then, by the transfiguration I saw taking place in Janaki's cracked full-length mirror—by the sari being wrapped around my body, the veil being pinned to my head, the rouge put on my cheeks, lipstick on my lips, kohl around my eyes—I was able to leave the constraints of myself and ascend into another, more brilliant, more beautiful self, a self to whom this day was dedicated, and around whom the world, represented by my cousins putting flowers in my hair, draping the palu, seemed to revolve. It was a self magnified, like the goddesses of the Sinhalese and Tamil cinema, larger than life; and like them, like the Malini Fonsekas and the Geetha Kumarasinghes, I was an icon, a graceful, benevolent, perfect being upon whom the adoring eyes of the world rested.

Those spend-the-days, the remembered innocence of childhood, are now coloured in the hues of the twilight sky. It is a picture made even more sentimental by the loss of all that was associated with them. By all of us having to leave Sri Lanka years later because of communal violence and forge a new home for ourselves in Canada.

Yet those Sundays, when I was seven, marked the beginning of my exile from the world I loved. Like a ship that leaves a port for the vast expanse of sea, those much looked forward to days took me away from the safe harbour of childhood towards the precarious waters of adult life.

* * *

The visits at my grandparents' began to change with the return from abroad of Kanthi Aunty, Cyril Uncle, and their daughter, Tanuja, whom we quickly renamed 'Her Fatness', in that cruelly direct way children have.

At first we had no difficulty with the newcomer in our midst. In fact we found her quite willing to accept that, by reason of her recent arrival, she must necessarily begin at the bottom.

In the hierarchy of bride-bride, the person with the least importance, less even than the priest and the page boys, was the groom. It was a role we considered stiff and boring, that held no attraction for any of us. Indeed, if we could have dispensed with that role altogether we would have, but alas it was an unfortunate feature of the marriage ceremony. My younger sister, Sonali, with her patient good nature, but also sensing that I might have a mutiny on my hands if I asked anyone else to play that role, always donned the long pants and tattered jacket, borrowed from my grandfather's clothes chest. It was now deemed fitting that Her Fatness should take over the role and thus leave Sonali free to wrap a bedsheet around her body, in the manner of a sari, and wear araliya flowers in her hair like the other bridesmaids.

For two spend-the-days, Her Fatness accepted her role without a murmur and played it with all the skilled unobtrusiveness of a bit player. The third spend-the-day, however, everything changed. That day turned out to be my grandmother's birthday. Instead of dropping the children off and driving away as usual, the aunts and uncles stayed on for lunch, a slight note of peevish displeasure in their voices.

We had been late, because etiquette (or rather my father) demanded that Amma wear a sari for the grand occasion of her mother-in-law's sixtieth birthday. Amma's tardiness and her insistence on getting her palu to fall to exactly above her knees drove us all to distraction (especially Diggy, who quite rightly feared that in his absence Meena would try to persuade the better members of his team to defect to her side). Even I, who usually loved the ritual of watching Amma get dressed, stood in her doorway with the others and fretfully asked if she was ever going to be ready.

When we finally did arrive at Ramanaygam Road, everyone else had been there almost an hour. We were ushered into the drawing room by Amma to kiss Ammachi and present her with her gift, the three of us clutching the present. All the uncles and aunts were seated. Her Fatness stood in between Kanthi Aunty's knees, next to Ammachi. When she saw us, she gave me an accusing, hostile look and pressed further between her mother's legs. Kanthi Aunty turned away from her discussion with Mala Aunty, and, seeing me, she smiled and said in a tone that was as heavily sweetened as undiluted rose-syrup, 'So, what is this I hear, aah? Nobody will play with my little daughter.'

I looked at her and then at Her Fatness, shocked by the lie. All my senses were alert.

Kanthi Aunty wagged her finger at me and said in a playful, chiding tone, 'Now, now, Arjie, you must be nice to my little daughter. After all, she's just come from abroad and everything.' Fortunately, I was prevented from having to answer. It was my turn to present my cheek to Ammachi, and, for the first time, I did so willingly, preferring the prick of the diamond mukkuthi to Kanthi Aunty's honeyed admonition.

Kanthi Aunty was the fourth oldest in my father's family. First there was my father, then Ravi Uncle, Mala Aunty, Kanthi Aunty, Babu Uncle, Seelan Uncle, and finally Radha Aunty, who was much younger than the others and was away, studying in America. Kanthi Aunty was tall and bony, and we liked her the least, in spite of the fact that she would pat our heads affectionately whenever we walked past or greeted her. We sensed that beneath her benevolence lurked a seething anger, tempered by guile, that could have deadly consequences if unleashed in our direction. I had heard Amma say to her sister, Neliya Aunty, that 'Poor Kanthi was bitter because of the humiliations she had suffered abroad. After all, darling, what a thing, forced to work as a servant in a whitey's house to make ends meet.'

Once Ammachi had opened the present, a large silver serving tray, and thanked us for it (and insisted on kissing us once again), my brother, my sister, and I were finally allowed to leave the room. Her Fatness had already disappeared. I hurried out the front door and ran around the side of the house.

When I reached the back garden I found the girl cousins squatting on the porch in a circle. They were so absorbed in what was happening in the centre that none of them even heard my greeting. Lakshmi finally became aware of my presence and beckoned me over excitedly. I reached the circle and the cause of her excitement became clear. In the middle, in front of Her Fatness, sat a long-legged doll with shiny gold hair. Her dress was like that of a fairy queen, the gauze skirt sprinkled with tiny silver stars. Next to her sat her male counterpart, dressed in a pale-blue suit. I stared in wonder at the marvellous dolls. For us cousins, who had grown up under a government that strictly limited all foreign imports, such toys were unimaginable. Her Fatness turned to the other cousins and asked them if they wanted to hold the dolls for a moment. They nodded eagerly and the dolls passed from hand to hand. I moved closer to get a better look. My gaze involuntarily rested on Her Fatness and she gave me a smug look. Immediately her scheme became evident to me. It was with these dolls that my cousin from abroad hoped to seduce the other cousins away from me.

Unfortunately for her, she had underestimated the power of bride-bride. When the other cousins had all looked at the dolls, they bestirred themselves and, without so much as a backward glance, hurried down the steps to prepare for the marriage ceremony. As I followed them, I looked triumphantly at Her Fatness, who sat on the porch, clasping her beautiful dolls to her chest.

When lunch was over, my grandparents retired to their room for a nap. The other adults settled in the drawing room to read the newspaper or doze off in the huge armchairs. We, the bride-to-be and the bridesmaids, retired to Janaki's room for the long-awaited ritual of dressing the bride.

We were soon disturbed, however, by the sound of booming laughter. At first we ignored it, but when it persisted, getting louder and more drawn out, my sister, Sonali, went to the door and looked out. Her slight gasp brought us all out onto the porch. There the groom strutted, up and down, head thrown back, stomach stuck out. She sported a huge bristly moustache (torn out of the broom) and a cigarette (of rolled paper and talcum powder), which she held between her fingers and puffed on vigorously. The younger cousins, instead of getting dressed and putting the final touches to the altar, sat along the edge of the porch and watched with great amusement.

'Aha, me hearties!' the groom cried on seeing us. She opened her hands expansively. 'Bring me my fair maiden, for I must be off to my castle before the sun setest.'

We looked at the groom, aghast at the change in her behaviour. She sauntered towards us, then stopped in front of me, winked expansively and, with her hand under my chin, tilted back my head.

'Ahhh!' she exclaimed. 'A bonny lass, a bonny lass indeed.'

'Stop it!' I cried, and slapped her hand. 'The groom is not supposed to make a noise.'

'Why not?' Her Fatness replied angrily, dropping her hearty voice and accent. 'Why can't the groom make a noise?'

'Because.'

'Because of what?'

'Because the game is called bride-bride, not groom-groom.'

Her Fatness seized her moustache and flung it to the ground dramatically. 'Well I don't want to be the groom any more. I want to be the bride.'

We stared at her in disbelief, amazed by her impudent challenge to my position.

'You can't,' I finally said.

'Why not?' Her Fatness demanded. 'Why should you always be the bride? Why can't someone else have a chance too?'

'Because . . .' Sonali said, joining in. 'Because Arjie is the bestest bride of all.'

'But he's not even a girl,' Her Fatness said, closing in on the lameness of Sonali's argument. 'A bride is a girl, not a boy.' She looked around at the other cousins and then at me. 'A boy cannot be the bride,' she said with deep conviction. 'A girl must be the bride.'

I stared at her, defenceless in the face of her logic.

Fortunately, Sonali, loyal to me as always, came to my rescue. She stepped in between us and said to Her Fatness, 'If you can't play properly, go away. We don't need you.'

'Yes!' Lakshmi, another of my supporters, cried.

The other cousins, emboldened by Sonali's fearlessness, murmured in agreement.

Her Fatness looked at all of us for a moment and then her gaze rested on me.

'You're a pansy,' she said, her lips curling in disgust.

We looked at her blankly.

'A faggot,' she said, her voice rising against our uncomprehending stares.

'A sissy!' she shouted in desperation.

It was clear by this time that these were insults.

'Give me that jacket,' Sonali said. She stepped up to Her Fatness and began to pull at it. 'We don't like you any more.'

'Yes!' Lakshmi cried. 'Go away you fatty-boom-boom!'

This was an insult we all understood, and we burst out laughing. Someone even began to chant, 'Hey fatty-boom-boom. Hey fatty-boom-boom.'

Her Fatness pulled off her coat and trousers. 'I hate you all,' she cried. 'I wish you were all dead.' She flung the groom's clothes on the ground, stalked out of the back garden, and went around the side of the house.

We returned to our bridal preparations, chuckling to ourselves over the new nickname we had found for our cousin.

When the bride was finally dressed, Lakshmi, the maid of honour, went out of Janaki's room to make sure that everything was in place. Then she gave the signal and the priest and choirboys began to sing, with a certain want of harmony and correct lyrics, 'The voice that breathed oh Eeeden, the first and glorious day. . . .' Solemnly, I made my way down the steps towards the altar that had been set up at one end of the back garden. When I reached the altar, however, I heard the kitchen door open. I turned to see Her Fatness with Kanthi Aunty. The discordant singing died out.

Kanthi Aunty's benevolent smile had completely disappeared and her eyes were narrowed with anger.

'Who's calling my daughter fatty?' Kanthi Aunty said. She came to the edge of the porch.

We stared at her, no one daring to own up.

Her gaze fell on me and her eyes widened for a moment. Then a smile spread across her face.

'What's this?' she said, the honey seeping back into her voice. She came down a few steps and crooked her finger at me. I looked down at my feet and refused to go to her.

'Come here, come here,' she said.

Unable to disobey her command any longer, I went to her. She looked me up and down for a moment, and then gingerly, as if she were examining raw meat at the market, turned me around.

'What's this you're playing?' she asked.

'It's bride-bride, Aunty,' Sonali said.

'Bride-bride,' she murmured.

Her hand closed on my arm in a tight grip.

'Come with me,' she said.

I resisted, but her grip tightened, her nails digging into my elbow. She pulled me up the porch steps and towards the kitchen door.

'No,' I cried. 'No, I don't want to.'

Something about the look in her eyes terrified me so much I did the unthinkable and I hit out at her. This made her hold my arm even more firmly. She dragged me through the kitchen, past Janaki, who looked up, curious, and into the corridor and towards the drawing room. I felt a heaviness begin to build in my stomach. Instinctively I knew that Kanthi Aunty had something terrible in mind.

As we entered the drawing room, Kanthi Aunty cried out, her voice brimming over with laughter, 'See what I found!'

The other aunts and uncles looked up from their papers or bestirred themselves from their sleep. They gazed at me in amazement as if I had suddenly made myself visible, like a spirit. I glanced at them and then at Amma's face. Seeing her expression, I felt my dread deepen. I lowered my eyes. The sari suddenly felt suffocating around my body, and the hairpins, which held the veil in place, pricked at my scalp.

Then the silence was broken by the booming laugh of Cyril Uncle, Kanthi Aunty's husband. As if she had been hit, Amma swung around in his direction. The other aunts and uncles began to laugh too, and I watched as Amma looked from one to the other like a trapped animal. Her gaze finally came to rest on my father and for the first time I noticed that he was the only one not laughing. Seeing the way he kept his eyes fixed on his paper, I felt the heaviness in my stomach begin to push its way up my throat.

'Ey, Chelva,' Cyril Uncle cried out jovially to my father, 'looks like you have a funny one here.'

My father pretended he had not heard and, with an inclination of his head, indicated to Amma to get rid of me.

She waved her hand in my direction and I picked up the edges of my veil and fled to the back of the house.

That evening, on the way home, both my parents kept their eyes averted from me. Amma glanced at my father occasionally, but he refused to meet her gaze. Sonali, sensing my unease, held my hand tightly in hers.

Later, I heard my parents fighting in their room.

'How long has this been going on?' my father demanded.

'I don't know,' Amma cried defensively. 'It was as new to me as it was to you.'

'You should have known. You should have kept an eye on him.'

'What should I have done? Stood over him while he was playing?'

'If he turns out funny like that Rankotwera boy, if he turns out to be the laughing-stock of Colombo, it'll be your fault,' my father said in a tone of finality. 'You always spoil him and encourage all his nonsense.'

'What do I encourage?' Amma demanded.

'You are the one who allows him to come in here while you're dressing and play with your jewellery.'

Amma was silent in the face of the truth.

Of the three of us, I alone was allowed to enter Amma's bedroom and watch her get dressed for special occasions. It was an experience I considered almost religious, for, even though I adored the goddesses of the local cinema, Amma was the final statement in female beauty for me.

When I knew Amma was getting dressed for a special occasion, I always positioned myself outside her door. Once she had put on her underskirt and blouse, she would ring for our servant, Anula, to bring her sari, and then, while taking it from her, hold the door open so I could go in as well. Entering that room was, for me, a greater boon than that granted by any god to a mortal. There were two reasons for this. The first was the jewellery box which lay open on the dressing table. With a joy akin to ecstasy, I would lean over and gaze inside, the faint smell of perfume rising out of the box each time I picked up a piece of jewellery and held it against my nose or ears or throat. The second was the pleasure of watching Amma drape her sari, watching her shake open the yards of material, which, like a Chinese banner caught by the wind, would linger in the air for a moment before drifting gently to the floor; watching her pick up one end of it, tuck it into the waistband of her skirt, make the pleats, and then with a flick of her wrists invert the pleats and tuck them into her waistband; and finally watching her drape the palu across her breasts and pin it into place with a brooch.

When Amma was finished, she would check to make sure that the back of the sari had not risen up with the pinning of the palu, then move back and look at herself in the mirror. Standing next to her or seated on the edge of the bed, I, too, would look at her reflection in the mirror, and, with the contented sigh of an artist who has finally captured the exact effect he wants, I would say, 'You should have been a film star, Amma.'

'A film star?' she would cry and lightly smack the side my head. 'What kind of a low-class-type person do you think I am?'

One day, about a week after the incident at my grandparents', I positioned myself outside my parents' bedroom door. When Anula arrived with the sari, Amma took it and quickly shut the door. I waited patiently, thinking Amma had not yet put on her blouse and skirt, but the door never opened. Finally, perplexed that Amma had forgotten, I knocked timidly on the door. She did not answer, but I could hear her moving around inside. I knocked a little louder and called out 'Amma' through the keyhole. Still no response, and I was about to call her name again when she replied gruffly, 'Go away. Can't you see I am busy?'

I stared disbelievingly at the door. Inside I could hear the rustle of the sari as it brushed along the floor. I lifted my hand to knock again when suddenly I remembered the quarrel I had heard on the night of that last spend-the-day. My hand fell limply by my side.

I crept away quietly to my bedroom, sat down on the edge of my bed, and stared at my feet for a long time. It was clear to me that I had done something wrong, but what it was I couldn't comprehend. I thought of what my father had said about turning out 'funny'. The word 'funny' as I understood it meant either humorous or strange, as in the expression, 'that's funny'. Neither of these fitted the sense in which my father had used the word, for there had been a hint of disgust in his tone.

Later, Amma came out of her room and called Anula to give her instructions for the evening. As I listened to the sound of her voice, I realized that something had changed forever between us.

A little while after my parents had left for their dinner party, Sonali came looking for me. Seeing my downcast expression, she sat next to me, and, though unaware of anything that had passed, slipped her hand in mine. I pushed it away roughly, afraid that if I let her squeeze my hand I would start to cry.

The next morning Amma and I were like two people who had had a terrible fight the night before. I found it hard to look her in the eye and she seemed in an unusually gay mood.

The following spend-the-day, when Amma came to awaken us, I was already seated in bed and folding my bride-bride sari. Something in her expression, however, made me hurriedly return the sari to the bag.

'What's that?' she said, coming towards me, her hand outstretched. After a moment I gave her the bag. She glanced at its contents briefly. 'Get up, it's spend-the-day,' she said. Then, with the bag in her hand, she went to the window and looked out into the driveway. The seriousness of her expression, as if I had done something so awful that even the usual punishment of a caning would not suffice, frightened me.

I was brushing my teeth after breakfast when Anula came to the bathroom door, peered inside, and said with a sort of grim pleasure, 'Missie wants to talk to you in her room.' Seeing the alarm in my face, she nodded and said sagely, 'Up to some kind of mischief as usual. Good-for-nothing child.'

My brother, Diggy, was standing in the doorway of our parents' room, one foot scratching impatiently against the other. Amma was putting on her lipstick. My father had already gone for his Sunday squash game, and, as usual, she would pick him up after she had dropped us off at our grandparents'.

Amma looked up from the mirror, saw me, and indicated with her tube of lipstick for both of us to come inside and sit down on the edge of the bed. Diggy gave me a baleful look, as if it was my fault that Amma was taking such a long time to get ready. He followed me into the room, his slippers dragging along the floor.

Finally Amma closed her lipstick, pressed her lips together to even out the colour, then turned to us.

'Okay, mister,' she said to Diggy, 'I am going to tell you something and this is an order.'

We watched her carefully.

'I want you to include your younger brother on your cricket team.'

Diggy and I looked at her in shocked silence, then he cried, 'Ah! Come on, Amma!'

And I, too, cried out, 'I don't want to play with them. I hate cricket!'

'I don't care what you want,' Amma said. 'It's good for you.'

'Arjie's useless,' Diggy said. 'We'll never win if he's on our team.'

Amma held up her hand to silence us. 'That's an order,' she said.

'Why?' I asked, ignoring her gesture. 'Why do I have to play with the boys?'

'Why?' Amma said. 'Because the sky is so high and pigs can't fly, that's why.'

'Please, Amma! Please!' I held out my arms to her.

Amma turned away quickly, picked up the handbag from the dressing table, and said, almost to herself, 'If the child turns out wrong, it's the mother they always blame, never the father.' She clicked the handbag shut.

I put my head in my hands and began to cry. 'Please, Amma, please,' I said through my sobs.

She continued to face the window.

I flung myself on the bed with a wail of anguish. I waited for her to come to me as she always did when I cried, waited for her to take me in her arms, rest my head against her breasts, and say in her special voice, 'What's this, now? Who's the little man who's crying?'

But she didn't heed my weeping any more than she had heeded my cries when I knocked on her door.

Finally I stopped crying and rolled over on my back. Diggy had left the room. Amma turned to me, now that I had become quiet, and said cheerfully, 'You'll have a good time, just wait and see.'

'Why can't I play with the girls?' I replied.

'You can't, that's all.'

'But why?'

She shifted uneasily.

'You're a big boy now. And big boys must play with other boys.'

'That's stupid.'

'It doesn't matter,' she said. 'Life is full of stupid things and sometimes we just have to do them.'

'I won't,' I said defiantly. 'I won't play with the boys.'

Her face reddened with anger. She reached down, caught me by the shoulders, and shook me hard. Then she turned away and ran her hand through her hair. I watched her, gloating. I had broken her cheerful façade, forced her to show how much it pained her to do what she was doing, how little she actually believed in the justness of her actions.

After a moment she turned back to me and said in an almost pleading tone, 'You'll have a good time.'

I looked at her and said, 'No I won't.'

Her back straightened. She crossed to the door and stopped. Without looking at me she said, stiffly, 'The car leaves in five minutes. If you're not in it by then, watch out.'

I lay back on the bed and gazed at the mosquito net swinging gently in the breeze. In my mind's eye, I saw the day that stretched ahead of me. At the thought of having to waste the most precious day of the month in that field in front of my grandparents' house, the hot sun beating on my head, the perspiration running down the sides of my face, I felt a sense of despair begin to take hold of me. The picture of what would take place in the back garden became clear. I saw Her Fatness seizing my place as leader of the girls, claiming for herself the rituals I had so carefully invented and planned. I saw her standing in front of Janaki's mirror as the other girls fixed her hair, pinned her veil, and draped her sari. The thought was terrible. Something had to be done. I could not give up that easily, could not let Her Fatness, whose sneaking to Kanthi Aunty had forced me into the position I was now in, so easily take my place. But what could I do?

As if in answer, an object which rested just at the periphery of my vision claimed my attention. I turned my head slightly and saw my sling-bag. Then a thought came to me. I reached out, picked up the bag, and hugged it close to my chest. Without the sari in that bag, it was impossible for the girls to play bride-bride. I thought of Her Fatness with triumph. What would she drape around her body? A bedsheet like the bridesmaids? No! Without me and my sari she would not be able to play bride-bride properly.

There was, I realized, an obstacle that had to be overcome first. I would have to get out of playing cricket. Amma had laid down an order and I knew Diggy well enough to know that, in spite of all his boldness, he would never dare to disobey an order from Amma.

I heard the car start up, and its sound reminded me of another problem that I had not considered. How was I going to smuggle the sari into the car? Amma would be waiting in the car for me, and if I arrived with the sling-bag she would make me take it back. I could not slip it in without her noticing. I sat still, listening to the whir of the engine at counterpoint to the clatter of Anula clearing the breakfast table, and suddenly a plan revealed itself to me.

I took the sari out of the bag and folded the bag so that it looked like there was something in it and left it on the bed. Taking the sari with me, I went to the bedroom door and peered out. The hall was empty. I went into Sonali's room, which was next to my parents', and I crouched down on one side of the doorway. I took off my slippers and held them with the sari in my arms. The curtain in the open doorway of Sonali's room blew slightly in the breeze and I moved further away from it so that I would not be seen. After what seemed like an interminable amount of time, I heard

Amma coming down the hallway to fetch me from her room. I crouched even lower as the sound of her footsteps got closer. From below the curtain, I saw her go into her room. As she entered, I stood up, pushed aside the curtain, and darted down the hallway. She came out of her room and called to me, but I didn't stop, and ran outside.

Thankfully the rear door of the car was open. I jumped in, quickly stuffed the sari into Sonali's sling-bag, and lay back against the seat, panting. Diggy and Sonali were looking at me strangely but they said nothing.

Soon Amma came out and got into the car. She glared at me and I gave her an innocent look. I smiled at Sonali conspiratorially. Sonali, my strongest ally, was doing her best to keep the bewilderment out of her face. By way of explanation, I said, with pretend gloominess, 'I can't play with you today. Amma says that I must play with the boys.'

Sonali looked at me in amazement and then turned to Amma. 'Why can't he play with the girls?' she said.

'Why?' Amma said and started up the car. 'Because the sky is so high and pigs can't fly.'

Amma sounded less sure of herself this time and a little weary. Looking in front, I saw that Diggy had turned in his seat and was regarding me morosely. I was reminded that the sari in the bag was worth nothing if I couldn't get out of the long day of cricket that lay ahead of me.

All the way to my grandparents' house, I gazed at the back of Diggy's head, hoping inspiration would come. The sound of his feet kicking irritably against the underside of the glove compartment confirmed that, however bad the consequences, he would follow Amma's orders. The sound of that ill-natured kicking made me search my mind all the more desperately for a way to escape playing cricket with the boys.

When the car turned down Ramanaygam Road, I still had not thought of anything. Meena was standing on top of the garden wall, her legs apart, her hands on her hips, her panties already dirty underneath her short dress. The boy cousins were on the wall on either side of her.

As we walked up the path to pay our respects to Ammachi and Appachi, I whispered to Sonali to keep the sari hidden and to tell no one about it. When we went into the drawing room, Her Fatness, who was as usual between Kanthi Aunty's knees, gave me a victorious look. A feeling of panic began to rise in me that no plan of escape had yet presented itself.

Once we had gone through the ritual of presenting our cheeks to our grandparents, we followed Amma outside to say goodbye.

'You children be good,' Amma said before she got into the car. She looked pointedly at me. 'I don't want to hear that you've given Ammachi and Appachi any trouble.'

I watched her departing car with a sense of sorrow.

Diggy grabbed my arm. I followed reluctantly as he hurried across the road, still holding on to me, as if afraid I would run away.

The wickets had already been set up in the field in front of the house and the boys and Meena were seated under a guava tree. When they saw us come towards them, they stopped talking and stared at us.

Muruges, who was on Diggy's team, stood up.

'What's he doing here?' he demanded, waving his half-eaten guava at me.

'He's going to play.'

'What?' the others cried in amazement.

They looked at Diggy as if he had lost his mind.

'He's not going to play on our team, is he?' Muruges said, more a threat than a question.

'He's quite good,' Diggy answered halfheartedly.

'If he's going to be on our team, I'm changing sides,' Muruges declared, and some of the others murmured in agreement.

'Come on, guys,' Diggy said with desperation in his voice, but they remained stern.

Diggy turned to Meena. 'I'll trade you Arjie for Sanjay.'

Meena spat out the seeds of the guava she was eating. 'Do you think I'm mad or something?'

'Ah, come on,' Diggy said in a wheedling tone, 'he's good. We've been practising the whole week.'

'If he's so good, why don't you keep him yourself. Maybe with him on your team you might actually win.'

'Yeah,' Sanjay cried, insulted that I was considered an equal trade for him. 'Why don't you keep the girlie-boy?'

At the new nickname 'girlie-boy', everyone roared with laughter, and even Diggy grinned.

I should have felt humiliated and dejected that nobody wanted me on their team but instead I felt the joy of relief begin to dance inside of me. The escape I had searched for was offering itself without any effort on my part. If Diggy's best team members were threatening to abandon him he would have no alternative but to let me go. I looked at my feet so that no one would see the hope in my eyes.

Unfortunately, the nickname 'girlie-boy' had an effect which I had not predicted. The joke at my expense seemed to clear the air. After laughing heartily, Muruges withdrew his threat. 'What the hell,' he said benevolently. 'It can't hurt to have another fielder. But,' he added, as a warning to Diggy, 'he can't bat.'

Diggy nodded as if he had never even considered letting me bat. Since each side had only fifty overs, it was vital to send the best batsmen in first, and often the younger cousins never got a chance.

I glared at Muruges, and he, thinking that my look was a reaction to the new nickname, said 'girlie-boy' again.

Diggy now laughed loudly, but in his laugh I detected a slight note of servility and also relief that the catastrophe of losing his team had been averted. I saw that the balance he was trying to maintain between following Amma's orders and keeping his team members happy was extremely precarious. All was not lost. Such a fragile balance would be easy to upset.

The opportunity to do this arose almost immediately.

Our team was to go first. In deciding the batting order, there was a certain system that the boys always followed. The captain would mark numbers in the sand with hyphens next to each and then cover the numbers with a bat. The players, who had been asked to turn their backs, would then come over and choose a hyphen. What was strange to me about this exercise was its redundancy, for, when the numbers were uncovered, no matter what the batting order, the older and better players always went first, the younger cousins assenting without a murmur.

When Diggy uncovered the numbers, I was first, Diggy was second. Muruges had one of the highest numbers and would bat towards the end, if at all. 'Well,' Muruges said to Diggy in a tone that spoke of promises already made, 'I'll take Arjie's place.'

Diggy nodded vigorously as if Muruges had read his very thoughts.

Unfortunately for him, I had other plans.

'I want to go first,' I said firmly, and waited for my request to produce the necessary consequences.

Muruges was crouched down, fixing his pads, and he straightened up slowly. The slowness of his action conveyed his anger at my daring to make such a suggestion and at the same time challenged Diggy to change the batting order.

Meena, unexpectedly, came to my defence. 'He is the first!' she said. 'Fair is fair!' In a game of only fifty overs, a bad opening bat would be ideal for her team.

'Fair is fair,' I echoed Meena. 'I picked first place and I should be allowed to play!'

'You can't,' Diggy said desperately, 'Muruges always goes first.'

Meena's team, encouraged by her, also began to cry out, 'Fair is fair!'

Diggy quickly crossed over to Muruges, put his arm around his shoulder, turned him away from the others, and talked earnestly to him. But Muruges shook his head, unconvinced by whatever Diggy was saying. Finally Diggy dropped his hand from Muruges's shoulder and cried out in exasperation at him, 'Come on, men!' In response, Muruges began to unbuckle his pads. Diggy put his hand on his shoulder, but he shrugged it off. Diggy, seeing that Muruges was determined, turned to me.

'Come on, Arjie,' he said, pleading, 'you can go later in the game.'

'No,' I said stubbornly, and, just to show how determined I was, I picked up the bat.

Muruges saw my action and threw the pads at my feet.

'I'm on your team now,' he announced to Meena.

'Ah, no! Come on men!' Diggy shouted in protest.

Muruges began to cross over to where Meena's team was gathered.

Diggy turned towards me now and grabbed the bat.

'*You* go!' he cried. 'We don't need *you*.' He pulled the bat out of my hands and started to walk with it towards Muruges.

'You're a cheater, cheater pumpkin-eater! I chose to bat first!' I yelled.

But I had gone too far. Diggy turned and looked at me. Then he howled as he realized how he had been tricked. Instead of giving Muruges the bat, he lifted it above his head and ran towards me. I turned and fled across the field towards my grandparents' gate. When I reached it, I lifted the latch, went inside the garden, and quickly put the latch back into place. Diggy stopped when he reached the gate. Safe on my side, I made a face at him through the slats. He came close and I retreated a little. Putting his head through the slats, he hissed at me, 'If you ever come near the field again, you'll be sorry.'

'Don't worry,' I replied tartly, 'I never will.'

And with that, I forever closed any possibility of entering the boys' world again. But I didn't care, and just to show how much I didn't care I made another face, turned my back on Diggy, and walked up the front path to the house. As I went through the narrow passageway between the house and the side wall that led to the back, I could hear the girls' voices as they prepared for bride-bride, and especially Her Fatness's, ordering everyone around. When I reached the back garden, I stopped when I saw the wedding cake. The bottom layer consisted of mud pies moulded from half a coconut shell. They supported the lid of a biscuit tin, which had three mud pies on it. On these rested the cover of a condensed-milk tin with a single mud pie on top. This was the three-tiered design that *I* had invented. Her Fatness had copied my design exactly. Further, she had taken upon herself the sole honour of decorating it with florets of grandapahana flowers and trails of antigonon, in the same way I had always done.

Sonali was the first to become aware of my presence. 'Arjie!' she said, pleased.

The other cousins now noticed me and they also exclaimed in delight. Lakshmi called out to me to come and join them, but before I could do so Her Fatness rose to her feet.

'What do you want?' she said.

I came forward a bit and she immediately stepped towards me, like a female mongoose defending her young against a cobra. 'Go away!' she cried, holding up her hand. 'Boys are not allowed here.'

I didn't heed her command.

'Go away,' she cried again. 'Otherwise I'm going to tell Ammachi!'

I looked at her for a moment, but fearing that she would see the hatred in my eyes, I glanced down at the ground.

'I want to play bride-bride, please,' I said, trying to sound as pathetic and inoffensive as possible.

'Bride-bride,' Her Fatness repeated mockingly.

'Yes,' I said, in a shy whisper.

Sonali stood up. 'Can't he play?' she said to Her Fatness. 'He'll be very good.'

'Yes, he'll be very good,' the others murmured in agreement.

Her Fatness considered their request.

'I have something that you don't have,' I said quickly, hoping to sway her decision.

'Oh, what is that?'

'The sari!'

'The sari?' she echoed. A look of malicious slyness flickered across her face.

'Yes,' I said. 'Without the sari you can't play bride-bride.'

'Why not?' Her Fatness said with indifference.

Her lack of concern about the sari puzzled me. Fearing that it might not have the same importance for her as it did for me, I cried out, 'Why not?' and pretended to be amazed that she would ask such a question. 'What is the bride going to wear, then? A bedsheet?'

Her Fatness played with a button on her dress. 'Where is the sari?' she asked very casually.

'It's a secret,' I said. I was not going to give it to her until I was firmly entrenched in the girls' world again. 'If you let me play, I will give it to you when it's time for the bride to get ready.'

A smile crossed her face. 'The thing is, Arjie,' she said in a very reasonable tone, 'we've already decided what everyone is going to be for bride-bride and we don't need anyone else.'

'But there must be some parts you need people for,' I said and then added, 'I'll play any part.'

'Any part,' Her Fatness repeated. Her eyes narrowed and she looked at me appraisingly.

'Let him play,' Sonali and the others said.

'I'll play *any* part,' I reiterated.

'You know what?' Her Fatness said suddenly, as if the idea had just dawned on her. 'We don't have a groom.'

That Her Fatness wanted me to swallow the bitter pill of humiliation was clear, and so great was my longing to be part of the girls' world again that I swallowed it. 'I'll take it,' I said.

'Okay,' Her Fatness said as if it mattered little to her whether I did or not.

The others cried out in delight and I smiled, happy that my goal had been at least partially achieved. Sonali beckoned to me to come and help them. I went towards where the preparations were being made for the wedding feast, but Her Fatness quickly stepped in front of me.

'The groom cannot help with the cooking.'

'Why not?' I protested.

'Because grooms don't do that.'

'They do.'

'Have you ever heard of a groom doing that?'

I couldn't say I had, so I demanded with angry sarcasm, 'What do grooms do then?'

'They go to office.'

'Office?' I said.

Her Fatness nodded and pointed to the table on the back porch. The look on her face told me she would not tolerate any argument.

'I can't go to office,' I said quickly. 'It's Sunday.'

'We're pretending it's Monday,' Her Fatness replied glibly.

I glared at her. Not satisfied with the humiliation she had forced me to accept, she was determined to keep my participation in bride-bride to a minimum. For an instant I thought to refuse her, but, seeing the warning look in her eyes, I finally acquiesced and went up the porch steps.

From there, I watched the other cousins getting ready for the wedding. Using a stone, I began to bang on the table as if stamping papers. I noted, with pleasure, that the sound irritated Her Fatness. I pressed an imaginary buzzer and made a loud noise. Getting no response from anyone, I did so again. Finally the other cousins looked up. 'Boy,' I called out imperiously to Sonali, 'come here, boy.'

Sonali left her cooking and came up the steps with the cringing attitude of the office peons at my father's bank.

'Yes sir, yes sir,' she said breathlessly. Her performance was so accurate that the cousins stopped to observe her.

'Take this to the bank manager in Bambalapitiya,' I said. Bowing again she took the imaginary letter and hurried down the steps. I pressed my buzzer again. 'Miss,' I called to Lakshmi. 'Miss, can you come here and take some dictation.'

'Yes, sir, coming sir,' Lakshmi said, fluttering her eyelashes, with the exaggerated coyness of a Sinhala comic actress. She came up the steps, wriggling her hips for the amusement of her audience. Everyone laughed except Her Fatness.

When Lakshmi finished the dictation and went down the steps, the other cousins cried out, 'Me! Me!' and clamoured to be the peon I would call next. But, before I could choose one of them, Her Fatness stormed up the steps.

'Stop that!' she shouted at me. 'You're disturbing us.'

'No!' I cried back, now that I had the support of everyone else.

'If you can't behave, go away.'

'If I go away, you won't get the sari.'

Her Fatness looked at me a long moment and then smiled.

'What sari?' she said. 'I bet you don't even have the sari.'

'Yes, I do,' I said in an earnest tone.

'Where?'

'It's a secret.'

'You are lying. I know you don't have it.'

'I do! I do!'

'Show me.'

'No.'

'You don't have it and I'm going to tell Janaki you are disturbing us.'

I didn't move, wanting to see if she would carry out her threat. She crossed behind the table and walked towards the kitchen door. When she got to the door and I was sure she was serious, I jumped up.

'Where is it?' I said urgently to Sonali.

She pointed to Janaki's room.

I ran to Janaki's door, opened it, and went inside. Sonali's bag was lying on the bed, and I picked it up and rushed back out onto the porch. Her Fatness had come away from the kitchen door.

'Here!' I cried.

Her Fatness folded her arms. 'Where?' she said tauntingly. I opened the bag, put my hand inside, and felt around for the sari. I touched a piece of clothing and drew it out. It was only Sonali's change of clothes. I put my hand inside again and this time brought out an Enid Blyton book. There was nothing else in the bag.

'Where is the sari?' Her Fatness demanded.

I glanced at Sonali and she gave me a puzzled look.

'Liar, liar on the wall, who's the liarest one of all!' Her Fatness cried.

I turned towards Janaki's door, wondering if the sari had fallen out. Then I saw a slight smirk on Her Fatness's face and the truth came to me. She'd known all along about the sari. She must have discovered it earlier and hidden it. I realized I had been duped and felt a sudden rush of anger. Her Fatness saw the comprehension in my eyes and her arms dropped by her sides as if in readiness. She inched back towards the kitchen door for safety. But I was not interested in her for the moment. What I wanted was the sari.

I rushed into Janaki's room.

'I'm going to tell Janaki you're in her room!' Her Fatness cried.

'Tell and catch my long fat tail!' I shouted back.

I looked around Janaki's room. Her Fatness must have hidden it here. There was no other place. I lifted Janaki's mattress. There was nothing under it, save a few Sinhala love-comics. I went to Janaki's suitcase and began to go through the clothes she kept neatly folded inside it. As silent as a shadow, Her Fatness slipped into the room. I became aware of her presence and turned. But too late. She took the sari from the shelf where she had hidden it and ran out the door. Leaving the suitcase still open, I ran after her. The sari clutched to her chest, she rushed for the kitchen door. Luckily Sonali and Lakshmi were blocking her way. Seeing me coming at her, she jumped off the porch and began to head towards the front of the house. I leapt off the porch and chased after her. If she got to the front of the house, she would go straight to Ammachi.

Just as she reached the passageway, I managed to get hold of her arm. She turned, desperate, and struck out at me. Ducking her blow, I reached for the sari and managed to get some of it in my hand. She tried to take it back from me, but I held on tightly. Crying out, she jerked away from me with her whole body, hoping to wrest the sari from my grip. With a rasping sound, the sari began to tear. I yelled at her to stop pulling, but she jerked away again and the sari tore all the way down. There was a moment of stunned silence. I gazed at the torn sari in my hand, at the long threads that hung from it. Then, with a wail of anguish, I rushed at Her Fatness and grabbed hold of her hair. She screamed and flailed at me. I yanked her head so far to one side that it almost touched her shoulder. She let out a guttural sound and struck out desperately at me. Her fist caught me in the stomach and she managed to loosen my grip.

She began to run towards the porch steps, crying out for Ammachi and Janaki. I ran after her and grabbed the sleeve of her dress before she went up the porch steps. She struggled against my grip and the sleeve ripped open and hung down her arm like a broken limb. Free once again, she stumbled up the steps towards the kitchen door, shouting at the top of her voice.

Janaki rushed out of the kitchen. She raised her hand and looked around for the first person to wallop, but when she saw Her Fatness with her torn dress, she held her raised hand to her cheek and cried out in consternation, 'Buddu Ammo!'

Now Her Fatness began to call out only for Ammachi.

Janaki came hurriedly towards her. 'Shhh! Shhhh!' she said, but Her Fatness only increased the volume of her cry.

'What's wrong? What's wrong?' Janaki cried impatiently.

Her Fatness pointed to me.

'Janakiii! See what that boy did,' she replied.

'I didn't do anything,' I yelled, enraged that she was trying to push the blame onto me.

I ran back to where I had dropped the sari, picked it up, and held it out to Janaki. 'Yes!' Sonali cried, coming to my defence. 'She did it and now she's blaming him.'
'It's her fault!' Lakshmi said, also taking my side.

Now all the voices of the girl cousins rose in a babble supporting my case and accusing Her Fatness.

'Quiet!' Janaki shouted in desperation. 'Quiet!'

But nobody heeded her. We all crowded around her, so determined to give our version of the story that it was a while before we became aware of Ammachi's presence in the kitchen doorway. Gradually, like the hush that descends on a garrison town at the sound of enemy guns, we all became quiet. Even Her Fatness stopped her wailing.

Ammachi looked at all of us and then her gaze came to rest on Janaki. 'How many times have I told you to keep these children quiet?' she said, her tone awful.

Janaki, always so full of anger, now wrung her hands like a child in fear of punishment. 'I told them . . .' she started to say, but Ammachi raised her hand for silence. Her Fatness began to cry again, more out of fear than anything else. Ammachi glared at her, and, as if to deflect the look, Her Fatness held up her arm with the ripped sleeve.

'Who did that?' Ammachi said after a moment.

Her Fatness pointed at me and her crying got even louder.

Ammachi looked at me sternly and then beckoned me with her index finger.

'Look!' I cried and held out the sari as if in supplication. 'Look at what she did!'

But Ammachi was unmoved by the sight of the sari and continued to beckon me.

As I looked at her, I could almost hear the singing of the cane as it came down through the air, and then the sharp crack, which would be followed by searing pain. The time Diggy had been caned for climbing the roof came back to me, his pleas for mercy, his shouts of agony and loud sobs.

Before I could stop myself, I cried out angrily at Ammachi, 'It's not fair! Why should I be punished?'

'Come here,' Ammachi said.

'No. I won't.'

Ammachi came to the edge of the porch, but rather than backing away I remained where I was.

'Come here, you vamban,' she said to me sharply.

'No!' I cried back. 'I hate you, you old fatty.'

The other cousins and even Janaki gasped at my audacity. Ammachi began to come down the steps. I stood my ground for a few moments but then my courage gave out. I turned, and, with the sari still in my hands, I fled. I ran from the back garden to the front gate and out. In the field across the way, the boys were still at their cricket game. I hurried down the road towards the sea. At the railway lines I paused briefly, went across, then scrambled over the rocks to the beach. Once there, I sat on a rock and flung the sari down next to me. 'I hate them, I hate them all,' I whispered to myself. 'I wish I was dead.'

I put my head down and felt the first tears begin to wet my knees.

After a while I was still. The sound of the waves, their regular rhythm, had a calming effect on me. I leaned back against the rock behind me, watching them come in and go out. Soon the heat of the rocks became unbearable and I stood up, removed my slippers, and went down the beach to the edge of the water.

I had never seen the sea this colour before. Our visits to the beach were usually in the early evening when the sea was a turquoise blue. Now, under the mid-day sun, it had become hard silver, so bright that it hurt my eyes.

The sand burned my feet, and I moved closer to the waves to cool them. I looked down the deserted beach, whose white sand almost matched the colour of the sea, and saw tall buildings shimmering in the distance like a mirage. This daytime beach seemed foreign compared with the beach of the early evening, which was always crowded with strollers and joggers and vendors. Now both the beach and the sea, once so familiar, were like an unknown country into which I had journeyed by chance. I knew then that something had changed. But how, I didn't altogether know.

The large waves, impersonal and oblivious to my despair, threw themselves against the beach, their crests frothing and hissing. Soon I would have to turn around and go back to my grandparents' house, where Ammachi awaited me with her thinnest cane, the one that left deep impressions on the backs of our thighs, so deep that sometimes they had to be treated with Gentian Violet. The thought of that cane as it cut through the air, humming like a mosquito, made me wince even now, so far away from it.

I glanced at the sari lying on the rock where I had thrown it and I knew that I would never enter the girls' world again. Never stand in front of Janaki's mirror, watching a transformation take place before my eyes. No more would I step out of that room and make my way down the porch steps to the altar, a creature beautiful and adored, the personification of all that was good and perfect in the world. The future spend-the-days were no longer to be enjoyed, no longer to be looked forward to. And then there would be the loneliness. I would be caught between the boys' and the girls' worlds, not belonging or wanted in either. I would have to think of things with which to amuse myself, find ways to endure the lunches and teas when the cousins would talk to one another about what they had done and what they planned to do for the rest of the day.

The bell of St Fatima's Church rang out the angelus, and its melancholy sound seemed like a summoning. It was time to return to my grandparents' house. My absence at the lunchtable would be construed as another act of defiance and eventually Janaki would be sent to fetch me. Then the punishment I received would be even more severe.

With a heavy heart, I slowly went back up the beach, not caring that the sand burned the soles of my feet. I put my slippers on, picked up my sari, and climbed up the rocks. I paused and looked at the sea one last time. Then I turned, crossed the railway lines, and began my walk up Ramanaygam Road to the future that awaited me.

HIROMI GOTO

(b. 1966)

'Inscribing a place. A sensitivity, a sensibility which resists commonality,' says Hiromi Goto by way of explaining what motivates and informs her writing. 'Defining my position through language. The intensely personal becomes public in the process of addressing issues of racism and sexism as a woman of colour writing in Canada.'

Born in Chiba-ken, Japan, in 1966, she immigrated to Canada at the age of three with her family. After a short time on the West Coast, they settled in southern Alberta. A resident of Calgary, Goto received a B.A. in English (1989) from the University of Calgary, and has had her short stories and poetry published in literary magazines and anthologies.

A member of the editorial collective of *absinthe* magazine, Goto was one of the co-editors of *The Skin On Our Tongues* (1993), a special issue on writers of colour and aboriginal writers. In her editorial statement accompanying that issue, she expresses a 'certain mistrust of . . . anthologies which highlight writers from a specific racial/cultural background'. Still, while agreeing 'on the surface' that such anthologies tend to 'segregate "ethnic writing" from the mainstream', she believes it is important to resist the 'ingrained canon of literary acceptance which excludes most writing that does not adhere to a Western (Eurocentric) standard'. As she says, writing 'that steps outside of this category is immediately "othered" as *ethnic*, thereby creating a division between what is deemed literary and what is not.'

Goto has published a full colour postcard poem, *Tea* (1992), with DisOrientation Chapbooks, and a novel, *Chorus of Mushrooms* (1994), which will soon appear in Israel in a Hebrew translation. The winner of the Commonwealth Prize for First Novel in the region of North America, it is about the complexity of cultural differences as expressed by three generations of women in the same family.

NIGHT

When your sight tilts like that
You laugh out loud in your sleep, you know. Did you know? You laugh out loud in your sleep. There are heads of hakusai in the basement starting to dry out before they have a chance to rot because of the heat from the dryer in what would otherwise be a very cold basement. It would be a terrible waste to throw them out because they are not so bad that I couldn't peel away the topper leaves and use the rest, but I can't bear to touch them because they're garden hakusai, grown outside and there are bugs gone cocooned or chrysalides or whatever in the folds of crinkle leaves and it'll make me scream if any touch my hands. (Three women sit around a formica table in the kitchen)

Cup
I like to sleep with the window open but you prefer it closed and I have to stick my feet outside of the covers if I want to get any sleep at all, but the one drawback to sleeping with the window open is that the magpies squawk at sunrise and I have to get out of bed and slam my palm against the glass until they fly away while you go to the fridge for a cup of cold mugicha but forget to bring me any and the baby wakes up from all the noise. (Three women at 1:37 a.m.)

2 Linger

Sometimes you say a word out loud and it's just that there is only the one falling from your mouth like a small bone or a stone from a plum and there's nothing to hold it up against so I have to prod you with sticks of questions but you never say anything else and only nuzzle below my breasts with your fingers in your sleep. (The grandmother sips noisily, her cup of beer and sucks the residue from her teeth in smacks)

Tick Tock

It's loud, you know. At night.
Sometimes I hate you so much I can't bear to lie beside you and I wish you'd go and sleep on the couch but you never do so I have to leave if I want you to go.
It's loud, you know. At night.

Tick Tock

Three women sit around a formica table in the kitchen. Three women at 1:37 a.m. The grandmother sips noisily, her cup of beer and sucks the residue from her teeth in smacks. The mother turns to her daughter.

'You should go to sleep soon. The baby's going to wake up at least once.'

'Yeah, soon,' the daughter says, wanting to sit a while longer, in the quiet with the women.

'Of course, if your father has another dream like the other night, everybody'll be up,' the mother laughs.

'What happened?'

'Such a yelling and screaming! I thought my heart would burst!' says the grandmother. Sucking the last drops of beer from her cup.

'Your father started screaming at the top of his voice in the middle of the night. Thrashing around on his bed. I was sleeping downstairs, but it woke me up, it was so loud. I ran upstairs. Grandmother ran in from her room too.'

'I thought he was dying,' the grandmother says.

'He was awake by then and such sweating and panting! I asked him what he dreamt about. And he said, his voice all quivering, "Two women were trying to crawl into bed beside me while I was sleeping! Two strange women!"' The mother glances at the grandmother and they start laughing loudly, snapping the humming night silence.

'I said to him, "Well, what are you so frightened about? Most people would love to have two strange women join them in bed!" But he only shook his head, got a drink of water, and went back to bed.' They laugh again and the daughter joins them.

'The poor man,' she says. 'We shouldn't laugh.' She gets up and goes to the fridge for a beer. She twists it open, pours some into her grandmother's cup and takes a long swallow from the bottle.

Her mother says, 'I think I'll join you,' and pours herself some rye and Diet Coke. The women sit together, drinking.

'I had the most frightening one last night,' the mother says.

'What did you dream?' says her daughter, picking at the label of her beer with her fingernail.

'I dreamt I was sleeping in the spare bedroom, so I didn't realize I was dreaming because I was dreaming I was sleeping, which I was. Anyways! There I was, sleeping and something wakes me up. I hear this rustling rustling then tapping. Kon, kon, kon. Like a hammer or something. Kon, kon, kon. And I lay there for quite some time, just listening until I realize it's an awfully strange time of night to be doing any construction work. So I slowly opened my eyes and there, beside my bed, in the wall, there's a great jagged hole—like someone had tapped a hole in the wall with a pick axe. Inside the room it's night dark, but outside the hole, it's that grey dawn colour. I thought to myself, "That's strange," and then a German Shepherd sticks his head inside the hole to look at me! But I like dogs, so I wasn't frightened. I just thought, "Why, there's a dog looking at me." The dog pulled his head out and left and I could see a pair of legs just standing right outside the hole.'

'The dog's?' asks the grandmother.

'No, a man's! I could only see from his mid-thigh down to his feet, just outside my room, and there's a long wooden handle standing vertically beside his legs and I knew it was the pick axe. My heart is pounding in my ears, but I can't move at all, only watch, and he bends down, looks inside, and sees me watching. He crams his head inside, shoving his shoulders, trying to get his leg through and I yell! I yelled, "Dorobo! Dorobo! Dorobo!" until I woke myself up.'

'Well, I didn't hear a thing,' says the grandmother, peering at her daughter. 'And there's nothing much in this house a thief would want to steal,' she adds. Sips from her cup.

'What do you dream of, Grandmother?'

'Oh I have frightening dreams, girl. Something terrible!' She says nothing more, and her daughter and granddaughter sit, watching her, waiting for her to continue. Outside, a late cricket begins to thrum and the cat wanders in from the living room and jumps lightly onto the mother's lap. The mother snuggles the cat between her breasts, cat rubbing his head against her chin.

'A very strange thing, this. Every time it's a new dream. Every moment it's brand new, and I don't realize I've dreamt it a hundred, a thousand times before until after I wake up.' She gazes beyond her fingers clutching her cup. She strokes the plastic cup with her pebbled fingertips, her other hand a knuckle around the handle. The cat watches her stroking finger with half-closed eyes, his pupils full and black. The woman stares at the top of the cat's head and glides her hand down his gleaming back. Her daughter watches the grandmother's face. The sharp bone of cheek, the hollows around her eyes, her throat.

'I don't know why, but I have all my clothes on, you know. Everyone else is naked. And I think, "That's strange," but not because everyone is naked. There's something else that is bothering me, only I don't, can't recognize it.' She leans into her cup and takes a sip of beer. Smack. Smack. The young woman leans back in her chair and sets her feet on the seat opposite, between her mother's legs, still watching intently, her grandmother's face.

'So everyone starts kissing and touching each other. Men and women, women and women, men and men, and it's good. Healthy. Then a woman I've never met before comes to me and starts touching my breasts and neck and I feel fine. Yes fine. Then a man, a stranger, he pushes her away and starts to kiss me. I'm not sure how I feel, but he keeps on kissing me and kneels down and kisses my breasts. I'm still half excited from the woman touching me, but it's going away and I'm clearing my head. There's something wrong. I know it now so close. Very very wrong. I feel his erection against my thigh and he grabs me close close No! Something hard stabbing beneath my chin, pushing up and up against the bottom of my chin and I shove him back and back and I see him. I really see him. Oh god. . . He is deformed. He is deformed. He has two erections. One between his legs and ohgod, one at the base of his throat. A penis rising at an angle from the base of his throat and mat mat of hair and his scrotum sags where his collarbones meet. And I feel sick. I feel sick and turn and look at all the men. I can see. They are deformed. Every one of them. They have genitals growing from their chests, where their collarbones meet.'

The three women sit silently. Only the sound of the cat.

'It's funny,' the grandmother says, 'how frightening the dreams are when you are in them, but if you try to explain them, they never sound that way.' She sucks the last bit of beer from her cup and turns to her granddaughter. 'And what about you, child? What do you dream?'

'I don't dream,' says the young woman, rolling the bits of the beer label into tiny pills. She looks up and sees her mother and her grandmother watching her face. 'At least,' she adds, 'none that I can remember.' From upstairs there is a sleepy wail and three women are still. Perhaps the baby will go back to sleep. Perhaps . . . But the cry gathers momentum, no longer sleepy, but rising in pitch to anger. The young woman finishes the beer in three long swallows and burps. She picks up a baby bottle from the draining board and fills it with warm water from the tap, screws the nipple on.

'Well, see you in the morning,' she says and thumps softly upstairs.

The grandmother and mother sit at the kitchen table. They didn't notice the cricket had stopped chirping until it started up again. Upstairs, it is quiet.

ZAFFI GOUSOPOULOS

(b. 1967)

I grew up never really knowing where my "place" was,' says Zaffi Gousopoulos. 'Not home, with its excessive patriarchal customs; not school, with its "White middle-class" biases. I felt so divided by my two contradictory cultures that it became a metaphor to live by.'

Born in Toronto of Greek parents, Gousopoulos holds a B.A. Honours in English and Psychology (1992) and a B.Ed. (1994) from York University. She has worked as educational assistant, as well as drama and cooperative games specialist, for many schools in Toronto. Her poetry, which has appeared in many literary magazines and in two chapbooks, *crazy lady* (1991) and *The Playing Field* (1993), reflects her ongoing process of both 'rejecting' and 'reclaiming' her heritage. 'I still take issue with the patriarchal customs that make me angry, but I have also developed a deep compassion, lamenting the hardships that my people have faced in this country. Capitalism has operated on the Greek spirit in ways that have made us live out the tensions between comedy and tragedy.'

Talking about her poem, 'Four Greek Men', she says that it was 'a gig as a waitress in a Greek nightclub/restaurant' that helped her 'come to terms with the contradictions. The Greek-Canadian culture is the place where I come from, my writing booting back like spawning salmon, trying to beget coherence.'

Gousopoulos is currently at work on a book-length poetry project called *Facing the Moon*.

FOUR GREEK MEN

the four Greek men
who came to the bouzoukia this weekend
for the tastes and sounds of their homeland
talked about money non-stop.

they talked about the miseries of this land
and its lifelessness
and they cursed in their mother tongue
Canadians and their coloured money
and the english language and the english tongue

and then they cursed all the colours that came to this country
their funny customs and their funny tongues
ruin the suburbs the schools the economy

these coloured immigrants who come
to this cursed colourful country
to make coloured money
but the four Greek men came
for nothing.

another round of *metaxas*
and they hit the dance floor
do the *zembekiko* to a modern song
order from me out loud
at the bargain price of
one hundred dollars
20 plates for the breaking

a hundred dollars more or less
thrown at the feet of their loved ones
you poor rich Greeks
who don't have enough money
throwing ten sets of two dollar bills
all over each other
your arms spread like tipsy branches

and all that god awful coloured money
falling around you
all that cursed Canadian money
falling to the floor
like the vibrant leaves that fall in this country
from the limbs of immigrants rooted in this soil

covered by broken plates and shoeprints
and the residue of Rothman's tobacco.

all that left for the musicians
who squat like youthful pigeons
when everyone has gone

EVELYN LAU

(b. 1970)

'One of the reasons I so enjoy work by [John] Cheever and [John] Updike is that they write about something that I don't know,' says Evelyn Lau. 'They write about something that is very exotic to me: well-off people having affairs, going out to parties and getting drunk and behaving badly, a real moral structure, family, secure housing, job, a privileged white class. A lot of younger writers rebel against that but to me that is sort of an ideal, something I'm very attracted to, it's a landscape I wish I could explore.' It is this kind of social landscape, more often than not seen from the outside, that Lau's writing attempts to capture. 'I don't have much interest in politics yet, or "the world",' she says. 'I guess I'm most interested in people's emotional states. And the emotional states of a middle-aged man are the ones I identify most with—outside of my own.' Her short stories, widely published in literary magazines and anthologies, depict this emotional terrain, usually from the point of view of young female characters who are involved with married men.

Born in Vancouver, Lau escaped from her strict and overprotective family by running away at fourteen. The journals she kept during the two years she spent on the street were published as *Runaway: Diary of a Street Kid* (1989). Translated into six languages and turned into a film, *The Diary of Evelyn Lau* (1994), it became an instant best-seller. This autobiographical narrative is, as Lau says, 'the most honest thing I could do, and the best thing I could do, at the time'. She has resisted being 'treated as a spokesperson for street kids'. As she states, 'I was horrified by that prospect and I refused opportunities like speaking to kids about drug abuse or anything like that, because I knew that would just be death to me and my own development as a writer.'

Her reluctance to be seen as a spokesperson or a writer who engages social and political issues also includes her resistance to being seen as a Chinese-Canadian writer. While she enjoys reading works by writers like Salman Rushdie and Rohinton Mistry—'I identify with the family life that's portrayed in them'—Chinese poets do not 'make any sense to' her. 'If I feel different from other people, I think of being different in terms of my background,' she says. 'That leaps to mind much sooner than being Chinese. Because I don't have contact with my family, or with that sort of community, I don't feel that in my character. It's quite irrelevant in my work.' Along the same lines, she also feels 'horrified and outraged that there should be [the] assumption' that she should write from a specifically feminist perspective. Lau succinctly articulates the independent stance she wants to maintain: 'I hate writing about politics. Amateurs who write about politics are so clumsy and so earnest, and all they want to do is get the message across. The writing has to be the most important, not the message, to my mind.'

Despite this disavowal, Lau has published three poetry collections that reflect her fascination with desire and sexuality. *You Are Not Who You Claim* (1990), which won the Milton Acorn People's Poetry Prize, *Oedipal Dreams* (1992), a finalist for the Governor General's Award, and *In the House of Slaves* (1994), all express the complexity of gender roles and class differences. Her collection of short fiction, *Fresh Girls and Other Stories* (1993), which includes the story that follows, is about young women involved with—usually older—men, about the hard realities of prostitutes and the comfortable lives of prostitutes' middle-class clients. 'If these stories were told by the man,' Lau says, 'they would be pornography.' But, narrated as they are by the women themselves who are aware of their ambivalent and tentative positions, the stories become an exploration of split as well as complicit subjectivities. The sensuous writing style of these stories is also present in her first novel, *Other Women* (1995), but the erotic and sexual imagery that has become characteristic of her work is less evident there.

Lau, the recipient of the Canadian Authors' Association Air Canada Prize as 'the most promising writer under thirty' (1990), resides in Vancouver.

MARRIAGE

His gold wedding band catches the light between the two walls of flesh that are our bodies in bed. It is a wide band with a perforated design, and it fits loosely on his finger. When he draws his hand up between us to touch me, the hand seems to take on a separate entity—as though it is a stranger's hand encountered in a crowded bus or an empty alley, the ring as hard as a weapon. I feel the coldness of it branding my skin. Yet I am drawn to it compulsively, this symbol of his commitment to another, as though it is a private part of him that will derive pleasure from my touch: rubbing it, twisting it, pulling it up to his knuckle and back down again.

In the morning we go for a walk in Queen Elizabeth Park, where a wedding is taking place. There are photographers bent on one knee in the grass, children with flowers looped through their hair, a bride in her layers of misty white. We watch from a bridge over a creek nearby, and then from the top of a waterfall. From that height the members of the wedding appear toy-like, diminished by the vast green slopes, the overflowing flower beds. When I glance sideways, I see him serenely observing the activity below, his hands draped over the low rail. I want then to step behind him, put my hands between his shoulders, and push him over, if only to recognize something in his face, some anxiety or pain to correspond with what I am feeling.

The people we pass in the park see a middle-aged man in a suit with his arm around a nineteen-year-old girl. They invariably pause, look twice with curiosity. At first I look back boldly, meeting their eyes in the harsh sunlight, but as the walk wears on my gaze falters. I keep my eyes trained on the ground, my pointy white high heels keeping step with his freshly polished black leather shoes. I don't know what people are thinking; I know they don't think I am his daughter. Their stares make me feel unclean, as if there is something illicit about me. Suddenly I wonder if my skirt is too short, my lipstick too red, my hair too teased. I concentrate hard on pretending that there is something natural about my odd pairing with this man.

He is oblivious to their looks; if anything, he is pleased by them, as though people are looking because the girl his arm holds captive is particularly striking. He does not see that the looks are more often edged with pity than any degree of approval or jealousy.

He tells me afterwards that he is proud to be seen with me.

Sometimes when he visits me he is carrying his beeper. He has just completed the crawl to the foot of my bed, drawn up the comforter tent-like over his head and shoulders, and is preparing in the fuzzy dark to attack my body with his tongue. And then from deep in the grey huddle of his pants on the floor rises the berating call of the beeper, causing the anonymous bulk under the covers to jump and hit his head against the soft ceiling of the comforter. I resist the urge to reach out and rub that dome under my comforter, like it is a teddy bear or my own bunched-up knees.

Naked, he digs into the mass of material on the floor, extracts the beeper, and seats himself on the edge of the bed. I tuck my hair behind my ear and examine his back as he dials a series of numbers to access his answering service, the hospital, other doctors.

'Good afternoon,' he says. 'Is this Dr Martin? Yes . . . yes . . . how is she? All right, one milligram lorazepam to be administered at bedtime . . .' while he remains half-erect between his long white thighs, one hand groping behind him 'til it finds and begins to squeeze my breast and then its nipple. Even though he has tucked the phone between his ear and shoulder so that the hand that flaps the air is not the one that wears the ring, I still feel it belongs to someone other than him as it rounds the blank canvas of his back and pats air and pillow before touching skin. I am reminded of the card in my desk drawer: on Valentine's Day four months ago he gave me a card that read, in a floral script, 'I Love You'. He said, almost immediately, 'I hope you don't get vindictive and send that card to my wife. It's got my handwriting on it.'

It never would have occurred to me to do so if he hadn't told me. What he said inspired me to keep the card in a special drawer, where I will not lose it. I put it away feeling reassured that at last I had some power over him. I had something I could hurt him with. I now know I saved the card because it was my only proof of his love for me, it is the only part of him that belongs to me.

The night before his wife's return from the conference she's attending in Los Angeles, we drive to our usual restaurant where the Japanese waiter smiles at us in a way he interprets as friendly, while I recognize amusement dancing at the corners of his mouth. I lift my purse into my lap and politely ask permission to smoke.

'I'd rather you didn't. My wife has a good nose for tobacco.'

How much I want his wife to come home to the smell of smoke in the family car. After she has walked off the plane and through the terminal to where her luggage revolves on the carousel, after she has picked out his face among the faces of other husbands waiting to greet their wives and take them home, I can see her leaning back in the passenger seat, rubbing her neck, tired after her flight and eager for sleep—then the trace of smoke acrid in her nostrils, mingled perhaps with my perfume. In my fantasy she turns to him, wild-eyed and tearful, she demands that he stop the car, she wrenches the perforated wedding band from her finger and throws it at him before she opens the door and leaves. *Give it to that slut*, she will say.

'Maybe I'm subconsciously trying to ruin your marriage,' I smile as I light a cigarette and watch the smoke momentarily fill up the front of the car.

'Please don't,' he says calmly. I think a man whose marriage is in my hands should sound a little more desperate, but in the dark I can only see his profile against the stores and buildings blurring outside the window, and it is unreadable. I wish afterwards that I had looked at his hands, to see if they tightened on the wheel.

He tells me that we will have lots of time together over the years but I have no concept of time. I ask him to leave the city with me.

'Would you really do that?' he asks. 'Run off with me?'

'Yes.'

'I'm very flattered.'

'Don't be. It wasn't meant to be flattering.' I pause. I want to say, *It meant more than that*. 'Why can't we just take off?'

'I can't do it right now,' he says. 'I have people depending on me—my patients. I'd love to. I can't.'

'I have just as much to lose as you do, you know,' I say, but he doesn't believe me. He has been feeding me whisky all evening, and I am swaying in a chair in front of him. He places my hands together between his own and pulls me out of the chair, collapsing me to my knees. Kneeling, I sway back and forth and squint up at him, my hands stranded in his lap.

'You should go,' I say.

'Yes, I have to work tomorrow morning.'

'And you have to pick your wife up from the airport,' I say, struggling to my feet to press the colour of my lips against his white cheek.

I do not realize I am clutching the sleeve of his suit jacket until we have reached the door, where he chuckles and pries my fingers loose. He adjusts his beeper inside his pocket and walks out into the rain-misted night.

Back inside the apartment I am intent on finishing the bottle of Chivas he left behind on the kitchen counter, but when I go to it I find an envelope next to the bottle, weighted by an ashtray. I tear it open, my heart beating painfully—it could be a letter, he could be saying that he can no longer live without me, that tonight he will finally tell his wife about us. Instead I pull out a greeting card with a picture on the front of a girl standing by a seashore. She is bare-legged, with dimpled knees, wearing a loose frock the colour of daffodils. She looks about twelve years old.

Inside are no words, just two new hundred-dollar bills.

He tries to alleviate his guilt by giving me money: cheques left folded on the kitchen table, crisp bills tucked inside cards. He takes me shopping for groceries and clothes, he never visits my apartment without bringing me some small gift, as though all this entitles him to leave afterwards and return home to his wife. But I have no similar method of striking such bargains with my conscience. The dregs of our affair stick to my body like semen. Because I do think of his wife—of the way she must sink into bed beside him in the dark, putting her face against his chest and breathing him in, his scent carried with her into her dreams. I do think of the pain she would feel if she knew, and I am frightened sometimes by the force of my desire to inflict that pain upon her—this wife who is to be pitied in her faithless marriage, this wife whom I envy.

And tonight I want more than anything to take those smooth brown bills between my fingers and tear them up. Does he think I'm like one of those teen hookers in thigh-high boots and bustiers he says he used to pick up downtown before he met me? My hands are shaking, I want so badly to get rid of his money. Instead I go over to the chest of drawers beside my bed and add this latest contribution to the growing stack of cards and cash I have hidden there.

He often says to me, 'If you were my daughter . . .' My lips twist and he has to add each time, 'You know what I mean.' If things were different, he means. If we weren't sleeping together. We cultivate fantasies for each other of what a loving, doting father he would have made me; of what a pretty, accomplished daughter I would have made him. 'I adore you,' he says to me. 'I wish I could marry you.' And then, 'I wish you were my daughter,' as he kisses my neck, my shoulders, my breasts, his fingers slipping between my thighs. As things are, I see we don't have anything that comes close to the illusion.

His cologne has found places to lodge in my blankets, clothing, cushions. No matter how many loads of laundry I carry down the back stairs, the smell of him has taken up residence in the corners of my apartment, as though to stay.

He tells me little about his activities, but the spare portraits he paints grow vivid in my mind. This weekend he will visit Vancouver Island with his family. I picture them on the ferry, with the possibility of grey skies and rain, the mountains concealed by veils of fog, the treed islands rising like the backs of beasts out of the ocean. I wonder if his family will venture onto the deck and look down at the water, I imagine them falling overboard and being ground to pieces by the propellers, staining those foamy waves crimson.

He's told me about his three sons and I know they are all teenagers. I know that the oldest is stronger than his father, handsome with a thick head of red hair, and that this son's feisty girlfriend reminds him of me. I know they tease him with the eyeball-rolling exasperation and embarrassment that I've felt towards my own parents.

'Oh, Dad,' they'd groan in restaurants where he'd be teasing the waitress. 'Don't *do* that. She's in our class at school!'

I imagine him clambering up the grey steel ladder leading to the top deck of the ferry. He reaches down towards his wife. When she grips his hand his ring bites into her palm, a sensation she has grown used to, as though the ring is now a part of his body.

They walk together behind their children, past rows of orange plastic chairs in the non-smoking section, past the cafeteria selling sticky danishes and styrofoam cups of hot coffee, past the gift shop with the little Canadian flags and sweatshirts in the window. They wrestle open the heavy door leading onto the deck and the blast of air sucking them out separates his hair into pieces plastering forward, backward, tight against his cheek.

His family races in their sneakers and jeans towards the edges of the ferry, clinging to the railings, and he fights his way through the wind towards them, laughing and shouting. I know for certain that, for once, he is not thinking of me.

TEXTS CITED

Allen, Lillian. 'Preface' and 'Introduction' in *Women Do This Every Day: Selected Poems* (Toronto: Women's Press, 1993), 9–21.

Armstrong, Jeannette. 'The Body of Our People', interview by Victoria Freeman. *Paragraph* 14, 3 (1992): 9–12.

Arnason, David. 'Arnason Prefers Storytelling', *Winnipeg Free Press* (29 August 1992): B21.

——. 'Introduction.' In *Isolation in Canadian Literature*, ed. David Arnason (Toronto: Macmillan, 1975), 1–2.

Bannerji, Himani. 'Returning the Gaze: An Introduction' in *Returning the Gaze: Essays on Racism, Feminism and Politics*, ed. Himani Bannerji (Toronto: Sister Vision Press, 1993), ix–xxiv.

——. Interview by Arun Mukherjee in *Other Solitudes: Canadian Multicultural Fictions*, eds. Linda Hutcheon and Marion Richmond (Toronto: Oxford University Press, 1990), 145–52.

Begamudré, Ven. 'Process, Politics and Plurality', interview by Zool Suleman. *Rungh* 2, 3 (1994): 14–18.

——. 'A Life in Revolution', profile by Allan Casey. *Books in Canada* 20, 9 (December 1991): 16–18.

Birdsell, Sandra. 'Taking Notice: An Interview', by Joan Thomas. *Prairie Fire* 15, 1 (Spring 1994): 80–5.

——. 'Falling into the Page: An Interview', by Laurie Kruk. *Quarry* 40, 3 (Summer 1991): 92–9.

Bissoondath, Neil. 'Escaping the Cultural Imperative', interview by Ali Lakhani. *Rungh* 1, 4 (1993): 8–13.

——. 'Interview', by P. Scott Lawrence. *Matrix* (Autumn 1994): 2–7.

Brand, Dionne. Interview by Dagmar Novak in *Other Solitudes*. 271–7.

——. 'In the company of my work', interview by Makeda Silvera in *The Other Woman: Women of Colour in Contemporary Canadian Literature*, ed. Makeda Silvera (Toronto: Sister Vision Press, 1995), 356–80.

Brandt, Di. 'letting the silence speak' in *Language in Her Eye: Views on Writing and Gender by Canadian Women Writing in English*, eds Libby Scheier, Sarah Sheard, and Eleanor Wachtel (Toronto: Coach House Press, 1990), 54–8.

——. 'The sadness in this book is that I'm reaching for this story . . .' in *Sounding Differences: Conversations with Seventeen Canadian Women Writers*, Janice Williamson (Toronto: University of Toronto Press, 1993), 31–45.

Brant, Beth. 'Preface: Telling' in *Food and Spirits* (Vancouver: Press Gang, 1991), 11–17.

——. Statement cited in *An Anthology of Canadian Native Literature in English*, eds Daniel David Moses and Terry Goldie (Toronto: Oxford University Press, 1992), 369.

Clarke, Austin. 'A Black Man Talks About Race Prejudice in White Canada', *Maclean's* (20 April 1963): 18, 55–8.

——. 'Introduction' in *Nine Men Who Laughed* (Markham, Ont.: Penguin, 1986), 1–7.

——. Interview for York University Television Series, 'Counterparts', July 1980. As cited in Leslie Sanders, 'Austin Clarke' in *Profiles in Canadian Literature*, vol. 4, ed. Jeffrey M. Heath (Toronto: Dundurn, 1982), 100.

Clarke, George Elliott. 'Fire on the Water: A First Portrait of Africadian Literature', introduction to *An Anthology of Black Nova Scotian Writing*, Vol. One, ed. George Elliott Clarke (Lawrencetown Beach, N.S.: Pottersfield Press, 1991), 11–29.

Crusz, Rienzi. *Oppositional Aesthetics: Readings from a Hyphenated Space*, Arun Mukherjee (Toronto: TSAR, 1994).

D'Alfonso, Antonio. 'The Road Between: Essentialism. For an Italian Culture in Quebec and Canada' in *Contrasts: Comparative Essays on Italian–Canadian Writing*, ed. Joseph Pivato (Montreal: Guernica, 1985), 207–29.

Di Cicco, Pier Giorgio. 'Virgin Science: The Hunt for Holistic Paradigms', interview by Robert Billings, *Poetry Canada Review* 8, 1 (Fall 1986): 3–4, 8.

Di Michele, Mary. 'Stealing the Language: An Interview with Mary di Michele', by Ken Norris, Essays on Canadian Writing 43 (Spring 1991): 2–13.

——. 'Conversations with the Living and the Dead', *Language in Her Eye*, 100–6.

El–Gabalawy, Saad. 'Introduction' in *Crash Landing of the Flying Egyptian*, Saad Elkhadem; trans. El–Gabalawy (Fredericton, N.B.: York Press, 1992), i–iv.

Faludy, George. 'Interview', by Jacqueline d'Ambroise, *Canadian Literature* 120 (Spring 1989): 42–5.

Friesen, Patrick. '*hooked, but not landed*: A Conversation with Patrick Friesen, part II', by Hildi Froese Tiessen, *Prairie Fire* 11, 2 (Summer 1990): 152–9.

——. Cited in 'Closing Panel', in *Acts of Concealment: Mennonite/s Writing in Canada*, eds Hildi Froese Tiessen and Peter Hinchcliffe (Waterloo: University of Waterloo Press, 1992), 223–42.

Grove, Frederick Philip. 'Canadians Old and New' in *A Stranger to My Time: Essays by and About Frederick Philip Grove*, ed. Paul Hjartarson (Edmonton: NeWest, 1986), 169–76.

——. 'Assimilation', in *A Stranger to My Time*, 177–87.

Gunnars, Kristjana. 'Myriads of Stars', interview by Jennifer Eagle, *Prairie Fire* 15, 1 (Spring 1994): 22–6.

Harris, Claire. 'Choosing Control: An Interview with Claire Harris', by Monty Reid, *Waves* 13, 1 (Fall 1984): 37–41.

_____. 'Why Do I Write?' in *Grammar of Dissent: Poetry and Prose by Claire Harris, M. Nourbese Philip and Dionne Brand*, ed. Carol Morrell (Fredericton, N.B.: Goose Lane, 1991) 26–33. Cited here from an unedited version entitled 'Why I Write'.

Hassan, Marwan. 'On and Around the Raft: An Interview with Marwan Hassan', by Will Straw, in *The Raft of the Medusa: Five Voices on Colonies, Nations and Histories*, Julian Samuel and Jocelyne Doray (Montreal: Black Rose Books, 1993), 89–110.

Jonas, George. 'An Interview', by Linda Sanders, *Canadian Literature* 73 (Summer 1977): 25–38.

King, Thomas. 'Interview with Thomas King' by Jeffrey Canton, *Paragraph* 16, 1 (1994): 2–6.

Kiyooka, Roy. Cited in 'Inter–Face: Roy Kiyooka's Writing, A Commentary/ Interview' by Roy Miki, in *Roy Kiyooka* (Vancouver: Artspeak Gallery and Or Gallery, 1991), 41–54.

——. 'We Asian North Americanos: An unhistorical "take" on growing up yellow in a white world', *West Coast Line* 3 (Winter 1990): 116–18.

——. 'Dear Lucy Fumi: c/o Japanese Canadian Redress Secretariat', *West Coast Line* 3 (Winter 1990): 125–6.

Klein, A.M. 'The Bible's Archetypal Poet' in *A.M. Klein: Literary Essays and Reviews*, eds Usher Caplan and M.W. Steinberg (Toronto: University of Toronto Press, 1987), 143–8.

——. (On Quebec.) Cited in *Like One That Dreamed: A Portrait of A.M. Klein* (Toronto: McGraw–Hill Ryerson, 1982), 149.

Kogawa, Joy. 'The Literary Politics of the Victim', interview by Magdalene Redekop, *Canadian Forum* (November 1989): 14–17.

Kryvoruchka, Alexandra. 'Introduction' in *Yellow Boots*, Vera Lysenko (Edmonton: NeWest, 1992), xi–xxiii.

Kulyk Keefer, Janice, interview by Jars Balan in *Other Solitudes*. 290–6.

——. 'From Mosaic to Kaleidoscope: Out of the multicultural past comes a vision of a transcultural future', *Books in Canada* 20, 6 (September 1991): 13–16.

Ladha, Yasmin. 'Circum the Gesture' in 'Wanting It Other/Wise: Race, Sexuality, Bodies, Texts'. Special Issue (Part 2) *Open Letter* 9, 3 (Summer 1995): 53–73.

Lau, Evelyn. 'The Economies of Language', interview by Brian Fawcett, *Books in Canada* 22, 4 (May 1993): 13–16.

——. As cited in 'Reading Evelyn Right', by Misao Dean, *Canadian Forum* LXXIV, 837 (March 1995): 22–6.

Layton, Irving. *Irving Layton: A Portrait*, Elspeth Cameron. Toronto: Stoddart, 1985.

Lee, Corinne Allyson. 'An Asian Lesbian's Struggle' in *Piece of My Heart: A Lesbian of Colour Anthology*, ed. Makeda Silvera (Toronto: Sister Vision Press, 1991), 115–18.

Lee, Sky (Sharon Lee). Untitled, in *Jin Guo: Voices of Chinese Canadian Women*, ed. The Women's Book Collective, Chinese Canadian National Council (Toronto: Women's Press, 1992), 91–8.

——. 'Is there a mind without media any more?' A talk with C. Allyson Lee, in *The Other Woman*, 382–403.

Maracle, Lee. 'The "Post–Colonial" Imagination', *Fuse* 16, 1 (Fall 1992): 12–15.

——. 'Native Myths: Trickster Alive and Crowing', *Fuse* 13, 1/2 (Fall 1989): 29–31.

——. 'Preface: You Become the Trickster', *Sojourner's Truths & Other Stories* (Vancouver: Press Gang, 1990), 11–13.

——. 'Just Get in Front of a Typewriter and Bleed' in *Telling It: Women and Language Across Cultures*, eds The Telling It Book Collective (Sky Lee, Lee Maracle, Daphne Marlatt, and Betsy Warland); (Vancouver: Press Gang, 1990), 37–41.

——. 'an infinite number of pathways to the centre of the circle', interview by Janice Williamson, in *Sounding Differences: Conversations with Seventeen Canadian Women Writers*, Janice Williamson (Toronto: University of Toronto Press, 1993), 166–78.

Marlatt, Daphne. 'On *Ana Historic*', interview by George Bowering. A Special Daphne Marlatt Issue; eds. Smaro Kamboureli and Shirley Neuman, *Line* 13 (Spring 1989): 96–105.

——. '"When we change language . . ." Interview', *Sounding Differences*. 182–93.

——. 'Meeting on Fractured Margins'. Introduction, *Telling It: Women and Language Across Cultures*, 9–18.

Mathur, Ashok. 'The Desisting Reader', *West Coast Line* 10 (27/1) (Spring 1993): 67–73.

Miki, Roy. 'From Exclusion to Inclusion', *Canadian Forum* LXXIII, 832 (September 1994): 5–8.

Mistry, Rohinton. 'An Interview with Rohinton Mistry' by Geoff Hancock, *Canadian Fiction Magazine* 65 (1989): 143–50.

——. 'Interview', by Dagmar Novak in *Other Solitudes*, 256–62.

Moses, Daniel David. 'The Rumour of Humanity', interview by Wanda Campbell, *Windsor Review* 27, 2 (Fall 1994): 55–63.

——. 'Interview with Daniel David Moses and Drew Hayden Taylor', by Terry Goldie, *Open Letter* 8, 8 (Winter 1994): 41–51.

—— and Terry Goldie. 'Preface: Two Voices' in *An Anthology of Canadian Native Literature*, eds Daniel David Moses and Terry Goldie (Toronto: Oxford University Press, 1992), xii–xxii.

Nourbese Philip, M. 'The Raft of the Medusa: Five Voices on Colonies, Nations and Histories' in *The Raft of the Medusa: Five Voices on Colonies, Nations and Histories* (with Thierry Hentsch, Amin Maalouf, M. Nourbese Philip, Sara Suleri, and Julian Samuel); Julian Samuel and Jocelyne Doray (Montreal: Black Rose Books, 1993), 1–85.

Ondaatje, Michael. '"The Germ of Document": An Interview with Michael Ondaatje', by Gerry Turcotte, *Australian–Canadian Studies* 12, 2 (1994): 49–58.

——. 'An Interview with Michael Ondaatje', by Eleanor Wachtel, *Essays on Canadian Writing* 53 (Summer 1994): 250–61.

——. 'Michael Ondaatje: An Interview', by Catherine Bush, *Essays on Canadian Writing* 53 (Summer 1994): 238–49.

Paci, Frank. 'An Interview with Frank Paci', by C.D. Minni, *Canadian Literature* 106 (Fall 1985): 5–15.

——. 'Tasks of the Canadian Novelist Writing on Immigrant Themes' in *Contrasts: Comparative Essays on Italian–Canadian Writing*, 35–60.

Petrone, Penny. *Native Literature in Canada: From the Oral Tradition to the Present.* (Toronto: Oxford University Press, 1990).

Rashid, Ian Iqbal. Untitled introduction, in *Beyond Destination: Film, Video and Installation by South Asian Artists.* Curated by Ian Iqbal Rashid (Birmingham, England: IconGallery, 1993), np.

Redekop, Magdalene. 'The Pickling of the Mennonite Madonna' in *Acts of Concealment: Mennonite Writing in Canada*, eds Hildi Froese Tiessen and Peter Hinchcliffe (Waterloo, University of Waterloo Press, 1992), 100–28.

Ricci, Nino. 'Recreating Paradise', interview by Jeffrey Canton, *Paragraph* 13, 3 (1991): 2–5.

——. 'A Big Canvas', interview by Mary Rimmer, *Studies in Canadian Literature/Etudes en littérature canadienne* 18, 2 (1993): 168–84.

Rodriguez, Nice. 'Innocent Lust' in *Piece of my Heart* (Toronto: Sister Vision Press, 1991), 82–7.

Salverson, Laura Goodman. *Confessions of an Immigrant's Daughter* (first ed. 1939), intr. K.P. Stich (Toronto: University of Toronto Press), 1981.

Selvadurai, Shyam. Cited in 'Personal and Political', by Leona Gom, Joyce Marshall, and John Steffler, *Books in Canada*, 24, 3 (April 1995): 9.

——. Cited in 'A Tale of Two Prizes', *The Globe and Mail* (29 October 1994): C7.

Silvera, Makeda. 'The characters would not have it' in *The Other Woman*, 405–19.

Skvorecky, Joseph. 'Reflecting on Exile: An Interview with Joseph Skvorecky (1989–92)', by Sam Solecki, in *The Achievement of Joseph Skvorecky*, ed. Sam Solecki (Toronto: University of Toronto Press, 1994), 3–14.

Schermbrucker, Bill. 'Preface' in *Chameleon and Other Stories* (Vancouver: Talonbooks, 1983), 9–13.

Spettigue, Douglas O. *FPG: The European Years* (Ottawa: Oberon,1973).

Stobie, Margaret R. *Frederick Philip Grove* (New York: Twayne, 1973).

Ternar, Yeshim. 'Writers Belong to World, not to Exclusive Groups', *Montreal Gazette* (2 July, 1994): H2.

——. Interview by Linda Leith, *Other Solitudes*, 328–33.

Suknaski, Andrew. From 'Rose Far in the East'. An envelope of nine *Poem/Drawings*, 1971.

Vassanji, M.G. 'An Interview' by John Clement Ball, *Paragraph* (Winter 1993–Spring 1994): 3–8.

——. '"Broadening the Substrata": An Interview with M.G. Vassanji', by Chelva Kanaganaykam, *World Literature Written in English* 31, 2 (1991): 19–35.

Waddington, Miriam. 'Rochl Korn: Remembering a Poet', in *Apartment Seven: Essays Selected and New* (Toronto: Oxford University Press, 1989), 190–9.

Wiebe, Rudy. '"Looking at our Particular World": An Interview with Rudy Wiebe', by Om P. Juneja, M.F. Salat, and Chandra Mohan, *World Literature Written in English* 31, 2 (Autumn 1991): 1–18.

Wong Chu, Jim. 'Jim Wong Chu', interview in *Voices of Change: Immigrant Writers Speak Out*, Jurgen Hesse (Vancouver: Pulp Press, 1990), 184–201.

INDEX